Amelia Ann Blanford Edwards

Barbara's History

A Novel

Amelia Ann Blanford Edwards

Barbara's History
A Novel

ISBN/EAN: 9783337033163

Printed in Europe, USA, Canada, Australia, Japan

Cover: Foto ©Andreas Hilbeck / pixelio.de

More available books at **www.hansebooks.com**

BARBARA'S HISTORY.

𝔄 Novel.

BY

AMELIA B. EDWARDS,

AUTHOR OF

"MY BROTHER'S WIFE," "HAND AND GLOVE," "THE STORY OF
CERVANTES," &c., &c.

NEW YORK:

HARPER & BROTHERS, PUBLISHERS,

FRANKLIN SQUARE.

1864.

BARBARA'S HISTORY.

I AM about to tell the story of my life—that is, the story of my child-hood and my youth; for the romance of life is mostly lived out before we reach middle age, and beyond that point the tale grows monotonous either in its grief, or its gladness. Mine began and ended when I was young.

When I was young! They are but four words; and yet, at the very commencement of what must prove a labour of many months, they have power to arrest my pen, and blind my eyes with unaccustomed tears. Tears partaking both of joy and sorrow; such tears as those through which we all look back to childhood and its half-forgotten story. Oh, happy time! so islanded in the still waters of memory; so remote, and yet so near; so strange, yet so familiar! Come back once more—come back, though never so briefly, and light these my pages with the pale sunshine of a faded spring.

I am answered. A pleasant calm steals upon me; and, as one might step aside from the troubled streets, to linger awhile in the quiet sanctuary of a wayside church, so I now turn from the eager present, tread the dim aisles of the past, sigh over the inscriptions graven on one or two dusty tablets, and begin with the recollections of infancy this narrative of my life.

CHAPTER I—REPORT.

BARBARA'S HISTORY.

CHAPTER I.

EARLY RECORDS.

"On rajeunit aux souvenirs d'enfance
Comme on renaît au souffle du printemps."
BÉRANGER.

SOMETIMES, in the suburban districts of London, we chance upon a quaint old house that was, evidently, a country-house some hundred years ago; but which has been overtaken by the town, and stands perplexed amid a neighborhood of new streets, like a rustic at Charing Cross. There are plenty such. We have seen them in our walks, many a time and oft. They look sad and strange. The shadows gather round them more darkly than 'on their neighbors. The sunlight seems to pass them by; and we fancy their very walls might speak, and tell us tales. In just such a house, and such a suburb, I was born.

Overgrown for the most part with a mantle of dark ivy, inclosed in a narrow garden that sloped down to a canal at the back, and shut sullenly away from the road by some three or four dusky elm-trees and a low wall, our home looked dreary and solitary enough—all the more dreary and solitary for the prim terraces and squares by which it was on all sides surrounded. Within, however, it was more cheerful; or custom made it seem so. From the upper windows we saw the Hampstead hills. In the summer our garden was covered with grass, and the lilac bushes blossomed where they leaned toward the canal. Even the shapeless coal-barges that labored slowly past all the day long had something picturesque and pleasant about them. Besides, no place can be wholly dull where children's feet patter incessantly up and down the stairs, and children's voices ring merrily along the upper floors.

It was a large old house—thrice too large for any use of ours—and we had it all to ourselves. Most of the top rooms were bare; and I well remember what famous play-grounds they made by day, and how we dreaded to pass near them after dark. Up there, even when my father was at home, we might be as noisy as we pleased. It was our especial territory; and, excepting once a year, when the great cleaning campaign was in progress, no one disputed our prerogative. We were left, indeed, only too much to our own wayward impulses, and grew wildly, like weeds by the wayside.

We were three—Hilda, Jessie, and Barbara. I am Barbara; and the day that gave me life left us all motherless. Our father had not married again. His wife was the one love of his existence, and it seemed, when she was gone, as if the very power of loving were taken from him. Thus it happened that from our first infancy we were left to the sole care of one faithful woman-servant, who spoiled us to her heart's content, and believed that we, like the king, could do no wrong. We call her Goody; but her name was Sarah Beever. We tyrannized over her, of course; and she loved us the more for our tyranny. After all, hers was the only affection we had, and, judicious or injudicious, we should have been poor indeed without it.

Our father's name was Edmund Churchill. He came of a good family; had received a collegiate education; and, it was said, had squandered a considerable fortune in his youth. When nearly arrived at middle life, he married. My mother was not rich—I never even heard that she was beautiful; but he loved her, and, while she lived, endeavored, after his own fashion, to make her happy. Too far advanced in years to apply himself to a profession, had even the inclination for work not been wanting, he found himself a hopeless and aimless man. He could not even console himself, like some fathers, in the society and education of his children, for he was not naturally fond of children; and now all the domestic virtues were gone out of him. Wrecked, stupefied, careless alike of the present and the future, he moped away a few dull months, and then, as was natural, returned to the world. He fell in with some of his former friends, now, like himself, grown staid with years; entered a club; took to dinner-parties, politics, and whist; became somewhat of a *bon vivant;* and, at forty-four, adopted all the small and selfish vices of age. At the time of which I write, he was still handsome, though somewhat stout and florid for his years. He dressed with scrupulous neatness; was particularly careful of his health; and prided himself upon the symmetry of his hands and feet.

His manners, in general, were courteous and cold; yet, in society, he was popular. He possessed, in an eminent degree, the art of pleasing; and I do not remember the day on which he dined at home. Yet, for all this, he was a proud man at heart, and dearly cherished every circumstance that bore upon his name and lineage. An observer might have detected this by only glancing round the walls of our dusky dining-room, and inspecting the contents of the great old carved bookcase between the windows. Here might be seen a "History of ye Noble and Ancient Houses of Devon," with that page

turned down wherein it treated of the Churchills of Ash. Here a copy of that scarce and
dreary folio entitled "Divi Britannici," written
and published by Sir Winston Churchill in 1675.
Several works on the wars of Queen Anne; five
or six different lives of John Churchill, Duke of
Marlborough; the Duchess of Marlborough's
"Private Correspondence;" Chesterfield's Letters; Mrs. Manley's "Atalantis;" the "Me-
moirs of the Count de Grammont;" various
old editions of Philips's "Blenheim," and Ad-
dison's "Campaign;" the poetical works of
Charles Churchill of Westminster; and twenty
volumes of the "London Gazette," (said to be of
considerable value, and dating from the year
1700 to 1715,) filled all the upper shelves, and
furnished my father with the only reading in
which he ever indulged at home. Nor was this
all. A portrait of the brilliant hero, when Lord
Churchill, and some fine old engravings of the
battles of Ramillies, Oudenarde, and Malplaquet,
were suspended over the chimney-piece and
side-board. A large colored print of Blenheim
House hung outside in the hall.

But far more impressive than any of these—
far more dignified and awful in our childish
eyes, was a painting which occupied the place
of honor in our best parlor. This work of art
purported to be the portrait of a second cousin
of my father's, one Agamemnon Churchill by
name, a high authority upon all matters connected with the noble science of heraldry, a
Knight of the Bath, and one of his Majesty's
most honorable heralds. Depicted here in all
the glory of his official costume, and looking
as like the knave of clubs as if he had just been
shuffled out of a gigantic pack of cards, Sir
Agamemnon Churchill beamed upon us from
the environment of his gilded frame, and filled
our little hearts with wonder and admiration.
We humbly looked forward to the possibility of
some day beholding our illustrious kinsman.
We fancied that his rank could be only second
to that of King William himself. We even
encouraged a secret belief that he might succeed
to the throne at some remote time or other;
and agreed among ourselves that his first exercise of the royal prerogative would be to
create our father Duke of Marlborough; or, at
the least, Commander in Chief and Lord Mayor
of London.

It was but seldom, however, that we were
allowed to contemplate the splendor of Sir
Agamemnon and his glittering tabard; for the
best parlor had been a closed room ever since
my mother's death, and was only thrown open
now and then for cleaning purposes. But this
very restriction; this air of mourning and
solitude; the darkened windows; the sheeted
furniture; the thick white dust that crept in
month by month; and, above all, the sense of
a mysterious loss which we were all too young
to comprehend, only served to invest the room
and the picture with a still deeper interest. I
well remember how often we interrupted our
garden-games to peep, with suspended breath,
through the chinks of the closed shutters, and
how our voices sunk to a whisper when we
passed the door.

I have said that we were three; but I have
not yet explained how nearly we were of one
age, or how, being the youngest, I was only re-

moved by three years from my eldest sister,
Hilda, and by fourteen months from my second
sister, Jessie. My father's little girls had, indeed, sprung up quickly around him, and our
mother was taken from us at the very time when
we most needed her.

Jessie was fair, and somewhat pretty; but
Hilda was the beauty of the family, and our
father's favorite. She was like him, but darker
of complexion, and more delicately featured.
She inherited the same pride; was willful and
imperious; and exercised, withal, after her
precocious fashion, the same power of ready
fascination. Besides, she was very clever—
much cleverer than Jessie or I—and learned
with surprising facility. My sister Jessie was
in many respects less forward than myself. She
had neither Hilda's talent nor my steadiness, and
was altogether deficient in ambition. To our
eldest sister she was entirely devoted, submitting
to all her caprices, and accepting all her opinions
with a blind faith worthy of a better cause.
This alliance was not favorable to my happiness.
Hilda and Jessie were all in all to each other,
and I found myself excluded from the confidence of both. Forgetting, or seeming to forget, how little our ages differed, they treated
me as a mere baby; called me "little Barbara,"
and affected to undervalue whatever I said or
did. When I tacitly rejected this mortifying
patronage, and with it, a companionship which
was only offered to me during a game of blind-
man's-buff, or puss-in-the corner, I was reproached for my indifference, or set aside as simply
dull and tiresome.   •

To be just, I do not believe that my sisters
had any idea of how they made me suffer. I
was too proud to let them see it, and my grief
may at times have worn a sullen aspect. Often
and often have I stolen away to one of the great
upper rooms, sobbing and lamenting, and wishing
that my heart might break and put an end to my
sorrows—and yet I kept my secret so bravely
that it was not even suspected by the dear old
servant whom I loved and trusted above all the
world.

The grievances of infancy lie mostly on the
surface. Time heals them, and they leave no
scar. But this was not my case. I was more
sensitive than the generality of children, and,
I believe, more affectionate. I could have
loved my sisters with my whole heart; but they
rejected me, and so the estrangement, which at
first might have been healed by a word, widened
with years and became at last almost irreparable.
By the time that I had reached the age of nine or
ten, I was no longer a child. My freshness of
feeling was gone — my heart was chilled.— my
first impulses were checked and driven back.
The solitude which was once my refuge became
my habit; and, grown indifferent to opinion, I
heard myself called "strange and unsociable"
without emotion. I appropriated one of the
garrets to my special use, and, being left in undisturbed possession, lived there among occupations and amusements of my own creation.
Thus it happened that, unless during the hours
of meals or tuition, I lived almost entirely
alone. My father knew nothing of this; for
he was always out, and troubled himself very
little about our domestic managements. Goody
knew and wondered, but loved me too well to

interfere with any thing I chose to do; and my sisters, after teasing and laughing at me to their hearts' content, at last grew weary, and abandoned me to my own solitary ways.

It was a sad life for a child, and might have led to many evils, but for a circumstance which I must ever regard as something more than mere good fortune.

Having wandered up-stairs one day with nothing to read and nothing to think of, and being, moreover, very listless and weary, I bethought myself of a pile of old boxes which lay stored together in a certain dark closet close at hand, and so set to work to turn out their contents. Most of them were empty, or contained only coils of rotten rope, pieces of faded stuffs and damasks, and bundles of accounts. But in one, the smallest and least promising of all, I found a dusty treasure. This treasure consisted of some three or four dozen worm-eaten, faded volumes, tied up in lots of four or six, and overlaid with blotches of white mold. A motley company! Fox's "Martyrs;" the Works of Dr. Donne; Sir Thomas Browne on "Urn Burial;" a Translation of Pliny, with Illustrations; Defoe's "History of the Plague;" Riccoboni on the Theaters of Europe; "Hudibras;" Waller's Poems; Bolingbroke's "Letters on English History;" the Tatler, Guardian, and Spectator; Drelincourt on Death, with the History of Mrs. Veal; an odd volume or two of the Gentleman's Magazine, and some few others, chiefly farming books and sermons. It was a quaint library for so young a reader, but a most welcome one. I necessarily met with much that I could not understand, and yet contrived to reap pleasure and profit from all. I had boundless faith to begin with, and believed, like the Arabs, that every thing printed must be true. I was puzzled by Sir Hudibras, but never doubted either his courage or identity. I was interested by the letters in the Tatler, and only wondered that so many ladies and gentlemen should have ventured to trouble that nice good-natured Mr. Bickerstaff with their unimportant private affairs. As for Edmund Waller, Esquire, I was quite sorry for his distresses; and could not conceive how the beautiful Sacharissa could bear to be told that she had "a wild and cruel soul" without relenting immediately. To me, happy in my credulity, the Phœnix and Mrs. Veal were alike genuine phenomena; and had Sir Agamemnon Churchill himself attempted to convince me that the History of the Plague was written by any other than "a citizen who lived the whole time in London," I should have made bold to reserve my own opinion on the subject.

Other books I had as well — books better suited to my age and capacity; but these, being common property, were kept in the school-room, and consisted for the most part in moral tales and travels, which, read more than once, grow stale and wearisome.

Fortunate was it that I found this second life in my books; for I was a very lonely little girl, with a heart full of unbestowed affection, and a nature quickly swayed to smiles or tears. The personages of my fictitious world became as real to me as those by whom I was surrounded in my daily life. They linked me with humanity. They were my friends, my instructors, my companions. I loved some, and hated others, as cordially as if they could love or hate me in return; and, in the intensity of my sympathy with their airy sorrows and perplexities, learned to forget my own.

But I had still another happiness — a half-developed taste, which, fed by such scant nutriment as fell now and then in my way, ripened, year after year, to a deep and earnest passion, and influenced beyond all calculation the destinies of my later life. Art — art called the Divine, but known to me under its meanest and most barren form — fed the dreams of my childhood, and invested with an undeserved interest the few wretched prints scattered here and there through the pages of Fox's Martyrs, Goldsmith's Geography, and other works of the same "mark and likelihood." Sometimes, after my own imperfect fashion, I strove to reproduce them in pencil or charcoal. Sometimes, even, I attempted to illustrate the adventures of my favorite heroes, or the landscapes described in books of travel. The whitewashed walls of my garret, the covers and margins of my copybooks, and all the spare scraps of paper that I could find, were scrawled over with designs in which the love of beauty might, perhaps, have been discernible; but in which every rule of anatomy, perspective, and probability was hopelessly set at naught. But of this, more hereafter.

Happy art thou, O little child, to whom is granted the guidance of loving parents! Happy, thrice happy, in the fond encouragements, the gentle reproofs, the tender confidences and consolations lavished on thy first uncertain years! I lost one of mine before my lips had ever been hallowed by her kisses; and by the other I was, if not wholly unloved, at least too much neglected. How I yearned and wearied for those affections that I now could never have; how I used to steal to dear old Goody's knees in the dim twilight, and beseech her to tell me something of my mother; how I listened with tears that I was ashamed to show, and stole away to hide them; how, thinking over all these things, I sometimes gave way to fits of bitterness and anger, and sometimes sobbed myself to sleep, with my head resting on a book, matters little now, and except as it may throw a light on certain passages of my inner life, is scarcely deserving of mention. Alas! I have yet much more to tell. The long story of my workings and wanderings lies all before me like a summer landscape, with its lights and shadows, its toilsome plains, and its places of green rest, mapped out, and fading away together in the blue distance.

Here, at all events, let me end my first day's record; for I am weary, and these pictures of the past lie heavily at my heart.

CHAPTER II.

DEPORTMENT AND DISCIPLINE.

My father's bell rang sharply.

It was about eleven o'clock on a brilliant May morning. Miss Whymper, who attended to our education between the hours of nine and twelve daily, presided at the head of the table, correcting French exercises. We, respectfully withdrawn to the foot of the same, bent busily over our books and slates, and preserved a decorous silence. We all heard our father close his bed-room door and go down-stairs; but it was his habit to rise and breakfast late, and we took no notice of it. We also heard him ring; but we took no notice of that either. Scarcely, however, had the echo of the first bell died away, when it was succeeded by a second, and the second was still pealing when he opened the parlor door, and called aloud.

"Beever!" said he, impatiently. "Beever! am I to ring for an hour?"

The reply was inaudible; but he spoke again, almost without waiting to hear it.

"When did this letter arrive? Was it here last night when I came home, or was it deliver-ed only this morning? Why didn't you bring it up to me with the shaving water? Where is Barbara?"

Startled at the sound of my own name, I rose in my place, and waited with suspended breath. My sisters, with their heads still bent low, glanced first at me and then at each other.

"Be so good, Miss Barbara, as to concentrate your attention upon your studies," said Miss Whymper, without even raising her eyes from the exercises.

"I—I—that is, papa—I heard——"

"Be so good as to hear nothing during the hours of education," interposed Miss Whymper, still frostily intent upon the page before her.

"But papa calls me, and——"

"In that case you will be sent for. We will proceed, if you please, young ladies, to the analyzation of the Idiom."

We pushed our slates away, took each our French grammar, and prepared to listen.

"The Idiom," said Miss Whymper, sitting stiffly upright, and, as was her wont, cadencing her voice to one low monotonous level, "is a familiar and arbitrary turn of words, which, without being in strict accordance with the re-ceived laws of——"

"Barbara! Barbara, come here. Tell Miss Whymper I want you!"

I started up again, and Miss Whymper, inter-rupted in her discourse, frowned, inclined her head the very least in the world, and said:

"You have my permission, Miss Barbara, to retire."

I was always nervous in my father's presence; but the suddenness and strangeness of the sum-mons made me this morning more than usually timid. I ran down, however, and presented myself, tremblingly, at the door of the breakfast-parlor. He was pacing to and fro, between the table and the window. His coffee stood untasted in the cup. In his hand he crushed an open letter. Seeing me at the door, he stopped, flung himself into his easy chair, and beckoned me to come nearer.

"Stand there, Barbara," said he, pointing to a particular square in the pattern of the car-pet.

Shaking from head to foot, I came forward and stood there, waiting, like a criminal for his sentence.

"Humph! Can't you look up?"

I looked up; looked down again; turned red and white alternately; and felt as if the ground were slipping from under my feet.

My father uttered an exclamation of impa-tience.

"Good heavens!" said he, pettishly. "What gaucherie! Are you taught to hold yourself no better than that? Are your arms pump-handles? What stranger would imagine—well, well, it can't be helped now! Tell me—did you ever hear of your great-aunt, who lives in Suffolk?"

"Heard of Mrs. Sandyshaft!" exclaimed Goody, who had been standing by the door, twirling her apron with both hands all the time. "I should think so indeed! Often and often; and of Stoneycroft Hall, too—haven't you, my lamb?"

Too confused to speak, I nodded; and my father went on.

"I have had a letter from your great-aunt this morning, Barbara. Here it is. She asks me to send you down to Suffolk; and, as it may be greatly for your good, I shall allow you to go. Though at a great inconvenience to myself, remember. At a great inconvenience to myself."

Uncertain what to reply, I looked down, and stammered:

"Yes, papa."

"I have not seen Mrs. Sandyshaft for many years," continued my father. "In fact, we—we have not been friends. But she may take a liking for you, Barbara—and she is rich. You must try to please her. You will go this day week, if Beever can get you ready in the time. What do you say, Beever?"

"Less than a week will do for me, sir," said Goody, promptly.

"No, no; a week is soon enough. And, Bee-ver, you are not to spare for a pound or two. I must have her look like a gentleman's child, anyhow. Not but that it is excessively incon-venient to me, just now. Excessively incon-venient!"

He paused, musingly, and then, leaning his chin upon his hand, looked at me again, and sighed. The sight, I suppose, was unsatisfactory enough; for the longer he looked, the more his countenance darkened. Suddenly he rose, pushed his chair away, and planted himself in the middle of the hearth-rug with his back to the fire.

"My compliments to Miss Whymper, Beever, and I request the favor of a moment's conver-sation."

Beever departed on her errand. After a few seconds of uneasy silence, during which I never ventured to stir from that particular square upon the carpet, Miss Whymper came.

My father bowed profoundly. Miss Whymper courtesied to the ground. I always noticed that they were amazingly polite to each other.

"Madam," said my father with his grandest air, and in his blandest accents, "unwilling as I am to trespass on your valuable time, I have ventured to interrupt you this morning in order to consult you upon——Barbara, place a chair for Miss Whymper."

Miss Whymper courtesied again, laid her head a little on one side, like a raven, and folded her hands together, as if she were expressing the letter M in the manual alphabet.

"I propose, madam," pursued my father, "to send Barbara on a visit to a relation—a rich and somewhat eccentric relation—who resides in the country, and with whom we have not held communication for many years. It is important, for several reasons, Miss Whymper, that the child should make a favorable impression; and

I feel sure that I shall not vainly entreat your coöperation during the few days that intervene between the present time and the period of her departure."

"With regard to any thing that *I* can do," murmured Miss Whymper, patting her hands softly together, as if she were applauding, "Mr. Churchill may at all times command me."

My father glanced at Miss Whymper's hands, which were somewhat red and bony, and at his own, which were particularly white and well shaped; and so, trifling carelessly with his watch-chain, continued.

"I am aware, of course," said he, "that much can not be done in so short a time; but that something may, I am induced to hope, knowing—ahem!—the talent and judgment to which I confide the task." ·

Miss Whymper smiled the iciest of smiles, and acknowledged the tribute by another bow, which my father returned immediately.

"You observe, no doubt, Miss Whymper," he continued, "that Barbara's carriage is essentially ungraceful. She never knows what to do with her feet. Her hands do not seem to belong to her. She enters a room badly. She has no self-possession, no style, no address—in short, there is nothing in her appearance which indicates either good blood or good breeding."

Whereupon my father glanced over his shoulder at the chimney-glass, and paused for a reply. Miss Whymper, perceiving that I had withdrawn behind her chair, as much out of sight as possible, shifted her position, and considered me attentively.

"It is quite true, sir," she sighed, after a few minutes of silence. "She is lamentably awkward! And yet her sister Hilda ——"

"Ah! if it had been Hilda!" exclaimed my father, regretfully. "Why could she not have invited Hilda?"

"So quick, so naturally graceful, such rapid perception!" murmured Miss Whymper, still noiselessly applauding.

"The only one of the three who is like me!" added my father, with another glance at the glass.

"A truly aristocratic cast of features," returned Miss Whymper, "and the very child to please a stranger! Well, well—we may do something with Miss Barbara, after all; and, perhaps, by confining our attention for the present to that one object ——"

"Precisely so, Madam. That is what I wish."

"And, if Mr. Churchill entertains no objection, by employing the aid of a few calisthenic exercises ——"

"Just so, Miss Whymper. Just so."

"I do not doubt being enabled to effect some slight improvement."

"In which case, Madam, you will confer a favor upon me."

"And should any trifling outlay be required ——"

"You will charge whatever is necessary to my account."

"A back-board, for instance, and a pair of dumb-bells?"

"I leave every thing, Miss Whymper, to your experience and discretion."

The tone in which my father uttered these last words, and the bow by which they were accom-

panied, concluded the interview. Miss Whymper rose; he held the door open while she passed through; more bows and courtesies were exchanged, and, when she was gone, he shrugged his shoulders contemptuously, and flung himself once more into the easy chair.

"Pshaw!" he muttered, "governesses and children—necessary evils! Barbara, you may go back to your lessons, and tell Beever to bring fresh coffee."

The result of this conversation was to make my life unbearably wretched for the next seven days. I was taught to walk, to stand, to shake hands. I stood in the stocks, and wore the back-board, till I was ready to faint. I was placed before a looking-glass, and made to courtesy to my own reflection for the half hour together. I went through the first interview with my great-aunt twenty times a day; my great-aunt being represented by a chair, and Miss Whymper standing by to conduct the performance. All this was very painful and perplexing, and, at the same time, very ludicrous. As for Hilda and Jessie, they allowed me no peace from morning till night; but, when our governess was out of the way, mimicked me with elaborate salutations, inquired perpetually after my health and that of my great-aunt, and humbly hoped that when I had inherited Stoneycroft Hall, and become a grand lady, I should not be too proud to take notice of my poor relations!

Thus the weary week went by, and but for dear old Goody, who comforted and consoled me under all my trials, I hardly know how I could have gone through it. Go through it I did, however; and, drilled and dislocated to the uttermost verge of endurance, hailed with a blessed sense of coming liberty the morning of my departure.

———◆———

CHAPTER III.

ON THE ROAD.

SEATED in a corner of the Suffolk Stage, with Goody clinging in an agony of tears to the door, and the guard insisting that she must get down, as the coach is going immediately, I feel that I am, indeed, a very lonely little traveler. I have left so early that no one in the house was awake to bid me good-by; I have scarcely slept at all throughout the night; and I have eaten no breakfast. Worse than all, my firmness is fast oozing away, and there is a lump in my throat that will surely break into sobs with the next word I utter.

"Now, ma'am, for the last time if *you* please," says the guard, impatiently.

"Eighty mile and more!" sobs Goody, clinging all the faster. "Oh! my dear lamb, eighty mile and more!"

"Well, it's your own choice," growls the guard, with an oath and a scowl, as he clambers to his seat. "You'll be thrown off the step, as sure as you're a Christian woman!"

Whereupon she smothers me in one last frantic embrace, and, being wrenched away by a humane bystander, disappears suddenly—only to reäppear, however, as suddenly; and, as the coach starts, to cry:

"Good-by! good-by! my darling! Eat your money, and take care of your sandwiches!"

Having no voice to answer, I can only hang from the window and wave my hand. We plunge out of the inn-yard and into the busy street beyond—the guard blows his horn—the loungers give a shout—and, looking after her to the last, I catch one parting glimpse of Goody in insane pursuit. Then a crowd of vehicles intervenes; we whirl sharply round a corner; and there is nothing left for me but to shrink back in my place and weep silently.

A long time goes by thus. My fellow-travelers, who are four in number and seem all to belong to one family, talk loudly among themselves, and take no notice of me. Looking up, by and by, when my first anguish has somewhat abated, I observe that they consist of a father, mother, and two daughters, all very cheerful and good-tempered-looking, and all busily engaged in the consumption of stout sausage rolls. Being pressed to accept one of these, and, to my shame, bursting into another flood of tears with the effort of declining it, I turn my face to the window, and they considerately speak to me no more.

The morning is cold and gray, and a melancholy damp, which is half rain, half fog, clings to the panes, and makes the prospect ghostly. We are not yet out of the great suburbs; but the houses, which run mostly in terraces, have an out-of-town look, and are presently succeeded by groups of twin-villas with gaps of market gardens between. Then come brick-fields, villas half built up, patches of waste ground, and lines of dreary pasture, which, seen through the drizzling mist, look more dismal than the streets.

Struck with the silence that has succeeded to the brisk conversation with which they began the journey, I venture once again to glance at my companions, and find that they have all four fallen asleep, with their heads tied up in pocket handkerchiefs—a proceeding so sensible and contagious, that I presently find myself also getting drowsy, and, before many minutes are past, have forgotten my troubles in a deep and dreamless slumber. Not having rested all the night before, I now sleep heavily—so heavily that nothing less than the opening of the door and the entrance of the sixth passenger (whose place has all this time been vacant) awakens me. It is now close upon midday. The mist has cleared off; the sun shines out gloriously; the sky is islanded with great solitary clouds; there are trees and trim hedges on either side of the road; and the country all about is green and pleasant. We are running on briskly, at the rate of ten miles an hour—so, at least, our last traveler observes—and the village at which we took him up is already left far behind.

"Ten mile an hour, a fine day, and five agreeable companions (four of 'em ladies,)" says the new comer, with a sniff at every comma, "what can the 'art of man desire more?"

He is a plump, smooth-shaven individual, with an unhealthy complexion, a black suit, a white neck-cloth, and a brown cotton umbrella. Despite the complacent smile with which he looks round upon the company, he is not by any means attractive, and nobody seems disposed to improve his acquaintance.

"Except conversation," he adds, after a long pause. "Yea—except godly conversation."

A dead silence follows, during which he smiles and looks round, as before.

"And godly conversation," says he, at the end of another interval, "is the refreshment of the sperrit."

Still no one answers, and this time the omission can hardly be misconstrued. By the fading of his ugly smile, and the gloom that gathers gradually about his heavy brow, it is plain that he sees the unpleasant truth at last. Finding presently that the father and daughters have resumed their chat in whispers, and that the mother has turned directly away from him, he pulls a greasy book from his pocket, lolls back in his place, and reads sullenly.

Thoroughly amused by the incidents of the road, and delighted with the country, I watch every thing that passes, and soon forget all about my traveling companions. The green fields rippling over with young wheat — the snug farm-houses, set round with yellow stacks and mossy barns — the wayside pond with its fleet of callow ducklings — the gray church tower that peeps above the willows — the weary peddler resting by the cross roads, with his bundle at his feet — the solitary inn, with its swinging sign, its old worn trough, and its sunburnt ostler lounging at the door — the traveling caravan that labors on with smoking chimney and close-shut windows, and is so soon left out of sight —the stretch of furzy common — the bridge where boys are angling — the drove of frantic pigs that rush under our very wheels, and seem bent on suicide — the plantations, mansions, toll-gates, wagons; in short, all these sights and sounds of country life fill my mind with pleasant pictures, and my heart with gladness.

Rattling at hot noon into a clean, bright, busy town, where it is market-day and the streets are thronged with farmers, we dash up to a large inn called the "Rose and Crown," and halt to dine. Having my basket of sandwiches at my feet, and being, besides, somewhat shy of the inn and the strange people, I remain in the coach alone; but the cheerful family hurry away as briskly as if the stout sausage-rolls had appealed only to their imaginations, and the sleek stranger saunters blandly up and down the yard under the shadow of his cotton umbrella. Seeing me engaged, shortly after, on the contents of my basket, he hovers about the door, smiles, lingers, and looks interested.

"What are your sandwiches made of, my dear?" he asks at length. "Ham or beef?"

"Beef, sir," I reply, coloring painfully.

The stranger smacks his lips.

"Dear me!" says he meditatively. "Only to think that they are beef! Why, I guessed they were beef from the beginning! They look very nice."

Scarcely knowing whether it be polite to do so, and fearful at the same time of offending this gentleman's delicacy, I hold out the basket with a timid hand, and try to falter forth some words of invitation. To my surprise, he accepts immediately; and not only accepts, but steps straightway into the coach, takes my basket on his knees, and, to show how little pride he has, helps himself as liberally to my sandwiches as though they had been his own. Thus powerfully aided, I soon arrive at the end of my dinner, and, somehow or another, leave off almost as hungry as when I began.

A sudden running to and fro, clattering of

hoofs, and crowding up of passengers, now indicates the renewal of our journey. The cheerful family hurries back, looking very warm and contented. The coachman clambers to the box, and has his last glass of ale handed up to him. The guard sounds a farewell blast; and away we go again, across the market-hill,· and out past the bank and the prison, and on once more along the dusty high road, with the fields on either side.

What, with the pleasant monotony of the landscape, and the heat of the sunny summer's day, and the general drowsiness of these and other influences, we are a very sleepy company this afternoon, and, unconsciously polite, nod to each other incessantly. At about four o'clock we come to a large town, where my cheerful neighbors are met by a roomy double-bodied chaise, and all shake hand with me at parting. Not so the sleek traveler, who, unmindful of the sandwiches, jumps out, as the coach stops, and goes his way without a word.

Handsome shops, wide streets, picturesque old houses, with projecting stories richly carved, solid public buildings, and glimpses of a noble river fringed with trees and villas, impress me with admiration as we pass, and make up a total that is more than commonly attractive. Having delayed here full half an hour, we start away again; and, just as we begin to move, I hear it said that the name of this town is Ipswich.

Being, by this time, very tired and hungry, and quite alone in the coach, I fall asleep once more, and, waking bewildered at every change of horses, forget where I am, and whither I am going. Sometimes, possessed with a vague notion that I must have slept for hours and passed the place long since, I start up in terror, and cry to be let out; but that is when we are going at full speed, and no one hears me. Thus two more weary hours lag by, seeming as long as all the other hours of the day together; and then, just as dusk is coming on, we pass through a straggling village, where the blacksmith's forge burns redly, and the children in the ivied schoolhouse are chanting an evening hymn. Dashing on between the straggling cottages, and up a hill so closely shaded by thick trees, that the dusk seems to thicken suddenly to night, we draw up all at once before a great open gate, leading to a house of which I can only see the gabled outline and the lighted windows.

The guard jumps ·down; the door is thrown open; and two persons, a man and woman, come hurrying down the path.

"One little girl, and one box, as per book," says the guard, lifting me out, and setting me down in the road, as if I were but another box, to be delivered as directed.

"From London?" asks the woman, sharply.

"From London," replies the guard, already scrambling to his seat. "All right, an't it?"

"All right."

Whereupon the coach plunges on again into the dusk; the man shoulders my box as though it were a feather; and the woman, who looks strangely gaunt and gray by this uncertain light, seizes me by the wrist, and strides away toward the house at a pace that my cramped and weary limbs can scarcely accomplish.

Sick and bewildered, I am hurried into a cheerful room where the table is spread as if for tea

and supper, and a delicious perfume of coffee and fresh flowers fills the air; and—and, all at once, even in the moment when I am first observing them, these sights and scents grow all confused and sink away together, and I remember nothing.

How long my unconsciousness may have lasted I know not; but when I recover, I find myself laid upon a sofa, with my cloak and bonnet off, my eyes and mouth full of Eau de Cologne, and my hands smarting under a volley of slaps, administered by a ruddy young woman on one side, and the same gaunt person who brought me from the coach, on the other. Seeing me look up, they both desist; and the latter, drawing back a step or two, as if to observe me to greater advantage, puts on an immense pair of heavy gold spectacles, stares steadily for some seconds, and at length says:

"What did you mean by that, now?"

Unprepared for so abrupt a question, I lie as if fascinated by her bright gray eyes, and can not utter a syllable.

"Are you better?"

Still silent, I bow my head feebly, and keep looking at her.

"Hey, now! Am I a basilisk? Are you dumb, child?"

Wondering why she speaks to me thus, and being, moreover, so very weak and tired, what can I do but to try in vain to answer, and, failing in the effort, burst into tears again? Hereupon she frowns, pulls off her glasses, shakes her head angrily, and, saying—"That's done to aggravate me—I know it is!"—stalks away to the window, and stands there grimly, looking out upon the night. The younger woman, however, with a world of kindness in her rosy face, touches my wet cheeks tenderly with her rough hands, dries my tears upon her apron, and bending low with her finger to her lips, whispers me "not to cry."

"That child's hungry," says the other, coming suddenly back. "That's what's the matter with her. She's hungry. I know she is, and I won't be contradicted. Do you hear me, Jane?— I won't be contradicted."

"Indeed, ma'am, I think she is hungry," replies Jane. "And tired, too, poor little thing!"

"Tired and hungry — Mercy alive! then why don't she eat? Here's food enough for a dozen people! Child, what will you have? Ham—cold chicken-pie—bread—butter—cheese—tea—coffee—ale?"

Too faint to speak aloud even now, I rather express the word "Coffee" by the motion of my lips than whisper it; and having done this, lie back wearily and close my eyes.

The first step is the great effort; but, being fed and waited upon by the younger woman, I soon get better and braver, and am able to sit up and be helped to a slice of chicken-pie. From pie to ham, from ham to a second cup of coffee, and from the second cup of coffee to more pie, are transitions easily understood, and pleasantly accomplished. Every thing tastes delicious; and not even the sight of the gaunt housekeeper, who sits all the time at the opposite side of the table with her chin resting in the palms of her hands, and her eyes fixed immovably upon me, has power to spoil my enjoyment.

For she is the housekeeper beyond a doubt. Those heavy gold spectacles, that sad-colored gown, that cap with its plain, close bordering, can belong to no one but a housekeeper. Wondering within myself why she should be so disagreeable; and why, being so disagreeable, my aunt should keep her in her service; then wondering where my aunt herself can be; why she has not yet come to welcome me; how she will receive me when she does come; and whether I shall have presence of mind enough to remember all the courtesies I have been drilled to make, and all the speeches I have been taught to say, I find myself eating as if nothing at all had been the matter with me, and even staring now and then quite confidently at my opposite neighbor.

My meal over, and the funereal silence, in which it has been conducted, remaining still unbroken, Jane clears the table, closes out the dark night, trims the lamp, wheels my sofa over to the fireside and is seen no more. Left alone now with the sleeping dogs and the housekeeper—who looks as if she never slept in her life—I find the evening wearisome. Observing, too, that she continues to look at me in the same grim, imperturbable way, and seeing no books anywhere about, it occurs to me that a little conversation would, perhaps, be acceptable; and that, as I am her mistress's niece, it is my place to speak first.

"If you please, ma'am," I begin, after a long hesitation.

"HEY!"

Somewhat disconcerted by the sharpness and suddenness of this interruption, I pause, and take some moments to recover myself.

"If you please, ma'am, when am I to see my aunt?"

"Hey? What? Who?"

"My aunt, if you please, ma'am."

"Mercy alive! And pray who do you suppose I am?"

"You, ma'am," I faltered, with a vague uneasiness impossible to describe. "Are you—are you not the housekeeper?"

To say that she glares vacantly at me from behind her spectacles, loses her very power of speech, and grows, all at once, quite stiff and rigid in her chair, is to convey but a faint picture of the amazement with which she receives this observation.

"I!" she gasps at length. "I! Gracious me, child!—*I* am your aunt."

I feel my countenance become an utter blank. I am conscious of turning red and white, hot and cold, all in one moment. My ears tingle; my heart sinks within me; I can neither speak nor think. A dreadful silence follows, and in the midst of this silence, my aunt, without any kind of warning, bursts into a grim laugh, and says:—

"Barbara, come and kiss me."

I could have kissed a kangaroo just then, in the intensity of my relief; and so, getting up quite readily, touch her gaunt cheek with my childish lips, and look the gratitude I dare not speak. To my surprise, she draws me closer to her knee, passes one thin hand idly through my hair, looks, not unkindly, into my wondering eyes, and murmurs, more to herself than me, the name of "Barbara!"

This gentle mood, however, is soon dismissed; and, as if ashamed of having indulged it, she

pushes me away, frowns, shakes her head, and says, quite angrily:

"Nonsense, child. Nonsense! It's time you went to bed."

And so, with Jane's good help, to bed I go, and thankfully, too; for I never was so weary in my life.

It is a large room, and a large bed stands in the center of it — a bed so soft and so extensive that I disappear altogether in its mighty depths, and am lost till morning.

———♦———

CHAPTER IV.

MY AUNT AND I BECOME BETTER ACQUAINTED.

Jours nâifs, plaisirs purs, emportés par le temps!"
J. REBOUL.

"YOUR name," said my aunt, with a little off-hand nod, "is Bab. Remember that."

She looked grimmer than ever, sitting up so stiffly behind the tea-urn; and this was all the morning salutation she vouchsafed me. A vacant chair awaited me at the foot of the table — such a chair! It had a high, straight, carved back, and huge elbows, to which my chin just reached, and legs like bed-posts, which, as they were very long, and mine very short, left my feet dangling half a yard from the ground. Unpleasantly conscious of my own diminutiveness, and still more unpleasantly conscious of my aunt's keen eyes, I endeavored to fill this piece of furniture as best I could, and to look as tall as possible.

"Bab," said my aunt, "what made you take me for the housekeeper?"

I had begun breakfast with a tolerable appreciation of the good things before me; but this question took away my appetite at a blow.

"I—I—I don't know, ma'am," I replied, falteringly.

"Nonsense, Bab. You know well enough. I see it in your face—and I won't be contradicted!"

"If—if you please, ma'am——"

"No, I don't please. What made you take me for the housekeeper? Was it my dress?"

"Yes, ma'am, I think so."

"Too shabby—hey?"

"N-no, ma'am—not shabby; but——"

"But what? You must learn to speak out, Bab. I hate people who hesitate."

"But papa said you were so rich, and——"

"Ah! He said I was rich, did he? Rich! Oho! And what more, Bab? What more? Rich indeed! Come, you must tell me! What else did he say when he told you I was rich?"

"N-n-nothing more, ma'am," I replied, startled and confused by her sudden vehemence. "Indeed, nothing more."

"Bab," said my aunt, bringing her hand down upon the table so heavily that the cups and saucers rang again, "Bab, that's false. If he told you I was rich, he told you how to get my money by and by. He told you to cringe, and fawn, and pay court to me—to worm yourself into my favor—to profit by my death—to be a liar, a flatterer, and a beggar! And why? Because I am rich! Oh, yes! because I am rich!"

I sat as if stricken into stone; but half comprehending what she meant, and unable to answer a syllable.

"Rich, indeed!" she went on, excited more

and more by her own words, and stalking to and fro between the window and the table, like one possessed. "Aha! we shall see! We shall see! Listen to me, child. I shall leave you nothing —not a farthing! Never expect it—never hope for it! If you are good, and true, and I like you, I shall be a friend to you while I live; but if you are mean, and false, and tell me lies, I shall despise you—do you hear? I shall despise you—send you home—never speak to you, or look at you again! Either way, you will get nothing by my death! Nothing—nothing—nothing!"

My heart swelled within me—I shook from head to foot—I tried to speak, and the words seemed to choke me.

"I don't want it!" I cried, passionately. "I—I am not mean! I have told no lies—not one!"

My aunt stopped short, and looked sternly down upon me, as if she would read-my very soul.

"Bab," said she, "do you mean to tell me that your father said nothing to you about why I may have asked you here, or what might come of it? Nothing? Not a word?"

"He said it might be for my good—he told Miss Whymper to make me courtesy and walk better, and come into a room properly—he said he wished me to please you. That was all! He never spoke of money, or of dying, or of telling lies—never!"

"Well, then, he meant it!" retorted my aunt, sharply. "He meant it!"

Flushed and trembling in my childish anger, I sprang from my chair and stood before her, face to face.

"He did not mean it!" I cried. "How dare you speak so of Papa? How dare——"

I could say no more, but, terrified at my own impetuosity, faltered, covered my face with both hands, and burst into an agony of sobs.

"Bab," said my aunt, in an altered voice, "little Bab!" and took me all at once in her two arms, and kissed me on the forehead.

My anger was gone in a moment. Something in her tone, in her kiss, in my own heart, called up a quick response; and, nestling close in her embrace, I wept passionately. Then she sat down, drew me on her knee, smoothed my hair with her hand, and comforted me as if I had been a little baby.

"So brave," said she, "so proud, so honest! Come, little Bab, you and I must be friends."

And we were friends, from that minute; for, from that minute, a mutual confidence and love sprang up between us. Too deeply moved to answer her in words, I only clung the closer, and tried to still my sobs. She understood me.

"Come," said she, after a few seconds of silence. "Let's go and see the pigs."

And with this she disengaged my arms from about her neck, set me down abruptly, and rang the bell.

"My pigs, Bab," said she, "are my hobby. I've a hundred of them out yonder, waiting to be fed. I always keep a hundred, and I see them fed myself, twice a day. Won't you like to go with me?"

"Oh! yes, ma'am, very much."

"Don't call me ma'am. I don't like it. Call me aunt. Jane, bring my boots and whip."

The whip was a short strong whip, with a leather thong, and the boots were the most amazing boots I ever saw. Jane brought them, quite as a matter of course, and my aunt put them on. They had iron heels, and soles half-an-inch thick, and reached, moreover, a long way above her ankles. They looked as though they might have been Wellingtons, originally, cut a trifle shorter, and opened down the fronts to admit of being buttoned. These on, my aunt proceeded to tie up the skirt of her dress all round, and completed her toilet by the addition of a huge green silk bonnet and vail, which hung on a peg in the hall.

"You see, Bab," said she, "I am a farmer. My property lies in farms. I cultivate this one, and I let the rest. I attend to my business myself; and as I never do any thing by halves, I buy, sell, go to market, keep my own books, and trust to nobody's eyes but my own. Some folks laugh about it; but I let them laugh, and wish them better amusement. This is my orchard, and yonder is the stack-yard; but we are not going there just now. The pigs are waiting."

Saying which, my aunt led the way across a broad grassy space, where the turkeys were strutting along with their heads in the air, and the hens were cackling about with broods of little yellow chickens at their heels, and the fruit trees made a green shade overhead. I could have staid in this delightful place for hours; but my aunt took me through a little gate to the left, and across a yard where a boy was chopping wood, and then through another gate into another yard which was littered all over with straw, and built round with neat brick sties, and as full of pigs as ever it could hold.

"There they are!" said she, with grim satisfaction. "There they are!"

There they were, indeed—pigs of all sizes, ages, and tempers. Black pigs, white pigs, spotted pigs, little pigs, big pigs, fat pigs, lean pigs, pigs with curly tails, and pigs with no tails at all. Quiet enough till we came into the yard, they no sooner beheld my aunt's green bonnet than they broke into the most appalling chorus imaginable, and came rushing up to us with an alacrity that soon brought the whip into service, and sent some of them shrieking away. But to see them fed was the great sight—to watch the perpetual replenishment of the great round troughs; the circles of tails, uplifted and quivering with excitement; the playful disturbances that broke out now and then among the younger members of the company, and the friendly bites, flights and scuffles that diversified the graver interests of the performance.

Meanwhile, my aunt stalked about with her whip in her hand; inspected the condition of the sties, and the quality of the food; rated the farm servants; discussed the question of bean-meal and pea-meal; gave orders that one youthful family should have their noses ringed; condemned two hapless porkers of middle growth to solitary confinement; and ended by taking me round to visit a very fierce dowager in an adjoining yard, who had the evening before presented society with no less than fifteen little ones, as black as jet, and not much bigger than kittens.

Having dismissed the pigs, we went into the stables and then round to the bullock yard; and, after that, went a long way off to a clover-field lying on the slope of a hill, where we saw the sheep and the little white lambs all feeding and gamboling about, to the number of three hundred and more. And throughout all this ramble, my aunt's vigilant eyes were on every thing and every body. Nothing escaped her; and not a servant on all the land but started into activity at her approach, and seemed to regard her not only with respect, but with some degree of terror.

At twelve o'clock we came home to lunch; at four we dined; and after dinner, my aunt put the *Times* into my hands, and desired me to read the debates while she sat and knitted in her easy chair. It was not amusing, but I acquitted myself creditably, and was praised for my enunciation. Having had tea at seven, we strolled about the gardens and orchard till nearly nine; and then I was sent to bed. Such was my first day at Stoneycroft Hall; and such was every day for weeks and months after. Sometimes we spent an evening at the parsonage—sometimes the vicar or the doctor dropped in to tea; but, with these slight variations, the programme remained unaltered. After a few weeks, my aunt taught me the leading rules of whist, and we played at double-dummy regularly for an hour after tea. It was a quiet life, but a very happy one—all the happier for its monotony, and all the pleasanter for its seclusion. The calm, the good air, the early hours, and all the circumstances of the change, seemed to strengthen and improve me. Every sight and sound of farm-yard or field delighted me. Every hour was a holiday—every breath enjoyment. Cured of my solitary habits, I grew daily more fresh and childlike, and more accessible to pleasant influences. To be released from Miss Whymper's government and my sisters' petty tyranny was much; but to live amongst green trees and kindly faces was even more. Day by day, my aunt and I became better acquainted—day by day I loved her and the old house, and all the surroundings of the place; more and more dearly. And this reminds me that I have not yet described Stoneycroft Hall.

Why it should ever have been called Stoneycroft Hall was altogether a mystery. A more inappropriate name could scarcely have been found for it, since it was justified by no trace of barrenness, by no poverty of soil, by no fragment of rock or boulder anywhere about. On the contrary, it would have been difficult to find in all the county a district more productive, or more highly cultivated. The great heaths, it is true, were in the neighborhood—vast sweeps of undulating moorland many miles in length, which traversed twelve or fourteen parishes, and ended at last upon that wave-worn coast where the tides of the German ocean ebb and flow between England and the shores of Holland. But these heaths lay at a considerable distance, and were not within sight from even our uppermost windows. They might have been a hundred miles away, for any show of waste land thereabout, and could scarcely have influenced the naming of Stoneycroft Hall.

It was a fine old Elizabethan homestead, and, in spite of its hard name, the very type of an ample, hospitable English dwelling. A little formal pencil sketch which I made of the place a few days after my first arrival, lies before me as I write. Meagre and childlike though it be, it yet brings back every quaint carving, every curved gable, twisted chimney, and fantastic weather-cock, as vividly as though they were the impressions of yesterday. There is the dear old porch with its environment of red and amber roses—there the window of my great formal bed-chamber—there the garret whither I so often stole away with my pencil and my books, and, from its narrow casement, watched the harmless lightnings of the summer dusk. Far and away, all round the house, studded by farm-buildings, varied by slopes and hollows, relieved by patches of brown fallow and tracts of radiant green, lay the pleasant Suffolk landscape. Our garden-gate opened on the highway—the church-spire peeped above the pollard-oaks close by—the pond stood in a grassy angle a few yards down the road. To the left (sheltered by a group of picturesque old trees, with knotted roots, and weird, wild-looking branches), lay the great pond, where the cattle were driven in to the water every evening, and many a traveler staid his horse to drink. To the right, we were inclosed by the stacks and out-houses. To the westward, skirting a ridge of rising-ground and filling the valley beyond with rich masses of rounded foliage, extended the park and preserves of Broomhill; while, farther away, in the midst of a stretch of open country, a bare gaunt poplar, with its lower branches lopped and only a few stray leaves left fluttering at the top, started up to an unusual hight, and served as one of the landmarks of the place. Concealed amid the plantations behind it, nestled a small white building, known as the Poplar Farm.

Such was the house, and such the neighborhood in which my aunt resided. It was no unusual scene. It would have interested the painter less than the agriculturist, and by many, perhaps, have been deemed but a tame specimen of even so tame a county as Suffolk. But I loved it. It possessed for me, at that impressionable age, a novelty and a charm beyond the power of words to utter. I studied it with a painter's instinct under every aspect of the year and all the moods of nature. Every thatched roof, every column of blue smoke, every lane, and drift, and hedgerow, contributed its own share of interest to the landscape. To watch the sunset burning through the boughs of the park trees, or the moonlight setting them in bronzed relief against the placid sky; to linger in the meadows till the very bursting of the purple storm-cloud; to lie at the foot of some far-spreading oak, and gaze up through the shifting leaves at the blue sky above; or on a summer's morning, to watch the waving wheat and rippling barley—these were among my keenest enjoyments. The good which they worked, and the tastes which they assisted to develop, have remained with me ever since. Familiar with every school of beauty, with scenes consecrated in song and associated with history, I can yet turn to the contemplation of this homely English pastoral with a freshness of admiration that never fades, and a love that knows no change.

CHAPTER V.

BROOMHILL AND ITS OWNERS.

"MARK yon old mansion frowning through the trees."
ROGERS.

ABOUT a mile to the east of Stoneycroft Hall, lay the park, mansion, and domains known collectively as Broomhill. The estate took its name from a picturesque sand-crag which rose to a considerable height at the back of the house and was all overgrown with furze and wavy ferns. The park, without being extensive, was finely situated; possessed some natural advantages; was broken up into dells and slopes, relieved by occasional gleams of water, and interspersed with oaks and cedars that were said to have been saplings in the reign of Elizabeth. Beyond the park lay a long line of plantations, and a tract of undulating common that reached away for more than three miles in the direction of Normanbridge. Normanbridge, be it observed, was the nearest market-town.

Antique, irregular, moated, and surmounted by a forest of quaint chimneys, the Hall at Broomhill was altogether a composite piece of architecture. It lay low in a warm hollow, surrounded by foliage and sheltered from all the winds of heaven. Begun about the year 1496, and carried on from century to century with such deviations from the original design as each successive owner was pleased to make, it could not be said to belong to any special order of architecture, but was a mixture of many. The octagonal tower, the bell-turret, and the whole of the east front, dated from the time of the early Tudors. The north wing, with its unsightly pediment and awkward Corinthian pilasters, was erected during the reign of James I., and designed by Inigo Jones. The courtyard, stone gateway, and offices were specimens of the worst Renaissance school; and the lodges were rustic Italian. If there ever was a plan, it had been abandoned and forgotten since the completion of the earliest part of the building. Indeed, it almost seemed as if the masters of Broomhill had striven, each in the fashion of his day, to encumber the old place with just whatever novelty was least in harmony with all that had gone before. Still it was as interesting a specimen of domestic architecture as one would wish to find; picturesque by reason of its very incongruity; and, in the fullest sense of the word, historic.

Conferred in fief upon some remote ancestor of the time of the Norman Kings, this estate had remained in the hands of his descendants for long centuries before a stone of the present edifice was laid. Given to a Farquhar, a Farquhar had held it ever since. There had never been a title in the family, and they prided themselves upon it. Independent Esquires, they had uniformly declined the lesser honors of nobility, and would not exchange the name and style of Farquhar of Broomhill for any rank below the peerage. They were not rich; but their descent was pure, and their honor unblemished. A Farquhar, followed by his fifty lances, fought with distinction in the third crusade under Richard Cœur de Lion, and was present at the siege of Acre. A Farquhar of the sixteenth century held a command under Sir Francis Drake, and was not only one

of the few among that gallant crew who returned to tell of a voyage round the world, but even bore a share in the pursuit of the Spanish Armada. The second Charles, in his long exile, had few adherents more faithful than one James Farquhar of Broomhill, who mortgaged his lands and melted his plate for the king's service, and was afterward rewarded with a captaincy in his majesty's new regiment of Coldstream Guards. True to the line of the Stuarts, a Farquhar was one of the first to follow the fortunes of the Pretender, and one of the last to abandon them. Later still, two of the house, father and son, fought for Charles Edward on the fatal field of Culloden, and fell side by side, just as his officers forced the prince away. Having by these means narrowly escaped the forfeiture of their estates, the Farquhar family lived henceforth in strict retirement, mingling but little in political or military questions, and, for the most part, devoting their attention to agricultural pursuits. To improve, to build, to cultivate, to purchase, had now been for more than three quarters of a century the pride and pleasure of the masters of Broomhill. Profiting by the economy of seclusion, they had added more than one farm to the heritage of their Norman predecessors, enlarged their preserves, and extended the boundaries of their park whenever the sale of adjacent lands enabled them to do so. How they had contended with my great grandfather for the purchase of Stoneycroft Hall; and how being defeated, they had ever since looked with a jealous eye upon those rich six hundred acres which would have added so materially to the value and importance of their own estates, was a story which my aunt delighted to relate. Somehow or another she disliked the Farquhar family. Not a deed that they had done, not an honor that they had achieved, found favor in her sight. To all that concerned them she was rootedly antagonistic; and there was not one of the name, from its earliest to its latest representative, of whom she could speak without prejudice. In all parish or county matters, she opposed their views on principle; and at election times it needed but the interest of a Farquhar in one scale to throw all the weight of her influence into the other. Thus, because they were Tories and advocated Church and State principles, my aunt inclined to Liberal views, and was hard upon Parliamentary Bishops; while, for no other reason than the devotion of their ancestors to the cause of the Stuarts, her hero of heroes was of course the Prince of Orange.

"The Farquhars, indeed!" she used testily to exclaim. "Don't speak to me of the Farquhars! I'm tired of hearing about their musty ancestors, and their Jacobite nonsense, and their trumpery pride. There hasn't been an ounce of brains in the family these two hundred years, Bab, and that's all about it. The old man was a fool—the last man was a fool—and the present man is a fool, or mad. Mad, I think. Mad as a March hare, Bab; and you may take my word for it!"

I did not take her word for it, however, but, having heard various opinions on the subject, entertained quite other views with respect to the sanity and capacity of the present master of Broomhill.

B

Hugh Farquhar happened to be abroad, making what was then called the "grand tour," when his father's sudden death left him without any close tie or near relation in the world. The news reached him at Genoa, and, to the amazement of all the parish, failed to bring him home. Instead of posting back to England, he took ship for the East, and had remained absent ever since. The house was shut up; the park gates were closed; the servants paid off or pensioned, according to their age and services. A housekeeper and one or two maids were left in charge of the mansion. A single gardener kept the walks and pastures from desolation. Year after year thus went by. Grass grew in the spacious avenues, and stonecrop along the coping of the garden walls. Birds built in the clustered chimneys whence no smoke issued. Rust gathered on the hinges of gates which were never opened except to the lawyer or the steward. Still the lord of Broomhill showed no care to revisit the home of his fathers; and, at the time when I first became an inmate of Stoneycroft Hall, his voluntary exile had lasted for nearly five years.

Tales of recklessness and profusion, of wild adventure, and of travels extended far beyond the beaten routes, were told of him throughout the county. That he had been heard of in Grand Cairo, and seen in Jerusalem — that he had boated up the Nile, and cut his name on the summit of the great Pyramid—that he had turned Mohammedan—that he had married a Persian princess with her own weight in gold and jewels for her dower—that he had fraternized with some savage Tartar tribe, and was living, a chieftain among chieftains, somewhere in Thibet — that, like Lord Byron, he had taken arms in the Greek cause; and that, like Lady Hester Stanhope, he had become a dweller in Arabian tents, were among the least improbable of these reports. How eagerly I listened to rumors which possessed for me more than the fascination of romance; how, in my childish way, I associated his name with those of my favorite heroes; how I compared him with Sinbad and Don Quixote, Tom Jones, Prince Camaralzaman and Robinson Crusoe, needs scarcely to be told here. Enough that Farquhar of Broomhill became my ideal of a *preux chevalier*, and that none of my aunt's sarcasms weighed with me for a moment. Indeed, I believe that the more he was maligned, the more I admired him; which added to the romance and made it nicer than ever. Nothing at this time gave me more delight than to scrawl imaginary portraits of him in the fly-leaves of my story books; or, more ambitious still, to cover whole sheets of foolscap with cartoons which represented him in the most bewitching fancy dresses, and the most stupendous situations, struggling with tigers, overcoming crocodiles, rescuing distressed princesses, putting whole tribes of Indians to flight, and otherwise conducting himself in a gallant and satisfactory manner.

Of all this, however, I was careful to let my aunt suspect nothing. She would surely have laughed at me, and I was keenly sensitive to ridicule. So I cherished my romance in secret; feeding my eager fancy with invention, and, from day to day, weaving fresh incidents upon the glowing tapestry of my dreams.

CHAPTER VI.

DOCTOR TOPHAM AND PAUL VERONESE.

"MORNING, Mrs. Sandyshaft," said Doctor Topham. drawing rein at our garden-gate and nodding to my aunt, who was pacing up and down the middle path with her hands behind her back, and the green bonnet inverted over her eyes like a flower-pot. "Famous weather for the crops—bad for the markets. Glass going up—prices going down. Always two sides to a question. Nobody ever satisfied—farmers especially. Eh, Mrs. S. ?"

Now Doctor Topham was my aunt's near friend and neighbor. He never agreed with her upon any subject whatever, and they seldom met but they quarreled; wherefore, apparently, they only liked each other the better. Incompatibility of taste and temper formed, indeed, the bond of their regard, and aggravation was the salt of their intercourse. Doctor Topham was sallow and saturnine, had long legs and a short pony, and rode with an umbrella.

"Humph! You'd better let farmers and farming alone," replied my aunt, testily. "Talk of something you understand, if only for variety."

"Can't make you my topic, then, Mrs. S.," retorted the doctor.

"I take it," said my aunt, "as no honor to be beyond *your* comprehension."

Whereupon the doctor scratched his ear, and, having no repartee at hand, changed the subject.

"Have you heard that story about Hugh Farquhar and the Paul Veronese ?" asked he.

"Yes. Is it true ?"

"I fear so."

"Hah—and a genuine picture ?"

"So they say; but old masters are dangerous folks to meddle with. No article going in the choice of which a man may be so cheated as a picture—or a wife."

"And worth six thousand pounds, too !" ejaculated my aunt, unmindful of this satire on her sex.

"Value is one thing and price another, Mrs. S.," said the doctor, drily. "Six thousand were paid for it. Randall told me so."

"Extravagant fool ! Picked it up somewhere in Venice, did he not ?"

"I believe so."

"Six thousand pounds for a picture ! Tut, tut ! We shall have Broomhill come to the hammer some day, at this rate ! The man's mad. I always said he was mad. Six thousand pounds for a picture ! Why, bless my soul, doctor, he could have bought the Bosmere property for that price !"

"And not have done so well, perhaps, after all," said Doctor Topham, differing for the mere sake of contradiction. "Travelers see strange things, and sometimes do wise ones by mistake. It's just possible that Farquhar may have given six thousand for an article worth twelve."

"Doctor," said my aunt, emphatically, "you're a greater idiot than I supposed."

"Much obliged, Mrs. S. Happy to return the compliment."

"And ought, at your time of life, to know better."

"My dear Madam, I'm a boy—seven years younger than yourself."

My aunt laughed a short dry laugh like a double knock.

"You'd give your head," said she, "to have the last word. Well—to return to the Paul Veronese. Will he send it to Broomhill, think you?"

"Send it! Why, it arrived yesterday! I met the procession myself, wagon, packing-case, Randall and all. That's how I come to know so much about it."

"And the subject?"

"Deal boards, Mrs. S.," said the doctor, with a grin, "are not generally transparent; and my eyes, however piercing, are not gimlets. Still, as far as size goes, I can relieve your mind. Our friend seems to have got plenty for his money."

"So! a large picture?"

"A quarter of an acre of it, I should say—high art, at so much per cubic foot."

My aunt shrugged her shoulders. The doctor looked at his watch.

"Mrs. Sandyshaft," said he, "I have a consultation at eleven, and you have made me lose ten minutes. By the way, you know the sad fate of poor Saunders?"

"Saunders? No—what of him?"

"It's all over with him."

"Over with him—mercy alive! is the man dead?"

"Worse, Mrs. S. MARRIED!"

And with this Dr. Topham drew up his knees, put spurs to the pony, and trotted away at a round pace, with his umbrella over his head, and his feet dangling about eight inches from the ground. My aunt looked after him, indulged in another double knock laugh, and presently resumed her walk. I could contain my curiosity no longer.

"Aunt," said I eagerly—"aunt, what is a Paul Veronese?"

Pacing to and fro, with her hands behind her back and her eyes fixed on the ground, Mrs. Sandyshaft neither heard nor replied. I plucked her by the sleeve, and repeated the question.

"Aunt, if you please—what is a Paul Veronese?"

"Bab, don't bother. I'm counting."

Used to these rebuffs, I drew back and waited quietly. Presently she looked up, met my asking eyes, and halted abruptly.

"Well, child," said she, "what is it?"

I repeated my inquiry for the third time. My aunt frowned and shook her head.

"I'll tell you what it is, Bab," said she, testily, "you ask too many questions. My life's a perpetual catechism: and for every breath you draw, one might write a note of interrogation. I won't stand it any longer. There's an Encyclopedia in the house—twenty-two volumes of it —and henceforth, when you want to know any thing, read it for yourself. Paul Veronese, indeed! Look for him under V, and there you'll find him."

Delighted to be made free of the locked-up book-case, I ran off, key in hand, and spent the rest of that morning poring over dusty quartos. I looked under V without success; but at length, after some trouble, found, under the head of Cagliari, all that I desired to know. Found that while this great artist was yet a youth, his competitors had themselves decreed him a prize for

which they were all contending—that in his maturity he created a school of art, and was the associate of ambassadors and kings—that whole churches and palaces had been enriched by his brush—that in life he achieved honors, and in death immortality. Brief and meager as it was, this biography made a profound impression upon me. It came to me like a revelation, and dazzled me with vague dreams of art-life and the splendor of the medieval painters. Allusions and references in the one article led me to the discovery of others, and the lives of Leonardo da Vinci, Titian, Rubens, and Vandyke were in turn eagerly devoured. Never having seen a really fine painting, my notions were perforce childish and confused, and the vocabulary of criticism puzzled me like Greek. I could not conceive the meaning of such words as "tone," "breadth," "chiaroscuro," and the like ; and my aunt was unable to help me.

"Don't ask me, Bab," she used to say. "I know more of pigs than pictures; and as for that art-jargon, I believe it's humbug—every word of it!"

For all this, however, I read, believed, and dreamed on. To be a painter became the single ambition of my soul; and a restless desire to behold Mr. Farquhar's Paul Veronese pursued me night and day.

CHAPTER VII.

MY GREAT ADVENTURE.

"WHO ever loved that loved not at first sight?"
MARLOWE.

BOLT upright, my aunt sat at her desk, writing; whilst I, waiting for the note, played with the dogs, and looked out the window.

"You'll see Dr. Topham, if he is at home, Bab," said my aunt, without looking up.

"Yes, aunt."

"And bring back an answer."

"Yes, aunt."

"And take the path over the fields. It's much the nearest."

"Nearer than the park, aunt?"

"Bless me! yes. Half a mile at least."

I sighed and was silent, while my aunt signed, sealed, and addressed her letter. Having done this, she beckoned me to her side, looked straight into my eyes, and said—

"Bab, if I were you I'd build myself a hut in Broomhill park, and live there, like Robinson Crusoe."

I felt myself blush up to the roots of my hair ; but made no reply.

"Wherever I send you, you contrive to make your way lie through the park. When you take a walk, it is always through the park. You haunt the park. To my knowledge you've been there every day for the last fortnight or three weeks. What's the meaning of it?"

I looked down; stammered ; had not a word to say. It was true that I had hovered about the place of late; but I had no courage for confession. How could I confide to her the wayward fancies of my idle hours? How acknowledge the "restless unsatisfied longing" that drew me daily to look from afar upon the walls which encompassed a Paul Veronese? Whether she guessed something of the truth, or thought me merely odd and unaccountable, I can not determine; but she took pity, at all events, on my confusion, and forebore to question me further. She looked at her watch, and gave me the letter. —"It's now nearly five o'clock," said she,. "and, by the fields, you have a mile to walk. I give you half an hour to go, half an hour to return, and half an hour for delays. It is quite far enough for you, and quite time enough; and if you are not punctual, I shall conclude that you have disobeyed me, and gone round by the park. Now go."

Thankful to be dismissed, I bounded across the hall and the garden, and was out of sight in a moment.

It was now August, and the sultry sun blazed fiercely, bending westward. There were reapers reaping wearily in the hot fields as I went by, and gleaners, footsore and dusty, resting under trees. Not a breath stirred. Not a cloud sailed. The hardened clods and languid grass looked parched and thirsty, and the very birds sang fitfully, as if pining for a shower. As for me, I delighted in the heat and bared my head to the sun, like a little Salamander; and danced on, rejoicing.

When I arrived at his house, Dr. Topham was out, and not likely to be back before dark. The servant would have had me rest awhile; but I looked up wistfully at the old clock in the hall, found that only twenty-five minutes of my allotted time were gone, and so left the note, and took my way slowly homeward. Only twenty-five minutes out of an hour and a half! To the right lay the fields—to the left, the stile and footpath leading to Broomhill. Supposing that I took the latter, it would be but half a mile added to my walk; and, after all, it was not the distance to which my aunt objected, but the delay. Granted that I reached home even now before the time, how could she be angry with me? Still hesitating, I lingered where the roads divided, and argued thus with my conscience. To convince ourselves according to our inclinations is not difficult. The debate was soon carried in my own favor; the stile soon crossed; the park soon gained.

And what a park it was! Putting Paul Veronese out of the question, it was the pleasantest spot in all our neighborhood. I loved nothing better than to lie under the shade of the gnarled oaks, and watch the deer browsing in herds along the grassy vistas round about. This afternoon the place seemed more sylvan than ever. The atmosphere, which all day had been dense with heat, was now traversed by currents of cool air, and fragrant with sweet scents. The hush that precedes the sunset had fallen upon every leaf, wild-flower, and blade of grass. Far away, distinct though dulled by distance, echoed the steady strokes of the woodman's axe; and, nearer, a party of disputatious rooks stalked gravely to and fro, and then rose, cawing, into the air.

Strolling idly on, and pausing every now and then to listen to the silence, I came to a point where the paths again divided. One led over the slopes where the horned oxen were feeding by scores, and opened out on the high road— the other was a right of way passing straight through the yards, and skirting the private gardens of the mansion. My horror of the cat-

tle decided me in favor of the latter, and I went on. On through the "checkered shade" that fell between the trees—on, past the two great cedars, and under the archway with its sculptured shield and motto overhead—on, past the coach-houses and stable-doors, and under the very windows of the Tudor gallery at the back of the house. Naturally a shy child, I hurried along as fast as my feet would carry me; dreading lest I should meet any of the servants, or see a face looking at me from some upper casement. Once past the iron gate, once clear of the yards and offices, I paused to take breath.

Before me stretched a fresh expanse of trees and slopes, bounded by a line of park-palings. To my right, inclosed by a high wall above which I could just see the tops of the pear-trees, lay the fruit and vegetable-gardens. To my left, half in light and half in shadow, stood the grand old house, with the red sunset burning on its panes, like "patines of bright gold." Brightest and nearest of all, blazed the great stained glass windows at the end of the Tudor wing; and strangely cool and calm, looked, by comparison, the narrow space of formal lawn in front. It was a little strip railed off from the park by a wire fence, and entered by a small gate that had been left partly open. An air of great quiet pervaded the place. A tiny fountain bubbled from a grassy mound in the midst, and a sun-dial on a time-stained pedestal stood before the window. Not a door banged—not a voice echoed—not a footstep crossed either courtyard or garden. It might have been an enchanted palace, with a spell-bound princess dreaming out her hundred years of sleep somewhere in the silence of those upper rooms, for any sign of life that one could see! Awed by the solitude and the hour, I held my breath, and wondered if the servants ever ventured among those suites and corridors above, and how they felt at night when it grew dusk.

And then I noticed for the first time that the shutters of the great bay window were unfastened, and stood some inches apart. Perhaps that very room held the Paul Veronese!

Struck, as it were, by a conviction, I hesitated; cast a hasty glance all around; and darted through the little open gate! To climb up by the aid of a honey-suckle, perch myself on the broad stone ledge, and press my face close against the glass, was the work of a moment. I had been out so long in the broad sunlight that for many minutes I could distinguish nothing. Then one object after another became visible through the gloom, and I found, to my disappointment, that I was peering into the library. Books, books, books—everywhere books! Books by hundreds, lining the walls, littering the tables, and piled in great heaps on the floor. The room, apparently, was being cleaned, or regulated. I gazed for a long time very earnestly, turned away presently with a sigh, and exclaiming—"Then it is not there, after all!"—swung myself down upon the lawn.

"What is not there?" said a voice close beside me.

Blinded by the change from dark to light, I could only see a tall figure standing between me and the setting sun.

'"What is not there? What are you looking for? Who are you?" asked the stranger, laying his hand upon my shoulder. "Why, what a frightened little trespasser it is!"

Frightened indeed! frightened almost out of my senses. Daring neither to look up nor speak, and feeling as though that touch had power to weigh me to the ground! He pitied my distress; for when he spoke again his voice was grave and sweet, like the deep notes of an organ.

"Fear nothing, my child," he said. "I am not angry with you. Come, speak—tell me why you were looking through that window?"

And still he kept his hand upon my shoulder —somewhat firmly, too, as if he thought I should presently dart away and escape him.

"So! still dumb? Nay, you will at least tell me your name?"

I faintly stammered—"Barbara."

"Barbara!" repeated the stranger musingly. 'A quaint old name! 'My mother had a maid called—Barbara!' Let me see—who says that? Desdemona?"

"I—I don't know, sir," said I, gaining confidence; but wondering at the question.

He smiled, put his hand under my chin, and turned my face to the light.

"I should think not, indeed!" replied he. "What should a little girl like you know about Shakspeare?"

"I have read of him," said I, stoutly. "He was a poet, and wrote plays."

"Per Bacco! A learned Barbara! A Barbara versed in the poets! Come, petite, you have a surname, surely—what is it?"

Uncomfortably conscious of something like irony in the stranger's manner, I hesitated and looked down.

"My other name is Churchill," I replied, after a minute.

"Churchill—Barbara Churchill! Good names both! They go 'tripplingly on the tongue,' and are pleasant to pronounce. There's something in a name, after all. Churchill is historical, too!"

And my new acquaintance, whose observation seemed like spoken thoughts and were scarcely addressed to me at all, began humming the old tune of—

"Marlbrook s'en va't en guerre!"

"The Duke of Marlborough was an ancestor of Papa's," said I, with great dignity. "We have ever so many lives of him at home."

"By Jove, now, this is wonderful!" exclaimed the stranger, laughing, and looking at me more attentively. "She's positively a genealogical Barbara!"

"Oh, we have the genealogy, too," said I eagerly. "It hangs in Papa's room. I have often looked at it—there's a great tree coming out of a man's body, and the apples all have names on them."

He looked at me again, and put his hand to his forehead.

"'Tis strange," he murmured, "but I—I don't remember any Churchills hereabout. Where does your father live, Barbara? In Ipswich?"

"Oh, dear, no! In London."

"So — so. Not a Suffolk family at all! I thought I could scarcely have forgotten that name. Who are you staying with, little one? The Grants of Bosmere?"

"I am staying with my great-aunt," said I, "at Stoneycroft Hall."

Having an immense idea of her social position, I announced this fact with quite a grand air, and expected to see it produce a wonderful effect. But the stranger only burst into a hearty laugh, and repeated my aunt's name over and over again, as if the very sound of it amused him.

"What, Mrs. Sandyshaft!" he cried. "Is she your great-aunt? Mrs. Sandyshaft of the hall! Mrs. Sandyshaft of the hundred pigs! Does she still keep a hundred pigs, Barbara?"

"Of course she does," replied I, half-affronted.

He laughed again — then became suddenly grave, and walked to and fro between the sun-dial and the gate for some minutes; lost, apparently, in thought.

"You have not yet told me what you were doing at the library-window," he said, stopping abruptly, and taking me again by the shoulder.

I felt the color rush to my face; but replied with tolerable self-possession that I was only "looking in."

"Yes; but what were you looking in for?"

"N — n — nothing at all," said I reluctantly.

"Non è vero, Barbara! You were looking for something. I heard you say 'it is not there, after all!' Come — I must know all about it, or I will take you home to your aunt and tell her you were trespassing!"

I knew he did not mean that; and I felt sure, somehow, that it would be best to confess at once. Besides, I was no longer afraid of him.

"I thought the picture might be there," I said hesitatingly. "I — I so wanted to see it?"

"Picture?" repeated the stranger, hastily. "What picture?"

"Oh, a beautiful, wonderful picture by Paul Veronese!"

"Paul Veronese!"

"Yes — did you never hear of him? He was a painter — a great painter, and he died a long, long time ago, somewhere in Italy," said I, with childish volubility. "I have read all about him in a book at home, and there's a picture of his somewhere in this house — a picture worth thousands of pounds!"

"And this picture you wish to see?"

"I have wished for nothing else, ever since Dr. Topham talked about it!"

"Humph! And pray what had Dr. Topham to say on the subject?"

"Nothing — except that Mr. Farquhar had bought it, and it was here."

"And Mrs. Sandyshaft — what did she say?"

"Oh, she said that Mr. Farquhar was an extravagant fool, and as mad as a March hare!"

The stranger laughed again; but with a dark flush on his cheek, as if the source of his amusement were scarcely a pleasant one.

"Not a very flattering verdict, upon my word?" said he. "Instructive, however, if taken as the measure of public opinion. 'A plague upon opinion! a man may wear it on both sides, like a leather jerkin.' 'Tis well for Hugh Farquhar that his hearing is duller than that of Signor Heimdale, of celestial memory!"

"Heimdale!" I exclaimed. "Who was he?"

"Heimdale, my dear little Barbara," said the stranger, "was a very respectable personage. He acted as watchman and light porter to the

Scandinavian Gods; and his ears were so inconveniently acute that he could hear the grass grow in the meadows, and the wool on the backs of the sheep."

It was now my turn to laugh.

"That's a fairy tale?" cried I. "What comes next?"

"More than I can tell you now," replied he, looking at his watch. "*Vediamo* — it is but seven minutes past six, and we shall have good daylight for more than an hour. Time enough, *petite*, for you to see the picture."

"The — the picture?" I faltered, incredulously.

He nodded, took me by the hand, and led me round to a low gothic door at the foot of an ivy-grown octagonal turret, facing the moat.

A tiny key, produced from his waistcoat pocket, admitted us into a small passage, which, so soon as the door was closed, became profoundly dark. He then took my hand again; warned me of some three or four stone steps, up which we felt our way cautiously; pushed aside a heavy curtain that seemed all at once to bar our farther progress; and led me into a bright eight-sided room, lined with books, fragrant with fresh flowers, and flooded with the glory of the descending sun. One large window with a rich heraldic bordering of stained glass, overlooked a broad sweep of park and open country; an elaborate bronze lamp swung by a triple chain from the middle of the ceiling; some three or four curious busts of Roman emperors and poets, done in colored marbles, occupied brackets over the chimney-piece and bookshelves. Something scholastic, something elegant and indolent, was expressed in every trifle about the chamber, from that luxurious piece of furniture which comprised reading-desk, reading-lamp, and easy-chair in one, down to the antique chased ink-stand on the table, and the delicate curiosities in porcelain and terra-cotta which crowded the mantle-piece.

"Oh, what a beautiful room!" I exclaimed, when my first surprise had somewhat abated.

"'Tis my study, Barbara," replied my new friend.

A strange suspicion for the first time flashed across my mind.

"*Yours?*" I echoed.

"Yes, I am Hugh Farquhar," said he; and rang the bell.

Hugh Farquhar! My hero, my Sindbad, my Prince Camaralzaman! Hugh Farquhar of whom I had heard so much and dreamed so much; whose rumored travels I had so often tracked upon old maps, and whose adventures I had illustrated upon foolscap without end! All the stories that had ever been told of him, and all the censure that idle tongues had passed upon him, came back in an instant to my memory — and then I recollected the speech that I had myself repeated, and, covered with confusion, knew not where to look.

"Well, *petite*," said he, after a brief pause, "now that you know who I am, have you nothing to say to me? Or, because I am as mad as a March hare, are you afraid of me?"

Afraid of him! Why I felt as if I had known him for years already. I did not dare, however, to say so; but, looking up, saw such a world of kindly merriment sparkling in his eyes, that

I smiled, and shook my head, and said quite confidently : —

"Not a bit."

"So much the better; for I have a mind, Barbara, that you and I should be good friends. Tippoo, desire the servants to unclose the shutters in the long gallery, and let the packing-case be sent for. I am going to have that packing-case opened."

"Yes, Sahib," said a low voice close behind me.

I turned somewhat nervously, and found a slender olive-colored man in a plain black suit and white neckcloth, with gold rings in his ears, standing at my elbow.

"And bring chisels and hammers, Tippoo; and be as quick as possible, for the daylight is going."

Tippoo bent his head; glided like a shadow to the door; and left the room as noiselessly as he had entered it. He had shown no surprise at my presence — he had not even seemed to see me. His glittering black-eyes had rested only on his master's face, and he moved like an automaton, obedient only to his master's will.

"Tippoo is my Hindoo servant," said Mr. Farquhar, explanatorily. "I brought him from Benares. He saved my life once, at the risk of his own, and we have never parted since."

"Saved your life?" I · exclaimed eagerly. "How? From a lion, or a tiger?"

"No, from the bite of a snake. But I will tell you all about that some other time, Barbara —let us now see after the Paul Veronese. I have not looked upon it myself since the day I bought it!"

And with this he took me away from the study in the turret, through some dreary rooms filled with sheeted furniture and out upon a spacious staircase hung with gloomy old paintings and broad enough for ten persons marching abreast. At the foot of this staircase we came upon a man with a basket of tools, who pulled off his cap respectfully, and stood aside to let us pass. Then Mr. Farquhar opened one half o. an oaken door, and I found myself in a long gallery lighted on one side by a row of windows, and closely hung with pictures on the other. The floor was laid down with matting; a large table covered with a dusty sheet was the only article of furniture in sight; and a huge deal packing-case, propped up at the back by wooden supports, stood in the very center of the room. Two women-servants who were busy opening the shutters when we came in, looked at me with unconcealed amazement.

"This, Barbara," said Mr. Farquhar, "is the picture-gallery. The pictures are mostly portraits, as you see. I could tell you lots of stories about these grim old ladies and gentlemen; but those will keep for some other occasion. Now, gardener—now Tippoo, we want this lid off. Here, give me a chisel, and let's see how quick we can be!"

And with this he snatched a tool from the basket, and set to work as actively as either of his servants. I stood by breathlessly and watched the process, counting nail after nail as it fell to the ground, and watching plank after plank as it was removed and laid aside. When the last was withdrawn, and only a covering of green baize intervened between me and the object of my desires, I turned cold and trembled.

"Now stand aside, all of you," said the master of the house, himself somewhat flushed and excited. "*Petite*, come forward to the angle of that window, and you will get the best light on it. So—there it is, safe and uninjured—my Paul Veronese!"

. He had plucked the baize away, and now came and stood beside me, contemplating his purchase. He was, at first, so absorbed in the pleasure of looking upon it, that he forgot to observe me. He advanced; he retreated; he shaded his eyes with his hands; he moved from right to left, from left to right, and exclaimed impatiently against the fading daylight.

As for me—how shall I confess it?—my first impression was—disappointment.

I had expected too much. I had expected, I know not what; but something, at all events, surpassing all the glow and glory of nature herself. The Paul Veronese of my dreams was an immortal vision — a resplendent mystery—a pageant of heroic forms more than half divine, and adorned in colors transcending the gold and purple of the eastern sky. The Paul Veronese of my awaking was, on the contrary, darkened and deepened by time; majestic, but somber; and flawed all over with those minute cracks, which are like wrinkles on the brow of ancient art. An aged man, robed and crowned, stood nearly in the centre of the picture surrounded by senators and nobles in dresses of ceremony, four of whom held a canopy above his head. At his feet knelt ambassadors with gifts, and in the distance lay the towers and cupolas of a great city, and a sea thronged with galleys. It was grand, but cold. It appealed neither to my imagination nor my sympathies, and even in point of color fell woefully short of my ideal.

Struck by my silence, Mr. Farquhar turned at length, and looked at me.

"Well, little one," said he. "What of the picture?"

I knew not how to reply.

"Does it equal your expectations?"

It needed some courage to confess the truth; but I contrived to stammer out a reluctant negative. He looked surprised, annoyed, disappointed. He frowned; glanced from me to the picture, and from the picture back to me; sighed impatiently, and said aloud:—

"Of course not—I was a fool to expect it! What should the poor child know about the matter? There, Tippoo, hang the baize over it again. The show's a failure."

Fain would I have begged to look longer; to have the subject explained to me; to learn why it was so good, and why I could not appreciate it—but I dared not. He was vexed with me—had over-estimated me—was disappointed in me. A choking sense of humiliation rose in my throat. I could not have uttered a syllable to save my life.

Fortunately for me, my vexation passed unnoticed. The covering of the picture and the reclosing of the shutters occupied all Mr. Farquhar's attention—then he made the servants go out before him, locked the door, and put the key in his pocket.

"Come along, Barbara," said he, "let us go back to the study."

And so we went back by the way we had come.

The place had been transformed in our absence. The fading daylight had been curtained out by a heavy crimson drapery—the table was laid for dinner—the lamp overhead cast a subdued light all around—and, despite the season and the heat, a pile of logs and pine-cones crackled on the hearth. My companion flung himself into his easy chair; bent shiveringly before the fire; and seemed lost in thought. I sat on a stool at the other side of the hearth, and looked at him.

Many and many a year has gone by since that evening, and I have long learned to distrust my preconceived ideas of men and things; but it puzzled me then to find myself so far mistaken. How unlike the Hugh Farquhar of my dreams! How unlike that brilliant hero with the Byronic collar whom I had been picturing to myself these four or five months past! I imagined him so handsome, so gallant, so fascinating — "a man rare as phœnix." I found him none of these; and yet, strange though it may seem, I was not disappointed. I had already a true instinct for character; and I am pleased to remember that, even then, I preferred originality and power to mere physical advantages. But I must describe him; and the task is one of no common difficulty. To go back to the first impression of a long-familiar face — to obliterate from cheek and brow the subtle finger-marks of time—to recall tones and gestures which seemed then to indicate so much, but which custom hath made no longer noticeable — all these and more, concur to baffle me.

I have never been a good judge of age; but at the time of which I write, my notions respecting it were of the vaguest possible description. So bronzed, so tall, so serious as he looked, sitting thus by the red fire-light, I believed Hugh Farquhar already to have arrived at middle-life —I now know that he was just twenty-seven years of age. It is possible, however, that he looked older—that varieties of climate, customs and food; adventures by land and sea; fatigue; exposure to weather; and all other contingencies of a wild and wandering life, had wrought some such effect upon him. Be this as it may, the year that followed worked, at all events, but little perceptible difference.

I have said that he was not handsome—nay, were I closely to analyze his features, I should perhaps be forced to confess that he was plain; and yet I never knew any one who thought him so. There was a certain grandeur in the poise of his head, a rugged power stamped upon his brow, a careless strength and dignity in his every gesture, that marked him for no ordinary man. Were I bidden to single out any well-known head, not as a likeness but a type, I should name Beethoven's. Yet it would then be necessary to efface those furrows of scorn and suffering, rage and bitterness, which plow the features of the deaf musician. The same loose, thick locks, however, were there -- the same characteristic prominences over the eyes — the same broad brow and massive jaw. Swarthy of complexion, dark-haired, dark-eyed, tanned by the wind and sun, and wearing such an amount of waving beard and moustache as was seldom seen in those days on this side of the Channel, Hugh Farquhar looked masculine and individual enough; but could scarcely have been more thoroughly the reverse of all that I had previously imagined. Men, as a rule, admired him more generally than women. Women, rarely indifferent, beheld in his countenance something more attractive than beauty. What was that something? How shall I define, how analyze it? Was it the impress of emotional, or the light of intellectual power? Or was it not, rather, that every glance and every tone conveyed some subtle record of an adventurous and reckless life, passion-worn, unsatisfied, and self-consuming?

I had intended to give my first childish impression of Hugh Farquhar, and I find that I have described him from my later experience. It is prematurely done; but let it be. Imperfect as it is, I can make it no better.

The fire blazed and crackled merrily all this time. My companion sat and looked at it with thoughts far distant. I crouched down in the shade, and watched him till I knew his face by heart. A quarter of an hour, or twenty minutes, went by thus, in silence. Then the door fell noiselessly back, and Tippoo came in with a small tray of silver-covered dishes. Mr. Farquhar sighed, and looked up for the first time.

"What," said he wearily, "is it already half-past seven?"

"It wants twenty-five minutes to eight, Sahib," replied the Hindoo, waiting his master's signal to remove the covers.

Mr. Farquhar rolled his easy chair round to the table, and glanced with a sort of abstracted wonder at the seat which had been placed for me.

"Do we expect any one, Tippoo?" said he.

Tippoo lifted his black eyes to his master's face, and then glanced meaningly toward the corner in which I was sitting. Mr. Farquhar turned half-round, started, laughed with something like confusion in his face, and said:

"Come, little one, the dinner is ready, and I should hope we are both hungry by this time!"

I came over without a word, and sat down where he bade me; but I was not hungry now. He had forgotten all about me!

How kind he was all dinner-time, and how he strove to compensate for his forgetfulness! He shook off his thoughtful mood, and I could see that it cost him an effort. He chatted with me; he exerted himself to make me laugh; he helped me to the choicest morsels, and insisted that I should taste every one of the dishes. They were all strange to me, and had a hot, spiced flavor which I did not like. Besides this, they were called the oddest names imaginable—mulligatawny, pilaff, caviare, curry, macaroni, and so forth—enjoying thereby the double advantage of being unpalatable and unpronounceable. By and by, the meats were removed, and strong black coffee, dried fruits, liquors and sweetmeats were brought to table. Mr. Farquhar then heaped my plate with dates, bonbons, and raisins; turned his chair once more to the fire; bade me do the same; and lighted a long Turkish pipe which had a coily tube like a green and golden snake, and a bowl of bell-shaped glass that rested on the ground.

"I am afraid, petite," said he, when Tippoo had left the room and we were once more left alone, "that you will not have much to say in praise of my cookery when you get home?"

Home! The word struck me like a blow. Like Hazlitt's "rustic at a fair," I had been all this time "full of amazement and rapture, and had no thought of going home, or that it would soon be night." Now it all rushed upon me in a moment.

"Oh, what o'clock is it, please?" I faltered.

"Nearly nine by my watch, petite."

I had risen; but, hearing this, laid aside the untasted fruits, and sat down again in blank dismay. Nine o'clock, and I was to have been home, at the latest, by half-past six! What was to become of me? What would my aunt say to me? How should I dare to face her? What excuse could I offer for my disobedience? Something of this I contrived brokenly to express, and Mr. Farquhar seeing my distress, rang the bell at once, and tried to reassure me.

"Fear nothing, my little friend," said he kindly. "I will take you home myself, presently, and bear all the blame as well. Tippoo, let Satan be saddled and brought round directly."

Tippoo bent his head, and disappeared. Mr. Farquhar glanced again at his watch, and smoked on with the utmost composure.

"In fifteen minutes," said he, "I promise to land you in your aunt's sitting-room. That allows me five minutes more to enjoy my pipe and coffee, and ten to ride from here to Stoneycroft Hall. Come, banish that melancholy look and trust to me for Mrs. Sandyshaft's forgiveness."

I would gladly have so trusted, if I could; but I too well knew what were my aunt's prejudices, and what her opinion of Hugh Farquhar and his family. However, I made an effort to be cheerful, and the five minutes went slowly by. As the last expired, my companion laid his pipe aside, and passed in an instant from the purest oriental languor to a state of genuine European activity.

To ring again for Tippoo, who immediately made his appearance laden with wraps—to envelop me in a cape lined with furs, and himself in a huge bearskin coat, fitter for the Arctic regions than for an autumn night in England—to pour out a glass of some delicious liquor, and compel me to drink it—to be booted, spurred and equipped, all in the twinkling of an eye—to take me up in his arms, and, preceded by Tippoo, carry me down-stairs and across the courtyard, as if I had been a feather—all this was the work of only a few seconds, and was done in less time than it takes to tell.

A groom holding a superb black horse, waited for us at the outer door.

"Soho, Satan—soho, boy!" said Farquhar, pausing an instant to lay his hand upon the glossy neck and mane, and then springing lightly into the saddle. The horse whinnied, and scraped the gravel impatiently with his fore-foot—Tippoo lifted me up, and placed me before his master on the saddle—Mr. Farquhar encircled me with his right arm, bade me hold tightly, gave a low whistle, and away we went at a gallop, dashing under the great archway, and making right across the park!

The rapid motion at first took away my breath, and I felt as if I must fall off and be dashed to pieces. This, however, soon passed away, and, feeling the clasp of his strong arm, I presently gained confidence, and enjoyed the speed with which we went. It was a glorious night. The moon shone with that yellow light which only belongs to her in the golden harvest-time; the dew sparkled, diamond-like, upon the grass; there were nightingales singing in the tall elms; and the deer, clustered in sleeping herds about the great oaks here and there, started at our approach and fled away by scores in the moonlight.

"Ha, little one!" said my companion, "see how they run! They believe we are hunting them to-night. Doesn't this remind you of Johnny Gilpin? It reminds me of one mistress Lenora who once rode a hundred miles somewhere in Germany at an unbecoming hour of the night, and lived to repent of it.

"*Graut Liebchen auch?—Der Mond scheint hell!*
Hurrah! die Todten reiten schnell!
Graut Liebchen auch vor Todten!"

By Jove! I shall begin to fancy presently that I am Wilhelm, and you Lenora. So—here the park ends, and there's a five-foot paling 'twixt us and the road. Hold on, little one, and hey for a leap! Soho, Satan—soho!"

Horribly alarmed, I clung to him as a drowning man clings to a plank; but Satan took the fence like a greyhound, and we were over before I knew where I was.

"Why do you call him Satan?" I asked, as soon as I had recovered my breath.

"Because he is black and wicked," replied Mr. Farquhar laughingly. "He is amiable to no one but me. He bites all the grooms, kills all the little dogs, and hates the sight of a woman. He tolerates Tippoo (but that's a prejudice of color), and he loves me—don't you, Satan, boy? He eats from my hand, kneels when I mount him, and follows me like a dog. I bought him from an Arab. He was a colt then, desert-born and bred. He will never tread the Arabian sands again—nor I either, perhaps. Bah! who knows? I may turn Bedouin, and make the pilgrimage to Mecca 'in most profound earnest,' as Claudio says, before I die!"

And with this he hummed more German lines, and urged his horse on faster and faster. The trees and hedges flew past—Satan seemed as if he would tear the road up with his hoofs—the sparks flashed from a flint every now and then; and our shadows sped beside us, like ghosts in the moonlight. Now we came upon a group of cottages, only hidden from Stoneycroft Hall by a bend in the road—now upon the pound, and the pond, and the old house, where lights were moving to and fro in the windows. We found the gate open—(I was glad of it, for we should certainly have taken the leap, had it been closed)—and dashed up to the door at full gallop. A touch of the rein, a word, and Satan, foaming and quivering as he was, stood stone-still, like a horse carved in black marble.

Mr. Farquhar dismounted with me in his arms, and raised his whip to knock upon the door; but it opened before the blow fell, and my aunt, candle in hand, narrowly escaped the whip-handle. She looked pale and stern; opened her lips as if to question; then, seeing my frightened face peep out from the furs, uttered a sharp cry, and dropped the candle.

"Found! found! Jane, come her! Oh!

Bab—naughty, naughty Bab, what an evening this has been!"

And with this, half-crying, half-laughing, she snatched me up, kissed, cuffed, and shook me all together, and knew not whether to be glad or angry. Then Jane came running up with lights, and there was more kissing and scolding; and then we all stood still, and paused for breath. My aunt turned from me to Mr. Farquhar.

"And it is to this gentleman that I am indebted for the return of my truant?" said she, fixing her keen eyes inquiringly upon him. "How can I ever thank him enough?"

"Simply by not thanking me at all," said he, standing by the porch with the bridle over his arm, and speaking for the first time. "Indeed, before we talk of obligations, I should beg your pardon; for, upon my soul, madam, I was near making your acquaintance by knocking you down!"

"Sir," replied my aunt with a stately reverence, for she could be immensely formal upon occasion, "I rejoice to make yours upon any terms."

"Then let me name them. Forgive this little girl for the alarm she has caused you. The fault was mine. I met her near my house, fell into chat with her, and thoughtlessly took her indoors to see a picture. How the time slipped by, I scarcely know; but we were amused with one another, and I believe that neither of us thought of the consequences till after dinner. It is now just twenty minutes since the word 'home' was first uttered, and I flatter myself that no time has been lost on the way. I promised to plead for her—nay, more, I promised her your pardon."

My aunt looked grave, or tried to do so. I believe she was almost glad to be obliged to forgive me.

"I redeem your promise, sir," said she, "in acknowledgment of the trouble you have taken in bringing her home; though, but for your intercession" (shaking her head at me), "I must have punished her. I exact obedience, and I will have it. Bab—thank the gentleman for his kindness. Sir, please to walk in."

"Not to-night, I thank you," said he courteously. "It is already late, and my little friend looks weary. If, however, I may call at some more reasonable hour——"

"You will be welcome," interrupted my aunt with one of her abrupt nods. "You will be very welcome. May I ask your name before you go? Your face is strange to me, and yet I seem to have some knowledge of it."

Mr. Farquhar smiled; drew a card from his pocket-book; gave it to me with a kiss; bade me hand it to my aunt; sprang into the saddle; took his hat quite off, and bowed profoundly; cried out "good night, *petite*," and dashed away at full speed down the garden.

"Humph!" said my aunt, shading her eyes from the candle and watching him to the turn of the road, "a fine horse, and a reckless rider. Let's see who he is. Mercy alive! FARQUHAR OF BROOMHILL!"

CHAPTER VIII.

A CITIZEN OF THE WORLD.

"THOU knowest I hunger after wisdom, as the Red
Sea after ghosts: therefore I travel."
DEATH'S JEST-BOOK.

SOME days went by, and Hugh Farquhar's promised visit remained unpaid. I rose every
morning with the hope that he would come before night, and I went to bed every night disconsolate. I waited for him—I wearied for him
—I was as much in love with him as any little
girl of ten years old could be! I brooded over
every word that he had uttered; strove to draw
his portrait, and tore up each abortive outline as
soon as it was made; recalled the last tones of
his voice, the last echo of his horse's hoofs, and
the parting kiss that he had given me in the
porch. He was still my hero, and a more
heroic hero than ever—Prince Camaralzaman,
with a'dash of Robin Hood now, and a spice of
the Wild Huntsman! I believe, on looking
back to this childish passion, that it was most
of all the power of the man that attracted me.
He was altogether older and plainer than I had
pictured him; and yet that sense of power
pleased me better than youth or beauty. It was
power of every kind—of health, and courage,
and daring—of the mind and the will—of freedom and fortune. His wealth I believed boundless; and Broomhill, with its portrait-gallery,
its corridors, and stately *suites*, reminded me of
Aladdin's palace. His mode of life, too, had
something strange and solitary in it. There
was a mystery and a charm in the gloom that
sometimes fell upon him. There was an oriental
romance in the very food he ate, in the pipe he
smoked, in Tippoo the noiseless, and in Satan
the swift! I could do nothing, in short, but
talk and dream of Farquhar of Broomhill.

My aunt said very little about him, and
listened with assumed indifference to all I had
to tell. That she was interested, however, and
that she not only listened but remembered,
I knew to a certainty; for I heard her repeating it next morning, word for word, as she and
Dr. Topham paced up and down the garden-
walk together. From this moment the train
was fired, and the news spread. Carried from
parish to parish, and from house to house, it
was known, as if by telegraph, throughout the
county. Alas for Hugh Farquhar!—his incognito was soon over.

At length there came a day when my aunt
and I were sitting together after dinner, beside
the open window. There had been rain, and
the atmosphere was damp and close, like that
of a hot-house. Not a breath stirred; not a
bird sang; not a leaf rustled. A voluptuous
languor pervaded all the drowsy air—a subtle
perfume uprose from the reeking earth—a faint
mist obscured the landscape. Yielding to the
influences of the hour, my aunt had fallen
asleep with the newspaper in her hand, whilst
I, perched on the broad window-seat with my
silks and sampler, suffered the work to lie unheeded in my lap, rested my chin upon my two
palms in an odd, old-fashioned way, and counted
the drops as they fell one by one from the broad
leaves of the heavy-headed sun-flower outside
in the garden. A long time went by thus, and
was meted out by the ticking of the old watch

over the fireplace—a long, long time, during
which only one solitary pedestrian trudged past,
with an umbrella over his shoulder. All at once,
remote but growing rapidly nearer, I heard
the quick echo of a well-remembered gallop!
Louder, closer, faster it came. I felt the blood
rush to my face—I held my breath—I strained
my eyes to that one spot where there was an
opening in the trees—then, springing suddenly
to my feet, I grasped Mrs. Sandyshaft by the
arm, and cried—

"Oh, wake up, aunt! wake up! Here he
comes at last! I knew he *must* come some day!"

"He? What? Who?" exclaimed Mrs. Sandyshaft, bewildered and half asleep. "What
noise is that?"

"That's Satan, aunt! Hark, how fast he's
coming!"

My aunt became rigid.

"Satan!" she repeated. "Mercy on us! The
child's demented."

I could only point triumphantly to the gate
where Mr. Farquhar had that moment dismounted, and was tying up his horse. My aunt relaxed, and smiled grimly.

"Oh, call him Satan, do you?" said she. "Not
a bad name, Bab—might suit the master as well
the beast, eh?"

Whereupon I rushed away without replying,
and, encountering him in the porch, became suddenly shy, and had not a word to say. Seeing
me, he smiled and held out both his hands.

"*Eccolà!*" said he. "The very Barbara of
my thoughts! How does your grace to-day?
Well, I trust, and undisturbed by the late fluc-
tuations in the funds, or the changes in the min-
istry? What news of the pigs and the fine
arts?"

Blushing and puzzled, I lingered with my
hand in his, and knew not what to answer.

"How! not a word? not a greeting? not a
mere '*give you good den, Sir Richard?*' Oh,
faithless Barbara!—and to think that I have
brought a box of Turkish sweatmeats for you,
in my pocket! Come, are you not glad to see
me now?"

And he took out a pretty little box of inlaid
woods, and held it playfully before my eyes. I
snatched away my hand and drew back.

"I am not glad for the sake of what you give
me," said I, grievously hurt; and so ran on to
the parlor door, and left him to follow. My
aunt held up her finger at me—she had heard
every word—and advanced to meet him.

"Sir," she began, "I am glad to see you; and
you are the first of your name to whom I ever
said so. Sit down."

Mr. Farquhar smiled, bowed, and took the
proffered seat.

"I hope, sir," continued my aunt, "that you
have come to settle amongst us. You have been
too long away. Traveling is a fool's Paradise;
and you must have sown your wild oats by this
time."

Mr. Farquhar looked infinitely amused.

"Madam," said he, "it is a branch of agriculture to which I have been assiduously devoting
myself for the last five years."

"Humph! And now you have come back
for good?"

"I should be sorry to believe that I have come
back for evil."

My aunt fixed her eyes sharply upon him, and shook her head.

"That's not what I mean, Mr. Farquhar," said she. "I want to know if you are going to live on your own lands, lead the life of an English gentleman, and marry a wife?"

"I had rather marry a maid," retorted he, with the same provoking smile, "and sooner than either, Mrs. Sandyshaft, I would remain a bachelor. As to living on my own lands, I may aver that I have done so ever since I left England; for as my steward can testify, I have drawn my rents with the most conscientious regularity."

"And spent them too, I'll warrant," said my aunt, grimly.

Whereupon Mr. Farquhar laughed, and made no reply.

"England is the best place after all," observed she, returning to the charge. "The *only* place!"

"For fogs and fox-hunts, granted."

"For liberty of the press, public spirit, domestic comfort, and national respectability! Find me the French for 'common-sense,' Mr. Farquhar!"

"Find me the French for the verb 'to grumble!'"

"I should be sorry if I could," said my aunt, rubbing her hands, and enjoying the argument with her whole heart. "'Tis a national characteristic—a national amusement—a national institution!"

"And the exclusive privilege of the British Lion," added Mr. Farquhar, with a shrug of the shoulders. "*Allons!* I am a citizen of the world—a vagrant by nature— a cosmopolitan at heart. I confess to little of the patriotic spirit, and much of the Bohemian. London porter tastes no better in my mouth than 'Hungary wine,' and between *Kabobs* and mutton-chops I find but little difference!"

My aunt held up her hands in amazement.

"Young man," said she, "your opinions are detestable. You don't deserve to have eight centuries of ancestors. No patriotic spirit, indeed! Mercy alive! What's your opinion, pray, of the English history?"

"My dear madam, I think it an admirable work—for the library-shelves."

"Have you ever read it?"

"Yes, in my boyish days, when I believed in Messrs. Hume and Smollett, looked on Charles the First as a genuine Royal Martyr, and pinned my faith upon the virgin purity of Queen Elizabeth!"

My aunt smiled in spite of herself.

"I fear," said she, "that you are a sad scapegrace, and believe in very little."

"*Que-voulez-vous?* The world has rubbed off most of my illusions."

"So much the worse for you. The happiest man is the most credulous."

"Then is the ass the most enviable of quadrupeds! I cry you mercy, madam! Let those be dupes who will—'I'll none of it.' Is it not better to see things as they are, and take them at their value?—to distinguish between base metal and gold, paste and brilliants? Now, for my part, I had rather know at the first glance that my mistress's front-teeth were false, than live to be told of it by some officious friend who met her at the dentist's!"

"Sir," said my aunt, emphatically, "I see nothing for you but a strict course of matrimony."

"Then your opinion of my case is, indeed, serious!"

"You must settle in England," continued my aunt. "You must see society. You must marry. A good-tempered, kind-hearted, well-educated English girl is what you want; and I know of four or five in this very county, all of whom would suit you to a T."

"Then I will marry them all."

"No, you won't, indeed! You are in a civilized country here, sir, and not among Turks and savages. Marry them all, hey? I like the idea!"

"*I* should prefer the reality!"

My aunt shook her head impatiently.

"Nonsense!" said she. "I am in earnest, and advise you as a friend. You want a wife, and, I repeat it, you must marry."

"Spoken *ex cathedrâ*," observed Mr. Farquhar, parenthotically.

"There's — let me see — there's Sir John Crompton's daughter," continued my aunt, telling off the young ladies on her fingers, "and there's Miss Heathcote, with thirty thousand pounds; and there are the two Somervilles, daughters of the Dean of Wrentham, and——"

"My dear lady," interrupted Mr. Farquhar, "before you go on with your list, tell me what chance I have of becoming acquainted with these Sirens? Shall I advertise myself in the 'Ipswich Herald,' or hang a label round my neck with the words 'TO LET' printed thereon in golden characters?"

"Neither, sir. You shall send for paper-hangers, upholsterers, and confectioners; put your house in order; and issue invitations to a ball."

"Not for a kingdom. What! pull the old place about my ears, and submit to an invasion of flirts and fiddlers? No, madam—I have too much respect for the spiders!"

"In that case," said my aunt, "I will give a party myself."

"I'll never believe it, Mrs. S.!" cried a voice at the door. "It's a fiction, a fable—

——'a tale
Told by an idiot, full of sound and fury,
Signifying nothing!'"

"Topham," observed my aunt, "you are a fool. Come in, will you, and be introduced to Mr. Farquhar of Broomhill."

Dr. Topham came in, hat, umbrella, and all, and solemnly deposited those properties on the table.

"You have mentioned that circumstance so often, Mrs. S.," said he, "that I begin to fancy I must be a fool, after all. I shall charge my cap and bells to your account. Don't trouble yourself, ma'am, to make me known to Mr. Farquhar. I can do that for myself. Sir, shake hands. You and I are old friends, and our acquaintance dates back for more than a quarter of a century. Introductions, forsooth! Why, sir, it was I who first had the pleasure of introducing you to your own father! I dare say you don't remember that event so accurately as I do?"

A shade, a trouble, an indescribable something flitted over Hugh Farquhar's sunburnt face, at these words.

"Indeed!" said he, in a low voice. "Then you knew my mother?"

"I did—a most excellent and beautiful lady, charitable, sincere, and earnest. She was beloved by rich and poor, and for many a year her name remained a household word throughout this countryside."

Mr. Farquhar bent his head gravely.

"You do her justice, sir," he said; and turned away with a sigh.

There was a silence of some moments, during which Dr. Topham and my aunt exchanged belligerent glances, and looked as if longing to begin their accustomed squabble. Presently Hugh Farquhar spoke again.

"It surprises me, Dr. Topham," said he, "that I have no recollection of your face. Your name I seem to have heard before; and yet, when I was a lad and used to come home from Eton and Oxford for the vacations, it was Mr. Stanley who——"

"Precisely so. Mr. Stanley of Normanbridge," interrupted the doctor. "Your father and I could never agree, Mr. Farquhar. We had a grand fracas, in fact; and though your mother did her best to reconcile us, the breach was never healed. Mr. Stanley is a very clever man—too fond of the lancet, though! Too fond of the lancet!"

"Hold your tongue, doctor," said my aunt, acidly. "You're all a set of murderers. Some prefer steel, and some poison—that's the only difference."

"Much obliged, Mrs. S. I reserve my vengeance till you next have occasion for my services."

Hugh Farquhar laughed, and rose to take his leave.

"War being declared," said he, "I will leave you to fight it out fairly. Dr. Topham, will you come up and smoke a pipe of Turkish tobacco with me to-morrow evening? At present I am but a hermit, and live in a turret by myself, like a mouse in a trap; but I shall be glad to see and know more of you. Mrs. Sandyshaft, you must let me know when you have chosen a wife for me. If you could allow me to see the lady before we meet at the altar, I should prefer it; but, for mercy's sake, don't marry me unawares!"

"You shall choose for yourself, Mr. Farquhar," replied my aunt. "I mean to give that party, I assure you."

"Not on my account, pray!"

"Yes, on your account, solely—therefore you will be bound to come to it."

And with this they shook hands, and parted. As Mr. Farquhar left the room, he beckoned me to follow, and walked with me silently to the garden gate. There he paused.

"Barbara," he said gently, "why were you so angry just now, when I offered you that box?"

I hung my head, and could find no words to reply.

"If you had known," he continued, in the same tone, "what trouble it gave me to find those bonbons, and how many hundreds of miles they have traveled with me, and with what pleasure I put them in my pocket to-day (hoping to please you), I don't think, petite, that you would have treated me quite so ungraciously."

I felt myself tremble and change color.

"I—I—it wasn't that I was ungrateful," I faltered. "But you said, 'Are you glad to see me now?'—I was glad before! I heard you when you were a mile away, and knew that it was you! I—I have been at the window looking for you all the week! Oh, pray forgive me—I was not ungrateful!"

Mr. Farquhar looked at me very earnestly, and with something like astonishment in his face.

"Why, Barbara mia," said he, "you are the most tender-hearted little maid that ever I met! Come, let us be friends. By Jove, I believe it was my fault, after all!"

And with this he stooped, and kissed away two large tears which were stealing down my cheeks.

"Will you take the box now, for my sake?" he whispered — then, with a last kiss, placed it in my hands, mounted, and galloped away.

I watched him out of sight, wondering if he would look back. He never so much as glanced to the right or left; but rode straight on, and vanished round the bend of the road.

CHAPTER IX.

A CHILD'S LOVE.

"Love sought is good; but given unsought is better."
                                        SHAKSPEARE.

HUGH FARQUHAR'S first visit was followed, not long after, by a second and a third; so that he soon became a recognized habitué of the house. His favorite time was twilight; and he used to ride up to the porch, tie Satan by the bridle, and walk in without announcement. My aunt then laid aside her paper; grumbled at him heartily, if he awoke her from her nap; and prepared for a chat. Sometimes I sat aside in a dark corner, and fell to my old occupation of watching him till it grew too dusk to see his face distinctly; after which I was content only to listen to his voice. Sometimes, for I was a great pet now, and highly privileged, I took a little stool at his feet, and laid my head against his knee, and was almost too happy. When, perchance, he interrupted his conversation to address a stray word to me; or, in the listlessness of thought, passed his hand through the wavy folds of my long hair, I trembled and held my breath, lest any motion of mine should cause him to take it away the sooner. What I would have given to dare to kiss that hand matters not now. It was a child's idolatry—an idolatry so innocent, unselfish, and spiritual, as few feel more than once, if once, in life.

My aunt and he suited each other, after their own odd antagonistic fashion. They always differed in opinion, for the sake of argument and the pleasure of wrangling; but I believe they often agreed at heart. My aunt had read much; and, despite her crotchets and prejudices, could both speak and think well when she chose. Books, history, politics, foreign life and manners, agriculture, and the arts, formed the staple subjects of their talk; and about each and all, Hugh Farquhar had something amusing and original to say. His conversation was peculiar, fragmentary, discursive, idiocratic. When thoroughly at his ease and "i' the vein," he wandered on from topic to topic, from jest to earnest, and thought aloud, rather than conversed. His memory was prodigious. He knew Shakspeare and his cotemporaries by heart, and was so thoroughly steeped in the spirit of that age that his very phraseology had oftentimes an Elizabethan flavor. Sometimes dreamy, sometimes sad, sometimes sarcastic—varying in his mood with every turn of the argument—breaking into "flashes of merriment" and unexpected sparkles of wit—abounding in quaint scraps of dry and dusty philosophies, and in quotations as apt as they were sometimes whimsical, Hugh Farquhar talked as few can talk, and fewer still can write. To record his conversation is, therefore, singularly difficult — to preserve its aroma, impossible. I should conceive, from what we read of those tea-table talks at the little waterside house in Islington, that Charles Lamb's familiar parlance may have been somewhat similar—more exquisitely playful, perhaps, and more sensitively sympathetic—certainly less caustic. Both, at all events, were in the rapidity of their hues and changes, kaleidoscopic. I learned much from these twilight gossips; and though I might not always understand, I always enjoyed them. Granted that the topics and opinions mooted on both sides were generally in advance of my actual knowledge, they set me thinking, and perhaps did more toward the premature development of my intellect than could have been effected by any set system of training. At the same time it must be confessed that my actual education was, in some degree, at a standstill. A couple of hours devoted each morning to Gibbon, Goldsmith, or Buffon, and another hour or so to the Parliamentary debates every afternoon, scarcely deserves the name of education; and, but for other circumstances, would have done little to improve me. I was free, however, of my aunt's book-case, of the fields, the sunlight, and the fresh air. I read more, saw more, felt more than I had ever read, seen, or felt in all my life before. Above all, I was happy; and happiness derived from, and dependent on, the love of those who are better and wiser than we, is, in itself, an education.

Thus the weeks went by, and the autumn waned, and still Hugh Farquhar dwelt alone in his solitary tower, and became, as I have already said, a frequent guest at Stoneycroft Hall. As the days grew shorter and the twilight encroached upon our dinner-hour, he took to coming later, and often rode over between eight and nine to drink coffee and play piquet with my aunt. Scarcely a week passed that he did not send her a present of game, or the latest parcel of books and magazines from London; while to me he never failed to bring some pretty trifle—a tiny Swiss Chalet bought at Berne, a coral toy from Naples, a Chinese puzzle, or a string of Indian wampum. He certainly spared no pains to place himself upon the footing of an intimate; though why he should have done so, and what pleasure he could find in the society of an eccentric old lady and a shy little girl of ten, seems unaccountable enough. Whether he meant to stay in England, or whether he was here for only a few months, remained as great a mystery as at first. He would either give no answer when questioned,

or declare that he knew no more than we — cared, perhaps, even less—had no wish to settle, and preferred to keep "one foot in sea, and one on shore," for, at least, a few years longer.

"But surely," said my aunt, assailing him one evening on this her favorite topic, "surely you have some definite plans?"

"Plans, my dear Mrs. Sandyshaft?" he exclaimed. "Not I, indeed. Heaven forbid!"

"Well, then, some regard for the future?" My aunt shook her head gravely, and looked shocked.

"None. *Oggi* is my motto, and *domani* may go to the devil!"

My aunt shook her head gravely, and looked shocked.

"You are wrong," said she; "young, wrong, and headstrong. You don't look at life seriously enough. You don't——"

"Pardon me, I look at it, perhaps, too seriously. If you imagine that I make of it one idle holiday, you mistake me altogether. I do no such thing. I look upon it as a very sad, wearyful, unsatisfactory affair; and because to-day is so burdensome, I care little for the events of to-morrow. I love to drift from day to day, like a weed from wave to wave; and it seems to me that the philosophies of all time are comprised in that sentence of Sadi the Persian:—

> ' 'Tis better to sit than to stand;
> 'Tis better to be in bed than sitting;
> 'Tis better to be dead than in bed.' "

"Wherefore," observed my aunt dryly, "you choose a life of incessant activity. Nonsense! Drift here, if drifting suits you; and if lying in bed be so very philosophical, lie in bed at Broomhill."

"First provide me with that model wife, Mrs. Sandyshaft!"

"Besides," continued my aunt, "there are duties arising from your position. You have a stake in the country, and——"

"And a very tough one it is!" interrupted he, laughingly. "I prefer a *côtelette à la Soubise*, served at the *Maison Dorée!*"

Whereupon my aunt waxed wroth, cited Dr. Johnson's opinion on the making of puns and the picking of pockets, and abandoned the siege for that evening.

Not many nights after this, he came again. It was the first frost of the season; and, though he had ridden fast and wore his great fur coat, he complained bitterly of the climate.

"Climate!" repeated my aunt, "Bless the man! what better climate can he desire, I should like to know? Climate, indeed, with such a coat as that on his back!"

"'The owl for all his feathers was a-cold!'" quoted Hugh Farquhar, hanging over the fire like a half-frozen Kamschatkan.

My aunt piled on more coals, rang for coffee, and muttered something about "salamanders" and "fire-worshipers."

"Do you wonder that I freeze," said he, "when for five years I have known no winter? My Decembers and Januarys have all been spent in South Italy, the East, or the tropics. Last Christmas Eve I lay awake all night in the deep grass on a ledge of one of the Chilian Andes, looking up to the Centaur and the Southern Cross, with not even a cloak for my counterpane. The year before that, I ate my roast-beef and plum-pudding with the officers of the Fourth Light Dragoons in Calcutta. 'Tis no laughing matter, let me tell you, to come back to this infernal land of fog and frost, after wandering for five long years

'where Universal Pan,
Knit with the Graces and the Hours in dance,
Leads on the Eternal Spring!'

Pshaw! Dante was of my mind when he made the lowest circle of hell an icy region, and imbedded His Majesty in the midst of it!"

"If you had been content to live respectably in your own country," said my aunt, testily, "you'd never have felt any difference. Will you take some brandy with your coffee? I hate to hear people's teeth clattering like castanets!"

"'Tis 'a spirit of health,' and I will not refuse to entertain it. *Barbarina mia*, will you vouchsafe to kiss me this evening? So! There's a shy little salute! Your ladyship is chary of your rosy lips, methinks! Ah! did you but know what I have brought to show you, and which of my pockets it is in! A sketch book, *petite*—a sketch-book full of pictures!"

My hands were diving into his pockets in an instant; for, by this time, those pockets were familiar ground. The first thing I brought out was a little square packet, sealed at both ends—the second, a book with a silver clasp.

"Stop," said he, taking the former from me, and breaking the seals that fastened it, "this is a pack of cards, Mrs. Sandyshaft, which I propose to play our piquet with to-night. Pray observe them, and tell me which are trumps."

Saying, which, he dealt out some twenty or thirty visiting cards in rapid succession, laughing heartily the while to see my aunt's amazement.

"General Kirby—Mr. Fuller—Mrs. Fuller—The Rev. Edward Grote—Sir John and Lady Lady Crompton—Miss Price—Lord Bayham—Captain Carter—Mr., Mrs., and the Misses Capel—the Hon. and Rev. Augustus Petersham—Why, where, for gracious sake, did you get all these?"

"They have been accumulating for the last month at compound interest; and I gathered them out of a basket in my study this afternoon. A famous pack for playing, with a suitable sprinkling of court cards and, doubtless, the usual allowance of knaves!"

"Have you returned any of these visits?"

"Not one. I thought of sending Tippoo about the country, as my representative."

"Absurd!"

"Not at all. He need only lie back in a corner of the carriage, wear lavender kid gloves, and hand visiting cards through the window. If any one caught a glimpse of his face, it would only be thought that traveling had spoiled my complexion. You may depend he would do it capitally, and be far more majestic than myself."

But my aunt only shook her head, took out a pencil and the back of an old letter, and began gravely making a list of all the names.

"Have you any idea," she said, presently, "of the number of folks which these cards represent?"

"Not I!"

"Well—from eighty-five to a hundred."

"Impossible!"

"Do you doubt it? Look here, then. The Cromptons have five daughters, so their tickets stand for seven people—the Fullers have two

sons and one daughter, so they stand as five—the Misses Capel are four—the Reverend——"

"Hold, enough! You are going on into unknown quantities, and my brain reels already. Must I be civil to all these people?"

"Oh, that's as you please!"

He took the list, read it through several times, and, resting his head upon his hand, dropped into a brown study. By and by, my aunt brought out her little walnut-wood table, trimmed her lamp, and sorted the playing cards. This done, they fell to piquet, and so spent the evening.

As for me, to sit on a stool at Hugh Farquhar's feet and pore over the book with the silver clasp, was delight and employment enough. Here were sketches indeed!—some in water-colors, some in pencil, some in sepia. Now a page of mere rough memoranda, faces seen from the window, fragments of capitals and cornices, and the outline of a boat with lateen sails—now a group of Tyrolean peasants, with green hats and embroidered jackets—now a snow-capped mountain, a wild plain scattered over with strange plants, an indigo sky, and the word *Chimborazo* written in the corner. Next, perhaps, came a cluster of old houses—a bit of coast and sea—an Indian head, studied from the life—a curious plant, leaf, flower, and bud, all side by side—a caricature of a priest, with a gigantic black hat and a pair of spindle legs—a ruined tower and ivied arch; a bridge; a tree; a vase; and so on for, perhaps, a hundred pages! When I came to the end, I went back again to the beginning; and save now and then to steal a glance at the bronzed face which I so loved to look upon, never lifted my eyes from the sketches. For here, at last, was the Art of which I had been dreaming all my little life—Art comprehensible, tangible, real and ideal in one! Here were places and people, vitality, action, color, poetry, intention. The Paul Veronese was too much for me. It needed an art-education to pierce the mysteries, and appreciate the beauties, of that marvelous Lombardic school. Not so with Hugh Farquhar's sketches. They were amateur's work; often faulty, no doubt, but full of character and effect, and just suggestive enough to stimulate the imagination, and supply all that might be wanting in them as works of art.

At length the clock struck ten, and my aunt threw down her hand. Though in the middle of a game, or at the most exciting point of the contest, she always stopped inexorably at the first stroke of the hour, and put the cards away.

"You are pleased with that book, Barbara?" asked Mr. Farquhar, speaking to me for the first time since they had begun to play.

"I never saw any thing so beautiful," said I; and my face, I doubt not, was more eloquent of praise than any words I could have uttered.

He smiled and took the volume from me.

"Show me which drawing you like best," he said, turning the leaves rapidly.

I stopped him at a sketch of a ruined fountain, with a background of misty mountains, and an Italian contadina filling her pitcher in the foreground.

"I like that best of all!" I exclaimed.

"And so do I, *petite*. You have pitched on the best thing in the book."

Saying which, he opened his penknife, cut the leaf out, and placed it in my hands.

"Mercy alive!" cried my aunt, "you're never going to give the child that picture?"

"Indeed I am; and if it had been fifty times better, she should have had it! *Carina*, I have more of these, and bigger ones, at home. You shall come and spend a day with me, and go through them all — and, perhaps, you may like the Paul Veronese better when you see it again. No thanks, little one — I hate them. Mrs. Sandyshaft, I have made up my mind!"

"To what, pray?"

"To the solemn duty of entertaining my dear eighty-five unknown acquaintances! What shall it be — a ball, or a dinner? Or both?"

"Both, by all means, if you really intend it!"

"Amen. And when?"

"How can *I* tell? You must put your house in order."

"And prepare to die! My dear Madam, your phraseology smacks of 'funeral baked meats,' and suggests uncomfortable results. Well, I must turn this matter over in my mind, and hold a cabinet council with my housekeeper — after that, *nous verrons!*"

With this he took his leave. I followed him to the porch, where Satan was waiting, fiery and impatient. There was no moon; but the stars shone keenly through the frosty night, and the stable-boy's lantern cast a bright circle on the path.

"Good night, little friend," he said, and touched my forehead lightly with his lips.

I could not bid him "good night" in return — my heart was too full; but I followed him with my eyes long after the dark had swallowed him up, and listened for the last faint echo of his horse's hoofs. That night I took my darling picture up with me to bed, and placed it where I might see it when I woke. I was very, very happy; and yet I remember how I cried myself to sleep!

CHAPTER X.

THE BALL AT BROOMHILL.

OVERSHADOWED by a huge pear-tree in a snug corner of the orchard behind the house, stood a low wooden building, the roof whereof was clustered over with patches of brown moss and ashy lichens. The padlock on the doors was red with rust, and the spiders had woven their webs over the hinges. It looked like a place disused; but it was my aunt's coach-house; and contained my aunt's carriage. Never brought out, unless once a year to be cleaned, or on occasions of solemn ceremony, this vehicle reposed in dust and dignity, like Lord Nelson's funeral car in the vaults at St. Paul's, and led, on the whole, an easy life of it. The first time that I ever had the honor of being jolted in it, was on the day of Hugh Farquhar's great dinner and evening party, about five weeks after the events last related.

I say jolted, and I say it advisedly; for surely a more obstinate and springless piece of furniture never went upon wheels. When set in motion it uttered despairing creaks; going down-hill it staggered from side to side, like a drunken giant; and we never turned a corner but it threatened to pitch over. Notwithstanding these little eccentricities, it was the object of my special veneration; and Mrs. Inchbald's hero never saluted the wig of his uncle the judge, nor Friday the gun of Robinson Crusoe, more reverently than I did homage to this antiquated "leathern conveniency." Our difficulties on the present occasion were increased tenfold by the condition of the roads; for there had been snow the night before, and a frost toward morning.

"Bab," said my aunt, "I never thought I should have lived to do this."

My aunt was very grand this evening, and wore her black brocaded silk dress, her black and gold turban, and the *suite* of oriental amethysts which were given to her by her husband on her wedding-day.

"To do what, aunt?" I asked, clinging to a carriage-strap; for we were just going over a piece of road where the snow had drifted somewhat deeply, and our conveyance was laboring onward, like a lighter in a gale.

"Why, to dine at Broomhill, to be sure! Have you not often and often heard me say that I never exchanged a civility with the Farquhars in my life, or crossed the threshold of a Farquhar's door? And yet here I am, at my time of life, actually going to Broomhill to dinner!"

"But then you like this Mr. Farquhar," I suggested, "and ——"

"Don't say I like him, Bab. I tolerate him. He's an amusing madman with a remnant of brains; and I tolerate him. That's all, and a good deal, too; for he's the first of his name that I ever endured, living or dead! So! I never drove through these gates before, old as I am. Bab, sit still."

But I was all excitement, and could not have sat still for the world. We had now entered the park, and yonder, framed in by the gleaming snow and sable sky, stood the house, lighted from basement to attic, like a huge beacon of welcome. The avenue had all been cleared; but the great old oaks stretched their snow-laden arms overhead, and looked, by the ghostly light of our carriage-lamps, like gigantic branches of white coral. There was another vehicle some little way in advance of us; and when we came to within a few feet of the arched gateway, we found ourselves at the end of a line of carriages, each advancing a few steps at a time, and setting down its occupants one by one. How my heart beat when it came to be our turn at last, and we drew up before the bright perspective of the lighted hall!

A powdered footman stood just within the entrance—a second took charge of our cloaks—a third announced us at the drawing-room door. I had never been to a party in my life before, and as we passed into the great room all ablaze with chandeliers and mirrors, I trembled and hung back. There were some twenty people or so, scattered about on sofas, or gathered round a table laden with engravings. From this group a gentleman disengaged himself at the sound of my aunt's name, and came forward to meet us. I scarcely knew him at first, in his close black suit and white cravat—he looked so unlike the fur-coated, careless Hugh Farquhar of every day! He bowed profoundly—so profoundly that I, in my ignorance was quite astonished—and led my aunt to an arm-chair by the fire.

"I look upon this as a high compliment, Mrs. Sandyshaft," said he, "and rejoice to bid you welcome, for the first time, to my home."

The formality of this 'address, the stately politeness with which my aunt received it, and, above all the sudden hush of curiosity that seemed to fall upon the assembled guests, struck me as something very strange. Not till years after, when I was old enough in the world's usages to interpret the enigma, did I understand why Hugh Farquhar paid her such public courtesy that evening, and how her presence there stood for a recognition of friendship, and the healing of old feuds.

Amid the brief silence that followed, more visitors arrived; and then the hum of talk began afresh. One after another, all the persons present came up and paid their compliments to my aunt, and, with very few exceptions, every face was strange to me. Most of them asked her who I was; some shook hands with me, and hoped I was a good little girl; and one old gentleman with white hair, looked at me attentively when he heard my name, and said that I was like my mother.

Presently the dinner was announced. Mr. Farquhar gave his arm to my aunt; the rest followed, two and two; and I found myself conveyed with the stream, and seated beside that same white-haired old gentleman, near the bottom of a very long table covered with glass and silver, glittering candelabra, and vases of delicious flowers such as I had never seen in winter-time before.

This meal was a stately solemnization, and, like that of matrimony, ended (so far as I was concerned) in amazement. Soup, fish, flesh, fowl, game, sauces, and sweets, succeeded each other in bewildering variety, and promised never to come to an end. Being no great eater at any time, and, like most children, averse to rich and highly flavored dishes, I amused myself by listening to the conversation that was going on around me, and observing every thing and every body in the room. There was Hugh Farquhar at the head of the table, with my aunt at his right hand and Tippoo standing stone-still behind his chair. He looked, I fancied, somewhat pale, and, though studiously courteous, was both grave and silent. Perhaps, having been so long a dweller in tents, he found these formalities irksome. Perhaps he felt himself a stranger in his own house and among his own guests, living another life, thinking other thoughts, and conversant with other topics than theirs. At the foot of the table where sat Sir John Crompton (a stout, jovial, fox-hunting, country baronet, in a blue coat with brass buttons and an expansive white waistcoat) there was ten times more enjoyment. Here the wine circulated more freely and the talk went briskly on, and all were neighbors and intimates. Captain Carter's blood mare and the marriage of Miss Rowland, the quality of Mr. Farquhar's Moselle, and that sad affair near Ipswich between the rural police and the Tenth Lancers, formed the staple subjects of their conversation. Meanwhile the ladies listened and chimed in; and the younger people spoke low, and flirted; and the fat gentleman with the bald head took two helpings of every thing;

and the lady in the amber satin dress had the gravy spilt in her lap, and was so cross that she scarcely knew how to behave herself; and the clergyman at the opposite corner talked of 'hunting and shooting, and drank more wine than any other gentleman at the table. All this I noticed, and much more beside. Nothing escaped me—not even the new liveries on the footmen, or the new furniture that decorated the room, or the new paper on the walls—least of all the lovely Poussin that hung just opposite my seat, fresh as if newly dipped in the dews of "incense-breathing morn," and opening a vista into Arcadia. Having feasted my eyes on this till they grew dim, and having listened with delight to the pale-faced young man who made puns, and having asked endless questions of the kind old gentleman beside whom I had the good luck to be seated, I came at last to the end of my resources, and longed for liberty again. I looked at my aunt, and wondered whether she also was not tired of the dinner by this time; but she was talking to an elderly gentleman in glasses, and evidently not only enjoying her argument, but triumphantly getting the best of it. I looked all round the table, and saw none but smiling, flushed, and occupied faces. To eat, drink, and be merry was the order of the hour; and, save in the countenance of the giver of the feast, I could nowhere read any lack of entertainment. He talked, it is true, but abstractedly. Once he looked up and found my eyes upon him, and so smiled, put his glass to his lips and nodded to me gayly; but that was the only moment when he seemed genuinely himself. And thus the dreary order of things went on and on; and what with the buzz and hum of conversation, the clatter of knives and glasses, the monotonous gliding to and fro of attentive servants, and the amalgamation of savory scents which rose like "a steam of rich distilled perfumes" and hung over our heads as an oppressive canopy, I became quite weary and confused, and well-nigh dropped asleep.

At last Sir John Crompton proposed the health of the "ladies"—for toasts were not yet gone out of fashion—and after that my aunt and Lady Crompton arose from table, and we all went out in a rustling procession of silks and satins, and left the gentlemen to their claret. By this time it was nearly nine o'clock, and we could hear the musicians in the long gallery tuning their instruments and making ready for the ball that was to follow. It was now duller than ever. Some of the elder ladies gathered into little knots, and chatted of their families, and their friends. The younger lounged about, and yawned over the engravings, or tried the tone of the piano. My aunt sat bolt upright in a high-backed chair, and had forty inflexible winks. I stole over to a distant window, and looked out at the snow which was falling fast again. Every now and then, strangely discordant with the white sepulchral calm of the scene without, rose the peals of laughter, and the "three-times three," of the revelers in the dining-room below. By and by, a carriage with gleaming lamps rose noiselessly past the window; and then another, and another, till the room began to fill with fresh arrivals, and the gentlemen came upstairs. Then coffee was handed round; and card-tables were opened for those who chose to play; and the rest dropped away by twos and twos, at the summons of the band-music, which now rang merrily out across the broad vestibule, and along the echoing staircases. My aunt sat down to loo, and my white-haired friend to whist. Nobody offered to take me into the ball-room, and no one spoke to me; so I kept by the window and listened longingly, and felt almost as lonely as I used to feel in my self-chosen solitude up in the old garret of my London home. A long, long time went by thus, and still more guests kept coming — chiefly young people, radiant in delicate gauzes and flowers, and full of life and gayety. Some of the girls were beautiful, and three or four of the gentlemen wore military uniforms. How I longed to see them dancing, and what a glittering scene I fancied that ball-room must be! At length the anguish of disappointment and neglect quite overcame my fortitude, and I leaned my forehead up against the window, and let my tears flow silently.

"What, Barbara here, and all alone!" said Hugh Farquhar's voice. "Why are you not in the ball-room, *mignonne?*"

Ashamed to be found weeping, I pressed my face closer to the glass, and made no answer. He laid his hand upon my shoulder, and bent down till I felt his breath upon my neck.

"Something is the matter, *carina*," he said gently. "Turn round and look at me, and tell me what it is!"

I could not bear his touch, or the tenderness of his voice; but trembled all at once from head to foot, and sobbed openly. In another instant he had taken a chair beside mine, had drawn me to his knee, folded his arms about me, and kissed me twenty times.

"Hush, hush, *Barbara mia!*" he murmured soothingly — "hush, for my sake, my bright-eyed Princess! I see how it is—she was forgotten—left all alone here in this dull room, and so grew sad and wanted company. Hush, no more sobs, *petite!* You shall come with me to the housekeeper's parlor, and she shall wash away those tears from your cheeks, and then we will go into the ball-room together and have a dance!"

"Dance!" I repeated in the midst of my sorrow. "Shall *I* dance?"

"To be sure you shall, and I will be your partner! *Eccola!* I thought the sunshine would soon come back again!"

With this he took me out of the drawing-room, and along a passage, and into a snug little apartment where an old lady in black silk filling out scores of cups of tea and coffee to send up to the visitors. At a word from Mr. Farquhar, this excellent old lady carried me off into an inner chamber, and there washed my face, brushed my hair, tied my sash afresh, and made me quite smart and presentable. Then he once more took my hand, and we went into the ball-room together.

The ball-room was the portrait-gallery; but the portrait-gallery transformed — transfigured — changed to fairy-land. It looked like a huge bower. The old portraits smiled out from environments of myrtle and holly — the walls, chandeliers, and music-gallery were festooned with devices of evergreens, crysanthemums,

and winter heaths—there were colored lamps and Chinese lanterns nestling in the leaves and suspended along every pillar and cornice—the orchestra was hung with flags of many nations; and at the upper end of the room, filling with its single dignity nearly all the space of wall, hung the Paul Veronese. Add to all this a joyous crowd floating in couples through the mazy circles of that dreamy waltz which has disappeared of late years with all the poetry of motion; superadd the intoxicating music of a military band; and then conceive the breathless delight with which I paused at the threshold, hand in hand with the master of Broomhill, and gazed on the scene before me!

We had not been there an instant when a couple of waltzers stopped near us to rest.

"Fie, Mr. Farquhar!" said the lady, "you engaged me for this dance, and, like a recreant knight, failed to claim me when it began. What apology have you to offer?"

"One so insufficient that I shall throw myself on your mercy, Lady Flora, and not even name it," replied my companion. "My only consolation is in seeing that you have found a partner better worth your acceptance."

The lady laughed and shook her head—she was very lovely; a dark beauty, rich complexioned and haughty, like Tennyson's Cleopatra.

"That mock humility shall not serve you!" said she. "I mean to be implacable."

"Nay, then, I have indeed no resource left but exile or suicide! Choose for me, since you condemn me—shall it be arsenic or Algeria, Patagonia or pistols?"

"Neither. You shall expiate your sins on the spot, by finishing the waltz with me."

Hugh Farquhar smiled, bowed low, and encircled her waist with his arm.

"For so fair a Purgatory who would not risk perdition?" said he, gallantly.

She laughed again, excused herself to her late partner with a careless nod, rested one tiny hand and an arm sparkling with jewels, on Mr. Farquhar's shoulder, and so they floated away together, and were lost in the maze of waltzers. I sighed, and followed them with my eyes. The gentleman with whom Lady Flora had been dancing, saw that wistful glance, and took pity on me.

"Too bad to leave you standing here alone, little lady!" said he with some affectation, but much real kindness. "Where would you like to sit? Near the music?"

"Up yonder, by the Paul Veronese," I replied eagerly.

"Don't know him," said my new friend with a yawn; "but if he's there we can find him. What's his name?"

I could not have kept from laughing to save my life.

He stared and looked down upon me, and twirled his mustachios with his thumb and forefinger.

"The Paul Veronese—the big picture," I explained. "I should like to sit where I could see it."

"Oh, the six-thousand pounder!" said he. "Like to sit and look at *that*, eh? What an original idea! Come along!"

Saying which, he took my hand, piloted me

C

in and out among the dancers, and placed me in a vacant chair by a window, at the upper end of the room.

"Will that do?" he asked. "Can you see it well? Are you comfortable?"

"Oh, yes, thank you!"

"All right!" said he; nodded languidly, and sauntered away.

Left to myself now, I watched the waltzers and looked out for the couple in which I was most interested. They swept past me presently, circling amid a number of others, and were gone almost before I had time to recognize them. Then the music ceased; the dancers fell into promenading order; and I waited and watched till they should again pass by. It was not long before the stream brought them round a second time. They were talking, and Hugh was bending down and looking in her face with such an expression on his own as I had never seen there before.

"I have had no motive to keep me here," I heard him say, "and without ties all men are Bohemians. If, however——"

They went on, and I caught no more. Alas! I had heard enough, and, child as I was, that unfinished phrase woke me to a sudden passion of jealousy. I thought of his speaking eyes and the tender earnestness in his voice—I remembered the flushed smile with which she listened and looked down—I compared her with the rest, and saw that she was the loveliest in the room! Oh! a child's jealousy is as poignant, after its kind, as man's, or woman's — perhaps more poignant, because more unreasoning!

They came round a third time, and paused before the Paul Veronese. I was just near enough to hear, and listened eagerly.

"It is well placed," said she, "but not well hung. The light falls on it disadvantageously. Why not let it lean more forward? The effect would be infinitely better."

"I think so, too," replied Mr. Farquhar. "Would you like to see it done at once? Nothing could be easier."

"I shall be delighted."

"To delight you, Lady Flora," said he, "I would move every picture in the house."

With this he stepped aside, and spoke to a servant who was in waiting. The man left the room, and presently returned, bearing a set of library steps and followed by Tippoo. Some few of the guests smiled and thought it odd; but the greater number took no notice, and kept on dancing merrily.

"Now I really hope this is not very troublesome—or very difficult," said Lady Flora, standing by and toying with her fan.

"Did I not say before that nothing could be easier?" returned Hugh. "They have but to let the cords out longer, and the thing is done. Every inch added to the length of the cord, is an inch added to the incline of the picture. Gently, Tippoo — gently. Are those staples safe?"

"If it were to fall and get injured, I should never forgive myself," said Lady Flora.

"Good Heavens! I never thought of that," ejaculated he. "Stand aside — it would kill you!"

She laughed carelessly, and stepped back.

"I was not thinking of myself," said she. "But would it not be well to support it on this side?"

He nodded, was advancing to lend his aid, had his hand uplifted, when a shrill, inarticulate cry broke from the lips of the Hindoo, and the whole mass surged forward, like a falling house!

A universal shriek of horror—a sudden rush of feet—the closing up of an eager crowd and a hubbub of frightened voices, is all that I remember for many moments.

"Dr. Topham!" cried some one. "Where is Doctor Topham?"

He was in the card-room. Before the words were well nigh spoken, some half-dozen gentlemen had flown to fetch him, and he, pale but self-possessed, came running in. They opened to let him pass, and closed after him directly, like parted water. Sick, trembling, standing on my chair, and yet scarce able to support myself, I leaned against the wall, and watched the crowd. I could see nothing of what was being done—hear nothing, when all were speaking—guess nothing, or dare to guess nothing, of what might have happened!

But I was not long kept in suspense. Presently the crowd swayed back and fell apart, and from the midst of it issued—oh, Heaven!—the inanimate body of Hugh Farquhar, pallid and blood-stained, and borne by two of his servants!

They carried him out, slowly and carefully, with Dr. Topham walking beside them. Then a dead silence fell on all the room—faces, lights, walls and ceiling seemed to rock to and fro before my eyes — a confused sound, as of many waters, came rushing to my ears, and I fell without the power to save myself.

I was lying in the same spot, partly hidden by the window-curtains, when I recovered consciousness. No one had heard me fall, and in the general trouble no one had noticed me. Feeling very cold and faint, I sat up, rested my heavy head against the wall, and recalled the accident that had just happened. Was he dead? Or dying? Or only badly hurt? I dreaded to ask, and yet I felt that I must know; so I got, somehow, to my feet, and made my way over to a couple of gentlemen who were talking softly together in the embrasure of the nearest window. The elder of the two looked kind and serious. I plucked him by the sleeve to attract his attention.

"Oh, sir, if you please," I faltered imploringly, "is—is he dead?"

He looked at me very gravely, and shook his head.

"No, my dear," he said, "Mr. Farquhar is not dead; but——"

"But what?" I implied rather than said, for my lips moved, though my voice died away.

"But we fear he is seriously injured. The picture knocked him down, and the frame came against the side of his head—in which case——"

"In which case there is probably a fracture; and brain-fever, or something worse, may ensue," said the other gentleman, shrugging his shoulders. "Tush! we are here to-day, my dear fellow, and gone to-morrow—gone to-morrow! What a vile night for one's horses! I believe 'tis snowing again!"

With this they looked out of the window, and

I, sick at heart and trembling still from head to foot, crept away into a far corner and sat down in dumb despair.

One by one, the groups of whispering guests broke up and dispersed. One by one, the carriages drove noiselessly away through the falling snow. The musicians lingered awhile; then gathered up their music and their instruments, and departed likewise. At length only three or four stragglers remained, and when these were gone, a silence and solitude as of death fell upon the place.

Crouching all alone upon a form, I closed my eyes on the empty room and wondered wearily where my aunt could be. Now and then I heard the shutting of a distant door, and so held my breath and listened eagerly. Once I saw a servant flit through the hall; but he was gone in an instant, and never even glanced in to see whether any guest remained. Then the wax-lights in the sconces guttered and flickered, and went out here and there amid the fading flowers; and by and by, what with cold, fatigue, and weariness of spirit, I was fain to stretch myself along the comfortless form, pillow my flushed cheek on my arm, and fall asleep.

It was an uneasy slumber, and pervaded by a feverish sense of trouble. Was it a dream?—or did I wake once for a moment, to find myself being carried up a dimly lighted staircase, with Tippoo's olive face bent close to mine?

CHAPTER XI.

THE CRISIS.

"Grief makes one hour ten."—SHAKSPEARE.

Hugh Farquhar was indeed very ill, and it continued doubtful for many days whether he would live or die. To the torpid insensibility which weighed upon him for long hours after his fall, succeeded a burning fever accompanied by delirium. In this state he remained, with intervals of restless sleep or outworn exhaustion, for nearly a fortnight, during which time Dr. Topham staid in permanent attendance at Broomhill, and my aunt went daily. Now that the time of trial was come, she proved, indeed, that if she could be a good hater, she could also be a good friend and true. On the third day, a famous physician came down from London—a very stout and pompous gentleman, who saw the patient for about ten minutes; offered no particular opinion one way or the other; dined enormously; drank two bottles of old port; slept in the best bedroom; and went off next morning by the early coach, with a fee of fifty guineas in his pocket and an air of the utmost condescension and unconcern.

Oh, the weary days, how slowly they lagged by! From the morning after the Ball, when I awoke with that strange sense of unexplained trouble at my heart, up to the time when Hugh Farquhar's illness came to a decided issue, seemed like the interval, not of days, but of months. My recollection of it is confused, like that of a dream, or chain of dreams dreamt long ago. Having slept at Broomhill on the night of the accident, I was sent home the next morning to Stoneycroft Hall, and there left alone till evening, when my aunt came home. The sight of my white face and swollen eyelids, and the housemaid's story of how I had lain moaning on the rug before the fire, eating nothing all the day and refusing to be comforted, opened Mrs. Sandyshaft's eyes to the danger of leaving me alone. She decided, therefore, to take me with her for the future; and by ten o'clock the next morning, we were both at Broomhill. There we remained till the carriage came for us at four; and so on for every succeeding day while he lay ill.

Not being allowed to enter his room, I passed away the hours as best I could. To linger aimlessly about the gardens, unconscious of the cold —to wander through the wintry park, watching the silent fading of the snow and wondering vaguely how it would be with him when all was melted and gone—to stand by the half-hour together looking up to the windows of his sick-room, and trembling if a hand but stirred the blind—to steal up when none were looking, and crouch down silently upon the mat at his chamber-door, listening and alert, like a faithful dog—to make my way fearlessly along the upper floors where the sheeted furniture stood ghost-like in dark corners, and so penetrate to the little room in the ivied tower where the books that he had last been reading were yet left piled upon the table, and his pipe lay beside his vacant chair, curled round like a green and golden snake laid asleep by the Charmer—to hope, till hope itself became agony—to despair, till despair became intolerable and tears brought something like relief—to count the ticking of the great clock on the stairs, or the drops that fell from the thawing snow in the fantastic gargoyles by the casement—to lie in wait for those who came out from his chamber, and entreat for tidings, though all tidings were but a reiteration of the same doubts and fears—to wake every morning, and fall asleep every night, sad and sick at heart—this was my life, and this was how I loved him!

Those who had been his guests that fatal night sent frequently at this time to inquire for him, and Lady Bayham and Lady Flora came more frequently than any. They passed me once as I was wandering along the leafless avenue, and I turned aside at the sight of that beautiful dark face, and shrank from looking on it. Was she not the cause of all this evil, and had not I, according to my childish logic, the right to hate her?

At length there came a day—I think it was the twelfth or thirteenth—when Hugh, having been worse than ever all the previous night, fell into a deep sleep that endured for hours. Dr. Topham said the crisis was come, and we all knew that he would waken by and by to life or death. The long morning and the brief afternoon passed thus. Then the early dusk came on; and still my aunt sat motionless beside his bed, and still the servants crept noiselessly about with slippered feet, and voices bated to a whisper. The carriage came for us at four, as usual, and went back empty. Visitors were stopped at the courtyard-gate, and not suffered to approach. The striking weight was taken off the great clock on the stairs. It might, indeed, have been an enchanted palace now, and all the living creatures in it phantoms!

The dusk thickened and became dark, and

there was yet no change. Unable to watch there longer without rest or refreshment, my aunt stole cautiously away, and the nurse and doctor remained with the sleeper. She came down to the housekeeper's parlor and placed herself silently at table. She looked paler and sterner than usual, and took no notice of my presence. Something in her face awed me, and I said nothing. She poured out a glass of wine and drank it, with her elbow resting on the table. Then she helped herself to meat. As she did this, I saw that her hands trembled. Presently she pushed the plate away, and drew her chair to the fire.

"I can't do it, Bab," said she. "I can't do it. The food seems to choke me."

I crept over to her feet, and rested my head against her knees. The sympathy of a mutual grief was between us, and not another word was spoken. She laid her hand upon my hair, and left it there. By and by the hand slipped off, and I knew by her breathing that she slept. Some time went by thus—perhaps three quarters of an hour—during which I watched the red caverns in the fire, and dared not move for fear of waking her. Once a coal fell, and she moaned uneasily; and, after that, the French clock on the sideboard struck the hour. But she slept through it, and scarcely seemed to dream. All at once there came a footstep along the passage, and a hand upon the handle of the door. I started to my feet; but it was too late —my aunt was already aroused, and Dr. Topham was in the room.

"The danger is past," said he, breathlessly. "He is awake—he has asked for you—the delirium is gone—he will live!"

Whereupon my aunt rose up, sat down again, covered her eyes with her hand, and, after a moment's pause, said very softly and distinctly: "Thank God!"

As for me, I burst into a passion of tears, and thought my heart would break for very joy!

CHAPTER XII.

CONVALESCENCE.

HERE is a pleasant room overlooking a garden. The ceiling is lofty, and the cornice shows traces of faded gilding. Where the walls are not covered with pictures, they are lined with serious-looking books in suits of sober calf and classic Russia. Above the mantlepiece hangs an oval portrait of a dark-eyed lady, with her hair in powder. The likeness of a gentleman in a peruke and ruffles is suspended over the door. A small old-fashioned harpsichord stands in one corner, laden with *rococo* dragons in porcelain, and nicknacks in ivory and Japan. A huge screen of gilded leather, vaguely representative of Chinese life and manners, reaches across the lower end of the room. A cheerful fire burns in the grate, and the black cat on the rug enjoys it sleepily. So does the gentleman on the sofa close by, as he lies with half-closed eyes, forgetting the newspaper which fell, just now, neglected from his hand, and the orange, ready-peeled, which waits on the table beside him. Without, the sun shines brightly; but here it is deliciously subdued, save where one long sun-

beam slants between tl the green Venetians, a bended head of a little half-lying, in the middl ed by a wilderness of s invalid is Hugh Farqub myself.

Alas! he is but the w sadly changed. The br has all faded, and lef place. His cheeks are unnaturally large; and about his temples, wh thunderbolts. His bear er; and his hands loo and feebler than a chil gether, between his str physical weakness is p framework is there, bu gaunt, and ruined, an and flaccid muscle—a strength. Looking up i sidering these things, I quite closed, and that h sleep. Let him rest. contentedly over the di are they not all the wo:

Italian skies and c scraps of desert-scene camels trampling their foot; glimpses of Alg strange curves of Indi gle grows down to the i all these and more, fan a dream!

At length I came up my curiosity, and set snow scene among Alp of figures on a ledge c hanging precipice. Or the snow, and three oth skins, stood round hin like poles. The wande their feet, and the e above and around th Where were they? W Was he dead? What l

"Why so earnest, s waking presently. "W I turned it toward l off his lips.

"Ah," said he, " *petite!* Put it away."

I laid it aside, and si by the couch. It was a

"I knew it was a tru coaxingly. "Tell me i

He closed his eyes, sight, and shook his be

"Oui bono? 'Twoul replied he.

"I like to be melan

"Nay then, *mignonn* liking, and we share it must be Beaumont wh(

'There's naught Were men but But onl Oh, sweetest }

Heigho! Barbara, you and I find myself talki a woman of forty! Sl

I brought it to him, and he looked at it for some seconds without speaking — then drew his finger along a little pathway which seemed as if trampled through the snow.

"This ledge of rock," he said, "stands four thousand feet above the valley, and the valley lies down yonder. That narrow track leads to a mountain village called Grieux, many hundred feet lower. There it is green and sheltered; but up here the snow often falls, even in summer. These people are Tyroleans. I know them well, and lodged in their cottage for many months; fishing and sketching, and chamois-hunting every day. François was always my guide and fellow-sportsman."

"Which is François?" I asked, eagerly.

He pointed to the prostrate figure, and then, in an altered tone, went on;

"That man with the white beard is old Loizet, the father of these three. François was his favorite son. The other two, Jean and Jacques, were good lads enough; but François was a fine intelligent fellow, brave as a lion, and so tender-hearted that I have known him bring home a wounded bird, and tend it in his own chamber till it could fly again. One day, when he and I were out, I brought down a chamois that stood poised on a solitary peak overhead. It fell, and, falling, became entangled in a clump of bushes, half-way down the precipice. Nothing would serve François but he must go and fetch it. To do this, he was forced to make a circuit of more than a mile, and when he was gone I took out my book, leaned against a rock, and sketched this scene. By and by, I saw him on the peak. I waved my hat to him; and he began clambering down, agile as a monkey. On he came, a step at a time, lower, lower, lower, till within a foot or so of the chamois! Then he grasped the upper branches of the bush with one hand, planted his foot on a projecting stone, stooped, uttered a wild cry, and — I did not see him fall, Barbara. I saw the rotten branch give way and all his body sway forward — and I closed my eyes in horror, and *listened!*"

"Listened!" I repeated, in a low, awe-struck tone. "What did you hear, Hugh?"

"I heard a dull sound, as of something rebounding from ledge to ledge. When I looked up again he lay there, as you see him in the picture, dead—dead, within a few yards of my feet!"

I covered my eyes with my hands, and shuddered.

"What did you do then?" I asked, after a long pause.

"I went down, somehow, like one half-asleep, and found the old man cleaning his gun before his cottage-door. I can not remember what I said. I only know that we went up the mountain together, Loizet, Jean, Jacques, and I, and that it was sunset when we reached the fatal spot. Then we bound our Alpine staves together, and bore the corpse down into the village. That was three or four years ago, Barbara; and his grave was quite green when I saw it last."

As he spoke these words, his voice sank almost to a whisper, and he laid his head back wearily. I sat still, thinking of the story I had heard, and wondering why and when he added the figures to the sketch. After a few moments, he came to it of his own accord, and said—

"The scene of that accident haunted me, Barbara, for months. I had it always before my eyes, and I dreamt of it nearly every night; so one day I took out my sketch and put all the figures in, as you see them. I thought it might take away something of the vividness of the impression—transfer it, in fact, from my brain to the paper. And it did. I thought less and less of it from that time, and at last it faded altogether. Now hide the picture away. I had rather not see it again."

I obeyed; gathered all the drawings into a folio; and crept back to my old place. To crouch there by the hour together, with no other occupation than now and then to fetch his medicine, or find the book he wished for, or peel his oranges, made me the happiest of creatures! Hugh had now resumed his paper, and we were silent for a long time. Presently the door opened, and Tippoo came in, with two cards on a salver.

"Lady Bayham and Lady Flora Percivale are at the door, Sahib," he said. "They wish to know if you are yet able to receive visitors."

Hugh looked at the cards, hesitated, and seemed as if he knew not how to answer.

"I had not intended to see any one," said he, "till I could get down to the rooms below."

"I can say that the Sahib has not yet left his chamber," said Tippoo, moving away. Hugh stopped him with a gesture.

"No, no," he exclaimed. "Tell them I regret — no, that I hope — Pshaw! that won't do — and they have called so often, too. Wheel the easy-chair round to the fire, and put that medicine out of sight, and say that if they do not mind an extra flight of stairs, Mr. Farquhar will have the honor of receiving them! 'Lord Warwick, on thy shoulder will I lean,'— come, Barbara, I am not going to be found on the sofa, anyhow!"

To help him across the room and put the table in order, was the work of a moment. As the ladies were announced, he steadied himself by the arm of the chair, and rose to welcome them.

I recognized Lady Bayham immediately. She had been one of the guests at the dinner-party, and even there, in the presence of many younger women, I was struck by her exceeding loveliness. Dark, queenly, rich-complexioned, like her daughter, she had probably been even more beautiful than Lady Flora at Lady Flora's age. Standing thus, side by side, it would have been difficult, even now, to say which was the most fascinating.

"Alas, Mr. Farquhar," said Lady Flora, when the first greetings were spoken, "I have never forgiven myself—never forgotten that I was the unhappy cause of all your suffering!"

"You ought never to have blamed yourself," replied Hugh, smilingly. "The fault, if fault there were, was mine only. Since, however, it has procured me the pleasure of this visit, I will not be so ungrateful as to regret even your remorse. You are very good to come up all these stairs to see me."

"It is a cheerful room for an invalid," said Lady Bayham looking round observantly, "and has a quaint old-fashioned aspect, as if you had stolen it out of Kensington Palace, or furnished it after an interior by Hogarth."

"As a question of date, Lady Bayham," said

Hugh, "your discrimination is perfect. This room was my grandfather's ' closet,' and he still occupies it in effigy. Yonder hangs his portrait. All that you see here was of his purchasing. He was a disciple of Horace Walpole and Beckford — a lover of ugly china, and a worshiper of idols. These were his favorite authors; some few old Romans, but mostly his cotemporaries — Sterne, Fielding, Richardson, Thomson, and so forth. The room is fairly illustrative of the taste of that time. It became, after his death, my father's own peculiar den, and —"

"And is now yours," interrupted Lady Flora. "Are you an idol-worshiper, also?"

Hugh shook his head, and smiled.

"We all have our fetishes," he said; "but I believe that mine are few. Old china, at all events, is not one of them."

"I wish I knew them, few as they are," said Lady Flora, musingly; "but I see nothing here which might serve to indicate them."

"If you would discover my tastes, you must first discover my *sanctum*," said Hugh, "and that, Lady Flora, lies beyond your ken."

"Ah, you have a *sanctum* also?"

"The holiest of holies."

"Where lies it?"

"That is a secret known only to Tippoo and myself."

"A blue closet! Oh, delightful! We will go in search of it, while you are too ill to prevent us."

"*Inutile!* This old house is a wilderness, full of dark corners, subtle staircases, and ' passages that lead to nothing.' You would only get lost, like Ginevra."

"That you might discover my skeleton, fifty years to come, and put it in a glass case for the world to wonder at! Mr. Farquhar, you are an agreeable prophet."

"Nay, the conclusion is your own."

"*Allons*, Sieur de Broomhill! do you defy me to discover your retreat?"

"Heaven forbid! I believe that you would then leave no stone unturned, and no door untried until you had succeeded! I have too much respect for my own peace of mind ever to cast my gauntlet at a lady."

"Mr. Farquhar is a wise soldier," said Lady Bayham, with a languid smile, "and knows discretion to be the better part of valor. That is a charming head over the mantlepiece, and painted, if I mistake not, by Sir Thomas Lawrence."

"You are right, madam," replied Hugh, "Sir Thomas Lawrence's brush, and none other."

"Indeed, an exquisite head. What a touch! what coloring!"

"And what a subject! Really, mamma, you might spare some of your admiration for the nature on which this art has been bestowed. I never saw a more bewitching expression, or more speaking eyes! Who was this lady, Mr. Farquhar?"

"That lady," said Hugh seriously, "was my mother."

Both visitors uttered an exclamation, and rose to examine it more nearly.

"I have seen Mrs. Farquhar many times," said Lady Bayham, after a brief silence; "but she was older than this, and much altered. She had bad health, I believe, for some years before she died?"

Hugh bent his head, and looked pained.

"Powder, too, was quite gone out before I married, and it was not till I came down here with my husband that I ever met your mother. Fashion, Mr. Farquhar — fashion, and a few years more or less, make all the difference to our sex!"

At any other time, and *àpropos* of any other topic, Hugh would probably have made the polite speech which her ladyship expected; but he contented himself with another bow, and silence. Lady Flora bit her handsome lip, and flashed a warning glance at her mother; but it was of no use. Her ladyship was obtuse, and went on scrutinizing the picture through her eyeglass.

"The eyes, Mr. Farquhar, are like yours," she said. "The eyes and chin—but I see no other resemblance. She was more like you when older. You must have been young when she died. I should think you hardly remember her?"

"I remember her, madam," said Hugh, with a mixed grief and impatience in his voice, "more distinctly than I remember the events and people of a year ago. So distinctly that the subject is inexpressibly painful to me. Lady Flora, you have traveled, I think, in Italy—these sketches may, perhaps, interest you. Barbara *mia*, place the folio on the table."

I obeyed, and her ladyship, looking at me for the first time, asked who I was. He drew me fondly to his side, and kissed me on the forehead before replying.

"Her name is Barbara," said he, keeping his arm round me. "Barbara Churchill; and a very formidable little damsel she is. Descended from no less a person than the great Duke of Marlborough, and mighty proud of it, also!"

Lady Flora smiled, raised her eyebrows, said "Ah, in-deed!" and became absorbed in the folio. Hugh, however, went on, without seeming to care whether she was interested or not.

"It was to this little girl," said he, "that I first showed my Paul Veronese—nay, more, it was to please her that I first had the packing-case opened in which it came from Venice. She is a great connoisseur, Lady Flora; a reader of parliamentary debates; a player of whist, piquet, and écarté; and, besides all this, my most especial friend, nurse, playmate, and companion. Upon my honor, I don't know what I should do without her. She has been my right hand ever since my illness—ay, and my left, too, for that matter!"

Lady Flora looked up at this and expressed herself " immensely interested," while Lady Bayham honored me with such a long, cool, supercilious stare, that I felt myself grow red and hot, and knew not where to look.

"If your hatreds be as determined as your friendships are enthusiastic, Mr. Farquhar," said she, "I should be sorry to offend you. Is your *protégée* a paragon?"

He turned and took me by the hand.

"There is but one Barbara," said he gayly, "and Hugh Farquhar is her Trumpeter! Lady Flora, that sketch of an Italian vintage was done near Naples, where the famous Lagrima Christi is grown—a wine of which travelers talk more than they taste; for very little is made, even in the most favorable seasons. *Mignonne*, run down to Mrs. Fairhead for me, and desire her to send up a bottle of that old Lagrima with the yellow seal—nay, I will take no refusal, fair guest. Duly to appreciate my sketch, you must drink of the vintage which inspired it. 'Tis but an illustration of an illustration!"

Delighted to escape, I hastened from the room and bounded down the stairs. At the foot of the second flight, I came face to face with my aunt, who, with the privileged freedom of an intimate, was going up unannounced.

"Well, Bab," said she, "I've come to fetch you home. How is he?"

"Lady Bayham is there," said I, "and Lady Flora."

"Lady Bayhâm and Lady Flora!" echoed my aunt, sharply. "Mercy on us! the man's hardly saved from his grave yet, and they're here, husband-hunting, already! I won't go up. They're none of my sort—a poor, proud, pretentious, scheming lot, without even ancestors to fall back upon! If he marries that woman, I'll never forgive him."

"Marries her!" I repeated, with a strange sinking at my heart.

"Gracious goodness!" continued my aunt, working herself up and getting very angry indeed, "she's thirty, if she's a day, and has been on hand these thirteen years, in spite of her fine eyes and her flirtations! I knew what they were after, sending, and calling, and leaving their trumpery coroneted cards every day! She hasn't a farthing, either—not a farthing. Bayham's over head and ears in debt—every acre mortgaged, and every tree! Aha, Lady Flora! Broomhill would suit your ladyship pretty well, even though it belongs to a commoner! There was a time, too, when you wouldn't look at a commoner! Pshaw, Bab, I've no patience with them. Let's go home, child."

"You won't go away without seeing Hugh!" I exclaimed, almost ready to cry.

"Why not? He has his grand friends with him."

"But he'd rather see you than all the grand friends in the world!"

"I'm not so sure of that," said my aunt; mollified, but unwilling to seem so.

At this moment, his bell was rung impatiently. I had forgotten all about the Lagrima Christi! To fly past my aunt without a word of explanation, fulfill my errand, and run back again, panting and breathless, was the work of a few seconds. But I had remembered it too late. Before the last vibrations of the bell had died away, I heard the rustling of their silks on the stairs; and, looking up, saw them already coming down. My aunt muttered something which was certainly no compliment, and turned away abruptly. I, taken by surprise, stepped aside, and knew not whether to go or stay. Lady Bayham swept by, dignified and unconscious; but Lady Flora paused and graciously extended the tips of her fingers.

"Good-by, little girl," said she. "What is you old-fashioned name? Tabitha—Dorothea—Pamela?"

"Neither," I replied coldly. "I am called Barbara."

"Ah, true—Barbara. Well, good-by, Barbara. When Mr. Farquhar is better, he shall bring you some day at Ashley Park, to see me."

And with this she nodded and passed on, not without a prolonged stare at my aunt, who was, apparently, intent upon a painting at the further end of the corridor. No sooner were they gone than Mrs. Sandyshaft came striding back, very red and excited.

"I like that!" said she. "Mr. Farquhar 'shall' bring you—she answers for him already, hey? You shan't go, Bab. I'll not hear of it—I'll not allow it. An artful designing flirt! If I had my will, she should never enter these doors again. I repeat it, if he marries that woman I'll never forgive him!"

Whereupon, being very indignant, my aunt took three or four turns along the corridor to cool herself, and then went up two stairs at a time. As for me, sorrowful and unsettled, I wandered about below, wondering if Hugh would really marry Lady Flora some day, and thinking how sad a change it would make for me.

───────

CHAPTER XIII.

THE SILVER RING.

HUGH FARQUHAR was a long time getting well. Struck down when the snow lay on the ground, he was not able to mount his horse again till the primroses lay clustered at the roots of the old oaks in the woods. His first ride was to Stoneycroft Hall—his second to Ashley Park. It seemed natural to conclude, since his health was so far reëstablished, that our intercourse would be firmer, more frequent, more intimate than ever. It was now his turn to repay my aunt's long kindness—to drop in, as of old—to chat and squabble, and play piquet of an evening, and renew, with interest, all the pleasant meetings of long ago. And yet, from this time, we saw less of him. He was no longer a stranger in the county; and we were not, as formerly, his only friends. Now that he was better, visitors and invitations poured in upon him; and, though he cared little for society, he loved sport too well to decline the last hunting parties of the season. Still this was not all. A certain uneasy sense of change came over the spirit of our intercourse. Something of the old genial feeling was gone, and things were no longer quite the same. I believe, after all, that it was Mrs. Sandyshaft's own fault, and that from first to last she had but herself to blame. She had made up her mind that he should not like Lady Flora too well ; and she could not, for her life, forbear to taunt him with the pride, poverty, and matrimonial designs of the Bayham family. She could scarcely have done any thing more injudicious. He liked these people tolerably well, visited somewhat frequently at Ashley Park, and was received there as a welcome guest. What was it to him if Lord Bayham were in debt? His dinners were none the less pleasant, and his port tasted none the worse. Lady Flora might be thirty and a flirt ; but she amused him, and he could enjoy her society without incurring the peine forte et dure of either courtship or matrimony. When first attacked by my aunt's petulant sarcasms, he laughed, and parried them. When he found them persistently leveled at himself, he grew weary. By and by, seeing the same thing persevered in, he became impatient. Thus it happened that bitter things were sometimes said ; that argument too often approached the confines of disagreement ; and the old times never came back.

I missed him—oh, how I missed him ! Latterly, as he was recovering from his illness, Broomhill had become almost another home to me ! I was there nearly every day. I knew where to find his favorite books ; how to fill his pipe ; which flowers he liked best ; when to be silent ; and when to talk to him. Sometimes I almost wished that he could remain thus forever, that I might forever wait on him. Now, however, my occupation was gone, and I found myself forgotten. Let it not be thought that I blame him for it. I was but a childish handmaiden, and held but a childish claim upon him. He had all my heart, and gave me for it a kind word now and then ; a stray caress ; a passing thought when he had nothing else to think of. To him I was something less than a pastime— to me he was something more than my life. What wonder, then, that I grew pale and thin, and drooped like a neglected plant ?

"Bab, you don't walk enough," said my aunt one warm spring morning. "You've lost all your color, and you eat next to nothing. This won't do. Put on your bonnet, and lay in a stock of oxygen directly."

I obeyed, and took the path to the woods. To reach them, I passed first through a large field where a single plowman was driving fragrant furrows in the rich red earth, and then through a hop-garden, gaunt with poles, around which the young plants were just twining their first tendrils. Then over a high stile, and into the shade of the woods.

What words of mine shall describe the peaceful beauty of the place that day ? The sky was gray and low, and there was a soft air abroad, heavy with gathered odors of May-blossom and wild hyacinths. The close young leaves made a sylvan roof above, and steeped every vista in a green and dreamy gloom. The birds sang to distraction in the uppermost boughs. The clouds met every now and then, and melted into a warm and gentle shower. In some places the ground was all golden with primroses, and in others the banks were so blue with hyacinths that no artist dared to paint them. By and by, I came to an open space carpeted with springy turf, in the midst of which stood a gamekeeper's cottage and a group of horse-chestnuts covered with white blossoms. Here a bloodhound sprang out of his kennel, straining to the full length of his chain, and barking at me till I turned aside into the close paths again, and wandered out of sight. Now I chanced upon a spot where the woodcutters had lately been at work. They had left the saw half buried in the stem of one tall beech, and another lay felled and stripped beside it, like the skeleton of the giant Pagan, in the Pilgrim's Progress. Presently a tiny brown squirrel darted by, and ran up a larch-tree ; and, farther on, I saw a pheasant stalking through the faded ferns. Here it was more silent, more solitary, more sylvan than ever. I sat down to rest on an old mossy stump, listening to the silence and to those sounds that make such silence deeper. Now and then I heard the

cuckoo's two sad notes ; and, nearer, the cooing of a wood-pigeon.

"How pleasant it would be," thought I, "to live here in a thatched cottage with roses growing over the door, and drink new milk and eat wild strawberries every day. But then it should be always summer-time ; and one would want to know the language of the birds, like the Prince in the fairy-tale !"

And then I remembered that Hugh had told me that story—told it to me one morning with his arm about my waist and his pale cheek resting languidly against a pillow—and this remembrance brought tears with it. It is sometimes a luxury to shed tears ; and to-day, in this balmy solitude, with the last slow drops of the passing shower yet falling around me, it was both sad and sweet to weep.

Suddenly, in the midst of the stillness, and so close that it seemed to come from behind the tree against which I was sitting, I heard the crack of a rifle ! At the same instant something hissed past my ear ; a small bird fluttered to my feet ; a dog and a man came crashing through the underwood ; a well-known voice cried—"My God ! I might have killed her !"—and I found myself clasped in Hugh Farquhar's arms ; safe, frightened, trembling, but very happy.

For the first few moments he was even more agitated than myself. Then he flung away his gun, sat down upon the broken tree-stump, held me at arm's length, looked in my eyes till his own grew dim.

"Oh, Barbara—little Barbara !" said he tenderly. "What should I have done if I had harmed thee ?"

I nestled closer to him ; and, for answer, laid my cheek down on his shoulder.

"I marvel," he went on, "that the ball spared thee, deary. See where it grazed the bark yonder ; and see where the woodcock lies—why, it must have sped within an inch of thy head !"

"I heard something whistle by," I said, shudderingly ; "but it all happened so quickly that I had no time for fear."

He kissed me on the forehead, and was silent after this for several minutes.

"It must be three weeks since I saw thee last, mignonne," said he, at length. "How the time slips through one's fingers !"

"It has seemed very slow to me, Hugh."

"Because you are young, happy, unoccupied —because life is fresh to you—because you count by impressions, instead of deeds. Tush, child, the sands will run fast enough by and by ! Too fast—too fast !"

"Why too fast ?"

"Because the world is a mighty pleasant place, and one would like thoroughly to enjoy it ! Think of all the books that we must leave unread, all the pictures we must leave unseen, all the countries, people, sciences, experiences which we must forego for want of time to know them ! I hate to be hurried, Barbara mia,— especially by that relentless old gentleman who carries the hour-glass and scythe !"

The dog, which had all this time been snuffing the fallen woodcock, now took it in his mouth, brought it gravely up, and laid it at his master's feet. A strange flash of expression passed over Hugh Farquhar's face.

"Pompey," said he, "what have I done, oh,

most satirical of puppies! that thou should'st rebuke me thus? Lo! my very dog cuts jokes upon me, and turns up his tail in contempt of my philosophy! Pompey, I confess it. I am a humbug—an egotist—a base, one-sided casuist! I love life; I grumble at death—and I shoot woodcocks! 'Tis Wordsworth who bids us

'Never to blend our pleasures or our pride
With sorrow of the meanest thing that feels.'

That's very good poetry, and better morality—yet Wordsworth ate game, like many a worse man."

. All this was said mockingly, sadly, abstractedly, more to himself than to me. Having spoken, he paused with his chin in his hand, and sat for a long time, looking at the dog and the bird. His attitude was meditative, his complexion paler than before his illness, his expression more than usually thoughtful. I crouched by, looking at him, listening to him, treasuring up every syllable. Considering all things, I followed the intention of his words more nearly. than might have been expected.

"*Petite*," said he suddenly, "when you don't see me for three weeks or a month together, do you ever think of me?"

"Think of you, Hugh!" I faltered. I did not dare to tell him that I thought of nothing else.

He laughed, and passed his hand over my hair.

"If I were to go away again," he said, "you would forget me."

"Never, Hugh! Never so long as I live."

Startled by the earnestness of my voice, he turned half round, took my head between his two hands, and looked at me.

"My child! my little friend!" said he wonderingly. "Why, what a pale face is this!"

I tried to smile; but the effort was too much for me. I felt my lip quiver and my eyes fill up, and so dropped my head upon his knee, and sobbed aloud.

"You—you won't go away, will you?" I cried passionately. "You won't go away—or—or marry Lady Flora?"

"Marry Lady Flora!" he repeated quickly. "What put that into your head? Who says it? Nay, child, I *will* know!"

"Every body."

"And who is every body, pray?"

"I—I don't know—Doctor Topham told us that—that every body says so. Please, Hugh, don't be angry—I—I am so sorry; but it's quite true."

"Is it, by Jove?" exclaimed he, starting angrily to his feet, and striding to and fro. "What an obliging world it is, and how flattering is the interest with which it dives into one's private affairs!"

I saw that he was vexed, and so held my tongue and tried to subdue the sobs that kept rising in my throat.

Presently he came and stood before me.

"Upon my soul, Barbara," said he, with a bitter laugh, "I think I had better marry you, and stop the people's mouths that way! What say you? Will you be my little wife seven years to come?"

I knew it was a jest; and yet I felt my heart beat, and my cheeks grow scarlet.

"You don't mean it," said I; "and if you did——"

"Oh, but I do mean it, though," returned he. "Put your hand in mine, and say 'Hugh Farquhar, seven years hence, when I am old enough, I will marry you.' Come, that's easy enough!"

I trembled from head to foot. I longed to say it, but dared not. He sat down, still laughing, drew me on his knee, and began disengaging a curious silver ring from a variety of seals and other trifles that hung at his watchguard.

"See now," said he, "I mean to betroth you with all due form and ceremony. This is an ugly thing; but a curiosity. I got it from an Arab in the desert near the Dead Sea, and gave him my penknife in exchange for it. Now, Barbara *mia*, say the words I told you, and you shall have the Arab's ring." .

Seeing that I still hesitated, he went through the sentence again, and I repeated it after him, whisperingly and with averted face.

"Lady, by yonder blessed moon, I swear," said he, placing the ring with mock solemnity on the third finger of my left hand, "that tips, most appropriately with Arabic silver, all these fruit-tree tops —— unfortunately the moon is absent just now, on a visit to our antipodes; but we can do without it on the present occasion! Now kiss me, Barbarina, and promise not to say a word of this to any body."

I gave the promise readily.

"*Corpo di Bacco!*" said he, now I'll give 'every body,' something to gossip about! I'll proclaim that I am an engaged man—what a joke! what a mystery! what a test! By Jupiter, if the Bayhams have any design——"

He paused; put me gently aside; rose; and again paced backward and forward, his eyes fixed on the ground, and his hands clasped behind his back. Coming back presently to where I was standing he saw me still occupied with the ring.

"You can not wear it, *mignonne*," he said. "It is twice too large for your little slender finger."

"But I want to wear it, Hugh. Always to wear it."

"Do you? Nay, then, you shall have my guard, and carry it around your neck, like a locket. Do you see those curious characters engraved upon it? They are Arabic letters, and spell the name of Allah. So that's capitally contrived. Now remember, Barbara, if any one sees it, or asks you about it, say I gave it to you—not a word more or less."

It was a tiny elastic guard, no thicker than a thread, and, having attached the ring to it, he put it with his own hands round my neck.

"Life is made up," said he, "of curious chances. I began by nearly shooting you this morning, little one, and I have ended by—— Pshaw! a betrothal is better than a bullet, anyhow! Seven years—seven short, long, pleasant, miserable years. How much taller do you mean to be by then, Barbara? 'Just as high as my heart,' as Orlando saith of Rosalind? Why, body, o' me! how seriously the darling takes it! Pale one minute, red another, and trembling like a frightened fawn. Come, this won't do, Barbara. Cheer up, and bid me good-by; for I have brought down but this one bird to-day, and

I must offer up more sacrifices to Cupid before I go home."

I forced a smile, and put up my face to kiss him.

"Good-by, Hugh," I said.   "When are you coming again?"

"I'll come—let me see——I'm engaged for two days—three days this week, and to-day is Monday.   Well, *petite*, I'll come on Friday."

I flushed all over with delight.

"Will you, really?" I asked, with my whole heart on my lips.

"I will, really.   Now go home before the next shower comes up.   Adieu, my lady-love."

And with this he pressed his lips once again to my cheek, bagged the woodcock, whistled to Pompey, shouldered his gun, and, with a last wave of the hand, plunged into the copse and disappeared.

, I sat there a long time—long enough for the shower to come and go, and the shadows perceptibly to shift upon the grass.   Once I heard the distant echo of his gun; but I remember only that, and the strange, vague, dreamy wonder with which I sat looking at the ring. He had asked me to be his "little wife" seven years to come.   Was he not both in jest and in earnest?   What did it all mean, and how was it to end?

By and by I adjusted the chain in such a manner that no one could observe it, and went home.   The day thus went by, slowly, deliciously, like a perplexed but happy dream; and that night I fell asleep with the ring clasped tightly in my hand, and that name that he had given me yet lingering on my lips.

CHAPTER XIV.

THE ROUNDING OF THE YEAR.

"ADIEU, mes beaux jours!"—MARIE STUART.

THE Friday morning came—the morning of the day on which Hugh had promised to call. I had been conscious of it all night, in my dreams; and now, as the first sunbeams touched my window-panes, I woke, knowing that the weary days of waiting had gone by, and I should see him soon again.

The morning was brilliant, mistless, and crimson toward the East.   It was yet very early; for yonder, across a field just opposite the house, went the laborers to their work.   Although it was not yet time, I rose and dressed, opened the casement, and leaned out into the fresh air to gather a few leaves from the myrtle that clustered without.   Reaching forward thus, bathing my head in the sunshine and my little white arms in the dew of the dark leaves, it occurred to me all at once that this was the month of May again, and that I had been here just one year.

Yes, a year, a whole year, during which I had beheld all the changes of nature; seen the green things flourish and die, and be born again; witnessed the fading of the frost and the falling of the snow; and watched how the morning sun varied in his rising as the months rolled on.   It seemed but yesterday when yonder dusky fallow was yellow with corn—when the oak beside the pond wore a brief livery of scarlet and gold—

when the blackberries lay thick in the hedge, and the dead leaves rotted in the lanes.   What a happy year, and how quickly it had flown! I had heard little from London all this time.   A formal letter was once or twice exchanged between my father and my aunt; but excepting that my sisters were well, that Miss Whymper continued as usual to teach them, and that dear old Goody always sent her love, I knew nothing of my home or its inmates.   I fear I had not much thought or care to know more.   Happy and unrestrained, I only desired to stay here forever.

"Ah! con che affetto amore e il ciel pregai
Che fosse eterno si dolce soggiorno!"

By and by, finding that as yet there was no one stirring in the house, I got a book, curled myself up in the embrasure of the window, and began to read.   I remember the book as well as possible—it was Dodsley's translation of Boccaccio, and the story was Griselda—but I also remember that I could not keep my attention to the tale; that my thoughts wandered away to Hugh Farquhar and my hands to the silver ring, and that I fell into a long dream from which I was at last aroused by the swinging of the garden-gate, and the halting tread of the lame postman on the gravel walk.   Seeing me at the window, he touched his cap and smiled, then left the letters in the porch, and hobbled away again with his leathern satchel swinging at his side.   I watched him to the turn of the road, and then, knowing by this time the household must be awake and stirring, went down-stairs.

I found my aunt in the breakfast-parlor. She was standing at the window with her back toward me, and an open letter in her hand. An indefinable something in her attitude, in the way that she kept her head turned from me, struck me the moment I went in.   I was about to speak; but hesitated and stood still.   She then folded the letter up, slowly and deliberately, and came over to the breakfast-table.   Silently I took my accustomed seat in the great carved chair opposite.   I felt that something was wrong.   I saw that she was pale, and that her hand trembled.   She laid the letter beside her plate.   I could not see the writing; but the seal looked like my father's, large, round, and firm, with showy armorial bearings.

A weary quarter of an hour went by, during which I ate little, and my aunt nothing.   Now and then she cast a troubled glance at the letter; but she only once lifted her eyes to my face.   Had I done any thing to offend her?

The silence became oppressive, and seemed all the more intolerable for the sunshine and splendor of the outer day.   The hall was flooded with a golden light, and the pleasant farm-house sounds came mingled with the singing of the birds.   Oh, how I longed to be out in the free air, and what a relief it was when my aunt pushed back her chair and said:—

"Bab, I have letters to write this morning, and must be alone.   Go out and amuse yourself till ten o'clock."

Welcome permission!   To call the dogs, tie on my broad-brimmed country hat, and dance away, reveling like a butterfly in the sun, was for me but the work of a few seconds.   Down the "checkered shade" of the green lanes; across the meadow, yellow with buttercups;

through the churchyard where the vicar's old gray cob was grazing; up the drift where the hay which they had been carting late the night before was yet clinging to the hedges on either side; over more meadows and through more lanes we went, and thus came back toward home so warm and weary that I was glad to sit down, at last, under the shadow of a clump of young alders, and rest till it was time to go in.

"Cuckoo!" intoned the messenger of summer, from a copse close by; and then I remembered the old German superstition, and said to myself—"Yes, I shall be here next year! I shall still be here, and I shall still be happy!"

Presently the church clock far away chimed the three-quarters, and I went home. My aunt was waiting for me at the gate. She shaded her eyes with her hand when she saw me coming, and looked at me earnestly.

"Come here, Bab," said she, stalking up the path before me, and taking her seat in the porch. "Come and sit here. I have something to say to you."

I sat down, my heart fluttering with a vague apprehension; and my aunt presently began.

"Your father and I have been writing to one another lately, Bab," said she. "Our correspondence is over now, however. I had a letter from him this morning, and I've answered it, and sent my answer to the post; and there it ends. What do you suppose we have been writing about?"

I shook my head. How should I know what they had been writing about?

"Well, Bab, we've been writing about you."

"About me?"

"Yes, and as you must know the issue of it, it is only right that you should also know the foregoings. I wrote first, Bab. I wrote to ask your father to leave you with me always. You have been here a year, Bab, and somehow, I have got used to you—like, to have you about me—believe you to be a true child, and — and fancy you have some kind of love for me, old and disagreeable as I am. Hush! not a word. Listen to me patiently; for I have more to tell you. Well, Bab, I wrote to your father and told him something of this. I offered to bring you up, educate you, and be a mother to you. I never had a child of my own, and I should have liked to keep you while I live, provided you were willing, Bab — always provided you were willing."

"Willing!" I repeated, with clasped hands and tear-filled eyes. "Willing!"

"Ay—willing—which I believe you would be. Well, don't let's be foolish, child. There's more to come. Your father answered my letter, and said neither 'yes' nor 'no;' but bargained with me, Bab—bargained with me—tried to trade on the love I bore you, and turn it to his profit! Didn't I say it from the first? Didn't I guess it from the first? Didn't I tell you that I would be your friend for life, but bid you count on nothing—nothing—nothing at my death? Answer me, child—do you remember it?"

Trembling, I bent my head, but had no power to speak. It frightened me to see her in these moods, and I knew that this was, of all topics, the one which moved her most. She rose and took a turn or two outside the porch, looking strangely angered and excited—then came back, resumed her seat, and went on.

"Your father, Bab," said she, speaking very calmly, but with a quivering undertone in her voice, "is a very clever, worldly, calculating man —a little too clever, sometimes, and a little too worldly; apt to speculate over-far on other folks' weaknesses; apt to overreach himself, now and then—but no matter! Now what do you think your clever father proposed to sell you at—eh, Bab?"

"Sell me!" I exclaimed, the indignant blood flushing all my face. "Sell me!"

"Ay, 'tis a rough word, but the right one, Bab —chafe under it if you will! He proposed—listen to this—he proposed that I should not only keep, educate, and provide for you; but that I should will my property to you and your two sisters, share and share alike. Fancy that—share and share alike!"

Dumb with shame, I could only clasp my hands and hang my head.

"Well, the wonder is that I didn't tear his letter into a hundred bits, and send them back by the next post," said my aunt, getting excited again, but striving hard to keep calm. "But no—I waited two whole days, and thought it all out from beginning to end before I answered it. What I then said, Bab, I may as well tell you. I refused his conditions point-blank. I would have nothing to say to his two elder girls —they are nothing to me, and always will be nothing. I refused to bind myself to any promises, even on your account. But I told him that if he left you here and trusted to my justice and generosity, you should be no loser at my death. What I meant by that is neither here nor there, Bab. It might have been all—it might have been half—at all events it would have been enough; but what I insisted on was the trust; and what I hate most in all the world is to be dictated to!"

"Well—and his answer?" I asked eagerly.

"Tush, Bab, let's make a long story short! We argued, and bargained, and wrote three or four letters, and couldn't come to an agreement anyhow. This morning I received what he is pleased to call his *ultimatum ;* in which he distinctly states that I must either keep you on his terms or send you home. He counts on my love for you—he believes that sooner than part from you, I will consent to any thing! Well, to-morrow morning he will have my answer. It's written, and it's gone, and it's all over. Bab, I—I——"

She paused, and her lip trembled. As for me, I rose up, sat down, rose up again, and shook from head to foot.

"You won't send me away!" I cried. "You —you won't send me away!"

"Bab," said she, with averted face, "your mother was my favorite niece. I loved her dearly; but she married against my will, and from the day of her marriage I never looked upon her face again. It cost me a deep sorrow; but I did it, and I would have done it, had it cost me twenty times that sorrow. Your father and I have been enemies ever since, and our enmity will henceforth be deeper than before. I can not be his tool and plaything, Bab—I can not, and I will not!"

"Still you won't send me away!" I repeated with increasing agitation. "You won't, you can't send me away!"

She remained silent for a moment. Then, nerving herself to firmness, said:—

"You must go home, Bab. I have said it."

Go home! The words struck upon my ear, but bore no meaning with them. Stunned, despairing, dumb, I stood before her, and neither spoke nor wept. Presently she also rose and turned as if to go into the house; but our eyes met, and she paused with her hand on the latch.

"When?" I whispered, rather than said.

She shook her head, and sighed heavily.

"When the coach comes by to-morrow," she replied tremulously. "The sooner it's over the better, Bab—the sooner the better!"

An involuntary cry of anguish escaped me, and I sat down silently, looking at her.

"God help us, Bab!" said she; then stooped, kissed me hurriedly on both cheeks, and went into the house.

Oh, the weary, weary day! Oh, the heavy hours—the dreary dinner-meeting—the heart-ache, the languor of soul, the tears kept back, and ever rising! All that afternoon, I wandered like a restless spirit through the dear familiar places. I visited the orchard, the sheep-fold, the churchyard, the meadow where I heard the cuckoo in the morning, and the mossy stump in the woods, where Hugh Farquhar sat three days ago. To each I said "good-by;" and yet, though I looked and lingered, and tore myself away, I could not believe it was for the last time. My only hope was to see him in the evening; my only comfort was to clasp the silver ring more closely to my heart. Somehow or another, I had a vague idea that he alone could help me now, and till I had seen him, I would not quite despair. Was he not my ideal of goodness and bounty, wealth and power? Was he not still my hero and my prince, and was it not natural that, even in this strait, I should look to him for succor?

The day faded out of the sky; the twilight thickened; the stars came out one by one; and still I waited, hoped, believed. All the afternoon my aunt had been shut up in her own room, and now she and Jane were preparing for my departure. There was no one to forbid me; so I went out and stood by the gate in the dim starlight, listening for his coming. The night air fanned my forehead and cooled my eyes, weary as they were, and hot with weeping. Yonder gleamed the light at my chamber window, and now and then a shadow flitted across the blind. I could not help looking toward it, for I knew what was going forward within—knew that my box was being packed, and that to-morrow I must go. Alas! there was both grief and anger at my heart, as I turned away again and gazed into the gloom toward Broomhill. My only hope lay in Hugh Farquhar and his influence; and ever as I waited, counting the minutes and the beatings of my heart, that hope grew stronger.

But he came not. One by one the quarters chimed out from the church-tower over the meadows—then nine o'clock struck—then the quarters, one by one again—then ten o'clock, and I knew that the last chance was past.

He had forgotten his promise, and I must go without even bidding him farewell!

CHAPTER XV.

A DREARY WELCOME HOME.

WOULD she really let me go? Not till the last moment could I bring myself to believe it —not till the last moment, when the coach stood at the gate and the time had come to say "good-by." Then by her pallor, by her silence, by the stony determination written in every line of her countenance, I saw that it must be. Sick, giddy, quite worn out with sorrow and wakefulness, I suffered myself to be drawn to her bosom, and felt that she kissed me twice on either cheek.

"Good-by, Bab," she said, hoarsely. "Heaven bless you!"

But I had no strength to answer — I could not even weep. I could only put one little cold hand in hers, and dumbly, drearily, turn away and follow Jane to the gate. The guard was waiting with the door open, impatient to be gone; and in another instant I felt myself lifted in; heard the starting-signal given; caught one brief glimpse of Jane with her apron to her eyes; saw that my aunt was no longer at the porch; and found myself speeding away— away toward London.

I can recall little or nothing of what followed, except that the coach was empty, and that I lay back in a corner, stupefied and motionless. Once I put my hand up to my face and found my cheeks were wet; and I recollect wondering whose tears they were, and how they came there; but beyond this I seemed to notice nothing. At Ipswich we stopped, as usual, for an hour; and later in the day I remember waking up, as if from a deep dream, and finding the coach quite full of passengers. How or when they took their places, and of what age, sex, or station they were, I have no idea. I only know that they came and went like the hedges that flitted past the windows, and that, drowned in the Lethe of my discontent, I took no heed of any thing.

As the day waned we drew near London, and, toward twilight, came upon gas-lamps and a road bordered by villas. Presently the villas were succeeded by long rows of houses; by shop-windows blazing with lights; by streets crowded, noisy, narrow, and alive with traffic. Then we turned sharply down a by-street, dived under an archway, clattered into a gloomy yard, and were at the end of our journey.

The passengers alighted, and were met by those who awaited them. I also got out and looked anxiously around, expecting Goody. But no Goody was there. Bewildered by the unusual noise and bustle of the place, I wandered to and fro, scanning every countenance, and recognizing none. Then the luggage was unladen, and each passenger claimed his own. When my box was handed down, I sat on it and waited wearily. One by one, my fellow-travelers then dispersed and went away; and only the empty coach, the smoking horses, and the busy ostlers remained.

It was now quite dark, and a searching wind came blowing through the archway. No one looked at me; no one spoke to me — save once, when the coachman bustled past, a mountain of coats and capes, and gave me a rough "good night." Shivering, I sat perched upon my box, like the dwarf in Mrs. Shelley's story, and watched the stable-boys running to and fro with their lanterns, the grooms rubbing down the horses, and the chamber-maids flitting along the wooden galleries above. Surely Goody had mistaken the hour, and would be here presently! Could it be possible that my aunt's letter had never been delivered? What should I do, if no one came to fetch me home?

Whilst I was turning these questions over in my mind, and striving hard to be brave and hopeful, an old man came hobbling across the yard, and peered curiously into my face. He was the oddest, driest, dustiest little old man I ever saw; and which was strangest of all, had a boot drawn up on each arm and slippers on his feet, so that he looked as if his legs were in the wrong place.

"To be left till called for?" said he, in a hoarse interrogative whisper.

Vaguely conscious of his meaning, I nodded; whereat he desired me to "come on," and limped away, beckoning mysteriously with his boots, like the ghost in Hamlet. Wondering, and half unwilling, I followed him to a little open doorway under the foot of the great wooden staircase. On the threshold of this place I shrank back, and hesitated. I had fancied that he was taking me to some room where Goody was waiting; but this was a mere den, filled, like a cobbler's stall, with rows of boots and shoes, and lit by a rushlight in a bottle.

"Come in," said he in the same tone, half-growl, half-whisper. "Come in. Don't be afeard."

Saying which, he crouched down on a box, and pointed with the toe of the right boot at a wooden stool in the corner.

Somewhat reassured by this invitation, I ventured in and sat where he directed. A long silence followed, during which I balanced myself on the edge of the stool; gazed curiously at the shelves all laden with boots and shoes, old bottles, blacking-brushes, and broken candlesticks; and now and then stole a side glance at my entertainer.

"It's a queer place, an't it?" he observed, resting his elbows on his knees, and rocking himself slowly to and fro. "Better to wait in than the yard; but a queer place to live in. A queer place to live in."

The position in which he was now sitting and the action by which it was accompanied, projected so hideous and grotesque a four-legged shadow on the opposite wall, that for some seconds I could only sit and stare at it, like one fascinated.

"Do you live here, sir?" I asked, presently. It was the first time I had spoken, and, despite my politeness, my voice trembled.

"Live here!" he echoed. "Ay. All day—every day. From year's end to year's end."

I was more amazed than ever, and, not knowing what to say next, looked from him to his shadow, and thence up to the inverted stairs overhead, thick-set with cobwebs and studded with rusty nails.

"But I don't sleep here," said he, after another pause. "I sleep in the stables."

To which I replied timidly, that I was glad to hear it; and again the conversation dropped. The silence this time was so prolonged that I twice heard a neighboring clock chime the quarters; and still the wind moaned drearily; and still horses, and ostlers, and travelers came and went in the yard without, and busy footsteps passed up and down the stairs above our heads, over and over again. Feeling at length desperately tired and sleepy, I fell to counting the boots and shoes to keep myself awake. I counted them from left to right—then from right to left—then took each alternate one, and went backward for the rest, and only grew more drowsy than ever for my pains.

"You're looking at them," said the little old man, suddenly. "There's lots of 'em, an't there? Lot's of 'em."

"Ye—es, sir," I faltered, somewhat startled to find that he had been watching me. "A great many."

"Twenty-seven pair," said he reflectively. "Twenty-seven pair, not counting the odd Hessian belonging to number thirteen with the gout."

Greatly perplexed by this observation, I hesitated, wondered, and at last suggested that he surely possessed more than he wanted of these useful articles.

"Oh, you think they're all mine, do you?" croaked he, shifting quickly round, and peering at me again from beneath a pair of bushy white eyebrows. "Who d'ye suppose I am, eh? Who d'ye suppose I am?"

I shook my head doubtfully.

"I'm Boots," said he, striking himself impressively on the breast with the heels of the pair which still remained on his arms. "Boots" —and immediately tucked up his legs, and sat tailor-wise on the box.

Utterly discomposed and overwhelmed by this tremendous revelation, I sat with parted lips and stared at him breathlessly. Boots! Boots incarnate! Good Heavens, was he mad, and could it be his propensity to wear Wellingtons as other folks wear gloves?

"I've lived here, man and boy, going over sixty year," continued he. "I was a young chap when I first came. They picked me out of the gutter, and made Boots of me; and Boots I've been ever since."

I began fervently to wish myself out in the yard again.

"The place has changed names and masters more than once all that time," he went on; talking, indeed, rather to himself than me. "But I belong to it, like the sign outside, or the big clock on the stairs. Blue Boar, or Red Lion, or White Horse, it's all the same to me. I'm a part of it; and somehow, I seem to fancy that so long as the old house holds together, I shall hold with it."

He fell musing at this, and gazed at the boots and shoes for a long time without speaking.

"See them, now," he said at length. "See them. They've been my business, my companions, my amusement these sixty year and more. You'd never guess the stories they tell me, or the news I pick out of 'em. Shut me up from the light of day and give me only these, and I'll tell you the changes in the fashion, the season of the year, and the state of the weather."

Finding that he looked to me for a reply, I ventured to inquire if he always had so many as seven and twenty pairs.

"Sometimes more," said he briskly, "sometimes less. It depends on the time of the year and the state of the markets. Twenty pair a day is the average I make of it, my dear. Twenty pair a day."

I made up my mind that he was very mad indeed.

"Look here, now," he continued, untucking his legs, and getting up to hunt for a fragment of old slate and a morsel of chalk, which lay with a heap of other rubbish on an upper shelf — "look here. Twenty pair a day, counting seven days to the week, and fifty-two weeks to the year, and letting leap-years alone, makes just four hundred and thirty-six thousand, eight hundred pair in sixty years. Think of that! Four hundred and thirty-six thous —— I've a bad head for most things—'specially for figures — but I've done it hundreds of times, and it always comes to the same. It's right. I know it's right."

"That is a great many, sir, for one person," I observed nervously.

"Ay, a great many. Sometimes I wonder if I shall live to make it five hundred thousand, and then I think I'd like to have them write it up on my gravestone, for the queerness of it. Four hundred and thirty-six thousand, eight hundred, in sixty year!"

With this he again began rocking himself backward and forward, and fell into the old reverie. And still the wind howled, and the footfalls echoed, and I sat staring at him by the light of the flickering rushlight. By and by a bell rang close outside the door of the den—a shrill, impatient bell, with a vixenish tongue—and a voice somewhere in the galleries cried "Boots!"

My companion shook his head, and got up wearily.

"That's it!" he growled. "That's it. Nothing but ring, ring, ring, from morning till night, and from night till morning. Keep you there, little girl. I'll be back presently."

And so, with his head bent forward and his arms crossed behind, he shambled away, looking like a man who had folded his legs over his back, and was walking off on his hands.

Left alone now, and feeling very cold and tired, I shut the door, and curled myself upon the box where he had been sitting. Again the clock struck—this time four quarters, and nine strokes for the hour. Nine o'clock, and the coach came in at half-past seven! Was I quite forgotten, and must I remain all night in this strange place? What would my aunt say, could she but see me now? Would the little old man give me shelter, and let me sleep there with the boots and shoes while he went to bed in the stables? How should I find my way home in the morning? And what would Goody do, when she found that I had been left in this plight all the dreary night? Despite my fortitude, I could not forbear a few self-pitying tears. Then my thoughts wandered and my eyelids grew heavy, and I fell into an uneasy sleep, during which I dreamed that I was once more in the coach traveling to London; the only difference being that Goody was driving, and that we were drawn by a team of four hundred and thirty-six thousand pairs of polished Wellingtons.

I can not tell how long I slept. It may have been more than an hour, or it may have been but a few moments. Deep as my slumber was, however, the flashing of a sudden light across my eyes awoke me.

"Barbara," said a quick distinct voice, close beside me. "Barbara!"

Struggling drowsily upright, I looked round and saw my father. He had his hat on, and a large cloak with a fur collar and clasp. A waiter stood behind him with a candle, and Boots was peeping in at the door. At first I could scarcely recollect where I was; but no sooner did my father speak again than it all flashed back upon my memory.

"I am willing, of course," said he, in his old imperative tone, "to pay any thing you may demand for the—the accommodation you have afforded her. Faugh! what a hole!"

"Very sorry, sir," said the waiter, obsequiously. "Had no idea the young lady was here at all, sir. All Boots's doing, sir—not our fault, I assure you."

"Boots, Boots, indeed!" echoed my father, angrily. "Pshaw, where is the fellow? I'll teach him to—— Ho, you're there, are you, sirrah? Tell me how you dared to bring any gentleman's child into such a filthy cellar as this?"

Boots looked down and made no reply, which only irritated my father the more.

"You may be thankful," said he, "that I don't complain of this to your master. Stand out of my way!"

Saying which, he grasped me by the arm and dragged me across the yard, to where a hackney coach was waiting in the shelter of the archway. Sick with terror and cold, I shrank into a corner of the vehicle, while my father, still storming at the apologetic waiter, flung himself into the opposite corner, and bade the coachman drive on.

The wind had now brought rain with it, and the streets were wet and empty. Scarcely a shop was open, and scarcely a creature stirring. Sitting there opposite my father and feeling that I dreaded him more than ever, I gazed out at the dreary night, and dared not speak or stir. We had a long, long distance to go, and I remember as well as if it were yesterday, how we traversed street after street; how the water stood in dark pools on the pavement; how we crossed a bridge where the rain was misting down upon the river; and how we by and by entered a well-known road, and drew up before that solitary house which was once more to be my home. There were the elm-trees, dark and gaunt as ever, and there was the mournful ivy mantling half the basement. There, too, as we stopped before the gate, was dear old Goody, shading the light with her hand, and peering out at the first sound of our wheels!

Scrambling down as best I could while my father was settling with the driver, I threw myself into her arms.

"My lamb, my darling!" she cried, brokenly, and covered my face with tears and kisses.

While I was yet clinging to her and she to me, my father came in. He glanced angrily at us both, and bit his lip.

"Stop that noise, Beever, and put the child to bed," said he, harshly; and so brushed past, and went to his room.

But Goody, instead of doing any such thing, took me down to the kitchen, where there was a cheerful fire blazing in the grate, and a little table spread for supper. Here she chafed my cold hands, and my still colder feet—took off my cloak and bonnet—and, though weeping abundantly herself, entreated me not to cry.

"For it's no use taking on, my deary!" said she. "It's a weary world, and troubles come to the young as well as the old; but what's God's will is surely for the best. It's hard always to believe that, darling; but it's no use taking on. Try to eat a little bit of chicken, my lamb—come, you're warmer, now!"

Though very faint indeed, I was not hungry, and had to be persuaded and petted a great deal before I could make up my mind to taste any thing. Having once begun, however, I felt better; and then Goody brought out a bottle with some brandy in it, and gave me a little warm brandy and water, which refreshed and strengthened me greatly. This done, I went and sat on her lap as I used to do in the old time before I went away, and laid my head down on her shoulder. Much to my surprise, Goody once again broke out into a passion of sobs, clasped me to her bosom, and began rocking me to and fro, like one in deep distress.

"Don't cry so, Goody," I whispered, putting my arms about her neck. "Pray don't cry so!"

"I can't help it, my deary—I can't help it, when it comes across me," she moaned. "And you'll miss her so! You'll miss her!"

"I shall miss her every day of my life," said I, struggling hard now to keep down my own tears. "She was so kind to me, Goody; and I loved her so dearly!"

"Nay, she was not always so kind to you as she might have been; but she meant no harm by it, and you're a dear lamb to remember her kindly," sobbed Goody. "But it's been sudden—too sudden, my deary, for me to know how to bear it yet!"

"I never knew a word of it till yesterday morning," cried I, fairly breaking down. "Not a word, and—and I was so happy, and——"

"Yesterday morning?" repeated Goody. "Why, it never happened till close upon eleven last night!"

Struck by a quick conviction that she was lamenting another grief than mine, I lifted my head from her shoulder, and looked her in the face.

"Oh, Goody," I faltered, "what do you mean? Is any thing the matter?"

She turned a startled face upon me.

"What," said she, breathlessly, "don't you know? Didn't he—didn't the master tell you as you came along?"

"Nothing—he told me nothing!"

"Jessie—your sister—your poor, dear, sister Jessie——"

"Oh, Goody, what of her?"

"Dead, my dear!—dead and gone!—dead since this time last night!"

And she wrung her hands, and lifted up her voice, and lamented again as a mother might lament for her child!

Chilled and horror-stricken, I looked at her, and could neither weep nor speak.

"She was well in the morning," continued Goody, "well, and gay, and pretty as ever!

She only suffered a few hours. It was soon over, and she died in my arms—in my arms, the child that I had nursed at her birth, and loved——oh! I never knew how I loved her till now! God help us all, deary! God help and spare us!"

"What did she die of, Goody?" I whispered, shudderingly.

"Cholera—cholera, my darling!"

I had never heard the word before—I could not tell what it meant—I only knew that my sister Jessie was dead. Dead! I repeated the word vaguely over and over again, and could not bring myself to realize its meaning. I felt as if a heavy hand were laid upon my heart. My eyes burned, and my tongue was dry. I wondered why I could not weep like Goody. A thousand things flashed through my mind—things of long ago; words that she had spoken; gestures, trifles, traits forgotten till this moment. Poor Jessie!—dead.

"And papa?" I faltered.

"He was out," said Goody, wiping her eyes with her apron, and speaking somewhat bitterly. "He went out early, to dine at Richmond and spend the day in the country. I had no one to send after him, and could not tell where he was to be found. When he came home at night, little Jessie was gone. He was sadly shocked at first; and walked about his room for a long time before he went to bed. This morning he asked to see her, and then he took Hilda on his knee, and kissed and cried over her. Oh! if it had been Hilda——"

She checked herself, and our eyes met. After this we sat for some time without speaking—I with my cheek laid against hers, and she with her arms clasped lovingly about me. By and by, seeing the fire was almost out, she took me by the hand, and led me up to bed. We stopped at the door of a room on the first floor, two stories lower than the bedroom which used to be ours.

"Hilda is here," she whispered, with her finger to her lip. "I sat with her to-night till she fell asleep, and we must try not to wake her. She is worn out with sorrow, poor darling—they loved each other so dearly!"

I had not seen Hilda for a whole year. I had left home without even bidding her farewell, and I returned to find her as I had left her—sleeping. Except that her face wore an expression of suffering which I had never seen there before, she seemed but little changed. Her cheek was flushed and feverish, and the rich tresses of her hair lay in heavy masses over her neck and arms. Bending down more closely, I saw that her eyelashes were still wet, and her pillow stained with tears. All at once, she awoke, looked at me fixedly, half-fearfully, and murmured—"Barbara!"

I hung over her with clasped hands—with streaming eyes—with I know not what prayerful longing in my voice.

"Oh, Hilda!" I cried, "love me, dear! Love me a little! we are both so lonely!"

A languid smile flitted across her lips. She opened her arms to me, and, clasping me convulsively round the neck, sobbed as if her heart would break.

That night, for the first time in our lives, we slept in the same bed, each with an arm about the other's neck.

CHAPTER XVI.

RESULTS.

" EARTH to earth, ashes to ashes, dust to dust" — mournful and eternal words which find an echo in all human hearts, and are borne to us, sighing, on every breath we breathe, from the cradle to the grave ! As they had been spoken, years ago, over our lost mother, so were they spoken over our sister. . I remember all the circumstances of the funeral with painful distinctness to this day—the mutes standing at the door ; the heavy tread of the bearers on the stairs ; the strange silence that fell upon the house when all were gone ; the unclosing of the shutters in the afternoon, and the sickening glare of the sunset as it streamed once again into the rooms. The day after, things lapsed, somehow, back into their old track. My father went to his club : and Miss Whymper came, as usual, and took her seat at the top of the school-room table.

A week, a fortnight, a month went by ; and I never once heard of, or from, my aunt. I was too deeply shocked at first by what had happened in my home to think much of my own troubles ; but as time went on, and these impressions lost somewhat of their intensity, all the old bitterness came back. Sometimes I wondered if it could all be true ; and, waking from my sleep in the still night-time, asked myself whether I had been dreaming ? Then flashed the desolate conviction—then rose the burning tears—then, slipping softly from my bed in the dim starlight, I crept, breathlessly, to a certain drawer, and took from its hiding-place the silver ring. To steal back with it to my bed ; to lie with it pressed against my lips ; to place it on the finger where he placed it ; take it off and kiss it twenty times, and fall asleep at last in the midst of murmuring his name, was all the solace I had left.

As for Hilda, she was herself too unhappy to give much heed to me. Gentler and more affectionate than of old, she yet cherished a grief that refused to be comforted. I soon found that, devote myself as I would, the one place must yet remain vacant in her life. Jessie had been her second self, her companion, confidante, sister, friend. She lamented her with a passionate intensity, of which childhood alone is capable, and, so lamenting, lost sleep, appetite, and strength. In certain imperious natures, sorrow wears the aspect of despair and consumes like a wasting fire. So it was with Hilda. She spent her nights in weeping, and her days in a hopeless apathy, from which no effort of ours availed to rouse her.

Thus brooding away the weary weeks, she grew daily thinner, paler, and more unlike her former self.

One afternoon, when Miss Whymper had gone away and we were alone in the school-room, my father suddenly came in, followed by a strange gentleman. I was putting away the books, and Hilda. was lying on a couch beside the open window, pale and weary, and half-asleep. The gentleman went straight to the couch ; drew a chair quite close beside her ; and said, turning to my father—

"This, I presume, Mr. Churchill, is our young friend—our, ahem !—valetudinarian ?" ·

To which my father replied, " Yes, Sir Andrew, the same ;" and sat down likewise.

Sir Andrew was a bulky man, tall and stout, with a forest of gray hair, a knobby red nose and a voice husky, oleaginous, mellowed by port and maturity, like a Stilton cheese. In the brief silence that followed, he brought out a heavy gold snuff-box, and, with much solemnity, partook of three pinches. Presently he laid his hand on Hilda's little wrist, felt her pulse, and nodded to himself several times.

" Well, Sir Andrew," said my father anxiously, " well ?"

The physician drew a long breath through his teeth, and tapped the lid of the snuff-box with his knuckles.

" Well, Mr. Churchill," said he deliberately, " we are, ahem ! — debilitated — considerably debilitated. We evince an absence of that *vis anima* which is so desirable in youth — our pulse is intermittent — our nerves are unstrung — we — in short, we are not absolutely ill ; but — but we are by no means absolutely well."

" And the remedy, sir ?" suggested my father, impatiently. " The remedy."

" Tonics ; port wine ; change of air ; amusement."

My father shrugged his shoulders, and clinked the money in his pockets.

" In point of fact," continued Sir Andrew, reflectively, " I should say — that is, Mr. Churchill, if I may offer a suggestion ?"

" Offer fifty—fifty, if you please, Sir Andrew," said my father.

" Well, then, I should say that mineral baths — Kissengen, for instance, or Ems — would do more for our young friend than any course of medical treatment whatever. It is the nervous system that wants bracing, Mr. Churchill — the ner-vous sys-tem."

Saying which, he closed the snuff-box with a click, glanced again at his watch, patted Hilda patronizingly on the head, and rose to take his leave.

" Mr. Churchill," said he, "I attend you."

Whereat my father ceremoniously ushered him from the room, and we heard his boots creak ponderously all the way down-stairs.

The next morning, when we were summoned, as usual, to the school-room, a letter addressed to Miss Whymper was found lying on the table. I recognized my father's large armorial seal and careless superscription, and, smitten with an anguished recollection of how and when I had last seen a similar missive, could scarce restrain my tears. I watched her break the seal — I watched her as she read — I translated that almost imperceptible expression of surprise and disappointment, and the quick glance which reverted more than once to Hilda's downcast face.

" Hilda is to be sent away," thought I, sadly ; as Miss Whymper put the letter in her pocket, and said, in the same words that she had used every morning for the last four years —

" Now young ladies, if you please, we will resume our studies."

I had guessed the truth, though not all the truth ; as I discovered before the day was out. Miss Whymper was to be dismissed, and not only was Hilda to be sent away for change of air, but I was to be sent with her. Our destination was not yet decided upon; but that it would be somewhere abroad was certain. In the mean time my father had set inquiries afoot, and authorized Goody to make active preparations for our departure. Hilda received this news with indifference — I, with mingled pain and pleasure — Goody, with unspeakable despair.

"Was it not enough," said she, twenty times a day, "was it not enough to lose one of my darlings, and must I now be parted from the two that are left? May be I shall never live to see either of you again, and, sure, if you were my own flesh and blood, I couldn't love you more!"

In reply to which, I consoled her as well as I could, and promised never to forget her, though I should be a dozen years away.

Thus many days went by, and the routine of our life was interrupted by all kinds of novel cares and occupations. Our wardrobes, which were always scanty enough, had to be almost entirely renewed; and two young women were kept constantly at work in an upper room, making cloaks, dresses, and other necessaries, all of which had, every now and then, to be fitted, and made the subject of discussion. Our studies, at the same time, were no longer enforced with their accustomed regularity, and, at the expiration of a week or so, Miss Whymper took her final leave. We were called down, I remember, to papa's room, to bid her good-by. Although it was now mid-summer and there was no fire, my father was standing, as usual, in the middle of the rug, with his back to the grate. Miss Whymper was consigning some three or four crisp bank-notes to the capacious recesses of a large red pocket-book.

"I have been careful, madam," said my father, with that air of magnificent politeness which he assumed at pleasure, "to keep a memorandum of the numbers of the notes. You will, therefore, apply to me, in case of accident."

Miss Whymper, with her head on one side, thanked Mr. Churchill for his "courteous consideration."

"And should any thing occur to frustrate the success of those views which I at present entertain with regard to the education of my daughters," continued he, "I trust that I may again be so fortunate, madam, as to secure your invaluable coöperation."

Miss Whymper replied by a profound courtesy.

"At the close of a connection," said she, "which I think I may, without undue temerity, characterize as unusually productive of satisfaction to all parties concerned — may I say to all parties, Mr. Churchill?"

"Madam," replied my father, with a glance at his watch, "you may."

"And which," pursued Miss Whymper, all on one subdued note, and as if she were repeating every word by heart, "has afforded me from first to last such a degree of interest as I do not remember to have ever previously entertained throughout the course of a long educational experience — at the close, I beg to repeat, of so agreeable an intercourse, have I Mr. Churchill's permission to present my dear young friends with these trifling evidences of my regard?"

D

Saying which, she produced two very small books from the depths of her reticule; while my father, more grandly than ever, protested that she did us both infinite honor, and desired us to thank Miss Whymper for her kindness. Whereat Miss Whymper bestowed on Hilda a frosty kiss, and a copy of Joyce's "Scientific Dialogues;" on me a still frostier kiss, and Mrs. Marcet's "Conversations on Chemistry;" hoped that we might be industrious and happy, and that neither our morals nor our digestive organs might be injuriously affected by foreign influences; and so, being moved to an unusual display of emotion, applied the corner of her pocket-handkerchief to her left eye, and wiped away an imaginary tear. My father than rang the bell; accompanied her as far as the study-door; bowed his stateliest bow; wished her "a very good morning;" and so she followed Goody down the stairs, and we saw Miss Whymper no more.

Our fate was decided by a foreign letter which arrived the next morning. We were to be received in a large collegiate school at Zollenstrasse, and were to start in two days, so as to arrive at the beginning of the July term. Except the Zollenstrasse was somewhere in Germany, and that Germany, though it seemed near enough on the map, lay a long way off across the sea, I knew nothing further of our destination.

CHAPTER XVII.

BY LAND AND SEA.

My father went with us himself the morning of our departure, and put us on board the steamer by which we were to be conveyed from London to Rotterdam. The bridges, quays, and floating piers were all alive with traffic. The deck of the steamer swarmed with seamen, travelers, and porters. Having seen our luggage safely stowed, and ascertained the situation of our berths, my father handed us over to the care of the captain, who not only promised us his special protection during the voyage, but engaged, on landing, to consign us to the care of one Jonathan Bose, Esq., a merchant of Rotterdam with whom my father was acquainted, and to whom we carried a letter of introduction. Presently the bell rang, and warned those who were not passengers to leave the vessel. My father took Hilda's hands in both of his, and, kissing her first on the forehead and then on the mouth, bade her get well, be happy, and profit by her instructors. To me he only said, "Good-by, Barbara," touched my cheek coldly with his lips, turned away, and hastened on shore. Then the gangway was removed; the moorings were loosened; the steamer heaved slowly round; the quays and bystanders seemed to recede behind us; and away we went, past the Custom-house and the Tower, and the crowded masts, which clustered, like a forest of bare larches, down the midpath of the river.

The day was fine, and for some hours we enjoyed it intensely. The passengers were all kind to us. Some of the ladies gave us fruit and cakes; the gentlemen told us the names of the places that we passed; and the Captain, every now and then, came up and asked us if we meant to be hungry by dinner-time. Toward noon, we passed the red lighthouse at the Nore, and stood out to sea. The steamer now began to roll; the seagulls darted to and fro; and we saw a shoal of porpoises tumbling on the waves, about half a mile ahead. With these sights we were more amused than ever; till presently we both turned ill and giddy, and were glad to be carried down to our little narrow beds. Of this part of the journey I remember only that I lay with closed eyes, and felt more sick and miserable than I had ever felt before — that, in the midst of my suffering, I strove every now and then to say a consoling word to Hilda, which only made me feel worse — that the day seemed as long as ten, and was followed by a weary night, lit by a swinging lamp, and traversed by hideous dreams and semi-conscious wakings — that the morning dawned grayly, and that, by and by, somebody bade me try to get up, for we were in smooth water again. We then got up, looking both very pale, and ventured on deck to breathe the fresh air, and have a peep at Rotterdam.

The passengers were all claiming their luggage, and the boat was crowded with foreign porters who wore ear-rings and red caps, and gabbled a strange guttural language that I had never heard before. Close beside us lay the great quays bordered with trees and lofty houses; laden with bales of goods; and swarming with sailors of all nations. Beyond us stretched the broad river, crowded with merchant vessels; and all along the banks, as far as one could see, an endless perspective of warehouses, cranes, masts, and tapering steeples. The strangeness of this scene, and the confusion of tongues, made me so nervous, and filled me with such a desolate sense of exile, that when a little old gentleman presently came up with an account book in his hand, and a pen behind his ear, and asked if we were not going to land with the rest, I could with difficulty frame an intelligible answer. He then looked at the address upon our boxes.

"Zollenstrasse!" he exclaimed. "Zollenstrasse am Main! Why, that is a long way from here, little travelers! Who is to take care of you across the country?"

I shook my head, and said I did not know.

"And what shall you do when you get there? Have you friends in the Duchy?"

Hilda tossed back her curls, and lifted her dark eyes to his face.

"We are going to College," she said, proudly.

"Poor children! Have you no parents, that you should be sent so far from home?"

"We have a papa," replied Hilda.

The stranger shrugged his shoulders compassionately.

"How strange!" he murmured. "Had my children lived I could never have parted from them; and yet this man trusts his little girls——"

"Papa is not a man," interrupted Hilda indignantly. "He is a gentleman."

The stranger, with a melancholy smile, sat down on one of the boxes, and took her unwilling hand in his.

"Just what I should have supposed, my dear," he replied. "What is your father's name?"

"Edmund Churchill, Esquire."

"Churchill!" he repeated. "Edmund Church-

ill!" and so with a look of some surprise, took a book from his pocket, and began hastily turning over the leaves. Stopping presently, with his finger on one particular entry, he said—

"I know your father—at least, I know a Mr. Edmund Churchill, of London."

"Then perhaps you know Mr. Jonathan Bose?" I interposed eagerly.

"I believe I do. What of him?"

"Only that we are to give him this letter; and the Captain has promised to take us to his house by and by."

Our new friend put out his hand for the letter, and broke the seal.

"The Captain may spare himself that trouble," he said. "I am Jonathan Bose."

Before we had well recovered the surprise of this encounter, he had glanced rapidly through the contents of the missive, thrust it into his pocket, and darted off in search of the Captain. A huge porter then shouldered our boxes; and Mr. Jonathan Bose, who was quite breathless with excitement, gave a hand to each, and hurried us along the quays. He was delighted to have charge of us, and said so repeatedly as we went along; interspersing his conversation, at the same time, with scraps of information respecting himself, his household, and the places we were passing on the way.

"This river," said he, "is the Maas—my house lies yonder, just beside that large India vessel which you see unlading farther on. This building belongs to the East India Company. I wish you could stay with me for a week, my dears, that I might show you all the sights of Rotterdam; but your father desires me to see you off again to-morrow morning. Well, well, this afternoon, at least, we can take a walk and see something of the city. I'll be sworn you never saw so many bridges in one place before, did you? How pleased Gretchen will be! Gretchen is my housekeeper; and the best creature in the world. You will not understand a word she says; but you will be capital friends, nevertheless. This walk along the quays is called the *Boompjes*; which means '*the little trees*.' They may have been little when they first got that name; but they are very big trees now, anyhow."

Chatting thus, he went on to say that, though a Dutchman by birth, he was English by education; that he had been for many years a widower, and had lost two little daughters whom he dearly loved; that he delighted in the society of the young; and that the pleasure with which he received us was only diminished by the knowledge that we must leave so soon.

Being now arrived in front of a large house with a great deal of wood carving about the doors and windows, Mr. Bose ushered us into a little dark office, with rows of ledgers all round the walls, and a desk beside the window. He rang the bell, and a fat old woman, with a mob cap, and a plate of gilt metal on her forehead, came bustling in; embraced us rapturously, and took us up-stairs to breakfast. The breakfast was laid in a quaint paneled room with a polished floor, upon which we were not allowed to walk till we had exchanged our dusty shoes for some huge list slippers which lay outside the door. After breakfast, Mr. Bose took us for a walk; and a most perplexing walk it was, through labyrinths of streets, over scores of drawbridges, and beside innumerable canals; all of which were alike shaded by trees, crowded with vessels, and swarming with sailors. In the afternoon we came back, very tired and hungry; and at dinner had thin soup, and sour cabbages, and jam with our meat, none of which we liked at all, though we were too polite to say so. After dinner, our host went out again, and Gretchen was left to entertain us till evening; when we had tea and chatted by twilight, while Mr. Bose smoked his pipe, and drank Schiedam and Seltzer water.

I cannot recall the substance of our conversation, for I was tired and dreamy, and he spoke more to Hilda than to me; but I remember how I sat looking at him by the fading light, reading every line and lineament of his face, and photographing his portrait on my memory. I see him now—a little spare figure, with scant gray locks, and an eye blue, benevolent, and bright as day. "A man of God's making," with goodness and sorrow written legibly on his brow. When we wished him good-night, he kissed us both and bade us sleep well, for we must rise with the sun to resume our journey. And we did sleep well, sinking deeply down between the fragrant sheets, and lulled by the murmuring sounds that rose from quay and river.

With the first blush of early morning came Gretchen to wake us, and long before the people of Rotterdam were stirring we had bidden adieu to the stout old hand-maiden and the quaint house on the Boompjes, and were shivering on board a steamer which was to convey us to Mayence.

"I only wish I could spare time to go with you, my children," said Mr. Bose, as the last passengers came hurrying on deck. "However, you will be taken good care of all the way. I have paid for every thing in advance, and the steward of this boat engages to see you off by the diligence when your water journey is ended. In the mean time, I will write to your father. God bless you both, and good-by. I must go now, or they will carry me down the river before I know where I am!"

He then kissed us many times, gave me a paper which secured our places as far as the steamer could take us; and so, with glistening eyes, bade us a last farewell, and went away.

What with Hilda's continued weakness and fretfulness, the discomfort of living daily amongst strangers, and the exceeding dullness of the scenery, the journey was dreary enough. The travelers were mostly Dutch, and took but little notice of us; and, for the first two days at least, our journey lay between poplar-bordered dykes and dreary flats, with now and then a windmill to break the dull monotony of land and sky. That this river could be the Rhine, the beautiful, romantic, castled Rhine, of which I had read so much, and of which Hugh Farquhar had told me so many tales and legends, seemed impossible.

On the third day, I began to believe it. Past Cologne, the scenery became beautiful, and for the first time I beheld mountains, vineyards, and ivied ruins. Then a number of French and English tourists, and a band of itinerant musicians arrived on board; and, as it was very

warm and fine, the tables were laid on deck, and we dined in the open air. All this was novel and exhilarating, and the hours flew so quickly that the summer dusk came on only too soon, and we landed, quite unwillingly, at Coblentz for the night.

The perpetual traveling, however, now began to tell upon us, and although the weather was even brighter, and the course of the river more lovely than ever, we were so wearied when the fourth day came that we could not half enjoy the wonders of the journey. Landing late in the afternoon opposite Mayence, we found that the diligence had started hours ago; so the steward took us to a quiet inn close by, where we supped at a long table with a number of other people, and slept in a bedroom overlooking the river.

The next morning we were on the road betimes, occupying two opposite corners in a huge unwieldy diligence full of bearded travelers, none of whom spoke a word of English. About midday we alighted at a dirty inn in a dirty village, and dined miserably. Then on again for hours and hours, past woods, and mountains, and picturesque hamlets lying low in green valleys, where sometimes the road ran for miles together beside the eager and beautiful Main river. Toward evening we stopped at a little wayside building with a flag before the door, where our passports and luggage were examined by three or four soldiers in faded uniforms of blue and silver. About half an hour after this, we turned the shoulder of a hill and came suddenly in sight of a pretty town with steeples and towers, and white houses, and a quaint old bridge of boats. It was just dusk —dusk enough to show the lighted oriel in the Cathedral, and yet not so dusk as to vail the outlines of the hills, or the gleaming of the river. The road wound downward to the town, bordered on either side by a double avenue of gigantic poplars. At the foot of this avenue stood a great hotel, before the door of which the diligence drew up. Then a waiter came running out; the conductor flung our boxes on the pavement; the passengers gesticulated; and from half-a-dozen mouths together I heard the welcome name of "Zollenstrasse—Zollenstrasse-am-Main!"

We had no sooner alighted than the diligence rolled rapidly away, and left us standing face to face with the bowing waiter, who smiled, nodded, examined the address upon our luggage, darted back into the hotel, and presently returned with a man in a blue and silver livery, who put our boxes on a truck, and led the way. We followed him down a narrow side-road bordered with trees, and stopped before a huge wooden gate with two enormous knockers, and a lamp overhead. This gate was opened by a porter in the same livery, who preceded us across the courtyard, up a lofty flight of steps, and into a large parlor, where an elderly lady and eight young girls were sitting at needlework. The lady rose, extended a hand to each, and kissed us both upon the forehead.

"Welcome," said she, in good English, "welcome, my dear children, to your new home. Try to like it and to be happy with us, and we shall all love you."

She then made a sign to the rest, who immediately surrounded us. Some shook hands with us; some kissed us on the cheeks; some disembarrassed us of our cloaks and bonnets; and all had a kind word or two of broken English to bid us welcome—all, except one shy little dark maiden, who whispered "willkommen," in my ear, and then, blushing and laughing, ran away.

"Your names, I think," said the lady, referring to a letter which she took from the pocket of her apron, "are Barbara and Hilda Churchill. Now you must tell me which is Barbara, and which Hilda, that I may know how to call you."

"I am Hilda," said my sister, "and I am called Miss Churchill, because I am the eldest."

The lady smiled gravely.

"We have no Misses here," said she, "and no distinctions of age. Your companions call each other by their baptismal names, and it is our rule to recognize no superiority but that of merit. As for myself, I am the superintendent of this Academy, and you will call me Madame Brenner. But I daresay you are tired and hungry after your day's journey. Annchen, see if supper be ready."

Annchen courtesied and left the room, while Madame Brenner resumed her seat, and continued to address us.

"At present," said she, "our numbers are few; for the half-yearly term only commenced yesterday, and our students rarely assemble under a week. However, we shall have more arrivals to-morrow; and by Sunday our society, I daresay, will be complete. But here comes Annchen, telling us that supper is ready."

So saying she took me by the hand, left Hilda to follow with Annchen and the rest, and led the way into an adjoining room where there was a long table laid for supper. The meal was plain, but abundant, and consisted of soup, eggs, rice-puddings, coffee, cream-cheese, brown bread and salad. This over, we returned to the parlor, and one of the scholars read prayers aloud in German. When we rose from our knees, each scholar went up to Madame Brenner in turn and bade her good night; but when we followed their example, she shook her head, and said—

"To-night I will go with you, and show you where you are to sleep."

We followed her through a long corridor with a row of doors on one side and windows on the other.

"This," said Madame Brenner, "is one of our four dormitories. It contains six rooms, and in each room six students sleep. Every door is numbered, and your door is number five. Annchen and Luisa are at present your only companions; but as soon as the rest arrive, each bed will have its occupant. Do you like your room?"

It was a pretty, conventual, white-washed chamber, containing six little beds with white hangings, six rush-bottomed chairs, three large deal presses, and no carpet. It looked cheerful and airy, notwithstanding its simplicity, and we both liked it at a glance.

Madame Brenner then bade us good night, and our companions assisted us to open our trunks, showed us in which press to keep our clothes, helped us to undress, and made as much of us as if we had been long-expected guests.

"You shall have my bed, Barbara, if you like it best," said Annchen. "It is next the window, and overlooks the garden."

"In that case," cried Luisa, "I shall sleep next to Hilda, and that will be delightful! Hilda and I must be great friends. I am so fond of the English! There was an English girl here last year, and we were the fastest friends in the world. She gave me this locket with her hair in it; but she only wrote to me me once after she left, and I fear she has forgotten me. And so you have come all this way, and have crossed the sea! Ah, how I should like to travel! I have never seen the sea. I come from Mulhouse, which is only a day's journey; and yet that is the longest distance I have ever traveled."

"You speak English very well," I observed, sleepily.

"Speak English! I should think so, indeed! You will not be surprised at it when you have been here a few days, and have seen what our English classes are. Such tasks as we have to learn! Such themes, and dictations, and tiresome rules! Mein Gott! we are martyrs to English, and are never allowed to speak German except in the hours of recreation! And there is Madame Thompson, our English gouvernante! —Oh, Annchen, how Hilda and Barbara will be amused with Madame Thompson!"

"Madame Thompson is very good-natured," said Annchen, quietly.

"And then there is Mousieur Duvernoy, our French tutor, and we have two French governesses besides, and such lots of other professors for music, drawing, Italian, natural philosophy, elocution, and Heaven knows what beside! Have you been to school before? No! Ah, then, you have no idea of what hard work it is; and this is not a school, you know, but a College."

"What is the difference?" asked Hilda, sitting up in bed, and looking considerably dismayed at the prospect disclosed by her talkative neighbor.

"The difference? Oh, the difference is enormous! In the first place, this is a government establishment, founded and endowed; and there are upward of seventy students, thirty of whom pay nothing, but are taught for charity, and elected every five years. Then we have examinations twice a year; and when we leave College we take home a certificate signed by the Grand Duke himself. And we learn in terms; and we call our holidays vacations; and our dining-room a refectory; and our teachers are never masters or governesses, but always professors. Oh, a College is a very grand place, I assure you, compared with a school; but one has to work like a slave for the honor of being brought up in it!"

"I think I would rather have been sent to school, though," said Hilda, dolefully.

Of this observation, however, Luisa took no notice; but kept running on long after Annchen had put out the light, and I had grown too sleepy to listen.

"Silver medal — half-holiday — breakfast — milk and water—Madame Brenner — counter point—perspective——"

These were the last words I heard, sinking, sinking away into the ocean of dreams.

CHAPTER XVIII.

ZOLLENSTRASSE-AM-MAIN.

It is not my intention to dwell at any considerable length upon the first years of my College life. I have already lingered too long and too fondly over these early reminiscences, and I must now content myself with an outline of that pleasant interval which links childhood to youth, and youth to womanhood—which stores the mind with knowledge, and the heart with all good impulses—which touches already on the confines of Romance, and yet leaves the poem of life unwritten and untold. It will bear to be related rapidly. The sketch of a month, a week, a day, would suffice to paint the pleasant monotony of years which so nearly resemble each other. Be this chapter devoted, then, to an "abstract and brief chronicle" of our occupations and way of life abroad; and also of the dominions, the capital, and the Collegiate academy in which it had pleased fate and my father to establish us.

Situated in the very heart of Central Germany, traversed by a broad and beautiful river, and celebrated alike for its scenery and its mineral waters, the Grand Duchy of Zollenstrasse-am-Main occupies but a very small space upon the map, and only half a page of Murray's Continental Handbook. The truth is that the whole territory covers an area of only eighty square miles; that the population numbers somewhat less than eleven thousand souls; that the capital consists of a square and two streets, chiefly hotels and lodging-houses; and that but for the influx of visitors every summer and autumn, the inhabitants would long ago have died of inanition and become an extinct species. Under these circumstances, the court of Zollenstrasse can hardly be expected to exercise much influence upon the affairs of Europe, or, even in its matrimonial alliances, materially to affect the balance of power. And yet the Grand Duchy is a real Grand Duchy; and the Grand Duke is a real Grand Duke; and the comfortable white house in which he lives is called The Palace; and the two little soldiers who walk up and down before the door all day long are privates in that shabby regiment of which His Serene Highness is so proud, and which the townspeople, with pardonable patriotism, style the Military Establishment of the State. Besides this, the Duchy has its national coinage, stamped with a profile of LEOPOLD XVIII., DUX ZOLL: on one side, and the Ducal arms on the other; and its national costume, which is horribly unbecoming; and its national dialect, upon which the Zollenstrassers pique themselves more than enough, to the infinite amusement of their neighbors.

Zollenstrasse, the capital, consists, as I have already observed, chiefly of lodging-houses, the largest of which, however, belongs to no less a landlord than His Serene Highness himself. It was formerly one of the royal residences; but is now let out in suites, and is by far the most reasonable and best appointed establishment in the town. The fact is humiliating; but the Duke is poor and the speculation profitable. The other principal buildings are the Pump-room, Bath-house, Conversation Haus, Palace, Theater, and Collegiate Academy. The Pump-room, or Trinkhalle, is an open colonnade painted gaudily in fresco, and provided with a chalybeate tap at either end. The Brunnen Mädchen are pretty and obliging. The waters taste like hot ink and lucifer matches. The Conversation Haus is a superb building, containing news-rooms, gaming-rooms, and a large hall which serves for balls and concerts. It was built by the present Duke, and is by him let to a company of French speculators at a round rental of sixty thousand dollars per annum. All things considered, His Serene Highness is not, perhaps, quite so needy as one might suppose. He has many little perquisites, besides those already enumerated. He taxes the hotel-keepers, the visitors, and the itinerant dealers in stag's-horn brooches and Swiss carvings. He levies an impost upon pleasure-boats, omnibuses, and donkeys. He regulates the tariff for ices, coffee, and Strasbourg beer. He claims a per-centage on the sale of guide-books and newspapers; and exacts a dividend out of the visitors' washing-bills. Then all the flys and saddle-horses belong to him; and the theater is his property; and the Bath-house was his father's private speculation; so that, concisely to sum up the sources of the Grand Ducal revenue, His Serene Highness is lodging-house keeper, theatrical manager, job-master, bath-owner, landlord of gambling-houses, and general tax-collector to the state. You would never think this to look at him. At least, you would not have thought it had you looked at him so nearly and so often as I did, and seen what a fine, handsome, polite gentleman he was, with a ribbon in his button-hole, and a cream-colored moustache that hung over his mouth like a fringe of spun silk. He used to ride and drive about quite unattended, and walk in the public gardens after dinner with his two little boys, like a mere ordinary mortal, and many a time, when the French company came down and Madame Brenner took a select detachment of her scholars to the theater to witness a piece of Racine or Molière, I have seen his august Highness applauding with his own royal hands; or, like an affable potentate as he was, leaning back in his seat, and laughing till the tears ran down his cheeks. The theater, I should observe, was always over at nine; and the ladies in the boxes wore their bonnets, and took their knitting with them.

Then the Grand Duke was an amateur composer, and wrote classical cantatas which were performed by the pupils of our academy; and he played the violin, it was said, to admiration; and he turned the most exquisite little boxes in ivory for all his royal nieces and cousins, down to those of Saxe-Hohenhausen in the fortieth degree; and he painted in oils; and he wrote poetry; and at his chateau of Schwartzberg, a romantic old hunting-lodge about two miles from the capital, he kept a preserve of tame wild-boars, for the express purpose of getting up boar-hunts by torchlight, for the amusement of those distinguished visitors who came to stay with him in the season. So his tastes, you see, were in the highest degree refined, and one was only surprised to think how little they interfered with his duties as a sovereign and a tradesman.

His duties as a sovereign, however, were not onerous; but consisted chiefly of a due supervision of the perquisites before mentioned, and the expenditure of the same. He held a privy-council every morning after breakfast, and a levee once a month. He reviewed the Military Establishment of the State every two or three days; and, as President of our Academy, honored the Examinations with his presence at the close of each term. On court-days a flag was hoisted at the palace; the sentries were doubled; and the band played for an extra hour in the public garden. I remember now, as well as possible, how we school-girls were amused to see the ladies picking their way across the square in their court-dresses, with their maid-servants and umbrellas — how we used to make bets beforehand as to who would walk and who would hire a fly, and how many families would borrow the Gräfin von Steinmetz's old yellow landau — how daring our remarks were when Herr Secretary Ungar went by, because he was stone-deaf, and could not hear a word we said — and what fun we made of General Schinkel's pigtail, and the Town-Councillors' legs.

It at first surprised me to learn how strictly these little courts were confined to the nobles and dignitaries of Zollenstrasse proper, and how rigidly the etiquette was kept up with regard to strangers. No foreigner could be presented unless he brought proof that he had been presented at home; and not even a German baron from a neighboring state was received without first submitting his credentials to a privy-councillor. I own that I laughed at this for a long time, and thought it preposterous that an English commoner whose income numbered thousands when that of His Highness numbered tens, and whose house and gardens were probably as large as all the houses and gardens in the Duchy of Zollenstrasse put together, should be excluded from the honors of a Ducal lévee simply because he had never kissed hands at St. James's; but as I grew older I discovered the wisdom of this arrangement, and found that, after all, the precautions of the Zollenstrassers were not quite misplaced. The fact was that our annual visitors were of a very miscellaneous description. They came and went like the swallows; with this difference, that, instead of seeking a warmer clime, they frequently came from one which was already too hot to hold them. How was one to know who they were, whence they came, or whither they were going? How guess the antecedents of those elegant ladies who drank the waters in the morning; ate ices all day long in the public garden; and staked their five-franc pieces at the roulette-tables every evening? That French exquisite who calls himself a marquis and wears a diamond as large as a three-penny piece, is perhaps a convicted forger, with T. F. branded on his shoulder. That gallant English tourist with the military frock, may be a blackleg. That wealthy capitalist who has hired the best suite at the best hotel, a fraudulent bankrupt. To speak truth, a gaming spa offers many inducements to the equivocal of both sexes; and though his Serene Highness, Leopold XVIII., did condescend to provide the tables, furnish the lodgings, and accept the profits, he had no resource but to turn his august back upon those visitors by whom he lived.

But it is time that I said something of our own way of life, and of the establishment whereof we were members.

Excepting only the Conversation Haus, our Collegiate Academy was the handsomest building in the little capital of Zollenstrasse-am-Main. The house was large and imposing; and, with its long wings, occupied three sides of a spacious courtyard. It contained a concert-room, a library, eight class-rooms, two large dining-halls, apartments for the resident professors, dormitories for sixty scholars, a board room, and extensive offices. At the back of the Academy lay an extensive kitchen-garden; and to the left of the garden, a playground and gymnasium. The number of residents, exclusive of teachers and servants, was limited to sixty; thirty of whom were boys, and thirty girls. Fifteen of each sex were admitted on the foundation. Out-pupils were also received to the number of sixty more; but these attended daily, made their payments half-yearly, and were neither permitted to dine at our tables, nor join us in our hours of recreation. A comfortable waiting-room was placed, however, at their disposal, where they could read, work, or practice; and those who came from a distance were allowed to have refreshments sent in from a Gasthof in the Theater-platz. The interior arrangements of the Academy were perfect. The male and female pupils were kept as thoroughly apart as if they had not been resident under the one roof. We had our separate class-rooms, dining-rooms, and occupations; and, save at the half-yearly fêtes, the concerts, the examinations, or the chapel on Sundays, never exchanged so much as a glance. For the maintenance of order and discipline we were also well provided. A matron attended to the housekeeping, and Madame Brenner had the supervision of all matters connected with the education and comfort of the female students. A president and master-librarian exercised supreme authority over the boys. The commissariat was liberal; a medical officer resided in the house; and six women-servants and two men were kept, besides the porter at the gate. These, with four resident professors, constituted the whole staff, and a highly efficient staff it was.

As for the education afforded by this institution, I can not better explain its aim and nature than by stating at once that it was essentially a school of art, devoted to the cultivation of native talent and regulated upon principles which subordinated all minor considerations to this one great object. Thus the free scholars were all brought up to the pursuit of either music, sculpture, or painting; and even those students whose means enabled them to dispense with a profession, were compelled, in like manner, to conform to the academic rules, and select some leading study. The head masters of each department resided in the house, and the rest of the teachers attended daily. Every year six advanced students of each sex were elected as monitors, whereupon it became their duty to overlook the studies of the rest; and, though none but Germans were admitted to the privileges of the gratuitous education, foreigners who were willing to pay for their instruction were not excluded. There were limitations, however, to both of these laws. No German who was a subject of either Austria or Prussia could, under any circumstances, be eligible as a free scholar; and this because Austria and Prussia were judged sufficiently rich and powerful to cultivate the fine arts for themselves.

Neither could any foreign applicant be received on paying terms, so long as there were native applicants of equal merit in the field.

This being the case, it was quite a rare and fortunate chance that Hilda and I should have succeeded so easily.

I have already said that the Grand Duke was our patron and perpetual president; but we also had honorary members and subscribers among most of the crowned heads and nobles of the German Confederation. We held yearly exhibitions, and concerts during the season; and besides the ordinary examinations at the close of every term, we had a grand triennial Competition, to which art-professors and amateurs from every quarter were invited. A committee of judgment was then formed; medals were distributed; and to those pupils whose term of study had expired, certificates of merit were delivered. Taken as a whole, I doubt if there be in all Europe an educational institute so methodically conducted, and so thoroughly repaying in its results as this Collegiate Academy which lies *perdu* in the heart of a remote German state, scarcely known even by name beyond the confines of the Rhine and Elbe; but destined some day to be famed in the fame of its disciples. May all prosperity and all honor be with it; and may other nations take example by it! Methinks there are one or two institutions in my native country, and, perhaps, one or two more in the gayest of neighboring capitals, which might with advantage be remodeled on the principles of our Zollenstrasse School of Art.

It was not long before I fell in with the prescribed routine, and became thoroughly at home and happy in my student-life. I liked my teachers, my friendly school companions, and the pleasant regularity of hours and occupations. Naturally eager for knowledge, I derived inexpressible satisfaction from the consciousness of daily improvement. To wake in the morning with all the day before me, and to know that every hour of that day was laid out beforehand for my benefit—to earn a smile from Madame Brenner, or a word of praise from Professor Metz—to work hard, while work was the order of the hour—to play heartily, when the interval of relaxation came—to steal by twilight into some quiet corner, and read till it was too dark to do aught but sit and muse with folded hands—to sup merrily off such pastoral fare as milk, and fruit, and fresh brown bread; and afterward to go to bed, tired, and happy, and at peace with myself and all the world besides—this was indeed a life such as I had never known before; such as I have never known since; such as none of us can know, save in our happy school-days.

Then the college was like a home, in the true meaning of that dear old Saxon word; and we house-students were to each other, for the most part, as the members of a single family. I had many friends, for we were all friends, and two or three special intimates. Amongst these latter were Annchen, and the dark-haired Luisa, and a tender-hearted impulsive Bavarian, called Ida Saxe, with a heart full of enthusiasm, and a head full of legends. I became much attached to her; and when Annchen and Luisa, who were both older than myself, had left the school, our affection grew even more exclusive than before. Our tastes, ages, studies, and ambitions were the same. We had each chosen painting for our principal pursuit—we studied under the same master—we drew from the same models—we worked in the same class, and we occupied the same bedroom. She was an orphan, and looked forward to art as her profession. I also cherished visions of ambition, and hoped that the time might come when my father would suffer me to turn my studies to their just account. For I had talent, and my talent was of the right sort—inborn, earnest, persevering, confident to strive, humble to learn, patient in defeat, and unsatisfied in success. Term after term, I won the approbation of my teachers, and felt the power growing stronger and clearer within me. By and by I carried off the third-class medal for the best drawing from the antique; and, at the close of my third year, the second silver medal for an original composition. To achieve the first silver medal, or even, at some far-off day, to become the victorious winner of the first-class certificate and the grand gold medal of the Triennial Competition, were glories that I could scarcely hope to compass; but which, though I hardly dared confess it to myself, had become the great aims of my life.

As for Hilda, she had no such ambition. Finding herself, according to the school regulations, obliged to make choice of some especial art, she took up that of music, in which she was already a tolerable proficient. I do not think she really loved music, or selected it out of preference; but because she disliked work, and believed that in this science she would find less to learn. She was mistaken, however; for music as it is taught in Germany, and music as it was taught by Miss Whymper, were two very different affairs. In the first place, she had to unlearn much of her previous knowledge, which is never easy; in the second place, she had to study counterpoint; and in the third place, she was forced to practice for a certain number of hours *per diem*. As for the light modern school to which she had hitherto been accustomed, it availed her nothing. Instead of Fantasias and Airs with amazing variations, she was condemned to the Sonatas of Beethoven and Mozart, and the fugues of Sebastian Bach. Cast adrift, thus, upon an academy where an arrangement of operatic airs by Hertz was looked upon with pious horror, my unlucky sister had but a hard time of it, and, for the first half year or so, made herself consistently wretched and disagreeable. The truth is that Hilda was not amiable. She was handsome, haughty, and ready-witted; and she possessed a remarkable facility in the acquirement of accomplishments. Up to a certain point, and for just so long as her curiosity held out, she succeeded rapidly; but she had no real industry; and as soon as she ceased to be amused, grew careless, impatient, and out of heart. With such a disposition, it is difficult to go creditably through any academic education; and indeed I hardly know how or where it would have ended, had not Professor Oberstein one day discovered that Hilda had a voice—a voice so pure, so extensive, so sweet and flexible, as had seldom before been heard within the walls of the college. From this time forth Hilda was content; and the masters had comparatively little trouble to make her work. To sing was easier than to play fugues, and study Albrechtsberger. Besides her vanity was touched. She longed for the time when she could take part in the academy concerts; and she found that when singing she looked even handsomer than when silent. Her progress soon surprised us; and though she continued to be but a moderate pianist and a very indifferent theorist, she improved so rapidly in her new study, that after about eighteen months of Professor Oberstein's tuition, she was competent to sing in a concerted piece at one of our *matinées musicales*. From concerted pieces she was promoted to solos; and though I am not certain that she continued always to advance at the same rate, she at least kept up her reputation in the vocal classes, and from time to time received, not only the applause of an audience, but the more solid testimonial of a second or third class examination medal. I do not suppose, however, that Hilda was ever so thoroughly happy in her school-life as I was in mine. Naturally proud and reserved, she made no intimacies, and was altogether less popular than myself. She never took me into her heart, as I had once hoped. We were good friends, but not much more; and our sojourn at Zollenstrasse drew us less together than one could have anticipated. She had but little sympathy with my pursuits, and none with my ambitions. That I, a Churchill, should dream of following my art as a profession, shocked all her prejudices; whilst I, on the other hand, entertained a profound indifference toward all those fashionable and matrimonial visions to which her present studies were by her regarded as mere adjuncts and preliminaries. And thus, alas! it was and must ever be. My sister was not to be my second self, pray for it, or strive for it, as I would!

So the years went on, and, being so far from home, we spent vacation-time as well as term-time at the college. We wrote to our father about once in every three months—he replied to us about twice in every eight or ten. His letters were always the same—so much the same that he might as well have had them lithographed. He was happy to hear that we were so well satisfied with our place of residence, and that we gave so much satisfaction to our teachers; he rejoiced to say that he was well, and that Beever was the same as ever; and he remained our affectionate father, etc. etc. This was the purport of his letters, one and all—not a word more, and not a word less.

For my part, I had ceased to care for home or England now. I felt that there was but one home in the old country that could ever be home to me—and into that I had no hope of ever entering again. To stay abroad, then, forever; to work out my life in the land of Kaulbach, Overbeck, and Lessing; to visit Rome and the Vatican some time before I died; and to end my days within the walls of that Academy of which I was a loving and reverent disciple, constituted all the substance of my prayers— "the *ultima Thule* of my wandering desires."

CHAPTER XIX.

AN UNEXPECTED EVENT.

"HAS any thing been heard about the excursion?"

"Yes, we are to go to-day, if Madame Brenner and the afternoon continue favorable."

"Oh, delightful! I declare I had almost feared that our country afternoons were never to begin again."

"That is because a whole winter has gone by since we took our last trip; and that—let me see—that must have been in October."

"And we are now in the middle of April! Well, never mind, the summer is coming again, and the time has not seemed so very slow, after all. Where do you think we shall go? To the Hermitage, or to the ruins of Königsberg?"

"Nay, that is more than I can tell; but I should say to the woods of Bühl. Professor Metz was there the other day, and I heard him tell Madame Brenner that he had never seen such wild-flowers in his life——"

"Hush! Here he comes. We must not be caught idling!"

And, as the door opened, the heads of the two speakers were bent busily over their easels. The Professor came in, tall, gaunt, and gray; stooping somewhat in the shoulders, as was his habit; and darting quick, searching glances all about the room. Not a whisper disturbed the profound silence of the crowded studio, and the buzzing of a fly against the skylight was distinctly audible. In and out, threading his way among the easels, the great master then made the round of the class. To some he gave a word of praise, to some a shake of the head, and some he passed by in silence. Pausing beside me for an instant, he uttered a short grunt of approbation; and the next moment bent over my unlucky neighbor, Emma Werner, took the brush from her hand, and at a single touch effaced the head upon which she had been toiling all the morning.

"Oh, sir!" she exclaimed, "is it so bad as that?"

"Bad?" he repeated. "So bad that I have more hope for you than before. Signal failures imply genius. A fool would have done better."

And with this equivocal encouragement, and a still more equivocal shrug of the shoulders, he passed on.

"That cherub," said he to one, "has the scarlet fever."

To another:—"Your Hagar looks like a female Ugolino. 'Tis a baker's conception of the subject."

To a third:—"This foreground labors under a green and yellow melancholy!"

To a fourth:—"Your Madonna is a coquette."

To a fifth:—"What is your subject—Bacchus and Ariadne? Humph! Which is Bacchus, and which Ariadne?"

At last, having finished his tour of inspection, he came back to where Ida and I were working side by side, and stood for some time between the two easels, silent and observant. We were copying a head of Christ by Guido, which the Grand Duke had lent for the advanced students.

"It is possible," said he, presently, "to copy too well. Try to think less of the painting, and more of the idea. Truth is not necessarily literal. The Divine never can be literal; and there is in all art a vanishing point where the real merges itself into the ideal. Have courage, and remember that to attempt much is to learn much. The horizon mounts with the eye of the climber."

Having said this, he strode to the door; bowed hurriedly ; and was gone in a moment. We had all risen in silence to return his salutation ; but the door was no sooner closed behind him than a Babel of chatter broke out, and every body was in motion. This afternoon visit concluded the day's work, and the Professor's exit gave the signal for breaking up the class. In an instant all was confusion, laughter, and bustle. Paintings were laid aside, easels shut up, brushes washed, pallets cleaned, and copies put carefully away ; while in the midst of it all came a message from Madame Brenner, desiring us to be ready to start at three o'clock upon an excursion to the woods of Brühl.

With what shouts and hand-clappings this information was received ; how quickly the studio was put in order ; what haste we made to dress ; and with what delight we poured out of the courtyard and took the road to Brühl, none but those who have lived in schools and enjoyed half-holidays can conceive. Ida and I walked together, and Hilda, as usual, with the French governess, Mademoiselle Violette. Whether she chose her companion from preference, or whether, being one of the elder girls, she thought it more dignified to be seen walking with a teacher, I can not tell—I only know that Mademoiselle Violette was a little elderly, frivolous, conceited Parisian, who talked of nothing but her high birth, her misfortunes, her lover who died abroad, and her everlasting *toilette.*

Having walked very soberly, two by two, all through the town and along the public road, we broke up the order of march as soon as we arrived at the low meadows, and became a very noisy company. Our way lay mostly beside the river. The trees were clad in their first pale feathery foliage ; the afternoon was hot and sunny like an afternoon in July ; and the swallows were darting hither and thither, as if they knew not how to rejoice enough in the returning summer.

The woods lay between two and three miles to the west of the town, and we reached them about half-past four o'clock. How pleasant to plunge into the shade, after walking for an hour and a half with the sun in our faces ! How delicious to tread the elastic moss between the trees ; to lie down upon banks literally mantled over with primroses, blue hyacinths, and the wild geranium ; to watch the shafts of sunlight piercing the green gloom here and there, and gilding the smooth boles of the silver ash ! Intoxicated with delight, we laughed, we ran, we pelted each other with wild flowers, and made the woods ring again with the echoes of our voices. By and by, being somewhat warm and weary, we strolled away by twos and threes, and found resting-places and green nooks to our fancy. An old felled trunk coated with gray moss, furnished Ida and me with a seat ; and there, at some little distance from the rest, we sat hand in hand, and talked, as only the young ever talk, of art, friendship, and the future.

"It was our old Frauenkirche in Munich that made me an artist," said Ida. "From the time when I was quite a little child, and my mother used to carry me in her arms to mass, I remember the bronze tomb of the Emperor Louis, and the painted windows behind the altar. I was never weary of gazing up at those gorgeous kings and saints. I remember, also, how the evening sun used to shine through, and stain the pavement of the side-aisles with flecks of purple and gold. I believe that my very soul thirsted for color, and that my eyes drank it in as eagerly as ever wayfarer drank from the springs of the desert. I little thought at that time that I should ever come to handle it familiarly, and make it the medium of my own thoughts !"

"But you hoped to be a painter from the first ?"

"No. My parents were humble folks, and chance alone determined my career."

"Chance ! What chance, Ida ?"

"I will tell you. My father kept a small fruit-garden on the left bank of the Isar, about three-quarters of a mile out of Munich on the Harlaching road. Our house stood by the wayside, and from the back we had a view of the Tyrolean Alps. We were very poor. The produce of the garden barely sufficed to keep us, though the land and cottage were our own ; and in the winter time we suffered many privations. Still my childhood passed very happily. I went to the Free-school every day, and to Mass every Sunday and Saint's-day ; and each October, when the People's festival came round, my parents made holiday, and took me with them to see the prize fruits and flowers, and the rifle-shooting in the Theresa-fields. Thus the years went by, and at thirteen I was less ignorant than might have been supposed. About this time, having by dint of severe economy saved a score or so of dollars, my parents contrived to furnish and let our two best rooms. Our first lodger was a clerk from some banking-house in the town, who went in to business every morning, and remained away all day. However, he only staid with us about three months, and was succeeded by an English artist, who had come to study in the galleries of Munich. This artist discovered, somehow, that I loved art ; became interested in me ; gave me a few lessons, and—and taught me, in short, to know my own destiny."

"Well ?" said I, finding that she paused in her narrative.

"Well, it went on thus for a year or more, till one day my kind friend suggested that I should become a candidate for one of the free scholarships of the Zollenstrasse School of Art, and himself offered to defray the expenses of election. I made the effort—I succeeded—I have been here, as you know, five years already, and I have two more years to remain."

"And the English artist—where is he ? Do you ever hear from him ? Have you seen him since you left Munich ?"

Ida shook her head, and turned her face away.

"He went back soon after, to his native country," she said, "and we have heard nothing of him from that day to this. But it is your turn now, Barbara. Tell me, when did you first recognize your vocation ?"

"In my cradle, I think," I replied, with a smile and a sigh. "Before I could speak plainly, I scrawled with a pencil : and when I was quite a little girl I could see more faces in the clouds, and more pictures in the fire, than either of my sisters. I never studied, however, till I came here."

"And that," exclaimed Ida, "was at the very same time that I joined, six years ago ?"

"Precisely."

"And you are one year younger than I ?"

"Yes," I replied, "I am just seventeen, and you are eighteen. You have the advantage of me in every way. You had a year's teaching before you came here."

"Bah ! What is that ? I have not half your genius !"

"Nay—if you talk thus we shall quarrel."

"For the first time, Barbara !" laughed Ida, putting her arms about my neck. "For the first time ! Besides, you know, we have promised each other never to disagree—never to love each other less—never to let any thing come between us, either in our friendship or our future !"

"Do you suppose, Ida, that I forget it ?"

"And then," continued she, "we shall some day go to Rome together—Rome, the artist's Paradise ! We shall lodge among the painters in the Via Margutta, and go to the artists' festival at Albano. We will hire a studio ; paint together ; study together ; wander together in the ruins of the Forum, and under the moonlit arches of the Coliseum ! Oh, Barbara, does it not make your heart beat to think of it ?"

"Alas ! dear, I am not so confident. Could I but believe it possible——"

"To those who rely upon their own industry, all things are possible."

"A most sententious maxim ; but how shall I apply it ?"

"You shall apply it by—let me see, by painting a great historical picture, a masterpiece of modern art !"

"Oh, by all means !"

"And the Grand Duke must buy it—stay, he could not afford to buy it. It will be too expensive for him ; and, besides, if he did buy it, where could he put it ? No—no, King Louis of Bavaria must buy it ! He will give you two or three thousand dollars for it, and it will be hung in the modern Pinacothek, in my own dear city of Munich, where all the world will see and do it justice."

"I desire nothing better. Pray go on."

"Well, with your three thousand dollars you can go to Rome, and voilà—the thing is done."

"Would that it were, Ida !" I exclaimed, laughing. "Unfortunately, however, something more than self-reliance is necessary to carry out this admirable project. At present, yours is but a programme, with no entertainment to follow."

"That does not prove that the entertainment never will follow. Oh, I have set my heart on seeing you famous !"

"Come, Barbara," said Hilda close behind me. "We are all going, and I suppose you do not wish to be left in the woods."

"What, already ?"

"It is six o'clock, and will be dusk before we reach home," replied my sister coldly. Then, dropping her voice so as to be heard by me only :—"What folly have you been talking ?" she added. "I have been standing here these five minutes, listening with amazement to all this nonsense about Rome and fame, and Heaven knows what besides ! One would think you were a free scholar, like your dear friend here, and had to work for your bread !"

"One may work for something better than bread, sister," I replied smiling.

But she turned angrily away, and we were presently surrounded by a troop of the younger girls, all shouting and dancing, and laden with wild-flowers, like a bevy of little bacchantes.

"Look here, Ida," said one. "Here is a daisy-chain that would reach across the river ! Did you ever see one so long ?"

"I have found a lovely maiden-hair fern, roots and all, for Madame Brenner's fernery !" cried another.

"Ah !" exclaimed a third, "I know something which none of you know — such good news !"

"Good news !" repeated a dozen voices at once. "What is it ? Oh, what is it ?"

"Guess—but you'll never guess. Shall I tell you ? Well, we are to have chocolate and cream-cakes for supper !"

And thus, chattering, laughing, and rejoicing, the merry crowd swept on homeward, and left the setting sun behind the woods of Brühl. By and by some elder girls began singing four-part songs ; and then the twilight came down ; and the stars gleamed out in the green-blue sky ; and the music mingled in with the lapsing of the river that ran beside us all the way.

It was almost dark by the time we reached the college. We were tired and silent enough now, and the wild-flowers had all been thrown away on the road. Still we were very happy, very hungry, very glad to be home again, and very glad to have been out.

The porter who opened the gate touched his hat and spoke to Madame Brenner. She left him, and came quickly into the midst of us.

"Barbara," said she, "Barbara and Hilda Churchill, where are you ? Some friends of yours are here. You will find them waiting in the parlor."

Friends ! Who could they be ? Whence had they come ? Save a flying call two or three years ago from dear old Mr. Bose, no one had asked for us ever since we had been in the College ! Could it be my aunt ? Could it be Hugh ? I felt myself flush, and then grow pale again. Going up the steps, I clung involuntarily to Hilda's arm, and when we reached the parlor-door trembled like a leaf.

The room was dimly lighted, and contained two persons, a lady and a gentleman. The lady was lying back in an easy chair, and turned her head languidly at the opening of the door. The gentleman was standing at the window with his hands behind his back.

"Madame," said he, addressing himself with a stately bow to Madame Brenner, "permit me to introduce myself—Edmund Churchill—the father of your pupils."

The superintendent courtesied, and looked from him to us, expecting to see us fly into his arms. My father, however, bowed again and glanced toward the occupant of the easy chair, who rose slowly, and threw back her vail.

"And Mrs. Churchill," added he very ceremoniously. He then turned toward us for the first time.

"My dear children," said he, touching our

foreheads lightly with his lips, "I rejoice to see you again. Be pleased to receive this lady with the affection and respect due to—ahem! your father's wife. Mrs. Churchill, I have the pleasure of presenting my daughters."

But that lady, instead of embracing us with maternal fervor, extended only the tips of two fingers, and said:

"I had no idea that your 'little girls' were grown up, Mr. Churchill!"

CHAPTER XX.

HILDA DISCOVERS HER VOCATION.

AND so my father had married again—married again at sixty, and brought his bride to Zollenstrasse-am-Main! It was their honeymoon. They had come up the Rhine viâ Brussels, and were returning by way of Paris; having at present been just ten days *en voyage.* This event was so unexpected that at first I could scarcely realize it. It took me, in fact, some two or three days to form an opinion of my father's choice, and in order to express that opinion I find myself referring not exactly to my first impression, but to the successive impressions of several interviews.

Mrs. Churchill was what is generally called a fine woman. That is to say, she was large, well defined and of a comely presence. She was about forty years of age. Her hands were small, her teeth admirable, her complexion well-preserved, and her taste in dress unexceptionable. Easy, indolent, self-possessed, and somewhat distant, her manner was that of a thorough woman of the world—or rather that of a woman who knew the world and herself by heart, and had determined to make the most of both. She was not clever—I soon discovered that—but she had tact. She knew what to admire, what tastes to profess, and how to give them effect. She spoke seldom, always slowly, and never unless she really had something to say. That something, if clever, was not original; and, if original, was not clever; but it was invariably judicious, and, like a paper currency, represented a value which was not intrinsic. Above all, she had studied the art of silence, and knew how to maintain a dignified repose. If that repose seemed somewhat artificial and over-elaborated—if she was, perhaps, on the whole, more fastidious than refined, more fashionable than highly bred, she could, nevertheless, be sufficiently gracious when she pleased, and was, beyond all doubt, well accustomed to the ways, means, and appliances of that little corner of society called "the world."

That she had also been previously married—that her first husband held a civil appointment in India under Lord Amherst, and there accumulated a considerable fortune—that he had been dead some fifteen years or so, and left her with a consolatory jointure of several hundreds per annum—that she had since then traveled hither and thither; gone extensively into society; spent every season in Paris; and preferred the interesting *rôle* of a wealthy widow to that of a wife twice wedded, were facts which we soon learned, and which she herself was not slow to announce. Where and when she had

first known my father, how she came to be wearied of her single life, and why she married him, were points left to conjecture. One thing, however, was evident—namely, that she was not prepared to find his "little girls" grown up; and I believe, to do him justice, that he was almost as much surprised himself. We were really little girls when he left us, six years ago, on board the Rotterdam steamer, and little girls, I have no doubt, he still expected to find us. Be that as it may, Mrs. Churchill was undisguisedly chagrined, and treated us for the first day or so with mortifying coldness. There is, however, a proverb in favor of second thoughts; and before a week was past, Mrs. Churchill had seen fit to reverse her tactics. Looking upon us, I suppose, as inevitable evils, she made up her mind to endure us with the best grace she could, and became, on a sudden, quite sympathetic and pleasant. She discovered that I had genius and originality; that Hilda's beauty and accomplishments were of the highest order; and that she (Mrs. Churchill) was unfeignedly proud of us both. I can not say that I was particularly elated by this tardy reception into my stepmother's good graces. I had neither sufficient respect for her understanding to value her praise, nor enough regard for herself to care much for her favor. But I received her advances with politeness, and endeavored, for my father's sake, to keep on such terms as might insure the comfort of our future intercourse.

Hilda, on the contrary, was completely won over by Mrs. Churchill's civilities, and tolerably well imposed upon by Mrs. Churchill's admirable manner. Having at first disliked our new stepmother ten times more bitterly than myself, she now found that she had judged too hastily of one who compared her singing to Persiani's and herself to Lady Clementina Villiers. Thus it happened that in the course of a few days they were on the best footing imaginable; and before the second week was over, had become almost inseparable. Mrs. Churchill declared that she could go nowhere without Hilda—Hilda was only too well pleased to go everywhere with Mrs. Churchill. So they lunched, dined, and drove out together every day, more like a pair of romantic friends than a middle-aged bride and a grown-up step-daughter. It is not impossible that Mrs. Churchill may have foreseen some such desirable effect, and acted accordingly.

Naturally fond of excitement, Hilda plunged with delight into this new life, and neglected every thing for it. Mrs. Churchill's Paris bonnets, Mrs. Churchill's fashionable acquaintances, and Mrs. Churchill's patronage, almost turned her head. She talked, thought, dreamed of nothing but dress, amusement, and the people whom she daily met. Remonstrance on my part was useless; for Madame Brenner, knowing that my father intended to remain only a month, thought fit to allow us every liberty during his stay, and voluntarily released us from our collegiate duties. To her surprise, I availed myself but sparingly of that privilege, pursuing my daily studies much as usual, and only spending an evening now and then at my father's hotel.

Going in there one afternoon about seven o'clock, I found the dessert still on the table;

Hilda trying on a bonnet before the glass; my father sipping his wine with half-closed eyes; and Mrs. Churchill lying on a sofa with her back to the light; and her head resting languidly on her arm. Mrs. Churchill always sat with her back to the light; and, having a white and very lovely arm, generally rested her head upon it.

My father looked up and nodded as I came in; Mrs. Churchill extended two fingers; Hilda turned eagerly toward me, and exclaimed:—

"Oh, Barbara, you are just in time to see my new bonnet! Is it not charming?"

"Yours!" I ejaculated, seeing what a thing of gauze and marabouts it was. "That bonnet, yours?"

"Mine—my own exclusive property! Is it not becoming?"

I hesitated. I had not yet reconciled myself to the metamorphosis in my sister's appearance; and though she looked handsomer than ever in these fashionable things, I could not help liking her old simple clothing best.

"It is stylish," I said, after a pause, "and, in a certain sense, becoming; but——"

"But what?"

"But I do not see of what use it will be to you when Mrs. Churchill is no longer here."

Hilda and my stepmother exchanged glances.

"In fact," I continued, "Madame Brenner will taboo it, as she tabooed Ildegarde's pink mantle last midsummer."

Hilda shrugged her shoulders.

"*Cela m'est égal!*" she said lightly. "I will, at all events, wear it while I can, and where I can. Sufficient for the day is the evil thereof—*n'est ce pas, ma belle mère?*"

Mrs. Churchill nodded a languid affirmative, and Hilda went on.

"What would be the good of the present," said she, "if one were always fretting for the future? Let the future take care of itself. It is bad enough when it comes, without being anticipated!"

"The future," said Mrs. Churchill, significantly, "sometimes exceeds our anticipations. But our dear Barbara is practical—immensely practical!"

"Only with respect to bonnets," I replied, laughingly. "In other matters, I fear, I am as visionary as most people."

"I should like to know what those other matters are."

"Nay—I am not fond of telling my dreams!"

"Except to Ida Saxe by sunset, in the woods of Brühl," said Hilda satirically. "Come, Barbara, confess that, on one occasion, you were any thing but practical."

But I was not disposed to enter on that subject before my father and his wife; so I only shook my head, and turned the conversation by asking what they had done since the morning.

"Done? Oh, not much to-day," replied my sister, still admiring the bonnet. "We promenaded in the gardens before lunch, drove to Wiesbach in the afternoon with papa, and dined at six. Why did you not come in time to dine?"

"The class broke up late to-day, and I could not leave sooner."

Hilda tossed her head impatiently.

"Be honest, Barbara," said she, "and say at once that you prefer the society of your easel to that of your relations."

"Be considerate, Hilda; and remember that satire is often neither witty nor true."

I answered sharply; for it seemed to me, somehow, that my sister was seeking either to provoke me, or to irritate the others against me. Be this as it might, Mrs. Churchill interposed before she had time to retort.

"My darling Hilda," said she, "I must positively find fault with you! Why blame your sister for a perseverance that does her so much honor? Our dear Barbara has genius, and the enthusiasm of genius. For my part, I adore art. I had rather have been Raphael than Shakspeare."

This was one of Mrs. Churchill's "effects." I began to know them now, and the little pause by which they were always followed.

"Besides," she added, after a minute, "Barbara is still very young, and youth is the season for study. Her industry, I am sure, is delightful. Perfectly delightful! Let us hope, however, that she will not overtax her strength. Art has its dangers as well as its fascinations; and I have heard that oils are sometimes bad for the chest."

Laughing, I scarcely knew why, at something in the tone of Mrs. Churchill's observations, I hastened to assure her that she need entertain no such apprehensions for me.

"Painters," I said, "do not die so easily. When they love art, they have the good sense to live for it."

"And you really do love it, I suppose?" said my stepmother interrogatively.

"With my whole heart."

"And prefer your studies to all the pleasures of the great world?"

"I can conceive no greater misfortune than to leave them off."

Again Mrs. Churchill and Hilda glanced at one another, and I detected something like a flitting smile upon the face of each.

My father, who had been dozing for the last ten minutes or so with his cheek on his palm, now woke up and looked at his watch.

"A quarter to eight!" said he. "A quarter to eight already! Will it be agreeable to you, Mrs. Churchill, to order coffee?"

Mrs. Churchill was agreeable, and Hilda rang the bell.

My father was the same as ever—a little stouter and greyer, perhaps, and a little more bald than when we left home; but the same man, every inch. He paced about the room; glanced in the looking-glass; and cherished his handsome hands just in the old way. He addressed his wife with as much stately politeness as he once addressed Miss Whymper. He was irritable with the waiters; despotic with the fly-drivers; and courteous to the chamber-maids. Above all, he planted himself on the rug, and turned his back to the fire with exactly the same air of commanding ownership; even though there were no fire there, but only an ugly, empty porcelain stove, with a blackened chimney reaching through the ceiling.

Having had coffee, and discussed the comparative attractions of the summer theater, the Hofgarten, and the concert in the grounds of the Conversation-Haus, Mrs. Churchill and Hilda made an elaborate walking-toilette, and insisted that I, for once, should make one of the party.

My father, not without a dissatisfied glance at my plain brown dress, then gave his arm to Mrs. Churchill, and we followed.

What with her new bonnet, and a lace shawl lent by our stepmother; and what with her own rich, haughty beauty, Hilda attracted all eyes, as we went along. Every one turned to stare after her; and my father, proud of the general admiration, glanced back every now and then with a well-satisfied smile, as if saying — "I am Edmund Churchill, and she is my daughter — my daughter, sir, and a Churchill, *pur sang !*"

Once arrived at the gardens, we were beset by a crowd of gentlemen.

"Friends of Mrs. Churchill," whispered Hilda. "And people of the highest fashion." She knew them all as they came up; had the name, rank, and profession of each at her fingers' ends; and seemed already intimate with most. Some she greeted with a jest, some with a shake of the hand, and for all had a bow, a smile, or a gracious word. I listened, looked on, and scarce believed my eyes. Ten days ago she was but a school-girl. Now I found her developed all at once into a consummate flirt; conscious of her advantages; and as thoroughly at her ease as Mrs. Churchill herself.

I cannot say that I was agreeably impressed by Mrs. Churchill's distinguished acquaintances; and yet they were very grand folks, Counts, Barons, Excellencies, and so forth, with nothing less dignified than a captain among them. They were all bearded, buttoned, frogged, and mustachioed, and wore little scraps of red or green ribbon at their breast. Perhaps the most striking amongst them, was a certain Captain Talbot, some thirty-five years of age and six feet two in height; bronzed, stalwart, assiduous; with something infinitely persuasive in his voice and manner, and something unpleasantly bold in the expression of his eyes. I liked him less, and Hilda seemed to like him better, than any of the rest. They kept up an incessant fire of raillery and flirtation; and by-and-by, when, weary of promenading, we sat down to eat ices and listen to the music, he usurped the seat beside hers, and succeeded in keeping all others at a distance. Then my father strolled away to the roulette-tables; and Mrs. Churchill sat like a queen amid her little court, and gave utterance every now and then to judicious observations on Rossini, politics, millinery, and the fine arts.

Thus the evening passed, and I was glad when it was over.

All that night, and for several days and nights following, I was restless and disquieted. I now scarcely saw Hilda at all, unless in the refectory at breakfast, or at night when she came in late and tired, after having spent the day with Mrs. Churchill.

"How will she endure the old life, when they are gone?" I asked myself continually. "How will she exist without excitement? What of these fashionable men with whom she has been flirting for the last three weeks? How will she conform again to the old rules and simple pleasures of the school?"

Troubled and apprehensive, I turned these questions over and over in my mind, and could arrive at no conclusion.

"Would that they were gone!" I murmured anxiously, as I saw the evil deepening day by day. "Would to Heaven that they had never come!"

At length there arrived a night when my doubts were brought to an abrupt conclusion. It was the evening of the twenty-fifth of May, and my father's departure was fixed for the twenty-seventh. Hilda had been all day with them as usual; the rest of the girls were gone for an evening walk; and I, tired and thoughtful, sat alone in the deserted class-room, looking out at the quiet garden and the gathering twilight. The banging of a distant door, the echo of a quick step in the corridor, and Hilda's sudden appearance at my elbow, roused me from my reverie.

"Well, Barbara," said she, "are you not surprised to see me so early?"

"It is early," I replied, "for you; but I suppose you are going back to spend the evening."

"No, I have come, on the contrary, to spend the evening with you and Madame Brenner. What do you think of that?"

"Why, that wonders will never cease; or that you are jesting."

"I am in earnest, I assure you."

"Then papa is not going away the day after to-morrow."

"He is going away, indeed, and—and I have something to tell you."

I looked up, and saw by the half-light that she was flushed and nervous. -

"Something to tell me?" I repeated.

"Well, they are going," said Hilda reluctantly, "and—and—promise not to be dreadfully hurt or angry, dear."

"Hurt! angry! What *can* you mean?"

"I mean that—that I am going with them."

"Going with them?" I faltered. "Impossible! In the middle of term—with the competition fixed for July—it is against the rules."

"What do I care for the rules, if I leave the College?" said Hilda, with a scornful gesture.

Leave the College! I sat down, bewildered, and looked at her silently.

"Why, you see," said my sister, speaking very fast, and plucking a pen to pieces, fiber by fiber, "I—I am not like you, Barbara. I don't love this place, as you do. I don't care for its rewards and honors, its medals, competitions, and petty successes, as you do. You desire nothing better than to be a painter—I would not be a singer for the universe. Work, in fact, is not my *metier*. I hate it. I am tired of it. I have had enough of it. Besides, I am three years your senior, and it is time I ceased to be a school-girl. Mrs. Churchill says I am destined to make a great success in society."

Mrs. Churchill. Ay, to be sure, this was her work.

"And then papa's plans are quite altered," she continued, finding that I remained silent. "Instead of going back to London, they mean to spend some months in Paris. Mrs. Churchill's Paris connection is immense; and she means to introduce me in all the best circles. It is not to be supposed, of course, with her means and position, that she will give up society just because she has married papa. Neither does he desire it. He has lived long enough out of the world, and it is time he returned to it, if only for your sake and mine. We must be introduced, you know,

Barbara; and, as I am the elder, my turn comes first. You cannot object to that surely ?"

I shook my head sadly.

"Not if you prefer it," I said, speaking for the first time. "Not if you think you will be happy."

"Happy!" echoed she. "Why, of course, I shall be happy. Society is my vocation !"

"Society is a phantom—a mockery—an illusion. Beware how you trust it. It will vanish some day, 'and leave not a rack behind.'"

Hilda shrugged her shoulders disdainfully.

"For mercy's sake, no moralizing!" exclaimed she. "I love life, and the little that I have seen disposes me to see more. You will like it, too, when you have the opportunity. Oh, how I long to be rid of this monotonous College routine, and all the art-jargon of our hum-drum professors !"

"Oh, Hilda !"

Touched by the reproach which my words conveyed, or moved, perhaps, by something like remorse for her own indifference, my sister bent down suddenly, and kissed me on the brow.

"I am sorry to leave you, dear," she said, apologetically; "but I cannot help rejoicing in my emancipation. I never was industrious or self-denying, like you; and papa and Mrs. Churchill are both very kind to me, and—and you have Ida Saxe, you know; and she will be here quite as long, or longer, than you—so you will not be lonely, or miss me very much when I am gone, will you ?"

"If I felt sure you would have no reason to repent the change," said I, speaking very slowly, and mastering the tears that rose unbidden to my eyes; "if I knew that your relations with Mrs. Churchill would continue to be as pleasant as they now are, believe, Hilda dear, that I should desire nothing farther."

"You will not even be vexed with me for going ?"

"Not in the least."

"Come, that is reasonable ! I had no idea that you would have taken my news so good-temperedly, or I would have told you long ago. Why, I have been hesitating for the last eight days, in the dread that we should have some horrid scene about it, and now—well, enough of that ! I wish you would come with me to my bedroom, and help me to make the inventory of my wardrobe. I must pack to-night before I go to bed; for they have made up their minds to go down the river to-morrow, and I shall not have a moment to spare."

About an hour after this we supped together for the last time at the general table, and in the morning she took leave of the school, and removed with her luggage to my father's hotel. Madame Brenner embraced her, and the girls bade her a kindly farewell; but there were no tears shed on either side, and the parting, altogether, was cool enough.

"The Fräulein might have done her teachers the justice to wait, at least, for the July competition," said Professor Oberstein, not without a touch of bitterness.

"Or have left us with something like regret," observed Madame Brenner.

"Oh, Barbara !" whispered one of the younger children, nestling close to my side, "had you been going away, how sorry we should have been !"

CHAPTER XXI.

A DIPLOMATIC INTERVIEW

"An artist, an organist, a pianist, all these are very good people; but, you know, not '*de notre monde*,' and Clive ought to belong to it."

The Newcombes.

"You are of course aware, Barbara," said my father, "that my income is circumscribed—exceedingly circumscribed—and that your educational expenses have been heavy."

Mrs. Churchill and Hilda were up-stairs, busied with their last traveling arrangements. My father and I were sitting at opposite sides of the breakfast table, with the hotel bill and the empty coffee-cups between us.

"You ought also to be informed," he added, "that although Mrs. Churchill is possessed of good private means, my own circumstances are not materially bettered by the alliance. I am even, in some respects, a poorer man than before. I must resume my position in society, reside in a better house, and inevitably increase the general ratio of my private expenditure."

Not knowing what reply was expected of me, or to what end this statement tended, I bowed, and was silent.

"I purpose, nevertheless," continued he, "to leave you here for the present. I believe that you have perseverance, and a certain amount of —of ability; and I have too much regard for your progress to withdraw you just yet from the College. This decision, understand, will put me to considerable inconvenience — very considerable inconvenience—which I am, however, disposed on your account to meet. On your account only."

Feeling almost overwhelmed, if not by the magnitude of the favor, at all events by the manner in which it was announced, I stammered a word or two of thanks.

"Circumstanced as I am," said my father, after a brief pause, "I can not provide for my family as I would. I am a poor man, and it is indispensable that the daughters of a poor man should marry well. For sons I could have made interest in high quarters; but to my daughters I can give only descent and education. Hilda, I feel sure, will do well. She has tact, style, conversation, and——"

"And beauty," I suggested.

"Exactly so. And beauty," said he, with something like a shade of polite embarrassment. "She will marry, no doubt, before the expiration of the year; in which case the field will be open to you. In the mean time I desire to draw your attention very particularly to one or two matters."

He was as formal to me now that I was grown up, as he was brusque and harsh when I was a child ! It was strange, but, sitting opposite to each other at eight o'clock this bright May morning, with the traveling *calèche* waiting at the door, and the certainty of a long separation before us, we were carrying on our conversation as distantly as if, instead of being father and daughter, we were a couple of ambassadors discussing affairs of state !

Finding that he was now coming to the point, I bowed again and waited anxiously.

"In the first place," said he, "you must cultivate manner. As a child you were awkward; and even now you are deficient in that style which your sister appears instinctively to have acquired. Style is the first requisite for society; and on society a young woman's prospects depend. I have sometimes feared, Barbara, that you do not sufficiently appreciate society."

"I—I must confess, sir, that for me it possesses few attractions."

My father shook his head, and trifled diplomatically with his snuff-box.

"So much the worse for you," he observed, drily. "I have no fortune for you; remember that. If you do not marry, what is to become of you?"

"I should hope, sir, that my profession will at all times enable me to live."

He looked fixedly at me, as if scarcely comprehending the sense of my words.

"Your *what?*" he said at length. "Your—— say that again."

"My profession, sir," I repeated, not without a strange fluttering at my heart.

"Your profession!" he exclaimed, flushing scarlet. "Upon my soul, I was not aware that you had one! What is it, pray? The church, the law, or the army?"

The tears came rushing to my eyes. I looked down. I could have borne his anger; but I had no reply for his sarcasm.

"I suppose," he continued, "that, because you have been daubing here for the last few years, you fancy yourself a painter?"

"I—I had hoped——"

"Hope nothing!" interrupted he. "Hope nothing on that head, for I will never countenance it! Do you suppose that I—a Churchill—will permit my daughter to earn her bread like a dress-maker? Do you suppose, if I had a son, that I would have allowed him to become a beggarly painter? If you have ever dreamt of this (and I suppose it has been instilled into you at this confounded College), forget it. Forget it once for all, and never let me hear another word about it!"

Still trembling as I had so often trembled before him in my early childhood, I nevertheless dashed away the tears, and looked up into his face.

"But, sir," I said firmly, "if you have no fortune for me, and if I do not marry—what then?"

"I will hear of no alternative. You *must* marry. It is your duty to marry. Every well-born and well-bred young woman who is properly introduced, has opportunities of marriage. You are tolerably good-looking. There is no reason why you should not succeed in society as well as others. Let me hear no more of this sign-painting nonsense. It displeases me exceedingly."

Saying which, he rose coldly, moved toward the door, and was leaving without another glance at me; but I had something to say—something that I had not yet ventured to say, though I had seen him daily for a month.

"Stay," I cried, hurriedly. "One question, sir—it is the only moment, the last moment, I can ask it. What of Mrs. Sandyshaft? Is she still living?"

He flushed again, and paused with his hand upon the door.

"Yes," he replied, "I believe that she is living."

"And has she never written to you? Never asked for me? Never attempted to recall me?"

"Never," said he, with mingled impatience and embarrassment. "Never."

And so passed on abruptly, and left the room.

I dropped into the nearest chair and covered my face with my hands. Alas! I was quite, quite forgotten.

Presently they all came down, cloaked and ready for the journey. Hilda tried to look serious at parting.

"Good-by, darling," she said, kissing me repeatedly. "I am so sorry to leave you; but I will write from Paris as soon as we arrive. You wil not fret, will you?"

"Fret!" echoed Mrs. Churchill, taking my disengaged hand between both of hers. "How can she fret when she has Art, divine Art, for her companion? Adieu, dearest girl—we shall not forget you!"

They then stepped into the carriage — my father touched my cheek coldly with his lips, and as he did so, whispered "Remember"—the courier shut up the steps—the coachman cracked his whip—my sister waved her hand, and, amid jingling harness-bells, bowing waiters, and a world of clattering and prancing, they drove rapidly away, and vanished in a cloud of dust round the corner of the Theater-platz.

That night I went sorrowfully to bed and lay awake for hours, thinking of Hilda, of the future, of my old Suffolk home, and of all that had there befallen me. Was I never again to see her who had been more to me than a mother? Was I never more to clasp that hand which placed the silver ring on mine, long, long ago, in the far-away woods about Broomhill?

Heigho! There it lay—there, in the corner of my desk—the Arab's ring, with the old watchguard knotted to it still!

CHAPTER XXII.

THE STUDENT IN ART.

"Art's a service."—Elizabeth Barrett Browning.

There is something almost sacred in the enthusiasm, the self-devotion, the pure ambition of the student in art. He, above all others, lives less for himself than for the past and all that made it glorious. What to him is the ignorant present? What the world, and the pleasures of the world? Truth, excellence, beauty, are his gods; and to them he offers up the sacrifice of his youth. He is poor; but poverty is a condition of endeavor. He is unknown; but were it not better to wrest one revelation from failure, than be blinded by a foolish prosperity? For his remote and beautiful Ideal he is content to suffer all things—privation, obscurity, neglect. Should the world never recognise him, can he therefore be said to have lived in vain? Has he not acquired the principles of beauty; studied under Michael Angelo; adored Raffaelle from afar off? Humble, earnest, steadfast, is he; modest of his own poor merit; and full of wonder and admiration as a little child. Infinitely touching are his hopes, his fears, his moments of despondency and doubt—infinitely joyous and repaying are his first well-earned successes, No mean desires leaven as yet the unsullied aspirations of his soul. A copper-medal, a wreath that will fade ere night, a word of encouragement from one whose judgment he reveres, are more to him than an inheritance. Worth, not wealth, is the end of his ambition; and he is richer in the possession of these frail testimonies than in any of those grosser rewards with which society could crown him.

Surely there may be found in all this something admirable and instructive—something which bears unmistakable impress of the old heroic element! What but this same mood of simple faith and constancy inspired the masterpieces, the martyrdoms, the discoveries of the past? What but this sent Leonidas to Thermopylæ, and Montrose to the scaffold; held Columbus on his course across the waste of waters, and consoled Galileo for the ridicule and persecution of his age?

It is pleasant thus to consider the nature of the student; to accept him as our living representative of the heroic race of gods and men—as the last lone dweller on those "shores of old romance" which, but for himself and the poets, were now well-nigh blotted from our charts. Let us cherish him, for he is worthy of all cherishing. Let us praise him, for he is worthy of all praise; and this independently of any genius that may be in him, but for love of that which he loves, and in honor of that which he honors.

Dwelling in the Art-School of Zollenstrasse-am-Main; sharing the hopes, efforts, and daily life of the scholars; witnessing their generous emulation, and partaking their simple pleasures, I came insensibly to form these views of art and its influences; to regard it as a high, almost as a holy calling; and to idealize, to a certain extent, the mission of the student. Under other circumstances, and in any other land, I might have had reason to judge differently; but it is not in the German nature to be diverted from a lofty pursuit by petty passions. Reflective, persevering, somewhat obstinate and limited in his opinions, somewhat heavy and phlegmatic by temper, the German student lives in brotherly relations with his fellow-laborers; helps cheerfully where help is needed; praises heartily where praise is due; and is too much in earnest about his own work to envy the progress or scorn the efforts of others. So national is he, indeed, and so thoroughly does he identify himself with the general cause, that he rejoices honestly in their success, and finds in it matter for self-encouragement. Of this disposition I never beheld more proof than during the six or seven weeks which intervened between my father's departure and the date of our July festival.

It was a momentous epoch for us. Report said that it would be the grandest competition ever known since the founding of the school. We all had something to strive for, and something to hope. In every department the students were working like bees; and, though it be the tritest of similes, I defy you to have avoided comparing the whole college to one vast hive, had you stood at hot noon in the midst of the empty courtyard, listening to the hum that issued from the open windows all around. We had, indeed, abundant motive for industry, since a harvest of honor, and prizes for

every branch of study, awaited our success. Concerts and musical examinations were to take place, and an exhibition of fine arts was to be held in the great-room of the Conversation-Haus. Amateurs, professors, and strangers were expected from far and near. The names of Heine, Lamartine, Overbeck, Waagen, Schwanthaler and others, were already stated to be upon the list of judges. King Louis of Bavaria, it was said, was coming to visit the Grand Duke; and some even whispered of the probable presence of Danneker, the venerable Danneker, "whose hand sculptured the beauteous Ariadne and the Panther." What wonder, then, if every student were at work, heart, soul, and brain, for the coming trial? What wonder if the musicians deafened us all day; if we painters smelt of megilp and copal varnish from morning till night, and came into dinner as plentifully besmeared with yellow ochre and Venetian red as a society of Cherokees or Blackfeet; if the teachers were all in a state bordering on distraction; and if Professor Metz (grown more ruthless and satirical than ever) hovered about the studios like a critical Asmodeus, breaking our hearts daily?

"You are a colony of daubers," he used to say; "canvas-spoilers, caricaturists! Were I Dame Nature, I would bring an action against you for libel. Do you call these pictures? They are not pictures. They are senseless masses of color. What do they mean? What do they teach? What do they prove? Keep every other commandment as faithfully as you have kept the second, and you will do well; for these are likenesses of nothing that is in heaven or earth! *Gott im Himmel!* if I am on the hanging committee, I'll turn every canvas to the wall!"

Notwithstanding this cold comfort on the part of our imperious Professor, we worked merrily on, encouraging and helping one another, and looking forward to the coming trial with expectations far from despondent. Ida, whose talent for landscape was unrivaled among us, touched up the mountains in Bertha's "Flight into Egypt." Bertha, whose figures were capital, put in a group of shepherds for Gertrude, whose "Vale of Tempe" would have been nothing without them—Luisa, a very Pre-Raffaellite of finish, manufactured weedy foregrounds by the dozen—and Frederika, whose forte lay in aërial perspective, dashed in skies and blue mists and graduated flights of birds for almost every girl in the class. As for poor Emma Werner, who really had no talent whatever, we all helped her, and produced by our combined efforts a very tolerable picture, which, I may as well observe at once, carried off a third-class medal, and made the crowning glory of her life for ever after.

I have hesitated, up to this point, whether or no to dwell upon my share of the hopes and toils of the time—whether to describe my own picture, or leave all such details to the imagination of those who read my story. Yet this book is the true chronicle of my life; and that picture was more than my life for many and many a month. I had it before my eyes at all times of the day, and in all places. I saw it painted on the darkness when I woke, restless and feverish, in the midst of the summer night.

I knew every inch of it by heart, and could have reproduced it from memory, touch for touch, without the variation of a hair's breadth, right or left. My opinion fluctuated about it all this time to a degree that nearly drove me mad. Sometimes I delighted in it—sometimes I loathed it. Twenty times a day I passed from the summit of hope to the lowest depths of despair. Twenty times a day I asked myself, "Is it good? Is it bad? Am I a painter; or have I deceived myself with the phantom of a vain desire?" I could not answer these questions. I could only hope, and fear, and paint on, according to the promptings that were in me.

My subject was Rienzi; my scene, the ruins of the Forum. A solitary figure seated, draped and meditative, upon a fallen capital at the foot of the column of Phocas; a dim perspective of buildings with the Colosseum far away in the shadowy distance; a goat browsing in the foreground; and, over all, a sky filled with the last rose-tints of the sunken sun, steeping all the earth and the base of every pillar in rich shadow, and touching church-tower, pediment, and sculptured capital with a glory direct from heaven—this was the scene I strove to paint, the dream I strove to realize, the poem I strove to utter. How imperfect that utterance was, and how vague that dream, none now know better than myself; but all the romance and ambition of my youth were lavished on it; though I have painted better pictures since, yet, in one sense, have I never painted another so good.

And thus the weeks went by, and the appointed time came up with rapid strides, desired yet dreaded, and pregnant with events.

CHAPTER XXIII.

THE FESTIVAL OF FINE ARTS.

THE great week came at last, and with it such shoals of visitors as filled the town of Zollenstrasse-am-Main to overflowing. Every hotel, lodging-house, boarding-house, gasthaus, and suburban inn was crammed from basement to garret. The King of Bavaria was at the palace, and the King of Würtemberg at the Kaiser Krone over the way. Every boat, diligence, and public conveyance came laden daily with double its lawful freight. Traveling *calêches* multiplied so rapidly that the inn-yards were in a state of blockade. The streets swarmed with officers of the royal suites, and every passer-by wore a uniform or a court suit. As for honorary ribbons, you saw as much in half an hour as might have stocked a haberdasher's shop, and stars were as plentiful as if the milky way had dropped in upon a visit.

The Competition lasted just a week, and was arranged according to programme, thus:—

On Monday and Wednesday the musicians competed in the Academy concert-room for the best orchestral symphony, instrumental quartet, and four-part song. On Tuesday and Thursday, the solo players and vocalists gave a public concert. On Friday and Saturday was held an exhibition of paintings and sculptures by the art-students. Sunday, however, the grandest day of all, was set apart for the distribution of prizes. For this ceremony the Assembly-room of the Conversation-Haus was to be fitted up, and no visitor could be admitted without a card of invitation. Then, besides all this, we had a French company at the theater; a review; a boar-hunt; a ball every night at the Conversation-Haus; and a fair in the public gardens—to say nothing of the extra roulette tables which Messieurs Fripon and Coquin found it necessary to provide for the occasion. A fine time, truly, for Zollenstrasse-am-Main—a fine time for the Grand Duke, the hotel-keepers, and the blacklegs!

Nor were we students one whit less excited than the rest of the community; for till the Sunday we knew no more than others what our fate would be. Every second day the committees of judgment met, discussed, passed resolutions, and recorded decisions of which we could in no wise foretell the purport. Whose would be the first prize, and whose the second? Would the medal be his, or hers, or mine? For my own part, when I saw the works of art assembled together in one hall, and came to compare my picture with those of my competitors, I lost all heart, and believed it to be the most egregious failure there.

At length the six days and nights were past, and the Sunday morning dawned, bright and hot, and flooded with intensest light. The ceremony was announced for two o'clock in the afternoon; so we went to church, as usual, in the morning, though none of us, I fear, attended much to the service. By half-past one we were at the Conversation-Haus, and in our places. It was a magnificent room, some eighty feet in length, decorated with alternate panelings of looking-glass and fresco-painting, and hung with superb chandeliers, like fountains of cut glass. At the upper end, on a dais of crimson cloth, stood a semicircle of luxurious arm-chairs for the Duke and his chief guests; to the left of the dais a platform of seats, tier above tier, for the accommodation of the minor nobility; and to the right of the dais, a similar platform for the artists and men of letters from among whom the different committees had been organized. Directly facing this formidable array, on benches that extended half way down the room, and were divided off from the lower end by a wooden barrier, we students were seated—the youths on one side, and the girls on the other, with a narrow alley between. In the space behind us and in the gallery above the door, were crowded all those spectators who, having procured cards, were fortunate enough to find places.

For the first half-hour all was confusion and chatter. Every body was staring at every body else, asking questions which nobody could answer, and making wild guesses which somebody else was sure to contradict immediately. "Where will the Grand Duke sit?" "Who is that stout man with the crimson ribbon on his breast?" "Which is Baron Humboldt, and which the Chevalier Bunsen?" "Do you see that old man with the silver locks?—that is Longfellow, the American poet." "Nonsense, Longfellow is quite a young man. It is more likely Danneker, or Beranger, or Dr. Spohr!" "See, there is Professor Metz—there, yonder, talking to that strange-looking animal with the red beard and the brown court suit!" "Animal, do you call him? Why, that is Alexandre Du-

E

mas." "Alexandre Dumas? Absurd! Do you not know that Dumas is a negro, and did you ever see a negro with red hair?"

And so forth, questioning, guessing, and contradicting, till two o'clock struck, and the Grand Duke, preceded by a couple of ushers and followed by five or six gentlemen in rich uniforms, came in and took his seat upon the center chair. The others placed themselves to his right and left.

A low buzz, that subsided presently into a profound silence, ran round the room. Then the Duke rose, and pronounced that celebrated speech which, after being printed on pink glazed paper, and distributed gratuitously to the visitors, reading-room subscribers, and academy students, was not only reprinted on coarse white ditto, and sold at the price of three kreutzers per copy, but was also reviewed, extracted, criticised, ridiculed, praised, quoted, and commented upon by every journal, magazine, and literary organ throughout the thirty-eight independent states of the Germanic Confederation.

I am not going to incorporate that speech, eloquent as it was, with my personal narrative. I shall not even recapitulate the heads of it, or dwell, however briefly, on those brilliant passages wherein his Serene Highness was pleased to enlarge upon the pleasures and advantages of the arts; to cite Plato, Fichte, Lord Bacon, and Sir Joshua Reynolds; to compare our Academy with the School of Athens; and finally, in drawing a skillful parallel between the Grand Duchy of Zollenstrasse-am-Main and that other insignificant Grand Duchy of Central Italy where Michael Angelo dwelt, Giotto painted, and Dante was born, to liken himself, with infinite modesty, to no less a patron and promoter of learning than Lorenzo of Tuscany, surnamed the Magnificent.

Enough, then, that his Highness spoke the speech "trippingly on the tongue;" that it was applauded as loudly as etiquette permitted; and that, at the close thereof, receiving a written paper from one of the ushers, he began the business of the day by summoning one Friedrich Bernstoff, of Würtemberg, free scholar, to receive a first-class medal for the best orchestral symphony.

"Herr Friedrich Bernstoff," echoed the usher, "Herr Friedrich Bernstoff is requested to advance."

A pale slender boy rose from the ranks of his companions, and stepped forward to the foot of the dais. The Duke addressed him in a few congratulatory but scarcely audible words; presented him with a small morocco case containing a gold medal; and then, stooping slightly forward, placed a fillet of laurel leaves upon his brow. The boy blushed, bent low, and returned to his seat, glad to escape observation and to snatch the wreath away as soon as nobody was looking.

The same ceremony then continued to be repeated with little or no variation, as the musical candidates were called up, one by one, throughout the sultry hours of the July afternoon.

Next came the sculptors, of whom there were but few in the school, and whose audience was proportionately brief. Lastly, after a tantalizing pause, during which his Serene Highness chatted with provoking nonchalance to his left-hand neighbor, Professor Metz came hurriedly to the foot of the dais, and, bowing, placed a paper in his Highness's hand. A whispered conference ensued. The Duke smiled; the professor retired; the usher cleared his throat, and waited the word of command; instead, however, of giving, as before, the name of the successful competitor, his Highness rose and addressed us, somewhat to the following effect:—

"Ladies and Gentlemen of the Academy — As regards the prizes which remain to be presently awarded, we have been placed — ahem ! — in a position of some doubt and difficulty — which position, ladies and gentlemen, I hasten — that is to say, I feel it due to yourselves to — in short, to explain."

(There were ill-natured tongues in the room which compared this speech with the preceding, and hesitated not to point out the difference between things studied and things extemporized.)

"Our rules," continued his Highness, "are exact with regard to most emergencies — for instance, ladies and gentlemen, we cannot admit a foreigner to — to the advantages of a free scholarship. You are all aware of that. We have, however, had very few foreigners as yet among our numbers — at present, I believe, we have but only two. The difficulty to which I allude has arisen out of — of the fact that one of these foreigners has been judged to — to deserve a prize which up to this time has never been awarded to any but a native of Germany. Divided between the desire to be just, and the fear of — of overstepping the laws of our institution, the committee of criticism have hesitated up to this moment, and I have but now received their decision through the hands of our friend, Professor Metz. The prize in question, ladies and gentlemen, is for the best historical painting in oils. Were we to be swayed by prejudices of sex or nation, that prize would be awarded to Herr Johann Brandt, whose 'Siege of Corinth' is, in point of drawing and composition, inferior to only one picture in the hall; but, ladies and gentlemen, having considered the matter under all its — under every aspect, the committee decides that, although the first prize for the first historical painting has never yet had been decreed to a foreigner or — or a lady, it must on the present occasion in justice be bestowed upon ——"

Here he referred to the paper —

— "Upon Mademoiselle Barbara Churchill, native of England, and six years a resident student in this Academy."

"Mademoiselle Barbara Churchill," repeated the usher, with an accent that left my name almost unrecognizable. "Mademoiselle Barbara Churchill is requested to advance."

Utterly confused and skeptical, I rose up, stood still, and, conscious of the eyes of the whole room, dared not leave my place.

"Come, my pupil," said a kind voice close beside me. "Fear nothing."

It was Professor Metz, who had made his way down the central alley, and offered me the support of his arm.

I do not remember if I took it — I do not even remember how I came there; but I found myself the next moment standing at the foot of the dais, and the Duke bending over me, with the laurels in his hand. He spoke; but I heard only the sound of his voice. He placed the medal in my hand, and the wreath upon my head. I stooped, instinctively to receive it; and this done, turned tremblingly and awkwardly enough, to return to my place. As I did so, I looked up, and there, amid the visitors to the right of the dais — there, bending earnestly forward, conspicuous among a hundred others, pale, eager-eyed, dark-haired, with the old impetuous glance, and the old free bearing, I saw — oh joy! — for the first time since that morning in the woods long years ago — my childhood's idol, my hero, Farquhar of Broomhill!

It was not the suddenness of the announcement — it was neither confusion nor fatigue, nor the emotion of an unexpected triumph — it had nothing whatever to do with prizes, examinations, or Grand Dukes — it was the sight of that one swarthy face, and the shock of those dark eyes shining into mine, that sent the room reeling, and made me lean so heavily on the professor's proffered arm.

"You need air," he whispered, and led me to an ante-room, where Madame Brenner brought me a glass of wine and water, and insisted on taking me back at once to the College. I went to my bed-room and entreated to be left quite alone.

"If I sleep," I said, "I shall be better."

But it was not sleep that I wanted. It was solitude and silence.

CHAPTER XXIV.

A WELCOME VISITOR.

He took my hands in his, and led me to the window.

"What, Barbara?" said he. "Little Barbarina, who climbed a certain library window one fine afternoon, and rode home upon Satan! By my soul, I can hardly believe it."

"Believe or disbelieve as you will, Sahib," I replied, half-laughing, half-crying; "it is none the less true."

"I suppose not," he said, seriously. "I suppose not. There could scarcely be two Barbarinas in so small a world as this! And then to find you here—here, of all nooks and corners in Europe! Why, I should as soon have thought of meeting you 'where the Chinese drive their cany wagons light!' So tall, too—so clever—such a capital artist! *Peste!* the sight of you makes me feel a dozen years younger. How long is it, *carina*, since you and I were at Broomhill together?"

"I left Stoneycroft Hall," sighed I, "just six years and three months ago."

"It seems like six centuries. I have been from Dan to Beersheba in the mean time; and I can not say that I am much the better for it—whilst you—by the by, you always had a taste for art. Do you remember choosing the best drawing in my sketch-book, Barbara? And do you remember how I unpacked the Paul Veronese for your connoisseurship's special delectation?"

"Indeed, yes—and I also remember how that same picture very nearly proved your death."

"Shade of Polyphemus, and so do I! A little more, and I should have been crushed as flat as Acis, without even a Galatea to weep for

me. Poor old Paolo! Heaven grant that mine ancestral rats have not quite eaten him up by this time. But, Barbarina, how came you here? And why? Have you adopted art as a profession? What are your plans, prospects, and so forth? Why, you have a thousand things to tell me."

"Not half so many as you have to tell me, Mr. Farquhar. From Dan to Beersheba is a journey worth relating, and you must have had many adventures by the way."

"As many as the Knight of La Mancha! As many as Don Diego, on his road to and from the Promontory of Noses! As many as any Sir Galahad that ever sat in the Siege Perilous, or brake bread at Arthur's round table! But let my stories lie and rest awhile longer Barbarina. They are scarcely worth the breath it costs to tell them. Sit down here, instead, and talk to me. Tell me all that has happened, and what your life has been since we parted."

"Will you answer me one question first?"

"Willingly—if I can."

"How long is it since you left Broomhill? Did you often see my aunt after I was gone? Did she miss me? Was she sorry for me? Did she never speak of me, or think of me again? Why did she not write to me after I went home? What had I done that she should utterly abandon me?"

"My child, instead of one question, here are a dozen; none of which I can satisfactorily answer. In the first place, I do not even know in what month you went away."

"In May."

"And I in September. In the second place, I never saw Mrs. Sandyshaft more than twice during that time. It was my own fault, and I was a fool for my pains. I behaved like an uncivilized savage; played with edged tools; very nearly fell into the hands of a female Philistine; discovered my error before it was too late, and fled the country. Pshaw! you remember her, Barbara?"

"Lady Flora——" I faltered.

"Now Countess of somewhere or another, with a castle in the west of England and a husband as old as Methusalah! Well, to return to Mrs. Sandyshaft—I saw her but twice. Once soon after you left, and again when I called to bid her good-by, the night before I started for the East."

"And what did she say of me?"

"Very little the first time, and nothing the second."

"Did she know that Papa had sent us to Germany?"

"I fancy not. I think she would have told me, had she known it."

"Do you think she missed me?"

"I am sure of it — the surer because she never said a word about it. Janet missed you sadly, and cried when she heard your name."

"Poor Janet!"

"For my own part, Barbara, I felt as if the house were not the same place at all. The daylight seemed to have gone out of it, and silence to have settled on it like a spell. When I was shown into the old familiar parlor, and saw your aunt in her old familiar place, and looked round for you as usual, and then heard that you were gone — gone right away never to return — I felt—by Jove, I felt as if a cold hand had been laid upon my heart!"

"Oh, Mr. Farquhar, did *you* miss me also?"

"Miss you? My little girl, I could not have missed you more bad I —— *Parbleu!* it was for that I staid away. Do you suppose I would not have spent many an hour with the old lady in her solitude, had I not been a selfish monster and hated to go near the place? And so you have never seen her since?"

"Never."

"Nor heard from her?"

I shook my head.

"And you do not even know whether she is alive or dead?"

"I have seen my father; and he says that she is living."

"But why not write to her?"

"I can not. I loved her, as though she were my mother, and her house was more to me than home had ever been. She exiled me from herself and from all that made me happy, and—and I can not write to her now—I can not write to her now!"

He shrugged his shoulders, and looked as people look when they blame you and refrain from saying so.

"Well, well," said he, "we will talk this over some day! In the mean time, Barbarina, tell me something of yourself. Tell me what has become of the wild, bright-eyed little girl whom I once knew at Broomhill, and what possible affinity can exist between her and you?"

I took the chair he placed for me, and obeyed him as literally, and in as few words as I could. I went back to that darkest day in all my calendar, when my aunt told me I must leave her. I recalled my weary journey home, and how I found my sister Jessie dead. I sketched the circumstances of my arrival in Germany; the routine of my school life; the growth of my taste for art; and all that I thought could interest or amuse him, down to my father's second marriage, and the departure of my sister Hilda for Paris. He listened attentively; sometimes interrupting me with exclamations, and sometimes with questions. When I had done, he pushed his chair away, and paced restlessly about the room.

"Strange!" said he, more to himself than me. "Strange, how all things shape themselves to the ends of genius! The old, new story, over and over again! The old, new story of how heartbreak, and exile, and neglect develop the nature of the artist, and arm him for his future career. Tush, Barbara, you may congratulate yourself upon your troubles! Had you vegetated till now in the bucolic atmosphere of Stoneycroft Hall, you had never carried off a gold medal or painted Rienzi in the ruins of the Forum!"

"Perhaps not," I replied sadly; "but then my childhood would have been cared for, and the first impulses of my heart would not have faded among strangers. I should have known the happiness of home, and——"

My voice failed, and I broke off abruptly. He finished my sentence for me.

"And, like a foolish virgin, you regret the good the Gods have sent you! Pshaw, child, beware of these longings—beware of such empty words as home, or love, or friendship.

They mean nothing—worse than nothing—disappointment, bitterness of soul, restlessness, despair! Forget that you have a heart, or begin life afresh with the determination to regard it merely as a useful muscle employed in the circulation of the blood. Steel yourself to this, and you may have some chance of happiness in the future. Devote yourself to your art. Make it your home, your country, your friend. Wed it; live in it; die for it; shut your eyes and your ears against all else; and if ever a fool comes talking love to you, laugh at him for his pains, and bid him 'go a bat-fowling!'"

"And if I cannot do all this? If the humanity that is in me demands something more than paint and canvas—what then?"

"What then? Why, shipwreck, child. Shipwreck on the deep sea, without a compass, without a morrow, without a hope."

There was a fierce and bitter regret in his voice, that struck me like a revelation.

"You speak as one who has suffered," I said, almost without intending it.

He smiled drearily.

"I speak," said he, "as one who has tried all things, and eaten of the Dead Sea apples—as one who, having wealth, is poor, and, having a home, is homeless! As one, Barbara, to whom 'this goodly frame, the earth,' seems but a sterile promontory, and this 'brave o'erhanging firmament no other thing than a foul and pestilent congregation of vapors!' But this is nonsense. *Parlons autre chose!*"

"If I dared," said I sadly, "I would ask you to talk to me of yourself alone; but ——"

"But you are too young to be my confidante, Barbara—too young—too innocent, too hopeful. Nay, it is useless to ask—Heaven forefend that I should burden your memory with the record of my faults and follies!"

I had no reply for this, and a long silence followed, during which he continued to pace to and fro, with his hands clasped behind his back and his eyes fixed gloomily upon the ground. For the first time since our meeting, I found myself at liberty to observe him closely. He was but little changed, if at all. Somewhat browner, perhaps; somewhat broader and more vigorous; but the same Hugh Farquhar, every inch! If the lines of the mouth seemed to have grown sterner and the brow more thoughtful, six years of traveling were sufficient to account for it; but would they also account for that deeper fire, so weary, wistful and consuming, that burned in his dark eyes, like the flame of a smouldering volcano? He had asked me what my life was since we parted: I asked myself what had been his? A thousand questions started to my lips; but I dared not utter one. I longed to ask him why he had again wandered away from Broomhill; where he had been traveling; whence he came; and whither he was going. I longed, also, to tell him that I kept his silver ring, and had kept it, ever since, as a sacred relic; but a strange reluctance tied my tongue, and kept me silent. In the midst of my reverie, he looked up suddenly and found me watching him.

"Barbara," said he, "you think me a strange being; fitful, perverse, good for nothing! Well, you are right; and if I puzzle you, I puzzle myself as much, and more. Some day or another, when you and I are both older and wiser, I will tell you the story of my inner life from first to last — if only to show you how a man may gamble away Heaven's precious gifts, and find himself, at thirty-four, bankrupt of all that makes the future not wholly desperate !"

" Bankrupt !" I faltered, bewildered by his vehemence, and fearing I knew scarcely what.

" Pshaw, child, bankrupt in hopes — not acres !" he exclaimed, impatiently. " What is life but a game of chance, and what are we but the players ? We stake on the future — it may perhaps be a prize; perhaps a blank. Who knows till the card turns up, or the ball has done rolling ?"

" I can not bear that you should feel thus," I said, the tears starting to my eyes. " You are still young — you are rich — you might make yourself and so many others happy; and yet ——."

" And yet, Barbara, I envy you with my whole soul !"

" Envy me, Mr. Farquhar ?"

" Ay, as Edmund envied Edgar ! When I came to-day into the calm atmosphere of this house, — when being conducted through yonder corridor, I passed an open door, and saw some twenty young girls sitting round a table with their books and samplers, all industrious, innocent, and happy — when I was shown into this pleasant, simple parlor, with its matted floor and open window, and flower-laden balcony — when I see you in that plain brown gown and snowy collar, looking so good and purposeful, and working out the problem of a studious and ennobling career; when I see all this, Barbara, and compare it with my wandering, aimless, hopeless, futile life, I envy you and such as you, and wish myself something worthier — or something worse — than I am ! Nay — do not interrupt me. I know what you would say. I know all that can be said upon the subject — but I am too old now to turn the current of my ways !"

" You are unjust to yourself," I suggested, scarcely knowing what to reply. " He who travels much, learns much; and I can conceive nothing finer than the life of one who studies history from the ruins of Greece and Rome, geology from the mountains and mines, and human nature from association with all the races of mankind."

He laughed, or forced a laugh ; and, taking a volume of Bacon from the table, read aloud —

" ' Travel in the younger sort is a part of education ; in the elder, a part of experience ' — why, Barbarina, you are a Verulam in petticoats ! Now, look you, I am of the ' elder ' sort, and travel is not only a part of my experience, but all my experience. For more than twelve years I have been wandering about the world, and what do you suppose I have learned for my pains ?"

" I should exceedingly like to know."

" In the first place, then, I am convinced that English ale is better drinking than train-oil ; and that Burgundy and Bordeaux are better than either."

" I think I could have told you that, without going from Dan to Beersheba, Mr. Farquhar."

" Miss Churchill, you are satirical ! In the second place, I have come to the conclusion that the world really is a round world, and not a flat surface with the Celestial Empire in the midst."

" Amazing discovery !"

" Be pleased not to interrupt the court. And in the third place, madam, I am persuaded that it is my destiny to dangle about diligences, be a perigrinator in post-chaises, and a diner at table d'hôtes throughout the term of my natural life. Surely this is experience and wisdom enough for one mortal man, and as much as my worst enemies have a right to expect from me !"

With this he snatched up his hat, and pointed to the time-piece on the mantle-shelf.

" I have been here an hour and a half," he exclaimed. " If I make my visits too long, the Academic powers will, perhaps, have the bad taste to object. Adieu, Barbarina. I shall come again soon.".

" Do you remain long at Zollenstrasse ?"

" Chi lo sa ? Yes — no — perhaps. 'Tis as the fancy takes me, and the mood lasts. Farewell !"

He shook hands; hesitated a moment, as if doubtful whether I were too old to be kissed ; laughed ; drew back ; and throwing wide the window, which opened on a balcony only three or four feet from the ground, leaped lightly down into the courtyard, without troubling himself to go round by the corridors, and out at the front entrance, like a respectable and orderly visitor. At the gate he turned again, waved his hand, and was gone in a moment.

I hastened to the solitude of my room, locked the door, and sat on the side of my bed, for a long time, thinking of many things. Was I happy? or sorrowful ? or both ? I know not—I only know that when I was summoned down to supper, I heard one of my schoolfellows whisper to her neighbor :

" Look at Barbara's eyes. She has been crying. The dark stranger from England brought bad news to-day !"

CHAPTER XXV.

I SHINE WITH A REFLECTED LUSTRE.

THE competition over, Zollenstrasse subsided into its normal state of semi-fashionable quiet. The King of Würtemberg drove away in a barouche and four, preceded by his outriders and followed by three carriages containing his *suite*. The other illustrious visitors, with the exception of a few who remained to drink the waters, departed with more or less of magnificence to their several destinations. The paintings and casts came back to the studios ; the benches and red hangings were cleared out of the Assembly room ; the theater, which for a whole week had been crowded every night, was advertised, as usual, for Sundays and Wednesdays only, and the waiters might once more be seen loitering with their hands in their pockets at the doors of the hotels. In the Academy, an unnatural calm succeeded to an unwonted confusion. The present was the long vacation, when every one, save a melancholy minority, packed up and went joyously away. Hilda and I, Ida Saxe, and one or two others, were among those who always staid behind. Now Hilda, too, was gone, and the great building was more desolate than ever. Had it not been for Hugh, my triumph, after all, would have been a sad one.

Still it was a triumph ; and my heart throbbed

with pleasure when my companions thronged about me that Sunday evening, asking to see my medal—my beautiful gold medal, in its case of morocco and velvet. I even went to sleep with it under my pillow that first night; and looked at it, I need hardly say, as soon as I opened my eyes in the morning.

"You will be made a sub-professor, now, Barbara," said one.

"And take out a double first-class certificate, when you leave the College!" added another.

"And sit at Madame Brenner's right hand at table and at chapel," said a third.

All of which came to pass; for at supper that very same night, I was installed in the seat of honor; and next day received my appointment as sub-professor, with a salary of two hundred florins per annum. Nor was this all. Professor Metz, the critical, the formidable, he who never praised or pitied, summoned me a few days later to his private studio, and graciously proclaimed his intention of employing me to assist him, during the vacation, in painting the panels of the Grand Duke's summer pavilion. I confess that I was more elated by this mark of distinction than by any other of my successes. Of course I wrote to Hilda by the first post, and filled four large pages of letter-paper with details of the Competition, not forgetting my own good fortune. I omitted, however, though I scarcely knew why, all mention of Farquhar of Broomhill.

The school was nearly empty when he next came to see me, and Madame Brenner, who was somewhat scandalized by the manner of his departure on the first occasion, received him in her own parlor, and remained there till he left. When he was gone, she said—

"Your friend, Barbara, is a very strange person."

To which I replied:—

"Strange, Madame?"

"Is it his custom to prefer the window to the door, when he leaves a house?"

"He — he has been a great traveler, Madame," I stammered. "He has eccentricities. He——"

"Have you known him long?"

"Since I was a little girl, Madame."

"And his profession?"

"He is a gentleman, Madame—a *propriétair* —very rich—a connoisseur of the fine arts."

"Evidently a connoisseur," said Madame. "I should have supposed him, from his conversation, to be a painter."

Here our little colloquy ended; but Madame Brenner was not quite at ease upon the subject of my English visitor. That any man should run, when he might walk; jump from a window, when he might go round by a door; stand up and pace about a room, when he might sit in a chair; and travel about the world, when he might live at home in a chateau of his own, were peculiarities entirely beyond the radius of her comprehension. All that he said, all that he did, was at variance with her German decorum; and henceforth she made a point of being present at our interviews. One day, however, when we were walking along the Weimar Strasse, we met the royal *cortége* face to face, with Hugh riding beside the Grand Duke, in familiar conversation. He took off his hat first to Madame,

and then to me. I observed that this incident produced a deep impression on her.

"Your friend is a man of rank?" said she, interrogatively, when the Ducal party was out of sight.

"No, Madame."

She looked perplexed.

"Of high position, then?"

"He is a gentleman, Madame, of ancient family."

"And enormously rich?"

"No, Madame—not rich for an English *proprietaire*. He has about a hundred and fifty thousand florins a year."

This was a piece of malice on my part; for the Grand-Ducal revenue amounted to about one third of the sum, perquisites included. Poor Madame Brenner murmured "*Mein Gott!*" sighed meekly, looked more perplexed than before, and was silent during the rest of the walk.

A day or two after this, one of the girls showed me his name in the Zollenstrasser Zeitung. He had been dining with the Duke and Duchess, and was written down an "Excellency."

"He must be a very great man," said she.

"He is a very wonderful man," I replied. "He has been all over the world. He speaks as many languages as you have fingers on your hands. He has a horse that kneels down to let him mount; and a black valet who saved his life from the bite of a serpent in India. He has a house four times as big as the Ducal Residenz; and a park larger than the woods of Brühl; and some years ago he bought a Paul Veronese, for which he gave thirty thousand florins."

"*Wunderbar!* And with all this he has no title?"

"None at all."

"And is not even a Geheimrath?"

"Nothing of the kind, dear. Nothing but an English gentleman, *pur et simple.*"

I did not think it necessary to say that we deemed that the better title of the two.

These things created an immense excitement in the Academy. Those few pupils who remained behind were very inquisitive about the marvelous Englishman, and listened eagerly to all that I could be brought to tell them on the subject. Whatever I said was repeated, with exaggerations, to Madame Brenner; Madame Brenner communicated it, with placid amazement, to the resident professors; the professors carried the news to all the æsthetic teas in Zollenstrasse; and Hugh Farquhar became the Monte Christo of the day. In the mean time, I shone with a reflected lustre, and was almost more revered by my fellow-students for my friend than for my medal.

Still, he came but seldom. Sometimes I met him going out of the public library, with a book under his arm. Sometimes I saw his horse and groom waiting before the door of his hotel. And one morning he came armed with an order to see the College, on which occasion Madame Brenner, whose respect and perplexity were ever on the increase, informed me that Her Excellency was an extraordinary man, and made extraordinary observations about every thing!

----◆----

CHAPTER XXVI.

THE GRAND DUKE'S SUMMER PAVILION.

THE Grand Duke's summer pavilion was in shape an oblong parallelogram, built in imitation of the celebrated Casino Rospigliosi. The façade was incrusted with tasteful bas-reliefs, and the interior divided into paneled compartments, filled alternately with mirrors and paintings. The old designs, of a bastard Watteau school, had been lately removed; and Professor Metz was replacing them by subjects descriptive of German life and landscape. His plan was to "lay in" the broad effects of each picture, and then leave me to carry it forward, guided by a small original sketch. When I had done as much as he deemed necessary, he took it in hand again, and finished it. Thus the work progressed rapidly.

One morning, when the Professor had gone home to lunch, and I was painting alone, Ida came in with a letter in her hand. She was flushed with running, and sat down, quite out of breath, in an old fauteuil in the middle of the room.

"I saw by the post-mark," said she, "that it came from Paris, and I knew by the writing that it was a letter from Hilda; so I put on my hat, and brought it directly. I have also brought you a roll, and some slices of liver-sausage! I was sure you must be hungry, and equally sure that you would never take the trouble to come back for the college dinner."

"Thanks, Ida dear. I believe I really am hungry; but it is so tiresome to go all the way back to College, across that wearisome Hof-garten in the broiling sun, and——"

"Nonsense! Genius must eat. No, Barbara —roll and sausage first, and letter afterward!"

"Nay, please let me have my letter!"

"Not till you have eaten!"

"Tyrant! How can I eat while you keep me in suspense? Remember, I have not heard from Hilda since I wrote to tell her that I had the medal!"

Ida gave it with a kiss.

"There," said she, "you are always to be spoiled! I shall amuse myself by looking at the pictures, What a charming place this would be for a studio!"

I broke the seal eagerly, and read my letter.

"My dearest Barbara," wrote Hilda, "Paris delights me more every day. I can not tell you how happy I am. My life is a perpetual fête. Every day we drive out and pay visits; and every evening is devoted to society. Mamma receives once a week, and, as she knows only the best people, our circle is of the most unexceptionable kind. Last evening we went to a ball at the Tuileries. I wore white lace over white gros de Naples, and mamma white lace over blue satin. The President received his guests, standing. He is a cold, resolute-looking man, of about the middle hight. He bears himself like a soldier, and looks taller than he is. He and Prince Napoleon strolled about the ball-room in the course of the evening. He was very polite to mamma, whose first husband, I find, held some appointment which brought him into communication with the French Government. She presented me; and, later in the evening, I had the honor of dancing with Prince

Napoleon. I was engaged for that dance, as it happened, to the Count de Chaumont; but a royal invitation supersedes every other, so I danced the next quadrille with the Count instead. The Count de Chaumont and papa are old acquaintances, and knew each other years ago in Brussels, before the Count had succeeded to his title. He is a highly distinguished man, still handsome, and very dignified. He holds an important office in the royal household, and admires me most particularly. Indeed, my dear sister, you would be surprised to see how I am flattered and fêted wherever I go. The Count told papa last night that I was the belle of the season. I have been taking riding-lessons, and next week am to ride with papa in the Bois. He says I shall create an immense sensation en Amazone; and Mrs. Churchill, who no longer rides on horseback, has given me her habit, which, with certain alterations, fits me to perfection. In short, I never was so happy. I can not understand how I lived through the monotony of our life at Zollenstrasse; and the mere recollection of that weary College overwhelms me with ennui. I ought not to forget, however, that I owe my knowledge of singing to Professor Oberstein; and my singing is one of my successes. I should tell you of an exquisite compliment paid to me the other day by Monsieur de B——, the celebrated historian. 'Mademoiselle,' he said, 'the race of Churchill is fatal to our nation; and I foresee that you are destined to carry still farther the conquests which your ancestor began.' And now, my dear Barbara adieu. This is a long letter, and must conten you for some weeks; for my life is a perpetua engagement, and I never have an hour that I can call my own. Mamma desires her love to you. Papa is gone to call on the Count de Chaumont, or he would doubtless desire some message. Once more, adieu, dear sister, and believe me, etc., etc."

I read it to the end, and sat silent.

"Well, Barbara," cried Ida, "what does she say to your success? How did your father receive it? Oh, I wish I had been there when they opened the letter!"

"Hilda says nothing at all about it," replied I, trying to look indifferent.

"Nothing at all?" repeated Ida. "But you wrote the day after the competition—you wrote on purpose!"

"Quite true."

"Then the letter miscarried!"

I shook my head.

"But—but are you sure she does not mention it?" persisted Ida.

I folded the letter, and put it in my pocket.

"Hilda names the College but once," said I, "and then only to wonder how she could have endured it so long. She never mentions the competition."

"Unkind! ungenerous!" exclaimed Ida, passionately. "If I were in your place——"

"If you were in my place, dear, you would forgive it as I forgive it—forget it, as I shall try to forget it; and—and——"

"And become famous in spite of them!" cried the warm-hearted little Bavarian, throwing her arms about my neck. "Yes, Barbara, you shall force them to care for it! You shall force them to be proud of you! Think of the future that lies before you. Think of all that you have already done—think of all that you have yet to do. What matter if Hilda is careless of your success—Hilda or any one—so long as the success is fairly achieved? Come, cheer up! Let us forget all about the letter and think only of this exquisite panel with the vintagers in the foreground!"

Saying thus, she took my hands in hers, and dragged me playfully back to my work. But the charm of the task was gone. The color that I had laid in half an hour ago looked muddy and indecisive, and I effaced my morning's labor at the first touch.

"Oh, Barbara!" cried my friend. "All those lovely vine-leaves sacrificed!"

"And quite rightly," said a voice at the door.

It was Professor Metz, returning from his one o'clock dinner. He wore a round straw-hat and a holland coat, and carried a red umbrella to shade him from the sun.

"And quite rightly," he repeated, walking straight up to the picture, umbrella and all. "I had a vast mind to draw my brush across them before I went out; but I thought it best to let Mademoiselle make the discovery herself."

"What discovery, mein Professor?" said Ida, timidly. "They were very like."

"*Too* like, Fräulein."

"Too like, mein Professor?"

"Yes. Too labored, too literal, too minute. Flowers, young ladies, should be treated like heads—with character and freedom. Compare the leaves which were painted here just now with that Van Huysum that you had in the class-room last spring. The one is a Denner; the other a Titian!"

Having said this, he laid aside the hat and umbrella, seized his own brushes, and plunged into his work. A dead silence followed. The Professor never spoke when he was painting, and so hated interruption that we often worked on for hours in the pavilion without exchanging a syllable. Presently Ida rose, and went quietly away; and then nothing was audible save the moist dragging of our brushes, the humming of the insects outside, and the distant rumble of an occasional vehicle.

Hilda's letter had pained me more than I cared to confess. It came between me and my work, and I could not banish it. I felt that I was very lonely, and I knew that I must accept my solitude sooner or later. Then Hugh's bitter warning came back to my memory, as if written there in letters of fire. "Beware of such empty words as home, or love, or friendship. Devote yourself to your art. Make it your home, your lover, your friend. Live in it—die for it." Alas! were they really "empty words?" Must I, indeed, make up my mind to the barrenness of life, and forget that I have a father, a sister, and a home?

Profoundly dejected, I painted on, effacing each touch as soon as made, and pausing every now and then for very lassitude. Startled from one of these pauses by the pressure of a heavy hand upon my shoulder, I found the Professor standing by my side.

"What is the matter, Fräulein?" he asked, bending a searching glance upon me. "Why do you weep?"

"I am not weeping, sir."

He touched my cheek significantly. It was wet with unconscious tears.

"I—I did not know—I am not well," I stammered.

He shook his head.

"You are not happy," he said, with unusual gentleness. "There—put away your work for to-day. One can not paint when the mind is out of tune."

"I am very sorry —— "

"Nay, you will do better to-morrow. Have you bad news from home?"

"No, mein Professor."

"What is it, then? Come, Fräulein, tell me your trouble, and let me help you if I can."

"You can not help me," I said, brokenly. "You are very kind, but —— "

The Professor frowned, and shook his head again.

"Fräulein Barbara," said he, "you have common-sense. Yours is not a merely sentimental trouble. You are not one of those young ladies who think it pleasant to be melancholy, and cry for want of something better to do. You have a grief. Well, fight through it alone if you are able. You will be all the wiser and stronger hereafter. But if you want counsel, or help, or any thing that I can give you, come to me."

Greatly touched by this unusual *démarche* on the part of our terrible Professor, I tried to express my thanks, but he stopped me at the first word.

"Hush, hush, nonsense!" said he abruptly. "Put away your work. Put away your work, and go for a walk. Make haste, and leave me in peace."

I made what haste I could; but while I was yet cleaning up brushes and pallet, I heard voices in conversation close beside the open window.

"The cactus," said one of the speakers, with a strong German accent, "is doubtless of the same family as the Euphorbias. Have you seen any specimens of the melon genus? They have one, I understand, in Paris."

"I have not seen it in the Jardin des Plantes," replied a second speaker, whom I at once recognized as Hugh Farquhar; "but I have had my mule lamed by its thorns in the deserts of South-Africa."

"But the juice is not unwholesome."

"By no means. Traveler and mule are alike thankful for it. Bernardin St. Pierre calls these succulent cacti 'the vegetable fountains of the desert.' I have a sketch of the melon-cactus which I shall be happy to place at your Highness's disposal."

The Grand Duke thanked him, and the voices passed away. Before I could tie on my bonnet and escape, they became audible again, and again approached the window.

"And the sketcher," said the Grand Duke, "has the privilege of perpetuating his travels. He can revisit his favorite scenes, and renew his first impressions, whenever he chooses to open his folio."

"The memory needs some such assistance," replied Hugh. "Impressions of scenery fade from the mind, like imperfect photographs, and the keenest observer can not long continue to recall them. Who, for instance, after the lapse of half a year, could accurately reproduce the outline of a chain of Alps?"

"Who, indeed! But shall we step in here, and see how the panels are progressing in my pavilion?"

They came in. The Professor rose to receive them.

"What, Barbara?" said Hugh, with outstretched hand, and a smile of frank surprise. "I never thought to find you here!"

"Sit down, sit down, Herr Metz," said the Duke, with voluble good-humor. "Do not let me interrupt the work. Ha! the English Fräulein who carried off our gold medal the other day! Good — good! Young lady, you have but to work hard, and obey Professor Metz, and you can not fail to become a fine painter. Remember that perseverance is to genius what fuel is to the locomotive. However perfect the machine, it is of no value without the fire that propels, or the engineer who guides. What say you, Professor? What say you?"

"Your Highness has defined perseverance as the fuel," said the Professor, bluntly; "but who is the engineer?"

"Yourself — myself — the Academy," replied the Duke, somewhat embarrassed by the detection of a flaw in his simile.

The Professor looked as if he should have liked to say something about this plurality of engineers; but he bowed instead, and held his tongue.

"And what progress has been made?" continued the Duke. "Has the Herr Professor succeeded in striking out any spark of picturesqueness from our stolid peasant-folk? So — the vintage — the Kirmess — the Schützen-fest — excellent subjects — excellent subjects! Herr Farquhar, permit me to introduce to you Professor Metz, our Director of Fine Arts, Hofmaler, and Academic Lecturer — a Zollenstrasser of whom Zollenstrasse is proud. This gentleman, Professor Metz, is a connoisseur, a sketcher, and a traveler, who has exhausted every quarter of the globe."

The Professor bowed again; and, having taken the Duke at his word, went on painting. He was evidently in no mood for chatting, and wished his visitors further.

"That is a charming sky," said the Grand Duke with the air of a *dilettante*.

"Yes; a sky under which one could breathe, without feeling that all above the clouds was a dome of blue paint," replied Hugh.

"That's very true," said the Duke. "Why *do* our landscape painters make their cobalts so solid?"

"Because they will not take the trouble to remember that we have fifty miles of atmosphere above our heads. The spectator should be able to look *through* an open sky, as we seem to look through this; conscious of depth beyond depth, and distance beyond distance."

The Professor glanced up sharply; but still said nothing.

"What do you mean to have for your foreground object, Professor Metz?" asked the Grand Duke, presently.

"Nothing, your Highness."

"Nothing! Why, I thought it was a canon of art to have some foreground object to throw back the distance. A — a figure, for instance; or a fallen tree; or a piece of rock; or something?"

"I trust my distance will keep its place without needing any device of that sort, your Highness," growled the Professor.

Leopold the Eighteenth smoothed out his cream-colored moustache and looked puzzled.

"Still there are canons," persisted he; "such as the division of a picture in three parts; the proportions of light and shadow as three to five; the pyramidal grouping of principal objects; the introduction of ——"

"All mischievous pedantry, your Highness," interrupted the Professor. "Such canons may do very well for cooks. They ruin painters."

The Duke smiled furtively, and offered the Professor a cigar.

"Thanks, your Highness. I never smoke till evening."

"Then put it in your cigar-case. It is of a very rare quality."

Sulkily polite, the Professor accepted it.

"And I have a folio of etchings to show you — just arrived from Paris — containing some fine proofs of Rembrandt and Albert Dürer. Will you join the dinner-party at the Residenz this evening, Professor Metz, and oblige me with your opinion on my purchase?"

"Impossible, your Highness," blurted out the Professor, utterly disregardful of the etiquette attaching to a royal invitation. "I am not used to court dinners — I'm — I'm a very plain man — your Highness must excuse me."

His Highness looked infinitely amused.

"As the Herr Professor pleases," said he. "But if I excuse him at dinner, I hold him engaged to join our party at coffee."

"I am at his Highness's command," replied the maestro, reluctantly.

The Duke led the way to a door at the farther end of the room.

"Before we go, Herr Farquhar," said he, "I should like you to see the view from the Belvedere. Will you follow me?"

Whereupon Hugh followed, and they both went up-stairs.

"Mein Gott!" exclaimed the Professor, wiping his forehead with every sign of trepidation. "Why won't these confounded aristocrats leave a man alone? Ah, Fräulein Barbara, you are escaping while you can. Quite wise. I have a vast mind to do the same."

"Oh, no, mein Professor! What would the Grand Duke think, if he found no one here?"

His eyes wandered affectionately toward the red umbrella.

"I'm afraid you are right; and yet——"

"Good morning, sir."

"Humph! good morning."

I ran down the steps of the pavilion, and turned into the first shady side walk that offered. The Professor had given me a half-holiday, and I scarcely knew what to do with my liberty. I had no inclination to spend it in the Academy; and still less to waste it in the park, or the Hofgarten, or any frequented place. After a few moments' consideration, I decided upon the Botanic Garden; a secluded, quiet spot, just beyond the Leopold Thor, where the public could only obtain admission by favor, and where we Academy students had a right of perpetual *entrée*.

I had not far to go. As I passed in at the little side-gate, the old doorkeeper said—

"You have it all to yourself, Fräulein. There hasn't been a soul here to-day."

It was just what I would have asked for. Restless and dissatisfied, I needed solitude; and the solitude here was perfect. I walked to and fro for some time among the deserted paths, and presently sought out a grassy slope where the garden went down to the river's edge. Sitting there in the shade of a group of foreign trees, and lulled by the gentle rippling of the stream among the reeds, I fell into a profound train of thought.

The future—what should I do with the future? I felt like one who has climbed the brow of a great hill, and finds only a sea of mist beyond. Go forward I must; but to what goal? With what aim? With what hopes? My father had already distinctly forbidden me to adopt art as a profession. My sister, by ignoring all the purport of my last letter, as distinctly signified her own contempt for that which was to me as the life of my life. Neither loved me; both had wounded me bitterly; and I now, almost for the first time, distinctly saw how difficult a struggle lay before me.

"If I become a painter," I thought, "I become so in defiance of my family; and defying them, am alone in the wide world evermore. If, on the contrary, I yield and obey, what manner of life lies before me? The hollow life of fashionable society, into which I shall be carried as a marriageable commodity, and where I shall be expected to fulfill my duty as a daughter by securing a wealthy husband as speedily as possible."

Alas! alas! what an alternative! Was it for this that I had studied and striven? Was it for this that I had built such fairy castles, and dreamt such dreams?

Lost in these thoughts, I heard, but scarcely heeded, a rapid footstep on the graveled walk above. Not till that footstep left the gravel for the grass, and a well-known voice called me familiarly by name, did I even look up to see who the intruder might be. It was Hugh.

"Why, Barbara," said he, running down the slope, and flinging himself upon the bank by my side, "I almost despaired of finding you. I have been twice round the gardens already; and but for the gatekeeper, who declared he had not let you out since he let you in, I should certainly have given you up, and gone away."

"How did you know I was here?"

"Easily enough. I saw you from the Belvedere up yonder—traced you down the path, and all along the road, and in at the side-gate—and here I find you, sitting by the river-side, like Dorothea in the Brown Mountain."

"It is my favorite nook," I replied; "the quietest spot in all this quiet garden."

"Quiet enough, certainly," said Hugh, yawning. "Might one smoke here, think you?"

"I should say so. The gardeners do."

"And your majesty has no objection?"

"My majesty has filled your hookah often enough at Broomhill, Hugh, to be tolerably well seasoned by this time."

"So you have, Barbara mia—so you have."

And with this he lighted his cigar, lay down at full length on the grass, and amused himself for some time by sending up little spiral wreaths of smoke into the still air.

"I expected to find you sketching," said he, after a long interval of silence.

"Sketching? Why, there is nothing here to sketch."

"Plenty, I should say—tropical plants, strange trees, orchids, cacti——"

"But I am not a flower-painter."

"Nonsense, Barbarina. That is just one of the rocks that so many painters split upon. They fancy they must be either flower-painters, or landscape-painters, or figure-painters; and that in order to be one of these, they are bound to be ignorant of the other two. And yet no man was ever truly great who could not, to a certain extent, combine all three. If Raffaelle but places a lily in the hand of a Madonna, or introduces a paroquet among the ornaments of an arabesque, he paints them as though flowers and birds had been the study of his life. If Rubens undertakes a landscape background, he almost makes us regret that he ever painted any thing else. The mind of the artist should be the mirror of nature, reflecting all things, and neglecting none."

"That sounds terribly like the truth, Hugh; and yet who can hope to be universal?"

"That which has been, may be," said he oracularly; and closed his eyes, and smoked like a lazy Pacha.

After this, we both sat for a long time in silence, with the golden sunlight creeping toward us, inch by inch, across the fragrant grass. Insensibly, my thoughts flowed back to their old channel, and I felt quite bewildered when Hugh broke in suddenly upon my reverie.

"I have been indulging in the queerest chain of fantastic speculations during this last quarter of an hour," exclaimed he; "and all à propos of those same orchids and cacti. There will be a great revolution in the world some day, Barbara mia!"

"Will there?" said I, dreamily. "When?"

"Ten or twelve thousand years hence, perhaps."

"Then what can it matter to us?"

"Matter, child? Why, in a scientific point of view, every thing. You might as well say what do the stars matter to us? There are few subjects more interesting than the variations of climate."

"Variations of climate!" I repeated. "What do you mean? You were speaking of revolutions just now."

"True; but it was a revolution of vegetables—not men."

"How absurd! Who ever heard of a revolution of vegetables!"

He laughed, flung away the end of his cigar, raised himself on his elbow, and said kindly:—

"What a child you are still, Barbara! Come, I will explain myself more clearly, and tell you what my fantastic fancies were. Would you care to hear this?"

"Yes, Hugh; very much."

"In the first place, then," said he, "our mother Nature is by no means so consistent a lady as one might suppose; but, like the rest of her sex, is apt to change her mind. She is continually shifting sea-bords, varying the beds of rivers, and experimenting upon the mutability of matter. Thus we find ammonites' and oyster-shells upon ridges of the Andes thirteen thousand feet above sea-level; and fossil fish imbedded below strata of petrified forests. Thus, also, we know that land and sea are but transferable commodities in her hands; that where the tides of oceans now ebb and flow, continents may some day be upheaved; and that Europe, with all her treasures, may yet be obliterated from the surface of our globe, and leave not even a legend of her glory."

He paused; passed his hand over his forehead, as if to collect his thoughts; and then, finding me attentive, resumed the thread of his discourse.

"Of all Nature's conditions," pursued he, "climates and products are among the most variable. Fossilized remains, indicative of torrid heats, are found underlying the upper strata of our northern lands, and the beds of many European rivers are paved with the bones of elephants and other 'very strange beasts.' I have myself been present at the opening of a cave in South Devon, where the skeletons of hyenas, tigers, and even crocodiles were found in abundance. Now these facts can only be explained in one of two ways. Either the climates of the globe have varied from age to age; or some vast motive power has transported these remains from one hemisphere to the other. For my part, I go with those who attribute the phenomena to mutability of climate, consequent on the shifting of the poles. I believe that they have not only shifted, but are shifting; that the face of the world has not only changed, but is changing; and that what once was, will surely be again."

"Yet these great changes were Pre-adamite," I ventured to suggest, "and perhaps only prepared the world for man's habitation. Is it likely they would be renewed now, when——"

"Listen," interrupted Hugh, with sudden vivacity; "for this is precisely my pet theory. The cactus is a plant indigenous to the tropics, and to certain districts of the new continent. In Peru, in Chili, on the table-lands of the Andes, and on the banks of the Amazon, it is equally familiar to the traveler; and yet of late years—nay, within the last quarter of a century—it has spread mysteriously through North-Africa and Syria, and naturalized itself in Greece and Italy. What is the evident deduction? What if this migration be the herald of strange changes? What if we are about to return by gradual but perceptible degrees to that temperature which, in ages past, is known to have fostered the bamboo and zamia on the plains of France, peopled with apes the Isle of Sheppey, and crowned the promontories of Portland with forests of the Indian palm?"

"It is a large inference to draw from the migration of a single plant," said I.

"And then think of all that it would lead to," continued he, with unabated eagerness. "Think of the difference it would make in our manners and customs, our civilization, our *morale*, our politics! Fancy the Belgian flats turned into rice-fields, and crocodiles sunning themselves on the meadow-islands of the Rhine! Fancy a lion-hunt in the New Forest! Fancy honorable members going down to the house in palanquins, and the premier taking out his stud of elephants for a little tiger-shooting in September!" ·

"Fancy yourself with a shaved head and a turban," said I, laughing. "Fancy Broomhill fitted up with punkahs and musquito curtains; and think how its master would look reposing on a divan, with slaves fanning him to sleep!"

"Oh, prophet Mohammed!" exclaimed he, "I should buy beautiful Circassians in the Marché des Innocents!"

"But, Hugh, supposing that all these things really took place, and we could live to see them, should we, or our descendants, get brown, or copper-colored, or black? What a dreadful thing that would be!"

"Ah, that is another and more difficult question still," said he, gravely. "It involves the vexed topics of race and climate; and leads one into a thousand labyrinths of speculation. I believe that color and type result from custom and locality. I believe that we should degenerate in form, darken in hue, and, after a few generations lose every trace of our Caucasian origin. Take the Americans for instance. Gathered together from all the shores of the old world, they have, as it were, received a type of nationality from the very soil on which they dwell — a type which becomes apparent in every second generation of emigrants."

"In short, then, to change climates would simply be to change states with the Asiatic."

"Ay; and some day the Hindoo race, grown warlike and hardy, would pour down upon our feeble millions, ransack our treasures, farm out our royalties, and lord it over us as we now lord it at Calcutta. Faith! the picture is complete."

Whereupon, we rose, for the sun was now full in our eyes, and strolled toward the hot-houses. There Hugh showed me some strange plants; described the places where they grew; the uses to which they were put; and the circumstances under which he had seen them when traveling in the far East. Anecdote, illustration, and jest, flowed from his lips that afternoon with the same freshness and abundance that used to charm my childish imagination years ago; and I almost fancied, as I listened, that I was back again sitting at his feet in my aunt's quiet parlor, or turning over the folios in the Hogarth room at Broomhill.

By and by, the clocks of Zollenstrasse struck five, at which hour the students had coffee, before going for their evening walk; so I bade Hugh a hurried good-by, and we parted at the gate. Before I had gone many yards, however, I paused, looked round, found that he was still gazing after me, and so turned back again.

"One more word, Hugh," I said, breathlessly. "What would it cost to go to Rome?"

"To Rome? From what point?"

"From here."

"Why do you ask?"

"No matter — I want to know."

"Well, I can hardly tell. It would cost me, perhaps, a hundred pounds; but then I'm not an economical traveler. I dare say a modest, quiet, steady-going fellow, who did not stop to sketch and dawdle on the way, might do it for half, or even a quarter of that sum."

"And I suppose one might live and lodge there for about a pound a week?"

"Yes, no doubt. I question if many of the

poor devils of artists in the Via Margutta have as much."

"Thank you. Once more, good-by."

"But, Barbara — I say, Barbara——"

However, I did not want to be questioned, so I only shook my head, and ran away.

"Twenty pounds!" said I, unconsciously thinking aloud, as I sat on the side of the bed, that night, before putting out the candle. "Twenty pounds, at least, for the journey, and then fifty more for a year's living! Oh, dear me! how could I ever save all that out of sixteen pounds per annum?"

"What did you say, Barbara?" murmured Ida, sleepily, from her bed in the corner.

To which I only replied —

"Nothing, *Liebchen*. Good night."

CHAPTER XXVII.

THE PIPER OF HAMELIN.

"HAMELIN town's in Brunswick,
By famous Hanover city;
  The river Weser, deep and wide,
  Washes its wall on the southern side;
  A pleasanter spot you never spied;
But, when begins my ditty,
  Almost five hundred years ago,
  To see the townsfolk suffer so
  From vermin was a pity.
      Rats!"   ROBERT BROWNING.

"Bring me back yoursel', Jamie."
                         SCOTCH SONG.

"MY dear little Barbara," said Hugh, taking possession of the Professor's painting stool, and advantage of the Professor's dinner-hour, "I am very glad to find you alone; for I have come to say good-by. I am going to St. Petersburgh."

I felt myself turn scarlet and then pale.

"To St. Petersburgh?" I repeated.

"Ay. It is one of the places I have not yet visited, and I have a mind to become acquainted with our friend the Russ, in his own capital. I want to see what is the actual difference between Ivan the prince, who rents his hotel in the Chaussée d'Antin and runs his horse at Newmarket, and Ivan the boor, who leads the life of a beaten hound, and drinks brandy from his cradle."

"Is this a sudden resolution?"

"Yes — all my resolutions are sudden, *carina*. I am the slave of a demon whose name is Whim; and when he casts his spells about me, I can not choose but obey. Did you never hear of the Piper of Hamelin?"

I shook my head.

"Then, Barbara, your education has been neglected. Listen, and I will tell you the story. Once upon a time, and a very long time ago, the town of Hamelin in Brunswick was infested by a plague of rats. There were, in fact, more rats than townspeople; and the race of cats was exterminated. So the mayor and council met to discuss the matter, and decide what was best to be done. In the midst of their conference, in came a little gnome-like creature clad in yellow and red, carrying a flageolet in his hand — but you are not listening, *carina!*"

"Yes, yes, I am listening. Pray, go on."

"And this queer little piper offered to spirit the rats clean away, for the small consideration of one thousand guilders. The Mayor was only too glad to close with him; the bargain was struck; the piper set up a quaint melody; and out came the rats from cellar and sewer, garret and basement — red rats, gray rats, black rats, rats of all ages, sizes, and colors—and followed the piper by thousands through the main street of the town, right down to the banks of the river Weser, where they all plunged in and perished, like the host of Pharaoh."

"But what has this to do with your journey to St. Petersburgh?"

"Let me finish my legend in peace, and then I will tell you. Well, when the rats were all drowned, and not even a tail of one was left behind, the Mayor repented his liberality, and declined to sign the order for the thousand guilders. 'You shall have ten,' said he, 'and a bottle of wine; but when we talked of paying a thousand, it was only for the joke of it.' 'Is that your last word on the matter, Herr Mayor?' asked the piper. 'It is our last word,' replied the Mayor and Councilors, all together. So the piper made a bow, more in mockery than in reverence; flung the ten guilders on the floor; put his pipe once again to his lips; and walked straight to the middle of the market-place, where he took up his station, and began playing the most beautiful tune that ever was heard in Hamelin before or since. No sooner, however, had he begun to play, than such a pattering of little feet, such a clapping of little hands, and such bursts of ringing laughter filled the air, that the piper's music was nearly silenced in the hubbub. And whence came all this riot, do you suppose? Why, from all the children in the town — from the children who came trooping out, like the rats, by scores and hundreds, with their fair hair all fluttering behind them, and their little cheeks flushed with pleasure—from the children who escaped from mothers and nurses at the sound of the pipe, and followed the piper, as the rats had followed him, all down the main street, and out by the old gate leading down to the Weser! Only, Barbara, he had not the heart to drown the pretty babies. He led them into a valley at the foot of a great black mountain, about half a league from the walls; and the side of the mountain opened to receive them; and there they all are to this day, shut up in the granite heart of it, waiting till the piper shall relent from his vengeance and bring them back to the town. Now what say you to my legend?"

"That it is charming, as a legend, but very perplexing as an explanation of your St. Petersburgh journey."

"Is it possible that you have not found out that my demon and the goblin piper are one and the same; and that when he pipes, I am bound to follow, like one of the rats of Hamelin? It pleases him, just now, to pipe to a Russian tune, and off we go together, 'linked with the Graces and the Hours in dance,' and cutting the most ludicrous melancholy figure imaginable!"

Something in his manner, something in the telling of the story and the comment with which it ended, convinced me that he was ill at ease.

"Do not treat me quite as a child, Mr. Farquhar," I said, earnestly. "You have some deeper motive for undertaking this journey. I do not desire to know what that motive may be; but I am sure it is not whim alone."

He turned suddenly, and looked at me—then turned as suddenly away.

"You are wrong," he said, "I am the soul of whim—the sport of a restless fancy—the creature of my own morbid imagination. There are in me neither motives, nor purposes, nor principles of action. Like the thistledown, I veer with every wind; and, like the wind, am 'every thing by turns, and nothing long.' I have the fancy to go to St. Petersburgh, and I am going. *Voilà tout !*"

"Then I wish you had the fancy to stay here, instead," said I, sadly.

"Stay here? Not for the world. I have staid too long already."

As he said the words, a shadow darkened the doorway, and Professor Metz came in. He looked unusually grave; saluted Mr. Farquhar with a nod and a scowl; and, ungraciously turning his back upon us, began painting away as if his life depended on it.

"A fine day, Herr Professor," said Hugh, vacating the stool with an apologetic bow.

"A confoundedly disagreeable day, to my mind," growled the Professor.

"Nay, with this glorious sunshine, and this refreshing breeze——."

"Lapland in the shade, and the infernal regions in the sun," interrupted the Professor. "I hate such weather."

"The panels progress rapidly, Herr Professor," observed Hugh, after a brief pause. "The effect, when complete, will be charming."

"I don't think so," retorted the Professor.

"May I ask why?"

"Because the shape of the room is bad, and the light is bad, and the designs are bad, and the whole thing is a failure."

Hugh laughed outright.

"The Herr Professor has certainly left his rose-colored glasses at home to-day," said he good-humoredly. "Happily, he will find no one to agree in his verdict."

The Professor muttered something inaudible about "public opinion," and then became so obstinately silent that, after one or two abortive efforts to keep up the conversation, Hugh was fain to take up his hat and say "good morning."

"I shall come round to-night, and bid you a last good-by, Barbara," whispered he, as we shook hands.

"Will you really—really?" said I, the tears starting to my eyes.

"I will indeed, my dear," he replied very gently, and hurried away without once looking back.

I watched him out of sight, and was just returning to my own work, when the Professor flung down his pallet and brushes, faced suddenly round upon his stool, and said—

"I must give you another holiday to-day, Fräulein Barbara."

"Why so, mein Professor? I had rather get forward with that sky."

"It isn't a question of 'rather,'" grumbled he. "You're to go back to College; Madame Brenner wants you."

"What can Madame Brenner want with me at this hour of the day?"

The Professor tugged gloomily at his moustache and glared at me without replying.

"Still I suppose I must go," said I, with a sigh.

"Ay," said he; "you must go."

I put on my bonnet and gloves, and went toward the door.

"Good-by," said the Professor.

"Good-by, sir," I replied. "I shall be back again very soon."

"No you won't" said the professor, holding out his hand.

That Professor Metz should offer to shake hands with me was in itself such a wonderful occurrence, that I had scarcely any power of astonishment left; but that the tears should be standing in his fierce little gray eyes when our palms met, was a phenomenon so utterly and overwhelmingly unexpected, that I stared at him in blank amazement, and had not a word to say.

"Adieu," said he, holding my hand loosely, and yet not letting it go. "God bless you."

"Mein Professor," I exclaimed, with a sudden presentiment, "what is the matter? You are bidding me farewell!"

"Yes—go—" he replied, abruptly. "Go. I am bidding you farewell."

"But I will not go! What is it? What does it mean?"

"You will soon know what it means. It means that I am a superstitious old fool, who believes that his little scholar will never come back again. There, go, I tell you! Go to Madame Brenner. She is waiting for you."

I ran back all the way across the Hof-garten; but, when within a few yards of the College gates, lingered, hesitated, and dreaded to go in. I felt that something strange and sudden was at hand, and would gladly have deferred it, if I could.

"The Fräulein is to go up to Madame's room," said the porter at the gate; and so, with my heart beating fast, I obeyed.

Madame received me with open arms.

"Come hither, mein Kind," she exclaimed, "I have news for you. I have received a letter from the Herr, your father. Such news! Your sister Hilda is about to be married."

"Married!" I repeated. "Hilda married?"

"Yes, and in ten days; and you are to go immediately to Paris, to be present at the wedding."

I sat down in the nearest chair, speechless. I could not believe it.

"Though how you are to travel alone, Gott im Himmel only knows," said Madame, shaking her head, despairingly. "If the girls were not all coming back this week, I would go with you myself; but it is impossible—impossible! There are the Pfeffers, to be sure; but they can not start till next week; and the Bachs went yesterday. What is to be done?"

"May I see the letter, Madame?"

"Ay, to be sure. And then there are your things to be packed; and the letter says you are to go immediately. How are you to go immediately, my child, without even a passport—much less an escort?"

I took the letter, written in my father's dashing hand, and sealed with his massive seal. It ran as follows:—

"Esteemed Madame,

"I have the honor of informing you that my daughter, Hilda Churchill, your late pupil, was last evening betrothed to His Excellency the Count Hippolyte Amadée de Chaumont, late plenipotentiary at the Court of Brussels, Chevalier of the Order of St. Esprit, etc., etc., etc. My daughter's marriage will take place in ten days from the present date. We desire the immediate presence of my youngest daughter, to whom be pleased to communicate the foregoing intelligence. I regret that it is not in my power personally to conduct her from Zollenstrasse to Paris; but I trust that it may be found possible to place her under the protection of some respectable family traveling in the same direction. Be so obliging, if you please, Madame, as to let me know by an early post, at what hour, and by what conveyance, I may expect her arrival.

"Accept, Madame, my distinguished compliments, and believe me to be your obedient servant.

"EDMUND CHURCHILL."

"It is a grand match," said Madame Brenner, admiringly; "a wonderful match! She will be Madame la Comtesse — only think of that, Barbara! No mere 'Gnädige Frau,' or 'Frau Geheimrath;' but Madame la Comtesse de Chaumont!"

"I hope she loves him dearly," said I.

"Loves him? You may depend, she adores him," replied Madame, whose tender German heart was brimful of sentiment. "Young, noble, handsome, distinguished — how can she help loving him?"

No one had said that he was young or handsome; but Madame Brenner conceived it must be so, and believed it accordingly.

"Ah, well, well," continued she, "and we all thought she would be a singer at one time! How little we can guess what a few months may bring forth! I have told Professor Oberstein of his pupil's good fortune; and —— "

"And Professor Metz also; have you not, Madame?"

"Yes, to be sure; because I begged him to send you home at once; but I forbade him to tell you the news, because I wanted to have that pleasure myself. But, dear heart! here we are standing and chattering, while there is such a world of things to be done, and no time to do them! I have already sent Gretchen down to the laundry with all the things that want getting up; and Ida is gone into the town to buy a new ribbon for your bonnet — for you could never have gone to Paris, my dear, in this shabby old hat! — and Professor Oberstein has kindly offered to see about your passport; and I have sent down to Kräuter, the carpenter, to come and look at your boxes; for it's years and years since you came among us, and they've been lying up in the lumber-rooms ever since, and are almost tumbling to pieces by this time, I shouldn't wonder! But, Barbara, my child, I thought you would have been more pleased to hear of Hilda's betrothal?"

"I do not know, Madame. It is so sudden — I hope she may be happy."

"How can she help being happy?"

I shook my head, sadly.

"Then, are you not yourself delighted to visit Paris?"

"I had rather stay here, dear Madame Bren-

ner, a thousand times. There is the pavilion, you know — I was so proud to help Professor Metz in the pavilion. And then Ida — how she will miss me!"

"How we shall all miss you, Liebchen!" said Madame, tenderly. "I don't know what we shall do when you're gone."

"Oh, but I shall hurry back as soon as the wedding is over."

Madame looked incredulous.

"Paris is a city of enchantment," said she. "You may like it too well to leave it; or you, also, may find a husband. Who knows?"

"But I intend never to marry! I have resolved to devote my life to painting."

"The resolutions of seventeen are easily broken," replied Madame, smiling.

"You forget how happy I am here. You forget that the College is my home."

"I forget nothing," said she; "but the hours are precious, and you will have to start early in the morning. Come up-stairs, my child, at once, and let us look over your wardrobe."

But I was in despair that she should believe it possible that I could prefer Paris and matrimony to Zollenstrasse and Art.

"You are mistaken, Madame," I repeated, as we went up the great stone staircase. "Indeed, indeed, you are mistaken."

To which she only replied — "We shall see."

We worked hard all the rest of the day and far into the evening, trimming, repairing, and packing my little outfit. At about half-past eight o'clock, Hugh came, according to his promise, and was shown into Madame Brenner's parlor, where we were all sitting together, still busy with our needles.

"I come to bid Barbara a last adieu," said he; "for we are very old friends, as you know, Madame Brenner; and do not like parting."

"I know you are, Herr Farquhar," replied Madame; "but you are not more sorry than we are, for all that."

"Upon my word, Madame," said Hugh, looking very much surprised, and bowing politely, "you are too good."

"The place will not seem the same to any of us," continued Madame, with the tears in her kind eyes.

"I — believe me I really do not know how to —— "

"And as for this poor Ida," said Madame, laying her own plump hand affectionately on Ida's slender fingers, "she will nearly break her heart, poor child."

Hugh looked from one face to another in such bewilderment and consternation, that I could forbear laughing no longer.

"And all because poor little Barbara is summoned away to Paris to her sister's wedding!" I exclaimed, purposely destroying the thread of the double entendre. "You did not know, Mr. Farquhar, that if you are off to-morrow to St. Petersburgh, I also start for Paris."

"You—you are going to Paris?" said he, with a deep breath of satisfaction. "This is sudden, is it not?"

"Yes, Hugh," I replied, demurely. "All my resolutions are sudden. I am the slave of a demon whose name is Whim. Did you never hear of the Piper of Hamelin?"

"The Piper of Hamelin!" repeated Madame Brenner. "Who is he, pray?"

"Oh, a friend of the Herr Farquhar, Madame. But, indeed, Hugh, I have very important news from Paris. My sister Hilda is to be married in ten days to the Count de Chaumont; and my father insists that I shall be present at the ceremony."

"But you are not going alone, little one?"

"Indeed I am."

"It is very unfortunate," said Madame; "but we have so short a notice that it is impossible to find any family traveling in the same direction."

"I am about to leave Zollenstrasse," said Hugh; "and a few days sooner or later would make no difference to me. I shall be happy to take care of Barbara as far as Paris, if Madame pleases."

The superintendent held up her hands in horror.

"Mein Gott! impossible," said she. "Such a thing was never heard of. The Herr Farquhar is a foreigner, and probably is not aware——"

"Oh, *les convenances*, I suppose!" replied he, laughing. "Madame, I confess to you frankly that I am a savage. I know no more of the by-laws of life than an Esquimaux; and if I conceived that, having known Barbara Churchill since she was no taller than my cane, I might with propriety volunteer to protect her during so short a journey, blame, if you please, my ignorance only. Why, *petite*, you have never been anywhere ·by your own little self, ever since you were born!"

"I beg your pardon. I traveled alone to and from Suffolk, when I was a very little girl," I replied; "and Hilda and I came alone from London Bridge to these College gates, six years ago."

"And how do you propose to make your way to Paris?"

"I leave Zollenstrasse to-morrow morning by the steamboat that goes down the Main as far as Frankfort. At Frankfort I am to sleep, and thence shall go on by diligence and railroad, according to the plan that Madame will write out for me."

"Can I be of any assistance in that matter, Madame?" said he. "I know every route, road, boat, rail, and diligence by heart; and every rood of the ground between this place and Paris. In me, without vanity, I may say you behold an accomplished courier, a steamboat directory, a hotel guide, a fluent vocabulary, a polyglot interpreter, a circumstantial handbook for travelers on the Continent; and, in short, all that the most inexperienced tourist can desire in a work of reference."

"Indeed I shall be very grateful," replied Madame; "for I never can understand these new-fashioned ways of traveling. Ten years ago, one never went by any thing but schnell-wagens, or steamboats; and now one hears of nothing but railroads springing up in every direction."

So Hugh pulled out his guide-book and time-tables, and he and Madame sat down quite cosily, side by side, and planned my journey for me. I was to go by boat to Frankfort; from Frankfort by diligence to Mayence; from Mayence to Cologne by steamboat; and from Cologne by railroad to Paris. As soon as all this was written down, with the fares and hours of starting, and the names of the hotels at which I was to stay, Hugh rose and took his leave.

"Good-by, *petite*," said he, quite gayly. "When I am tired of Russia, I shall come back to Zollenstrasse and hear all about Hilda's wedding, and the visit to Paris. What shall I bring you from St. Petersburgh?"

"Nothing, thank you."

"Nonsense—I will bring you a set of sables; or, if you like it better, a bracelet of gold roubles."

"What do I want with bracelets or sables, Hugh? Bring yourself back. I am very lonely here, now that Hilda is gone."

"Ah, Barbarina, that is more difficult! Adieu, and God bless you. Adieu, gracious Madam. I hope some day to have the pleasure of paying my respects to you again."

And with this he went away. I was very sad that evening; and I felt it hard, somehow, that he could go so cheerfully.

CHAPTER XXVIII.

A KIRMESS AND SCHUETZEN-FEST.

It is almost as difficult to part from places that we love, as from people who are dear to us. I scarcely knew, indeed, whether my tears fell faster for the Academy, or for the friends whom I left in it. Twenty times I turned back to take a last look at the pretty bedroom which Ida and I had shared so long between us; at the familiar studio ·in which I had worked so happily; at the half-finished painting which I was leaving on the easel. To one I said : "Take care of my mignonette, and water it for me every morning before breakfast." To another : "Let no one take my seat in the studio, or move my easel from the corner it always occupies." · To me there was something significant in every petty detail of the localities I loved—something precious in the very patterns of the furniture, in the weather-stains upon the old flags in the courtyard, in the rough chalk outlines scrawled here and there on the walls of the class-rooms.

They were all sorry to part from me, and crowded round to bid me a thousand last good-bys. Professor Metz came out from his private room to shake hands with me; Madame Brenner accompanied me to the wharf; and Ida, and two or three others who had not gone home for the vacation, went down to the bridge to see me off. To every one I kept repeating: "I shall be back soon! I am sure to be back, at the latest, in a month, or five weeks." But my heart failed me all the time; and the more I strove to console others, the more inconsolable I became. At length the bell rang, and Madame left me, with many embraces; and the steamer hove slowly round, and carried me away. My school-friends on the bridge waved their handkerchiefs. Madame Brenner put hers to her eyes, and turned away; and Ida's pale, tearless face grew less and less distinct, till the bend of the river carried us out of sight, and the last spire of Zollenstrasse disappeared behind the woods of Brühl.

The morning was dull and chilly. The decks

were still damp from recent swabbing. The passengers were few, and the scenery looked ghostly through the white fog hanging low upon the banks. Whenever we came to a little river-side village, which happened about four or five times in every hour, the bell rang, and the steamer lay to for the purpose of receiving and landing passengers. These were chiefly market-women and washer-women, who piled their picturesque baskets in the middle of the deck, and sat knitting and chattering together as long as they remained on board. Some brought crates of live poultry; some, glittering brass milk-cans, slender and graceful as antique vases; and one was accompanied by a very noisy and disobliging pig, who protested loudly against the manner of transit, and was landed by force at a squalid little hamlet about eight miles down the river. By and by, shortly after mid-day, we arrived at an ancient walled town standing on a granite cliff high above the stream, with a line of quaint watch-towers reaching down to the water's edge. Here we stopped, as usual, and took in some soldiers, a few peasants, and a pair of splendid horses, covered with horse-cloths from their ears to their fetlocks. Sad and weary as I was (for the four hours that I had already been on board seemed like sixteen) I saw, but scarcely heeded, these fresh arrivals. What, then, was my amazement, when a gentleman came and flung himself familiarly on the bench beside me, and said—

"Shall we go down together to the cabin, and have some lunch, Fräulein?"

Without even turning my head to look at him, I rose indignantly, and was about to move away, when he seized me by the wrist, and added—

"Barbarina!"

"What, Hugh?"

"Of course. Who else?"

"But—but how——"

"How came I here? Well, by a post-chaise, if I am bound to render up an account of my proceedings. I sent my horses to this place last night—it is only fourteen miles by the road—and followed them this morning, just in time to catch the boat, and place myself at your Highness's service. I had no mind that my little Barbarina should travel to Paris alone."

"Oh, Hugh, how good of you—how wrong of you! What would Madame say if she knew it?"

"What she pleased, carina. I have a right to travel when and where I choose. Would you like to come and look at the horses?"

Of course I liked to look at the horses. I should have liked to look at a pair of basilisks, by his invitation. I knew nothing about horses; but that was of no consequence. I admired them because they were his; and a smart English groom, whose top-boots were the wonder of all the German rustics on board, stepped forward and unbuckled the horse-cloths for my especial satisfaction. This done, we went into the cabin and had sour claret and tough cutlets for lunch; by which time the fog had cleared away, and the sun was shining, and it became quite a pleasant thing to go on deck again, and enjoy the scenery.

All that day, Hugh exerted himself to keep me amused and cheerful. He pointed out every picturesque effect, every ruin, boat, and incident on the way. For me he ransacked the store-houses of his memory; for me raked up every dry and dusty legend of the Franconian land—legends of the Fichtelgebirge, and the magical mountain filled with halls of gold and jewels; and the story of Conrad the devil; and the history of the Empress Cunigunda, whose petticoat is kept to this day in the Cathedral of Bamberg, as a cure for the toothache.

Besides all this, I found myself traveling *en princesse*, and surrounded with unaccustomed luxury. At Frankfort, where we stopped for the night, Tippoo suddenly made his appearance, and, after his old noiseless fashion, took the charge and conduct of every thing. He seemed neither to see nor recognize me; but, having quietly searched out our luggage, and delivered over the groom and horses to an ostler who was waiting on the quay, preceded us to a spacious hotel, where we were received by a crowd of bowing waiters, and ushered into a pleasant parlor opening upon a garden, at the foot of which flowed the river Main. Here the table was ready laid with glittering glass and silver, and flowers that filled the air with fragrance.

"What a charming room!" I exclaimed.

But Hugh flung his hat impatiently upon a sofa, and said:—

"How is this, Tippoo? Did I not tell you the pavilion?"

"Sahib, the pavilion is engaged."

"*Mille diables!* Remember, then, that to-morrow I have the Green Drawing-Room overlooking the river."

"Yes, Sahib."

"You see, Barbara," explained Hugh, "I have my favorite apartments, wherever I go; and it is Tippoo's duty to secure them. I have also my own especial taste in the matter of *cuisine*. I can not eat these innocuous European dishes. I must have my Indian spices, and, like Sir Epicure Mammon, bargain for 'the tongues of carp, dormice, and camels' heels:'—so Tippoo always travels in advance, and prepares both the rooms and the dinner. Nay, never look so dismayed, little one! For you I have provided

Syllabubs, and jellies, and mince-pies,
And other such lady-like luxuries.'

I have no mind to starve you between this and Paris."

"And where is this green-parlor of which you spoke just now?"

"At Coblentz, where we break our journey again to-morrow evening. But will you not go to your room now; for we are already somewhat after the time at which I ordered dinner?"

So I hastened to take off my bonnet, and make such scanty toilette as I could; and then came back to the pretty parlor, where we dined in great state, with Tippoo standing behind his master's chair, and two waiters in attendance. Despite this grandeur, the dinner passed off merrily, thanks to my companion's inexhaustible gayety. After the cloth was removed, we strolled for an hour through the old dusky streets in the summer twilight, and saw the Cathedral, and the house where Goethe was born, and the Ober-Main Thor, and the gilt weather-cock at which the child-poet loved to gaze in the sunshine. Then, when it grew quite dark, we came back to our hotel; and coffee was served; and Tippoo produced the never-failing hookah, and the spirit-lamp in its stand of frosted-silver. So I bade good-night, and left Hugh to enjoy his pipe and his book.

The next morning we were breakfasting before six; for the railway at that time was only just commenced between Frankfort and Mannheim, and we had a long day's work before us. Instead of the weary schnell-wagen, a smart open carriage and four post-horses, with bells upon their collars, and red-worsted tassels and rosettes upon their heads, waited at the hotel-door to convey us on our journey. The landlord and waiters bowed us out, calling Hugh "my lord," and me "my lady;" the little boys set up a feeble cheer as we stepped in and drove away; and I remember feeling quite sorry that the good people of Frankfort were not up and stirring, to witness the grandeur of our departure.

It was a glorious summer day, and we had nothing to do but to enjoy it to the music of the horses' bells, and the singing of the birds. We had it all to ourselves. Tippoo, as usual, had gone on before; the groom and horses were left behind, to follow by easy stages; and if a remorseful thought of Madame Brenner did now and then cross my mind, I banished it as quickly as possible. About every two German miles we changed horses; and at eleven in the forenoon reached a quaint little town where there was a *Kirmess*, or fair, and a shooting festival going forward. Here our arrival created an extraordinary excitement; for the streets were full of rustics, to whom the sight of a traveling-carriage with four horses and two postillions was an event of some magnitude. The market-place and chief thoroughfare were lined with booths; the eating-houses were full of customers; the free-shooters, in their gray and green coats and steeple-crowned hats, were standing in knots at the doors of the wine-shops; the bare-headed, broad-shouldered peasant-girls were crowding, gossiping, and eating gingerbread in the broiling sunshine; and the air was all alive with laughter, music, shouting, shooting, and the creaking of merry-go-rounds. Having with difficulty procured a disengaged parlor, we stopped at the principal inn to take lunch, and while it was being prepared, went out to see something of the fair.

It was a thorough German Volks-Fest, and the booths were stocked with thorough German wares. Here was a stall for combs, probably made at Heidelberg, and beside it a fantastic little temple piled high with compact brown bundles of "Brennen Cigarren." Beyond these again, came stalls for the sale of untanned leather, soft and velvety, with a curly surface, like brown tripe—stalls for mock jewelry and bead necklaces, dear to German Mädchens—stalls full of Tyrolean knapsacks, faced with goatskin and ornamented with fringes of knotted twine—stalls of Nüremberg toys; beer-jugs gray and blue, with hieroglyphic patterns; tin oil lamps, preserving something of the antique Roman shape; Bavarian glass; umbrellas, chiefly of colored chintz and scarlet gingham; gorgeous gingerbread; brooms; brushes; spectacles; clocks;

F

cutlery; Lutheran hymn-books and Roman Catholic missals; stationery; china; silver hair-arrows; pumpernickel; cravats; and wooden shoes. One stall was exclusively devoted to the sale of mouse-traps. But foremost in attraction, and most characteristic of all, were the pipe-stalls. Here were carved wooden pipes; great porcelain pipes with colored pictures of huntsmen and maidens on the bowls; pipes with metal stoppers, and little German silver chains; pipes without stoppers; pipes of cherrywood, clay, meerschaum, red earth; pipes with twisted stems, elastic stems, short stems, long stems; comic pipes with queer faces on the bowls; solemn pipes, like grinning death's heads; portly aldermanic pipes; slender, genteel ones—in short, pipes of all shapes and complexions, sizes, prices, and colors. The love of the German for his pipe is almost a sentiment; and he puts into the pattern and painting of it such small change of fancy, humor, and poetry, as passes current with the honest Gottliebs and Heinrichs of every-day life.

Mingling still with the noisy crowd, Hugh and I passed through these long avenues of stalls till we came to the old medieval town-gate. Beyond this lay a meadow, part of which was partitioned off for the shooting ground, while the rest was filled with booths of a larger size than those within the walls. Here were tents with the words "*Tanz Musik*" painted up conspicuously over the entrance; in each of which we saw some twenty or thirty stalwart couples whirling and stamping about as merrily as if the midday sun were not shining down with almost tropical splendor. Here, too, were Punch and Judy shows, where the showman appeared on the stage in person, as far as his head and shoulders, and exchanged thumps with his quarrelsome hero—peep-shows containing views of London, Paris, and the Rhine—*manèges*, in which grown-up folks were going gravely round—and the great "Puppet-theater from Vienna," recommended to public admiration by a huge external fresco representing two gentlemen in Paul Pry costume with labels issuing from their mouths, on one of which was inscribed, "I have been in to see it, and it is splendid!" To which the other replies, "I would go; but I haven't a groschen!"

Beyond the shows lay the refreshment booths; ambitious edifices of planks and canvas, surmounted by flags, and disclosing vistas of tables and benches occupied by jovial holiday folks, feasting on German sausages, black bread, Swiss cheese, and flagons of thin Rhenish or sparkling Baïerisch. These booths bore all kinds of high-sounding titles, such as Bavarian Beer-Halls, Jäger's Refreshment Halls, Free-shooters' eating-rooms, Kirmess Gasthofs, and the like; whilst in their neighborhood hovered professional touters who filled our hands with printed advertisements and our ears with vociferate praises of the establishments to which they were severally attached.

"Try Mollberg's 'Temple of Cookery,' gracious Excellency!" cries one Jewish-looking fellow with gold rings in his ears. "Venison, nödel soup, grape-cakes, and the best Lager-bier in the world, for thirty-six kreutzers per head!"

"Come to Schwindt's Restauration, Herr Graf!" shouts another. "The best hotel in Frankfort couldn't serve you better!"

"Read this, *gnädiges Fräulein*," says a third, thrusting a slip of paper into my hand. "Read this, and persuade the Herr Excellency to bring you to the 'Hunter's Delight.'"

The slip of paper proves to be an advertisement in doggerel rhyme, over which Hugh and I have a hearty laugh together; and which, roughly translated, would run as follows:—

ESSER'S KIRMESS RESTAURANT.

"*The Hunter's Delight.*"

Come, neighbors, 'tis our yearly fair ;
Let all to Esser's booth repair !
There every friend and honored guest
May freely feast upon the best.
Cutlets, and sucking pigs, and veal,
Hams, jellies, capons, ducks, and teal,
Plums, peaches, melons, figs, and pease,
All kinds of sausages and cheese,
Anchovies, sardines, oysters, steaks,
And (for the women) sweets and cakes ;
All these, and more (if you've the mind)
At Esser's eating-rooms you'll find.
As for my stock of wine and beer,
I can not dwell upon it here ;
Enough that there will be, as well,
An extra cask of prime Moselle ;
So good that it would be a shame
If but a single schoppen came
To palates dulled by beer and spirits,
And, therefore, tasteless to its merits.
So come, my friends, and try my famous cheer:
A bottle and a capon, who need fear !
Remember, Kirmess comes but once a year !

Resisting the attractions held out by these beery and smoky temples of festivity, we crossed to the free-shooters' ground, where some eighty riflemen were gathered together at the lower end of the field ; each man with his gun in his hand, and all wearing the characteristic hat and coat of the brotherhood. At the upper end of the inclosure stood three large targets. In a small tent close by were ranged the prizes to be shot for. In a large booth against the place of entrance, a young woman dispensed wine and beer, and an old man collected the shooting-fees. These were about twopence each for entrance, and a penny for every shot.

"Stand aside, *meine Herren*," cried the old money-taker, as we passed the wicket, and came in. "Stand aside, and let His Excellency have a shot!"

But Hugh laughed, and shook his head.

"I have no gun, friend," said he.

"Eh, *mein Gott*, Excellency, here are guns in plenty. See—one, two, three, four, five, six !"

And the old man pointed to a row of well-used rifles ranged on a stand behind his counter.

"The Herr Excellency is welcome to mine," said a handsome free-shooter, standing close by.

Something in the man's tone, perfectly civil though it was, brought the angry color to my cheeks.

"Take it, Hugh ; take it," I whispered. "These men think you can not shoot."

"And what matter if they do, *carina*? They are the best rifle-shots in the world, except the Tyroleans ; and they know it."

"But you are quite as fine a marksman as any Tyrolean in Tyrol."

"I am a very fair marksman," replied Hugh ; "but——"

"But they do not believe it ! See, they are smiling. Do — do take the man's rifle."

He laughed, and took it.

"The young lady wishes it," said he ; "so I accept your offer, friend, with thanks. A heavy

gun to carry on a long day's shooting, upon my word !"

"We mountaineers think nothing of heavier rifles than this," said the free-shooter, with a slight curl of his handsome lip. "I come from the Black Forest ; and I carry that gun on my shoulder all day, where the mountains are steepest. Take care, Excellency. When cocked, a breath is almost enough to free the trigger."

But Hugh, balancing the rifle in his hand, seemed scarcely to hear the warning.

"What is the distance of your farthest target ?" asked he. "Three hundred paces ?"

"Two hundred and fifty, Excellency," replied the old man at the counter.

Hugh lifted the rifle to his shoulder and fired, almost without seeming to take aim.

"Stop !" shouted he, as some half-dozen free-shooters . began running toward the target. "Stop ! Another shot first ! Will any one lend me another rifle ?"

One of the recalled runners handed his own immediately.

Hugh fired again.

"Now," said he carelessly, "find the two balls."

The target was presently surrounded. There was a moment of silence ; then a shout ; then a sudden waving of caps, and a general rush toward the further end of the field.

"What *have* you done, Hugh ?" cried I, scarcely able to forbear following the example of the rest. "What *have* you done ?"

"Fired the second ball precisely upon the first, if I am not strangely mistaken," answered he. "I could have done the same thing at nearly double the distance. Why, you excitable little monkey, you are quivering from head to foot ! Surely the firing does not frighten you ?"

"Frighten me ! Do you suppose I tremble from terror ? But this must be a wonderful feat ?"

"They seem to think so."

"How glad I am you fired !"

"So am I, Barbarina, since it has given you pleasure ; but I did not desire to do so. There is something 'snobbish' in exhibitions of skill, merely as exhibitions."

By this time the men had thronged back again, and were pressing round us ; all eager to shake hands with Hugh at the same moment.

"We never saw such a shot."

"The Herr Excellency is —— come back again !"

"*Wunderbar !*"

"*Unerhört !*"

And the bullets, completely ·socketed the one in the other, were passed from hand to hand among the crowd.

In the mean time, the young woman at the counter had fetched a heavy earthenware drinking *Krug* with a still heavier German-silver lid, representing a free-shooter sitting astride on a beer-barrel, and presented it to Hugh with much ceremony.

"What am I to do with this, mein Fräulein ?" asked he, gallantly. "Shall I drink your health in it ?"

"It is the first prize, Excellency," replied the young woman with a courtesy.

"Nay, nay, I do not wish for a prize !"

"But his Excellency has won it."

"Yes! Yes! Fairly won it! Take it! Take it!" was echoed on every side.

"I had rather leave it still to be shot for," said Hugh; "but I will gladly drink a health out of it, to my friends the German free-shooters. They, in return, must, however, allow me to offer them some of the Fräulein's best Lager-bier. Fräulein, have you enough of the best to furnish all these Herren with two *Schoppen* each?"

"With three, if the Herr Excellency pleases," replied the young woman, briskly.

"Then three let it be. Gentlemen, to your health and success."

Saying which, Hugh Farquhar drained a measure in their honor; returned the cup to the Mädchen with a broad gold-piece lying at the bottom; shook hands once more with the honest riflemen all round; and, giving me his arm, hastened away from the meadow and the fair, and round by a pretty field-path to the gate by which we had first entered the town. Long before we left it, which was in less than an hour from the time we regained our inn, the fame of Hugh's achievement had flown all over the place; so that there was quite a crowd about the door when we drove away. Their last shout rings in my ears to this moment. I never was so proud and happy before; indeed, I doubt whether, at any period of my life, I have been so proud and so happy at the same instant of time. It was one of those rare and transient gleams of pure, unalloyed, unselfish, perfect pleasure that glance now and then, like mysterious *étoiles filantes*, across the dark horizon of our lives.

That afternoon, we took the Rhine steamer at Mayence, and went with the rapid river as far as Coblentz, where we had the green-room with the balcony overlooking the river, just as Hugh had directed. Here we found the table laid, and the dinner ready; and after dinner, being too tired to stroll about as we had done the night before, we sat outside, and watched the late steamers coming in; and the people going to and fro across the bridge of boats; and the lights along the banks coming out brighter and brighter as the twilight crept up from the west, and the stars stole out overhead. Then coffee was brought; and, after coffee, the spirit-lamp and the hookah; but Hugh laid the pipe aside, and said—

"Stay a little longer, Barbarina. By this time to-morrow we shall be in Paris; and then, who knows when we shall meet again?"

So I sat down again, and he talked to me. Such talk! At that time, though tolerably well read in German literature, I was but slightly acquainted with any, except Shakspeare, among our English poets. Of Coleridge, I knew only that he was the author of "The Ancient Mariner," and a brother-in-law of Robert Southey. Had I then read any of those written testimonies in which his friends and hearers bear witness to the wonders of his eloquence — that eloquence which was reported to "marshal all history, harmonize all experiment, and probe the depths of all consciousness" — I might perhaps have been able to measure Hugh Farquhar's conversation by something of an ideal standard. As it was, I lost myself in listening; and he went on from topic to topic, from speculation to speculation, like an inspired dreamer.

I can recall only fragments of what he said — mere waifs and strays of splendid reasoning and gorgeous metaphor. To put them into any thing like an intelligible form would, at this distance of time, be altogether impossible. He began, I think, by some observation on the night-landscape before our windows, and thence diverged into Shakspeare's sonnets, Goethe's Theory of Plants, the influence of poetry, the Arcadia of Sir Philip Sidney, and the Utopia of Sir Thomas More. Hence he plunged into a strange theory of the fundamental unity of the arts, and related some wild adventure of his own in the depths of a South-American forest, where he chanced one days upon the ruin of a primeval temple, and found, yet standing erect above its portals, a sculptured figure with uplifted arm and broken bough; rude, imperfect, but embodying the identical conception of the Belvedere Apollo.

Supposing, even, that I could remember his very words, reconstruct his very sentences, how should I then express the power and variety of his style? It was like the flowing of a royal river; now broad and strong — now narrow, and wild, and eager — now bearing the sunlight along with it like a freight of jewels — now gliding subtly through the shadow — now winding round some sweet green isle of fancy — and anon breaking forth into foam, and hurrying on, on, till it leaps over the rocks with a mighty voice of triumph.

But to describe all this, "one should write like a god."

When, at length, he came to a pause, and saw how earnestly I was listening, he smiled sadly, rose from his chair, and began pacing to and fro, as was his wont, when moved by strong excitement.

"Barbara," said he, "to-night my thoughts run away with me, and I, like a foolish Phæton, can not hold them in. Do I weary you?"

"You can not weary me," I replied. "Even when I was a child, and less able to understand you, I used to think that I could go on listening to you forever."

"And do you understand me now?"

"Yes—in a certain sense."

"What do you mean by 'a certain sense'?"

"I mean that even when your ideas are too deep, or too high, for my following, I always feel their beauty; as I might feel the melody of a language that I had never heard before."

Suddenly, before I could guess what he was about to do, he clasped me in his arms, and kissed me twice or thrice upon the eyes and forehead—kissed me so wildly, so passionately, so strangely, that I could neither speak nor move, nor be any thing but passively and tremblingly amazed. Then, releasing me as suddenly—

"Child! child!" he exclaimed, "forgive me! I am not myself to-night. Leave me. Go to bed—forget this folly. Pshaw! I am old enough to be your father. There—shake hands. I am not going to kiss you again. Good-night."

Without a word, I left him and went to my room. I felt strange and bewildered, as if I were walking in my sleep; and my heart beat painfully. To shed tears might have been a relief; but no tears came—so I sat, half undressed, upon the bed, with my face buried in my hands, and the moonlight streaming in through the uncurtained casement. By and by, my eyes grew heavy and my thoughts more vague, till at last I was fain to lay my tired head upon the pillow, and fall fast asleep.

CHAPTER XXIX.

PARTING AND MEETING.

WE met the next morning, and resumed our journey, as if nothing had taken place. Finding that Hugh in nowise alluded to the events of the previous evening, I gradually recovered my self-possession, and came to look upon them as the results of a fantastic ebullition—a freak—a suggestion of the Goblin Whim ; and so ceased to puzzle myself about the matter.

Still, things were not quite the same with us. I observed that he was more grave and silent than heretofore, and that he frequently roused himself to talk on subjects from which his thoughts were, far distant. Thus a shade of restraint interposed between us, and our third day's journey seemed ten times longer than either of those by which it was preceded.

We left Coblentz very early in the morning, while the mists were yet hanging about the armed hights of Ehrenbreitstein, and, landing at Bonn, thence took the railway to Paris. I had never traveled by railway before! My journey to Zollenstrasse had been accomplished nearly all the way by water ; and most of the great Continental and English lines had sprung into existence during the time of my quiet academic life. I remember that I was very much impressed by the speed, and smoothness, and mysterious strength of this new power. I was even somewhat nervous, though I would not confess it ; and felt that it was a great additional security to have Hugh Farquhar sitting by my side.

It was a weary journey, and we did not come in sight of Paris till past ten o'clock in the evening. All the afternoon, while it was yet day, I had been wondering when these monotonous corn-flats and lines of melancholy poplars were to be relieved by something green and hopeful—and now that the dusk had closed in, and the lights glared up to the sky, and the blurred outline of a mighty city seemed to gather round us, with towers and spires uplifted here and there through the darkness, a great depression fell upon me. Yet a little farther, and the houses grew thicker, and the lights nearer. Then came nothing but stone walls on either side, and a glass roof over head, and a blaze of brilliant gas ; and it was Paris at last.

We alighted, and there, as usual, was Tippoo waiting to receive us.

"Look round, Barbara," said Mr. Farquhar, "and see if there be any face you know."

I looked round ; but, though the platform was not crowded, I saw no one who I could suppose was there to meet me. We went into the waiting rooms ; but they were empty. We came back to the platform ; and still with the same result.

"They have either forgotten you, Barbarina, or made some mistake about the time," said my companion. "And yet the train is true to a minute."

"And I wrote last evening from Coblentz," said I, "as soon as we arrived. It is not flattering to be forgotten."

"At all events you remember your father's address?"

"No—but I have his letter in my pocket."

"Then we need only send Tippoo for a cab. Here, Tippoo—a *voiture de place !*"

But, to my dismay, I could not find the letter One by one, I took out all the contents of my pocket, and found that, beyond a doubt, I had left the letter on my bedroom table at the hotel in Coblentz. I had no need to tell of my loss —my face told it for me.

"Never mind !" said Hugh, smiling. "The misfortune is not irreparable. We must e'en go to Meurice's together, and be fellow-travelers for twelve hours longer."

"But——"

"But I engage to find your father before noon to-morrow ; so think no more about it. Come, it is of no use to linger here."

Just at this moment, as we were preparing to leave the station, a servant in livery came hurrying up the platform. He compared his watch with the railway-clock, looked at me, looked at my companion, hesitated, looked at the clock again, and finally, touching his hat, came forward and said—

"Pardon, Madame ! Je cherche Mademoiselle Churchill."

Which statement put an end to all my difficulties.

Mr. Farquhar gave me his arm ; the servant preceded us ; a porter followed with the luggage ; and Tippoo brought up the rear. To my surprise, I found a carriage drawn up and waiting for me at the entrance—a superb carriage, with blazing lamps, and crested hammer-cloths, and a pair of magnificent bays.

"Adieu, Barbara," said Hugh, as I turned to say good-by. "Our companionship is ended."

"For the present, Mr. Farquhar."

"Ay—for the present. Who cares for the past, and who dare answer for the future ? Thou wilt forget me when I am gone — eh, little Barbara ?"

"No, sir."

" ' *No, sir*,' indeed ! Why you are as spc-ing of protest as Cordelia herself ! I shall send Tippoo on the box, to see you safely home. Is this your father's carriage ?"

"I do not think so."

"Nay, then, whence comes it ?"

"I neither know nor care ; but, if you are curious, you can inquire."

"Of course I shall inquire. There may be witchcraft in it. Good Heavens ! it might turn to a pumpkin before you were half-way home — who knows ?"

And with this he asked the servant to whom the equipage belonged.

"*A Monsieur le Comte de Chaumont.*"

"To your future brother-in-law, Barbarina ; who, it appears, is as good a judge of a horse as of a bride. Now, fare-you-well, since I know that you are in safe custody."

"Good-by — but do not send Tippoo with me. It is quite unnecessary." ·

"It is not unnecessary, if I choose to be satisfied of your safety. Besides, I shall then know your address."

"And will you make use of it ?" I asked, eagerly. "Will you come and see me, before you go to St. Petersburgh ?"

He lingered for a moment with my hand in his, and his foot on the carriage-step.

"I do not know — perhaps !" he said abruptly ; and so shut the door upon me, and turned away.

In another moment I was whirling through

the busy Paris streets — streets bright as day, lined with foliage, crowded with pleasure-seekers, and noisy with the multitudinous life of a great city! Dazzled and bewildered, I knew not at which side to look, or what most to admire; and in the midst of it all, the scene changed to what seemed like a huge park traversed by innumerable avenues of lamps, and filled with one moving mass of carriages and riders. Here we proceeded for some distance at a foot-pace, till we came to a large circular opening with a fountain in the midst, and then turned aside into an avenue, comparatively dark and empty, with houses peeping whitely through the trees. Before one of these we stopped. It was a handsome residence, with a garden and a high wall dividing it from the road, and heavy wooden gates, that opened to admit the carriage.

An English page, in a plain black suit, was waiting in the hall. I alighted and looked round for Tippoo, but he was already gone; so I followed the servant up-stairs, not without some little agitation, and wondered with what kind of reception I should meet. At the first landing he paused, threw open a door, and stood aside to let me pass.

It was a spacious drawing-room, dimly lighted and richly furnished.

"Mrs. and Miss Churchill are gone to the opera," said the lad, seeing me look round.

"Gone to the opera?"

"Yes, miss, with the Count de Chaumont. The Count's carriage went to fetch you after setting them down."

"And my father?"

"Master is at his club, miss. Would you please to have any refreshment?"

I sat down, wearily, upon the nearest sofa; scarce able to keep down the rising tears.

"You can bring me some coffee," I replied. "And desire some one, if you please, to show me to my bed-chamber."

I looked round the room. A few illustrated books with indifferent engravings and rich bindings lay scattered here and there upon the tables. The card-baskets were full of cards. A pile of Hilda's music lay upon the piano. A shawl of Mrs. Churchill's showed from which couch she had last risen. A superb bouquet in a vase on one of the side-tables told of the last night's party. I sighed.

"What would I not give that it were all over," thought I, "and I going back to Zollenstrasse to-morrow! Well, at all events, I shall see the Louvre!"

My reverie was interrupted by the return of the page, who brought me a very small cup of coffee on a very large salver. This youth was closely followed by a smart French lady's maid, who wore her hair drawn back à la Chinoise, and conducted me up-stairs to a small ill-furnished room on the fourth story. Her name, she informed me, was Juliette, and she was Mrs. Churchill's femme de chambre. Being abundantly loquacious, she then went on to say that she hoped to transfer herself and her accomplishments to the service of that charmante demoiselle, my sister, on her auspicious marriage with M'sieur le Comte de Chaumont. As for Hilda, Mademoiselle Juliette averred that she had never known any lady upon whom the arts of dress were more satisfactorily bestowed. She

was so beautiful — she had such enchanting taste — she so amply repaid all the pains that one could take to adorn her charms to the greatest advantage. Then her hair — Ah, ciel! it was a real pleasure to dress such hair as Mademoiselle Hilda's! She looked ravishing with it in every style you could name — whether à la Grecque; or in bands; or in ringlets à l'Anglaise; or à la Sevigné; or drawn simply back, à l'Espagnole, with one little mignonne curl on each cheek; or even with it powdered à la Marie Antoinette, as Mademoiselle wore it last Thursday week at the Préfet's fancy-ball. Ah! let one figure to one's self — powdered, positively powdered! But then Mademoiselle Barbara's hair was lovely, also. And Mademoiselle's was of the finest quality; soft, glossy, abundant, and of that exquisite brown (the brown with the chestnut flush) which is so greatly admired in the beau monde! Decidedly, Mademoiselle Barbara would find the new rouleaux very becoming.

But I protested that I had no wish to change the familiar fashion of my hair; whereat Mademoiselle Juliette held up both her hands, and refused to entertain any such possibility. Of all the essential points connected with a lady's toilette, said she, the art of arranging the hair was the most important. To judge of styles and their application to individuals, was in itself a study — a study to which she, Mademoiselle Juliette, had devoted herself from her youth upward, and in which, without vanity, she believed herself without a rival. This being the case, and as it was likewise the express desire of Madame Churchill and Mademoiselle Hilda that she should make it her especial care to transform me as speedily as possible into a faultless Parisienne, she must begin by entreating that I would permit her to dress my hair to-morrow morning à l'Espagnole, which she was persuaded would improve the contour of my head, display the moulding of my throat, and bring out the intellectuality of my forehead in a most unprecedented and surprising manner! To all of which, being excessively tired and preoccupied, I replied briefly enough; and brought the subject to an end by dismissing Mademoiselle Juliette for the night.

From my window I could see down to the end of the road, where it opened upon the great Park through which I had passed on my way. The carriages were still going by in one continuous stream, and I leaned out for a long time, watching the bright lamps flitting through the trees, like a current of fire-flies. It was strange to think of how much love and how much hate, what youth, what age, what eager pleasure-seekers, and what wearied world-worn hearts those lamps were lighting through the dusk of the sweet summer night. Stranger still, that this should be Paris, and that hundreds of miles hence, deep down amid the pine-grown hills that leaned above the waters of the Upper Main, kind hearts and loving lips were, perhaps, at this very moment, busy with my name.

At twelve o'clock the scene was still the same, and the moving lamps were undiminished in number; so, weary and sad, I closed the casement, and went to bed.

I fell asleep immediately, and had slept for

a long time — or for what seemed a long time, so dreamless was my sleep—when I was awakened by a hand on my shoulder, and a sudden light throughout the room.

"Barbara!" said a familiar voice. "Barbara, dear! we are just home, and I would not go to bed without seeing you."

"Hilda!" I exclaimed, forgetting where I was, and looking up with a vague wonder at the radiant creature beside my bed. "Why, where have you been?"

"To the opera first, and then to a reception at the Prussian embassy. Did not Bruce tell you?"

"To the opera?" I repeated. "Ah, true — I remember. And the Count?"

"The Count de Chaumont was with us, of course. He goes everywhere with us. To-night he gave me this bracelet — see, is it not beautiful?—a snake in blue enamel, set with diamonds!"

I looked at the bracelet, and then at her.

"I scarcely know which is the more beautiful," I said, smiling. "He may well be proud of you!"

She laughed, cast away the lace cloak from her shoulders, and sat down on the edge of my bed.

"He *is* proud of me," she replied, well pleased with my admiration. "He already introduces mamma to every one as his *belle-mère*, and not a day passes that he does not bring me some splendid gift. On Thursday it was an ornament for my hair, and yesterday it was his portrait set as a brooch. Would you like to see it?"

"Indeed, yes — if you do not mind the trouble of bringing it!"

"Oh, my bedroom is next to yours, and the case lies on the table. I shall not be a moment!"

And with this she flitted away, and came back with the portrait in her hand.

"Mind," said she, with a somewhat embarrassed gayety, "you must tell me exactly what you think of him — I bargain for that."

I took it, glanced at it, and, taken by surprise, uttered an exclamation of dismay.

"Is it possible," I cried, "that he is as old as this?"

She looked down, and bit her lip.

"He is not old," she said. "At least, not *so* very old! He is a year younger than papa."

"A year younger than papa," I repeated. "Oh, Hilda!"

"And his features are very fine. Indeed, he is still considered a remarkably handsome man."

"And you love him?"

"Yes—that is to say, I love him—of course I love him. Quite as much as—as I ought. Why not?"

I continued looking at the portrait, and made no reply.

"Besides," added my sister, getting more and more piqued, "we do not live in the times of the Troubadours and Crusaders, or expect to find Leanders and Romeos every day at our feet. Matters are differently managed in the *beau monde*, my dear; and people who marry for rank and wealth are not supposed to be dying for love! The Count is very generous, very gentlemanly, highly *distingué*, and quite rich enough for my ambition. What more could one desire?"

"What more? Nay, no more, if this be sufficient."

"Sufficient? Why, Barbara, how absurd you are! Do you think I would marry, if I were not quite sure of being happy? I tell you that I like the Count very much, and that he adores me. I know that, as his wife, I shall never have a desire ungratified. I shall have a Hôtel in Paris, and a villa in Florence; I shall travel; I shall go into the best society; I shall become a leader of the fashion; and have as much money as I care to spend!"

"And that will make you happy?"

"Happy? Perfectly happy. Oh, you do not know all that I intend to do! I mean to dress better than Madame de Bernard—to give more elegant *soirées* than the Vicomtess de St. Etienne—to—but I have not told you where the Count is to take me for our wedding tour! Guess."

"How should I guess, dear? Perhaps to Naples and Sicily."

"Naples and Sicily at this time of the year? Why, one might as well take apartments in the crater of Vesuvius, at once! No—no, Barbara. Guess again."

"Well, Switzerland."

"Too vulgar. Every one goes to Switzerland in the autumn."

"Nay, then, I am utterly at a loss. Spain, I suppose, would not be cool enough, nor Scotland genteel enough, to please you. If it be not Vienna and the Danube, I will give it up."

"It is neither Spain, nor Scotland, nor Vienna; but Norway! What say you to Norway? Is it not a magnificent idea?"

"It is indeed. Was it your own?"

"Entirely. The Count asked me where I should like to go, and so I took the map, and studied the matter thoroughly. It must not be very far South, I said, on account of the autumnal heat; and it must not be on the beaten track, because I should like to do something original. And then I decided upon Norway."

"*Eh bien!* When does the wedding take place?"

"To-morrow week—or, rather, this day week; for it is three hours past midnight!"

"And it will be a grand affair, no doubt?"

"Yes—as grand as we can afford to make it; but papa's means, you know, are not great, and though Mrs. Churchill is well off, one does not like to owe too much to her bounty. However, the Count will bear a part of the expense. We shall be married first at the Protestant Chapel in the Rue du Chaillot, and from thence go on to the Church of Nôtre Dame de Lorette for the Roman Catholic ceremony. I am to wear white Brussels lace over white gros de Naples, and a vail to match. The lace is a present from the Count, and Mrs. Churchill says it can not have cost less than three thousand francs! But it is shamefully late, and I am tired to death, and you, by the by, have been traveling."

"Yes, I have come between four and five hundred miles in three days."

"Poor child! And all alone, too."

"Not alone. I had an escort all the way."

"That was fortunate. Some acquaintance, I suppose, of Madame Brenner? Ah, *mon Dieu!* I had almost forgotten the existence of Madame Brenner. Does the College still stand in the old place, and are the rolls on Monday mornings as stale as ever?"

"Every thing is as you left it," I replied, with a sigh.

"*Ainsi soit il!* Now good-night!"

I embraced her silently, and, as she left the room, followed her with my eyes, and sighed again. Was it possible that she could be happy? She seemed so—and yet—and yet it was but a bartering of her youth and beauty! Money, dress, position, and the empty vanity of a title—these were her gods, and to these she offered herself as a sacrifice. For her, neither the woman's dream of love, nor the artist's lofty ambition—for her, neither the poetry, nor the purity, nor the passion that makes life beautiful, and marriage holy! Instead of home, she has chosen society—instead of love, the admiration, or envy, of a careless world—instead of Paradise, the mirage of the desert, fruitless as the sands, and fleeting as the mists that paint it on the poisoned air.

Alas, poor Hilda!

CHAPTER XXX.

AT THE OPERA FRANÇAISE.

THE next day, when we were assembled in the drawing-room before dinner, waiting the arrival of the Count de Chaumont, my father took a card from his waistcoat pocket and handed it to Hilda, saying—

"This was left for you to-day, by a gentleman on horseback. Who is he? I do not remember the name."

"Nor I," replied my sister, and passed it to Mrs. Churchill. "It must have been for mamma."

Mrs. Churchill looked at it languidly, through her double eye-glass, and shook her head.

"Never heard of him in my life," she murmured, and leaned back again in the corner of the sofa.

My father put on his spectacles, and took the card over to the window.

"I feel convinced, Hilda," said he, "that the visit was for you. You must have been introduced to this person last evening at the Prussian embassy; for I was in the breakfast-room when he called, and I heard him inquire if you were fatigued this morning. Just consider. Whom did you meet last evening?"

"Very few English," said she, "and none whom I had not met before."

"Humph! It is scarcely an English name—more likely Scotch, by the sound of it. Farquhar! Farquhar—let me see, there was a Captain Farquharson of—no, that can have nothing to do with it. How singular!"

My heart beat, and my color rose in spite of me.

"If it be Mr. Farquhar of Broomhill," I said, nervously, "the card was left for me. He accompanied me from Zollenstrasse to Paris."

They all turned and looked at me, and Hilda burst out laughing.

"Brava, Barbara!" she exclaimed. "You begin well. Why, how you blush! Who is this Mr. Farquhar?"

"Yes, who *is* this Mr. Farquhar?" repeated my father, drawing himself to his full hight, and assuming his most dignified deportment. "Who *is* this Mr. Farquhar, that he should think fit to call at my house without an introduction? What did Madame Brenner know of him, that she should intrust my daughter to his care? I am not fond of these English frequenters of petty German spas."

"Mr. Farquhar is a gentleman of family and fortune," I replied; "a great traveler, and a patron of the fine arts. He was constantly in the society of the Grand Duke; and dined frequently at the Residenz, during his stay at Zollenstrasse."

"And that is all that any one knows about him, eh?"

"By no means, sir," I said, firmly. "His estates join those of Mrs. Sandyshaft; and I know every inch of Broomhill as well as I know the College in which I have been brought up."

My father coughed, and looked disconcerted.

"Is this old friend of yours a young man, Barbara?" asked my sister, satirically.

"About thirty-four."

"And tolerably well off?"

"I remember that he once gave six thousand pounds for a picture."

Mrs. Churchill and Hilda exchanged glances. My father rang the bell, and desired Bruce to fetch a certain book from a certain shelf in the little closet which they dignified by the name of the study. It was a thick volume in an old-fashioned calf binding with red edges, and my father, as he turned over the leaves, took occasion to inform us of its contents.

"This book," said he, "gives a brief account of the old county families of England. It goes wherever I go. So does the peerage, and so does the baronetage; but this, in ordinary cases, is the most useful of the three. It tells one who is who, which is no trifling advantage abroad, and——Ah! here we have it. 'Farquhar of Broomhill'—humph!—take Broomhill as a kind of title, like the Scotch lairds; very curious that! 'One of the oldest families of East Anglia.'—'possessions considerably increased during the last half century'—'present owner married to Lucy, eldest daughter of J. Clive, Esq., M. P.—rental from twelve to fourteen thousand per annum'——So, your friend is married, Barbara?"

"No, sir. I think if you look to the date——"

"True—the book has been published these twenty-five or thirty years. Then the present man is the son of this Farquhar and Lucy his wife—I see! And what do you say is his age?"

"About thirty-four, I believe."

My father looked at me thoughtfully, and clinked the money in his pockets.

"Fourteen thousand a year is no such undesirable income!" said he, more to himself than to me. "Ha!—four—teen thou—sand; and thirty-three years of age!"

Mrs. Churchill smiled, and nodded—(she had the art of implying a nod with her eyelids, which saved trouble, and looked *distingué*)—but Hilda, with a satirical laugh, repeated my father's last words.

"Fourteen thousand and thirty-three years of age would alone be a guarantee of respectability!" said she. "No occasion to look in your county book, papa, when a man is his own ancestry, and dates himself back to the Pre-Adamite world!"

My father's brow darkened. According to his creed, all jesting was undignified ; but a jest at his expense, or a play upon his words, was an offense little short of treason. Just, however, as he was about to speak, the door opened and Bruce announced—

"Monsieur the Count de Chaumont."

A tall grave man, with a conical bald head and a huge white moustache, came into the room with his hat under his arm, and one glove dangling in his hand. Any thing more stiff, polite, and diplomatic it would be impossible to conceive. He bowed profoundly to Mrs. Churchill ; he bowed profoundly to my father ; he carried Hilda's hand to his lips ; and, being introduced to me, he bowed again. This done, he sat down and said nothing, till we were summoned to the dinner-room.

The dinner passed off grimly. My father was still annoyed ; Hilda seemed out of temper with herself and every one ; and the Count, who had no conversation, stared incessantly at Hilda with his round light eyes, and adored her in silence.

After dinner, we went up to dress for the opera.

It was an event in my life, and I had been anticipating it the whole day long ; so, when Mademoiselle Juliette insisted upon dressing me in a pink silk of my sister's, with trimmings of flowers, and ribbons, and all kinds of unaccustomed fineries, I submitted with slight resistance. In one matter only I would have my will ; and that was in wearing my hair as I had always worn it, twisted plainly round a comb, and waving round my forehead in its own uncontrolled luxuriance.

At half-past eight o'clock we all went down to the theater in the Count's carriage, and the overture was just ending as we came into the box.

Mrs. Churchill and Hilda took the front seats, and I placed myself behind them, where I had a good view of the stage. The curtain rose upon a crowded scene—the first chords of a chorus broke forth at once from a couple of hundred voices—a procession of monks and soldiers came winding down a rocky pass at the back—and one singer, more richly dressed than the rest, advanced to the footlights. I could scarcely breathe, for wonder and delight ; but listened in a kind of ecstasy.

"Is this Mario ?" I asked, laying my hand on Hilda's shoulder.

"Mario ?" she repeated. "How absurd ! This is the Opera Française. Don't you hear that they are singing in French ?"

"I had not observed it. I thought it was the Italian theater. How should I know ?"

"How should you know ? Why, every one knows that the Italian season only lasts from October to March ! How stupid you are !"

I drew back, pained and surprised.

"Two months ago, Hilda," I said, "you knew as little of these matters as myself."

And so the conversation dropped. Her mood puzzled me. Last evening, when she came to my bedroom in her ball-dress, she seemed kind, and gay, and, as I then thought, more than usually affectionate ; but now——But now the novelty and splendor of the theater gave me no time for any thing but admiration ; so I dismissed the subject.

To this day I remember nothing but the bewilderment with which I gazed and listened. I can recall neither the names of the singers, nor the plot, nor the title of the piece, nor any thing but the result produced upon myself. Perhaps had I never seen any kind of theater, I should have expected more, and have been less delighted ; but I had formed my notions of the stage upon our little establishment at Zollenstrasse, and the contrast took me by surprise. These masterly effects of light and distance ; the grandeur of the grouping ; the variety of costume ; the richness and harmony of color ; and, above all, the wonderfully artistic beauty of the scenery, dazzled me on the side of pictorial illusion, and carried me out of myself. I could hardly believe that all was not real—that these moving masses of soldiers, nobles, and priests were not actual characters, swayed by actual passions, and acted upon by the very "form and pressure" of the time ! I could still less believe that these airy distances and Claude-like vales, these palace-fronts, and endless corridors, were mere daubs of paint and canvas, to be looked upon from afar. All seemed perfect, real, wonderful ; and when the curtain fell upon the first act, I felt as Ferdinand might have felt when Próspero suddenly dismissed "into thin air" his masque of spirits.

Mrs. Churchill tapped me on the cheek, and smiled benevolently.

"It is quite a luxury, my dear child," said she, "to witness your pleasure. Come now to the front of the box, and look round the house. This is the interval when every body criticises every body. What say you to the Parisian *toilettes ?*"

"I like the play much better," I replied. "Will they soon begin again ?"

"Yes—in about ten minutes. Hilda, my sweet love, who is that distinguished-looking man in the second row of stalls ? His glass has been leveled at our box for the last three minutes."

Involuntarily, I looked in the direction indicated. The gentleman lowered his glass, and bowed immediately.

"It is Mr. Farquhar," I said, with something of a childish triumph ; and returned his salutation.

"Mr. Farquhar ?" repeated my father, and Hilda, and Mrs. Churchill, in one breath. "Is that Mr. Farquhar ?"—and pressed forward to look at him.

"A very gentlemanly person, upon my word," said my father, approvingly. "Really, a very gentlemanly person."

"But excessively plain," added Hilda.

"Nay, not 'excessively,' my love," said Mrs. Churchill. "Not 'excessively' by any means. Rather a—if I may so express it—a prepossessing plainness ; and decidedly aristocratic !"

"*Mais oui—c'est un Monsieur très comme il faut,*" chimed in the Count, with a glance toward the mirror at the side of the box.

"I—ahem !—I really am of opinion," said my father, "that, considering all Mr. Farquhar's attention to Barbara, I might, with propriety, go down and express my sense of obligation in person. What do you say, Mrs. Churchill ?"

"That it would be only correct to do so ; and, Mr. Churchill, bring him here if you can !"

So my father took his hat, and went down,

and we saw him presently in conversation with that very Mr. Farquhar who had "thought fit" to call at his house without an introduction. So much for position, and a rental of twelve or fourteen thousand per annum! In the course of a few minutes they left the stalls and came up to our box; where Hugh Farquhar was formally introduced.

"Delighted, I am sure," murmured Mrs. Churchill, with the most benignant smile. "Gentleman of Mr. Farquhar's position and taste—kind attentions to our darling girl—charmed with the opportunity of expressing our gratitude. Barbara, my love—a seat for Mr. Farquhar!"

"I think," said he, "that I have had the pleasure of seeing Mrs. Churchill before."

Mrs. Churchill suspended the dexterous flutter of her fan, and expressed interrogation with her eyebrows.

"At Homburg," replied Hugh, "if I remember rightly; about four years ago."

"I did once visit Homburg in the spring," hesitated Mrs. Churchill, "and it was probably about that time; but I am ashamed to confess that——"

"Oh, Madam, I did not imply that I had had the honor of an introduction! There are persons whom to see is to remember."

Mrs. Churchill bowed, and tried to look as if she blushed. Her good opinion was won forever. Hugh turned to me as the curtain rose, and withdrew to the back of the box.

"Why, Barbarina," he said, "you are transformed to-night! Where is the Jenny Wren dress? I seem scarcely to know you in any other."

"I scarcely know myself, Mr. Farquhar," I replied. "I like my brown feathers better than all this gay plumage."

"So do I—and yet, somehow, it pleases me to see you thus. It looks young and bright; and heaven knows that you are young and bright enough! Never so bright, I fancy, as to-night."

"That is because I have been so much excited."

"By the music?"

"No—strangely enough; not so much by the music, as by the grandeur of the scenes and costumes. I can not describe to you how these have affected me. Each time the curtain rises, I feel as if a window were opened into fairy land!"

"That is because your artistic perceptions are more highly educated than your ear. Your sense of color, of form, of composition, is being perpetually gratified; and each scene presents you with a gallery of living pictures. For my part, I am more influenced by the music; and yet I love art almost as well as you love it. How do you account for that?"

"Easily enough. Your tastes are variously cultivated, and your judgment is matured. Amid many things, you know how to choose the best, and, having chosen, accept the rest as adjuncts."

"Excellently reasoned!" exclaimed Hugh; "and truly reasoned, too. How is it that you are so good a logician?"

"I am no logician, Mr. Farquhar. How should I be?"

"Nay, how should you not be, being an artist? It is the power of rightly seeing Nature that makes the painter; and to see rightly with the eyes of the body, is surely but a stepping-stone to seeing rightly with the eyes of the mind."

"I am not so sure of that," I replied laughingly. "Between a landscape and a proposition there is a considerable difference. But the scene changes—oh, how lovely! See, the light absolutely flickers on that water—the gondola casts a reflection that moves with it—the moon goes behind a cloud! Can this be art?"

"Not high art, certainly," replied Hugh.

"Because it is higher than art! It is nature herself! Oh, Mr. Farquhar, I feel as if I should never care to paint again, after this!"

"You are a foolish child, and know not what you say," said he, impatiently. "I tell you this is not pure art—nay, it is but one third art, and two-thirds machinery. This ripple is produced by moving lights behind the canvas, and that moon is made of muslin and gas! All that you see here is imitation; and art does not imitate—it interprets."

"Hush—do not destroy the illusion!"

"I am willing to leave you the illusion, Barbarina; but I can not suffer you to mistake illusion for art."

"Suffer me, then, to mistake it for nature."

"Worse again! Learn to accept it for what it is. Accept it as an ingenious and beautiful background to a fine story; and remember that mock moons and practicable waves bear to true painting the same relation that wax-modeling bears to sculpture. But silence for a moment. I want you to hear this *duo*."

I leaned back, and listened. The audience was profoundly silent, and a semi-darkness prevailed in every part of the theater. In the orchestra only a single harp was heard, and to this accompaniment the two voices rose and fell, mingled and parted, threaded all the involutions of harmony and all the mazes of passion, and died away at last, tremblingly, throbbingly, wearily—like a whirlwind wasted of its fury, or a heart of its desire!

Then came a moment of intense suspense, and then, before the last vibration seemed quite to have faded from the air, a storm of applause that shook the very chandeliers above our heads!

"Well, Barbara," murmured Hugh, bending so low that I felt his breath upon my shoulder; "is this true art, think you? But, child, you are weeping!"

I raised my hand to my cheek, and found it wet with tears.

"I did not know it," I faltered. "It was so wild and sad, that——"

"That,' like Jessica, you are 'never merry when you hear sweet music!' Tender little heart! it is as susceptible to all the influences of feeling, as a flower to the changes of the sky!"

There was a strange, caressing gentleness in his voice, as he said this, which brought my color back and made me tremble. Involuntarily, I looked up to see if any one were listening; but my father was gone; the Count de Chaumont was talking in an undertone to Hilda; and Mrs. Churchill's eyes were discreetly fixed upon the stage.

"I did not think to see you here to-night, Barbara," he continued — "still less to be so near you."

"I am very glad—it was so good of you to come up. You had a much better place in the stalls."

"That is a matter of opinion, *carina*. I have the bad taste to prefer this. But, tell me, were you up this morning when I called?"

"Yes; but I never heard of your visit till many hours after. Papa thought at first that you left your card for Hilda."

"Cupid and the Count forbid! *Mais, dites donc*, how do you fancy your future brother-in-law?"

I sighed, and shook my head.

"Yes," he said, "it is a sacrifice.

'Crabbed age and youth
Can not live together.'

I never could understand the loves of Goethe and Bettina! Your father, by the way, is polite enough to invite me to the wedding; and also to dine with him to-morrow."

"And you will come?"

"To-morrow—yes."

"And to the wedding?"

"If I can; but I may be far, far hence, ere then; where no echoes of marriage bells can follow me!"

"So soon, Mr. Farquhar?"

"So late, you mean! There, let us say no more of it. I am not yet gone."

"But you are going!"

"I am going — yes, I am going, 'sith I have cause and will, and strength, and means to do it.' Strength, do I say? Pshaw! the words are not mine, but Hamlet's!"

Startled by the vehemence of his manner, I drew back and looked at him; but he turned his face quickly away, and said no more. Just at this moment the curtain fell again, and he took the opportunity to leave us. As he made his adieux, I saw that he looked pale and disturbed; but no one else observed it. Mrs. Churchill gave him her hand.

"Then to-morrow, at seven o'clock, Mr. Farquhar," said she, "we may expect to be indulged with the pleasure of your society?"

"To-morrow at seven, Madam, the indulgence will be yours—the pleasure mine."

Saying this, he bowed over her hand, as though it had been the hand of an Empress, and touched it with his lips. To Hilda he bowed also, but more distantly, and from me he parted silently, with a warm pressure of the hand.

"My dear Barbara," sighed Mrs. Churchill, as the door closed behind him, "that is the most elegant, the most aristocratic, the most gentlemanly man I have met for many a season! I am not given to sudden prepossessions—far from it!—but I protest that with Mr. Farquhar I am positively fascinated!"

"*Mais oui*," repeated the Count. "*C'est un Monsieur très comme il faut*."

"Quite the tone of high society!" said Mrs. Churchill.

"*Tout-à-fait*," replied the Count sententiously.

"And evidently a person of education and judgment. But, my darling Hilda, you say nothing?"

"Because I have nothing to say," retorted my sister, with a scornful smile. "Your *rara avis* appears to me to be a very ordinary biped."

Mrs. Churchill's color rose. She leaned back, toyed with her glass, and said, in her most measured accents—

"Your mistake, my love, arises from ignorance of the world. You have yet much to learn; but you are improving."

Hilda bit her lip, and turned to the stage with an impatient gesture; the Count looked puzzled; and Mrs. Churchill smiled in the calm consciousness of victory.

As for me, I scarcely heeded their conversation. My eyes were fixed upon Mr. Farquhar's vacant stall; but he occupied it no more that night.

———

CHAPTER XXXI.

DOMESTIC DETAILS.

"WE are appreciated," writes a cynic, "not for what we are, but for what others think of us."

And my belief in that maxim dates from the time when Hugh Farquhar became known to my family. They respected him on account of his position; they liked him because he was pleased to exert himself to make them do so; and the result of all this was that I came in for some share of their good opinion. He was attentive to me; and they became considerate. He loved to talk with me; and therefore they began to suppose that I might have some kind of cleverness. He praised me; and they discovered that I was amiable. In a few days my position at home was radically changed. I found myself listened to, consulted, placed on an equal footing with Hilda, and in all respects treated as it was pleasant to be treated. The morning after we had been to the theater, my father called me into his "study," and gave me a check for six hundred francs, intimating that I was to use that sum for my present necessities, that I should have more in the course of a couple of days, and that I was to be sure and make "as good an appearance" as my sister. Mrs. Churchill, not to be outdone in generosity, presented me with a bracelet of mosaic-work, and devoted one whole morning to accompany me in my shopping—on which occasion, however, I persisted, to her great dismay, in preferring a plain brown silk of rich quality, to all the delicate light fabrics which were put before me. In vain she argued that it looked too sober, and old, and somber for my wearing. I was determined to adhere to my "Jenny Wren" colors, at all events on ordinary occasions, and only consented to purchase lighter materials for the wedding, on condition that I retained the one dress in which I knew *he* would prefer to see me.

Altogether, I was much happier in my home relations than I had ever been before; I should have been happier still, but for the daily and increasing coldness with which Hilda treated me. Communicative and pleasant on the night of my arrival, she was now fretful, impatient, and reserved. Nothing that I did was right—nothing that I said pleased her. She could scarcely hear Hugh Farquhar's name without some sarcastic or depreciatory remark. One might almost have believed that she hated him for being my friend, and me for the consideration with which he treated me. As for the renovation of my wardrobe, and my father's recommendation to make as "good an appearance" as herself, she laughed it to scorn, and protested that it was the most ridiculous arrangement she had heard in her life. Considering that she was to be married within a week, and that none of these domestic trifles could be of import to her in her new sphere, I thought her remarks on this head singularly illiberal. Even the poor Count received his share of her displeasure, and led, at this time, the most miserable life in the world. She quarreled with him continually; if quarreling it can be called, where on one side all is tyranny, and on the other all submission. I even fancied, more than once, that she had conceived some strange and sudden dislike to him, and would fain have got rid of him if she could!

In the mean time the days went by, and the eventful one drew nearer. The breakfast was ordered from Tortoni's—the passports of M. le Comte and Madame la Comtesse de Chaumont were made out for Norway. The light traveling-carriage which was to accompany them for their use in a country where railroads and comfortable post-chaises were unknown, had been brought round for Hilda's inspection, and dismissed with approval. The guests were invited to the number of forty in the morning, and one hundred in the evening. And, above all, Sir Agamemnon Churchill — he whose glory had been the tradition of our childhood; whose portrait (as the knave of clubs) hung in the place of honor in our London home; whose position as a knight, a herald, and an archæologist placed him at the head of all that now remained of our branch of the great Marlborough family — Sir Agamemnon Churchill himself, was coming, in his own august person, to grace our wedding feast, and give the bride away!

And all this time Hugh Farquhar came and went as he pleased, and became our frequent guest. He talked politics and the wars of Queen Anne with my father. He was gallant to Mrs. Churchill. He was polite and stately with the Count. Sometimes I fancied that he knew how his friendship had led them to be kinder to me —at all events I heard no more about St. Petersburgh!

CHAPTER XXXII.

IN THE FOREST OF VINCENNES.

It was the morning of Hilda's wedding day. The bride was dressed; the carriages were at the door; the guests were assembled; and we only waited for Sir Agamemnon Churchill. A messenger from Meurice's had brought word of his arrival late the night before; and as it had been arranged that Hilda was not to make her appearance till he came, she and I remained up-stairs listening to the echo of every passing wheel. Now and then one of the bridesmaids came up, or we heard my father's impatient voice upon the landing; and still we waited, and still the great man of the family kept us in suspense.

Hilda looked ill and agitated; but haughtily

beautiful as ever. She had scarcely slept at all the night before. I had heard her in her room, and seen the light under her door long hours after midnight; but deterred by her coldness, had not ventured to intrude on her privacy.

Now, white and silent, with her hands locked fast together, she stood before the glass, seeming to look at her own image, but seeing only vacancy. Thus the last anxious quarter of an hour ebbed slowly away; and then, at the very moment when to have delayed longer would have been impossible, a carriage dashed up to the door, and a servant came running breathlessly to tell us that "Sir Agamemnon was come!"

Finding my sister still unmoved, I went over and repeated the message.

"Sir Agamemnon is here," I said. "We must go down."

She started, and, as it were mechanically, took her gloves and bouquet from the table.

"And it is very late," I added.

"Late indeed," she echoed, drearily. "Too late!" and moved toward the door. At the threshold she paused, stooped forward all at once, and kissed me.

"Sister," she said, hurriedly, "forgive me! I have not been kind; but my life has been a hell this past week! I have hated myself and all the world!"

"Oh, Hilda!"

"Yes—I see it all now; but it is too late—too late! Your future is bright, Barbara. You love each other—you will be very happy. My future is dark enough—God help me!"

And with this she drew her vail about her face, and went down-stairs.

I followed her, with her last words echoing in my ears, and my heart beating painfully. The first face I saw as I went into the room was Mr. Farquhar's. He was standing just inside the door, and, as I came in, put out both his hands, and smiled joyously.

"Eccolà!" he said, surveying me from head to foot. "Why, what a dainty, coquettish, charming little Barbara it is to-day! Quite a dangerous Barbara, I vow! But why so pale and nervous, petite? Your hands tremble—you are not well! Is any thing wrong?"

I shook my head—I dared not look at him, remembering the words that Hilda had just spoken.

"Nothing is wrong," I said, and turned hastily away—too hastily as I fancied; for when I had threaded my way half-across the room, I turned, and saw him following me with his eyes, so gravely, so inquiringly, that had I known how to say it, I should have gone back and asked his pardon. As it was, our eyes met just as my father took me by the hand and said:

"My second daughter, Sir Agamemnon. Barbara, make Sir Agamemnon Churchill welcome to Paris."

A shrunken, under-sized, dissipated-looking old beau of the Prince Regent type, was my illustrious kinsman; with little, bold, bloodshot eyes, and a flushed face, and a withered double chin buried behind a huge white satin cravat sprigged with gold. He had been a 'ladies' man,' a 'buck,' and a leader of the 'ton,' some five and forty years ago; and now, wigged, laced, padded, scented, dyed, and 'used-up,' he clung fondly to the traditions of his youth and his 'bonnes fortunes.' He tied his neckcloth in the Brummel bow, and wore three inside waistcoats and a mulberry coat with a velvet collar as high as his ears. In short, he looked as if he might just have stepped out from the Pavilion at Brighton, or have come straight from a breakfast at Carlton House!

Courtesying, I murmured something, I scarcely know what; but he interrupted me by kissing first my hand, and then my cheek, and protesting that he was "devilish glad" to see me, and that "a fellow might be devilish proud of two such pretty cousins—begad!"

One wedding is just like another, and the only respect in which this differed from most lay in the fact that it was celebrated in two churches, in two languages, and in two religions. Nobody shed tears, for we were late and had no time for sentiment. As it was, we dashed through the streets at a pace better becoming an elopement than a wedding, and overturned a flower-stall at the corner of the Place de la Madeleine. Then the bride and bridegroom drove back alone in the Count's carriage, and we, having quite lost the order of going, followed as we pleased, taking whatever vehicles and companions we could get. Thus it happened that Mr. Farquhar found his way to the bridesmaids' carriage, and came back in the seat beside my own.

Then came the congratulations, the breakfast, the champagne, and the speeches — most notable of all, that speech of Sir Agamemnon Churchill's, in which he brought a very rambling oration to a close by saying that he had that morning performed the most disagreeable task he had ever undertaken in his life:—

"For, ladies and gentlemen," said he, looking round to enjoy the surprise with which this observation was received, and nursing his final joke till the last moment, "when I came to give the bride away, begad! I was devilish sorry I couldn't keep her myself!"

Which delicate and ingenious witticism was greeted with immense applause (as well by the foreigners who didn't understand it, as by the English who did) and covered Sir Agamemnon with glory.

Then the Count de Chaumont, in three or four very brief and solemn sentences, returned thanks for himself and his bride; and then, my father, with a great deal of self-possession and dignity, made a speech full of point and emphasis, which threw all the rest into the shade, and produced the great effect of the day. After this the ladies withdrew, and Hilda went up to change her dress for the journey.

Her pallor, her agitation, her despair, were all gone now; but her cheek was flushed, and her eye strangely bright and restless. In vain I looked for any trace of the emotion which had so startled me a few hours back. Not a glance, not a tone, betrayed that she even remembered it. Thus she dressed and went down in all the splendor of her proud beauty. Thus she embraced us, was handed into her carriage by the husband of her choice, and drove away. The game was played out. The stakes were won. She was Madame la Comtesse de Chaumont!

After this, the guests mostly dispersed — some to their avocations, and some to amuse themselves, till it became time to dress for the even-ing party. My father and Sir Agamemnon, and three or four of the elder men, chiefly members of my father's club, went out to play at billiards or stroll in the Champ Elysées. Mrs. Churchill, whose delicate nervous system was supposed to be overwrought by the morning's excitement, retired to her room, and had a sound sleep on the sofa; whilst we three bridesmaids, Hugh Farquhar, a pretty widow named Julie de Luneville, the Count de Charlot, Monsieur de Fauval, and some three or four other young men, all of whom were frequent guests at Mrs. Churchill's receptions, drove over to Vincennes. When we reached the forest, we left our vehicles at a certain spot, and alighted. It was now between three and four o'clock, and the slanting light came goldenly through the trees, and lay in broad patches on the open glades. The place was very quiet and lovely, and we sat on the fragrant grass under the shade of oaks as old as the faraway towers of Nôtre Dame. Here the young men lit their cigars, and the ladies took off their bonnets; and some flirted, and some ate bonbons, and we were all as sociable as if we had known each other from childhood. As for Hugh Farquhar, I had never before seen him give such play to his exuberant animal spirits. He jested; told stories; talked as readily in French as in English, and in German as in either; and was the very life of the party. Buoyant, almost boyish, in his gayety, he seemed as if he had that morning drunk of the Elixir of Life.

My recollection of the general conversation as we sat there on the grass, like a group by Watteau, is now somewhat confused and fragmentary; but we had been talking, I think, of park and forest scenery, and Hugh had been telling us something of his wild wanderings in South-America.

"It always seems to me," said he, as he lay reclining on his elbow, "that a forest is a school of etiquette, and that nothing could be more natural than for Hazlitt to take off his hat to a certain majestic oak whenever he passed it, as he tells us somewhere in his Essays. See the great elms, how polite they are! How they bow their plumed heads, and stretch out their stately arms to one another! For my part, I never enter a forest without feeling at once that I am moving in the best society."

They smiled at this; and some one observed that "it was a pity the trees limited their courtesies to their own circles."

"How agreeable it would be, for instance," said Monsieur de Fauval, a dramatic author and feuilletoniste, "if some of the more hospitable among our present hosts would unpack their trunks just now, and oblige us with a few ices and a dozen cups of coffee!"

"Or if the woodpecker would make himself useful, and tap us some good old Burgundy from his 'hollow beech tree!'" added Hugh. "But whom have we here? A Jongleur of the olden time?"

"Say, rather, an Orpheus of shreds and patches!"

It was a wandering musician, with a guitar slung over his shoulder. Seeing our carriages before the gates, he had sought us out through the pathways of the forest. Timidly, he took off his battered cap, and passed his fingers over the strings of his instrument.

" *Chantez donc !*" said one of the young men, tossing him a franc for encouragement.

He looked up, bowed, preluded a few chords, and sang, with a slightly foreign accent, three or four verses of a plaintive ballad, the refrain of which was always —

" Flle, flle, pauvre Marie,
    Pour secourir le prisonnier ;
Flle, flle, pauvre Marie, -
    Flle, flle, pour le prisonnier !"

The guitar was cracked; but the song had truth of feeling, and the singer, voice and sentiment. After he had finished, we were silent.

Then somebody signed to him to continue, and he sang a little rhyming Biscayan romance about a fisherman and a phantom ship — a mere story to a fragmentary chant; but wild as the winds, and melancholy as the moaning of the sea.

When he had done, Mr. Farquhar beckoned to him to come nearer.

"Your music is of the saddest, friend," said he. "Can you sing nothing gay ?"

The man shook his head.

" *Monsieur,*" he replied, "*je ne suis pas gai.*"

The answer provoked our curiosity, and we urged him to tell us his history; but we urged in vain.

"I have nothing to ' tell," he said. "I am poor, and a wanderer."

" But are you French ?" asked one.

"I do not come from these parts," he replied, equivocally. " *Bonjour, Messieurs et Mesdames.*"

He was going ; but Mr. Farquhar stopped him. "Stay, *mon ami,*" said he. "I have a fancy to try your guitar."

The musician unslung and handed it to him, with an apologetic shrug.

"It is not good," he remonstrated humbly.

"Nay, it has seen honorable service," said Hugh, "and has been excellent. It was made, I see, in Naples."

The man looked down, and made no reply.

"Sing something, Mr. Farquhar!" cried three or four together.

He smiled, and ran his fingers over the strings with a touch that evoked more tone than one could have expected from so poor an instrument.

" What shall I sing ?" said he.

Some asked for one thing; some for another. I who had never dreamt till this moment that he had any musical knowledge, remained silent.

" *Eh bien !*" he exclaimed. "I will give you a Spanish *ballata* — something very savage about a bull-fight. It is supposed to be sung by a girl who is sitting among the spectators, and whose lover is a matador in the arena. You will hear how she cries to him to kill the bull, ' *por l'amor de Dios !*'"

And with this he struck the strings with the side of his hand, producing a strange barbaric jangle, and broke out into the wildest rush of words and notes that I had ever heard in my life. Well might he call it " something savage !" It made my heart throb, and my blood run cold, and, which is more, produced some such effect on the rest ; for, when it was over, we looked in each other's faces, and drew a long breath of relief.

" *Mais, mon Dieu !* Monsieur Farquhar," said Madame de Luneville, " do you wish us all to be afraid of you ? Where, in Heaven's name, did you learn that diabolical song ?"

"In Madrid," replied he, laughingly, " where it is as popular in the most refined *salons* as in the lowest *posadas.* My teacher was an Andalusian water-carrier, who, after plying his trade all day long in the Puerta del Sol, used ' to sing songs o' nights,' sitting on the steps of a public fountain, and surrounded by all the ragamuffins of the quarter."

"How picturesque !" I exclaimed ; for the whole group came at once before my eyes.

"Yes ; it was an animated Murillo. But, since I have shocked you with my savage performance, I will soothe you with something sweet and sentimental."

Whereupon he modulated through a succession of keys, and, to a soft *arpeggio* accompaniment, sang, with infinite tenderness and passion, the following

SERENADE.*

" The winds are all hushed, and the moon is high,
    Like a queen on her silver throne !
Tranquil and dusk the woodlands lie ;
Scarcely a cloud sails over the sky ;
None are awake, save the stars and I—
    Sleepest thou still, mine own ?

" The song of the nightingale stirs the air,
    And the breath of the brier is blown !
Come forth in thy beauty beyond compare ;
I'll clasp thee close, and I'll call thee fair ;
. And I'll kiss off the dew from thy golden hair—
    Sleepest thou still, mine own ?"

Again there was a long-drawn breath when he had ended, but this time it was a breath of approbation. Monsieur de Fauval was the first to speak.

"That song," said he, "breathes the very soul of passion. Whose is it ? Where can it be purchased ?"

"It can not be purchased at all," replied Hugh, smiling. "It is an unpublished manuscript."

"And the author ?"

"Unknown." ،

"Unknown !" repeated Madame de Luneville. "But you are in the secret ?"

"Of course I am, or else how should I have known it ? But enough of *al fresco* music. The grass is already getting damp, and we must not suffer these ladies to take cold. Many thanks, friend, for the use of your instrument."

And with this he returned the guitar to its owner, and took out a handful of loose silver.

The musician drew back.

"Thanks, Monsieur," he said. "I am already sufficiently paid."

"Nay—for the loan of the guitar."

The stranger drew himself up, and with a gesture full of dignity, again refused.

"My guitar," said he, " is not only my *gagnepain ;* but my friend. Monsieur did me the honor to borrow it."

Hugh rose from his half-recumbent attitude.

"In that case," he said, courteously, "I wish you *bon voyage.*"

The stranger murmured something of which we lost the purport ; and, with one low, comprehensive bow, slung his guitar once more across his back, and turned away. At the bend of the path, he paused, looked back and then disappeared among the trees.

"There is something odd about that man !"

* The words of this song are copy-right, and have been set to music by Mr. J. F. Duggan.

said the Count de Charlot. "I would give a hundred francs to know his story."

"If you gave a thousand, he would not tell it," said De Fauval. "I believe that he is an escaped convict from Toulon or Brest."

"And I, that he is a political exile," said Madame de Luneville.

"He certainly is not a Frenchman," observed another. "Did you notice how he evaded the question, when he was asked his country?"

"Yes—and how silent he was when Mr. Farquhar examined his guitar!"

"Poor fellow!" said Hugh. "He is no common adventurer; and by his accent, I should say he is Italian. He refused my little *obolus* with an almost Roman dignity. But what is your opinion, Barbarina?"

"Indeed I scarcely know," I replied. "The expression of his eyes struck me painfully. I feel sorry for him, and—but you will laugh at me, if I tell you that!"

"No—I promise not to laugh. Pray tell me."

"Well, then, I feel as if—as if the sight of him were unlucky—as if—I scarcely know what I mean, or how to say it; but as if he brought some shadow of trouble with him! Do you understand me?"

"Perfectly; and think I can account for it, too. We were very gay when he came and sobered us. Those sobering processes are not pleasant. The time has gone by when a skeleton was looked upon as an agreeable addition to a dinner-party. But we may as well talk of something more agreeable!"

He had given me his arm, and we were now strolling, two and two, in the direction of the gates. Being somewhat in the rear of the rest, we had our conversation quite to ourselves, and could chat without reserve.

"With all my heart," I replied, smiling. "Of your singing for instance. I never knew that you were a musician before; and still less that you were a poet!"

"A poet!" he repeated. "What do you mean?"

"Simply that your unknown author, Mr. Farquhar, has no *incognito* for me. That Serenade is yours."

"In the name of St. Ursula and her eleven thousand virgins! how could you tell that?"

"Nay, I am not wise enough to analyze my impressions! I only know that I recognized you in the verses—should have even known them to be yours, had any other person read or sung them to me."

He came to a sudden halt, and laid his hand heavily upon my shoulder.

"Barbara," he said, in a low vibrating tone, scarce louder than a whisper. "What can *you* recognize of the *Ego* in that song? What experience have *you* of any power of passion that may be in me? You neither know how I can love, nor how I can hate. I am a sealed book to you."

Was he a sealed book to me? I began to doubt it.

"You are silent," he said, and I felt that he was looking at me. "You are silent; and I dare not interpret that silence, lest I deceive myself. Is it possible that you know me too well? Is it possible that your eyes have read that page which I had vowed they should never read,

though to blot it out were to erase the fairest passage from my life? Speak child; for I must know!"

"I—I have read nothing—I know nothing," I stammered. "I never wish to know any thing that you do not choose to tell me! Pray do not be angry with me, Mr. Farquhar!"

"Angry!" he echoed. "Angry, my darling?"

His voice, as he spoke these words, took an accent so sweet and tender that I looked up and smiled involuntarily, like a child forgiven.

He passed his arm about my waist, and drew me gently toward him.

"We have misunderstood each other, Barbara mia," he said, soothingly. "Nothing was farther from my mood, heaven knows! than to pain or terrify you. It was not anger, but—but, child, can you not understand that there might be something—something written down in that same book of my soul, which I would not place before you for a kingdom; and yet—if you guessed it——Am I talking enigmas?"

Saying this, he held me still more closely, and looked down into my eyes with such a burning light in his that I could not meet them.

"I—yes—you bewilder me," I faltered. "See —we are left quite behind! Let us go on."

"Yes, let us go on," he repeated; but, instead of going on, bent down, and pressed his lips upon my forehead.

For a moment I rested in his arms, willingly, wearily, and allowed my eyes to close, and my cheek to lean against the beatings of his heart. Only for a moment; and yet in that moment, the sense of the mystery grew clear to me, and life began in earnest!

Then he suffered me to disengage myself from his embrace, and we went on our way without another word.

The rest of that walk, the drive back to Paris, the ball that followed in the evening, all passed over me like a dream. I remember nothing of the incident, nothing of the conversations that took place. I only know that he was there; that he danced with me; that he looked at me; that he held my hand many times in his; and that once during the evening he praised my looks, and the fashion of my hair, and told me I was like some picture of Jephtha's daughter that he had seen abroad. And then, when it was all over, and the guests were gone, and I had gained the solitude of my own room, I was happy—so happy, that I threw open my window and leaned out into the cool night, and wept for joy!

And then I thought of Hilda, and my heart bled for her. I had pitied her in the morning; but I now pitied her far more. A whole world of feeling had been revealed to me since then. I had passed in a few hours from childhood to womanhood; and now, measuring her loss by my sweet gain, shuddered at the life to which she had condemned herself.

And all this time I never paused to reason on my own feelings or my possible future. I never once asked myself "what next?" or wondered at aught that had hitherto been ambiguous and strange in the tenor of our intercourse. It was enough happiness to love and be loved—and enough knowledge, also!

———◆———

CHAPTER XXXIII.

THE NEXT MORNING.

Mr. Farquhar called the next morning, about noon. My father had gone to see Sir Agamemnon off by the midday train, and Mrs. Churchill was reclining on a sofa, absorbed in a novel by George Sand. When our visitor came in, she laid her book aside, welcomed him graciously, and assigned him a seat beside her sofa. To me he gave only a glance, and a pressure of the hand.

First they talked of the wedding, the ball, the *belles toilettes*, and such other matters. Then the conversation fell upon Norway, and they traced out Hilda's route upon the map, and calculated the probable whereabouts of the bridal pair at that present moment. In all this I took no part, but sat by silently, content to listen to his voice. I had been sketching a little subject in Mrs. Churchill's album, and I endeavored still to seem occupied upon it; but my hand grew unsteady, and my attention wandered. By and by Mrs. Churchill left the room on some trivial pretext, smiling as she passed me; and I suddenly remembered that she had done the same thing once or twice before. The blood rushed to my face, and, half in shame and half in anger, I rose to follow her.

He was at my side in an instant.

"Whither away, my child?" he said. "Are you afraid of me to-day?"

I murmured something unintelligible — I scarcely know what — but passively resumed my seat. He stooped over the back of the chair, and looked at my half-finished sketch.

"What have we here?" he exclaimed. "A fountain and a group of beggars—one stalwart figure high above the rest—a mandolin in his hand—a pair of buckets at his feet——*Per Bacco!* 'tis my Andalusian water-carrier of the Puerta del Sol! Whose album is this?"

"Mrs. Churchill's."

"Then Mrs. Churchill must resign the water-carrier in my favor. Nonsense, child! I have half a right to him already. He is the creature of my experience."

"But he is also the creature of my imagination," I remonstrated, seeing him take his penknife from his pocket; "and as such I have already given him away."

"A reason the more why I should have him! I mean to take possession of your imagination, your heart, your past, your future, and all that is yours! So! when Madame *la belle mère* comes to examine her album, she will wonder what conjurer has been at work upon it."

And with this he very deliberately and dexterously cut the page away, and put the drawing in his pocket-book.

"Indeed, Mr. Farquhar," I said reproachfully, "this is not fair. What shall I say to Mrs. Churchill?"

"Nothing whatever. I engage to make it right with her myself. You look tired, Barbara *mia!*"

"I am tired," I replied. "I have been out with Mrs. Churchill all the morning."

"And slept too little last night!"

"Nay, it was not a very late party. They were all gone by one o'clock."

"True; but you were not in bed till after three."

"How should you know?" I exclaimed, startled into involuntary confession.

"Ah, that is my secret. Guess it if you can."

"How should I guess it, unless you possess a magic mirror, or Doctor Dee's crystal, or travel over Paris at night, like the Devil on two Sticks!"

"Neither of the three, *carina*. What will you give me if I tell you?"

I smiled, and shook my head. I was painfully nervous; and, strive as I would, could not control the changing of my color, or the trembling of my hand.

"Will you give me this curl of brown hair?"

"No; for it is the most unlucky of gifts."

"My child, you are superstitious. However, I am not difficult. Give me this little golden cross from round your neck, and I will promise to kneel to it every night before I sleep, and every morning when I rise, like the best of Catholics!"

"No, for the cross was Ida's, and I have promised to keep it for her sake. Besides, you should kneel to better purpose."

"Ay—to yourself. Well, give me yourself, and I will lie forever at your feet!"

"Tell me without asking to be paid at all," I stammered. "It would be far more generous."

"But I am not generous! I am jealous, exorbitant, insatiable—a very Shylock at a bargain! Well, well, Barbarina, since you are so hopelessly mean, give me what you will; or give me nothing. I will tell you all the same!"

"I have already given you the sketch, Mr. Farquhar."

"Given me the sketch! Hear that, oh Gods of Olympus! Why, you have no conscience, Barbara, if you call that a gift! I stole it—'tis 'the captive of my bow and spear,' and I owe you no thanks in the matter. Come, I will make you a present of my information, and leave you to reward me as you will. I know that you were not asleep till three o'clock this morning, because it was not till three o'clock that you extinguished your candle. Now, if you want to be told whence I obtained that knowledge, we will begin bargaining over again!"

"Indeed, we will do no such thing. I believe it is but a chance guess, after all!"

"A chance guess! Alas! shall I confess to a piece of arrant folly?"

"Nay, I am not your father confessor."

"No matter — supposing now — supposing that I, 'potent, grave, and reverend signor' as I am, had actually been romantic enough to linger last night, like Romeo, in the shade of yonder trees, watching that little taper light of yours for two mortal hours—what then?"

What then, indeed! I felt my lip quiver, and dared not trust my voice with words! The whole tone of this conversation, half jesting, half passionate, was inexpressibly trying. I felt as if I would have given the world to escape.

All at once he rose, and stood before me.

"Little Barbara," he said, earnestly, "let us trifle no more. I am a conceited monster — granted. And I am as unworthy as I am conceited—granted again. But, when I saw that light burning in your window — when once I even fancied that I saw the very flutter of your drapery—I had the vanity, the stupid, ignorant vanity, to believe that you were wakeful for my sake—just as I was wakeful for yours. I was wrong. I know I was wrong—and yet I shall not be quite at rest until I have my answer from yourself. Give it to me in a single word, a single look, and let me go!"

I felt my color rise and then ebb quite away; and still I spoke not. He bent over me, lower and lower.

"What! silent, Barbara? Have you no word of banishment for me?"

I shook my head.

"Why should I banish you?" I faltered.

"Why should I banish you, when your presence makes my happiness?"

With a sort of wild sob, he fell down before me, and covered my hands with kisses.

"My darling! my darling!" he cried, "can you really love me?"

"I have loved you," I whispered, "ever since I was a little child. Do you remember our last meeting in the woods?"

"I remember it," he said, softly.

"I have cherished the ring ever since. It was too big for me then—it is too big for me still. Do you remember it?"

"Yes," he repeated, in the same low tone. "I remember it."

We were silent for some moments.

"How much has happened," I said, "since then! I never thought to see you again."

"And now you really love me? You are sure—sure you love me, Barbara?"

"Quite sure," I replied, laying my hand timidly upon his brow. "Quite sure, Hugh—and quite happy."

He shuddered, and buried his face in my lap.

"Happy!" he echoed. "Happy!—oh, my God!"

"What do you mean?" I faltered. "Are you not happy?"

"I—I happy?" he cried, hoarsely. "I am utterly miserable—I hate myself! Oh, Barbara, tell me that you love me no longer, and let me go!"

"That is the second time that you have bade me send you from me!" I said, becoming greatly agitated. "The second time within a few moments! What do you mean? You are free to go—you were free never to have come! Why can not my affection make you happy? If it be fault of mine, I will amend it; but do not torture me with vague fears, or tell me that you are miserable. If you love me, why desire to leave me? If you do not love me, why come here to humble my pride, and wrest from me an avowal——"

"I do love you!" he sobbed. "I love you better than earth or heaven!"

His anguish disarmed me.

"Oh, Hugh," I said, "your love is the blessing of my life!"

He sprang to his feet, and turned upon me a face so haggard and disfigured that it seemed scarcely the same.

"But it is the curse—the curse of mine!" he exclaimed bitterly, and, with wavering steps, turned toward the door. About half-way he paused, ran back, caught me in a wild embrace, and was gone in an instant.

Terrified, half-fainting, sick at heart, I followed him to the landing, and heard the echo of the closing door—then sat down on the stairs and wondered why I could not weep, or whether I were dreaming?

"I shall never see him again," I said to myself. "I shall never, never see him again!"

CHAPTER XXXIV.

BEFORE BREAKFAST.

THREE days went by, and I neither saw nor heard any thing of him. I believed that he was gone forever, and so gave myself quite up to a passive despair which I can not now recall without a shudder. I seemed to live "'twixt asleep and awake," and, on the plea of some minor indisposition, kept chiefly in the solitude of my chamber. There I lay for hours at a time, with closed eyes and clasped hands, scarcely moving, scarcely breathing, scarcely conscious of living, save for the dull weight upon my heart, and the perpetual throbbing at my temples. All my thought was but of the one theme — *he was gone!*

I never once asked myself whether he was gone. I never once hoped that he would come back. I simply said—"it is over."

On the evening of the third day, I made up my mind that I would return to Zollenstrasse. This resolution did me good, and gave me temporary strength. I thought of Ida; and I endeavored to persuade myself that while art and friendship remained to me, all was not wholly dark in life. I did not really believe in my own reasoning, and I was not really comforted by it. Like all who mourn, I had a conviction that the present shadow must lie upon my soul forever; but still the mere contemplation of action brought with it something like the relief of change. That night I slept for several hours, and on the morning of the fourth day rose, still weak and pale, but resolved to carry out my design, and to acquaint my father of it without delay.

"If I can but start this evening!" I kept repeating to myself. "If they will but let me go without torturing me with questions!" The questioning was all I dreaded.

Having awoke early, and dressed with all the haste of this project on my mind, I found that it yet wanted an hour and a half to our usual breakfast time, and that none but the servants were stirring. An unconquerable restlessness had taken possession of me, and, in my present mood, inaction was no longer possible. What was I to do for an hour and a half? The morning was cool and bright, and the trees rustled pleasantly in the breeze. I fancied the air would brace my nerves for all that was to come; so I put on a thick vail, wrapped a shawl hastily about me, and went out.

I walked fast, and the quick motion did me good. I think I went as far as the gates of the Bois; but I remember nothing distinctly, save that a detachment of troops came marching past, with a band playing merrily before them, and that the music to my sick ears sounded sadder than a requiem. As I came back to the Round Point and turned down the avenue in which we lived, the clocks were striking nine.

While I was yet listening to their echoes, and hesitating whether to go home or turn back again, a man rose from a stone bench close at hand, and called me by name.

"Barbara!" he said. "I am here, Barbara!"

Oh, the dear voice that I had thought never to hear again! It seemed for a moment to stop the pulsations of my heart, and then sent it beating so fast that I could scarcely breathe.

"Hugh!" I faltered. "I thought you were gone!"

"And so I was; but at Liège my strength failed me. I could not leave you, Barbara."

"Let me sit down," I said, clinging to him. "I am giddy."

He passed his arm about my waist, and carried me to a bench farther in among the trees.

"My own darling!" he exclaimed brokenly. "Look up—look up—smile upon me—tell me that I am welcome! Oh, I have suffered, Barbara! I have gone through an eternity since we parted!"

"And is it really you?"

"It is really I. I, thy friend, thy lover, thy husband!"

"And you will never leave me again?"

"Not till you bid me go!"

I smiled at this, and laid my head upon his shoulder like a tired child.

"Yesterday," he went on, "all Belgium lay between us. I was mad — utterly mad, and broken-hearted. I should have been glad to die —I felt I must die if I went farther!"

"And so you turned back again?"

"Turned back—traveled all the afternoon, all the night, and reached this place five hours ago. It was just dawn, and I have been walking up and down these roads ever since, waiting till it was late enough to claim admittance."

"One day more, and you would not have found me. I had made up my mind to return to Zollenstrasse to-night."

"What of that? I should have followed you."

"So far?"

"Cruel! Have I not fled from you, come back to you, traveled without rest or pause since I last saw you; and do you doubt that I would follow you, though Zollenstrasse lay at the ends of the earth?"

"Ah, but why did you fly from me at all?"

He looked down, and hesitated.

"My darling," he said, pressing his hand nervously to his brow, "I am a strange fellow, and have led a strange life. I—I can not look at things as others do—I am but half civilized, you know, and — and reason upon ordinary events more like a red Indian than a man of the world. You can not understand what I have felt of late —I can not even explain to you what I mean! I have fantastic scruples—self-torturing doubts —all sorts of hesitations — weaknesses, if you choose so to call them. You must not question me too closely—you must make allowances and excuses for me, and be content with knowing how I love you. It would puzzle me, indeed, to reply distinctly to all that you might ask. My motives are not always clear to myself, and I act more frequently from impulse than reflection."

"Then impulse took you from me," I said reproachfully, "and reflection brought you back!"

G

"By heavens! the reverse. I left you because—because I felt unworthy of your fresh, pure love. I came back, because I could not live without it!"

"And yet——"

"And yet you are not satisfied! Oh, Barbara, bear with me, bear with me; for I love you! I love you with a love beyond love; with all my strength and all my weakness—with every breath that I draw, and with every pulse of my heart! To dedicate my life to your happiness; to be the author of your future; to build up all your joys; shield you from all sorrow; and turn aside every shaft of evil fortune as it flies — these, these are now the only privileges for which I pray to heaven!"

Feeling how thoroughly every word came from his heart of hearts, what could I do but listen and believe?

"I never thought," continued he, "to love again. I never hoped to win a nature so sweet, so fresh, so innocent as yours. My experience, dear, has been fierce and stormy; and my very soul is scarred with self-inflicted wounds. Would you know the secret of my restless life? Read it in my bitterness of heart, my weariness of soul, my inward rage of disappointment, my unsatisfied longings! Begun in the first buoyancy of youth, these wanderings became at last my sole resource. Change of scene, intercourse with strangers, accident, danger, activity—these things alone rescued me from utter lassitude of spirit, and preserved me from becoming a mere misanthrope. He who dwells always in the world can never wholly hate it; and I, thank God! have lived too much among my fellow-men to judge them harshly. Still, Barbara, I have suffered—suffered disappointment, and solitude, and that feverish recklessness of past and future that has already hurried many a better man to perdition. But it is over — over forever; my sweet child! You love me, and I am at rest! You love me, my love, and that knowledge is the undeserved blessing of my life."

I had listened, till now, in a dreamy content, paying less heed to the sense of what he said than to the low, passionate music of his voice; but at these last words I started. My love "the undeserved blessing of his life!" Alas! four days ago—only four days ago—in accents that I never could forget, had he not cried against it as "a curse?" A curse! The recollection was horrible, and flashed across me like an evil prophecy.

"Oh, Hugh," I faltered, "are you sure that I can make you happier?"

"As sure," said he, "as of my own existence."

"But I am so young and ignorant — what power of blessing can there be in me?"

"As much as in any saint that ever visited the visions of an anchorite! Power to bless, to heal, to save! Power, dear heart, to bring me back to the earnestness of life, and teach me all the meanings of that sweet word 'home,' which as yet I have never, never learned!"

"Home!" I repeated, musingly. "Home! Home means Broomhill — oh, Hugh, how strange that seems!"

His hand closed sharply and suddenly on mine.

"Home, my dear love," he said, hurriedly,

"means any corner of God's earth where you and I may care to pitch our tent together. We carry our home in our own true hearts, and neither country, nor climate, have aught to do with it!"

"But—but will you still care to be always wandering?" I asked, somewhat dismayed.

"Heaven forbid! Nay, darling, why that troubled face! My wanderings are done, my anchor cast, my haven found! Your presence is now become my only need; and where you are, there is home for me! Do you not believe that loving you thus, I could be as happy with you in Siberia as in England—in a prison as at Broomhill? Now, for my part, I should ask nothing better than to live with you forever in a secluded *châlet* on the borders of some blue Swiss lake, isolated and unknown! Or, better still, in some old Italian villa looking to the sea, with gardens half in ruin, halls once painted by the hand of Mantegna or Bordone, and a name recalling all the faded glories of a race long passed away! What say you, Barbara *mia?*"

"That I could be happy anywhere with you, needing neither châlets, nor villas, nor any kind of probation to prove it, Hugh; but that, above all imaginary homes, I prize and prefer your own dear substantial, actual English house at Broomhill!"

He turned his head away, still playing caressingly with my hand.

"Do you so love and remember it?" he asked in a low constrained tone.

"I remember it, as if it were but yesterday when last I saw it; and I love it better than any spot in all the world!"

He was silent, and, in the midst of his silence, the clocks again began striking.

"Ten o'clock!" I exclaimed. "Ten o'clock, and we always breakfast punctually at half-past nine! What will papa say?"

"That he has no objection, I hope, to receive me for a son-in-law! Come, shall we go in and tell him that he has this morning lost another daughter?"

And so we rose from our bench among the trees, and went back along the Allée des Veuves. At our own gate we paused, and Hugh put out his hand to ring the bell. I laid mine on his wrist, and stopped him.

"But tell me," I said, half-laughing, half-crying—"shall I really not go back to Zollen-strasse-am-Main?"

"No more, dearest, than I shall go to St. Petersburgh!"

———◆———

CHAPTER XXXV.

THE SILVER RING IS TURNED TO GOLD.

THREE weeks went by—only three weeks of betrothal between that morning and our marriage day! An interval too brief, considering how mere a child I was; but, even so, too long for his impatience. Bewildered by a thousand womanly cares and preparations and hurried on by his feverish entreaties, I saw the time glide past, almost without comprehending how utterly my future was transformed, or how grave a care I had taken into my life. I was about to become Hugh Farquhar's wife—that was the one thought filling all my being, starting up before me at every turn, and informing my very dreams with a strange joy, half wonder and half prayer. His wife! There were times when I could not believe it—when not even that little ruby ring, "heart-shaped and vermeil-dyed," with which he had commemorated our first vows, seemed proof enough—when only the pressure of his warm, strong hand, and the repeated assurance that he loved me, and only me in all the world, could bring conviction of the truth. His wife! How should I deserve, and how do honor to that name? What was I, that he should have chosen me to be the friend and companion of his life? I loved him, it is true; and I had loved him from my childhood upward. Before I had ever seen him, he was the hero of every fairy-tale and every wild adventure that I read—the prince in disguise, the avenger, the conqueror, the chevalier "*sans peur et sans reproche.*" At Broomhill, from that night when first we met, he became the idol of my dreams; and, engrafting upon my knowledge of the man as I then saw him all that had before been visionary and romantic in my conception of him, I loved him as only a child can love—purely, passionately, humbly, like a dog, or a devotee. Remembering how I lay at his door when he was ill; how I prayed for him; how I watched his every look; anticipated his merest wish; and was repaid a thousand-fold by only a smile or a word, I could but acknowledge that I deserved, after all these years, to win his love in return. Yes—I had loved him all my life, and he had chosen me to be his wife at last!

Still I was very young — very ignorant of the world and its duties — very doubtful how to make him happy, and how to be worthy of his choice. Fain would I, for these reasons, have prolonged our engagement for a year; but my father objected to the delay, and Hugh himself could scarcely have pleaded more eagerly had I desired to break it off altogether. Even when I had given up this point, and the day was close at hand, he tormented himself and me with a thousand apprehensions.

"I feel," he said, "as if something *must* happen to rob me of my happiness — as if an invisible hand were outstretched, even now, to snatch you from me! I never leave you without a vague dread lest it should be the last time that I behold you; and I never return to the house without asking myself what I should do if you were gone, no one knew whither! At night I start from sleep, calling upon your name, and fancying we are parted forever. I know that these are absurd terrors; but is it my fault if I suffer from them? Till you are wholly and irrevocably mine, it must be thus. Without you I am nothing — not even myself. Tortured by a thousand fears and follies, I count every day and every hour that lies between me and the fulfillment of my hopes. Do you wonder at it? I have never yet been happy, and happiness is just within my grasp. I have thirsted; and an angel holds the cup to my lips. I have wandered all my life in the desert; and Paradise is opening before me! If I am a coward, it is because I love you, and because to lose you were to lose all that makes existence precious!"

Saying thus, he would clasp me wildly to his heart; or seize my hands and cover them with kisses.

Sometimes he was absent, silent, oppressed, as it were, with an overwhelming melancholy. Sometimes he almost terrified me by his frantic and unbounded gayety. More than once, when we were sitting quietly alone, talking as lovers talk by twilight, he started from my side like one possessed, and paced the room in uncontrollable agitation. If I questioned him upon these wayward moods he laughed the subject off, or went back to the old theme of his presentiments and his impatience.

During these three weeks my father was kinder to me than he had ever been before. Knowing what my views had been with regard to art, I think he was agreeably surprised by the turn affairs had taken — at all events, he took occasion to show me that I had risen in his good opinion, and that he looked upon my present conduct as the result of his own paternal cares and counsels. He considered that to marry advantageously was the duty of every well-bred young woman, and that to achieve this duty as early as possible, evinced on her part only the more gratitude and discretion. I had fulfilled both these conditions, and he was pleased to regard me with proportionate favor. In all matters connected with my trousseau he was liberal to a degree that surprised me; for I knew that Mrs. Churchill's fortune was settled on herself, and that our means had never been large; but he explained this by telling me that he had some years ago sunk his capital for an annuity, reserving only a few hundreds in case of sudden need. These hundreds he had now divided between Hilda and myself; judging it better for ourselves, and more creditable to his own name and position to equip his daughters richly, than to bequeath them, at his death, a sum too small to be regarded in the light of a dowry. His own pride, in short, colored all my father's opinions, and governed every action of his life.

From the manner in which he received Mr. Farquhar's proposals, and the readiness with which he consented to our speedy union, I could not help thinking that he had, from the first, foreseen how this intimacy might end, and was glad to get me married as soon as might be. Certain it was that both he and Mrs. Churchill had afforded every facility to our attachment; and I now remembered a thousand trifles that had escaped me at the time, if not without observation, at all events without suspicion. Now they recurred to me distinctly enough, and despite my present happiness, irritated and humiliated me almost beyond endurance.

Thus the three weeks ebbed away, and it came to the eve of our wedding.

We had had news that day from Hilda. Her letter was dated from Drontheim, and full of the scenery of the Dovrefjeld, over which they had just passed. In a brief message she desired her love and her congratulations to her "sister Barbara;" but it read coldly and grudgingly, as if she could scarcely forgive me for my happiness. This impression, added to the cares and excitements of this busy time, made me sad and weary; and I was thankful when Hugh came at length to tempt me out for a last stroll among the dusky avenues of the Champs Elysées.

It was twilight, and the evening air tasted already of autumnal frosts. We were glad to walk fast and get warm, exchanging just a word from time to time, and finding as much companionship in silence as in speech. How gay it was here among the crowded pathways! How the lamps glittered, and the music echoed in the illuminated gardens of the Cafés Chantants! Here were carriages, "thick as leaves in Vallambrosa." Yonder, with a helmet on his head, and a trumpeter at his side, stood a quack doctor, gesticulating like a marionnette. A little farther on was gathered a ring of applauding spectators, with the dancing dogs performing in the midst. It was Paris epitomized — pleasure-seeking, feverish Paris, with all its wealth, its poverty, and its unrest!

Strolling idly hither and thither; hazarding guesses as to where we two might be this day week, or this day month; talking now of Rome, now of Venice, and now of the great Alps which I was soon to see for the first time, we came all at once upon a space to the left of the Cirque, where an itinerant ballad-singer stood, surrounded by his little audience. Something in the voice, something in the melody struck me, and we paused to listen.

"Surely," said Hugh, "it is our guitarist of Vincennes!"

And so it was. We did not care to go nearer; but, lingering beyond the circle, could just catch the plaintive burden of his song: —

> "*File, file, pauvre Marie,*
> *File, file, pour le prisonnier!*"

When this was ended, he sang another as sad. Then there was a stir among the listeners, and some dispersed, and we saw a woman collecting such stray contributions as three or four of the more liberal were pleased to offer.

"Poor Orpheus!" ejaculated my companion, taking out his purse. "I had not supposed that there was a Eurydice in the case!"

Scarcely had the words escaped his lips, when she came a step or two nearer; but hesitatingly, as if too proud to solicit. Hugh slipped a five-franc piece into my hand.

"Be my almoner," he whispered, and drew back to let me give it.

She took it, unconscious of its value; then paused, examined it wonderingly, and looked up in my face. At that moment I felt my arm crushed in Hugh's grasp, as in a vice!

"Come away! come away!" he said, dragging me suddenly, almost savagely, into the road. "My God, child! why do you hold back?"

Too frightened to reply, I suffered myself to be hurried between the very wheels of the carriages, and lifted into the first empty fly that came past.

"*Où allez vous, Monsieur!*" asked the driver.

Hugh flung himself back, with a kind of groan.

"Anywhere — anywhere!" he exclaimed. "Out beyond the barriers — round by the Invalides. Anywhere!"

The man touched his hat, and took the road to Neuilly. For a long time we were both silent; but at length, weary of waiting, I stole my hand into his, and nestled closer to his side.

"Oh, Hugh," I said, "what ails you? What has happened?"

He shook his head gloomily.

"Was it my fault, Hugh?"

"Your fault, my darling? What folly!"

And, taking my head in his two hands, he kissed me tenderly, almost compassionately, like an indulgent father.

"Nay, then, what ailed you just now?"

He shuddered, hesitated, sighed heavily.

"I — I scarcely know," he said. "It was the sight of that — that woman's face when the light fell on it — a resemblance, Barbara — a resemblance so strange and ghost-like, that — Pshaw, child, can you not understand that, when a man has traveled about the world for twelve or fourteen years, he may sometimes come across a face that startles him—reminds him perhaps of some other face thousands of miles away? It has happened to me before—fifty times before."

"And was that all?"

"All. All and enough."

"But you frightened me — and my arm will be black and blue to-morrow."

"Oh, Heavens! Have I hurt you?"

Laughing, I rolled up my sleeve, and, by the light of the lamps, showed him the red marks on my arm. He overwhelmed himself with reproaches and me with pity, till, satisfied with the excess of his penitence, I silenced and forgave him.

"But," I began, "you have not yet told me whose face ——"

He interrupted me by a gesture.

"My dear love," he said earnestly, "spare me that question. By and by, when you have known me longer and better, I will tell you from end to end, the story of my life — all its follies, all its weaknesses, all its errors. But this is not the time or place, Barbara. Wait — wait and trust; and till then ask no more. Will you promise this?"

I promised it, readily enough; and there it ended.

The next morning we were married. Married very early, and very quietly, in the little Marbœuf Chapel of the Rue du Chaillot. We had neither bridesmaids, nor carriages, nor wedding-guests. We walked down to the chapel before breakfast, my father, Mrs. Churchill, and I, and found Hugh waiting for us, and the clergyman chatting with him over the rails of the chancel. I can see the place now; the morning sun shining slantwise through the upper windows; the turned cushions in the pews; and the old sextoness, in her mob-cap and sabots, dusting the hassocks on which we were to kneel. I even remember how, in the midst of the service, my eyes became attracted to a tablet beside the altar, recording the early death of a certain Eleanor Rothsay, "one year and three days after her marriage;" and how, with a strange pang, I wondered if she were content to die; if her husband soon forgot her; and whether he loved another when she was gone?

When the ceremony was over, and the great books had been signed in the vestry, we went home again on foot, and breakfasted together, as usual. As for me, my thoughts still ran on that poor Eleanor and her brief year of happiness. It haunted me, like a sad tune, and set itself to every sight and sound of the "garish day;" nor did I quite forget it till, having bade them all good-by, I found myself alone with my husband, speeding, speeding away, with Paris

already far behind, and the eager train bearing us on toward Italy — the "azure Italy" of my old desires.

"My wife!" murmured Hugh, as he folded me closer and closer to his heart. "Mine — my own — my beloved! never, never more, by day or night, to be parted from me!"

CHAPTER XXXVI.

OUR HALCYON DAYS.

"Ye glittering towns with wealth and splendor crowned;
Ye fields where summer spreads profusion round;
Ye lakes whose vessels catch the busy gale."
GOLDSMITH.

WE are traveling — have been traveling for many days — and find a second summer among the hights of the Bernese Oberland. The sky hangs over us like a dome of blue and burning steel; and for a week we have not seen a cloud. Every night we rest at some hamlet in a valley among mountains; and every morning are on the road again. How happy we are, wandering like children, hand in hand, amid this wild and beautiful nature! Italy lies yonder, behind those farthest peaks; but we are in no haste to climb them while this rare autumn lasts. Free to go, free to stay, free to loiter away our halcyon days where or how we will, we linger among the upper Alps, and can not bear to leave them. Sometimes our path lies across brown, heathery slopes, blazing with sunlight; sometimes through gorges dark with firs and deep in shade, where the night-dews rest till noon. The other morning, we saw the sunrise from the Righi. Yesterday we rowed across the blue-green lake of Brientz, and slept within hearing of the waterfalls in the vale of Hasli. To-day we have the Wetterhorn before us, piercing the calm sky like an obelisk of frosted silver. By and by, crossing a plateau of bare rock, we stand where the glacier of Rosenlaui reaches a frozen arm toward us down a chasm in the mountains. Tossed in huge peaks, and precipices, and crests of cruel ice, it lies with the blue light permeating through its uppermost blocks, and the sun shimmering over all its surface, like a moving mantle of intolerable splendor. Silently we traverse a mere plank across a rushing cataract, and tread the solid ice. Great crevices and pinnacles are around us. We enter a cavern in the glacier — a cavern blue and glassy as the grotto at Capri — and open in places to the still bluer vault of heaven. Strange passages of ice branch from it right and left, leading no one knows whither; but our mountaineers whisper together of one who ventured to explore them and returned no more.

"Supposing, now, that these ice-walls were to give way," says my husband, leaning composedly upon his Alpenstock, "our remains might be preserved here for centuries; like the Mammoths that have been found from time to time imbedded in the ice-fields of Siberia! Only conceive, Barbarina, how the *savants* of a thousand years to come would be delighted with us!"

Seeing how the sides of the cave drip in the sun, and to what frail points of junction they have melted here and there, I confess to having but little relish for such speculations.

"This place," continues he, "reminds me of

Dante's lowest circle. Here are the '*gelate croste*;' but where is Lucifer, with his mouthful of sinners? By the way, had Dante ever seen a glacier? It is possible. He traveled to Germany and Paris, and studied theology at Oxford. He might have crossed the Alps, Barbarina — who can tell?"

Who, indeed? But we have now once more emerged upon the outer world, and stand looking up toward that mysterious and immeasurable ice-field reaching away from plateau to plateau, from peak to peak, from Alp to Alp, of which the mightiest glaciers are but fringes on the mantle of winter. Before this sight, we both are silent; and, as we go down again into the valley, I remember those solemn lines, "written before sunrise at Chamounix":—

"'Ye Icefalls! Ye that from the mountain's brow ·
Adown enormous ravines slope amain —
Torrents, methinks, that heard a mighty voice,
And stopped at once amid their maddest plunge!'"

It is a glowing golden afternoon, and this "summer of All Saints" has not yet been troubled by a sign of change. We are staying now at Interlaken, whence all the summer visitors have long departed; and this morning have come up the Valley of Lauterbrunnen, and seen the rainbow on the Staubbach. Hence, a steep zig-zag in the cliff has brought us to a plateau of pasture-lands nine hundred feet above the valley. Far beneath, threaded by a line of shining torrent, and looking so white, and still, and small, that I fancy I might almost cover it with my hand, lies the tiny village with its wooden bridge and antique painted spire. High above and before us, with only the fir-forests of the Wengern Alp between, rise the summits of the Jungfrau and the Peak of Silver.

"How strange it is up here!" says Hugh, as we pause to rest and look around. "What a delicious sensation of light and freedom! This plateau is a mere shelf midway up the mountain, and yet we have streams, and meadow-lands, and all the verdure of the valleys. Faith, love, I had rather live in such a scene, with the Alps for my neighbors, than in any family mansion that disfigures the face of the earth!"

"Had you been born to the inheritance of a châlet and a couple of meadows, husband, you would tell a different tale!"

"Nay, wife, you should have milked the cows, and made the cheeses; and I would have carried them to market on my back, like that stalwart fellow who went by just now. It would have been a pretty piece of pastoral for us both!"

And so, laughing gayly together, we go forward in the sunshine, and at every step the scene becomes more lovely. We are in a district of farm-lands and pastures. Every now and then, we come upon a cluster of cottages built in red-brown wood, with great sheltering eaves, and carven balconies, where long strings of Indian corn hang out to dry in the sun. Some of these cottages have proverbs and sentences of Scripture cut in German characters all across the front; and at the doors sit old women with their distaffs, and young girls who sing as we pass by. Now we turn aside to gather the wild gentians hidden in the grass, and fill our mountain flasks at a pool among the rocks; and

now, on a mound overgrown with briers, we find an Alpine strawberry. Here, too, are purple whortleberries and star-leaved *immortelles*, and whole shrubberies of the Alp-rose, with its myrtle-like leaf. But the roses are faded, and will bloom no more till the snows have fallen and melted again!

Now the cliffs close round more nearly, and the plateau narrows to a space of rock-strewn heath, a mile or so in width. The spot is strangely desolate, and looks as though it might have been the battle-ground of the Titans. Huge blocks of slate-gray granite here lie piled and scattered — each fragment a rock. Some are brown with moss; some are half-buried in the turf; and some are clothed with shrubs, the growth of years. A few goats browsing here and there, with bells about their necks, and a few rude cowsheds built in sheltered corners, "all in and out of the rocks," only serve to make the place more solitary.

"I remember this spot," says Hugh, eagerly. "I descended upon it from the mountains, years ago, when I walked through Switzerland on foot. It was more wild and savage then — and so was I. Ah, little wife, you can not fancy how wild and savage I was!"

"Nay, it is not difficult. You are half a barbarian now!"

"Am I? Well, so much the better; for it shall be your occupation to tame me! But look up yonder — do you see a tiny rift there, on the face of the crag; like a scar on a soldier's brow?"

"Yes, I see it."

"Well from that rift fell a rock, which, shattering from ledge to ledge, covered these acres with ruin. It happened, fortunately, toward midday, on the anniversary of some country festival, when the farm-folks were all gone down into the valley. What must they have felt, poor souls, when they came up at sunset, and found their homes desolate!"

"Oh, Hugh! when did this happen?"

"Long, long ago—twenty years, or more. The grass has grown, and the shrubs have sprung up since then, making destruction beautiful. But it was not thus when I first saw it. Those green hillocks were then mere mounds of stones and rubbish, and all the ground was sown with rugged fragments. Hark! what sound is that?"

Startled, we hold our breathing, and listen. First come a few hoarse discordant notes, and then, as if in the air above our heads, a silvery entanglement of such rare cadences as we have never heard before. What can it be? We hear it die away, as if carried from us by the breeze, and, looking in each other's faces, are about to speak, when it breaks forth again, mingling, echoing, fading as before, upon the upper air!

"We are on enchanted ground," whispers Hugh; "and this is the music that Ferdinand followed in the Island of Prospero!"

"Say, rather, that there are Eolian harps hidden somewhere in the rocks," I more practically suggest. "Let us look for them!"

"Look for them yourself, prosaic mortal—I shall seek Ariel. What ho! my tricksy spirit!"

But lo! a sudden turn in the rocks brings us face to face with the mystery; and our fairy music, so wild and sweet, proves to be a wondrous echo, tossed from cliff to cliff. As for Ariel, he is only a tiny cow-boy blowing a horn seven feet in length for the entertainment of a solitary traveler, who rides by, like Doctor Syntax, with a mule and an umbrella.

———

Thun, Berne, the Gemmi, Leukerbad—we have seen all these, and left the Oberland behind us; and now our route lies through the valley of the Rhone. We came from Leukerbad to Leuk last evening by the gorge of the Dala; and this morning drive gayly out through the one desolate street of this crumbling old Vallaisan town, passing the church, and the antique castle with its four quaint turrets, and the covered bridge over the Rhone. Hence we journey for some distance among stony shrub-grown hillocks, and plantations of young trees; and then we cross the river again into a district of vineyards, with our road reaching straight into the dim perspective, miles and miles away. How like a painting of Turner's it opens before us, this broad and beautiful valley! Rich sloping vines "combed out upon the hillsides" skirt the mountains on either hand; sometimes divided from the road by flats of emerald meadow, and sometimes trailing their ripe fruits within reach of the passing wayfarer. Behind us, the stupendous precipices of the Gemmi still tower into sight; and in advance, far as we can see, the valley is bounded right and left by the Vallaisan Alps, which mingle their snow-peaks with the gathering cumuli, and fade away to air. Midway along the shadowy vista rise two steep and solitary hills, each crowned, like a Roman victor, with its mural coronet of ruins. A glorious landscape, so stately with poplars, so garlanded with vines, so thoroughly Italian in its beauty, that it might well be on the other side of the Alps, for any difference that the eye can see!

Thus, as we go forward through the plain, passing villages, and towns, and vineyards where the merry vintage is at its hight, the scene becomes more and more Italian. In Sierra, through which our postillions rattle at full speed, the houses are high and dilapidated, with arcades running along the basement stories, and Italian signs and names above the doors. In Sion there are Capuchins at the corners of the streets; and sullen, handsome women, who throw up their windows, and lean out to look at us, in true Italian fashion. Even the farm-houses scattered all about the valley are stuccoed white, or built of stone; with loggias on the roof, and sometimes a trellised vine before the door. We are now, it would seem, in the very heart of the grape-district. Here are vineyards in the valley, vineyards on the hillsides, vineyards down to the road on either hand! From some the harvest has already been gathered — some are still heavy with white and purple fruit — and some are filled with gay groups of vintagers, sunburnt as the soil. By and by we come upon a long procession of carts, all laden with high wooden cans of grapes; then upon an open shed, where some five or six swarthy fellows, armed with short poles, are mashing the red fruit; then upon a couple of grave shovel-hatted Abbés, and a stalwart friar, who prints the dusty road with the firm impress of his sandaled foot at each impatient stride. Then come more farms, more villages, more

"Wains oxen-drawn,
Laden with grapes, and dropping rosy wine;"

and presently we pass a blind beggar sitting by a roadside cross, who asks charity in the name of the Blessed Mary.

Thus the day wanes, and, toward afternoon, we reach a famous vineyard of the Muscat grape, where the vignerons load our carriage with armfuls of the perfumed fruit. Here the cottages are more than ever Italian, with tiled roofs, and jutting eaves, and ingots of Indian corn festooned about the upper casements. Here, also, the wild peaks of the Diablerets come into sight —grim sentinels of the legendary Inferno of the Vallaisan peasant.

And now, as the sun sinks westward, we hear the chiming of the chapel-bells far away, and see bands of vintagers trudging wearily home; and still the long road lies before us, bordered by tremulous poplars, dusty, direct, interminable as ever! Being by this time very weary, I nestle down "like a tired child," in my husband's arms, and implore to be amused; so Hugh proceeds to ransack the dusty storehouse of his memory, bringing forth now an anecdote of one who was buried alive by a landslip among the Diablerets— now an incident of his own travels—now a weird Hungarian legend of a vampire-priest who slaked his fearful thirst upon the fairest of the province, and was stabbed at last upon the steps of his own altar. Thus the tender gloom of early twilight steals over the landscape. Thus the first pale stars come forth overhead. Thus, loving and beloved, we journey on together toward that still distant point where yonder solitary tower keeps watch above the village of Martigny.

———

We are in Italy. The snows of St. Bernard and the plains of Piedmont are passed. We have visited Turin, the most symmetrical and monotonous of cities; Alessandria, the dullest; and Genoa, where hail and sunshine succeeded each other with every hour of the day. Now it is fine again; but clear and cold, and we are traveling by easy stages along the delicious Riviera. All day long, we have the blue sea beside us. At night, we put up at some little town in a nook of sandy bay, and are lulled to sleep by the sobbing of the waves. Sometimes, if the morning be very bright and warm, we breakfast on the terrace in front of our osteria, and watch the fishing-boats standing out to sea, and the red-capped urchins on the beach. Sometimes, as we are in the mood for loitering, we do not care to go farther than twelve or fifteen miles in the day; and so I spend long hours climbing among the cliffs, or coasting hither and thither in a tiny felucca with fantastic sails.

"Truly," says Hugh, as we sit one afternoon upon a "sea-girt promontory," watching the gradual crimson of the sunset, "Plutarch was a man of taste."

"Plutarch!" I repeat, roused from my dreamy reverie. "Why so?"

"Because he has somewhere observed, that 'on land, our pleasantest journeys are those beside the sea; and that at sea, no voyage is so delightful as a cruise along the coast.' And he is right. Contrast and combination — these are the first elements of the picturesque. Salvator Rosa knew well the relative value of land and sea, and, whatever his faults, made a wise use of both. I am often reminded of his pictures by the scenery about us!"

"Why, Hugh, I have heard you condemn Salvator Rosa by the hour together!"

"Yes, for his blue mountains and his unnatural skies; for every thing, in short, save the choice of his subjects, and the tone that time has helped to give them. See those overhanging cliffs, and that natural arch of rock above the road; could *he* have painted that, think you? Or yonder village with its open *campanile*, and background of ilex groves sloping almost to the water's edge? But this reminds me, dear, that you have not made a single sketch since we left Paris!"

"I have been very idle, it is true."

"Extremely idle! Come, you shall do penance to-morrow morning, and make me a sketch from this very spot; taking in that fragment of red cliff, that group of fan-palms, and that exquisite cove with the old broken boat drawn up upon the beach! The coloring of that rock, Barbarina, with the dark cacti growing out of every cliff, is a study in itself!"

"Yes; but you would do it as well, and, perhaps, more patiently than I. Do you never draw now, Hugh?"

"Seldom or never."

"And yet you are a true artist. I have not forgotten those great folios full of sketches at Broomhill! They were in sad disorder, too—Algiers and Brighton, the Thames and the Nile, Devonshire and the Andes, all thrown together in most admired disorder. I shall regulate them when we go home, Hugh—ah, how strange it will seem, after so many, many years!"

"Yes," replies my husband, gloomily, "you were a little girl then, and I——Heigho! *Tempora mutantur.*"

"And then I shall see my aunt once more, and——"

"Your aunt, child!" says Hugh, turning his face away. "Pshaw! she has forgotten you."

"I know it. She has cast me out of her heart, for a sin not my own. That is very bitter; and yet I believe I love her as dearly as ever! I have been tempted a thousand times to write to her; and then again I have checked the impulse, believing that—that she cares for me no longer."

"My poor little Barbara!"

"Hush! I am not poor now, dearest! I am rich—very rich, and very happy."

And, with this, I nestle closer to his side, and the dear, protecting arm is folded round me.

"Can you not guess, Hugh, why I have been so very, very idle?" I whisper, presently.

"Nay, little wife, am I a sorcerer?"

"Yes—no—sometimes I think you are!"

"Well, then, I am a sorcerer no longer. I have broken my wand, burned my book, dismissed my goblin messengers, and become a mere mortal, like yourself. *Eh bien*, why is it?"

"Because—because I am too happy to sketch. Too happy for even Art to make me happier!"

"My darling!"

"And—and Love is so new to me, Hugh, and life so fair; and I feel as if to be grateful and happy were occupation enough."

"And so it is, wife—so it is! The gods do not often come down from Olympus; but when they do, let us entertain them royally, and put all else aside to do them honor!"

"But—but sometimes, Hugh, when I consider what a perfect love is ours, I tremble, and, ask myself, 'shall I always be so happy?'"

"Ah, Barbara, that is a question that we all ask once, perhaps twice, in life. But who can answer it? Neither you nor I! The present is ours—let us be content with it."

"I could not be content with it, Hugh, unless I accepted it as a prophecy of the future."

"Nor I, dear wife—nor I; but I believe that, with God's help, it will be so. And yet I have learned to mistrust the morrow, to mock the past, and to value the present moment at no more than its worth! These are hard lessons, love, and I have not yet unlearned them!"

"Hush," I cry, shudderingly. "To doubt our morrow is to blaspheme our love!"

"Child, I do not doubt—I speculate; and this only because I am so happy. Because I would fain stay the glory of the passing hour, and, like one of old, bid the Sun and Moon stand still above our heads. But I can not—I can not!"

"Alas! no. We must grow gray, and old, and change as others change; but what of that? We shall love on to the last, and die, as we have lived, together."

"Dear love, we will! *Amo, Amas, Amamus, Amaverimus.* Ah, what a pleasant verb, and how readily we learn to conjugate it!"

By this time the sunset has faded quite away, and the vesper-bell chimes from the campanile on the hight; so we rise and go homeward by the beach, and find our landlady sitting on the threshold of her house with her infant at her breast, like one of Raffaelle's Madonnas. Within, a little brazen hand-lamp, by which Virgil might have sat to write, half lights our dusky chamber. The window is open and looks upon the sea; and beside it stands a table with our frugal supper. How sweet is the flavor of our omelette to-night, and how excellent this flask of Orvieto! Like children on a holiday, we find every thing delicious, and turn all things "to favor and to prettiness." The glorious world itself seems made for our delight; and the phenomena of nature appear, to our happy egotism, like spectacles played off to give us pleasure. For us the moon rises yonder, and the silver ripples break upon the beach—for us the evening air makes music in the pines, and wafts past our casement the last lingering notes of the Ave Maria!

"Ah, me! how sweet is love itself possessed,
    When but love's shadows are so rich in joy!"

Time went on, and the New Year found us dwelling in the shadow of that marble tower that leans forever above the Holy Field of Pisa. We liked the strange, old, lonely city, and lingered there for some weeks, sketching the monuments in the Campo Santo, wandering by moonlight among the grass-grown streets and silent palaces, and watching the sluggish Arno winding from bridge to bridge, on its way toward the sea. At length, as February came, the calm, bright skies and distant hills tempted us forth again; so we resumed our pleasant traveling life; turning aside, as heretofore, when it pleased us, from the beaten track; pausing on the road to sketch a ruin, or a lake; sleeping sometimes in a town, and sometimes at a farm-house among olive-groves; and loitering away our happy time, as though, like Sir Philip Sydney's Arcadian shepherd-boy, we should "never grow old."

By and by, however, there comes a day long to be remembered. Last night we were upon the sea, having taken a felucca at Orbitello. This morning we are slowly traversing a brown and sterile region. Our road lies among shapeless hillocks, shaggy with bush and brier. Far away on one side gleams a line of soft, blue sea—on the other, lie mountains as blue, but more distant. Not a sound stirs the stagnant air. Not a tree, not a housetop breaks the wide monotony. The dust lies beneath our wheels like a carpet, and follows us like a cloud. The grass is yellow; the weeds are parched; and where there have been wayside pools, the ground is cracked, and dry. Now we pass a crumbling fragment of something that may have been a tomb or a temple, centuries ago. Now we come upon a little wild-eyed peasant-boy, keeping goats among the ruins, like Giotto of old. Presently a buffalo lifts his black mane above the brow of a neighboring hillock, and rushes away before we can do more than point to the spot on which we saw it. Thus the day attains its noon, and the sun hangs overhead like a brazen shield, brilliant, but cold. Thus, too, we reach the brow of a long and steep ascent, where our driver pulls up to rest his weary beast. The sea has now faded almost out of sight—the mountains look larger and nearer, with streaks of snow upon their summits—the Campagna reaches on and on and shows no sign of limit or of verdure—while, in the midst of the clear air, half way, as it would seem, between us and the purple Sabine range, rises one solemn, solitary dome. Can it be the dome of St. Peter's?

I have been anticipating this for hours, looking for it from the top of every hill, and rehearsing in my own mind all the effect that it must produce upon me; and yet, now that I have it actually before my eyes, it comes upon me like something strange, sudden, unreal!

"Yes, little wife," says Hugh, answering my unspoken thought, "Rome lies, unseen, in the shadow of that dome—Rome, and the Seven Hills! That mountain to our left is the classical Soracte. Yonder, amid the misty hollows of those remotest Apennines, nestle Tivoli and Tusculum. All around us reaches the battleground of centuries, the wide and wild Campagna, every rood of which is a chapter in the history of the world!"

I hear, but can not speak; for I am thinking of Raffaelle and Michael Angelo, and the treasures of the Vatican.

"How often," continues my husband, musingly, "have the barbaric foes of early Rome paused thus at first sight of the Eternal City—paused, perchance, upon this very spot, with clash of sword and spear, eager for spoil, and thirsting for vengeance! And how often—ah! how often, may not the victorious legions of the Republic and the Empire have here staid the torrent of their homeward march, to greet with shouts of triumph those distant towers where the Senate awaited them with honors, and their wives and children watched for their return! Faith, Barbara, I never come to Rome without wishing that I had lived in the period of her glory!"

"Absurd! You would have been dead hundreds of years by this time."

"A man can live but once, *petite;* and 'tis hard that he may not, at least, make choice of his century. Now, for my part, I would give up all that has happened since, only to have heard Mark Antony's speech over the dead body of Cæsar, and to have dined with Cicero at his villa in Tusculum!"

"Whilst *I* prefer to read Shakspeare's version of the former, and to-picnic at Tusculum with Farquhar of Broomhill!"

"That is because times are degenerate, Barbarina!" replies Hugh, laughingly. "Had you been educated at Magdalen College, Oxford, instead of at Zollenstrasse-am-Main, you would have had better taste, and more respect for the classics. "*Oh, Roma, Roma, non e più come era prima!*' Have I not seen a traveling circus in the Mausoleum of Augustus, a French garrison in the Mole of Hadrian, and a Roman audience at a puppet-show?"

We have now lost sight of St. Peter's, and entered upon a narrow, dusty road, with moldering white walls on either side. 'Tis a dreary approach to a great city, and for more than three miles is never varied, unless by a wayside trough, a ruined shed, a solitary juniper tree, or a desolate *albergo* with grated windows, and a rough fresco of a couple of flasks and a bunch of grapes painted over the door. Then comes a steep descent, a sharp bend to the right, and the great dome again rises suddenly at the end of the road, so near that it seems as if I might almost touch it with my hand! And now the gates of Rome are close before us; and a cart comes through, driven by a tawny Roman peasant who guides his oxen standing, like a charioteer of old. Now we pass the piazza and colonnade of St. Peter's, and the Castle of St. Angelo, with St. Michael poised above in everlasting bronze—ah, how well I seem to know it! Then the bridge guarded by angels; and the Tiber, the classic Tiber that Clelia swam! Alas! can this be it—this brown and sluggish stream, low sunk between steep banks of mud and ooze? Ay, it is indeed the *flavus Tiberinus*, the golden river of the poets; and these narrow streets, these churches, palaces, and hovels are ROME!

CHAPTER XXXVII.

ROME.

"I AM in Rome! the City that so long
Reigned absolute, the mistress of the world;
The mighty vision that the prophets saw,
And trembled."

ROGERS.

IN Rome, the artist feels impelled to stay forever and be at rest. For him, other cities lose their old attractions; modern art, progress, personal ambition, cease alike to be of importance in his eyes; effort and emulation pass from him like mere dreams; "he walks amid a world of art in ruins," and would fain loiter away the remainder of his days among the wrecks of this antique world. Nor does he even feel that a life thus spent were unworthy of the genius that is in him. Self-forgetting, reverential, absorbed, he stands in the presence of the "Transfiguration," like a mortal before the

Gods. If ever he chances to look back upon his former aspirations, it is with a sense of inferiority that is neither humiliation, nor envy, nor despair; but only lassitude of spirit, and the willing homage of the soul. Thus he comes to live more in the past than the present, more in the ideal than the real. Thus, too, all that is not Rome gradually loosens its hold upon his heart and his imagination. He feels that certain statues and pictures are henceforth necessary to him, and that certain ruins have become almost a part of his being. He could scarcely live away from the Vatican, or the Campidoglio, or the sweet sad face of Beatrice Cenci in the Barberini palace; and not to be within reach of Caracalla's Baths, or the solemn corridors of the Colosseum, would be exile unbearable. In this mood, he suffers the years to go by unheeded, and voluntarily blots his own name from the book of the Future; for Art is to him a religion, and he, like a monastic devotee, is content to substitute worship for work.

But for the strong tie binding me to the present, and but for that love which had of late become more to me than art or fame, I should have yielded utterly to the influences of the place. As it was, the days and weeks seemed to glide past in one unceasing round of delight and wonder. I was never weary of villas, palaces, and galleries; of Raffaelle's violinist, or the dying gladiator, or the Archangel of Guido in the little church of the Cappucini. I filled my sketch-book with outlines, and spent whole days in the Halls of the Vatican, copying the figures on a frieze, or the *bassi relievi* of an antique sarcophagus. In these studies Hugh was my critic, associate, and guide; and, although his practical knowledge fell short of mine, I learned much from him. His taste was perfect: his judgment faultless. He was familiar with every school, and had all the best pictures in the world by heart. The golden glooms of Rembrandt, the "rich impasting" of Van Eyck, the grand touch of Michael Angelo, were alike "things known and inimitable" to his unerring eye. He detected a copy at first sight; assigned names and dates without the help of a catalogue; and recognized at a glance

"Whate'er Lorraine light touched with soft'ning hue,
Or savage Rosa dashed, or learned Poussin drew!"

To the acquisition of his critical knowledge he had, in short, devoted as much study as might have fitted him for a profession; and to use his own words, had spent as many years of life in learning to appreciate a picture as he need have spent in learning to paint it. Thus I acquired from him much that had hitherto been wanting to my education, and made daily progress in the paths of art. Thus, like many another, I could have gone on for ever from gallery to gallery, from church to church, from palace to palace, dreaming my life away in one long reverie of admiration before

"The grandeur that was Greece, and the glory that was Rome."

We lived on the Pincian Hill, close by the gardens of the French Academy. Far and wide beneath our windows lay the spires and house-tops of the Eternal city, with the Doria pines standing out against the Western horizon. At the back we had a *loggia* overlooking the garden-

studios of the French school, with the plantations of the Borghese Villa and the snow-streaked Apennines beyond. Ah, what glorious sights and sounds we had from those upper windows on the Pincian hill! What pomp and pageantry of cloud! What mists of golden dawn! What flashes of crimson sunset upon distant peaks! How often "we heard the chimes at midnight," rung out from three hundred churches, and were awakened in the early morning by military music, and the tramp of French troops marching to parade! After breakfast, we used to go down into the city to see some public or private collection; or, map in hand, trace the site of a temple or a forum. Sometimes we made pious pilgrimages to places famous in art or history, such as the house of Rienzi, the tomb of Raffaelle, or the graves of our poets in the Protestant Burial-ground. Sometimes, when the morning was wet or dull, we passed a few pleasant hours in the studios of the Via Margutta, where the artists "most do congregate;" or loitered our time away among the curiosity shops of the Via Condotti. Later in the day, our horses were brought round, and we rode or drove beyond the walls, toward Antemnæ or Veii; or along the meadows behind the Vatican; or out by the Fountain of Egeria, in sight of those ruined Aqueducts which thread the brown wastes of the Campagna, like a funeral procession turned to stone. Then, when evening came, we piled the logs upon the hearth and read aloud by turns; or finished the morning's sketches. Now and then, if it were moonlight, we went out again; and sometimes, though seldom, dropped in for an hour at the Opera, or the Theatre Metastasio.

Oh! pleasant morning of youth, when these things made the earnest business of our lives — when the choice of a bronze or a cameo occupied our thoughts for half a day, and the purchase of a mosaic was matter for our gravest consideration — when the reading of a poem made us sad; or the sight of a painting quickened the beating of our hearts; or the finding of some worthless relic filled us with delight! We could not then conceive that we should ever know more serious cares than these, or take half the interest in living men and women that we took in the Scipios and Servilii of old. We loved Rome as if it were our native city, and thought there could be no place in the world half so enchanting; but that was because we were so happy in it, and so solitary. We lived only in the past, and for each other. We had no friends, and cared to make none. Excepting as we were ourselves concerned, the present possessed but little interest for us; and dwelling amid the tombs and palaces of a vanished race, we seemed to live doubly isolated from our fellow-men.

Thus the winter months glided away, and the spring-time came, and Lent was kept and ended. Thus Rome made holiday at Easter; and the violets grew thicker than ever on the grave of Keats; and the primroses lay in clusters of pale gold about the cypress glades of Monte Mario. Thus, too, we extended our rambles for many a mile beyond the city walls, trampling the wild-flowers of the Campagna; tracking the antique boundaries of Latium and Etruria; mapping out the battle-fields of the Eneid; and visiting the sites of cities whose history has been for long centuries confounded with tradition, and whose temples were dedicated to a religion of which the poetry and the ruins alone survive.

It was indeed a happy, happy time; and the days went by as if they had been set to music!

───◆───

CHAPTER XXXVIII.

CARPE DIEM.

> "DESERTED rooms of luxury and state,
>   That old magnificence had richly furnished
>   With pictures, cabinets of ancient date,
>   And carvings gilt and burnished."
>   THOMAS HOOD.

I NOW hardly know in what way the idea first came to me; but, somehow or another, I began about this time to suspect that my husband had no wish to return to Broomhill. The discovery was not sudden. It dawned upon me slowly, vaguely, imperceptibly; and was less the result of my own penetration than of evidence accumulated from a thousand trifles.

He never named Broomhill, or any circumstance that might lead to the subject. If I spoke of it, he was silent. If I exacted a reply, he gave it as briefly as possible, and turned the conversation. When sometimes we talked, as lovers will, of how this love should run through all our days, like a golden thread in the rough woof of life, he avoided all mention of that ancestral home which should have been the scene of our romance; but laid it ever under foreign skies. Sometimes he talked of buying land in Switzerland, and cultivating a model farm. Sometimes of purchasing a villa at Castellamare; or of building one upon the borders of Lake Como; or of buying some old deserted *palazzo* in the environs of Rome, and fitting it up in the Renaissance style. Then, again, he would have a project for the extension of our tour through Hungary, Bavaria, and the Danubian provinces; or propose to equip a vessel for a lengthened cruise in Mediterranean waters touching at all the chief ports of the Turkish and Dalmatian coasts, threading the mazes of the Isles of Greece, and ending with the Nile or the Holy Land. At first I only used to smile at these restless fancies, and attribute them to his old wandering habits; but a time came, by and by, when I could smile no longer — when a strange uneasy doubt stole gradually upon me, and I began to wonder whether there might not be, in all this, some purpose of intentional delay; some design to keep longer and longer away, and, perhaps, never to return.

How this doubt deepened into certainty, and in what manner it affected me, are transitions of thought and feeling which I now find it difficult to trace. I only know that I was bitterly disappointed; perhaps not altogether without reason, and yet more so than the occasion warranted. In the first place, my expatriation had already lasted many years. I longed to be once more surrounded by cheery English faces, and to hear the pleasant English tongue spoken about me. In the next place, I felt hurt that my love was not enough to make my husband happy, even under our gray skies in "duller Britain." Nay, I was half jealous of these foreign climes that had grown so dear to him, and of those habits which had become necessities. Besides, Broomhill, of all places in the land, was now my lawful home. Broomhill, of which I had been dreaming all these years. Broomhill, where, as a little child, I had contracted the first and last love of my life! It was no wonder, surely, that I yearned to go home to it across the Channel — and yet I might have been content with the sweet present! Except Hugh, no one loved or cared for me; and I had better have accepted my happiness *per se*, without a care or desire beyond it. Ah, why did I not? Why, when I had most reason to be glad, did I suffer myself to be tormented by the phantasm of a trouble? What mattered it whether we dwelt in England or Italy, Rome or Broomhill, so that we were only together? He was with me; he loved me; and where love is, heaven is, if we would but believe it! Eve made Adam's paradise, and Robinson Crusoe's isle was a desert only because he lived in it alone. But, alas! it is ever thus. We cavil at the blessing possessed, and grasp at the shadow to come. We feel first, and reason afterward; only we seldom begin to reason till it is too late!

One day, as the spring was rapidly merging into summer, we took a carriage and drove out from Rome to Albano. It was quite early when we started. The grassy mounds of the Campo Vaccino were crowded with bullock-trucks as we went down the Sacred Road; and the brown walls of the Colosseum were touched with golden sunshine. The same shadows that had fallen daily for centuries in the same places, darkened the windings of the lower passages. The blue day shone through the uppermost arches, and the shrubs that grew upon them waved to and fro in the morning breeze. A monk was preaching in the midst of the arena; and a French military band was practicing upon the open ground behind the building.

"Oh, for a living Cæsar to expel these Gauls!" muttered Hugh, aiming the end of his cigar at the spurred heels of a dandy little *sous-lieutenant* who was sauntering "delicately," like King Agag, on the sunny side of the road.

Passing out by the San Giovanni gate, we entered upon those broad wastes that lie to the south-east of the city. Going forward thence, with the aqueducts to our left, and the old Appian way, lined with crumbling sepulchers, reaching for miles in one unswerving line to our far right, we soon left Rome behind. Faint patches of vegetation gleamed here and there, like streaks of light; and nameless ruins lay scattered broadcast over the bleak slopes of this "most desolate region." Sometimes we came upon a primitive bullock-wagon, or a peasant driving an ass laden with green boughs; but these signs of life were rare. Presently we passed the remains of a square temple, with Corinthian pilasters — then a drove of shaggy ponies — then a little truck with a tiny pent-house reared on one side of the seat, to keep the driver from the sun — then a flock of rusty sheep — a stagnant pool — a clump of stunted trees — a conical thatched hut — a round sepulcher, half-buried in the soil of ages — a fragment of broken arch; and so on, for miles and miles, across the barren plain. By and by, we saw a drove of buffaloes scouring along toward the aqueducts, followed by a mounted herdsman, buskined and brown, with his lance in his hand, his blue cloak floating behind him, and his sombrero down upon his brow — the very picture of a Mexican hunter.

Now the Campagna was left behind, and Albano stood straight before us, on the summit of a steep and weary hill. Low lines of white-washed wall bordered the road on either side, inclosing fields of *fascine*, orchards, olive-grounds, and gloomy plantations of cypresses and pines. Next came a range of sand-banks, with cavernous hollows and deep undershadows; next, an old cinque-cento gateway, crumbling away by the road side; then a little wooden cross on an overhanging crag; then the sepulcher of Pompey; and then the gates of Albano, through which we rattled into the town, and up to the entrance of the Hotel de Russie. Here we tasted the wine that Horace praised, and lunched in a room that overlooked a brown sea of Campagna, with the hazy Mediterranean on the farthest horizon, and the tower of Corioli standing against the clear sky to our left.

By and by, we went out through the market-place, and up a steep road leading to the lake. Ah, how well I remember it! How well I remember that table-land of rock on which we stood, with Monte Cavo rising high before us, and the blue lake lying at our feet in a steep basin clothed with forests! Scrambling down upon a kind of natural terrace several feet below, we pushed our way through the briers and found a grassy knoll at the foot of an ilex, just on the margin of the precipice. Here we sat sheltered from the sun, with the placid lake below, the mountains above, and the pines of Castel Gondolfo standing like sentinels between us and the landscape. The air was heavy with fragrance, and a golden haze hung over Rome. We had brought sketch-books, but they lay untouched beside us on the grass. The scene was too fair for portraiture; and all that we could do was to drink deeply of its poetry, and talk from time to time of our great happiness.

"'Twas by the merest chance that you and I ever met again, love," said Hugh, taking up the broken threads of our conversation. "A feather might have turned the scale and carried me direct to St. Petersburgh; and then, good heavens! what a miserable wretch I should have been to this day!"

"A good angel brought me to you, Hugh," I murmured, leaning my head against his shoulder. "I can not bear to think that we might never have met. I can not believe but that we must some day have come face to face, and been happy!"

"Alas! we should have been strangers, Barbara *mia*. We might have looked in each other's eyes, and passed on for evermore!"

"Nay, that at all events would have been impossible! I should have known *you* anywhere."

"Perhaps so, little wife; but time, remember, has changed me less than you. You have journeyed all the way from Lilliput to Brobdignag; whilst I have only grown rougher, browner, and uglier than ever. But you look grave, *mignonne*. What have I said to vex you?"

"Nothing, dearest—and yet—and yet I am grieved to think that you could have passed me without one gleam of recognition. Surely some old thought must have come knocking at your heart—some vague picture of the little girl who loved you so dearly, long and long ago!"

My husband smiled, and laid his hand upon my head, as he used to lay it in that far-off time.

"*Enfant!*" he said, tenderly, "what matters it to thee or me, since we have met, and are happy? Think what it would have been had our meeting happened many a year to come, and happened too late!"

"Or if all things had come to pass just as they did, and yet you had not cared for me! Oh, Hugh, that would have been the cruelest of all."

"And the least likely. Why, Barbara, you came to me at the time when I most needed you. You revived my trust in heaven, and my faith in man. You reconciled me to the present and the future; blotted out the past, and turned to wine the bitter waters of my life! How, then, could I choose but love you? Ay, with every pulse of my heart, and every nerve of my brain—with my hopes, and my dreams, and all that is worthiest in me! Hush you are weeping!"

"For joy," I whispered, brokenly; "for joy only. Speak to me thus forever, and I will listen to you!"

He pressed his lips upon my forehead, and for some minutes we were both silent.

"Tell me," I said at length, "how and when you first began to love me. Did it come to you suddenly, or steal imperceptibly upon your heart, like the shadow over the dial?"

"Neither, and yet both," replied he, musingly. "I never knew the moment when it first befell me; and yet, like one of those mysterious isles that are upheaved in a single night from the depths of the great ocean, it rose all at once upon my life, and became my Paradise. Now it is ours, and ours alone. None but ourselves shall enter into that Eden—none but ourselves gather its flowers, or feed upon its fruits! Pshaw! what children we both are! With what delicious egotism we treasure up each 'trivial, fond record,' and tell the old tale o'er and o'er again!"

"Say rather the tale that is never old," I suggested; "the poem that is never ended; the song that can not be sung through! Ah, Hugh, I almost fear, sometimes, that to be so happy is not good for me."

"Not good, my Barbara—why so?"

"Because I seem to live for love alone, and to have forgotten all that once made the pleasure and purpose of my life. I have neither strength nor ambition left; and my 'so potent art!' has lost its magic for me. I fear that I shall never make a painter."

He smiled and sighed, and a look half of regret, half of compassion, passed across his face.

"Art is long, and life is short," he said. "We can never compass the one; but we may at least reap all that is fairest in the other. Look yonder, child, beyond the boundary of the pines—look yonder, where Rome glitters in the sun, and remember that Raffaelle lies buried in the Pantheon."

"I do remember it."

"Ay, and remember that love is here, but fame is hereafter—that to be great is to be exposed to all the shafts of envy; but that to love thus is to wear an 'armoure against fate!' What to us are the changes of the years, the wars of kings, the revolutions of empires? We dwell in the conscious security of our love, as

" In a green island far from all men's knowing;"

and, happen what may in the wide world beyond, there abide 'till our content is absolute.' Heigho! I also used to dream, once upon a time, of art, and poetry, and fame; but that was before I knew how much had already been done—how little was left to do! Now I am wiser, and more indolent. Satisfied to appreciate, I wander from Shakspeare to Goethe, from Raffaelle to Rembrandt, from Plato to Bacon. I taste of all arts and all philosophies. 'Seneca can not be too heavy, nor Plautus too light' for me; and yet what hope have I of ever compassing one half of the accumulated riches of the past? Ten lives would not be enough to read all the best books, and see all the best pictures in the world!"

"Nor ten times ten," I added, sadly. "Alas! to what end are we working, and of what avail is any thing that we can do? Why paint pictures that can achieve no fame, or write books that will never be read? Why multiply failure upon failure; and why 'monster' our 'nothings' in the face of all that has been done by the greatest and the wisest? For my part when I think of these things, I am hopeless."

"And for mine, Barbarina, I believe that the life of the *connoisseur* is as well spent as that of any other man on earth! It is for him that the author toils, and the painter mixes his colors; and neither of them could well live without him. He reads the books that others write. He buys the pictures that others paint. He represents popular opinion, embodies the taste of the age, and keeps us in mind of all that we owe to the past. *Per Bacco!* I begin to have quite a respectful admiration for myself when I think of it!"

I could not help smiling. "This is mere sophistry," I said. "You love an idle life, and are 'nothing if not critical;' and now you want to make your very idleness heroic. No, no, Hugh—confess that it is pleasanter to dream in libraries and galleries than to contribute to either; and that enjoyment is more agreeable than work!"

He laughed, and sprang lightly to his feet. "Be just, Barbarina," he said. "Be just, if nothing more. A reckless dare-devil, such as I have been this many a year, scarcely deserves to be accused of idleness or dreaming. I am an Epicurean, if you will; but not a Sybarite."

"Be both," I cried, hastily; "be an idler, a dreamer, a trifler—any thing you please; but never, never wander away into dangers and deserts again! You once talked to me of the pleasure of peril. Oh, I have never forgotten that phrase!"

"Foolish little wife! Forget it, dear, at once and forever. Henceforth I shall only travel where I can take you with me, and that is guarantee enough for my own safety. But the afternoon is waning, and I have still something to show you in Albano."

Upon this, we went down again into the town, passing our hotel by the way, and stopping before the heavy double doors of what seemed to be a handsome private residence. Here Hugh

rang, and a very old woman admitted us. A paved carriage-way intersected the ground floor, and led out upon a graveled space at the back. Beyond this lay extensive grounds, richly wooded, with vistas of lawn, and winding walks between.

"This is the Villa Castellani," said Hugh passing through with a nod to the portress. "We will go over the gardens first, and then see the house. It is a strange, rambling, deserted place, but there is something romantic about it—something shady, quiet, and medieval which takes a peculiar hold on my imagination, and possesses a charm which I scarcely know how to define."

"Then you have been here before?"

"I once lodged in the house for two months. It was a long time ago—six or eight years, I suppose; but I remember every nook and corner as well as if I had left it only yesterday. Stay—this turning should lead to the ruins!"

We went down a broad walk, wide enough for a carriage drive, and completely roofed in by thick trees. Weeds grew unheeded in the gravel, and last year's leaves lay thick on the ground. Here and there, in the green shade, stood a stone seat brown with mosses; or a broken urn; or a tiny antique altar, rifled from a tomb—and presently we reached a space somewhat more open than the rest, with a shapeless mass of reticulated brick-work, and a low arch guarded by two grim lions in the midst. Here the leaves had drifted more deeply, and the weeds had grown more rankly than elsewhere; and a faint oppressive perfume sickened on the air. We pushed our way through the grass and brambles, and looked down into the darkness of that cavernous archway. A clinging damp lay on the old marble lions, and on the leaves and blossoms of the trailing shrubs that overgrew them. A green lizard darted by on a fragment of broken wall. A squirrel ran up the shaft of a stately stone pine that stood in the midst of the ruins. I shuddered, and sighed.

"The place is strangely melancholy," I said. "What ruins are these?"

"Probably those of Pompey's villa," replied my husband; "but their history is lost. The estate now belongs to a noble Roman family, one of whose ancestral Cardinals built the house yonder, about a hundred and sixty years ago. They are now too poor to keep it in repair, and they let it whenever they can get tenants to take it. The whole place is going fast to decay."

"And you once lived here for two whole months?"

"Ay, for two very pleasant months, during which I spent all my time wandering about these lakes and ruins, with a carbine on my shoulder and a book in my hand—like a literary bandit. How often I have lain among these very trees, with a volume of Tasso in my hand, dreaming and reading alternately, and peopling the shady avenues with Armida and her nymphs!"

But I hardly listened to him. I was fascinated by this gloomy arch leading away into subterranean darkness, and could think of nothing else.

"I wonder where it goes, and if it has been explored," I said. "These lions look as if they were guarding the secret of some hidden treasure. There ought to be a dreadful tale connected with the place!"

"There shall be one, if you wish it, *carina.* Let me see—we have a Cardinal, who is an intellectual voluptuary, fond of learning and pleasure, and in love with a beautiful peasant girl down in the village. We have gardens, with ancient ruins lying in the shadows of the trees —a jealous lover lurking in the archway—twilight—an ambuscade—a revenge—a murder— oh, it would make a charming story!"

"Then you shall put it together, and tell it to me as we drive back to Rome."

"Willingly; but come a few yards farther, where you see the light at the end of the avenue."

I followed, and we emerged upon a terrace that bounded the gardens on this side. The Campagna and the hills lay spread before us in the burning sunset, and a shining zone of sea bounded the horizon. Long shadows streamed across the marble pavement, and patches of brilliant light pierced through the carved interstices of the broken balcony. A little fountain dripped wearily in the midst, surmounted by a headless Triton, and choked with water-weeds; whilst all along the parapet, with many a gap, and many a vacant pedestal, the statues of the Cæsars stood between us and the sun.

When at length we went back, we took a path skirting the ridge of a deep hollow, where a forest of olives shivered grayly in the breeze. The house stood before us all the way, stately but dilapidated; with closed windows and shattered cornices, and an open Belvedere on the top, where one shuddered to think how the wind must howl at night. Something of this I must have shown in my face, for Hugh, looking at me, said anxiously:—

"The place is solemn, but not sad; and to my mind, is only the more beautiful for its desolation."

"Yes," I replied, "it is very beautiful."

But I felt a strange oppression, nevertheless.

"And one might paint twenty pictures from these gardens alone."

"Yes, truly."

He glanced at me again, and seemed about to speak; but checked himself, and walked on silently. The same old woman was waiting at the house to receive us—such a weird, withered, tottering creature, that one might have fancied her as old as the building.

"The Hall of the Hercules, *signora,*" said she, in a shrill treble, that quavered like the tones of a broken instrument.

It had once been a stately vestibule; but was now a lumber-room. Ladders, gardening tools, and rubbish of all kinds lay piled in the corners; and at the farther end a store of fagots and *fascine* was stacked against the wall. The frescoes on the ceiling were broken away in patches here and there. The tesselated pavement was defaced and soiled. Busts, black with the dust of years and draped with cobwebs, looked down from their niches overhead, as if in solemn pity "for a glory left behind." Altogether it was a mournful place—still more mournful than the grounds and the ruins.

From this erewhile "Hall of the Hercules," we passed on through the chambers of the lower floor, preceded by our guide, with her bunch of rusty keys. They were all dusty and solitary alike. The daylight filtered drearily into them through half-opened shutters, and the doors complained upon their hinges. In some were broken mirrors, worm-eaten remains of costly furniture, and funereal hangings which fell to pieces at a touch and sent up clouds of dust. Others were bare of every thing save cobwebs; and all were profusely decorated with tarnished gilding; marble pilasters, rich cornices, panelings from which the delicate arabesques were fast disappearing, and ceilings where "many a fallen old divinity" still presided, amid faded Cupids and regions of roses and blue clouds.

In the second story, the rooms were smaller and cleaner, and contained, moreover, a scanty supply of uncomfortable modern furniture. It was this part, said the old *cicerone,* which his. noble Highness graciously condescended to let during the season, reserving the lower floor to his own masterful use, or disuse, as the case might be.

"Then it must have been here that you lived, Hugh," I said, as we took our way from suite to suite.

"No—like a true hero I sought to climb above my fellows, and secured the top of the house. Up there, 'my soul was like a star, and dwelt apart.' I could do as I pleased, had a terrace to myself, and the key of the Belvedere. Oh, what songs and sonnets I scribbled by moonlight on that terrace-top, and how I used to twist them into pipe-lights the next morning!"

By this time we had reached the foot of the last staircase, and Hugh, springing forward, took the lead.

"See," said he, "these are my old quarters. What do you think of them?"

It was like passing from dark to light—from winter to summer—from a prison to a palace. The private apartments of a princess in a fairy tale could not have been more daintily luxurious. Ante-room, *salon,* library, and bed-room led one from another; and the library opened on a marble terrace with orange trees in tubs at all the corners, and a great stone vase of mignonette before the window. Exquisite furniture, glittering with pearl and ormolu; mosaic tables; walls, paneled with mirrors and paintings; gauzy hangings; carpets in which the feet sank noiselessly; precious works of art in marble and terra-cotta; books, flowers, and all those minor accessories which give grace and comfort to a home, were here in abundance.

"Well," repeated my husband, laughingly, "what do you think of them?"

"I scarcely know what to think," I replied confusedly. "I—surely I—I seem to recognize some of these things — that bronze, for instance; and those vases—and this cabinet— nay, I am certain this is the cabinet that we bought the other day, in the Via Frattina! Why are they here? — and what does it all mean?"

"It means," said he, taking me by the hand, with a strange mixture of doubt and eagerness, "it means that all wise people will soon be leaving Rome for the hot season, and—and that I have reëngaged these old rooms of mine for your reception. See, here are all our recent purchases—our pictures, our statues, our mosaics. These shelves contain copies of your favorite authors; and in the next room you will find an easel, and a stock of artistic necessaries. Our bedroom windows overlook the hills about Gensano—our *salon* commands the town and market-place—our library opens toward the Campagna, with Ostia in the distance, and the gardens at our feet. Here, with all Latium mapped out before us, we can spend our happy summer in absolute retirement. Here, wandering at will among lakes, forests, and mountains, we can sketch—we can read—we can ride—we can study this beautiful, half-savage Roman people, and trace in the present the influences of the past! Ah, dearest, you know not yet the enchantment of an Italian summer amid Italian hills! You know not what it is to breathe the perfume of the orange gardens—to lie at noon in the deep shadow of an ilex-grove, listening to the ripple of a legendary spring, older than history—to stroll among ruins in the purple twilight! Then up here, far from the sultry city and the unhealthy plains, we have such sunrises and sunsets as you, artist though you be, have never dreamed of—here, where the cool airs linger longest, and the very moon and stars look more golden than elsewhere! Tell me, dear heart, have I done well, and will my bird be happy in the nest that I have made for her?"

Seeing how flushed he was with his own eloquence, and how he had anticipated all things for my pleasure, I tried to seem glad—even to smile, and thank him. But, for all that, my heart was heavy with hope deferred; and, as we drove back to Rome in the gray dusk, I wept behind my vail, thinking of home, and seeing the term of my exile growing more and more indefinite.

Not many days after this, we moved out to Albano, and established ourselves in *villeggiatura* at the Villa Castellani; taking with us for our only attendants two Italian women-servants and our faithful Tippoo. Alas! why was I not happy? Why was I restless, and why did I cast aside canvas after canvas, unable to settle to my art, or to enjoy the paradise around me? Wherefore when the transparent nights were radiant with fire-flies, did I yearn only for the red glimmer of one far-off village smithy; and wherefore, when the sun went down in glory behind the convent-crested brow of Monte Cavo, could I only sigh, and picture to myself how it was burning even now upon the Tudor windows at Broomhill?

CHAPTER XXXIX.

A VICTORY.

THE year wore on, and, toward autumn, my health gradually declined. I suffered no pain, and my physicians could discover no disease; but a strange mental and physical lassitude had taken possession of me, and I faded slowly. I seemed to have lost all my old strength and energy—all my love of life—all my appreciation of beauty. Lying languidly upon a sofa on the terrace, I used to listen to the noises in the market-place without ever caring to look down on the picturesque crowd beneath; and many a time I closed my eyes upon the landscape and the sky, in utter weariness of spirit, because "I had no pleasure in them." Thus day after day went by, and at length it was said that I must have change of air.

Unanimous upon this one point, my advisers could agree upon no other. One recommended Nice. Another was of opinion that Nice would be too mild, and advocated Florence. A third insisted upon the waters of Vichy. When they were all gone, I called Hugh to my side, and as he knelt down by my couch in the light of the golden afternoon, I clung to his neck, like a sick child, and whispered—

"Take me home, dear—only take me home!"

"Home?" he repeated, vaguely.

"Yes—to Broomhill. I shall never get well here, or anywhere, unless you take me to Broomhill!"

I felt him shudder in my arms, and that was all. After waiting some moments for the answer that did not come, I went on pleading.

"You don't know, Hugh, how I have longed for it, or how I have been thinking of it, these last months. If we had gone there first of all, though only for a few weeks, I believe I should have been content—content to stay with you here for years and years; but now—you will not be angry with me, dear, if I tell you how I have yearned to go back?"

He shook his head, and drew my cheek closer to his own, so that I could not see his face.

"And you will not fancy that I have been unhappy, or discontented, or ungrateful?"

He shook his head again, with a quick gesture of deprecation.

"Well then, I—I feel as though I could never get well anywhere but at home, and as though I must die if you do not take me there. You see, dear, I have thought of it so much—thought, indeed, of nothing else for months. When you told me you loved me, my first thought was for you, and my second for Broomhill. Ever since our marriage, I have looked forward to the happy day when we should go back there together, and make it our own, dear, quiet home. Ah, Hugh, you can not know the charm there is for me in that word, Home! You can not know how often I have lain awake in the pauses of the night, repeating it to myself, and trying to call back every tree in the old park — every picture, and corridor, and nook in the old house, till memory seemed to grow too vivid, and became almost pain!"

"My poor child," said my husband, tenderly, "this is a *mal de pays*."

"Perhaps so. I have fancied that it might be, more than once. No Swiss, I am sure, could sicken for his own Alps more than I sicken for Broomhill. But then, you see, dear, the happiest days of all my past life were linked with it—and I have been so many, many years away from England—and—and, like Queen Mary, I fancy if I were to die now, you would find the name of Broomhill engraven on my heart!"

He drew a long breath that sounded almost like a sob, and, disengaging himself from my embrace, got up, and paced about the room.

"How strange it is!" he said. "We love each other—why can we not live anywhere, be happy anywhere together? I have heard of those who were happy in a garret—a prison—a desert—and this is the garden of the world! What is it? Fate? No—no—no! We make our own ends—our own pitfalls—our own sorrows. All might be well, if we would have it so—but we cannot rest—we are fools; and the fool's punishment must follow, sooner or later—sooner or later! Turn aside the lightning from heaven, and it comes up through the ground on which one stands!"

"Oh, Hugh! Hugh! you are angry with me!" I cried, terrified by these wild words. "Forgive me—pray forgive me! I could be happy with you in a dungeon—indeed, indeed I could. Only say that you forgive me!"

He mastered his agitation by a strong effort, and drew a chair, quite calmly, beside my couch.

"I have nothing to forgive," he said, in a low, measured voice. "Nothing whatever, Barbara. You desire only what is just and reasonable. You have married the master of Broomhill, and you have a right to live at Broomhill."

"No, no—not a right!" I interrupted. "I wish to have no rights, save those which your dear love gives me!"

"And you have a right to live at Broomhill," he repeated, as if he had not heard me. "But, on the other hand, I dislike England. I prefer a continental life, and a continental climate; and I had hoped that you, educated and almost naturalized abroad, would share my tastes, and conform gladly to my wishes."

"I have tried to do so," I said complainingly; for I was very weak, and felt hurt to hear him set it forth so coldly. "I have tried; and while my strength lasted, I succeeded. But though I was silent, I was always longing to go back—and now—and now my longing has worn me out, and, with me, all my power of resistance!"

He looked at me, and his forced coldness melted all at once.

"My Barbara!" he said. "My poor, pale Barbara!" And so leaned his forehead moodily in his two palms.

A long time went by thus—he bent and brooding; I anxiously watching him. By and by I raised myself from my pillows, and crept close to his knees.

"You will take me home, dear, will you not?" I said once more, trying to draw his hands down from his face.

"Yes. If you must go—yes," he answered, looking up with a face that startled me—it was so much whiter than my own. "I can not let you take, my Flower; but—God help us both!"

And with this he kissed me, and lifted me from the floor, and laid me tenderly upon the couch again; and then went out upon the terrace.

I had prevailed. The desire that had been upon my mind for so many months was spoken at last, and granted; and yet I felt uneasy, apprehensive, and but half satisfied. Was it well, I asked myself, to succeed against his will? Was it well to have evoked the first hint of dissension for my gratification? Might not ill come of it; and might I not, at least, have tried the air of Nice, or Florence, first? Wavering thus, I was more than once upon the point of calling to him—then I checked myself, and thought how happy I would make him at Broomhill; and how he should thank me by and by for having brought him there; and what a pleasure it would be to see him once more in

the home of his fathers, respected and honored, and bearing, as became him, 'the grand old name of gentleman.' Thus the moment, the precious moment of concession, went by; and I wandered away into a train of dreams and musings.

It was almost dusk before Hugh came in again; but he had regained his composure, and spoke cheerfully of England and our journey. His nature was too generous to do a kindness by halves, and, since he had yielded, he yielded graciously. For all this, however, I saw the dark shade settle now and then upon his brow, and noted the effort by which it was dismissed.

In a few days more, we were on our way home.

<hr>

CHAPTER XL.

THE FIRST CLOUD ON THE HORIZON.

WHAT with waiting some days for finer weather at Civita Vecchia, and what with the delays occasioned by my fatigue at different points of the journey, we were more than three weeks traveling from Rome to London. I had begun to mend, however, from the day that we left Albano—I might almost say, from the hour that our return was resolved upon—and by the time I stepped on shore at Dover, I had already recovered my spirits, and much of my strength. We came home without having met any whom we knew, having rested a few days in Paris in a solitude as complete as that of Albano. Hilda and her husband were with the court at Fontainebleau; and Mrs. Churchill, who could not exist throughout the autumn, even in Paris, without the excitement of a German Spa, had gone with my father to Homburg some ten days before. So we went our way like strangers, welcomed only by the hotel-keepers along the road; and, arriving in London toward the latter end of August, put up at Claridge's in Brook Street.

On the evening of the second day, as we were sitting at desert, Hugh looked up suddenly, and said—

"You are going to make a pilgrimage to-morrow to your old home, are you not, Barbara?"

"To my old home and my old nurse, dear. I want to bring poor Goody to live with us at Broomhill."

"Do so, darling, by all means. She shall have one of my model cottages; or, if you prefer it, a nook in the old house, somewhere."

"Then we will let her choose, please, Hugh; but I think she will prefer a little cottage of her own to a great house full of servants."

"And in the mean time," said my husband, with something like a shade of embarrassment in his manner, "I think of running down to Broomhill myself to-morrow, for a few hours; just to—to see that all is in order before its little mistress makes her triumphal entry."

"What folly, dearest, when we are both going the very following day!"

"Ah, but that is no longer possible, carina. I have an appointment here with my lawyer for that precise evening; and my business may, perhaps, detain us in town till Monday or even Tuesday next."

I looked down to conceal the tears which I could not prevent from springing to my eyes. This delay was almost more than I could bear; and I should have been ashamed to confess how keenly I felt it.

"Besides," continued he, "the servants do not yet know that we are in England. I ought to have written to Mrs. Fairhead by this day's post."

"Is Mrs. Fairhead the same housekeeper whom I remember?"

"The very same—an excellent old soul, whom I have tormented in various ways ever since I was born. By the way, she does not even know that her vagabond master brings a wife home with him; so, you see, it would never do to take her by surprise."

"You have not told her that we are married?"

"Not a bit of it. I wrote home a few weeks ago, to say that I was on the point of returning to England, and desired the house might be thoroughly ready in every part. I suppose, however, that I am bound to reveal the fact before you make your appearance."

"And—and shall you really go to-morrow?"

"I think so," replied he, carelessly. "And I also think that Mr. Claridge might find us a better wine. Tippoo, go down and inquire if they have any genuine white Hermitage, which they can particularly recommend."

Tippoo glided away; and for some moments we were uncomfortably silent.

"I—I hope you will not be long away, Hugh," I faltered, presently. "I do not like being left all——"

"Left?" echoed he. "Why, you little goose, I shall come back by the last train."

"What, the same day?"

"Of course—in time for supper, if your highness will consent to dine early and sup late."

"But how is it possible——"

"Every thing is possible where there are railways and steam-engines. The station, carina, is within eleven miles of home; and the express whirls me over all the rest of the distance in two hours and a half. I'll be bound, now, that you had forgotten all about the railway, and thought I should be two or three days away from you!"

"I had forgotten it. Remember, I have been living a conventual life these last years, and the face of the world is changed since I looked upon it last. But don't you think we might go home on Saturday, husband? It is so long to wait till Monday or Tuesday next?"

He passed his hand caressingly over my hair, as if I were a spoiled child, and sighed.

"Perhaps," he said; "perhaps. We shall see."

"And tell me," I whispered nestling closer to his side, "is Satan quiet enough for me? I should so like to ride that dear, beautiful creature."

"Satan? Oh, poor old Satan! I don't even know if he is still alive. He must be sixteen years old by this time, at the least."

"But if he is alive——"

"If he is still alive, he is so old that he is sure to be quiet enough for a baby. But I shall buy my Barbarina a dainty cream-colored Arab, fit for a princess's mounting; and a little chaise and pair of Shetlands that Cinderella might envy."

"Oh, no, Hugh—not for me."

"Not for you, you foolish birdie? And why

not, pray? Can any thing be too good or too rare for you? Why, I mean my wife to be the best dressed and the best mounted, as well as the best loved little woman in the county! And that reminds me that you must be measured for a new habit before we leave town; and the day after to-morrow we must go shopping together, and I will show you what a lady's man I can be, and how learned I am in silks, satins, laces, cashmeres, and chiffonnerie."

"But, dear husband, what do I want with laces and satins—I, a poor little painter, whose only happiness is to be quite alone with you, and quite unnoticed?"

"My child," said Hugh, with a look half of sad reproach, "we should have staid away, if we desired to live on in our solitary paradise. In Suffolk, every one knows me. I can not live incognito on my own acres. When it is known that I am at Broomhill, and that I have brought a wife to my hearth, we shall be inundated with visitors and invitations. Ah, Barbarina, you had not thought of that."

I was dismayed.

"But—but we need not see them," I said. "We can refuse their invitations."

"Only to a certain extent. I can not suffer my neighbors to suppose that my wife is not presentable. There are families whom we must receive and visit, or we shall appear ridiculous. Uncivilized as I am, carina, I have no mind to become the laughing-stock of the county."

"But——"

"But there is no help for it, little wife. I am willing, even now, if you desire it, to go back to Italy—or travel in any direction you please, East, West, North or South, without going one mile farther on the road to Suffolk; but if the master of Broomhill returns thither with his wife at his side, he must not forget that he is the last representative of a long line of English gentlemen who never yet closed their doors in the faces of their neighbors, or neglected the good old English virtue of hospitality."

It was the first time he had ever spoken to me thus. It was the first time he had ever used a tone even bordering upon authority. It was the first time that I had ever heard him express any thing like pride of birth, or respect for the observances of society. Startled, confused, almost abashed, I knew not how to answer.

"You—you did not think thus seven years ago," I faltered. "You shut yourself up like a hermit; and it was Mrs. Sandyshaft who——"

"Who dragged me into society," interrupted he, impatiently. "I know it. But I was not a married man; and I was just seven years younger than now. As I said before, Barbara, I can not let the world suppose that I have made a mésalliance, and am ashamed to introduce my wife in the county. We will turn back, if you please. God knows, I came here only for your sake, and would far rather retrace the pleasant road that leads to liberty; but, if we go forward, we must be prepared to occupy our home in a manner consistent with our own dignity. Which shall it be—Broomhill or Italy?"

"I—I don't know," I replied, feeling half-hurt, half-angry, and bitterly disappointed. "I must have time to consider—I will tell you when you come back to-morrow evening."

"Nay, that will hardly do, my child; because

If we turn back, there will be no need for me to go down at all."

I went over to the window, and looked out for some minutes in silence.

"Well," said Hugh, after a considerable pause, "have you made up your mind, Barbarina?"

"Yes, Hugh, I have made up my mind. We will go to Broomhill."

CHAPTER XLI.

A PIOUS PILGRIMAGE.

It was a dull, gray day, when (having breakfasted very early, and seen Hugh step into the cab which was to convey him to the Eastern Counties Station) I ordered a fly to be brought round, and desired to be driven to that familiar suburb, every street and house of which I knew by heart. The way, however, was long, and the approach from this side of London so new to me, that till we turned into the High Street, I scarcely recognized any of the old topography. Even there, nothing seemed quite the same. New houses had sprung up; the trades in the shops were many of them changed; a smart terrace occupied the site of the stone-yard by the canal; and a church stood on the waste ground where the boys used to play at cricket on summer afternoons. Seeing all these changes, I began to fear lest the old house might be gone; but just as the doubt occurred to me it came in sight, gloomy as ever, behind the dusty trees.

Finding myself so near, I stopped the carriage and went forward on foot, with a strange sensation of being still a child and having left the place but yesterday. I looked up at the windows — they were blacker and blanker than ever. I rang the bell, and its echoes jangled painfully in the silence. Then, after a long, long pause, a footstep slowly crossed the paved space between the house-door and the gate; a key grated rustily in the lock; and not Goody, but a dark and sullen-looking woman stood before me. I asked for Mrs. Beever.

"Mrs. Beever?" repeated she, holding the door jealously ajar. "I never heard the name."

Never heard the name! This answer so confounded me that I scarcely knew what to say next.

"She had charge of the house," I faltered.

"I have charge of the house," replied the woman, "and it's let."

With this she seemed about to shut the door; but I staid her by a gesture.

"Let?" I reiterated. "Let! Mr. Churchill——"

"Mr. Churchill is gone to live abroad," said she. "If you want his address, I have it on a card, indoors."

I shook my head, and, being still weak, and somewhat overcome, leaned against the doorway for support.

"I want the old servant," I said; "the old servant who was here before the house was given up. If you can tell me where to find her, I shall be very thankful."

She shook her head impatiently. She knew nothing of any such person. She could give me Mr. Churchill's address, if I wanted it; but

not his servant's. That was no part of her business. And again she made as if she would shut the door.

I took out my purse and spoke gently to her, ungentle as she was.

"Will you let me go over the house?" I said, placing a half-crown in her hand.

She glanced sharply at me, and at the coin.

"But the house is let," she said again.

"I know it. Still, if you are alone here, you can let me go through the rooms. I — I lived here once; and I should like to see the place again."

She seemed about to refuse; but looked again at the money, and put it in her pocket.

"Well, come in," she said, a little more civilly. "I suppose there can be no harm in that."

So I passed in. She locked the door behind me, like a jailer, and followed me into the house. With this I would willingly have dispensed; but she kept me in sight, suspiciously, from room to room, through all the lower floors. They were mostly bare, or contained only worthless lumber. I asked her what had been done with Mr. Churchill's furniture, and if there had been a sale; but found that she knew, or would know, nothing. At the foot of the garret-stairs she paused, thinking it useless, I suppose, to follow farther. I went up alone.

Alas! my lonely garrets, where we used to play as little children, half fearful of the silence when the ringing of our baby-laughter died away! Where, a few years later, I spent so many bitter solitary hours, blistering my books with tears, and rebelling against the fate that made me younger than my sisters. Where I come back now, after long years, to find upon the walls strange traces of my former self, scribbled sentences of childish writing, and charcoal outlines, half-defaced, but full, to me, of their old meanings! This, I remember, was a landscape; this, Sir Hudibras and Sidrophel; this, the vision of Mirza — all suggested by the books I had read, and all bearing, at the least, some stammering evidence to my inborn love of art. I looked at them sadly, as one long freed might decipher his own writing on the walls of what had been his cell, and sighed, with a retrospective pity, for my bygone self— then, turning to the window, saw the strip of weedy garden, and the foul canal with its sluggish barges creeping by, just as they used to creep in that old time; and far away, beyond the spires and house-tops, those well-remembered hills that had mocked me so often with their summer greenness. I had trodden the snows and glaciers of the Alps since last I looked on them — I had dwelt with Rome and the Tiber before my windows, and seen the sun go down behind Soracte, "his own beloved mountain;" but I question if I ever looked on either with such emotion as I felt this day in sight of the only glimpse of nature that gladdened my childhood.

I seemed to have been here only a few moments, but I suppose the time went quickly; for the woman presently came up, as if to see what I could be doing there so long. So I hurried down again, almost glad to be spared the pain of staying longer. At the house-door I paused, and gathered a few leaves of dusty ivy.

H

"And you have no idea of where I can find the servant?" I asked for the last time.

She shook her head sullenly, and unlocked the outer door.

"Perhaps they may be able to tell you over there," she said, pointing to a baker's at a distant corner.

I passed out, and would have bade her good morning; but she shut the door behind me in an instant, and turned the key. I never crossed that threshold again. Never again.

At the baker's they could tell me nothing; but referred me to a grocer's next door. The grocer directed me to Pink's Row, the third garden on the right. Mrs. Beever, he said, had been there—might be there still, for aught that he could tell. At all events I should there learn all particulars. So, still leaving the carriage in sight, I took the grocer's little daughter for my guide, and went in search of Pink's Row.

It opened from a noisy by-street, all alive with stalls, and consisted of some eight or ten poor dwellings, each with a narrow space of garden railed off in front. In one or two of these stood blackened skeletons of trees, and rotting summer-houses, and, perhaps, a sickly sunflower tied, like a martyr, to a stake. But most of them were mere uneven patches of rubbish and waste ground, trodden out of all productiveness, and gone utterly to ruin.

Though very small—smaller, it even seemed, than the others—the third house to the right looked clean and decent. A white blind, and a flower in the window, gave it an air of cheerfulness; and a little child playing on the threshold added that precious link that binds poetry to life in the poorest home. I dismissed my guide, and went up to the door alone. There were two women in the little room; one by the window, stitching busily—the other attending to something on the fire. Though her back was turned, I knew the last directly.

"Goody," I said, forgetting at once all that I had meant to say by way of preparation. "Goody, dear, don't you know me?"

And Goody, with an inarticulate cry, dropped her saucepan, and stared at me as if I were a ghost—then laughed, and sobbed, and flung her arms about me, and said all the loving, foolish things that she could think of.

"But sure, my lamb," she said, when the first outburst was over, "sure you've not come home, thinking to find the old house as it was, and with nowhere else to go? May be you didn't know your father was still in foreign parts, and never likely to return? Or is he with you, deary? And have you left the school for good? And has he changed his mind, meaning to live in England, after all; and you with him? Then, to think of his having married again — ah, my pretty, I never thought he would have done that! And to think of little Hilda being married too, and to a fine foreign gentleman with a title to his name! Dear, dear, how things have changed! How things have changed!"

"And we also," I answered, holding her hands in mine, and smiling to think how much I had to tell her. "And we also, Goody. Don't you think I am changed, since you last saw me?"

"Changed! Why, you were a little child—a little, pale, wee, delicate child, when you went away, my deary; and now——Why, I can hard-

ly bring myself to believe it is the same little Barbara! And yet I knew you—should have known you anywhere—anywhere! You have the same brown eyes, and the same smile, and the same wave in your hair—oh, my darling, what a happy day for me!"

I drew a chair beside her, and prepared for a long chat. The younger woman had left the room, taking the child with her; and we were quite alone. First I drew her simple story from her, and then I told her mine.

Of all that had befallen me I found her still ignorant, and of my father she had only heard through the agent who from time to time transmitted money to her. The house, it seemed, had been given up six months ago, and she, after her life's devotion, dismissed with a year's salary and a message that Mr. Churchill intended, for the future, to reside abroad. But of this she did not even complain. She had saved money, and was now living, happily enough, with her married niece, whom I remembered as a tall girl who played with us sometimes when we were children. As for the furniture, some had been sold, and some was stored away in a warehouse in the neighborhood. More than this she could not tell me.

Then I bade her prepare for a great surprise, and so took off my glove, and, smiling, held my left hand up before her eyes. Ah, me! what laughing and crying, what broken exclamations and eager questions! Was I really married? Was I happy? Was my husband also a fine foreign gentleman with a title to his name? Where did I see him? How long was it ago? And so forth, in an endless tide of questions. But her delight when she found that he was an English gentleman, and her wonder when I told her the circumstances of our first acquaintance, knew no bounds; so I gave her the whole story from beginning to end. When I had finished, she drew a long breath, and said—

"Now, my lamb, please begin, and tell it to me all over again; for I'm confused in my head, you see, and can hardly bring myself to believe it at first!"

Whereupon I, repeated my narrative, with some abridgments, and having brought it once more to a close, found that it was more than time to go. But she would hardly part from me.

"I will come again to-morrow, Goody," I said, lingering on the threshold with her hand upon my shoulder. "I will come to-morrow, and take you with me to our hotel. You must see my husband, and love him, for my sake."

"Bless his heart!" said Goody.

"And by and by, when we are quite settled at Broomhill, you shall come and live with me, dear; and never, never leave me again!"

"If I might only live to nurse another little Barbara!" ejaculated Goody, with her apron to her eyes.

"So good-by, till to-morrow."

She shook her head, and embraced me again, and seemed so sad that, when half-way down the garden, I turned back and repeated—

"Only till to-morrow, remember!"

"May be, my lamb. May be," she sobbed; "but I feel as if to-morrow would be never! I don't fare to feel as if I should see you again!"

But I waved my hand and hurried away, and

she stood watching me as long as I remained in sight.

The evening was very lonely without Hugh. It was the first time that we had been parted by so many miles and so many hours, and it seemed as if the moment of his return would never come. I sent down for a railway-book; and, when it was brought, could not fathom the mystery of the time-tables. I took up a novel, and found my thoughts wandering far away from the story. I threw aside the novel for the 'Times,' and the first column that met my eyes recorded a "terrible railway accident and fearful loss of life." Thoroughly restless and nervous, I then took a seat by the window, and watched every vehicle that came and went, till impatience became agony, and I felt as if I must go down to the station to be sure that nothing had happened on the line that day. Just at the very last moment, when it was about five-and-thirty minutes past eleven, and I had made up my mind to ring for a fly without further delay, a cab dashed up to the door; a gentleman jumped out; there was a rapid footfall on the stairs; and Hugh burst into the room.

"Oh, husband, at last! Thank heaven, at last!"

"At last, my darling, and in capital time, too," he replied, cheerily. "The train was in to a moment, and my cabman had a famous horse, and here I am, hungry as a hunter! Why, you look quite agitated — what is the matter?"

"You were so late, Hugh; and I have been reading about a dreadful accident in the newspaper, and ——"

He interrupted me with a kiss, rang loudly for his supper, closed the window shiveringly, and muttered something about "this diabolical climate."

"Nonsense, sir," I said, "you ought to like your native temperature. It is a delicious night, coming after an oppressively hot day."

"A delicious purgatory! I'll buy a suit of bearskins."

"Do, dear. It will be quite in character. But have you no news for me? What did Mrs. Fairhead say, when you told her? How does the old place look? Were they not very glad to see you? Is Satan still alive?"

"I will not answer a single question till I have had my supper."

"Nay, one, dearest — only one. Did you hear any intelligence of — of my aunt?"

Hugh looked grave, and shook his head.

"I am sorry to say that I did, my Barbarina," he replied. "Mrs. Sandyshaft is ill — very ill."

"Ill!" I echoed, all my gayety deserting me in a moment. "What is the matter with her?"

"I don't know. Some kind of low fever, I fancy. They told me she had been confined to her bed for the last fortnight or more."

"Low fever — so old as she is — so strong and healthy as she has always been! Do they say she is in danger?"

"Indeed, I fear so. Doctor Topham, I am told, is far from sanguine, and ——"

"Let us go," I interrupted, vehemently. "Let us go at once. Oh, I thank God that we are in England!"

I had risen, in my excitement, and moved toward the door; but he brought me back to my chair, and took my hands gently between his own.

"Be patient, my darling," he said. "I have already considered what must be done."

"Considered! Oh, heavens! as if there were time for considering!"

"Plenty of time, if one be only calm. Mrs. Sandyshaft is very ill, but I have not heard that she is dying. Besides, we can not go at once. It is impossible."

"Nothing is impossible! with post-horses ——"

"With money and post-horses," said my husband, "we could certainly travel all night, very uncomfortably; but to-morrow morning, by the better help of the railway, we shall reach Ipswich in three hours and a half. Besides, we can telegraph in advance, and have a post-chaise waiting for us at the station."

"You are right, Hugh," I admitted, after a brief silence. "Forgive my impatience."

"As heartily as you forgive your aunt for her long neglect."

"Hush, Hugh! I remember only her love."

Just then, the supper was brought, and we sat down to table. Hungry as he said he was, Hugh ate but little, and made no effort to resume his temporary cheerfulness. By and by, the supper was removed, and the hookah brought; but the hour of our most genial intercourse went by in unbroken silence; and the cloud that had brooded over Hugh for the last few weeks came and settled more heavily than ever on his brow: settled like the darkness on the earth; like the weight on my own heart.

Alas! dear Goody, there are such things as presentiments, let those deny them who will! I shall be far away to-morrow — far away!

———

CHAPTER XLII.

THE OLD FAMILIAR FACES.

IT was between three and four o'clock, and we had been traveling by rail and road for nearly five hours; so we left our spattered post-chaise down at the inn, and walked up the hill together. There had been rain during the greater part of the day; but the clouds were now clearing off rapidly, and the red sunlight of the autumnal afternoon glittered on the wet leaves in the hedges, and in the rain-pools on the road. Presently a laborer passed us, driving a tumbril with the name of ANN SANDYSHAFT painted on the side.

"Good evening, friend," said Hugh. "Is your mistress better to-day?"

The man touched his cap, and stared at us vacantly. Hugh repeated the question.

"Oh, ay," drawled he, "she's bad enough, and to spare, master. Yon comes the Doctor. Ask him."

And with this, and a prolonged shake of the head, he plodded on his way. At the same moment a single horseman came round the bend of the road behind us, and was about to pass on with a civil salutation, when Hugh stepped forward and took the pony by the reins.

"Dr. Topham," said he, "I hope you are not going to pass me like a stranger?"

"God bless my soul, sir!" exclaimed Dr. Topham. "Is it — is it possible that I see Mr. Farquhar, of Broomhill?"

"Such as he is, you do," replied Hugh. And they shook hands heartily.

"You—you come upon us, Mr. Farquhar, like an apparition," said the little man, still flurried and surprised. "Egad, sir, you did the same thing a few years ago, and startled the whole county by appearing suddenly, like a jack in a box! What part of the globe do you come from now, pray?"

"From Italy," replied Hugh, "where I have been residing for nearly a year."

"Italy! Why, Randall told me the other day that you were in America!" ejaculated the Doctor, with a side glance at myself. "'Pon my life, the fellow said America to hoax me!"

"Randall is an excellent steward," said Hugh, quietly, "and knows that I do not care to let 'the stones prate of my whereabout.' America does well enough for an answer."

The Doctor scratched his ear, and looked puzzled. Then glanced at me again.

"I suppose," said he, pointing with his whip-handle in the direction of the hall, "I suppose you have heard the sad news over yonder, Mr. Farquhar? Our poor friend, Mrs. Sandyshaft—very ill, very ill, indeed. Low fever—debility—my second visit to her to-day, sir—my second visit."

"Indeed I have heard of it," replied Hugh, "and that brings me to the subject of my sudden arrival. But I have not yet introduced you to my wife. Barbara, I think you are not unacquainted with the name of Doctor Topham?"

Dr. Topham took off his hat, and bowed profoundly.

"I—I really had no idea," he stammered. "This is surprise upon surprise! The—the honor—the pleasure—the—the congratulations ——Egad, I'm so amazed that I don't know what to say!"

"Amazed to find Benedick a married man, or amazed that Beatrice should turn out to be an old acquaintance, eh, Doctor?" laughed my husband.

The little man looked more bewildered than ever.

"Excuse me," he said, "but, proud as I am to become acquainted with a lady so—in short, with Mrs. Farquhar—I can not presume to—to lay claim to any previous——"

"For shame, Dr. Topham!" I interposed. "Do you forget Barbara — little Barbara Churchill?"

Dr. Topham deliberately dismounted, put his hat on the pony's head, and kissed me on both cheeks.

"From this time forth," said he, "I will never be astonished at any thing."

In a few moments more he had passed his arm through the bridle, and we were all walking on slowly, side by side, with the gables of Stoneycroft Hall peeping over the trees some little distance ahead.

"I am glad you are here," he said; "more glad than I can tell you. And I am also very glad to have met you before you went up to the house. The shock might have excited her too much, and this enables me to prepare her for it. The sight of your face, Barbara, will do her more good than all the physic in my surgery. I beg your pardon—old habit, you see! Mrs. Farquhar, I should say."

"No, no, Doctor—please call me Barbara."

"Well, then, Barbara, I look upon you as a great tonic to be employed for my patient's benefit. Poor soul! how she has longed to see you!"

"Oh, Doctor Topham! has she ever really said so?"

"Said so? Hundreds of times."

"Then she has not forgotten me?"

"If she had forgotten you, would she have sent for you?"

"What do you mean? Sent for me?"

"Why, of course. If not, how should you be here now? You—surely you received my letter?"

It was now my turn to be puzzled.

"I know of no letter," I said; "and if you have written to my father, I have heard nothing of it. He is at Spa, and very seldom writes to me."

"Then mine, being addressed to his old club in London, has most likely followed him," said the Doctor; "which explains both his silence and yours. But what lucky accident brought you home? And how did you know that Mrs. Sandyshaft was ill? And—and, above all, how is it that at the very time when we believed you to be still learning your lessons in some foreign school, you turn out to be married and settled—married, by all that's incomprehensible, to Farquhar of Broomhill?"

"Is that so wonderful?" asked Hugh, amused at the Doctor's mystification. "You forget that Barbara and I have known each other ever since I was last in England. It is quite an old attachment."

"An old attachment?" repeated Doctor Topham, incredulously. "Humph! I should as soon have expected to see her married to the Wandering Jew."

"Thank you; but the disparity is hardly so great."

"I don't allude to your age, Mr. Farquhar, but to your habits," said the Doctor, quickly. "You must remember that we are accustomed to think of you as the Flying Dutchman. We hear of you as being everywhere by turns, and nowhere long; and that you could ever commit any thing so civilized as matrimony, never entered the sphere of our calculations. Then to think that Barbara, our little Barbara should be ——Upon my soul, Mr. Farquhar, I believe it would have surprised me less if you had married an Indian begum, or a North American squaw!"

"You do my taste but little honor, then," said Hugh, "and give me credit for nothing but my love of locomotion. A pretty reputation for a county gentleman! But see, Barbara, here we are at the garden-gate, where you so often ran to meet me. The place looks just the same."

Ah me! it did, indeed. Nothing was changed. There were the same roses on the porch—the same swallows' nests under the eaves—the same laurels at the gate—the same old trees showering down their russet leaves upon the pond!

The doctor tied his pony to the staple in the wall, as he used to tie it years ago, and preceded us up the path. In the porch he paused, and laid his hand upon my shoulder.

"God bless you, Barbara," he said earnestly. "If any thing can save her now, it will be your presence. I scarcely hoped to see you, child; and had it depended on your father, I don't believe you would have been here now. But it depended on a higher will. There is a Providence in the chance that brought you—a great and gracious Providence."

Saying which, he reverently took off his hat, and I noticed for the first time how his hair had silvered since last I saw him.

"She is my oldest friend," he added, sorrowfully, "and the best I ever had. Hush! go into the parlor, and wait till I have been upstairs."

We went into the little parlor with the deep bay window, which I remembered so well. A strange servant was preparing the doctor's tea, but dropped a startled courtesy at the sight of strangers, and vanished. There stood my aunt's chair and footstool, and yonder, in its old place, the bookcase half filled with the ponderous Encyclopædia. I sat down in the nearest seat, faint with agitation and fatigue; while my husband, absorbed in his own thoughts, stood looking out upon the garden.

"Of course, Barbara," he said, after a long silence, "you will not think of leaving here for the next day or two?"

"I suppose not," I answered, with a sigh.

"I have sent Tippoo to Broomhill for a horse," he added.

"For a horse, Hugh?"

"Certainly. You did not suppose that I could establish myself here without invitation?"

I had not thought about it; but it seemed like an evil omen that my husband should go home this first night to his own roof, alone.

"No, no," I said, "do not do that. Stay here, or take me with you."

"I can not stay here," he said hastily, "in a sick-house—uninvited—unexpected—it would be impossible. And as for taking you with me—why, you are no longer a child to ride before me on the pummel!"

"We could get the postchaise which we left in the village!"

But he waved his hand impatiently.

"Nonsense, darling," he said, "you talk like a child. It is clearly your place to stay, and mine to go. I shall be down here again to breakfast, and you will scarcely have had time to miss me. Why, what folly is this? Tears for such a trifle!"

"It is no trifle to me. Call it folly, superstition, if you please; but I can not bear that you should go back to Broomhill without me. I feel as if it were a bad beginning to our home-life; and—and we have never yet been parted——"

The door opened, and Dr. Topham came in.

"I have kept you waiting a long time," said he; "but I was obliged to prepare her by degrees. She knows now that you are here, Barbara, and is ready to see you; but we must be careful not to excite her. She is very weak to-day."

"But not in danger?"

"In no immediate danger. If, however, she were not to rally within the next twelve hours, I should begin to fear seriously for the result. But you have been giving way to nervousness, and unfitting yourself for the interview. That is very wrong, Barbara. Tears and trembling do no good to an invalid, and often a great deal of harm. You must compose yourself before you go up."

Seeing how Hugh persisted, and how lightly he put my remonstrance aside, I felt angry with myself and him, and forced myself to be firm.

"I am not nervous now," I said. "You may trust me to go up."

"I think I may," he replied approvingly. "You are a brave little woman. Please to remember, however, that your aunt is not in a state to bear any farther surprise or excitement. You are still little Barbara Churchill, and Mr. Farquhar here is still at the Antipodes. Let this be understood between us."

"With all my heart."

"Then follow me."

So we went, leaving Hugh still loitering gloomily about the parlor, with the twilight thickening fast, and the rain beginning to pelt against the panes. The next moment I was on the threshold of the sick-chamber, forgetting all my lesser troubles in the sight of that curtainless bed, and the gaunt figure reclining on it, like a statue on a tomb. Her face was turned toward the window, so that her profile came for an instant between me and the light, stern as ever, but sharpened by time and sickness. Her hands lay listlessly upon the counterpane. Her hair was drawn back beneath the same plain cap that she always used to wear. After all, she was not so much changed as I had expected. As the door closed, she turned her head and said, faintly and slowly:—

"Bab, is it you?"

In answer to which I kissed her on the brow, and said, as composedly as I could:—

"Yes, aunt, it is I."

She waved me back by a feeble gesture, and pointed to the foot of the bed.

"Stand there, Bab," she said, "and take that bonnet off. I want to look at you."

I obeyed her, and stood there, holding my breath lest it should break into sobs. When she had looked long enough, she beckoned me back, and bade me sit beside her. Then, turning her face again to the window—

"The light is going," she said. "Put the blinds back, that I may watch it to the last."

A servant sitting by the fire rose and drew them back; but the sky was wild and dark, and the rain continued to come in heavy gusts.

"A bad night at sea," observed the doctor, briskly. "I don't envy those who are beating about the Atlantic in this treacherous wind."

But she seemed scarcely to hear him, and kept her eyes fixed upon the fading twilight. When it was quite gone, and all beyond the casement looked darker than within, she sighed heavily, asked for lights, and complained that the darkness seemed to weigh upon her.

"Bab," she said after a while, "you look older than I expected."

"I am eighteen, dear aunt," I replied, "and it is seven years since you saw me."

"Tush, you are a child still. Only eighteen! But you look older."

To which, being warned by a sign from the doctor, I made no answer.

"You have had no troubles?" she asked after another pause. "You are not unhappy?"

"No—my troubles have been few, and I shall be quite happy when you are well again."

Something like a faint smile passed over her face, as I said this, and took her hand in mine. Alas! how thin and weak it was, and I remembered it so firm and masculine!

"Poor Bab!" she murmured. "Poor little Bab! I knew you would come back to me at last!"

And with this she closed her eyes, and seemed to fall suddenly asleep. The doctor laid his finger on his lip, and drew a chair softly to the fire; but I could not stir, for her hand remained in mine, and I feared to wake her. And still the wind moaned round the gables, and the rain came and went in stormy bursts; and save the dropping of a cinder on the hearth, or the ticking of my aunt's great watch upon the chimney-piece, all within was silent as the grave. A long time went by thus; and at last, being myself very weak and tired, I also fell into an uneasy sleep, from which I woke up every few minutes without the power to keep myself from dropping off again. By and by, something, I knew not what, roused me all at once, and seeing that my aunt still slept, and that Dr. Topham was nodding in his chair, I sat up and listened. Hush! is it a horse's footfall on the wet road? Is that the latch of the side-gate? Do I not hear a sound like the cautious opening of a door downstairs?

Breathlessly, and by the gentlest degrees, I drew my hand away without waking her, crept to the door, felt my way along the corridor, and ran down in the dark, taking, by a kind of instinct, the passage leading to the back of the house.

I found him standing by the open door, penciling some words on a leaf torn from his pocket-book, while the servant stood beside him with a lantern. Seeing me, he crushed the paper in his hand and flung it away.

"I was bidding you good night, *carissima*," he said, in Italian; "but paper farewells are not worth the having. I am glad you have come, though I would not send for you."

"Cruel! Then you will go?"

"I must. Hush! do not try to persuade me. It is better thus, and yet—and yet I am weak enough to yield, if you look at me with those imploring eyes. No—no—I must go, for your sake more than mine. Oh! Barbara, Barbara, why did you bring me back to England?"

"What can you mean?" I cried. "For God's sake, stay with me. You are not well, Hugh!"

"Nor ill, my love. Pshaw! it is hard to kiss and ride away, like a knight in a novel — but the rain beats in upon you, and if I close this door I shall not have courage to open it again! Good-by, my wife, my own—the night will be long without thee!"

Thus, clasping me closely in his arms, he kissed me twice or thrice; broke away, as if he dared not trust his resolution; sprang into the saddle; and was gone.

All without was intensely dark. I could see nothing—nothing but the groom leisurely preparing to follow his master, and the rainpools lying round the door. I could not even hear his horse's footfalls for the raving of the wind. So, cold and heavy-hearted, I came in and closed the door, and thought how empty the house seemed now that he was no longer in it—how empty life would be without him—and, above all, how strange his moods had been of late, how irritable, how impatient, how wayward! Musing and wondering thus, perplexing myself with questions that I could not answer, and with doubts that I could not solve, I made my way slowly back to the door of my aunt's chamber —then, remembering the scrap of writing he had thrown away, stole down again to look for it. It was but a tiny crumpled leaf, and the wind had blown it into a distant corner; but I found it, for all that, and rescued it from the dust, and smoothed it out tenderly, as if it were a sentient thing to be prized and comforted.

There were only a few words scrawled hastily in pencil—a few Italian words, beginning with "anima mia," and breaking off abruptly before the ending of the first sentence; but the "anima mia" was enough. It consoled, it made me happy. I felt that I was no longer alone, and that his love and his thoughts would be with me all the weary night. "Anima mia"—my Soul! Was I indeed his soul? his very soul? more than his heart—more than his wife—more even than himself? Nay, better than himself—his soul, the spiritual and divine part of his nature—the gift of God! I kissed the paper, hid it in my bosom, and went up again to my place by the bedside. Alas! on what trifles do our smiles and tears depend, and how eagerly we interpret all things to our comfort! I had already forgotten much that was unexplained in his conduct, much that had pained me in his speech; and, child that I was! blamed only myself for my past uneasiness.

My aunt continued to sleep all that evening, and Dr. Topham to sit before the fire, drinking strong tea to keep himself awake. At ten o'clock, seeing how worn out I was, he insisted on dismissing me for the night, and so I found myself once more occupying the same bedroom which was mine years ago. Perhaps I fell asleep dreaming the same dreams, and, waking, found myself whispering the same name as of old!

CHAPTER XLIII.

MY AUNT AND THE DOCTOR CONTINUE TO DIFFER.

"Mrs. S.," said Dr. Topham, "you are considerably better this morning."

"Nothing of the kind," replied my aunt. "I feel much weaker."

"That is because the fever has left you."

My aunt shook her head.

"And for that very reason," persisted the doctor, "you are better."

"I am a great deal worse," said my aunt, "and worn out for want of sleep."

"But you have slept profoundly all night long," urged the doctor.

"Not a wink," said my aunt.

"Thirteen hours, by my watch," said the doctor.

"Thirteen fiddlesticks!" ejaculated my aunt contemptuously.

The doctor turned red, and took up his hat with great dignity.

"I presume, Mrs. Sandyshaft," said he, "that I may be allowed to trust the testimony of my senses. I tell you that you have slept, and I tell you that you are better. If you do not

u are at liberty to call
please."
| my aunt, tartly. "I
elling me."
stiffest bow.
r of better or worse, I
udge of my own feel-

n.
i my business, and con- .
—ch ?"

'e——"
're, Mrs. Sandyshaft,"
'elling somewhat satiri-
'ill also *choose*, I hope,
credit for my share in

umoredly.
' you are an idiot, and
so. I suppose I am
re the spirit to quarrel

much as you please, my
little man, with a sud-
id an odd quivering of
your heart's content—
i a fool to be irritated.
—I am glad—I—I am
iow to express. Bless
ve aggravated me yes-
pended on it!"
i," admitted my aunt;
time ?"
i had been listening
strong inclination to
ong inclination to cry,
I spoiled the situation
iesses at once.
' said my aunt testily,
:han the doctor! Be
and don't make your

is Barbara, don't you
neither agreeable nor
ie doctor, rubbing his
ow that sentiment is
aunt wants her break-
' breakfast, don't you,
iencing a return of ap-
i.?"
needed the point, and
, and ordered a supply
ely.
is, ma'am," he said,
i sleep have been the
hat you now want is
es, tonics
we can think of; and
id well in three weeks
id."
:," observed my aunt,

pham," she continued,
the cup which I was
warn you at once. I
son."
doctor, aghast.
.d enough of it—too
so, I forgive you. At
mother drop of it; and

if you send me any more, I'll make you drink
it."
"Mrs. Sandyshaft," began the doctor, "you
are the most unreasonable, and the most——"
"Topham," interposed my aunt, "hold your
tongue. If you were to talk till midnight it
would make no difference. Bab, my dear, you
don't look nearly so old this morning."
"My dear aunt," I replied, "that is because
I am so happy. Yesterday, you know, I was
both very tired and very anxious—and besides
I, also, am only just recovering from an illness."
She looked at me tenderly, and patted my
cheek, just as she used to pat it when she was
pleased with me, years ago.
"Poor Bab!" she said. "Poor little Bab!
What has been the matter with you? Over
study ?"
"No—home-sickness, I think. I pined to
come back to England again, and fell ill."
"Ay—true. They sent you to some foreign
school, did they not? Yes, yes. I remember.
I wrote to you, and your father sent me back
my letter. He would not tell me where you
were, Bab, and he would not send my letter to
you. I wonder he has allowed you to come to
me at all; but I suppose he thought I was
dying, and it couldn't matter!"
"Oh, my dear aunt, did you really write to
me ?"
"Write to you, child! Ay, to be sure I did
—and, after you were gone, would have given
all I possessed to get you back again. Not that
I ever confessed so much, however! No—I
was too proud to do that. Mercy on us, what
fools we all are!"
"And I who thought you had forgotten me!
I who was also too proud to—to—— I shall
never forgive myself!"
My aunt, who had all this time been progressing with her tea and toast in the most matter-of-
fact manner, dealt me a smart blow with the
spoon, and bade me hold my peace.
"Here you are," said she, "and that's enough.
Don't let us have any whimpering about it.
Now tell me, were you happy at the outlandish
place they sent you to? And did they treat
you kindly when you were ill? And did you
learn any thing worth knowing, besides their
gibberish? Come, you have plenty of news for
me, Bab."
"All of which must for the present be reserved," interposed the doctor. "Mrs. S., I am not
going to let you talk yourself into a relapse of
the fever. Miss Barbara, I forbid every thing
like news. Suppose that you and I take a turn
in the garden together, while your aunt rests
from the fatigue of this last half-hour?"
Saying which, and despite my aunt's remon-
strances, he drew my arm through his, and led
me from the room. In the parlor below, we
found Hugh waiting. He had come round
quietly by the back-way, and, true to his promise, was in time for breakfast.
"Well, little wife!" said he. "Well, doctor,
what news of your patient?"
"The best—the best in the world," replied
Dr. Topham, joyfully. "A reäction has taken
place, and the danger is past. I believe we
must thank Mrs. Farquhar for some share in this
result."

My husband smiled, and drew me fondly to his side.

"I have more than once found her to be the best of physicians," he said.

"Well, last night she surpassed herself, for she sent Mrs. Sandyshaft to sleep for thirteen consecutive hours. But you, by the by, look as if you had scarcely slept at all."

"I ?" said Hugh, with some embarrassment. "Oh, I am right enough. I sat up late with my steward, looking through the accounts."

"Very foolish, very foolish, indeed !" said Dr. Topham. "What business has an independent man to work by night, when every hour of the day is at his disposal ? Barbara, my dear, you must not let your husband do these inconsiderate things. See how haggard and ill he looks to-day !"

"Nonsense, doctor, I tell you I am well enough," exclaimed Hugh, impatiently. "I do not habitually sit up beyond midnight, but last night ——"

"Last night you had no one to call you to order, eh ?" suggested the doctor. "Well, well, we must bind you over to keep good hours for some few nights yet to come — that is, if you will spare us our physician till the patient is out of all danger ?"

"Nay, for how long will that be ?"

"Four or five days, at the most."

"Four or five days !" repeated my husband. "Steal my little Barbara from me for four or five days — why, I shall be lost without her !"

But though he sighed as he said this, and played reluctantly with my hair, a strange, improbable notion flashed across my mind. Could it be a relief to him that I must stay for some days longer at Stoneycroft Hall ?

CHAPTER XLIV.

THE FIRST NIGHT AT BROOMHILL.

Hamlet.—Do you see nothing there ?
Queen.—Nothing at all ; yet all that is I see
SHAKSPEARE.

"WELL, Bab, what's done can't be undone," observed my aunt, "and marriages, they say, are made in heaven — though, for my part, I believe they are much oftener concocted in t'other place. I suppose we must just try to make the best of it."

"Try to make the best of it !" I repeated. "Why, my dear aunt, there is no effort needed. I am perfectly happy."

My aunt shook her head, ominously.

"Poor child — poor little Bab !" said she. "So young ! Such a tender, foolish, inexperienced baby ! Oh, dear ! oh, dear ! She ought to be at school now. Farquhar of Broomhill, indeed ! A man old enough to be her father ——"

"I beg your pardon, aunt," I interposed, somewhat warmly. "Hugh is only thirty-four, and, for freshness of feeling, might be ten years younger."

"Freshness of fiddlededee !" said my aunt. "What freshness of feeling can any man retain, after knocking about the world for ten or fifteen years ? Why, child, he is the most unsettled, uncivilized, uncertain of God's creatures ! He'll be taking you here, and there, and everywhere

all your life long, just
and as to a quiet life
never know what they
ther. I confess to y
pointed. I thought t
to have kept you with
years as I may have to
whipped off by a fello
week to the antipodes
or do to prevent it !

"But, my dear aunt
this to you, and told
settle permanently at
can you desire than to
and united to the ma
world — whom I have

"You might as wel
the weathercock on
aunt. "But it was m
made his acquaintanc
name of Farquhar !
crossed his father's
pounds !"

"But you liked hi
visited him !"

"He amused me,"
"And when he was
"I would have do
else."

"But not in the sa
Hugh is my husband,
him — I honor him.
he is. I know how st
ledge, and what deep s
beneath the careless s
read his noble nature t
and I know how it w
and want of sympath
treat you ; and if you
ship you once felt for
respect the goodness
him !"

My aunt shrugged h
though she pitied me

"He must do som
knowledge his greatn
respect——"

"And as for respec
am not aware that
feited his just claim
him. You seem to
birth and fortune, a g

"Oh, I forget nothi
which he squanders a
and a fool !"

I remained silent.

"Nor his talents, w
—nor the idle life th
dangling about pict
name upon pyramid
in American forests !
of a career do you ca
man ? I tell you, B
philosophy, nor wan
a man vagabondizing
mad way — it's the m
nothing else. The
passion that drives a
and a rogue to the g
it."

What language to
lips ! I dared not tr

lest it should utter something unforgivable; but I turned away, and, standing in the deep embrasure of the window, shed tears of mortification. It was the fourth day of my stay at Stoneycroft Hall, and my aunt was so far recovered that Hugh had arranged to come for me in the evening, and take me home to Broomhill. In the mean time I had told her the story of my love and my happiness, and she, in return, had spoken words too bitter, ah ! surely too bitter to carry with them any leaven of the truth ! And yet—what if his love for me *were* only to last till the excitement had burnt out, and were then to crumble away into dust and ashes ? What if he *were* to grow weary and restless, and go back some day to his old wild life, and leave me weeping ? The thought was too terrible. I dared not dwell upon it.

Alas ! life knows no darker moment than that which first disturbs our faith in the fair romance of the future. Happily our incredulity is brief. The shock is too rude, and the arrow, like vaulting ambition, "o'erleaps itself" and flies beyond the mark. The idol of a woman's love is not so easily hurled from its pedestal. For my part, I believed only the more implicitly for having wavered, however momentarily, in my faith; and so lifted my idol from the dust, and kissed it reverently, and fell down again, and worshiped it.

It was but the revolution of a few moments; yet in those few moments I passed through a whole cycle of feeling, and became, by some strange alchemy of passion, other than I was before. What had happened to me ? I could scarcely tell. I only felt calmer, better, more worthy of myself and him. Ten years seemed to have flown suddenly over my head, and to have brought with them clearer convictions of duty, and deeper resources of self-help. My pride as a woman, my dignity as a wife, were developed, as it were, spontaneously, from this ordeal of doubt; and I felt that, happen what might, no deed or thought of mine should ever seem to sanction the injustice of others. Whose tongue so fit as mine to "smooth his name," though all the world should mangle it ? Whose faith so necessary, whose respect so justly due to him ? In less time than it has taken to write, these things succeeded each other in my mind, and determined my line of conduct for the future.

I put back the curtain behind which I had concealed my trouble, and returned quietly to my seat beside the bed.

"Aunt," I said, "for our mutual peace and love, let this conversation never be renewed. It is my place to silence those who censure my husband—not to defend him, for he needs no defense. His honor and mine, his interests and mine, are one; and who wrongs him, injures me. He will be here in a few moments to take me home for the first time since our marriage—have you nothing kinder, nothing more just, to say to me before I go ?"

My aunt stirred uneasily, but remained obstinately silent. I heard a carriage draw up at the gate.

"He is here," I said, earnestly, "He is here, and I must leave you—but not thus ? Surely, not thus ?"

My aunt opened her lips, as if to speak, and shut them again quickly, like a trap. I moved toward the door.

"Good-by, then," I faltered.

"Bab," said my aunt, "come back."

I was at her bedside almost before the words were out of her mouth.

"I am an old woman," she continued, turning her face from me, "and no wiser, I dare say, than my neighbors. As for my politeness, or my good temper, the less we say about either, the better. Remember, child, that I am disappointed. I didn't want you to marry, and I didn't dream you'd marry for many a year to come; and it aggravates me that you should have chosen a man who never lives on his acres, and who may carry you off to Timbuctoo any day, at a moment's notice."

"My dear aunt," I began; but she stopped me with a gesture.

"Don't interrupt me, Bab. I hate it. Now, listen to me. I dare say I said some harsh things just now—if I did, forget them. I dare say they were true enough, too; but that's not to the purpose. You may think 'em all false, if you please; and as to this precious husband of yours, why, I dare say he is not so bad as he seems. If he only makes you happy, Bab, I'll forgive him."

"If he did not," thought I to myself, "I would never tell *you*, Aunt Sandyshaft !"

"But you must make him live in England," she continued. "Be sure you make him live in England."

"Nay," said I, "of that you may be certain. Is it not my own dearest wish ?"

"Ay, then you may go. Stay, though—one may as well be civil, even to the devil. Let him come up and see me."

"Who, aunt ? The devil ?"

"Nonsense, child ! Your husband, of course. Who else ?"

It was an ungracious invitation; but I worded it more pleasantly, and brought him to her room.

"So ! Hugh Farquhar," she began, before he had time to open his lips, "what business had you to steal my Bab ? What have you to say for yourself ? What have you been after all these years ? Mischief, I'll be bound ! There, I know what you are going to say, by the expression of your face—that is, by what's visible of it. Why, man, you look like a Skye terrier, with all that hair about you !"

Hugh laughed, good-naturedly, and took a seat by the bedside.

"Complimentary as ever, I see, Mrs. Sandyshaft," he said. "I am glad, however, to find you well enough to be sarcastic. You are looking better than I expected."

"Looking, indeed ! I look like a lemon, and feel as sour. What right had you to marry my Bab ?"

"No right at all, my dear Madam; but great good fortune," replied Hugh.

"That's very true," said my aunt, "and good luck always falls to those who don't deserve it. She's too good for you, by half, Hugh Farquhar; and that's the long and short of it. Come, tell me what you've been doing all these years? Buying more pictures at six thousand pounds apiece, eh ?"

"On the contrary, I have been improving myself in arithmetic and self-denial, and learning how to balance my love of art against my banking book."

"Humph! so much the better. And where have you been? What have you been doing?"

"Since when, Mrs. Sandyshaft?"

"Why, since you left England six or seven years ago, after so nearly making a fool of yourself with Flora Bayham."

A dark flush mounted to the very roots of his hair; but he repressed the rising answer, and said —

"I have been to more places, and had more adventures than you would care to hear, or I to tell. I have shot buffaloes in North-America, and tigers in the Indian jungle — I have smoked my pipe in a Nile boat, and my paper cigarette in a Mexican wine-shop — I have thrown my harpoon at a whale; caught turtles at Ascension; left my visiting card on the peak of Teneriffe; and supped with Mr. Layard among the ruins of Nineveh. _Enfin_, I have packed away my 'sandal shoon and scallop shell;' and taken unto myself the responsibility of a wife. Will that do, Mrs. Sandyshaft; or shall I go into details of latitude and longitude, ships' names, private expenses, and so forth?"

"No, thank you. I had much rather hear you say that you've done with all such freaks for the future. Traveling, without any useful object in view, is folly, sir, and nothing short of it."

"Traveling, like love, my dear madam, is the folly of the wise man, and the wisdom of the fool. Now I am modest enough to fancy that it has been my wisdom."

"Well, supposing that I admit this proposition, can you tell me what have been the fruits of your wisdom? What you have gained by all this gadding about, and what you have learned?"

"Unquestionably. I have acquired an admirable judgment of old masters and cigars — learned the art of playing the castanets, and throwing the lasso — studied every variety of war-whoop, under the best native teachers; and practiced the art of fishing by night with a lamp and a knife, till I defy the most practiced mountaineer to excel me."

"Meritorious and useful in the highest degree!" said my aunt. "Pray, is that all?"

"Not half," replied Hugh, determined not to observe the growing bitterness with which she listened. "I can interpret a Turkish love-letter, and frame an answer in return. I can eat rice with chop-sticks, and dine off _caviare_ without holding my nose. I can dance like a dervish, fling a lance like a Bedouin, cook chowder like a Yankee ——"

"Enough," interrupted my aunt. "Don't fatigue yourself with more examples. In a wigwam, or a desert, I have no doubt that you are a delightful companion; but here, I fear, your accomplishments will not meet with the respect they merit. The conversation and habits of our English gentry will be intolerable to you, after the wit and refinement of your Choctaw and Tartar friends."

"True; but when I weary of civilized society, I can take refuge in yours."

My aunt smiled grimly. Like a good fencer, she could applaud her adversary's "very palpable hit," and like him the better for it.

"Done," said she. "My barbarity will always be at your service. In the mean time, I recommend you to let your Asiatic talents lie dormant for the present. Don't be throwing the lasso at your neighbor's cows, or the javelin at my pigs, or you may find the sport expensive. Now, good night to you."

Thus abruptly dismissed, we took our leave, and as I kissed her, she whispered, "Come back to-morrow, Bab. I'm a cross old woman, but I can't do without you."

An old-fashioned yellow chariot was waiting at the gate, with lighted lamps and a pair of patient horses. The coachman started from a doze at the sound of our voices. He was a very old man, and touched his hat to me as I got in; then feebly gathered up the reins, and drove us at a foot pace down the hill. Hugh flung himself impatiently into a corner, and found fault with every thing.

"A delightful mode of progression, certainly!" he exclaimed. "It carries us back, Barbarina, to the time of our forefathers, and proves the possibility of going from London to York in four days by the 'Flying Coach.' Did you ever see such a musty old vehicle? It was my father's coach, built for him on his marriage. Faugh! it smells of cobwebs! I unearthed it yesterday, and had it furbished up for your ladyship's state progress. That relic of antiquity on the driving-box was my father's coachman, and my grandfather's also, I believe. I had to unearth him as well; for he has been lodge-keeper these last fifteen years. As for the horses, they are as old and out of date as the rest of the equipage, and have been doing duty at the plow this many a year. _Corpo di Bacco!_ if we stay in this place, what a revolution I'll effect! I'll build a billiard-room, and a private theater. I'll keep hunters, and a French cook, and teach you to follow the hounds! How will you like that, my little wife?"

I shook my head. His restless gayety jarred upon me, and my heart was full of a very different future.

"I should not like it at all, Hugh," I said, sadly. "I had far rather transfer to Broomhill the quiet life we led in Italy—that happy life of books and art, that suits us both so well."

"Tush, child!" he answered, lightly, "the _dolce far niente_ needs a Southern sky. In this bitter North, men are driven to rough stimulants, and need something more than books to stir the currents of their blood. For my part, when in England, I almost lived in the saddle. By the by, you were asking about Satan!"

"Satan," I repeated, vaguely; thinking less of the question than of what had gone before. "What of him?"

"He's dead, poor brute. A good horse he was, too—pure Arabian."

"But surely," I said, anxiously, "surely you do not mean to tell me that you can never again be satisfied to share my quiet pleasures, simply because this is Broomhill, and not Rome. Oh, Hugh, when I think how perfectly happy we have been up to this moment——"

He laid his hand, laughingly, upon my mouth.

"_Silenzio, Barbarina mia!_" he exclaimed. "We have been happy—we are happy—we may, can, shall, and will be happy, _etcætera, etcætera,_

etcætera! Now look out, and tell me if you know where we are!"

Where indeed! Under the arching branches of the dear old avenue—passing the great gnarled oaks, the centenarians of the park—approaching the cedars, and the Tudor gateway, and all the hallowed places photographed for years upon my memory! It was dark, and the moon had not yet risen; but I could trace their outlines through the gloom. We turned the western angle, and passed under the archway.

"One word, Hugh," I faltered, "one word before we reach the door. Is it *no* pleasure to you to bring me home to your own ancestral roof? Absolutely none?"

"My dear love," he said, hastily, "why revive that vexed question at such a moment? Here we are, and we must make the best of it. Stay, I will get out first."

Make the best of it! For the second time that afternoon I heard those unsatisfying words. Was there, indeed, "something rotten" underlying every condition of my life, that I must always be warned to "make the best of it?" What was wrong? What was wanting? Whence this vague trouble, the very source of. which I knew not?

Discouraged and oppressed, I crossed the threshold of my husband's home, and passed the servants in the hall without even observing that they were assembled there in my honor. Tippoo preceded us with a pair of wax-lights, and we followed in silence. I scarcely noticed to which part of the building he was leading us. I scarcely remarked through what a number of corridors, and up how many flights of stairs we had to go. Not till he stopped before a gothic door, and drew aside the curtain by which it was shrouded within, did I even guess that we were to dine that first evening in the turret-chamber! Ah, the snug, secluded, pleasant turret-chamber! There it was, just as I remembered it, with its books, and its busts, and its swinging lamp, and all its graceful accessories—ay, even to the green and golden hookah in the corner, and the table glittering with glass and silver. Seeing all this brought back, as it were, suddenly, out of the past, I uttered an exclamation of joyful recognition.

"That's well," said Hugh. "I fancied I should please you by bringing you to my old snuggery, where we dined together the day of our first acquaintance. Ah, wifie, do you remember how frightened you were when I came behind you at the library window?"

"Ah, husband, do you remember how you forgot all about me, though I was sitting in that corner all the time; and how you asked Tippoo why he laid a second cover?"

"Nay, did I? I had forgotten it. I recollect, however, that you had the bad taste not to like my dinner, and ate scarcely any thing."

"And the still worse taste to be disappointed in the Paul Veronese! Tell me, am I yet forgiven that offense?"

Hugh laughed, and shook his head.

"Not yet," said he. "Not till you have seen it again with your own, dear, sensible artist-eyes, and performed a heavy penance of admiration. But see, here comes our dinner. Tippoo, desire Mrs. Fairhead to send us up a bottle of the old Romanée, and a pint of the special Tokay with the yellow seal. Come, wife, we will feast to-night, and make "high holiday." What say you? Shall we dismiss that awkward supernumerary in the white cravat, and keep only Tippoo to wait upon us?"

"Only Tippoo, of course."

So the servant was dismissed, and Tippoo waited on us as noiselessly and dexterously as the slave of the lamp. We jested, we laughed, we drank toasts, and were as gay as children out of school. Every thing that evening seemed delicious, and life all rose-color. My husband exerted himself solely to amuse me; and if it did once or twice occur to me that he made an effort to be gay—that if he ceased one moment to make that effort, he would relapse into the sullen gloom which had of late become his frequent mood—I banished it, and flattered myself that I was mistaken.

After dinner we sat long over our coffee and dessert, and talked of Italy, and Rome, and our wanderings in the Alps; and looked through a portfolio of rare etchings that he had brought from the library to show me; and planned how we would go to Venice and the Tyrol some day, and perhaps as far as Constantinople. Ah, what a child I was, and how little made me happy! Thus the pleasant evening passed away, and it was almost midnight before we went to bed. This brings me to something which I must tell in its place—something so strange, so uncomfortable, that merely to recall it brings back the shuddering disquiet of the moment when it happened.

The house was very still. As I have already said, it was just midnight, and the servants, used to country hours, had long since retired. Tippoo waited, as usual, in my husband's dressing-room, ready, if we rang, to attend upon us. To-night, however, being still in merry conversation, we did not care to summon him; so Hugh took the lamp himself and led the way. It was a very powerful lamp, with a shade over it, which concentrated the light into one intense circle, and left all beyond in darkness. As we went out into the corridor, suffering the door of the turret-chamber to swing back with a reverberating echo, I laughingly compared the effect of this light to that of a lantern in a fine Rembrandt etching of the Nativity, which we had been admiring a little while ago. Whereupon Hugh, profanely humoring the idea, fell into the majestic attitude of the chief shepherd, and intoned the first verse of a drawling Christmas carol. It was a boyish trick, boyishly done — one of those foolish jests that arise when two people are in high spirits, and no third stands by to keep them within the bounds of common-sense.

At that very moment I saw something darker than the darkness glide down the gloom of the corridor. I looked at Hugh; but he had evidently seen nothing.

"Hush!" I said shudderingly. "Don't wake the echoes of these great wandering passages, at such an hour of the night. Let us go on. I shall never dare to walk about this house alone, after dark!"

"Why not, child? We have nothing so vulgar as a ghost in the family. But you tremble!"

I muttered something about the cold, and he put his arm around me, quickening his pace the while. We were now at the head of the great well-staircase, and again, if I were not strangely mocked by my own terrors, I saw the dark shadow stealing swiftly down before us. To keep silent longer was impossible.

"What's that?" I cried, clinging to the balustrade, and pointing downward with unsteady finger. "What's that? See!—see where it goes!"

He snatched the shade from the lamp, and held it at arm's length over the deep shaft.

"Where what goes?" said he, shifting the light so that it fell from flight to flight, and from side to side, down all the windings of the stairs, till lost in the lower darkness. "I see nothing."

"Nor I—and yet I am positive—just now—a figure—it could not have been fancy!"

"It was fancy, then, and nothing else. Why, Barbarina, I never dreamed that you were such a coward. You shake from head to foot!"

So I did, and was too thoroughly frightened to be even ashamed of my terror. I only clung to his arm, and implored him to hurry on; and, when we came to our own bright, snug bed-room, with its cheerful lights and crackling wood-fire, bolted the door, and sank into an easy-chair with a deeper sense of relief than I had ever known in my life before.

Was it fancy—fancy and nothing else?

Revolving that question in my mind, I lay awake long after Hugh had fallen into his first deep sleep: and all through the night, at intervals that seemed, in my restlessness, to follow each other with scarcely a moment's intermission, started from uneasy dreams to listen, and wonder, and ask myself the same thing over and over again.

CHAPTER XLV.

THE SHAKSPEARE FOLIO OF 1623.

"Out, damned spot!"—*Macbeth.*

"Fear is a night-bird, and vanishes, like the owl, at sunrise. Come, wife, are you not ashamed to have been such a coward?"

Seeing the bright day pouring in at every window and lighting up the brown and amber foliage of the sere woodlands round about, I was thoroughly ashamed, and owned it freely.

"As for apparitions," continued Hugh, alternately sipping his coffee and examining the lock of his gun, "we decline to harbor any such spiritual rogues and vagabonds. We leave them to the tender mercies of Messrs. Dumas and Co., to be dealt with according to the law of public taste. Broomhill, my child, abounds in game—not ghosts. Now it is my firm belief that I shall shoot a dozen pheasants before dinner."

"Not till you have first made the tour of the house with me, Hugh—and I am longing to explore every nook and corner of it."

"Nonsense, love; the house will not run away. You are mistress here, and can see it at any time."

"And because I am mistress, I mean to see it at once. There, lay your gun aside. Grant the pheasants a reprieve for my sake, and indulge me this one morning with your company."

"And why will not Mrs. Fairhead do as well? She knows the house and its history far better than I."

"Mrs. Fairhead may come too; but I can not do without you."

"*Quatre-vingt mille tonnerres!* What *do* you want with me?"

"A hundred things. I want you to show me the Paul Veronese; and the ball-room where the accident happened; and the library. And I want you to introduce me to your ancestors in the matted gallery——"

"I hate my ancestors," said Hugh, irreverently.

"And I want you to tell me the history of all that old armor in the west wing, and——"

"Then it is quite evident, Barbarina, that your wants far exceed my resources. Come, let us compound the matter. I will go with you through the library and the matted gallery, and you must be content with Mrs. Fairhead's company the rest of the way. She is a wonderful old lady, I assure you, and has all the genealogy of the Farquhar family at her fingers' ends. She will show you every thing, and explain every thing, from the plate-closet to the picture-gallery, with the accuracy and elegance of a catalogue *raisonnée*. Bid her discourse, and she will enchant thine ear for hours on the fashion of a morion, the tone of a Murillo, or the pattern of a Majolica service. Archæology is not too heavy, nor court scandal too light for her. She will relate all about the battle of Worcester better than the Boscobel tracts, and tell sad stories of the freaks of kings, when de Querouailles became Duchesses in the land, and orange-girls rode in coaches to Whitehall. As for architecture——"

I put my fingers in my ears, and refused to hear another word.

"Enough of Mrs. Fairhead's accomplishments!" I cried, impatiently. "Let us have her up in person, and begin at once."

We rang for her, and she came—a fair, portly sedate old lady, in an ample gray silk dress, with a small key-basket in her hand, and in the key-basket a book with a red cover. She courtesied profoundly, first to me, then to Hugh, and then to me again.

"We want you—that is, your mistress wants you, to take her over the house, Mrs. Fairhead," said Hugh.

"I concluded as much, sir," replied Mrs. Fairhead, with a glance at the key-basket, and a side-glance of curiosity at myself.

"We came so late last night, Mrs. Fairhead," continued Hugh, "that I forgot to present you to my wife. Barbara, in Mrs. Fairhead you see an old and attached servant of the family. One whom we can not value too highly."

Mrs. Fairhead, with the gravity of a Mohammedan at his genuflexions, courtesied three times, as before.

"When your lamented father brought home *his* lady, sir," she said, "it was in a carriage and four, to the ringing of the church-bells; and we servants, fourteen of us, received our mistress in the hall, and very happy and proud we were. But now, sir, the house is more than half shut up, and we had so little time to prepare, and your establishment for the last twelve or fifteen years has been so small, that——"

Hugh stopped her with a quiet gesture.

"Mrs. Farquhar knows all that," he observed, "and will make every allowance for the neglected state of the place. My dear, you understand that we are only on a peace footing here, with all our cannon rusted, and our soldiers out at elbow. Shall we begin with the matted gallery?"

We began with the matted gallery, and Mrs. Fairhead led the way. It was a noble room, oak-paneled, lit from the left by a long line of windows, and diminishing to a fine perspective. On the side opposite the windows hung a double row of paintings, chiefly family portraits, with a sprinkling of old masters; and between each window stood a bracket with a bust on it. At the farther end, like a note of admiration at the close of a fine sentence, stood a pedestal, and a superb Roman vase of dark green marble.

"This gallery, ma'am," began Mrs. Fairhead, "occupies the upper floor of the Tudor wing. The library occupies the ground-floor, immediately beneath our feet. This wing was built in the year fifteen hundred and——"

"Spare us the dates, my good Mrs. Fairhead," interrupted Hugh, "and tell us about the pictures. Who is this scarecrow in the brown cloak and muffin cap?"

Mrs. Fairhead looked shocked, and said, with increased gravity:

"That, sir, is a portrait of Marmaduke, fourth Baron de Grey, whose second daughter, the Lady Mary, married John Farquhar of Broomhill, the head of this house, in the year fifteen hundred and eleven. That is John Farquhar's portrait above, painted by the celebrated Holbein. He appears in a fancy costume, supposed to be the dress worn by him at a court-entertainment given in honor of King Henry the Eighth's marriage with Queen Anne Boleyn."

"No more painted by Holbein than by me!" said Hugh, between his teeth. "Well, Mrs. Fairhead, go on. Number seven, in a ruff. Who is number seven?"

"Number seven, sir," replied the housekeeper, "represents Madam Eleanor Farquhar, wife of Richard Farquhar of Broomhill, eldest son and heir of John Farquhar, just mentioned. Madam Eleanor was the daughter of a wealthy London merchant, and brought a considerable fortune to her husband. She was a great beauty, and her portrait is considered to be very curious."

"And so it is—for a beauty! Well, Mrs. Fairhead, number nine?"

"The eldest son of Madam Eleanor, and Richard Farquhar, sir. This young gentleman went out with the Earl of Essex's expedition in fifteen hundred and seventy-six, and was killed at Cadiz. The next three portraits represent the next three generations—Edward Farquhar, high sheriff of the county under James the First; William Farquhar, his eldest son and successor; and Richard Farquhar, eldest son of the last, who commanded a squadron at the battle of Naseby, and died in London of the great plague, in the year sixteen hundred and sixty-five."

"Ay, I remember. One of the few men who, having succored the exile, were remembered by the king. He got a commission in the Coldstream Guards, then first levied. What business had he to be painted thus? He ought to have left us the portrait of his uniform, if only to give some flavor to his own! Go on, Mrs. Fairhead!"

"Portrait of the celebrated Inigo Jones," began the housekeeper, "by whom the elegant façade of the east wing was designed in the year sixteen hundred and nineteen, and——"

"And the effect of the whole building destroyed!" interposed Hugh, shaking his fist at the portrait. "You mischievous, meretricious old scoundrel, I have a great mind to make a bonfire of you, next fifth of November!"

Mrs. Fairhead turned pale with horror.

"What, sir!" she exclaimed, "burn a painting that has been in your family for generations?"

"The more shame to my forefathers, for not sparing me the trouble. And this jovial-looking warrior in the blue and buff livery?"

"The portrait of Lionel Farquhar, Esquire, who was made a major in the Suffolk militia in the year 1759; which was the first year of the militia being raised in all parts of England, in consequence of the expected invasion of the French under King Lewis the Fifteenth."

"Oh, such marchings and counter-marchings, from Brentford to Ealing, from Ealing to Acton, from Acton to Uxbridge," laughed Hugh. "Ah, Barbarina, I quote Major Sturgeon; a hero with whom you are not acquainted. Well, Mrs. Fairhead, number fourteen?"

"Lionel Farquhar, Esquire, junior, son of the last, and Lieutenant in the Royal Navy, under Admiral Lord Rodney," pursued the housekeeper, keeping steadily on, catalogue in hand, and evidently scandalized by our levity. "Number fifteen; the infant family of Lionel Farquhar, junior, with the family mansion in the background. The little boy in the blue gown is Alexander, the eldest son and heir, whose portrait you observe above, painted some years later by Sir Joshua Reynolds. Alexander Farquhar, Esquire, was the first of the name who represented the Borough of Ipswich in the House of Commons."

"Patriotic grandpapa Alexander!" ejaculated Hugh. "Shall I follow his example, wife, and present myself as a candidate at the next general election?"

"If your question were put seriously, I should ask time to consider, Hugh, before replying."

"Number seventeen, as I can tell without Mrs. Fairhead's help, is by Quintin Matsys — one of the most curious and valuable paintings in the house," said he, without seeming to have heard me. "It is a variation on his favorite 'miser' subject, one specimen of which is at Windsor, and the other at Antwerp. Look at that fellow's eager eyes and long greedy fingers. The picture is a sermon on avarice."

"But where," I asked, "is the Paul Veronese?"

"In the dining-room, I believe."

"And who is this in the blue coat, and white neck-cloth? What a candid, benevolent face!"

"That," said Hugh, a shade of sudden anguish passing over his face, "is my father — my dear father, from whom I parted in health, and hope, and joy, as I went out upon my first travels; and whom I never saw in life again."

I looked at the portrait with earnest interest, trying to trace in it some resemblance to my husband.

"You are not like him, Hugh," I said.

"Only my eyes are like his, and the vein upon my left temple. All the Farquhars have that vein upon the temple — invisible when they are calm, but starting into angry relief in moments of passion. But we have come to the end of the portraits."

"Your own should be added now," I sug-gested.

"Pshaw! I am too ugly."

"Ugly, *sposo mio!*"

"Ay; and too old."

"What folly! I believe you only want to be complimented on your youth and beauty. But, indeed, Hugh, I should like to see your portrait carrying on the line of Farquhars."

"Then we will both be painted, *carina*, when we next go up to London for a few weeks. You are looking at that vase. It is veritable *verde antico*. I bought it in Rome, on my first visit to Italy, and had shipped it home as a present to my father, only a few days before I received intelligence of his death. But these are sad memories. Mrs. Fairhead, we will follow you to the library."

His gayety was gone, and we left the gallery in a mood very unlike that in which we had entered it. Mrs. Fairhead preceded us down the great stone staircase, and paused to direct my attention to a large battle-picture in the hall.

"That subject ought to interest you, Barbara," observed Hugh, seeing me turn away with scarcely a glance at the huge dull canvas. "It represents the siege of Nimeguen."

"Why should I be interested in the siege of Nimeguen?" asked I. "I am no admirer of battle-pieces."

"Because it was at Nimeguen that your hand-some ancestor first distinguished himself, and Turenne predicted his future greatness. You must know, Mrs. Fairhead," added Hugh, turn-ing to the housekeeper, "that my wife is de-scended from the famous Duke of Marlborough."

Mrs. Fairhead dropped a profound courtesy.

"The same who won so many battles against the French, in the reign of Queen Anne, and whose portrait, in miniature, hangs in my father's study."

Mrs. Fairhead courtesied lower than before, and declared she could see a likeness to Madam about- the forehead and eyes. These facts evidently went far to raise me in her good opinion.

"And now, Barbarina, for the room of which I am proudest in this old house — the library accumulated by my forefathers from generation to generation during a term of nearly four hun-dred years. We have here a manuscript Horace of the seventh century; a genuine copy of the Shakspeare folio of 1623; a first edition of Chaucer; a volume of unpublished manuscript notes and extracts of Jeremy Taylor; and I know not — what's the matter with the lock, Mrs. Fairhead?"

"Nothing, sir, to my knowledge," replied the housekeeper, turning the key with some little difficulty. "It opened quite easily this morning."

She and Hugh staid back a moment, examin-ing the lock, while I pushed the door open, and went in.

To my surprise, I heard another door, at that instant, closed sharply and suddenly at the farther end of the library. It was a very long, narrow room, corresponding exactly in shape and length to the matted gallery above, and lined with books from end to end. I looked, naturally, for the door that I had heard; but there was no second door visible. Windows there were all along one side, like the windows

in the picture gallery; but not one that opened to the ground, and could therefore be used as a means of entrance or exit. And yet I was con-fident that my ears had not deceived me. I heard the creak of the hinge and the click of the lock as distinctly as I now heard Hugh walk up to my side, and say:

"A goodly show of literature, is it not, *petite?*"

"Goodly, indeed. It makes me feel like a traveler in sight of a strange country."

"Or a discoverer about to journey round the great world of books, in search of unknown continents. Ah, wife, what exploring voyages we will make together — what strange specimens of 'barbaric gold and pearl,' scraps of crabbed verse, quaint rhyme, and flowery rhetoric, we will bring back, in testimony of our wander-ings!"

"Is there no other entrance to this library?" I asked, suddenly.

"My child, what an absurd question! Don't your own eyes answer you? Why do you ask?"

"Because I am confident I heard a door closed as I came in."

"In one of the upper rooms, no doubt," said my husband, turning abruptly aside and search-ing along the nearest shelves. "Mrs. Fairhead, do you know where that last lot of foreign books has been placed?"

"The large case, sir, that you sent from Ger-many?"

"Yes. I desired they should be bound before they were placed upon the shelves."

"I believe they are between two of the win-dows, sir, lower down," replied Mrs. Fairhead, "but I am sure I don't know which. By refer-ring to the catalogue ——"

"Yes, yes, of course," interrupted Hugh; "but I am sure to come to them presently. See, Barbara, here is the 1623 Shakspeare — a volume which dignifies a library like a patent of nobility."

"A grand folio, truly; and, I suppose, very valuable?"

"I gave three hundred pounds for it, and never spent my money with more hearty satis-faction. Faulty as the text is, if you once begin to read Shakspeare out of these pages, you will never tolerate him in any other edition. You can not think what a flavor of antiquity this old type gives to Macbeth and King Lear."

"But — but, Hugh ——"

"Yes, my darling?"

"I know you will think me very foolish; but I do assure you that sound was too distinct to be in any upper floor. It came, apparently, from the farther end of this very room, and ——"

"And was, no doubt, the work of that ghost which you fancied you saw on the stairs last night! What say you to this, Mrs. Fairhead? Your mistress would have me believe the old place is haunted!"

Mrs. Fairhead smiled respectful incredulity.

"I have lived in it all my life, sir," said she, "and this is the first time *I* ever heard of such a thing."

"Fancied she saw a ghost last night on the great staircase," continued Hugh, speaking rapidly, "and declares she heard a supernatural door closed in this very room, while you and I were examining that lock a moment ago."

But for the impossibility of such a thing, I could have believed that I detected a glance of intelligence between Mrs. Fairhead and her master. Anyhow, the smile vanished from the housekeeper's lips, and the color mounted to her face.

"I — I am sure," stammered she, "if — if Madam——"

"Mr. Farquhar only jests," I said, impatiently. "I have as little faith in ghosts, Mrs. Fairhead, as either himself or you; but I do believe that these old mansions have often secret doors and hiding places, the very existence of which is forgotten. Such a door there might have been in this room—nay, may be, and yet unknown to you. So simple a thing as the trick of a sliding panel might be accidentally discovered, any day, by a servant; and the sound I heard—but, there, it is of no consequence. You know of no door, and perhaps there is none. Most likely, I was mistaken."

"Most likely and most certainly, Barbara," said Hugh, shrugging his shoulders. "Where every shelf is full, as you see here, the best contrived sliding panel that ever medieval builder planned, would be of little service. And now let us have done with ghosts. Shall I put back the Shakspeare?"

"No, I should like to look through it for a few moments."

"Then I will place it on this table for you, while I find the manuscript Horace."

He placed it on the table—one of two, carved in oak and covered with green morocco, which stood at equal distances down the middle of the room — and I began turning over the yellow leaves with that reverent delight which is only known to the real book lover. As I did so, dwelling on the fantastic head and tail pieces, and spelling over the quaint address supposed to have been written by Ben Jonson, I saw with dismay that my finger left an ink mark on the page.

I looked at my hand, and found the stain yet damp upon it. How could this be? I had used no writing materials; written nothing; touched nothing on which there was writing this day! I anxiously closed the precious folio, and examined the cover; but the glossy old brown calf was dry and stainless. Puzzled, but relieved, I drew a chair to the table, and reopened the volume. Suddenly, I felt the blood rush to my face, like a fiery tide.

I saw a large ink-drop on the green morocco, close against my arm.

My first impulse was to utter an exclamation; my second to suppress it, and try whether the drop was really fresh, or whether the gloss had only dried upon it. I touched it, and the stain came off upon my finger, leaving a little half-dried circle outlined on the table. What mystery was this? There was an inkstand, it is true, upon each table; but what of that? The door was locked before we came in. There was no second door, and the room was empty. Empty? Was it empty? Was there no second door? Was Mrs. Fairhead absolutely certain that there was no second door? Was Hugh—No, no! if mystery there was, he had no share in it. He was deceived as well as I; and Mrs. Fairhead — I mistrusted Mrs. Fairhead. I remembered her embarrassment. I trembled, I

knew not why, and bending low above the book, leaned my head upon my hand, and concealed my agitation as well as I could.

"See here, Barbarina," said my husband, cheerily, coming up from the lower end of the library with an armful of dusty volumes, "here are treasures for your delectation — the early Chaucer; a queer old Tasso, clasped and bound in vellum; a very curious illuminated Greek testament of — but what is the matter? You look pale!"

"I do not feel very well, Hugh," I replied. "A slight faintness came over me just now, and——"

"This room is too cold for you, my child," he interrupted, anxiously. "I ought to have remembered that we are in the first days of October, and have ordered the stove to be lighted before you came into this great desolate library. Let us go up-stairs at once. I can bring the Shakspeare, if you wish it; and send one of the servants for these other books Do you still feel faint?"

"Not nearly so faint as I did. A walk, I think, would do me good; and it is quite time that I went over to Stoneycroft, if I would not make my visit too brief."

"I fear those four days spent at Mrs. Sandyshaft's bedside have done you harm, my wifie," said Hugh, encircling my waist with his strong arm, and leading me tenderly away.

"Oh, it is not that, Hugh!"

"Nay, I am not so sure. I shall not let you stay long with her to-day. Remember, my little one, you have but lately recovered from illness yourself, and are too precious a jewel to be imperiled, though all the aunts in creation clamored for your company."

"My poor aunt, Hugh, I tell you again, has nothing to do with it," I repeated, when we had reached our quiet up-stairs room, and were alone again.

"What was it then?"

"If I tell you, you will laugh at me."

"By Jove, now, if it's any thing more about your imaginary ghost——"

I laid my hand upon his mouth.

"It's about no ghosts," I said; "but an ink-drop."

"The ghost of an ink-drop?" laughed Hugh.

"No—a very material ink-drop, I am sorry to say," replied I; "for it has left a stain on the title-page of your 1623 Shakspeare."

"Confound it! How did that happen?"

"Sit down quietly, and I will tell you; but first of all, understand that although I was the unlucky transferrer of the stain, it was through no fault of mine. I would not have injured your precious folio, husband, for the world."

And with this I told my story with all my doubts, suspicions, and conclusions. When I had done, he laughed, patted me on the cheek, and told me I was a goose for my pains.

"But some one must have been in the room, Hugh," I persisted; "or how could the ink-drop have fallen on the table?"

"And some one had been in the room, no doubt—one of the housemaids, most probably. The place was dusted this morning, of course, before we went into it."

"But it was still wet, and——"

"A large drop, such as you describe, carina,

would take some time to dry in a room without a fire, this cool October morning."

"Then housemaids don't go into libraries to write."

"By no means certain, if the housemaid has a sweetheart; but it does not follow that she was writing. She may have set the inkstand roughly down, or have whisked her duster into it, or have spilled the ink in half a dozen ways, without using a pen for the purpose."

"And as for that sound that I heard, Hugh, I am as certain that it was not on an upper floor——"

"As I am, that it was the work of your own fancy!" interrupted he. "Pshaw, my darling, it needs no sliding panels, no ghosts, no diabolical machinery whatever to account for your marvelous ink-drop! As for poor, good, simple Mrs. Fairhead, I wish you joy of her, if she is to be your arch-conspirator! Be advised by me, you nervous unreasoning child, and banish all this nonsense from your mind. I declare, I thought you had more sense, and less German romance, in your dear little head!"

Silenced, but only half convinced, I gave up the point, and said no more about it.

"You do love your little Barbarina, even though you think her a goose, don't you, Hugh?" I said, presently.

"Love you, my darling! It is all I live to do."

"I believe it."

He was kneeling beside my chair; and I took his great shaggy head in my two hands, and kissed him on the forehead.

"Now may I go and shoot some pheasants?" asked he, with mock humility.

"Yes; and be sure you come and fetch me home at five o'clock, sir."

"Thy servant hears; and to hear is to obey."

I watched him go forth with his gun and his dogs, active and athletic as a prairie hunter. As he crossed the courtyard, he turned and waved his hat to me. That gesture, and the smile by which it was accompanied, staid by me all the day and made me happy. I knew that he loved me; and I knew that I loved him, and trusted him, perfectly.

CHAPTER XLVI.

OUR LIFE AT BROOMHILL.

HUGH'S prophecy came but too true. Our arrival at Broomhill was no sooner known through the county, than we were overwhelmed with visitors. They came day after day, and week after week, till I began to think we should never be at peace again. The gravel in the avenue was cut into furrows by their carriage-wheels, and had to be rolled continually. The card-baskets filled and overflowed, like perpetual fountains. Every evening I added fresh names to the list of visits which must be returned—some day. I need hardly say that this influx of strangers wearied and annoyed me beyond description. I knew that curiosity alone brought nine tenths of them to my door, and felt that I was the object of their criticism from the moment they passed its threshold till they went away again. That I was Mrs. Sandyshaft's niece;

that my father was descended from the Marlborough family; that my sister Hilda was married to the Count de Chaumont; that I had been educated in Germany; and that we had been married and living abroad for more than a whole year, were facts that seemed to have propagated themselves in the air, and spread, heaven only knew how! in all directions. Every body seemed to know every thing about me; and one of the county papers even went so far as to hint at "a romantic attachment of long standing;" though that could have been nothing but conjecture. In the midst of all this visiting, I confess that I did not regret the absence of Lady Flora Bayham, now married, and living in a distant county. That childish wound of jealousy had left its scar, and though long since healed over, was not forgotten.

In the mean time my husband lavished gifts upon me; and, sober and simple as were my tastes, insisted, though with a more substantial result than did Petruchio, on providing me—

> "With silken coats, and caps and golden rings,
> With ruffs, and cuffs, and farthingales, and things."

I had cashmeres brought by himself from the East, that a queen might envy; furs fit for a Russian princess; gold and silver filigrees from Genoa; coral ornaments from Naples; mosaics from Rome and Florence; silks and velvets so rich that I felt afraid to wear them, and which a stately London court-dressmaker came all the way to Broomhill to fit and adapt to my little person. Then I had a riding horse; and a new habit; and a dainty little whip set with turquoises. And, above all, there came one day for my approval the most exquisite lounge-chaise that Messrs. Turrill and Co. ever turned out from their workshops—a graceful shell-shaped thing, so light that it seemed to be hung upon nothing —and a pair of the shaggiest, tiniest, friskiest Shetland ponies that ever scampered in harness! This last gift delighted me more than all the rest, and went far to reconcile me to the stern duty of returning my neighbors' visits.

In spite, however, of all this luxury, and all these indulgences, my happiest hours were those which I spent in my painting-room, or alone with Hugh after dinner in our favorite turret-chamber. The painting-room had been a spare bedroom in the wing traditionally appropriated to visitors, and I chose it for my studio for two reasons; one of which was that it commanded a fine view and an excellent north light, and the other that it was only separated by a landing from that very turret chamber, the threshold of which no strange foot ever profaned. I had but little time; for the days grew short, and my interruptions were frequent; but it was very pleasant only to have a picture on the easel and a task in hand; and I contrived almost daily to secure the first two hours after breakfast.

My aunt, meanwhile, recovered rapidly; and, save such inevitable alteration as seven years must work, looked much the same as ever. Her step perhaps was a shade less firm, her carriage a trifle less erect, her voice a little less resonant, than when I first came to live with her at Stoneycroft Hall; but her eye was as vigilant, and her tongue as caustic, as of old. As for her temper, it had become far more sour and overbearing than I had ever known it before.

While she was yet very ill I began to suspect this; and as she got well, I saw it more and more plainly.

"I know I am cross, Bab," she used to say. "I know I am cross, and very disagreeable; but I can't help it. It's my infirmity. If you had never left me, I shouldn't have been half so bad. I had got used to you; and the loss of you soured me—I know it did; and now it's too late to be helped. I have lived too much alone these last years. It isn't in human nature to live alone, and improve. You must take me as you find me, and make the best of me."

I did take her as I found her, and I made the best of her; but, for all that, things would not go quite easily and cordially between us. Her temper was an infirmity; and I made every allowance for it. The loss of me had soured her —I did not doubt it for an instant. But that was not all. The fact was that she could never forgive me for marrying Hugh, nor Hugh for asking me. It had frustrated all her favorite plans; and time, instead of reconciling her to the disappointment, seemed only to aggravate her sense of the injury and injustice which she conceived had been dealt out to herself. Thus it came to pass that she was always saying some bitter thing which I could not hear without remonstrance, and which she was angry with me for feeling. To my husband she was so rude, that, with all his forbearance, he found it difficult to steer clear of open disagreement with her; and so staid away more and more, till at last his visits might almost be said to have entirely ceased.

These things were to me, of necessity, the sources of profound and frequent trouble. The two whom I loved best in all the world were gradually growing to dislike each other more and more; and nothing that I could do would avert the catastrophe. The breach widened daily before my eyes. I tried to patch it over continually; but in vain. In the attempt to justify Hugh to my aunt, or excuse my aunt to Hugh, I soon found that I did more harm than good; and so gave it up after a while, and sadly suffered matters to take their course.

The month of October, and the greater part of November, passed by thus, in receiving and paying visits, driving, riding, wearing fine clothes, and staving off that quarrel between my aunt and Hugh which seemed to be inevitable at some time or other. Active and restless by nature, my husband had been more than ever unsettled since our return to Broomhill, and now lived almost entirely in the open air. When not riding or driving with me, he was out shooting in his preserves. He rode to every meet, however distant; although in Rome he had never expressed a wish to follow the subscription pack. It appeared, indeed, as if he had lost his taste for all the quiet pleasures of indoor life; as if he never could never be happy unless out and stirring; as if, alas! he took so little pleasure in his ancestral home that it was a relief to him to get beyond its precincts.

There were times when I looked back with loving regret to our delicious life in Italy—when, but for the confident hope that better times must come, I should almost have wished that I had never brought him back to Broomhill.

In the mean time Goody—dear, faithful Goody

—came down and made her home in a little gothic cottage that had once been a game-keeper's lodge, situated on a pleasant green knoll, just where the woods bordered on the western boundary of the park. To furnish this little *maisonette* for her, to stock her presses with linen, her cupboards with crockery, and her poultry-yard with cocks and hens, afforded me many hours of unmixed pleasure. Possessed of all these luxuries, she thought herself a rich woman; and though it was almost winter when she came, looked upon Broomhill as little short of an Eden upon earth.

CHAPTER XLVII.

THE FAMILY DIAMONDS.

"BARBARINA mia," said Hugh, as we were sitting together one evening after dinner, "I forgot to tell you that the Bayhams are going to give a great ball."

"Who told you so?"

"Lord Bayham, himself; I met him as I was coming home."

"Oh, dear me! shall we be obliged to go?"

"Most undoubtedly; since it is to be given chiefly in honor of ourselves."

"I am so tired of society," said I, with a sigh.

"I am not 'tired' of it—I loathe it," grumbled Hugh, dealing a savage kick at the log upon the fire, and sending a shower of sparks, like a miniature firework, careering up the chimney.

"If we could only live here, Hugh, as we lived abroad!"

He shrugged his shoulders gloomily.

"We might if we liked, you know," I pursued, laying my hand coaxingly upon his. "We were bound to return the people's calls, and we have done so; but we are not bound to accept their invitations, or cultivate their acquaintance, unless we please."

"Bah! what else can we do? What else is there for us to do in a place like this?"

"More than life itself would be long enough to do satisfactorily, depend on it. In the first place, you have books; in the second, you have art——"

"My dear girl," said he, impatiently, "books and pictures are all very well in their way; but to an English country life they can add very little real enjoyment."

"You desired no other pleasures when we were in Italy."

"In Italy the case was different. In Rome we had all the art of the world. At Albano we had natural scenery. In both we had the climate of Paradise."

"But——"

"But, my darling, this is a subject which we see so differently, that it is useless to argue upon it. And now about this ball at Ashley Park. It is to take place in about a month from the present time—that is to say, a week before Christmas; and as it will be her first appearance in a large assembly, I am anxious that my little wife should make a good appearance."

"I want no more new dresses, Hugh," I exclaimed. "I have more now than I shall ever wear."

I

"What an amazing Barbarina it is!" laughed he, unlocking a quaint old carved bureau in a recess beside the fireplace, and taking thence a large red morocco case. "The lady of Burleigh herself could scarcely have regarded the haberdasher and dress-maker with a more pious horror. *Mais, rassure-toi, chérie.* It was not of your dress that I was thinking, but of these."

He touched the spring, and disclosed what looked like a constellation of diamonds.

"Oh, husband, how beautiful!"

"They were my mother's, and my father's mother's," said Hugh, somewhat sadly; "and some of the stones, I believe, have been in the family even longer. They are yours now, my darling."

"They are magnificent: but—but fancy me in all these diamonds!"

"Why not?"

"I should feel ashamed—my grandeur would overwhelm me. How well Hilda would become them!"

"Not better than thyself, *carissima.* But they are old-fashioned, and must be reset before my little woman wears them."

"Indeed, no! they will do beautifully as they are."

"Indeed, yes. Look at this aigrette. How would you like to go to Lord Bayham's ball with an aigrette perched upon your head, like an ornament on a twelfth cake? Then here are earrings. You have never worn earrings in your life; and do you think I could endure to see my wife's ears barbarously stilettoed, as if she were a Choctaw squaw? No, no—the aigrette and earrings will make a charming little tiara for her brow; and the necklace shall assume a more modern pattern; and the brooch—what shall we do with the brooch? Have it reset as a brooch, or turn it into a bracelet?"

"Turn it into a bracelet, by all means, with a miniature of yourself in the midst."

"*Bon.* I should not have trusted any one but myself to take the jewels up to town, and I can see about the miniature at the same time. I think I will go to-morrow by the early train."

"And come back by the last?"

"Humph! I don't know how to promise that, Barbarina. I shall have to choose the patterns for the diamonds; to find an artist, to give my artist a sitting, if he will take me on so short a notice; to—— well, I will do my best; and if I find I can not catch the train, I will telegraph."

"You will not telegraph," said I. "You will come. Remember the motto of Henri Quatre: '*à cœur vaillant, rien d'impossible!*'"

I drove him over to the station the next morning by starlight, and saw him vanish like Aubrey's ghost, to the "melodious twang" of the railway whistle. As I came back, the day was superb. The frosty road rang beneath the hoofs of my Shetlanders. The blue sky, unflecked by even a vapor, seemed immeasurably high and transparent. There was a magical sharpness in the tracery of every bare bough that rose into the sunlight; and the yellow leaves that still masked the nakedness of the woodlands, mocked the wintry landscape with autumnal hues. But for those yellow leaves, it might have been a morning of early spring-time.

Some such thought as this it was, perhaps, that led me back, during that homeward drive to old memories of the happy spring-tide that I spent here long ago. I thought of that last morning when I met Hugh in the woods; and remembered, almost with a sense of self-reproach, that I had not once revisited the place since my return. Then I looked at the silver ring, now transferred to my watch-chain; and wondered if the marks of the shot were yet visible on the beech-bark; and if the old mossy stump on which I was sitting when they whistled past, had been spared all this time by the woodcutters. Finally, when, at about the distance of a mile and a half from Broomhill, I met one of the grooms and two or three of the dogs, I alighted, desired the man to drive the ponies home, and announced my intention of walking round by the woods.

"If you please, 'm," said he, touching his cap, "I think Nap would like to go with you."

"Then he shall certainly do so, Joseph. Come, Nap! Come on, boy!"

And with this I struck down a side path, leading to the woods, with the great dog barking and galloping round me. The groom, the pointers, and the Shetlanders pursued their way by the high road.

Nap and I were great friends. He was a magnificent beast, of pure St. Bernard breed; powerful and tawny as a young lion, with a deep furrow on his brow, and a voice that sounded as if it came from an organ-pipe. His name was Napoleon, called Nap for shortness; and his pedigree was as illustrious as his name. He was, in fact, the last lineal descendant of an ancestor whose owner acted as guide to the First Consul in the celebrated passage of 1800; and who himself accompanied his master and the army through all the difficulties and dangers of the route. I used sometimes to think that Nap was conscious of his own nobility, and becomingly proud of his genealogical advantages. He accepted caresses as if they were his due; was dignified in his intercourse with small dogs; and had at all times such an air of easy grandeur that it would have been impossible to treat him with disrespect.

His first greeting over, and his satisfaction sufficiently expressed, Nap trotted calmly forward, some three or four yards in advance, with now and then a pause and a glance back. Thus we crossed the upland fallows, and skirted part of the Stoneycroft land, and entered the woods by a little rustic stile, the top-rail of which was carved all over with the initials of by-gone loiterers.

It was by this time nearly mid-day, and the wintry wood, carpeted with russet leaves, and interspersed here and there with ilex, holly and fir-trees, glowed in the sunshine with a beauty peculiar to the season. Unexcluded by foliage, the broad full light poured in upon every bank and hollow, and checkered the ground with shadows of interlacing boughs. There was scarcely a breath of air, and the calm of the place was perfect. The dry leaves crackled underfoot. Now and then, a bird twittered, or a pheasant rose, whirring, from the brushwood. Now and then, a leaf fluttered down through the sunshine. As I went forward, half uncertain of the way, and looking out on all sides for any indication of the rising ground which had been the scene of my childish romance, I could not help thinking of this passage in "Christabel:"—

> "There was not wind enough to twirl
> The one red leaf, the last of its clan,
> That dances as often as dance it can,
> Hanging so light, and hanging so high,
> On the topmost twig that looks up at the sky."

Suddenly, while I was repeating the last two lines dreamily over and over, the St. Bernard uttered a short joyous bark, bounded from my side, dashed away across a little space of open glade where several fallen trunks showed that the woodmen had been lately at work, and precipitated himself in a rapture of recognition upon the knees of a lady whom, but for this incident, I believe I should have passed without seeing. She was dressed all in black, and half hidden by the pile of log-wood on which she was sitting. I was just close enough to see her throw her arms passionately round the dog's neck, and kiss him on the furrowed forehead—glance quickly round—snatch up a book from the grass beside her—start to her feet, turning upon me a pale face with a strange flash of terror and dislike on it—and plunge hastily away among the trees. The dog plunged after her. Surprised and disturbed, I stood for a moment, looking after them. Then, while I could yet hear him crashing through the brushwood, I called "Nap! Nap! Nap!" repeatedly, but in vain. Once, after an interval of several minutes, I heard him give a faint, faraway, uncertain bark—then all was still again.

Somewhat unsettled by the loss of my four-footed companion, and perplexed by the strange manner of his disappearance, I followed the open glade till I came to a game-keeper's cottage, and thence inquired my way home. I was tired, and it was useless to think of searching the woods to-day for a spot which by this time, no doubt, had lost all its former characteristics. Besides, I did not quite like wandering alone, without even a dog to bear me company. So I went back, by the nearest path, to Broomhill, intending to send some one in search of Nap as soon as I got home; and feeling something like an uneasy doubt as to whether we should ever see him again.

What, then, was my relief when the first object I beheld as I approached the house on the library-side, was Nap himself, lying sphynx-like, with his nose upon his paws, in the midst of the sunny graveled space where the fountain was playing!

I opened the little iron gate—the same through which I had ventured, a breathless trespasser, that day when Hugh surprised me at the window—and went up to him, and patted him, and remonstrated with him on his late behavior. But he only thumped his tail upon the ground, and blinked at me lazily—and it was of no use to ask him where he had been, or with whom.

Then I went in, sent for Mrs. Fairhead, described the lady, and inquired if any one had seen the dog come home. But Mrs. Fairhead could tell me no more than Nap himself; so I betook myself to my painting-room, and proceeded to work away the weary hours before my husband's return.

———◆———

CHAPTER XLVIII.

IMPERIAL TOKAY IN VENETIAN GLASSES.

> "To have my way, in spite of your tongue and reason's teeth, tastes better than Hungary wine."
>
> DEATH'S JEST BOOK.

"Put the painting by for to-day, Barbara," said Hugh, thrusting his head just inside the door, "and come with me."

"Where, dear?"

"Into the next room."

"What for?"

"You shall know, when you get there."

"Well—in five minutes."

"No, carina—at once."

"Tiresome fellow! The light is just going, and I want to add another touch or two to this head, before leaving off."

"Never mind the head. I can show you something much better worth looking at."

"Your own perhaps?"

"May be. Chi lo sa?"

"Your portrait?" I exclaimed, starting up at once. "I am sure it is your portrait? Who has brought it? When did it come?"

"I have not even said that it is my portrait," replied he, laughing, and leading the way. At the door of the turret chamber, he paused and put his hands over my eyes, saying that I must go in, blindfolded.

"And now, one—two—THREE, and the curtain rises on the Halls of Dazzling Light, in the Refulgent Abode of the Fairy Crystallina!"

He withdrew his hands, and for the first moment I was really dazzled; for he had caused the fading daylight to be shut out, and two enormous branch candelabra and a powerful vesta lamp to be lighted; so that the little room seemed all ablaze. Then, as my eyes grew accustomed to it, I saw that these lights were ranged round a sort of fantastic altar draped with a rich oriental shawl of crimson silk and gold, supporting a velvet cushion on which were arranged a glittering tiara, necklace, and bracelet of diamonds.

I flew to the bracelet, and burst into exclamations of delight.

"Oh, husband, how charming! What an admirable likeness! What a treasure!"

"I am glad the portrait pleases you, Barbara mia."

"It enchants me! You never gave me any thing that pleased me half so much."

"Come, that's well. And the setting?"

"It has your very expression."

"My expression is brilliant, I confess," said Hugh; "but you mustn't be too flattering."

"I could declare that the mouth is just about to say 'Barbarina!' And then the eyes, looking up, half in jest and half in earnest——"

"Will it please your Majesty to turn your own eyes in this direction, and tell me what you think of the rest of the regalia?"

"I think it exceedingly beautiful—much too beautiful for my wearing. I shall feel like King Cophetua's bride, or Grisildis with the 'croune on hir hed,' when I wear that circlet upon mine."

"Never mind how you will feel; I want to see how you will look. Come, let me crown you."

"Nay, in this woolen gown——"

"Oh, the woolen gown is easily disguised. See, with this shawl flung over it — and fastened on the shoulder, thus — and the sleeve rolled up, out of sight—and the bracelet on the pretty white arm—and the tiara——"

"What a boy you are, Hugh!"

"Stop, here's the necklace yet to come. *Per Bacco,* I have seen many a genuine queen who looked not half so well in her finery!"

"But I can not see myself in this mirrorless room!"

"Then we will go into the drawing-room, *carina,* where you can flourish at full length in three or four mirrors at once."

"How absurd, if we meet any of the servants on the stairs!"

"Pshaw! what does that signify?" laughed Hugh, ringing the bell. "We will make a state procession of it. Tippoo shall precede you with the branches, and I will bring up the rear with the lamp. Shall we send for Mrs. Fairhead to carry your train?"

"Mercy on us! what mummery is this?" cried a voice at the door; and not Tippoo, but Mrs. Sandyshaft stood before us.

We both started at the sight of this stern apparition, and, for a moment, could find nothing to say.

"You must be mad," pursued my aunt, still on the threshold; "stark, staring mad, both of you! It's only charity to suppose it. Pray, may a sane person inquire what it is you're after?"

"My dear aunt," I stammered, divesting myself of the shawl, and pulling down my sleeves as fast as I could; "the—the diamonds—Hugh wanted to see how I should look in them. They have just come home."

"The diamonds?" repeated she, incredulously. "Stuff and nonsense—the fiddlesticks! What are they made of? Bristol paste, or bog crystal?"

"My dear Madam," said Hugh, shrugging his shoulders, "do you suppose I should allow my wife to wear mock jewels?"

My aunt snatched the tiara from my head, and examined it closely.

"If the stones *are* real, Hugh Farquhar," said she, "the more shame for you! No man in your position can afford to buy diamonds at this rate. They'd be worth eight or ten thousand pounds."

"They are valued at twelve," replied he, calmly.

"But he has not bought them," I interposed. "They are old family jewels, most. They belonged to his mother, and his grandmother; and some of them are older still."

"Humph! And are you going to be such a fool as to wear them, Bab?"

"I can not see where the folly would be, aunt."

"Nonsense! a child like you; young enough to be at school now—people will laugh at you."

"If they do, the folly will be theirs. As the wife of a gentleman, and the daughter of a gentleman——"

"Bab, don't argue with me. I won't stand it. I think one of you might have offered me a seat all this while, considering it's the first time I've called on you."

"Forgive me, Mrs. Sandyshaft," said Hugh, placing a chair for her, immediately; "but you took us so by surprise that——"

"That you forgot your good manners," interrupted my aunt, sharply; "though, goodness knows, they're not much to boast of at any time!"

"Always indulgent and complimentary, Mrs. Sandyshaft," retorted he with a bow of mock acknowledgment.

Having by this time thrust the shawl out of sight, and shut the jewels away in their cases, I hastened to divert the conversation by helping my aunt to loosen her great cloth cloak and boa, and telling her how glad I was to see her at Broomhill.

"You're not glad to see me, Bab," said she, suspiciously. "I don't believe it."

"My dearest aunt, why——"

"Because I'm old, and you're young. Because I'm crabbed and sour, and you're happy and gay. Don't tell me! I know the world; and I know you'd far rather have my room than my company!"

"You know nothing of the kind, aunt," I replied, giving her a hearty kiss; "and you don't mean a word of it."

"Every syllable," said she, obstinately.

"And you know that I have always loved you dearly, and that——"

"You care a deal more for your trumpery diamonds, and your ugly ponies, and your gauds of silk and satin, I'll be bound!"

"How dare you say so? I've a great mind to say that I don't love you a bit—that I am very sorry to see you—that I wish you would go away directly, and not even stay to dine with us, like a dear, good, sociable, welcome old darling, as you are!"

"I'm not good," said my aunt, grimly; "and I never was sociable."

"Be bad and unsociable, then, if you like; but at all events remain a few hours with us, now that you are here," persuaded I, with an impatient glance at Hugh to second my invitation.

"I think Mrs. Sandyshaft will stay," said he, smiling.

"Do you?" exclaimed she, with a determined little jerk of the head. "Then you're mistaken. *I* dine with you, indeed? No, thank you. None of your outlandish foreign messes for me! I go home to my plain beef and mutton—plain English beef and mutton!"

"But my dear aunt," I began, "you shall——"

"Bab," said she, "you're as bad as he is by this time, I've no doubt. I can't eat sour kraut, my dear. It's of no use to ask me."

"What shall we do, Hugh, to persuade her?" pouted I; fancying that she, perhaps, refused because he did not press her sufficiently. "How shall we make her believe that she would not be poisoned?"

"We—that is, *you,* can do no more than you have done, my child," replied he, drawing back one of the curtains, and looking out across the park. "Still I am of opinion that Mrs. Sandyshaft will stay."

"And why?" said my aunt.

"For two excellent reasons; the first of which is that it is now dark, and——"

"I have my old close carriage with me," interrupted my aunt.

"—and rather foggy," pursued Hugh; "and your old close carriage has just disappeared through the gates of the west lodge."

"Disappeared! Mercy on us! who dared to send it away?"

"I did. And the second reason——"

"But I tell you I can't stay, and I won't stay! I insist on having it called back! Bab, do you hear me?—I *insist* on having it called back."

"And the second reason," continued Hugh, with the same cheerful impassibility, "is that we have red mullet for dinner."

Now if there was one delicate dish which more than another tempted my aunt's frugal appetite, it was a dish of red mullet. Distant as we were from any large town, fish was at all times scarce in our part of the country; and red mullet especially so. It was not in human nature to resist such a combination of circumstances. My aunt's countenance softened. I suspect that she had wished, in her heart, to stay with us from the first; but the red mullet gave her an opportunity of doing so upon purely neutral grounds, and that was no small advantage.

"Red mullet?" said she. "Humph! Where did you get it?"

"From London—fresh this morning."

"And how d'ye have it cooked? Red mullet properly cooked is the best dish that comes to table; but messed up with foreign kickshaws——"

"It shall be dressed, my dear aunt," said I, "in any way you prefer."

"Well—what else will you give me?—not but what I can make my dinner off the fish, if the rest is uneatable."

"My dear Mrs. Sandyshaft," said Hugh, "you shall dine exclusively upon red mullet, if you please; though I think I can answer for a palatable pheasant as well. As for Barbara and myself, we, of course, habitually sit down to birds' nest soup, fricasseed frog, alligators' brains *à la sauce*, potted cobra-di-capello, and other foreign trifles of the same kind; but of these you need not partake, unless you please."

My aunt smiled grimly.

"You have a disgusting imagination, Hugh Farquhar," said she; "but you may depend that you have eaten things quite as bad, and worse, many a time without knowing it."

And so the dinner question ended, and she staid. How often and how vainly I afterward wished that I had never persuaded her to do so!

We dined at seven, and it was nearly six by the time she had agreed to remain; but that hour was actively employed by Mrs. Fairhead and the cook, and the result was an excellent dinner in the genuine English style; so well dressed and so well served, that it even elicited the approbation of Mrs. Sandyshaft herself. In addition to this, Hugh, of course, brought out the best wines that his well-stocked cellars afforded; and, at dessert, produced a very small, cobwebbed, ancient-looking bottle, which was placed upon the table in a silver stand, as reverently as if it had been a sacred relic.

"What have you got there?" asked my aunt, complacently.

"A patriarch," replied Hugh. "A patriarch that once dwelt in an Emperor's cellar, and was one of a hundred dozen presented by the Emperor to a great Jew capitalist. The Jew capitalist died, and his heirs put up to auction all his wines, plate, pictures, books, horses and personal property. At this auction the patriarch, with his surviving brethren, now only twelve dozen in number, passed into the hands of a great English physician, famed alike for his wit, hospitality, and learning. The physician and my father were friends and school-fellows. My father died first; but the physician remembered me in his will, and left me, among other items, a valuable chronometer, a very curious Latin library, and the last fifteen bottles of the wine now before you. Tippoo, draw the cork."

Tippoo stepped forward from behind his master's chair, where he had been standing like a bronze statue, and obeyed.

"Bring me three Venetian glasses."

And three Venetian glasses (quaint, delicate things, with bowls like finely blown soap-bubbles, and fantastic wreath stems of white and sapphire glass) were placed before him. Into these he slowly poured the precious liquid, which came out sullenly, like a liquor, and hung in heavy red drops about the brim.

My aunt tasted hers — set it down — tasted it again — sniffed it — held it up to the light; and finally said —

"The richest wine I ever tasted in my life. What is it?"

"Imperial Tokay."

"And is that all true that you've been telling us?"

"Every word of it. The Emperor was Francis the First of Austria; the capitalist was Goldschmidt, and the physician was Sir Astley Cooper."

"I've tasted Tokay before," said my aunt; "but it wasn't like this."

"I dare say not. This is the real Tokay essence, and is used by Austrian and Hungarian wine-merchants merely as a flavoring for the Tokay that is bought and sold. The genuine essence, in its unadulterated purity, is hardly to be tasted at other than royal tables. The name of this wine is the Mezes-Malé Tokay, and it grows in a small vineyard which is the property of the Emperor."

"It must be valuable," said my aunt, emptying her glass with infinite gusto.

"It is valuable. This wine is at least sixty years old. Sir Astley Cooper bought it for sixty-three shillings the bottle. The bottle contains six glasses, and each glassful is therefore worth half a guinea. The Venetian beakers out of which we drink it are three hundred years old; and the value of each beaker is about equivalent to a bottle of the wine. There's a pretty piece of arithmetic for you, ladies."

"It's drinking money," exclaimed my aunt. "It's sinful!"

"Pleasant sinning, however," replied Hugh. *"Péchons encore!"*

"Not for the world. Mercy on us! I wouldn't have drunk that, if I had know what it was worth."

"Nonsense. The patriarch is sacrificed in your honor, and you are bound to perform your share in dispatching him. Tippoo, fill Mrs. Sandyshaft's glass."

"No — no thank you; not another drop!"

And my aunt in the energy of her abstinence, clapped her hand so roughly over the top of her glass, that the delicate globe snapped away at its junction with the stem, rolled over the edge of the table, and shattered into a thousand fragments.

"Mercy on us! — a glass worth three pounds! I'll — I'll get you another like it!" gasped my aunt, aghast at her misfortune.

"Indeed you must not think of such a thing," said Hugh. "It is a matter of no importance. Tippoo, another glass for Mrs. Sandyshaft."

"But indeed I will! I'll have every curiosity shop in London ransacked till I find one. Give me the pieces for a pattern, please — dear, dear me, I wish people wouldn't eat and drink out of things that are too fine for use!"

"People who do so, dearest aunty, must be prepared for the possible consequences," laughed I. "Pray say no more about it."

"And pray do not attempt to replace the glass either," added Hugh; "for it would be perfectly useless. I bought that half-dozen at the sale at the Manfrini palace, and I know there are no others like them."

"How do you know it?" asked my aunt, snappishly.

"Because I am a *connoisseur* of antique glass, and am acquainted with all the best collections in Europe."

"I believe Hugh Farquhar," said my aunt, "that you know every thing that isn't worth knowing, and nothing that is."

"I know that this Tokay is too good to be refused. Let me persuade you to take a second glass."

"Not I! I only wish I hadn't taken the first."

"I should have been really vexed if you had declined it," said Hugh; "for it is a wine that I only produce on rare occasions."

"The rarer the better, I should say," retorted my aunt. "Especially if you give it to people in glasses that can't be touched without being broken; and which, when broken, can not be replaced. It may be a compliment — I dare say it is; but it's a very disagreeable one, let me tell you."

"I wish, upon my honor, Mrs. Sandyshaft, that you would think no more about it."

"But I can't help thinking about it. It annoys me."

"Well, let us, at all events, *say* nothing farther upon the subject."

"Oh, it's of no use trying to impose silence on me," said my aunt. "What I think of, I talk of. It's my way."

A slight flush of displeasure rose to my husband's brow, and he looked down without replying. He had been admirably polite and good-humored up to this time; but I could see that he had not liked the tone of her remarks for some minutes past.

"And besides," added she, working herself into a worse temper, as she went on, "I hate to incur obligations that I can't return. I feel I've cost you six guineas within the last half-hour; three of which at least, no money can make right again."

"I beg leave to assure you, Mrs. Sandyshaft," said Hugh, coldly, "that I am not in the habit of estimating the pounds, shillings, and pence which it may cost me, when I entertain a friend at my table."

"Perhaps, if you thought a little more about

the pounds, shillings, and pence, it would be better for you," replied she.

"Of that you must permit me to judge."

"A civil way, I suppose, of desiring me to mind my own business."

"My dear aunt," said I, growing momentarily more and more uneasy, "this conversation has wandered quite far enough from the subject. Pray let us talk of something else."

"Bab, it's neither your place, nor your husband's, to stop my mouth. What I think, I think; and what I choose to say, I say; and both Houses of Parliament shouldn't prevent me. When I see people extravagant, and ostentatious, and thoughtless, I tell 'em of it. If they don't like to hear the truth, it's not my fault."

"You must give me leave to say, Mrs. Sandyshaft, that I am really at a loss to understand your meaning," said Hugh. "If I could suppose that you intended those expressions for——"

"Intended? — fiddlesticks! Who else should I intend them for? *You* are ostentatious, and extravagant, and thoughtless, Hugh Farquhar; and you know it; there isn't another man in this county who has spent his money so wildly and foolishly as yourself — and not only his money, but all the most precious years of his life, into the bargain. Ah, Bab, it's no use to look at me like that! These things have been on my mind a long time, and now that I've begun, I'll just say my say out, and have done with it. I tell you I'm sick of your art-jargon, and absenteeism, and continental ways — of your Paul What-you-may-call-'ems, and your ponies, and your curiosities, and your nonsenses and follies. Nothing English is good enough for you. If you've a horse, he must be Arabian. If you've a dog, he must be a St. Bernard, or a Dutch pug, or a French poodle, or an Italian greyhound. If you buy a picture, it's never a Gainsborough nor a Sir Joshua Reynolds; but some miserable foreign daub got up in the back slums of Rome to dupe the English. Every sentence you speak is interlarded with parley-voos. The very servant that stands behind your chair is a nasty, sly, black, heathenish savage, more like a monkey than a man!"

"Stop, Mrs. Sandyshaft," interposed Hugh, the angry vein swelling on his temple, and an ominous flash lighting up his eyes. "I can make large allowance for your prejudices and your temper; but I will not suffer you to utter malicious untruths of the most faithful friend and servant I have ever known."

"Oh, Hugh!" I exclaimed, "she does not mean it! Pray, pray let this discussion be ended!"

"Bab, I *do* mean it," replied my aunt, whose long-repressed irritation had now burst forth in a fiery torrent, stronger than her own reason. "I do mean it, and it's true; and I only say what every body thinks, and nobody dares to say before his face. He's no Englishman. No man who lives as he has lived these last twelve or fifteen years, deserves the name of Englishman. He has performed none of the duties belonging to his position in the county. He has neither represented it in Parliament; nor served it as a magistrate; nor improved his acres; nor cultivated the good-will of his neighbors and tenants; nor done any one single thing but spend out of his country the money that his ancestors invested in it. Nothing but ruin can come of it—nothing but ruin !"

"Upon my soul, Mrs. Sandyshaft," said Hugh, rising angrily from his seat at the table, " this is insufferable ! By what right do you take the liberty of judging my conduct according to your standard ? I have yet to learn that——"

" By the right of my relationship to this poor, luckless, mistaken child !" interrupted my aunt. "A year ago, I would have said nothing about it. You might have gone to perdition your own way, for any interference of mine ; but now things are different. Your worthless lot is linked up with hers, and if you're ruined, she must be the victim. I wish she'd never seen you. I wish I'd never seen you. I'd as soon she'd married a strolling player, or a wandering Arab, as you, Hugh Farquhar ! You're the last man living whom I'd have given her to, if I'd had any voice in the matter ; and I don't mind telling you so !"

" Having told me so, Mrs. Sandyshaft, and having, I presume, insulted me sufficiently at my own table, you will now be satisfied, and permit me to wish you a good evening," said Hugh, looking very pale, and moving toward the door. " Barbara, I leave to you the task, or the pleasure, of entertaining Mrs. Sandyshaft during the remainder of the evening."

" That won't be for long, then, I can tell you ; and what's more, it will be many a day before I cross your threshold again."

" As you please, Madam.'

And with this, he left the room.

"Oh, aunt Sandyshaft ! aunt Sandyshaft ! What have you done ?" I cried, bursting into tears.

"Told him a piece of my mind, Bab ; and much good may it do him," replied she, stalking angrily up and down the room.

" But you will never, never be friends again !"

" I can't help that."

" But I—what am I to do ? I who love you both so well ! Remember how dear he is to me —my husband——"

" Bab, he's a scamp. He is not worthy of you."

" It is false ! You do not know him—he is the best, the bravest, the—the noblest——"

My sobs choked me, and I broke down. My aunt stopped short before me, and struck the table violently with her open hand.

"Bab," said she, " you're a fool. The man will break your heart some day, and then you'll believe me.'

A few minutes more, and she was gone ; never, as I felt in my heart, to return again.

CHAPTER XLIX.

THE MYSTERY IN THE HOUSE.

"———to be wroth with one we love
Doth work like madness in the brain."
CHRISTABEL.

SHORT as were the wintry days, and frequent my interruptions, I went on painting regularly throughout November and the greater part of December. The beloved occupation did me good in all ways, and helped to keep my thoughts from dwelling too constantly on that painful breach which now seemed as if it could never again be healed over. My aunt had been the aggressor ; and I knew her too well to hope that she would ever acknowledge herself wrong. She would have died, at any time, rather than apologize. This being the case, I found it more and more difficult to keep peace with her ; and so staid chiefly at home and at work, during the time that elapsed between the great Bayham ball, and the evening of her unfortunate visit. As that long appointed date drew nearer, my picture approached completion. The subject had been suggested by Hugh when we were traveling in Switzerland, more than a year ago, and had dwelt in my recollection as a hope and a project ever since. It represented Erasmus at Basle.

The great wit and theologian was seen standing, toward evening, on the terrace in front of the Cathedral, looking thoughtfully over toward the hills of the Schwartz-Wald. The sun had just set, and a calm light filled the sky. Far below coursed the Rhine, broad, green, and eddying. Between the chestnut trees on the terrace peeped the quaint red columns of the cloister which he loved to pace ; and on the ledge of the parapet, against the stone-bench on which he would seem to have been sitting, lay an antique folio, printed, perhaps, by Gutenberg of Maintz. On the figure of Erasmus I had bestowed infinite pains, having made a sketch from his portrait in the *Concilium Saal* for this purpose. Desirous of representing him as he appeared toward the latter end of his life, when he had returned to Basle for the second time, I took care to deepen the lines about the face ; and strove to light it up, as if from within, with that divine expression of hope and resignation which is said to have settled upon it, like a glory, during his last sufferings. He wore a long furred robe, and a flat, three-cornered cap of black velvet. One thin hand rested on the book, while with the other he supported his frail and failing form upon a stick with a transverse handle, like a short crutch. Close of day, and close of stainless life ; peace within, and peace on the world without ; night coming on, and the Great Dawn after the night :—these were the thoughts I sought to utter upon the canvas ; this was the tale I endeavored, however imperfectly, to relate.

It happened one morning, when Hugh was out with his gun, and I had settled down to a long day's work, that I became dissatisfied, somehow, with the folio on the parapet. I had taken the 1623 Shakspeare for my model—a fine old book, which looked as though it might have sat for its portrait to the author of these well-known lines descriptive of a medieval volume :—

" That weight of wood, with leathern coat o'erlaid,
 Those ample clasps of solid metal made,
 The close-pressed leaves unclosed for many an age,
 The dull red edging of the well-filled page,
 On the broad back the stubborn ridges rolled,
 Where yet the title stands in tarnished gold."

The Shakspeare's "leathern coat," however, was of dark brown calf, and looked too somber when seen in conjunction with the deepening shadows on the terrace, and the dark-robed figure of Erasmus. I placed the picture in various lights, and the more I looked, the more I became convinced that some less heavy color would improve the composition. What if I made it a binding of antique vellum, toned by age to a mellow golden hue, in harmony with the warm tints of the sky? I had seen one whole compartment full of such in the library below—great, ponderous, ancient folios of theologic lore, lettered "*Acta Sanctorum*," and extending through some thirty or forty volumes. Could I do better than take one of these? Could I, if I searched for a year, place in the hands of Desiderius Erasmus a work which he was more likely to have had in frequent use? Delighted with the idea, and eager to put it into immediate execution, I ran down at once to the library, to select my volume.

The circular stove within its trellis of wrought bronze, diffused a mild warmth throughout the great room. The wintry sunlight poured in at intervals through the lofty windows, and fell in bright patches on the floor. The long rows of books, shelf above shelf, in their rich and varied bindings, glowed with a friendly lustre, and gave out a pleasant odor of Russia and Morocco. The brass wire-work glittered like gold. It was a place to have made even a savage in love with books—a *columbarium* where there was found neither dust, nor ashes, nor funereal urns; but only caskets of rich workmanship embalming the souls of the wise.

The library, as I think I have already mentioned elsewhere, was divided into compartments of carved oak; each of which was about four feet in width, and reached all the way to the ceiling, where it terminated in a simple cornice supporting a small entablature. Of these compartments there were sixteen on the right hand side, divided half way by the stove, which stood somewhat back in an antique carved fireplace. On the opposite side, divided at regular intervals by five long windows, stood twelve similar compartments; while at the end the great Tudor window, through which I was caught peeping so many years ago, filled in the vista with rich heraldic emblazonments of stained glass, through which the daylight filtered in streams of purple and gold.

And all this was his and mine!

There were moments, now and then, when I seemed to wake up to a sense of sudden wonder and gratitude, scarce believing that my happiness was more than a dream; and this was one of those moments. I paused; looked up and down the noble gallery; and asked myself what I had done to deserve so much devotion, so much wealth, so great and many advantages? Truly, I had done nothing but love, and love perfectly; and my love had brought its own "exceeding great reward." Was not that reward too gracious and abundant? Was I old enough, and wise enough, to use it rightly? I could but try, humbly, earnestly, faithfully. I could but try; and I would try—and my eyes grew dim as I registered that silent resolution, which was a prayer and a promise in one.

Turning these things over in my mind, I passed slowly up the library, looking for the compartment of the "*Acta Sanctorum*." I found it at the farthest end, making the last compartment on the right hand side, on a line with the fireplace. I have said that the books were protected by wire screens. These wire screens worked upon hinges, and opened in the middle of each compartment, like folding-doors. I turned the key; took out the first volume on which I happened to lay my hand; and was about to close the book-case without further investigation, when it occurred to me that the folios on the left half of the compartment looked fresher and more attractive. I therefore replaced it; unbolted the other half of the wire-door; and proceeded to take down another specimen.

To my surprise, the book would not stir. I tried its next neighbor, and then one on the shelf below; and still with the same result. Looking more closely, I found that, although their vellum backs were gilt and lettered precisely like those on the adjoining shelves, they were, in fact, not books at all; but imitations put there to fill a vacant space. No wonder they looked fresher than their genuine brethren, which had withstood the wear of centuries!

Half smiling at the deception and its success, I was about to turn back to my former choice, when a thought flashed across me, like a revelation, and brought the blood in a torrent to my face. The door! The door that I had heard as I came in that morning, weeks and weeks ago! The secret door of which no one knew any thing, and for suggesting the very possibility of which I was laughed at as a romantic child!

Trembling with excitement, I eagerly examined the false half of the sixteenth compartment, in every part. If it were a door, it must open somewhere; and that opening would, most likely, be hidden in some part of the woodwork. Nevertheless, I scrutinized the woodwork in vain. I next looked for the hinges; but no trace of a hinge was visible. I then thought that one of the mock books might, perhaps, be movable, concealing a lock at the back; but having tested all in succession, I found all false alike. At last I began to think I must be mistaken, and that no door existed, after all.

Having come to this conclusion, I chanced to pass my hand, almost mechanically, along the under edges of the shelves. I did not even say to myself "there may be a bolt here;" but I did it, as if by a kind of instinct. Suddenly my finger slipped into a groove, and encountered a metal catch. I drew back, flushed and agitated, and scarcely able to stand. I had suspected the existence of the door; I had searched for it; and now that I had found it, I was terrified by my own discovery. What weakness! Half angry with myself, and half defiant, I pulled the catch quickly back, and, leaning my knee against the books, saw the five lower shelves yield at once to the pressure, swing back on concealed hinges, and reveal a narrow dark passage of about two feet in width. The passage once before me, I plunged into it without a second's hesitation; struck my foot almost immediately against the first step of a steep and narrow staircase; and felt my way cautiously upward.

I counted the steps, one by one, till I reached the eighteenth, and then my outstretched hand came suddenly against a door. It was totally dark, and only a faint gleam from below showed the way by which I had come; for the staircase seemed to have turned in ascending, and the hidden door had swung nearly close again, after I passed through. I felt the panels over, with the slow and careful touch of a blind person.

I found a small metal knob, which turned noiselessly within my grasp. I paused. My heart beat violently. My forehead was bathed in a cold perspiration. I asked myself for the first time what it was that I was about to see when this door was opened? What chamber, long closed—what deed of mystery, long forgotten—what family-secret, long buried, would be revealed to my eyes? Was it right, after all, that I should pursue this discovery? Ought I not, perhaps, to go back as I had come; tell my husband of the secret upon which I had stumbled; and leave it to him to deal with according to his pleasure? Hesitating thus, I had, even now, more than half a mind to go no farther. It was a struggle between delicacy and curiosity; but I was a mere woman, after all, and curiosity prevailed.

"Come what may," said I aloud, "I *will* see what lies beyond this door!"

And with this I opened it.

My disappointment was great. I had strung myself up for the sight of something strange and terrible—for closed shutters, through which a narrow thread of daylight should half reveal a room, in every corner of which the dust of years would lie like a mysterious mantle; for a floor stained, perchance, with blood, and furniture giving evidence in its disorder of some fearful struggle enacted long ago; for something, perhaps, even more ghastly still; and now—

And now I found myself, instead, upon the threshold of a pretty, cheerful, bright little sitting-room, with a good fire blazing in the grate, and a window overlooking part of the shrubberies. The walls were covered with books and pictures. In a cage hanging against the window, sang and fluttered a pair of little gold-colored canaries. Across the back of an easy chair beside the fireplace lay a woman's shawl of black cashmere, bound with black velvet; and on the table lay a pile of books, some of them open; a desk; writing materials; and a small work-basket.

I had made a wonderful discovery, after all! Here was, doubtless, some little *sanctum* sacred to the private hours of good Mrs. Fairhead; and a very snug little *sanctum*, too!

"She must be fond of reading," thought I, looking round at the books with some surprise. "Where can she have got all these? And what kind of literature does she indulge in?"

I went over to the table, smiling at my own thoughts, and expecting to find the works of Soyer and Miss Acton on the desk of my studious housekeeper. But the smile vanished and left me cold, motionless, paralyzed.

The first book on which my eyes fell was entitled "Storia d'Italia, di Francesco Guicciardini, *gentiluomo di Firenze*."

I sat down, mechanically, in the chair facing the desk, and closed my eyes, like one who is stunned by a sudden blow. A history of Italy, in Italian! How should this thing be possible? Who, in my house, could read that book, unless it were my husband or myself? Surely I must be mad, or dreaming.

I opened my eyes again; but the same words stared me in the face. Another book lay beside it, also opened—the celebrated "Storia della Letteratura Italiana" of Tiraboschi. Three or four others were within reach. These I drew toward me with shaking hands that could scarcely turn the leaves. I examined them in a kind of dull stupor. They were "Baretti's Italian and English Dictionary," "Waverley," the "*Prigioni*" of Silvio Pellico, and Rogers's "Italy."

Who, then, was the reader of these books? Who the inhabitant of this room? I looked round vaguely, with a sense of bewildered uneasiness, such as one feels in a dream, when on the verge of some unknown danger. There lay the shawl—here the work-basket. Then it was a woman. Merciful God! what woman? Why had I never seen her? Why had no one told me that she lived under my roof? What was her name? What right had she here? I felt as Hugh in the secret? Was Mrs. Fairhead? Were they both deceiving me; and, if so, for what purpose? I sprang to my feet. I felt as if my brain were on fire. Finding no name written in any of the books on the table, I turned to those on the shelves, and tore down volume after volume with feverish haste. They were chiefly Italian, some much worn, and some yet uncut—Manzoni, Alfieri, Metastasio, Ariosto, and the like. In none of them, any writing. There were pictures on the walls; colored prints and engravings, for the most part—Naples, Messina, Pæstum, and the Grotto of Capri. There were ornaments on the chimney-piece—a leaning Tower in alabaster, a bronze Temple of Vesta, a model of Milan Cathedral. Italy—everywhere Italy!

Then this woman was Italian.

The very thought that she was Italian seemed, somehow, to make the mystery less endurable than before. I felt that I hated her, unknown as she was. All my senses appeared to be unnaturally keen. Nothing escaped me. I saw everything, and reasoned upon all that I saw with a rapidity and directness that seemed like inspiration. Possessed by a kind of despairing recklessness, I searched every article of furniture, every shelf; even the shawl on the chair; even the work-basket on the table. Then I opened the desk. At any other time, the mere thought of such an act would have shocked me; but now, half insane as I was, I did it without even the consciousness of possible wrong.

The first things that I saw inside were a small book and a little oval velvet case, about the size of a five-shilling piece. I opened the book first; a dainty pocket volume of Petrarch's Sonnets, bound in scarlet morocco, with a gilt clasp. On the first leaf was written in Hugh's bold hand, somewhat cramped to suit the tiny page—

"*Maddalena, del suo amico*—H. F."

Maddalena! Her name was Maddalena.

Then I took up the oval case. A mist swam before my eyes. I scarcely dared to look at the portrait within, even when it lay open before me—but I did look. It was Hugh—a younger Hugh, beardless, boyish, different, and yet the same. Opposite the portrait, on a gold plate inside the cover, were engraved the words "*Hugo a Maddalena*."

I do not know how long I stood gazing down upon this in my dumb despair; but it seemed as if hours had gone by, when I at last dropped again into the chair, laid my head and arms on the table, and burst into an agony of sobbing.

Presently I became conscious that there was

some one in the room. I had heard no one enter; but I felt that I was no longer alone. Looking up in sudden terror and defiance, I saw my husband standing before me. He was very pale—lividly pale—and his eyes were full of tears.

"My poor Barbara," said he, softly, and held out his hand. I shrank back, involuntarily. He shuddered.

"No, no," he said, "not that I any thing but that." Then, as if recollecting himself, he resumed his former tone, and added, "I see it all, my Barbara. Come with me—trust me—and I will explain every thing."

I pointed to the portrait.

"Yes, every thing, my darling—every thing."

CHAPTER L.

THE STORY OF MADDALENA.

"Un pezzo di cielo caduto in terra."—SANNAZARO.

"POOR Maddalena!" said Hugh. "Her life is very solitary—her story very brief. An exile from her country, a fugitive from her family, she has for years taken refuge under my roof. It is her only home. Alone here with her books and her sad thoughts, she wears away the slow cycle of a companionless existence. She is no longer young; and she has no friend in all the wide world, but myself. You will pity her, my Barbara, as I do, when you have heard me to the end.

"You know that I chanced to be abroad when my father died. It was my first visit to the Continent, and I was making what was then called the 'grand tour.' I loved him very dearly, and could not endure to return to the home where I should have missed him in every room; so I prolonged my travels indefinitely; and, instead of coming back to England, went farther and farther East, leading a wild nomadic life, and seeking to forget my sorrow in deeds of peril and adventure. Wearying at length of the tent and the saddle, I retraced my steps, after a year and a half of Oriental wanderings, and re-turned westward as far as Naples; where I bought a yacht, hired a villa at Capri, and lived like a hermit. Here Tippoo and a female servant constituted all my establishment; while, for the management of my little yacht, I needed only one sailor and a pilot. The pilot's name was Jacopo. He lived in the island, and was at my service when I needed him. The sailor slept on board; and there was a sheltered cove at the foot of my garden, where we used to cast anchor.

"In this place I lived a delightful life. Every day I coasted about the enchanting shores and islands of the Neapolitan bay; sketching; fishing; reading Cicero, Suetonius and Virgil; landing wherever it pleased my fancy; and wandering among the ruins of Pæstum, Pompeii, and Baiæ. My books, at this time, were my only associates. I knew no one in the neighborhood of Naples, and desired only to be alone. It was a strange life for a young man, not yet twenty-three years of age.

"I have already mentioned to you my pilot Jacopo. He was a swarthy, handsome fellow, about three years older than myself, sullen, active, and taciturn as a Turk. All I knew of him was

that he was unmarried, and lived somewhere on the other side of the island. Accident, however, brought me to a knowledge of his family. Coming home one afternoon, about two hours before sunset, and running the yacht into our little harbor, I saw a young contadina waiting in the shadow of the rocks. As Jacopo sprang on shore, she ran to meet him, clasped him by the arm with both hands, and spoke with great apparent earnestness. He, in reply, nodded, muttered some three or four brief syllables, and kissed her on the forehead. She then ran lightly up one of the many rugged paths that here intersect the face of the cliff, and disappeared. As we went up to the house, I laughed at Jacopo about his innamorata. 'She' is no innamorata, signore,' said he. 'She is my sister.' 'Thy sister, Jacopo,' repeated I. 'Hast thou a sister, amico?' 'I have a sister, signore, and a brother, and a sister-in-law,' replied he; 'and Maddalena tells me that the sister-in-law has this day been delivered of her first-born. The babe will be baptized to-night, and if the signore wants me no more this evening——' 'No, no, Jacopo,' said I. 'Go to the baptism, by all means. Thou wilt act as godfather?' 'Sì, signore, and as father, too; Paolo being away.' 'Who is Paolo?' 'My brother, signore, who is at sea.' 'Friend Jacopo,' said I, 'do you think the sister-in-law would allow me to be among the guests?' Jacopo flushed up under his dark skin, and said she would think it a great honor. 'But,' added he, with a kind of proud shame, 'it is a poor place, signore.' To which I replied that I was a citizen of the world, and all places were alike to me; and so it was settled. We then started at once for his home, striking across the island by short cuts and sheep-tracks known to my companion, who preceded me in his accustomed silence. By and by we came again in sight of the sea, and, following the course of the shore, reached an open space, or high level plateau, on the very verge of which stood a small antique stone dwelling, bowered in with trellised vines, and almost overhanging the sea. A raised terrace in front; a little garden at the back, full of orange and fig-trees; a rude dove-cot clinging, like a parasite, to the walls of an outhouse; a few goats browsing on the herbage round about; and a flight of rough steps, hewn in the solid rock, and leading down to the beach, seventy feet below, made up the picture of this humble home. As we drew near the music of a zampogna and tambourine became audible; and Maddalena came out to meet us. Learning that I was the padrone, she kissed my hand, bade me welcome, and made me known to the guests. They were the priest; some fishermen and their wives; and one Matteo, a wealthy peasant, who kept the only little albergo in Capri. They all rose at our approach. The zampogna and tambourine players laid aside their instruments; the priest put on his alb and chasuble; the inn-keeper made his best bow; and we all went into the house, where, in a room opening on the garden, lay the young mother and her infant; their clean white coverlet strewn with sprigs of rosemary and fresh thyme, and a crucifix at the head of the bed. Jacopo and Maddalena then stood by as sponsors—the priest gabbled through the baptismal formula—the little Christian protested lustily against the mouthful of salt administered to him on the finger of the holy man; and so the ceremony ended. Maddalena then ran to prepare supper on the terrace, while we congratulated the mother, and made such little presents to the baby as each could afford. Thus the priest gave a tiny medal, blessed by the Pope; Jacopo a piece of linen; the innkeeper a string of coral beads; and I, in pledge of a gift to come, a broad gold coin, for which the mother and Jacopo kissed my hands. After this we we went out on the terrace, and supped by sunset, waited on, in Eastern fashion, by the women. I shall never forget the crimson splendor of that evening sky, nor the pastoral charm of that rustic festival, at which Plenty and Good-will presided, like unseen gods. There was white bread made from Indian corn, and wine in goat-skin vessels. There were crabs fried in olive-oil; quails, for which the island is famous; omelettes, dried fish, salad, fresh cucumbers, melons, green figs, macaroni, and the delicious *ricotta* of goat's-milk, which every peasant of South Italy is skilled in making. While we were yet feasting, the tender twilight came on, and the broad summer moon rose over the tops of the olive-trees, glowing and golden. Then the tables were cleared away; the priest took his leave; those who could play snatched up their instruments; and a circle was formed on the grassy plateau for the tarantella. I could dance it myself, then, as well as any Neapolitan among them; and so, by and by, took Maddalena for my partner, and delighted my simple hosts by performing their national dance like one 'to the manner born.' Would you know what Maddalena was like when I first saw her? Well, I will try to describe her. She was about eighteen years of age, and looked somewhat older. Her features were agreeable without being handsome. Her complexion was pale, her figure slight, her hair black and abundant. At eighteen, most Italian women were married or betrothed; but Maddalena was neither. Her life had, hitherto, been devoted to her brothers. Their will was her law; and if she feared Jacopo more than she loved him, she adored Paolo and his wife with her whole heart. I learned these things afterward, and by degrees; but I tell them to you now, *carina*, to make my story clearer and briefer. For a peasant—and you must remember, my Barbara, that she was nothing but a peasant—Maddalena had a more than ordinary air of intelligent thoughtfulness. Something of this she may have owed to her housewifely habits and secluded life; but much also to natural abilities of no common order. For all this, she could neither read nor write; and was as ignorant as a child of all the world that was not Capri. She had never been farther than Naples in her life. Her beads were her library; the Madonna was her religion; Tasso, as she had now and then heard him chanted by the *Canta Storia*, her only historian.

"I have always loved to identify myself with the life of the people in every land that I have visited, and my introduction to this family of simple islanders gave me unusual pleasure. I staid with them till nearly midnight, taking my turn at the guitar or the tarantella; helping Maddalena to mix lemonade for the thirsty dancers; and joining, between whiles, in the chorus of a *canto popolare*. When, at length, I bade them farewell, and went home, with Jacopo for my guide, the fishers were out in the bay with their nets and torches, like sea meteors, and the moon was declining with yet unabated splendor.

"'I shall go over to Naples to-morrow, Jacopo,' said I, as we went along. 'Sì, signore.' —'But you must tell me what gifts to buy.' Jacopo shook his head. 'Nay, but how can I guess what would be acceptable to the father and mother?' Jacopo, however, was as proud and shy as he was taciturn, and would only say that whatever the *padrone* pleased would surely be most acceptable; so, being thrown on my own resources, I suggested a pair of gold earrings for the mother, a piece of cloth to make a holiday suit for the father, and a necklace for Maddalena. To each of these, Jacopo bent his head, with a pleased '*grazie*, signore;' and to the last he said, '*La sorella* will keep it for her wedding.'—'Has she then a lover?' I asked. He shook his head again. 'Not yet,' he replied; '*ma vedremo* — we shall see.'—'And Paolo,' I said, 'where is he now?'—'At sea, signore, with his ship.'—'And where is his ship?'—'*Non so*, signore.'—'To what port was she bound?'— 'To Smyrna, signore, and the Greek Isles.'— 'You never hear from him while he is away?'— 'Never, signore.'—'Surely his wife is sometimes anxious?' Jacopo shrugged his shoulders. '*E buon giovane*,' said he; 'the Madonna will watch over him.'

"By this time we had come upon roads that I knew, and so I bade Jacopo good night, and we parted company.

"The next day, I sailed over to Naples, as agreed; made my purchases, spent my evening at the San Carlo, and returned to Capri just as the sun was rising behind Vesuvius. That same afternoon, I coasted round to the northwest of the island; cast anchor in a little creek at Point Vitareto, about half a mile below Maddalena's home; and went up to the cottage on foot. I found Jacopo there before me, tying up the vines; and Maddalena sitting in the porch, spinning, singing to the baby, and rocking the cradle with her foot. She rose and bade me welcome, fetched a wooden chair from the house, and placed before me a plate of fresh figs, and a small flask of wine. 'It is the *vino Tiberiano*, signore,' said she. 'The wine of Tiberius!' I repeated. 'A good wine, but deserving a better name.' She looked up inquiringly. 'Did you never hear of Tiberius, who lived on this island in the ancient times?' I asked. 'Yes, signore,' she replied, crossing herself; 'he was a magician.'—'Ay, and a Pagan,' added Jacopo, coming down from his ladder among the vines. 'He built twelve palaces here by enchantment; but they were all destroyed by the holy Saint Constantine.'—'*E vero—è verissimo*, signore,' said Maddalena, seeing the smile which I could not wholly suppress; 'one may see the ruins in all parts of Capri.'—'I have seen the ruins, Maddalena,' I replied; 'but Tiberius was no magician. He was a wicked Emperor, and all his palaces were razed to the ground by his successor.' At this moment, my sailor came up from the beach, bringing the box of gifts, and we went into the house to open it. The sister-in-law was sitting up in bed to receive me, and the room, as usual in South-Italy, when a woman is recovering from her confinement, was fragrant with sweet herbs. First, I took out the earrings; then a mug for the baby; then the cloth for Paolo; then a silver watch for Jacopo; and, lastly, a coral necklace for Maddalena. You would have thought, Barbarina, that I had given them the sovereignty of the island. The young mother called on the Madonna and all the saints to bless me. Jacopo, though he said little, was eloquent in gesticulation. As for Maddalena, almost childlike in her joy, she clapped her hands, laughed, danced, hung the necklace on the baby's little neck, and finally ran to the well, like a young water-nymph, to see how it looked upon her own. For my part, *carina*, I only felt ashamed to think at how little cost of money or effort I had made these poor souls so happy. Anxious, at last, to put an end to their thanks and praises, I proposed that Maddalena should go down to see the yacht.

"We went — Maddalena going first, rapidly and lightly as an island-born Diana—down the rock-hewn steep, and along the narrow path of amber strand that lay between the precipice and the sea. She had seen the yacht often, from afar off; but had never yet been on board. She admired every thing—the polished deck; the brass-swivel gun, shining like gold; the compass in its mahogany shrine; the dainty little cabin, with its chintz hangings, its mirror, its pictures, and its books. All was beautiful, all was wonderful in her eyes; and she would have taken off her shoes at the cabin-door if I had not prevented it. My book-case, which, like that of the clerk in Chaucer, stood at my 'beddes hed,' and contained about as many volumes, surprised her more than all the rest. '*Dio!*' said she, to Jacopo, 'can the *padrone* read all these?'—'*Certo*,' replied her brother; 'and ten times as many.' She shook her head, incredulously. 'What can they tell him?' exclaimed she. Jacopo shrugged his shoulders; but I came to his assistance. 'They tell me, Maddalena,' said I, 'of all kinds of strange and precious things, some of which happened hundreds of years ago, and some of which are happening every day. Here is a book that tells me about Italy in the time when all men were pagans, and no one had heard of Christ or the Madonna. Here is another which explains about the stars, how they come and go in the heavens, how far off they are, and what are their appointed uses. This one gives an account of all the seas and cities, islands, mountains, and rivers all over the face of the earth. This is poetry — not such poetry as the hymns and ballads which the fishermen sing; but long histories of war and love, all in rhyme, like the 'Rinaldo.''—Maddalena listened eagerly, devouring each volume with her eyes as I took it out, and almost holding her breath while I spoke. '*La guerra e l'amore!*' repeated she. 'How beautiful! What is it called, signore?' I replied, 'and it is written in Greek.'—'Did Homer write it?' she asked, quickly.—'Yes, Homer wrote it.'—'In Greek, signore?'—'Yes; Homer was a Greek by birth.'—'Then perhaps Paolo will see him; *chi lo sa?*'—I laughed, and shook my head. 'No, no, Maddalena,' I said, 'Paolo will not see him. Homer has been dead nearly three thousand years.' She clasped her hands, and her dark eyes dilated with wonder. 'Three thousand years!' she murmured. '*Madre beata!* three

thousand years!' And presently, when we were leaving the cabin, I saw her turn back to the book-case, and touch the volume timidly with one finger, as if it were a sacred relic, and had some virtue in it.

"After this, I landed now and then at Point Vitareto, and went up to the cottage to see Maddalena and her brother's wife. The affection of these women for each other, and for the sailor far away at sea; the patriarchal simplicity of their home; the calm sanctity of their lives; the antique songs which they sang to the baby in his cradle; the legends which they repeated with the credulity of children, were all, to me, sources of interest and pleasure. Even their household occupations charmed my imagination, like the details of an idyllic poem. The plying of the distaff, the pruning of the vines, the salting of the olive-harvest, the gathering of the honey, the preserving of the figs — what were these but commentaries upon Hesiod and Virgil? If only as a student of the poets and an observer of manners, I loved to familiarize myself with this pastoral interior, and to learn all that I could of the hopes, fears, and narrow ambitions of its inmates. Sometimes, however, we talked of Paolo, and then their hearts welled over with love and praise. Sometimes I told them tales of far-off lands, or translated into their own soft vernacular a page of the Georgics. Then would Jacopo pause in his work, and Maddalena's distaff lie idle on her knee; and when I left off, they would point across the bay toward Posilippo and the tomb of Virgil, and say, 'Yonder is his place of rest.'

"At length there came a day when Jacopo informed me, not without a certain air of subdued exultation, that *la sorella* had just been asked in marriage by Matteo Pisani of Capri. 'Matteo Pisani!' I repeated. 'Not the innkeeper, Jacopo?'—'Si, signore,' he replied. 'Matteo whom you saw on the night of the baptism of little Paolino.'—'But he is old enough,' said I, 'to be Maddalena's father!' Jacopo shrugged his shoulders. 'He is rich, signore.' I shook my head. 'Riches alone do not make a marriage happy,' I objected. 'Does Maddalena love him?' Jacopo laughed. 'Matteo is a good man,' said he, 'and if *la sorella* likes him well enough to marry him, the love will be sure to follow.' And with this he turned away, and said no more.

"It happened that this conversation took place as we were scudding before the wind on our way to Salerno, where I had made arrangements to remain for some days, for the purpose of sketching that part of the coast. During all this absence, neither my pilot nor myself recurred to the subject of Maddalena's betrothal, and by the time we returned to Capri I had almost forgotten it. Once home again, I found my time more than usually occupied; for the term of months for which I had hired my villa was on the point of expiration, and I had made up my mind to go to Algiers for the winter. Busy, therefore, in packing my books and sketches, and making such final arrangements as not even a dweller in tents like myself could wholly escape, I allowed nearly another week to elapse before visiting my humble friends at Vitareto. When at length I found time to do so, it was to bid them farewell.

"The afternoon was mild and delicious, when

I walked across the hights toward Jacopo's home. It was the third week in October. The yellow vine-leaves were withering fast in the grape-stripped vineyards, and the early snow already lay in faint streaks about the summit of Mount Solaro. As the ground rose, Naples and Ischia, Vesuvius with its plume of smoke, and the blue sea flecked with sails, came into sight. Half way to Vitareto, there was a point whence all the glorious bay might be seen on a day as clear as this. A stone seat and a solitary tree marked the spot. I pressed eagerly forward, remembering how many and many a year might go by before my eyes should rest upon that sight again. As I drew near I saw a woman sitting on the bench, with her face buried in her hands. At the sound of my approaching footsteps, she looked up. It was Maddalena.

"'Well met, Maddalena,' said I. 'I was coming to see you.'—She blushed; but the blush died away, and left her very pale. 'Our hearts always bid the signore welcome,' she replied.— 'I was also coming,' I added, 'to say farewell.' 'Alas!' said she, 'we have heard it. The signore is going away.'—'Yes,' I said, regretfully; 'I am going; but I am sorry to leave Capri.' She looked up with naïve wonder. 'The padrone is master,' said she. 'He can stay if he chooses.' 'True,' I replied; 'but I can also return when I please; and—and I have something of the Zingaro in my blood—I can not help wandering. I am going to Africa for the winter. Still, I should have wished to stay, Maddalena, for your wedding.'—She blushed again, more faintly than before, and turned still paler after. 'I hear that it is a fortunate marriage,' said I, hastily disengaging a small ornament from my watch-chain. 'You must accept my congratulations, and this little remembrance of your English friend.'— She murmured some scarcely audible thanks. I looked at her closely, and could see that she had been lately weeping. Her face, too, looked haggard, and her hands thin. 'I hope, Maddalena,' said I, 'that you may be happy.'— Her lips trembled; but she made no reply. 'Marriage,' I continued earnestly, 'is a very serious thing—almost more serious, Maddalena, for a woman than for a man. It is a bondage for life; and unless it be a bondage of love, not all the golden ducats in the world can make it happy. I hope you do not accept Matteo because he is rich?'—'No, no, signore,' she replied, turning her face from me.—'Nor in obedience only to the wishes of your family?' She shook her head. 'If you do not love him,' I said, 'which I fear may be the case, you at all events respect him, Maddalena? You have no personal objection to him?' She shook her head again, with something like a suppressed sob. I took her hand. It was cold and damp, and I could feel all the nerves of the palm vibrating with agitation. 'Cara Maddalena,' I said very gently and soothingly, 'I have no right—I know I have no right to question you thus; but I can not bear to think that you are, perhaps, about to sacrifice your whole life to some mistaken sense of duty. Confide in me, as in one who knows the world so much better than yourself; and be assured that I will spare neither money nor influence, if money or influence can help you. Is there—as I can not help thinking there may be—some

other with whom you believe you could be more happy?'—Maddalena covered her face with her hands, and burst into an agony of weeping. 'No one can help me!' she cried, brokenly. 'No one can help me!' 'Hush, Maddalena,' I said. 'Do not weep—do not despair. I am your true friend. I offer no more than I am ready to perform; and I believe that I can help you. Who is it that you prefer? If there are obstacles, what can be done to remove them?' 'Nothing, signore! nothing!'—'Is it that your lover is poor?' I asked. She shook her head. 'Is it that Jacopo dislikes him?' She shook her head again. 'Is it that you have quarreled, and parted, and are too proud to be reconciled; or is it that he is no longer free to claim you?'— Maddalena started to her feet, and for the first time since our conversation had begun, looked straight at me through her tears. 'Signore,' she said, rapidly and vehemently, 'ask me no more. You mean kindly; but you can do nothing, nothing, nothing! If my heart aches, no medicine can cure it! My lot is cast. I *must* marry Matteo. I have given my promise, and whether I keep or break it, can make no difference now. He is rich. He is our landlord. If I marry him, I can, at least, do something to help my brothers and our little Paolino. By refusing him, I could do nothing to help myself. If you desire to be kind to me, question me no more, and forget all about me! God and the Madonna bless and keep you, dear signore! I am not ungrateful, and—and I am not unhappy!'

"And with these words, Maddalena seized my hands, covered them with tears and kisses, and fled away before I could utter a word in reply. I sat for a long time on the stone bench, after she had disappeared, troubled and perplexed by what had taken place. I was sincerely grieved for her, my Barbara; and all the more grieved because I could see no way to serve her. The more I considered what she had said, the more I became convinced that it was now my duty to interfere no farther. I had sought her confidence, and she had refused it. I had offered my aid, and offered it in vain. If neither money nor influence could avail her, there remained but one conclusion. Maddalena, without doubt, loved a man who was already married; and in this case her best hope lay in honest Matteo. What readier cure, after all, for the heart-ache, than the love of a good man, the cares of a household, and the duties of maternity? As I sat and pondered thus, the sun sank lower and lower, till it was too late for me to go on to Vitareto that evening. So I rose and retraced my steps, resolving to send some farewell message by Jacopo the following day.

"The rest of my story, *carina*, may be summed up in a few words. I went no more to Vitareto; and, having only two days to remain in Capri, I discharged Jacopo. Having made arrangements to dispose of my little yacht and forward my superfluous books and drawings to England, I then bade farewell to the pretty villa; and on the third day after my interview with Maddalena, slept on board my boat for the last time, and steered for Naples. I had now only my one sailor to navigate the yacht; but it was all plain sailing enough, so, after remaining on deck till the little white house that had been my home for so many months was carried out of sight by the curve of the shore, I went down into the cabin. At the cabin-door I met Tippoo, with a strange startled look upon his face. 'Sahib!' he said, pointing over his shoulder. 'Sahib — do you know?' — 'Do I know what?' I asked. 'There, Sahib – in there!' Puzzled and impatient, I pushed past him into the cabin, and found — Maddalena! Maddalena, who fell at my feet, entreating me to forgive her, and imploring me to save her!

"I am almost ashamed to confess to you, Barbara, that my first impulse was one of anger. I felt that, having offered to help her when I could have done so without serious inconvenience, it was excessively annoying to find her claiming my protection just as I was starting on a long journey. However, I raised her up, soothed her as well as I could, and learned, to my amazement and distress, that she had been married to Matteo Pisani the day before. Once married, her friendly indifference changed, to use her own impassioned expression, to an unconquerable personal loathing. Feeling that she could never be his wife, she fled from his roof on her wedding night, and took refuge till daylight in a little oratory on Mount Solaro. Returning at dawn to her old home, she found Jacopo absent, summoned away to assist Matteo in the search for herself, and her sister-in-law in the deepest trouble. In vain she represented her aversion toward her husband. In vain she implored her sister's mediation and sympathy. She was told, and with bitter truth, that she should have known her own mind while there was yet time; that now her only course was submissively to apologize to Matteo, and return to his roof without delay; and that if she did not do so, none of her family would ever speak to her again. 'In this strait, signore,' said Maddalena, 'what could I do but fly to you for protection? I found your vessel ready to start — I chose a moment when there was no one within sight — I stole on board, and hid myself under your bed, till I knew that we were safely at sea. And now — now I am at your mercy! If you take me back, my husband and Jacopo will kill me. If they do not, I shall kill myself, sooner than be the wife of a man whom I abhor. You, and you only, signore, can save me now!' — Serious, almost tragic as the situation was, I could not help feeling that there was in it an element of the ludicrous. 'Good God! Maddalena,' said I, 'it is all well enough to ask me to save you; but what am I to do with you?' — 'Let me be your slave,' replied she. In spite of myself, I could not keep from smiling. 'You foolish little girl,' said I, 'what do I want with a slave? And why should you prefer slavery to a comfortable home with an honest, respectable husband, like Matteo Pisani? Come now, Maddalena, don't you think you have been somewhat rash and romantic, and that it would be better for us to turn the boat about, and steer for Capri? I will do my best to make your peace with Matteo, and ——' 'Enough, signore!' she exclaimed, flushed, and trembling, and indignant. 'I see that you despise me! Take me back, if you will. Take me back, and abandon me to my fate. I deserve your scorn.' I became serious in an instant. 'Maddalena,' I said, 'I no more despise you than I am disposed to abandon you. I offered you my help three days ago, and I will help you still. Give me a few moments to think what is best to be done; and believe that, whatever the difficulty or danger, I will, by the help of Heaven, save you if I can.'

"With this I went on deck, and looked out ahead. We were, as nearly as possible, halfway across between Capri and Naples, and the shores of the little island were already indistinct in the distance. I went up to my sailor, who was steering. 'Tommaso,' I said, 'what wind have we? It seems to me to be blowing due west.' 'Si, signore; due west,' replied Tommaso, with his eye on the compass. I took a turn or two on deck, and came back again. 'You are not a married man, I think, Tommaso?' said I. He looked surprised at the question, laughed and shook his head. 'And you have no particular home-ties, either — I mean you are a free man to come and go as you please; is it not so?' 'Si, signore; certo, certo,' replied Tommaso. I took another turn; again came back; laid my hand on his shoulder, and said, 'Supposing that I were to keep the yacht, after all, Tommaso, and change the whole of my plans, would you stay with me?' 'Gladly, signore.' 'And could you, do you think, pilot the boat safely as far as Palermo, without putting into Naples at all?' 'Yes, signore.' 'Are you certain, Tommaso?' 'Quite certain, signore. It is all open sea, and my whole life has been spent in these waters.' 'Then 'bout ship, my man, at once,' said I, 'and steer for Palermo. There we shall be sure to pick up a pilot; and we can go on to Greece, or Constantinople, or Grand Cairo, or to the deuce, if we choose!'

"And this, Barbarina, was how I came to know poor Maddalena, and how I made myself responsible for her protection. I took her first of all to Palermo; then up the Adriatic to Venice; and from Venice to Vienna, where I placed her in a private family, and gave her, in accordance with her own desire, every facility for the improvement of her mind. She had excellent abilities, and a passion for knowledge; so that she became educated, as it were, by a miracle. At the end of three years, she could not only read and write her own language with correctness, but had made good progress in English as well. Since then, she has gone on improving year after year. Her happiness is bound up, so to speak, in her favorite authors; and her whole life is one long course of study. For the last five or six years, she has lived under my roof here, at Broomhill; occupying two little rooms at the back of the house; maintaining the strictest seclusion; knowing no one, and known of none. It has pleased her, poor soul, to constitute herself my librarian. She loves, in her gratitude, to believe herself of some little service to her benefactor; and the arrangement, classification, and cataloguing of the books down-stairs have given her occupation and amusement together. As for the secret door, my Barbara, it has only been so disguised since she came here. It was originally contrived by my grandfather for his own convenience, and communicated with the rooms which he had in occupation. Those rooms, for that very reason, I assigned to Maddalena; and the door I caused to be masked by shelves of mock 'Acta Sanctorum,' partly for the better appearance of the library, and partly for Maddalena's satisfaction. She is haunted to this hour by a morbid fear of discovery. She believes, after all these years, that her husband or her brother, will some day track her to her hiding-place; and that she is, perhaps, a little safer in having a concealed door by which to escape to her apartments. She dreads every strange face—even yours, my wife; and would have kept her very existence a secret from you, had it been possible. Now you know her story, and my share in it. Was I not right when I said that, having heard it, you would pity her, even as I pity her myself?"

I have not here interrupted Hugh's narrative, as I continually interrupted it at the time, with questions, and anticipations of what was to come. I have given it as he would have given it to a less impatient listener; and, ever so, feel that my version fails to do his story justice. When he had quite finished, he took me in his arms and asked me if I was satisfied.

Was I satisfied? Yes—for the moment; and frankly gave him the assurance for which he asked. Listening to him, looking at him, how could I do otherwise than accept in its fullest sense every explanation given or implied? How could I pause to ask myself if, when all looked fair and open, there were any flaw, or gloze, or reservation? I did not pause, I believed. It was, therefore, in the simplest faith that, just as we were parting, I said,

"Oh, stop, Hugh! One thing more — did you never find out who it was that poor Maddalena loved, after all; and why she could not marry him?"

"I did, my darling, and a hopeless affair it was. She loved a man who no more loved her, or thought of her, than you love or think of the Grand-Duke of Zollenstrasse-am-Main."

"Poor, poor girl! But do you think, Hugh, that you could have done any thing if she had confided in you that day when you met her on the hights? Do you think——"

"My child, how can I tell? You might as well ask me if I believe that Tasso and Leonora would have lived happily together all their days in the bonds of holy matrimony, if the poet had not been mad, and the lady a duchess!"

"Still, if Maddalena could have procured a divorce——"

"Barbarina," interrupted he, laughing, "you are a goose, with your ifs and supposes! If Queen Cleopatra's nose had been an inch shorter, the face of the world would have been changed. We have that fact upon the authority of Pascal. Besides, the Holy Roman Catholic Church couples up her children very firmly indeed. I could more easily have procured a cardinal's hat for myself, than a divorce for Maddalena."

———

CHAPTER LI.

TOTAL ECLIPSE.

—— "TOTAL eclipse
Without all hope of day!"—MILTON.

THE eventful night came at last—the night on which I was to make my *début* in society. It was my first ball; excepting only the memorable night at Broomhill, years ago—but I am not, therefore, going to describe it. In brief, it was a ball like every other; crowded and stately, with blaze of lights and blush of flowers, with rustle of silk, and murmur of compliment, and, over all, the clash and clang of a military band. "Every ball," wrote one as wise as he was witty, "is a round; but not a perpetual round of pleasure." To me it was no pleasure at all, but a moral penance. I was the heroine of the evening, and I would fain have been unsought and unobserved. I was nervous; I was stared at; I was flattered by the men; I was criticised by the women; and I went through more introductions than I could ever hope to remember. Happy was I when, having taken leave of our noble entertainers, we were once more driving homeward.

"My little wife," said Hugh, circling me fondly with his arm. "My little wife, who has borne herself so well and gracefully, and of whom I have been so proud!"

"You would hardly have been proud of me, Hugh," said I, "if you had known how frightened I was the whole time."

"I did know it, *carissima*, and thought you went bravely through the ordeal — looking so pretty, and so pale, too, under that coronal of diamonds!"

"It is very heavy—it hurts my forehead."

"What! wearying already of the 'polished perturbation,' and sighing for the 'homely biggin,' my Barbarina? Tush! these are the penalties of splendor."

"Say, then, the penalties of a penalty."

"Do you mean to tell me seriously, wife, that you did not enjoy the homage lavished upon your little self this evening!"

"Seriously, husband, I did not."

"Nor the attentions of Lord and Lady Bayham?"

"Not in the least. I thought him very dull and pompous; and her so satirical, that I dared not open my lips in her presence."

"Still, my darling, you are but mortal; and I don't believe there ever lived the woman who did not love to be well dressed and admired."

"I love to be well dressed, *for* you; and I love to be admired, *by* you—and I love both because I love you. There, sir, are you satisfied?"

"If I were not more than satisfied," replied he, "I should deserve to have you carried off from my arms by some worthier knight. By the way, I have gleaned one wheat-ear of useful information out of the barren stubble of small-talk this evening. Holford tells me that Lord Walthamstow's library has come to the hammer, and will be on sale to-morrow and the four following days. It is an auction that I would not willingly miss. Will you come with me, Barbarina, in the morning?"

"Where will it be held?"

"At Christie and Manson's."

"What, in London?"

"Unquestionably. Where else would you have it? We should try to get our old rooms at Claridge's, and——"

"No, no, Hugh—not in December, thank you. I prefer Broomhill to a dreary hotel, where I should be alone all day, with nothing to do but watch for you from the windows. *Must* you go to-morrow?"

"If I do not go to-morrow, my darling, I may as well not go at all ; for the very books that I should, perhaps, most desire to purchase, may be the first offered."

"Then why go at all ? I am sure we have books enough—more than you or I will ever live to read."

"Books enough, Barbarina ! Can a hero have glory enough ? or a miser gold enough ? or a collector books enough ? Why, my child, there is one volume in the Walthamstow library for which I would go to Calcutta, if necessary ; an original copy of Meninsky's great Oriental Dictionary. It is a very scarce book. Shall I tell you the cause of its rarity ?"

"If you please, Hugh," I replied, sleepily.

"Well, then, Meninsky was a great Oriental scholar, who lived in Vienna toward the latter part of the seventeenth century. This dictionary, in four folios, was the result of seven years' labor and the studies of a life. In 1683, Vienna was besieged by the Turks. A bomb burst upon Meninsky's house. Nearly the whole edition of the Dictionary was consumed ; the very types from which it had been printed were destroyed ; and of the few copies which remain scattered through Europe, scarcely one may be found which is not either blistered by the fire, or stained by the water with which the flames were extinguished. Now, for a dabbler in all kinds of tongues, like myself, that book will be——"

I heard no more. Meninsky and his dictionary, Vienna and the Turks, seemed to shift confusedly by, in a stream of unmeaning phrases ; and when I next opened my eyes, it was to see Tippoo's olive face at the carriage-door, and the lighted-hall beyond.

Wearied out with fatigue and excitement, I went up at once to my dressing-room, whither my husband presently followed me.

"I have come, my darling," said he, "to say good-night, and implore you to go to bed as quickly as possible. For myself, I shall be late, for I have several letters to write."

"Letters?" I repeated. "Why, it is already two o'clock !"

"I know it ; but having to start by the early train, and be at the rooms by the time the sale commences, I must write now, or wait till to-morrow evening. You see, my love, I go so seldom to town, that I am compelled to make the most of my short visits ; and by writing now to my lawyer, my tailor, and such other persons as I may desire to see while in London, I save several posts, and provide for my more speedy return."

"And when will that be, husband ?"

"Perhaps the day after to-morrow ; but I shall know better when I have seen the catalogue, and learned on what days the various books will be sold."

"Which means, I suppose, that you may possibly be away till Saturday ?"

"Possibly ; but not probably."

"Oh, Hugh, what a long time ! Five days ! —five dull, dreary, miserable days ; and all for the sake of a stupid Oriental dictionary !"

"What an illogical Barbara ! In the first place, I do not go 'all for the sake of a stupid Oriental dictionary,' because that book is only one among many which I should wish to secure. In the second place, the dictionary is one of the

noblest works ever undertaken by a single laborer. In the third place, it is unlikely that the best lots should be left to the last, or that I should need to remain away later than Thursday. In the fourth place——"

I put my fingers to my ears, and refused to hear another syllable.

"Enough !" I cried pettishly. "If you had been Orpheus, and I Eurydice, you would have talked Pluto into compliance without help of song or lyre. Go write your letters, Hugh, and try to snatch, at least, a couple of hours' rest before starting."

He laughed, and pulled my ear.

"I forgot to mention," said he, "that there are some magnificent 'picture-books,' in the Walthamstow collection : — fac-similes of the drawings of Raffaelle and Michael Angelo ; engravings after Leonardo, Veronese, and Titian ; to say nothing of a complete set of Piranesi's Roman Antiquities."

"Oh, Hugh !"

"But they are sure to fetch a large price. Good works of art always do."

My enthusiasm went down to zero.

"Besides," added he, maliciously, "they will undoubtedly reserve the prints till the books are sold ; and by that time I shall have returned home again."

"Hugh, you are the most tormenting, tiresome, tantalizing——"

—"Indulgent, delightful, and admirable husband upon earth !" interpolated he. "*Eh bien, petite, nous ferons notre possible.* I shall see to what price these things are likely to amount ; and if I ruin myself, we will sell the family diamonds. Now, good night, my dear love—good night, sweet dreams, and happy waking."

And with this, and a kiss, he left me.

The ball-dress thrown aside, and the "warmed jewels" all unclasped and laid in their velvet cases, I then dismissed my maid, and sat by the fire for some time, in a delicious idleness. I was very happy, and dreamily conscious of my happiness. Every uneasy doubt that had of late been knocking at my heart seemed laid at rest ; every perplexing trifle, forgotten. I tried to think of the old time at Zollenstrasse, and to compare the dear present with that past which already seemed so far away in the distance ; but my eyes closed, and my thoughts wandered, and I sank away to sleep.

By and by, after what seemed like the interval of only a few minutes, I awoke. Awoke to find the fire quite out, the lamp dim, and myself ice-cold from head to foot. I sat up, shivering. My first thought was to hasten to bed, lest Hugh should come and find me waking. I next looked at my watch. It was half-past four o'clock. Half-past four already, and Hugh still writing ! Naughty Hugh, from whom I had parted more than two hours ago, and who would have to leave the house, at latest, by seven ! I rose ; exchanged my slight dressing-gown for a mantle lined with furs ; lit a small Roman hand-lamp ; peeped into his vacant dressing-room as I passed ; and went at once to seek and summon him.

In order to go from our sleeping-room to the turret-chamber, I had to traverse a corridor extending the whole length of one front of the house. All was very dark and still. My little lamp shot a feeble glimmer on each closed door that I passed. My shadow stalked awfully beside me. The very rustling of my garments had a ghostly sound. At the top of the great well-staircase I looked away and shuddered, remembering the shape that I saw, or fancied I saw, gliding down the darkness, the first night of my coming home. Once past this dreaded point, I went on more bravely and reached the door of the turret-chamber. Before lifting the inner curtain, I hesitated.

It seemed to me that I heard voices.

· I held my breath—I advanced a step—I paused.

" *Hugo—Hugo mio* "—these were the words I heard—" *guardami*—look at me, listen to me, for a moment !"

" *Pazienza, cara*," replied my husband, abstractedly.

" *Pazienza !*" repeated the other. " Alas ! is it not always *pazienza ?* What is my life but one long patience ?"

I had heard the scratching of his pen. I now heard it laid aside.

" My poor Maddalena !" said he.

Sì—povera Maddalena," she echoed, with a heavy sigh.

" You look very pale to-night," said he. " Are you tired ?"

" Of my existence—yes."

" Alas ! Maddalena, I know how weary it must be. And then I can so seldom see you."

" That is the worst—that is the worst !" replied she, eagerly. " If I could speak to you once or twice in each long day—touch your hand or your hair, thus—feel the sunshine of your eyes upon me, I should be almost happy. You do not know how I pine, sometimes, for the tones of your voice, Hugo. You do not know how often I creep out at dusk, to listen to them."

" But, *cara*," said Hugh, " it is not well that you should haunt about the house in such ghostly fashion, for fear——"

" For fear that I should meet *her ?*" interrupted Maddalena. " No—no, I am careful. I only venture near when you are dining or reading. There is no danger."

" You can not tell. Accident might——"

" Never. I have seen her once, face to face. I would die, sooner than meet her so again."

She had seen me once ? My heart was beating so heavily that I almost thought they must hear it. I blew out my lamp, advanced a step, and drew back a corner of the curtain. It was as I had already suspected. Maddalena and the lady in the woods were one and the same. Hugh was sitting at his desk, with his head resting on his hand. Maddalena was kneeling beside him, with just the same look of defiance on her pale face that I saw upon it first.

In the same moment the look faded and the face became gentle.

" And yet, *Hugo mio*," said she, " I do not hate her. I—I have even tried to love the thought of her, for thy sake."

" You would love herself, if you knew her," said my husband, quickly.

" She is very young, and fair, and true-looking," replied Maddalena. " I am glad she is so fair, for thee."

" She is as true as she looks," said Hugh. " She knows all your story now—at least, as

much of it as I could tell her—and if you would only see her——"

" See her !" interrupted the Italian, with a vehement gesture. " Are you mad to ask it ? See her—the woman who bears your name ?—who sleeps every night in your arms ?—who, perhaps, even now, bears a child of yours in her bosom ? Whilst I—*Dio !* how tame a wretch you must think me !"

" Maddalena——"

" The light in my eyes would wither her—the breath of my lips would poison her !" continued she, impetuously. Then, suddenly checking herself, " Pardon, pardon," she cried, " I do not mean to vex thee, Hugo ! Thou knowest how gentle I have been—how patient—how obedient ! Thou knowest how I have kept my word to thee !"

" Yes, yes, *poverina ;* I know it."

Maddalena took his disengaged hand and kissed it, and laid her cheek caressingly upon it.

" What do I live for, *idol mio*," murmured she, " if not to obey thee ? Why do I drag on this weary chain of years, unless to dedicate each day and hour to thy service ? And yet, I sometimes weep because I can do nothing for thee. Dost thou remember the time, Hugo, when I used to mend thy gloves ? It was long, long ago. It made me very happy. I have not even that happiness now. Dost thou remember a little purse which thou hadst thrown away one day, and I asked for it ? See—here it is, all worn with my kisses. Ah, do I not love thee ?"

Standing there, cold and trembling, with that horrible sensation of helplessness that one has in a dream, I saw my husband cover his eyes with his hand—heard him reply, in a voice altered by emotion :

" *Sì, sì, Maddalena—tu m'ami.*"

" Could any one love thee better ?"

He shook his head.

" Could any one—*any one*, Hugo, love thee so well ? Could *she* give thee up as I have done ? Could *she* sleep under the same roof, knowing another in her place, as I do ? Could *she* live, banished as I am, and yet love thee as I love thee, utterly and blindly ?"

" No—no, impossible !"

" And yet you avoid me ! Nay, do not shake your head ; for it is true. You keep out with your dogs and your gun, day after day, and never seek to see me of your own will. Is it that you fear my reproaches ? You need not ; for I never even think blamefully of you, now. Is it that you shrink from the sight of my sorrow ? You need not ; for, when I see you, I am happy. Are you not my king and my life ? Is not one such hour as this, my recompense for weeks of suffering ?"

" Maddalena, Maddalena, you torture me !" cried Hugh, brokenly. " When I think of thee, and of all the misery I have caused thee, I hate myself !"

" Nay, thou shalt not hate what I adore," said Maddalena, with a piteous smile.

Hugh laid his head down upon his desk, and covered his face with his hands.

" Hugo," she faltered ; " *Hugo mio*, there is one thing—one little thing, which thou couldst do, my love, to make me very happy."

" Then, in God's name, let me do it."

" Dare I ask it ?"

J

" Yes, if—if—what is it ?"

" Only this—only this,"—and I saw her throw her arms passionately about him, and press her head against his shoulder—"call me once—but once—by my old name. Let me, oh ! let me hear it, even though it be for the last time !"

He lifted his pale face from the desk, and took her head in his two hands. My heart stood still. I felt as if it were my sentence that he was going to utter.

He bent forward—his lips moved—he whispered, "*Sposa mia !*"

CHAPTER LII.

WEARY AND HEAVY-LADEN.

His wife !

He had called her his wife—I had heard it—and I lived. I remember wondering, vaguely, how it was that the words had not killed me where I stood. But they did not. They only paralyzed me, brain and body, and left me scarcely conscious of the blow by which I had been crushed. I have no distinct recollection of any thing that followed. I saw their lips move in speech, but the words had no sense for me. I saw Hugh resume his writing, and Maddalena trim the lamp, without at the time deriving any kind of mental impression from what passed, or being sensible that their conversation was ended. I can form no conception of how long I staid there ; or how I came to find myself, by and by, in my own room, standing before the empty grate. Here, for the first time, a wondering consciousness of misery dawned upon me. I began to remember, word by word, look by look, gesture by gesture, all the fatal evidence that had just been brought before me. I began to comprehend that Hugh had deceived me with a false story—that two words had changed all my past and all my future—that my world had suddenly became a chaos of ruin, and that I had better have died than survived it.

The room was almost dark. The lamp which I had left flickering had long since gone out ; and only a faint reflex of the outer starlight struggled through the blinds.

Cold and dark as it was, I crept to bed without relighting the lamp—a statue of ice with a brain of fire. The reaction had come now. My head burned ; my temples throbbed ; fears, possibilities, retrospections, thronged and surged upon me, like the waves of a tumultuous sea. I could not think ; for I had no power to arrest my thoughts. They racked me, tossed me to and fro, mastered, and bewildered me. I could weigh nothing, compare nothing. I only felt that I was wrecked and heart-broken—that he called another, Wife—that he was no longer my own—that I was alone in the wide world—alone for evermore !

Some time had gone by thus—perhaps hours ; perhaps minutes—when I heard a cautious footstep in the corridor, and a hand at the door. I buried my face in the pillow, and feigned sleep. He came in very gently. I heard him set his candle down upon the table and cross to the foot of the bed, where he stood some moments without moving. It then seemed to me that he went back, drew a chair to the table, and took something from his pocket. Once or twice,

during the silence that followed, I distinguished the rustling of paper. Presently he moved again, very cautiously ; and I distinctly heard him fold the paper over and over. He was writing to me—I knew it as well as if I had been at his shoulder—writing to bid me farewell, because he would not awake me ! I felt as if my senses were leaving me. I bit the pillow in my agony of anguish ; and felt my heart contract as if grasped by an iron hand.

Then he came back to the bed ; laid the note beside me ; bent over me silently. I felt the soft incense of his breath upon my neck—I heard him murmur my name fondly to himself—I knew what a loving light was in his eyes as he looked down upon me. Then he lifted a stray curl from the pillow, pressed it to his lips, lingered, sighed, and went away.

For one moment—one wild, delirious moment I felt as if I must call him back, open my arms and my heart to him, forgive all, and weep out my grief on his bosom. But the words "*Sposa mia,*" started up before me in letters of flame. The desperate question, " What am I to this man, if another is his wife ?" forced itself upon me with pitiless rigor. I crushed the impulse down —I let the moment pass. He was gone.

Then a deadly, sickening, stifling sensation rushed suddenly upon me. I tried to sit up in the bed ; but it seemed to sink away beneath me. I fainted.

I recovered my consciousness gradually and painfully. I think I must have lain a long time, for when I again opened my eyes, it was daylight. O God ! was I mad, or was it all a wicked dream ? My eyes fell upon the note which he had left on the pillow. I recoiled, as if I had been stung ; for it was directed in pencil, " *To my wife.*" His wife ? What wife ? Not I ! not I ! Another claimed that title—it was her " old name ;" whilst I — oh shame and sorrow ! I was only his mistress.

I had but one thought now ; one insane, desperate, overruling thought—flight.

Yes ; flight. I felt that I must go—that I could not sleep another night under his roof— that I never dare look upon his face again. I scarcely asked myself whither I should turn. I neither knew nor cared. Anywhere, so that it were but far, far away, where none who had ever known me should witness my misery !

This resolve once taken, I became possessed by a feverish haste which brooked no delay, and hurried me from step to step, from project to project, with an energy of will that, for the time, supplied the place of physical strength. I rose, weak and trembling, and dressed myself that cold December morning, without any thought of those luxuries of the toilette to which I had of late been accustomed. While I was dressing, the thought of my poor old faithful nurse flashed across my mind, and I determined, if she would go, to take her with me. Desperate as I was, the prospect of being utterly alone in my flight appalled me. As for my father, or my sister, or Mrs. Sandyshaft, I would sooner have died than seek a refuge with either. Their pity would have driven me mad.

I rang for my maid, who was amazed to see me up. From her I learned that Hugh had left the house at seven, taking Tippoo with him. It was already half-past eight o'clock. The next direct train left, I knew, at half-past one; therefore I had four hours before me. I desired the girl immediately to pack my smallest portmanteau, and said that I was going to London.

"To London, ma'am—to-day?" faltered she.

"You—you look so very tired—more fit to be in bed than to take a journey."

I glanced at the glass, and saw a haggard, white-lipped shadow of myself. I tried to smile, and answer carelessly.

"I am not used to balls and late hours, Ann," I replied. "I think I shall never go to another large party."

"What would you please to have packed, ma'am?" said Ann, still looking at me somewhat anxiously.

"Only necessaries — no laces, no jewelry. Nothing but some underclothing and one dress; the darkest and plainest I have."

"That will be your brown silk, ma'am. Nothing else?"

"Yes—my case of colors."

"And shall I require me to go with you, ma'am?"

"No; I go alone. I may, perhaps, take Mrs. Beever with me. I am now going across the park, to ask her about it."

Ann looked more surprised than before.

"Not without your breakfast, ma'am?" said she, seeing me with my bonnet in my hand. "May I not bring you a cup of coffee first? Indeed, you should not go out this bitter morning without it."

I told her she might bring it, and when she was gone, swept the jewels that were lying about into my jewel-case, stripped the rings from my fingers, took out the brooch with which I had mechanically fastened my collar, and locked them all in—all, except my wedding ring. I could not part from that. Mockery as it was, I felt I *must* keep it.

In a few minutes more, I was hurrying across the park. The day was dull and intensely cold; but I went forward like one under the influence of opium, heeding neither the moaning wind nor the wet grass about my feet. I should scarcely have hesitated in my path had a thunderstorm been raging. Arrived at the cottage, I went in without knocking, and found my old nurse ironing linen.

"Goody," I said, abruptly; "will you leave all this, and come with me? I am going away."

She looked at me, turned deathly white, and sank into a chair.

"Dear God!" stammered she, "what has happened?"

"Great wrong and sorrow," I replied. "I am leaving my—Mr. Farquhar, forever. Will you come with me?"

She wrung her hands, and stared at me piteously.

"Yes, yes — God love you, yes, my poor lamb!" she cried. "Where will you go?"

"I don't know. Somewhere abroad, far away."

"And when, my darling—when?"

"To-day—at once."

The old woman clasped her head with both hands, utterly bewildered.

"To-day!" she repeated. "Mercy! that's sudden."

"Yes, yes—today," I replied, impatiently. "Every hour that I linger here, is torture to me."

I wanted to be gone without delay. I felt as if the loss of every minute were irreparable. I would have set off for London, walking, by the high road, sooner than wait for the train, if she had proposed it.

"Oh, that it should all end like this!" moaned she, rocking herself to and fro. "My little lamb, that I nursed on my knees so often! Well, well, my poor rags are soon put together——What will the master say? And Miss Hilda, too! Oh, dear! oh, dear! we are here to-day and gone to-morrow. Where is he, my darling?"

"Gone."

"He'll support you in comfort, my deary, anyhow?"

"I would not accept a farthing from him, if I starved!" I cried, fiercely. "I have kept nothing of his—not a book, not a jewel. I can support myself, Goody, and you too."

"Well, well, deary, there's Mrs. Sandyshaft—she won't let you——"

"Mrs. Sandyshaft knows nothing—never will know any thing from me," I interrupted. "All I want is to hide myself far away, where none of them will ever see me, or hear of me, again. Don't ask me why. You shall know all, by and by. I have been cruelly deceived and wronged—there, not a word. Make haste, for God's sake, and let us be gone."

The old woman stood up mechanically, and began folding the linen that lay upon the table. All at once she stopped, and said:—

"But, my deary, have you any money?"

Money? In my distress and eagerness, I had never thought of it! I had none of my own; and I would not have taken his to save myself from beggary. I felt as if a thunderbolt had fallen at my feet.

"Not a farthing," I replied.

Goody shook her head sorrowfully.

"Alas, and alas! my lamb," said she, "where can we go, and what can we do, without it? I—I have a little bit of money laid by, myself; but it's only a bit, and when that's gone——"

"When it's gone, I can earn more, and pay you back tenfold!" I said, hurriedly. "How much have you?"

"Oh, very little, my deary; a—a matter, may be, of thirty pound," replied she, somewhat reluctantly.

Thirty pounds! We might travel a long way for thirty pounds, with economy. To Belgium, perhaps; or some obscure corner of Switzerland; or Rome—ah! no; Rome was too difficult of access. We could not go to Rome for thirty pounds; and yet in Rome, I could have earned money by my art more easily than elsewhere. What was to be done?

"Or—or, may be, it's pretty nigh as much as fifty," added Goody, after an anxious pause, during which she had watched all the changes of my countenance. "I'm pretty sure it's fifty; but no more."

"But it's enough," I said. "Yes—yes, quite enough."

Goody took a little withered stump of myrtle

from her window, set the pot on the table, and said, with a sigh :—

"It's all there, my deary—every penny of it. I'll give it to you at once, and it will be off my mind."

And with this, she turned the myrtle out, took a very small circular tin box from the bottom of the pot, cleansed it carefully from the loose earth, and laid the contents before me. There were some bank notes, and a few loose coins.

"Two twenties, my lamb," said she, smoothing them out tenderly, as they lay upon the table ; "two twenties, and a five, and four sovereigns, and two halves, and a lucky sixpence. It's the savings of a life, my deary, but you're welcome to them, that you are — kindly welcome."

The simple, generous fidelity of this honest heart melted the ice of my despair, and I burst into tears.

"God bless you, dear! God bless you, and thank you," I cried, throwing my arms about her neck, and laying my head down upon her shoulder, as I used when I was a little child. "You, at least, will never deceive me!"

They were the first tears I had shed since this blow fell upon me ; and they seemed to cool my brain, and slacken the unnatural tension of my nerves. They left me clearer to think and freer to act ; and it was well they did so, for now, alas! helpless and inexperienced as I was, I had to act and think for two.

In the mean time, the day was passing. A few more words, and we had arranged all. I was to keep the money ; we were to leave Broomhill at midday ; and I was to take her up at the lodge gate, on my way to the station. Thus we parted. I had scarcely passed the garden gate when she came running after me.

"You'll bid them mind the poor dumb things, my deary," said she, with her apron to her eyes. "There's the cat, and the bulfinch, and the cocks and hens—they all love me ; and I should be loth to think they were forgotten."

Struck with the selfishness of my sorrow, I turned back, took her by both hands, and said, earnestly—

"You shall not leave them—no, dear old friend, you shall not leave them. You—you love your little home ; you had thought, to end your days in it. I will not tear you from it, to share my sad and uncertain fortunes. I am young ; fitter and better able to battle with the world than you. Forget that I asked you to go with me. God bless you, dear, and good-by."

But Goody would not hear of this. I might say what I pleased ; but she would never leave me. If I refused to take her with me, she would follow me upon her knees ; beg her way after me wherever I might be ; pursue me to the ends of the earth with her love and her devotion. Finding her thus resolute, and feeling my own weakness and desolation, what could I do but thank her with my whole heart for the sacrifice, and gratefully accept it?

A few hours more, and we were speeding toward London ; Broomhill receding every moment farther and farther into the past, and the wide world opening, a desert, before me.

A weary journey! a weary, wretched journey,

made up of anxious days and dreary nights ; of bodily unrest, and nervous prostration ; of perpetual heart-ache, of broken sleep, and terrified wakings, and strange mental confusion! My recollection of it is indistinct and fragmentary. Scenes and incidents occur to me here and there, as one might remember glimpses of a half-forgotten panorama. Faces of fellow-travelers pass before my mind's eye, like faces seen in dreams. To this day, I shudder when I recall these scattered mosaics of things and places which are bound up in my memory with so much suffering.

Now, it is the dull room where we wait, hour after hour, till the starting of the Dover train. I see the gloomy fireplace with its cavernous hollow of sullen red fire. I see the reversed letters on the ever-swinging glass door. I see the table heaped with rugs and traveling-bags ; the travelers that come and go incessantly ; the colored flashes on the wall from red and green lamps which are carried past, lighted by hurrying porters. I see the widow-lady in the corner, with her little girl asleep on the sofa beside her, at the sight of whose pale face and mourning garb my tears fell without control. I hear the rumbling vehicles outside, and the shrill whistle of arriving trains ; and I remember, oh, how distinctly I the dread with which I turned to the door each time it opened, trembling lest some fatal chance should bring Hugh to the spot before we could get away from it.

Now it is midnight, and we are in Dover. We are late, and are hurried off to the boat, which is on the point of moving. A few wintry stars glimmer here and there overhead. The lights from the quays flicker down upon the troubled water in the harbor. The pier seems to recede. The steamer begins to lurch. We are at sea.

Now we are on shore again, in a dim office guarded by foreign soldiers. Here, all is confusion and dismay, for I have forgotten to provide myself with a passport. Interrogated, rebuffed, alarmed, I am forbidden to pursue my journey without the authorization of the resident English Consul. It is now between four and five in the morning, and the Consulate will not be open before nine ; so we are conducted to a huge gloomy hotel, like a prison, and there left till morning. Our room is immense, carpetless, damp as a vault, and furnished with two funereal-looking beds, antique oaken bureaus, dusty mirrors, and consoles that look as if they dated from the reign of Louis Treize. Weary and miserable, my poor old nurse and I sit, hand in hand, talking and weeping together till the neighboring clocks clash and clang the hour of six, and the market-folks begin to be noisy in the street below. Then, outworn with fatigue and sorrow, we both sleep heavily.

Now it is the railway again, and we are on our way to Marseilles. I am Mrs. Carlyon, British subject, traveling on the continent, attended by her servant. It is a good name, and belonged to some distant ancestor of our family. I remembered it in the old genealogical chart that used to hang in my father's sitting-room, and chose it for that reason. It is very trying and monotonous, this perpetual railway traveling. Hour after hour, in daylight or dusk, the same landscape seems to be forever flying past. Sometimes the lamp is flickering down upon the faces of our fellow-travelers, while without there are white villages dimly seen, steep cuttings, and wide flats crossed at intervals by lines of skeleton poplars that look ghostly in the moonshine. Sometimes it is daylight, and very cold. The country is lightly sprinkled with snow. Trees, hills, plains, and villages flit past us as before; and every now and then we come to a station near a large town, where passengers arrive and alight, and venders of roasted chestnuts and French journals cry their wares shrilly to and fro upon the platform. And all this time I travel like one who is flying from fate; jaded, benumbed, feverish, and sullenly silent. Sometimes I fall asleep; then wake, trembling, from fantastic dreams, in which Hugh and Maddalena and my old school-friends at Zollenstrasse are strangely associated. My head aches; my lips are parched and bleeding; my eyes are burning hot; and, sleeping or waking, an oppressive sense of woe weighs on my chest, and impedes my very breathing. There are times when, do what I will, I can not keep my thoughts steady; when all seems confusion in my brain, and I can not discover the things of the past from the events of the present. There are also times when I recall our life in Italy with strange distinctness—when I torture myself with reproaches and self-questionings, and repeat over and over again, in the silence of my heart, "Alas! why was I not content in my Paradise? Why could I not have been happy a little longer?"

Thus, with one night's rest at Châlons-sur-Saône, the long land journey passes, and we traverse all France from coast to coast. The poor old woman by my side sleeps nearly all the time; and bears it, on the whole, better than I could have hoped. For my own part, I have some recollection of wondering once or twice, in a passive confused way, whether acute mental suffering and bodily fatigue acted upon others as they were now acting upon me—whether this faintness and shivering, this alternate burning heat and freezing cold, this torpidity and languor, were common to all who, like myself, were weary and heavy-laden, and in need of rest?

Now it is a great crowded port; and high white buildings, forts, batteries, ships, piers, quays, light-houses, and traffic of all kinds, seem to pass multitudinously before me. Our luggage is placed upon a truck, and we follow it down to the place of embarkation, through streets crowded with vehicles, soldiers, sailors, and foot-passengers. Weak and trembling, I cling to Goody's arm for support; and, once on board, am thankful to go at once to my berth, and be at peace. By and by, the steamer begins to sway, and we are again at sea.

Then comes a troubled, restless time, of which I can remember nothing distinctly. A time when I lie, hour after hour, in a state which is neither sleeping nor waking—when I have dreams which seem scarcely to be dreams, but are mixed up, in some painful way, with realities—when not blood, but fire, courses through my veins—when my thoughts wander, and I try in vain to stay their wanderings—when I am conscious of uttering words over which I have no control—when my own voice sounds far away—when I fancy I can hear Hugh's footstep in the cabin; and there is something unfamiliar in Goody's well-known face beside my pillow; and the steamer is no longer the steamer, but the old house in which I was born; and the dashing of the sea against the port-hole is the flowing of the canal, through which the painted barges pass and repass all day long.

Then I hear a strange voice, which says that I am very ill—and then all is blank.

CHAPTER LIII.

GOODY'S SECRET.

"SURELY, dear Goody," said I feebly, "I have been very ill."

"Indeed you have, my lamb," replied Goody, wiping her eyes. "So ill, that I never thought to hear you call me by my right name again!"

I looked, languidly, round the room; at the painted arabesques on the walls and ceiling; at the print in a black frame over the fireplace; at the medicine-bottles on the table. All were strange to me.

"What place is this?" I asked.

"They call it a hotel," said Goody, contemptuously. "I call it a barrack."

"And where is it?"

Goody shook her head vehemently.

"There, then, my deary," exclaimed she, "don't you ask me, for I'm sure I can't tell you, no more than one of them cherubs on the ceiling! It's some outlandish name or another; and though I hear it twenty times a day, and though, when I do hear it, I know it, I couldn't fit my lips to it, if it was to save my life! All I can answer for is, that the Pope of Rome an't very far off, and all the travelers land here from the steamers."

I closed my eyes and lay silent for a long time, trying to remember how and why it was that I had left Broomhill, and by what chance my old nurse happened to be with me; but I was too weak to think, and in the effort fell asleep.

When I next woke, it was dusk, and there were two gentlemen in the room, talking softly together beside the fireplace. Finding that I was awake, one came to my bedside, and sat down; the other left the room.

"La Signora sta meglio," said the stranger, taking my wrist between his fingers, and smiling gravely. "Molto meglio."

"It's the doctor, my darling," whispered Goody, over his shoulder.

He was a tall young man, with a black beard, and a very gentle voice. Catching the sense of her explanation, he bowed his head slightly, and added—

"Sì, Signora; sono il medico."

I replied, in Italian, that I was much obliged to him; and asked how long I had been ill.

"The Signora arrived here," said he, "on the fifth of January, and it is to-day the second of February."

"And this, I suppose, is Civita Vecchia?"

"Sì, Signora. È Civita Vecchia," he replied.

I had been ill a month—a whole month, every day of which was as completely blotted from my memory as if it had never been! He turned away, examined the medicines in the bottles, and scribbled a rapid prescription. In that moment I remembered all that had happened; but, being so very weak, remembered it with no other emotion than a kind of languid wonder, as if it were a thing of long ago. The prescription written, the doctor came back to my bedside.

"The Signora must keep very quiet," said he. To which I replied—

"How soon, Signore, shall I be able to go on to Rome?"

He smiled, and shook his head.

"If you are impatient, not so soon as if you could, for the present, put all thought of it aside. You can not keep your mind too calm. You can not, just now, think or converse too little."

I promised to obey as literally as I could; whereupon he took his leave.

The next day, about noon, I suddenly recollected the second gentleman whom I had seen in the room the evening before, and asked Goody who he was.

"Second gentleman, my lamb?" said she, confusedly. "What do you mean? What second gentleman?"

"He left the room just as I woke," I replied. "He was standing by the fireplace, where you are, with his back toward the bed. Surely you must know whom I mean!"

"Eh? deary me! What was he like, darling?" said Goody, bending over the fire.

"I don't know. It was dusk; and he was gone immediately. Is he the doctor's assistant?"

"The doctor's assistant?" repeated she. "Ay, to be sure. Yes, yes, my lamb, I remember."

"Then he was the assistant?"

"Now, didn't I say so? But, bless your heart, deary, you know you're not to talk."

"Well, tell me one thing—what is the Doctor's name?"

"His name? Bless you! my lamb, I can't remember their outlandish talk. Why, they don't even call beef-tea, beef-tea; nor gruel, gruel—the poor heathens! I'm sure, I'm ready to go down on my knees, sometimes, and thank God that I wasn't born one of 'em. His name, indeed! No, no, my deary; but here's his card. May be you can make it out by that."

I looked at the card, which she held before my eyes, and read—"*Giorgio Marco, M.D.*"

I lay still, after this, for a long time; for my thoughts flowed very slowly. When I next spoke, it was to say—

"Goody—how much money have we left?"

To which Goody replied, briskly—

"Oh, plenty, my deary. Near five-and-twenty pound."

Near five-and-twenty pounds! I closed my eyes again, and tried to think how much we had spent before I lost my memory; but this was an effort of which I was quite incapable. I then tried to calculate what our expenses at Civita Vecchia might amount to; but with no better success.

"There's the doctor to pay, Goody," I suggested, after a while.

"That won't be much," said she.

"He has attended me for a month, has he not?"

Goody admitted the fact, reluctantly.

"And has called, I suppose, daily?"

Goody admitted this also.

"Indeed, there were some days," added she, "when he came twice—that was when you were at the worst, my deary. But, bless you! *his* bill won't be much, for all that. Why, he lives in two little rooms up at the top of a great white house over yonder; and he always comes walking; and when it's wet, he carries a red umbrella."

Another long pause.

"And then there's the hotel bill," I resumed, by and by.

"Ah, well; that can't be much either," said Goody. "We have only this one room, and I attend upon you myself; and as for eating and drinking—ugh! it's little enough *I* take of their nasty food. My living don't cost sixpence a day."

"Well, well, Goody," I sighed, quite wearied out by this long conversation, "I dare say the money will last out till I can earn some more. If not——"

"Don't you think of that, my lamb," interrupted she. "It'll be enough, and to spare; take my word for it. And besides, I know what I know—but there, the doctor says you're not to talk; so don't let's say another word about it."

And I noticed, after this, that whenever I began to speak about money, or my desire to reach Rome, or any other subject involving anxiety about the future, she invariably took refuge in Dr. Marco's prohibition, and reduced me to silence.

Day by day, though very slowly, I progressed toward recovery. My hours went by in a kind of passive languor. Sitting up in bed, or propped with pillows in an easy chair, I was content to watch Goody at her work; or to let my eyes wander from curve to curve, from wreath to wreath of the poor conventional arabesques upon the wall, with scarcely the accompaniment of a thought. As I grew stronger, however, my mind began to dwell more upon the future and the past; and the old perpetual sense of trouble resumed its hold upon my heart. I became restless and feverish. I pined for active occupation. I felt that the first great shock of my grief was indeed over; but that the weariness and desolation of life were mine forever.

My young physician, observant of every symptom, came to me one morning with a parcel of books under his arm.

"What have you there, Dr. Marco?" I asked.

"A tonic, signora," he replied. "Your thoughts want feeding, just as your body wants strengthening. Change of mental occupation is as necessary to health as change of scene or diet."

I thanked him, and untied the parcel. There were Sir Joshua Reynolds's Discourses; Lessing's "Laocoon" in German; Schlegel's "Letters on Christian Art," also in German; and Viardot on "Les Musées d'Italie." Every one upon Art! I was startled, and, looking up with the quick apprehension of one who has a secret to keep, said—

"This is a strange choice, Dr. Marco. Your books are all on one subject. How could you tell that that subject would interest me?"

He colored up to the roots of his hair.

"I—I did not know—I did not observe, signora," stammered he.

"You did not observe?" I repeated.

"The truth is, signora," replied he, "they are not my books. I borrowed them for you; and took them, as they were given to me."

"Then you borrowed them from an artist," I said, smiling.

"Even that I do not know," he replied, examining the volumes with some embarrassment. "They belong to a gentleman who was staying at this hotel when you were first brought here, and who is now in Rome. He still comes occasionally to Civita Vecchia. He may be an artist. It is very possible. Rome is always crowded with them."

"Ah, Signor Marco," I said, eagerly, "if I could but reach Rome I should be well. How soon, do you think——"

"As soon, signora," interposed he, "as you can take a drive without too much fatigue, and are strong enough to bear a journey of eight hours. In the mean time, I think it would be as well if you could remove into a more cheerful room. There are apartments in this house which look toward the south, and command the sea and the harbor. You would find one of those much pleasanter."

I thought of our scanty means, and sighed. Dr. Marco blushed again, like a girl.

"You have been here so long," said he, "that the landlord would, no doubt, let you have a front room for the same rent as this. May I negotiate for you with him?"

I thanked him, and accepted his offer. When he was gone, I took up a volume of Schlegel. Turning to the fly-leaf, I found the right hand top corner torn off. I turned to the next, and found it mutilated in the same way. I then examined all the rest; and from each the name of the owner had been subtracted in the same rough fashion. The strangeness of it awakened my curiosity.

"Goody," I said, "did you ever see that gentleman who was staying here when we first came?—the gentleman who lent these books to Dr. Marco?"

"How should I know, my deary?" replied Goody, carelessly. "I've seen a good many gentlemen, first and last, since we've been in this house."

"The one I mean has gone to Rome."

To which she only said, "Ay, indeed?" and so the subject dropped.

The next day we removed into a front room overlooking the harbor, where I could sit for hours in a southward window basking in the sunshine, and watching the fishermen's barks as they came and went with the tides. Leaning on Goody's arm, I could now walk about the room for a quarter of an hour at a time; and Dr. Marco proposed that I should venture on a drive the following morning.

Thus recovering, as it were, hourly, and seeing myself ever nearer and nearer to the end of my journey, I began to get seriously anxious lest our money should not be sufficient for the discharge of our debts at Civita Vecchia. I examined the contents of the purse, and found, as Goody had said, a sum equivalent to about twenty-four pounds and twelve shillings.

"What shall we do, dear, if it is not enough?"

I said, looking hopelessly at the money in my lap.

"It will be enough, and pounds to spare, my lamb, as I've told you before," replied Goody, oracularly.

"I might sell my watch and chain, it is true," I pursued, "though I should be sorry to do so."

"Did he give 'em to you, my deary?"

"He? Do you suppose I should have brought them away with me, if he had?" I asked, flushing at the mere mention of his name. "No, they were my father's gift, on—on my wedding-day."

"Ah, well; you won't have to part from 'em just yet," said Goody, with confident composure.

I was not quite so well satisfied; and so, by and by, wrote a little note to the landlord in my best Italian, and begged that I might have his bill made out up to the present time. To my amazement, Goody flatly refused to take it down.

"Goin' worrittin in this way about bills, and money, and watches, and what all!" exclaimed she, irritably. "It's just the way to make yourself ill again, and lay you on your bed for another month, it is! I wonder what Doctor Mark would say! No, no,—I'll have nothing to do with it. Wait a day or two longer, till you're strong enough to think of going, and then I'll take your messages, and welcome."

I rose, and rang the bell.

"I had not expected this from you, Beever," I said angrily. "But there are servants in the hotel who will obey my orders."

The door opened almost immediately, and a waiter, who was probably passing, came in.

"Is the landlord within?" I inquired.

"Sì, signora."

"Then be so good as to give him this note, and say that I shall be obliged by a speedy reply."

The waiter took it, and retired. He was no sooner gone than Goody burst into tears, and went over to the window in great agitation.

"Oh, dear! oh, dear!" moaned she, "what's to be done now? What's to be done now? I can't bear your anger, my lamb, and all I've done, I've done for the best; and because I love you as if you had been my own flesh and blood! And now you'll never trust me again—I know you won't; and whether I have done right or wrong, I know no more than the babe unborn!"

The vehemence and suddenness of her repentance quite took me by surprise.

"My dear old friend," I said, affectionately, "don't be grieved — don't say another word about it. You were wrong to refuse, but——"

"No, no, no," she interrupted, sobbing. "It isn't that, my dreary love; it isn't that at all! But you'll know quite soon enough—oh, Lord! oh, Lord! here's the landlord himself; and now it'll all come out!"

The landlord came in; a grave man dressed all in black, with a white cravat, and a profusion of jewelry. He held my note, opened, in his hand; and said, bowing profoundly——

"The Signora has done me the honor to write?"

I replied that I had written, and requested

him to be seated. Goody's last mysterious words had somewhat unnerved me, and I waited with some anxiety for what he should say.

He, however, bowed again, sat down, coughed, and ventured to hope that the signora's health was becoming reëstablished.

I thanked him, and said that my health was already much improved; for which I was largely indebted to the care of Doctor Marco.

"Doctor Marco, Signora," observed the landlord, "is a very clever young man. He is lost in Civita Vecchia. There is an opening in Rome for a physician of Doctor Marco's abilities."

I replied that I had no doubt there might be.

"The air of Civita Vecchia, signora, is highly favorable to invalids," continued the landlord. "Many come from Rome to recover. The signora, I will venture to affirm, would not have been restored so rapidly either in Rome or Florence."

I bowed, interrogatively; and was about to lead to the subject of my note, when the landlord, with polite fluency, resumed:—

"The signora," said he, "sees Civita Vecchia at its dullest season. At this period of the year, we stagnate. The signora should visit us in the bathing season. Then all is life and gayety. Every hotel and lodging-house is filled. The beach is covered with promenaders. We have music on the Molo, daily. _E molto piacevole._"

"I have understood," I replied, "that it is an agreeable _villeggiatura_. But——"

"The bathing, too, is excellent," said the landlord, "and is preferred by many to the Baths of San Giuliano. We were honored, last autumn, by a visit from His Holiness the Pope."

"To return, however, to the subject of my note," said I, resolutely stemming this tide of small talk. "The _padrone_ will do me the favor to make out my bill in full, up to the present time; after which, if he pleases, we can begin a new account. I purpose leaving Civita Vecchia for Rome in a few days, and I wish to form some estimate of what my expenses have been during my illness."

The landlord bowed again; referred to the note through a double eye-glass; darted a suspicious glance toward Goody, who was rocking herself restlessly to and fro in her chair at the farther end of the room; and said—

"The signora desires to have a—a copy of all her weekly accounts, dating from the fifth of January?"

"Precisely."

"We are not in the habit of copying former accounts," said the landlord; "but as this is not our busiest season, and the signora has been with us for some weeks, it shall be done, to oblige her."

"To oblige me?" I repeated, with a smile.

He darted another glance at Goody; looked somewhat embarrassed; and said, with a hesitation very unlike his former fluency—

"I am surely mistaken in supposing the signora to be ignorant of the fact that—that her accounts have been regularly paid during the period of her stay in my house?"

"Paid?" I echoed, scarcely believing my ears.

"Paid punctually, every Monday morning."

"By whom?"

"By the signora's own servant, who has all the receipts in her possession."

"Is this true?" I asked, rising, all in a tremble, and facing her where I stood. "Is this true?"

"Is what true?" whimpered Goody, with averted face.

Her voice and attitude confirmed it, without need of confession. I turned to the landlord, who was fidgeting with his eye-glass in the utmost perplexity, and wished him good-day.

"If I can be of any further service to the signora——" he began.

"Not of the least, thank you."

"The accounts," said he, lingering, "shall be copied forthwith."

"Pray do not take the trouble," I replied. "It is sufficient if my servant has the originals in her care. Good afternoon."

"Good afternoon, signora—good afternoon." And the padrone reluctantly took his leave, with his curiosity unsatisfied.

When he was gone, I went over and stood before her.

"Whose money was it?" I asked, in an agitated whisper. "Tell me at once. No lies—no equivocations. Whose money was it?"

"Oh, dear! oh dear!" cried she, "I did it for the best—indeed, indeed, I did."

Half beside myself with apprehension and anger, I took her by the arm and shook it violently.

"Speak at once," I said. "What wicked folly have you been committing? You have betrayed me—confess that you've betrayed me!"

"No, no, my dear lamb, not that! not that! I couldn't help his seeing you — you being carried up on a mattress, poor love, as helpless as a babe — how could I? But, there—only give me time, and don't frighten me, and I'll tell you every thing—that I will, my deary, true as Gospel!"

"_He!_" I faltered, catching at a chair for support. "Who? For God's sake, who?"

Poor old Goody wrung her hands together, and looked up, deprecatingly, through her tears.

"I don't know, my deary!" she sobbed. "I never saw him before, in all my life; but he said he knew you as well as if he was your own father—and—and I believed him—and I know I was very wrong to take his money; but I was all alone among strangers, my deary, in a — a foreign land—and you all but dying—and and I was so thankful to find a friend, that—that——"

I flung myself into her arms, and kissed her over and over again.

"Hush, dear, hush!" I cried. "I thought it was — you know who I thought it must be! Since it is a stranger, never mind. We can pay him back his money, whoever he may be. I was very, very harsh to you, dear — pray forgive me. There, now — dry your eyes, and try to describe him to me; and let us think how we can find him out, and how much we owe him, and who he can be. In the first place, what is his name?"

"I don't know, my deary."

"Did he never tell you? Or have you forgotten it?"

"He never told me, my deary."

"Was he old or young? Tall or short? Fair or dark?"

"Bless you, my lamb," said Goody, with a bewildered face, "I haven't the least notion."

"It isn't Dr. Topham?"

She shook her head, doubtfully.

"You remember to have seen him, dear, at Broomhill? The doctor, you know — my aunt's doctor, who used to come riding through the park on his little pony — a very cheerful, pleasant ——"

"It's no one I've ever seen before," replied Goody, decisively; "and the farthest off from cheerful and pleasant that I've come across this many a day. I don't mean to say but what he's very kind, my lamb — as kind as can be. He helped to carry you up-stairs himself; and he downright forced the money into my hand, saying you might want comforts, and that was to make sure of your having all that was necessary before he came again."

"And he did come again?"

"Bless you, yes — he was staying in the hotel for the first day or two; and after he'd gone away to the Pope of Rome, he came back once or twice; and would have had me take more money every time, only I knew we had enough without it, and wouldn't hear of it."

"Did he seem to be very rich and grand?" I asked next, with some vague idea of the Grand Duke floating through my mind. "Had he many servants with him; and did he seem like a nobleman?"

"Lord, no, my deary! as plain as could be."

"You are quite sure he was an Englishman?"

"Indeed I wouldn't be sure at all," replied she. "He had a queer way in his talk. To be sure, he might be from some other part of the country; but I can't help thinking the English didn't come quite natural to him."

My eyes fell upon the volumes. A sudden thought flashed across me.

"It is the same who left the books with Doctor Marco!" I cried, eagerly. "Run, dear — run down and ask the landlord to let me see the visitor's book. I'm sure I know who it is now!"

"How am I to ask for it, my deary?" said Goody. "You must write it on a bit of paper, please, and — Mercy! there he is!"

"Where? where?"

"There, my deary — down by those posts there — coming up to the house, with his face this way!"

I followed the direction of her finger; and saw, as I had already expected to see — Professor Metz.

CHAPTER LIV.

THE CHANGE 'TWIXT NOW AND THEN.

"Roma! Roma! Roma!
Non ò più come era prima!"

To an artist, the words "habitable Rome," convey few ideas beyond the Via Margutta and the Café Greco. In the former he lives and works; in the latter he smokes, sups, meets his friends, and with them discusses his bottle of Orvieto and the news of the day. From the café my inclinations and sex alike excluded me; but in its immediate neighborhood, if not in the street itself, my lodgings were situated. I lived, in short, in precisely that central house of the Vicolo d'Aliberti that looks down the Via Margutta. Those who know Rome will not need to be told that these two streets, in their relative positions, take the form of a T.

The Via Margutta is a street of studios and stables, crossed at the upper end by a little roofed gallery with a single window, like a shabby Bridge of Sighs. Horses are continually being washed and currycombed outside their stable-doors; frequent heaps of *immondezzajo* make the air unfragrant; and the perspective is too frequently damaged by rows of linen suspended across the road from window to window. Unsightly as they are, however, these obstacles in no wise affect the popularity of the Via Margutta, either as a residence for the artist, or a lounge for the amateur. Fashionable patrons leave their carriages at the corner, and pick their way daintily among the gutters and dust-heaps. A boar-hunt by Vallati compensates for an unlucky splash; and a Campagna sunset of Dessoulavey glows all the richer for the squalor through which it is approached. But I was not a resident in the street of painters. I only commanded it from my bedroom window; and I lived chiefly at the back of the house, in a room which served me for studio and parlor together. Just outside this room was a little loggia, where I could breakfast in the open air; and where Goody used to sit in the sun with her needlework while I was painting, and chat to me through the open window. The loggia was a great comfort to us; for there was no garden attached to the house in which we lived. We were, however, surrounded on this side by the gardens of others, overlooking, as we did, the great quadrangle formed by the backs of the houses in the Via Babuino, the north side of the Piazza di Spagna, the high ridge of the Pincian hill, and our own modest little Vicolo d'Aliberti. Within this quadrangle the air was always fresh, and the sunshine warm and lulling. The gardens below were full of orange and lemon trees; some of which (laden with yellow fruit, like the golden apples of the poets) were trained along the walls; while others, again, stood sturdy and wide-spreading, like mere northern apple-trees. Most of our neighbors kept poultry; and many were the contrivances of up-stair lodgers to hang linen from window to window, or balcony to balcony. In one garden close by, there was an old marble water-tank, that had once been a costly sarcophagus, and came, most probably, from the tomb of some noble Roman on the Appian Way. In another, were two crumbling moss-grown urns of stone, apparently of cinque-cento origin. Piled high upon a loggia nearly opposite, rose a pyramid of empty Orvieto bottles, in their wicker-coats. Lower down were the stables of a *remise;* and on the brow of the Pincian, closing in our horizon on the left, stood the twin-towered villa of the French Academy. Merely to lounge on this little loggia in the morning sunlight, throwing crumbs to the chickens in my neighbor's garden, watching the light and shadow on the green leaves and the broken urns, and listening to the military music on the Pincian, was pleasant and soothing to one whose health was so broken as mine. It was a quiet, cheerful nook — just the place in which to live a life of work and solitude; day repeating day, and year year, till the end should come.

This little home was found for me by my good friend, the Professor. Poor Goody, it appeared, had told him, in her perplexity and fear of possible consequences, that I had lost my husband, and come abroad for change of scene. He believed my name to be Carlyon; and he knew that I looked to my artistic talents for a livelihood. Finding all this to be the case, I suffered him to continue in the same convictions; and this with all the less difficulty, since he scrupulously abstained from even an allusion to my married life. Was I wrong to do this? I think not. I could have told him nothing, unless I told all; and my wounds were too fresh to bear reöpening. And then the shame of it! No—no; broken as I was, my pride sealed that confession on my lips, and gave me strength to suffer in silence.

The dear, rough, kind Professor! I had never known till now how gentle, how chivalrous, how generous a heart beat beneath that rugged exterior. I was unhappy, and he respected my sorrow. I was ill, and he succored me. I was alone, and he protected me. He brought me to my little home himself, all the way from Civita Vecchia; saw to the drawing up of the agreement by which I hired it; and was as careful of my interests and my comfort as if I had been his own child. He had come to Rome to collect works of art for the Grand Duke, and was lodging temporarily in the Piazza di Spagna. Closely as his time was occupied, he came to see me once in every day; and often, when he had been the whole morning among the print-shops or studios, would bring an open *vettura* in the afternoon, to take me for a drive along the meadows behind St. Angelo. As I became stronger, he introduced me to several of the best picture-dealers; one of whom at once commissioned me to copy a painting in the Schiarra Palace. From this moment, my modest future was assured. Once known in Rome as the pupil of so eminent a master, I was certain of employment as a copyist; and a copyist was now all that I desired to be. Ambition, hope, the desire of excellence, the love of praise, were all dead within me. The enthusiasm with which I once worshiped the painter's art, was dead also. I did not even look upon the masterpieces of the past with the same eyes as before. For me, the Magdalens of Guido had lost their languid charm. Something of its subtlety had fled from the syren smile of Johanna of Naples. A power was gone out from the walls of the Sistine, and a glory had faded from the Transfiguration. Not all the wonders of art, antiquity, or story had power now to hasten the pulses of my heart. I could wander among the colossal ruins of the Baths of Caracalla, or tread the chariot-worn pavement of the Appian Way, with an apathy at which I marveled. Nothing moved me, save the remembrance of when and with whom I had first visited each well-known site. In the Colosseum, I no longer saw Commodus, "the Imperial Sagittary," with his crescent-shaped shafts, decapitating the ostrich as it fled round the arena. Amid the gigantic desolation of the Palace of the Cæsars, I no longer remembered Caligula dancing madly before the trembling Consuls,

"in the second watch of the night," or Nero weeping on the bosom of his nurse. I thought only of Hugh, and of how we had wandered together in the shadow of these very walls and arches. I remembered how, for my pleasure, he used to ransack the stores of his learning, people each ruin with the men of antique Rome, and "unsphere" the spirits of Suetonius and Plutarch. "In Italy," saith a brilliant Essayist, "we leave ourselves behind, and travel through a romance." Alas! it was so with me, but in a sadder and a very different sense. I had indeed left far behind my former self of youth and happiness; and now, a mere shadow traveled mournfully through the romance of my own fair and faded past. Every broken column, every mouldering architrave, recalled some half-forgotten passage from its pages. On this fallen capital I sat to rest, while he filled my lap with violets. At this fountain we stooped and drank, in the mid-day sunshine. In this mosaic-paven nook we read aloud the fourth canto of Childe Harold. It was all over now. He whom I had worshiped as a child, dreamed of as a girl, adored as a wife, had deceived me, wronged me, embittered all my past, and laid waste all my future. Yet I lived, and knew that I must bear the burden, and set myself to the business of life. Life?—alas! what was life to me? Like the Campagna, on all sides a desert; at every step, a tomb. All the joy and the fullness of this life of mine had sunk, in one night, at a single blow; like a stately ship that goes down in the deep waters, with all sail set, and every hand on-board. Still I lived, and was calm;—so calm that I sometimes asked myself if my heart yet beat in my bosom, and the blood yet ran warm in my veins?

And thus the weary sands dropped, dropped, dropped daily, in the great hour-glass of Time.

CHAPTER LV.

TIME PAST AND TIME PRESENT.

"Parvum parva decent. Mihi jam non regia Roma
Sed vacuum Tibur placet."—Horace.

"Cyprus and ivy, weed and wall-flower grown
Matted and massed together, hillocks heaped
On what were chambers, arch crushed, column strown
In fragments, choked-up vaults, and frescoes steeped
In subterranean damps."—Byron.

There was a tap at the door.

"May I come in?" said a well-known voice.

The voice was followed by the shaggy gray head of the Herr Professor, and the head was duly succeeded by the rest of his gaunt person.

"Are you not always welcome?" I replied, answering a question with a question. "I am making the coffee, while Goody is gone to the Via Condotti for the rolls. Will you breakfast with us?"

"Breakfast! I breakfasted two hours ago, by candle-light."

"You are a Spartan, mein Professor."

"You are a Sybarite, *meine liebe Schülerinn.* Who ever heard of such an hour as eight for breakfast at the Zollenstrasse College? Madame Brenner would be ashamed of you."

"My dear friend," I said, smiling and sighing together, "that was at least fifty years ago — when I was young."

"Pooh! you are a child now," growled the Professor; "and because you are a child, I come to propose a holiday. Will you go to Tivoli?"

"To Tivoli? When?"

"To-day. It is still early enough, and will do you good. Yes or no?"

I had no desire to go, but feared to disappoint him by a refusal.

"If you can spare the time," I began, "and would enjoy it——"

"I can spare the time," he interrupted; "but my stay in Rome draws to an end; and in another week I may be no longer here. Shall I order a carriage to be at the door in half an hour?"

"In twenty minutes, if you like, mein Professor."

"No no—eat your breakfast in peace. And, remember, your friend Goody is a charming old woman; but she may as well stay at home, and keep house."

With this, he strode away down-stairs, three steps at a time, and I presently saw him in the yard of the *remise*, several gardens off, inspecting the condition of an open carriage which was being cleaned by one of the stablemen.

The drive was less beautiful than most of those which lie round Rome, and the Professor was more than usually silent. Thus two hours and a half went by, dully; and I was not sorry when, turning aside from the castellated tomb of the Plautia family, we passed down a shady lane, and stopped at the gate of Hadrian's Villa. Alighting here, we passed into that wide and wondrous wilderness of ruin, through avenues dark with cypress, and steep banks purple with violets. The air was heavy with perfume. The glades were carpeted with daisies, wild periwinkle, and white and yellow crocus-blooms. We stepped aside into a grassy arena which was once the Greek theater, and sat upon a fallen cornice. There was the narrow shelf of stage on which the agonies of Œdipus and Prometheus were once rehearsed; there was the tiny altar which stood between the audience and the actors, and consecrated the play; there, row above row, were the seats of the spectators. Now, the very stage was a mere thicket of brambles, and a little thrush lighted on the altar, while we were sitting by, and filled all the silent space with song.

Passing hence, we came next upon open fields, partly cultivated, and partly cumbered with shapeless mounds of fallen masonry. Here, in the shadow of a gigantic stone pine, we found a sheet of mosaic pavement glowing with all its marbles in the sun; and close by, half buried in deep grass, a shattered column of the richest porphyry. Then came an olive plantation; another theater; the fragments of a temple; and a long line of vaulted cells, some of which contained the remains of baths and conduits, and were tapestried within with masses of the delicate maidenhair fern. Separated from these by a wide space of grass, amid which a herd of goats waded and fed at their pleasure, rose a pile of reticulated wall, with part of a vast hall yet standing, upon the vaulted roof of which, sharp and perfect as if moulded yesterday, were incrusted delicate bas-reliefs of white stucco, representing groups of Cupids, musical instruments, and figures reclining at table. Near this spot, on a rising ground formed all of ruins overgrown with grass and under-

wood, we sat down to rest, and contemplate the view.

A deep romantic valley opened before us, closed in on either side by hanging woods of olive and ilex, with here and there a group of dusky junipers, or a solitary pine, rising like a dark green parasol above all its neighbors. Interspersed among these and scattered about the foreground, were mountainous heaps of buttressed wall, arch, vault, and gallery, all more or less shattered out of form, or green with ivy. At the bottom of the valley, forming, as it were, the extreme boundary of the middle distance, rose two steep volcanic hills, each crowned with a little white town, that seemed to wink and glitter in the sun; while beyond these, again, undulating, melancholy, stretching mysteriously away for miles and miles in the blue distance, lay the wastes of the Campagna.

The Professor pulled out his book, and made a rapid sketch.

"Why do you not also draw?" asked he.

"Because I prefer to be idle, and fancy how this scene may have looked eighteen hundred years ago."

"You can not fancy it," he said, abruptly. "It's impossible. Who could reconstruct, to the mind's eye, a group of palaces, theaters, barracks, temples, and gardens, such as once were here gathered together? Why, the outer wall measured between eight and ten miles round."

"It was not a villa at all," I replied. "It was a model city."

"And can you 'fancy' a city?"

"Perhaps."

The professor grinned, somewhat contemptuously; shook his head; and went on sketching.

Now it happened that I really could 'fancy' these things with a degree of accuracy that would have been surprising had the knowledge been my own. I had gone over this very ground with Hugh, when we were living in and near Rome, many and many a time. It had been one of our most favorite spots, and I knew every site, every path, and every historical conjecture of the place by heart. To reconstruct these buildings; to people temple, and palace, and amphitheater, with the life of eighteen hundred years ago; to identify each hill, and vale, and pile of ruin, had been precisely the object and the charm of our explorations. It was in studies such as these that Hugh's active mind found one of its highest satisfactions. They brought his vast reading to the surface. They exercised his imagination, stimulated his memory, and interested him on the side of poetry and art. I think I seldom knew him so communicative of his knowledge, and so happy in the exercise of his manifold powers, as when, strolling through these ruins, he used to think aloud, and enrich my mind with the precious overflowings of his own.

Of all this, however, the Professor knew nothing; and so, being this morning in a particularly amiable mood, began presently to banter me on my "antiquarian spirit."

"Why so silent?" said he. "Lost among the Romans—eh? Perhaps you knew the Emperor Hadrian in some state of preëxistence—who knows?"

"Perhaps I was a handmaiden of Julia Sabina."

"Julia Sabina! Who was she?"

" His wife, mein Professor."

" Humph! I wish your antiquarian inspiration would move you to discover what all these places were, that I'm putting in my sketch."

" Will you confess that I am a genuine Sibyl, if I really tell you?"

" Oh, of course."

" Well, then, this spot on which we are sitting was probably the site of an Academy. The valley before us was called the Vale of Tempe, and laid out in imitation of the celebrated Thessalian pass. Down yonder, where you see that line of bushes and deep grass, there runs a tiny rivulet which the Emperor caused to be led through the valley in imitation of the Perseus."

" You have got this from the guide-book," said the Professor. " False Sibyl! fill me this cup with water from your mock Perseus. I must just add a dash of color." ·

I took the little tin cup and filled it for him. When I came back he desired me to go on.

" What is the use of going on," said I, " if you deny my inspiration? No Sibyl ever brooked incredulity."

" Tell me something worth hearing, and I will believe in you to any extent you please."

" Upon your honor?"

" Upon my honor — if your Sibylline leaves are not stolen from Murray's Hand-book."

" Be silent, then, while I invoke the aid of the gods."

The Professor mixed a great pool of cobalt, and laid a flat wash of cloudless sky over all the upper half of his paper. Then humming an unmusical growl, touched in the shadow-sides of his ruins with a warm gray which seemed at once to put every thing in its place, and harmonize the picture. I, in the mean time, strove to collect my thoughts, and arrange my already half-forgotten learning.

" Come, my pupil," said the Professor, " you are a slow prophetess."

" I have to travel back through eighteen centuries," I replied, " and that is no light matter. Now listen, while I summon up remembrance of things past, and bring before your eyes the revels of the Cæsars!"

The Professor put his brush to his lips, and blew an imaginary trumpet. I proceeded with my narrative.

" Imagine, O learned Apelles, that it is now the tenth hour of the Roman day. There has this morning been a chariot-race, followed by a show of gladiators, and the victors have just gone down through the valley crowned with palm leaves and ribbons. Now we hear a sound of flutes and clarions. A company of the Pretorian guard advances, followed by musicians and fire-bearers, after whom comes the Emperor, clothed in a long white robe and crowned with roses. He is followed by some two dozen Roman nobles, all in festive dress; and another company of guards brings up the rear. They are going to sup in the Imperial Banqueting-hall, of which the ruins are now before your eyes. Imagine that hall——"

" Stop!" cried the Professor. " Those are the ruins of the Thermæ."

" They are called so, O Apelles, by the ignorant who compile guide-books," I replied; " but I, the Sibyl, tell thee that those ruined arches once echoed to the sounds of feasting. See the stuccoed flutes and garlands, the amphoræ, the groups of revelers yet fresh upon the hollow of that vault. To what end should decorations such as these be moulded upon the ceiling of a bath-room?"

" Humph! There's some reason in that," admitted he, now busy upon a cluster of dock leaves and a fallen trunk in the foreground.

" Let us follow the Emperor," continued I. " Let us pass, invisible, through the guards at the portal, and the crowd of Sicilian cooks, pantomimists, slaves, and dependents in the outer hall. Guided by the sound of music, let us penetrate to the cœnaculum itself. Here, on semicircular couches, recline the Emperor and his guests, their hair redolent of fragrant ointments, their fingers covered with rings, and their jeweled slippers lying beside them on the floor. Each man holds in his left hand a napkin with a gold and purple fringe. On the tables stand small images of the gods. At the lower end of the room is an elevated stage, on which a party of buffoons are performing a comic interlude. The visitors play at dice between the courses. Now and then, through revolving compartments in the ceiling, flowers and perfumes are showered down upon the feasters; while slaves stand by, whose duty is to fan away the flies, and bring fresh towels and scented water to the guests, after every dish."

" By Thor and Woden!" exclaimed the Professor, " how do you come to know all this?"

" The feast begins," said I, taking no notice of the interruption, " to the sound of trumpets; and slaves carry round cups of Falernian wine, flavored with honey. Then come oysters from the Lucrine lake, cray-fish from Misenum, mullets from Baiæ, lampreys, and perhaps a sturgeon, which is weighed alive at table, allowed to expire before the eyes of the guests, and then carried off to the kitchen, presently to appear again, cooked with a rich sauce of wine and pickles. Then come dishes of nightingales, thrushes, roasted shrimps, African cockles, Melian cranes, Ambracian kid, and a boar from the Umbrian forests, roasted whole, and stuffed with beef and veal. This is carved by the *carptor*, with pantomimic gestures, to the sound of music."

" But how do you know this?" repeated the Professor, fairly laying down his brush with astonishment.

" Next some jars of rare Massic and Chian wines are opened; a libation is poured out to the gods; and the Emperor pledges his guests. Then enter four musicians playing on double flutes, followed by as many servants crowned with flowers. They bring the royal dish of the entertainment—a peacock with all its plumage displayed, on a salver garlanded with roses. At this sight, the guests burst into murmurs of applause, and salute the Emperor. The buffoons now retire, and a couple of gladiators make their appearance on the stage, armed with helmets, bucklers, greaves, and short swords. The serious business of supper being now over, and the dessert about to be brought on, the feasters have leisure to enjoy this more exciting amusement. Additional cushions are brought; spiced wines are handed round; the tables are cleared; fresh cloths are laid; the guests lean back; the Emperor gives the signal, and the gladiators begin their combat. Now pistachio nuts, dates, Venafran olives, Matian apples, pears, grapes, dried figs, mushrooms, sweet cakes, preserves, and all kinds of delicate confectionery moulded into curious and graceful devices, are placed upon the tables. Conversation becomes animated. A gladiator falls, mortally wounded, the spectators cry '*habet!*' a fresh combatant replaces him; and the Emperor himself deigns to bet upon the victor. Thus amid bloodshed, dicing, wine and feasting, the hours pass by, and the entertainment draws to a close. Valuable presents are then distributed to the guests. One gets a precious ring, one a robe of Tyrian dye, another a sketch by Parrhasius, another a bust of Hadrian in colored marbles; and thus each takes his leave, enriched and feasted, and pours a last libation to the health of the Emperor and the honor of the gods."

"Is that all?" gasped the Professor.

"O Apelles! the Sibyl hath spoken."

He jumped up and flourished his umbrella menacingly before my eyes.

"Confess!" cried he. "Down on your knees and confess directly where you read all this! Name the book, the author, the publisher and the price! Tell every thing this moment, you impostor, on pain of death!"

"I have nothing to tell," replied I, composedly.

"False! inconceivably false! Where did you read it?"

"Nowhere."

"Who wrote it?"

"Nobody."

"Have you invented it?"

"By no means."

"Nowhere—nobody—by no means! Sphinx! Monster of negations! Speak, and be intelligible. If thou hast neither read nor invented these things, whence thy knowledge of them?"

"Inspiration."

"Humbug! humbug! humbug!"

"As you please, mein Professor," I replied, quietly smiling. "Is the sketch finished?"

The Professor flung away his umbrella, and resumed his seat by my side.

"Seriously, *meine Schülerinn*," said he, "I want the secret of your learning. I know you to be a sensible young woman, and a very tolerable painter; but a savant in petticoats, 'darkly, deeply, beautifully blue.' Pooh! it's impossible!"

"Wonder of wonders! Apelles quotes Byron?"

"You trifle with me," said the Professor, frowning darkly. "You do not choose to speak. Eh?"

"Can you not guess why?" I asked, turning away that he might not see the tears in my eyes. "Can you not guess that I trifle, because it would cost me so much pain to be in earnest?"

"I—I don't understand," stammered he.

"Then I will tell you. You do not know, perhaps, how familiar this place is to me. I have been here over and over again, in—in time past. I once staid at Tivoli for more than a week. I have sketched this very scene from almost the same point of view as yourself. I know every ruin in the place by heart—outwardly, in its form and color; inwardly, in its legend and history. The outward, I gathered

for myself. The inward, dear friend, I acquired from the lips of one who had

'——made a general survey
Of all the best of men's best knowledges,
And knew so much as ever learning knew.'

One to whom all art, all poetry, all history was dear and familiar—one——"

My voice failed, and I covered my eyes with my hand. The Professor coughed, fidgeted, and was for some moments silent. When he spoke it was with a voluble embarrassment quite foreign to his ordinary manner.

"I beg your pardon," said he. "I—I was an ass. I ought to have guessed—I might have guessed. If I am a fool, I can't help it. You —you see, I forget. I always think of you as my little scholar. It always seems to me that we are still at Zollenstrasse, and—and when I look at you and talk to you, I never remember that you—perhaps if you wore a widow's dress, it would be different; or if you sometimes talked about your late—but I beg your pardon. Of course it's a very sad subject, and—and, as I said before, if I am a fool, I can't help it!"

"You are my best friend in all the world," said I, putting out my hand.

He shook it, as if it had been a pump-handle, and blushed purple to the very tips of his great ears. Then, relapsing into sudden misanthropy, said—

"Nonsense! All men are fools, and all women are hypocrites. I don't believe you care a *groschen* for me. Ei, *schweigen Sie!* I won't hear a word you have to say. Do you see that man on the top of those arches? I wonder how he got there. What a famous distance I should get for my sketch if I could find my way up!"

"I can show you the path," said I. "It lies round behind those bushes. You must, however, follow it alone, for it is rough climbing."

He gathered up his sketching traps, and I led the way, pausing at the foot of the ascent, which was even more wild and inaccessible than when I last saw it. Leaving him there to fight his way through the brambles as well as he could, I then strolled back into the valley, and followed the little rivulet, as it gurgled and sparkled through cresses and pebbles, till lost among the deep grass farther down. Little rivulet that had been flowing on thus for so many centuries, singing the same low song forever and ever! For my ears that song had but one burthen. What to me were the Imperial feet that had once trodden its borders, and become dust? What to me were the ravages of Goth or Gaul? I remembered only Hugh, and how we had wandered there together in the sunlight of two short years ago. I plucked a little red flower from the bank, and watched it float away with the stream. "Is it not thus," I asked myself, "that a life floats down the stream of time? Is it not thus that those whom we love are snatched from our embrace, and hurried away forever? To what shore, oh flower? To what sea, oh stream? To what haven, oh my heart?"

It was one of those moments when I realized, in all its bitterness, the thought of how, on this fair earth, two could never meet in peace and love again; and it smote me with a sense of pain "too deep for tears."

The Professor came back covered with dusk and scratches, and looking much the worse for his excursion; but delighted, nevertheless, with all that he had seen and sketched from the roof of the Banqueting-hall. And now, as the day was advancing, and our time was fast ebbing away, we hastened back, found our vettura waiting at the gate, and drove on through the famous olive-wood, to Tivoli. As the town came in sight, the Professor pulled out his watch, shook his head, and sighed.

"All the inns are detestable," said he. "Heaven only knows what we shall get for dinner."

"Oh, never mind," I replied. "What does it matter?"

"Matter?" said he, sharply. "It matters every thing in this infernal country. My dinner has been the misery of my daily life ever since I have been in Rome. The sight of the trattore's list each morning drives me mad. I never know what any thing means; and when at length I mark off three or four things, they generally turn out to be loathsome messes, unfit for any but a Caliban. Yesterday, when I sat down to dinner, I found I had ordered nothing but a few saucers, and some scraps of half-raw potato, swimming in oil?"

"Well, I promise you that shall not be the case to-day," said I, smiling.

"Then they eat such unholy things," grumbled he. "What do you think I saw on the price-list at the *Lepre* the other day. It ran thus:—

' BEEF—the eye of.
  Do.—the tongue.
  Do.—the ear.
  Do.—the feet.

Fancy a people that can feed on such offal as this! What wonder that art dies out among them? What wonder that they are priest-ridden and degraded? Do you believe that Michael Angelo and Raffaelle nourished their mighty thoughts on the eyes and ears of Campagna bullocks? Faugh!"

We were by this time entering the dirty, ruinous alleys of Tivoli, followed by a lively crowd of beggars.

"What hotel, signore?" asked the driver.

"Hôtel!" growled the Professor. "Say hovel. Take us to the Sibyl. There, if we are starved, we shall at least have something to look at."

So we drove on into the yard of the Hôtel de la Sibylle, which was already crowded with carriages and coachmen, and were at once shown out upon the terrace overlooking the falls. Here, at a long table in the shadow of the loveliest of Roman temples, sat a merry party of ladies and gentlemen, dining in the open air. No sooner, however, had we made our appearance, than three or four started up from their seats, and, to my dismay, burst into exclamations of welcome.

"Why, it's Professor Metz!"

"What lucky chance has brought you here to-day, Professor Metz?"

"Just in time to dine with us, too!"

"Well, now, this is famous!"

"Couldn't have happened better!"

To all of which the Professor replied by shaking hands with nearly the whole party, and blurting out such commonplaces as first suggested themselves. This done, he came back to me, looking considerably embarrassed.

"What's to be done?" said he. "They want us to dine with them; and—and they've

such a capital dinner there, furnished by Nazzari. Every thing cold. Brought it with them from Rome. If we order a dinner at this vile place, we shan't be able to eat it. What do you say?"

"I say, do as you please, my kind friend."

"Humph! Ha! But—but you don't like strangers—I know you don't like strangers! Then you need not know them again to-morrow, you see, unless you choose. They are nearly all artists. Still, if it wasn't for the dinner——"

"I won't condemn you to die by starvation," said I.

"I'm afraid I'm selfish," hesitated the Professor.

"I should know I was, if I allowed you to refuse on my account."

While we were yet wavering, a lady left the party, and came toward us. Her person was large; her complexion fair; her face square, massive, full of power and frankness, and lit by a pair of wondrous eyes that seemed to flash and vary with every word she uttered.

"Will it not be possible, Herr Metz," said she, "to prevail upon your friend?"

"Oh, yes—I—that is, she—permit me to introduce Miss Dunham — Mrs. Carlyon," stammered the Professor.

Miss Dunham put out her hand with the sunniest smile in the world, and said:—

"You are very welcome. Our tables are ' but coldly furnished forth;' yet if you will balance our good-will against our baked meats, both shall be heartily at your service."

I thanked and followed her, while the Professor whispered hastily in my ear:—

"Miss Dunham, you know—the celebrated American tragedian. One of the most charming women in Rome."

Miss Dunham resumed her seat at the head of the table, made room for me at her right hand, and introduced me to the rest of the company. The Professor found a place at the farther end; and thus I found myself, for the first time since the fatal night of the ball at Ashley Park, surrounded by strangers, and listening to a whirl of conversation and laughter. Confused, bewildered, feeling strangely sad and out of place, I sat silently by, replying in monosyllables when spoken to, and scarcely able at first to disentangle the separate threads of talk. Presently, as my embarrassment subsided, I found that my neighbors at the upper end of the table were chiefly occupied with the present state of Roman art.

"That which shocks me most," said Miss Dunham, "is the fatal influence of Rome upon our young artists. Men who in London or New-York showed vigor and originality, here either sink into classical imbecility, or turn manufacturers of busts and medallions."

"Nothing more easily accounted for," replied a handsome young man with an open collar and long hair, at the opposite side of the table. "A fellow can but choose between the antique and the modern. The antique drives him to despair; and all he does is miserable imitation. The modern is a market, governed by the almighty dollar."

"If the artist did his duty, he might make that market what he pleased," said a bright-faced girl, whom they called Charlie. "It is his business to elevate the public taste."

"All very well when he has a fixed public to

deal with," replied the young man ; "but the public of Rome is a mere fluctuating tide of tourists, most of whom know no more about art than about Lindley Murray—wretches who prefer a marble record of their own ugliness to the bust of the young Augustus ; and see a finer study of color in a yard of Tartan than in a masterpiece of Titian."

"Penwarne," said Miss Dunham, "you grow misanthropic. That unsold Eve that I saw in your studio yesterday will prove the ruin of you. Remember the fall."

"I'd rather put the Eve into the fire than sell her to some of your countrymen," said the painter, coloring. "A Yankee monster asked me the other day what I would take for—' the gal eating oranges.'"

"I can tell you a better story than that," observed a quiet man at the lower end of the table. "An American capitalist came to me not many months since, and opened the conversation by saying—' Sir, your name is Robson.' I admitted that my name was Robson. ' And you air a Statuary,' said he. I admitted this fact also, substituting sculptor. ' Sir,' continued he, 'I will give you a commission.' I bowed, and begged him to be seated. ' Mr. Robson, sir,' said he, drawing a paper from his pocket, ' I am a remarkable man. I was born in the en-Vi-rons of Boston city, and began life by selling matches at five cents the bunch. I am worth, at this moment, one million o' dollars.' I bowed again, and said I was glad to hear it. ' Sir,' he went on to say, ' how I airned that million o' dollars —how from selling matches I came to running of errands ; to taking care of a hoss ; to trading in dogs, tobaccos, cottons, corns, and sugars ; and how I came to be the man I am, you'll find all made out on this paper, dates and facts correct. Sir it's a very Re-markable statement.' I replied that I had no doubt of it ; but that I could not quite see what it had to do with the matter in hand. ' Sir,' said my capitalist, ' every thing. I wish, sir, to per-petuate my name. You have a very pretty thing, sir, here in Rome—a pillar with a Pro-cession twisting up all around it, and a figger up at top. I think you call it Trajan's column. Now, Mr. Robson, sir, I wish you to make me one exactly like it—same hight, same size, and money no object. You shall re-present my career in all my va-ri-ous trades a-twisting round the column, beginning with the small chap selling matches at five cents the bundle, and ending with a full length figger of ME on the summit, with one hand, thus, in my Bo-som, and the other under my coat-tails !'"

"Won't do I won't do I" laughed a chorus of skeptics. "A palpable invention, Robson I Too good to be true."

"Does any b-b-b-body know what is to be done at the artist's fête this year ?" asked a slim youth with blue glasses and a stutter. "I c-c-can't find out any thing ab-b-b-bout it."

"There's nothing decided yet," replied Mr. Penwarne. "Murray was talking about a travestie of Sardanapalus the other day ; but the notion didn't seem to be popular."

"Why not pay the 'tedious-brief scene' of Pyramus and Thisbe ?" suggested Miss Dunham.

"Why not play the whole Midsummer Night's Dream ?" said another lady. "It needs no scenery that the Campagna will not furnish."

"Then Charlie should play Puck," said Miss Dunham, smiling.

"And yourself, Oberon," rejoined the young girl.

"I should wonderfully like to play B-b-b-bottom," stammered the youth in the spectacles.

"Yes, it would suit you capitally," said Penwarne ; "and no expense for the head."

"It has always seemed to me," observed an intelligent-looking man who had not spoken before, "that there is a poetical inconsistency in the remarks made by Bottom, after he is ' translated.' When he is introduced to Mustard-seed he makes a pungent allusion to ox-beef. When Titania presses him to eat, he asks for a peck of provender. How are these to be reconciled ? If he thinks as an ass, he would know nothing of beef and mustard. If he thinks as a man, he would not ask for oats."

"You can only reconcile it by remembering that he is both a man and an ass," replied Miss Dunham. "No uncommon phenomenon either."

"You might get up an annual exhibition, I should fancy, in one of the private galleries," said the Professor, in answer to some observation which I had not heard. "Where no comparisons can be made, the fire of emulation smoulders. A man ought to see his own works beside those of his cotemporaries at least once in every two or three years."

"We would gladly do so, if we could," replied the gentleman with whom he was conversing ; "but a thousand difficulties are thrown in our way by the government whenever it is proposed. We all feel the want of an exhibition room. We should be able to undertake larger works, if we had a large place in which to hang them. It is just this advantage that causes the historical school to be almost abandoned by our young artists, and drives so many into the realistic style."

"Realistic I historical I" repeated the Professor, impatiently. "Nonsense, nonsense, young man ! All true art is a form of history. If you paint but a tree, or a face, or a boat, faithfully —that is history. Don't lose yourself in a maze of words. Painting big pictures of medieval men and women from hired models in hired costumes, is not history. The real is your only historic ; and all art, to be beautiful, must first be true."

"But the best critics——"

"Critics be hanged !" interrupted the Professor, savagely. "God sent art, and the devil sent critics. Where were the critics when Raffaelle painted his Transfiguration, and Michael Angelo worked in the Sistine Chapel ? In those days, there were no critics. The best pictures the world ever saw were painted before the brood existed. Critics, indeed I Vultures feeding on the corpse of ancient art—fungi flourishing among ruins—ghouls I"

"Will any b-b-body go down to see the falls ?" asked the youth in the spectacles.

"No one who objects to being left behind," replied Miss Dunham, who was evidently the leader of the party. "It is half-past four already, and we have all our miles before us. The night-mists will have risen, as it is, before we are half across the Campagna."

"No danger of B-b-b-banditti, I suppose ?"

"Banditti ?" repeated Mr. Penwarne, carelessly; "why, I fear not. There are a few hordes about; but they chiefly haunt the Florentine and Neapolitan roads. Fancy falling in with a Fra Diavolo and his gang—wouldn't it be exciting?"

"I shouldn't f-f-f-fancy it at all," stammered the other, looking very uncomfortable.

"Nonsense! think of the romance of it."

"B-b-b-bother the romance of it," replied the stammerer, upon whose mind was dawning a dim consciousness of banter. "R-r-r-robbery and murder are acquired tastes, and I don't p-p-possess them."

The al fresco dinner was now over; the order was given for putting in the horses; and the gentlemen began gathering the knives, glasses, and unemptied bottles into two large baskets. In the mean time we made the tour of the little temple, and looked down upon the plunging waters of the Cascatelle, the distant roar of which had accompanied our voices all dinner-time, like a concert of solemn instruments.

"I wish I had gone to the b-b-bottom," said the stammerer regretfully, as he leaned over the parapet.

"I wish you had, with all my heart," replied Penwarne.

A few minutes more, and we were all on our road back to Rome. Mr. Robson and Mr. Penwarne shared our carriage, and chatted of Italian politics, books, art, and artist-gossip all the way; and as we went along, the sun set, and the mountains changed from rose-color to amethyst, and from amethyst to a cold and wintry gray.

———◆———

CHAPTER LVI.

THE PROFESSOR.

"Sweetest nut hath sourest rind."—As You Like It.

I HAD been all day, copying in the Sciarra Palace, and was cowering over my little wood fire after dinner, when the Professor walked in, unannounced, and sat down at the opposite side of the hearth.

"The evenings are still cold," said he. "I am glad you have a fire."

"They are very cold," I replied, throwing on a couple of pine cones, which blazed up immediately in a wavering pyramid of flame.

"That's cheerful," said the Professor, approvingly.

"So cheerful that I only wish it were possible to bear it all through the summer. There is real companionship in a fire."

"You are lonely here?"

"Sometimes."

He stirred uneasily in his chair, and stared at the fire.

"I am not more lonely," I said, after a long pause, "than I should be elsewhere. You must not suppose, kind friend, that I do not like the place."

"That's well," he said; and sighed.

And then we were both silent again.

"Rome is a melancholy place," he observed, after some five minutes' interval.

"I am not sure that I think so. It is melancholy, perhaps, to the heavy-hearted, in the sense that all visible history is melancholy;

but to those who are happy, it is one of the most charming places in the world."

The Professor looked up, sharply.

"Your definition?" said he.

"Of what?"

"Of 'visible history.' What do you mean by it? Ruins, monuments, records of past generations?"

"Yes, precisely."

"Humph! And do you suppose that a pair of honeymoon lovers would find the Appian Way a lively place of resort?"

"We were speaking of Rome, Herr Professor. Not of the road from Rome to Heaven."

"A pretty idea," said he, smiling; "but of doubtful application. Not many of those old Romans, I fancy, went to Heaven. Quite the reverse."

And then the conversation dropped again.

"I—I must go, *meine Schülerinn*," he said, by and by.

"Not till I have made you a cup of coffee?"

He shook his head.

"That's not what I mean. I must go back to Germany."

"Alas! when!"

"The day after to-morrow; or—or, perhaps, to-morrow."

"So soon?"

"Ay, so soon."

"How much more lonely it will be when you are gone!" I said, sadly.

He stared gloomily at the fire, and made no reply.

"You—you will sometimes take the trouble to write to me, mein Professor?"

"Ay—surely."

Another long silence.

"I have one favor to beg from you," I began, at length. "That is to say, one more favor, in addition to so many."

"You have only to name it, child," said he, still with the same intent look.

"Then I—I want you to promise me something."

"I promise. What is it?"

"To keep my name, my place of residence; my very existence secret. To deliver over to no living soul the key of my seclusion. To deny me, if need be, to my own father."

He looked up with a startled flash in his eyes.

"To your own father?" he exclaimed.

"To my own father—my own sister—all who ever knew me. To—to Mr. Farquhar, if he should visit Zollenstrasse again."

"Mr. Farquhar?" said he, quickly. "The rich Englishman who——"

"The same. Do you promise this?"

"I have promised," he replied, sinking back into his former attitude.

"Why I desire it," I continued, falteringly, "is—is of no consequence to any one but myself. I am not happy. I look back upon a very dreary past, and forward to a very dreary future. My only prayer now is for solitude. Let me be dead to all the world except yourself—dead and buried."

"Be it so," he said. "I will keep your secret faithfully."

"And—you are not vexed that I withhold my motive from you?"

"Not in the least."

I put out my hand to him in silent thanks. He took it; held it loosely for a moment, as if he did not quite know what he ought to do with it; and then dropped it.

"Do you really think you shall miss me?" he said, after another pause.

"Can you ask the question?"

"I'm but an old bear."

"You are the best friend—the only friend, I have."

"I would stay if I could," he continued, pulling contemplatively at his moustache. "If I gave up the Art-directorship and settled here in Rome, I might, perhaps, manage it."

"Gave up the Art-directorship!" I repeated, with incredulous amazement. "You can not be serious?"

"Humph! the Art-directorship is more honor than profit, and more plague than either. The salary is only twelve hundred florins a year."

"But the Academy—the Grand Duke—what would they do without you? How could you endure to live out of Germany?"

"I should do more for my own fame," said he.

"True—you would paint more pictures."

"And I should not be leaving you alone here in Rome."

"For heaven's sake, put that thought aside! If you take such an important step, my dear friend, let it be in consideration of your own prosperity and happiness only."

"As far as my prosperity is concerned, I should do well enough, no doubt. Whenever I have time to paint a picture, it sells at once. Besides, I have a little money put by. Then as for my happiness, I—why, the fact is, *meine Schülerinn*, I'm just as lonely as yourself, and—and I have no ties—and——why do you suppose I took you the other day to Tivoli?"

"To give me pleasure, I am sure; though I fear you could ill spare the time."

"Not a bit of it."

"Well, then, to give yourself pleasure."

"Not a bit of it."

"Oh, in that case I give up guessing."

"To—to ask you a question, *gnädige Fräulein*."

"A question? Nay, you are jesting."

He shook his head, and sat tugging at his moustache as if he meant to pull it off.

"I'm serious," said he.

"But what question?"

"One that I hadn't courage to put to you, after all. Can't you guess it?"

"Not in the very least; but if it be any thing that I can do for you—any thing in this wide world, no matter how difficult, or——"

"No, no, no—nothing of the kind. Bah! what a fool I am!"

"But why do you hesitate?"

"Because—because something tells me that I had better hold my tongue. And yet—I hate the thought of your toiling here year after year, with no one to work for you or watch over you. You're young, and you're poor, and you're—you're pretty; and the world will come hard to you in many ways that you've not yet thought of. You want some one to take care of you. I'm—I'm a disagreeable old fellow—rough and gruff, and tough as a bear; but—will you marry me?"

Marry him! Marry the Professor! Were my senses deceiving me?

"I—I don't expect you to love me," he went on, hastily. "I know that isn't possible. I quite understand that your heart is buried with the husband you have lost. But if you can esteem me, take me for what I am, and put up with my companionship for life, why—just say so at once, and let us make an end of the matter."

"If I thought that you loved me, my kind friend," I began, "and if——"

"I do love you," interrupted he, with his eyes still fixed unwaveringly upon the fire.

"Yes, I know you do, as a dear friend; but if I thought you loved me as a lover——"

"Well? If you thought I loved you as a lover,—what then?"

"Then I should have one more bitter grief to bear; because I could never be your wife."

"I expected this," he muttered, more to himself than me.

"I can not tell you why. It makes part of my unhappy secret; but——"

"But I know why," said he, with an impatient movement. "Because I am old, and gray, and ugly."

"Before heaven, no!"

He shook his head.

"Do you not believe me?"

"I don't believe that the Beauty would ever have loved the Beast, if he had not turned into a handsome prince at last."

"Alas! you did not ask me for love, two minutes since. You asked only for my hand, and my esteem. My esteem you know you have—nay, more; my warmest gratitude—my friendliest affection."

"Then why——"

"Do not ask me why! Is it not enough if I say that it is impossible?"

"Oh, it is quite enough," he replied bitterly.

I started up, stung by his incredulity.

"Ungenerous!" I exclaimed. "Ungenerous and unkind! Know, then, if you *will* know it, that I am no widow. He whom I wedded, lives. He deceived me—I fled from him. I have neither hand nor heart to give. Now you know all. Are you satisfied?"

He looked up, for the first time; and his eyes met mine. He rose.

"I beg your pardon," he said; so softly that his breath seemed to tremble, and not his voice. "I beg your pardon. I was greatly in the wrong."

"You were, indeed!"

"You will forgive me before I go? You will shake hands with me?"

I put out my hand, somewhat reluctantly. He took it between both his own. They were damp, and cold, and trembled palpably.

"Good-by," he said.

"Good-by."

He went toward the door, paused half-way, and stood irresolute.

"We part friends, surely?" he asked, almost in a whisper.

"Friends!" I repeated, the last shade of vexation vanishing in an instant. "The best and truest friends in all the world. Never doubt it, while we both live!"

"Thank you," he said; and moved a step farther.

"And you will not leave Rome to-morrow? You will come and see me again?"

K

"Well—I will not leave Rome to-morrow," he replied, after a moment's hesitation.

There was something strange in his manner; something that I could not entirely understand.

"You would not, surely, be here another whole day without seeing me?" I persisted.

He put his hand to his brow, as if in pain.

"No, no," he said. "I will not be in Rome another day without seeing you. Good-by—God bless you."

He made but one step to the threshold—looked back with a face, oh, so pale!—moved his lips without uttering any sound; and was gone.

I listened to his footsteps going down the stairs, and then went back to my seat by the fire. His empty chair stood opposite. The pine-cones had long since burnt to ashes, and my little room looked lonelier than ever. I sat with clasped hands, sadly thinking.

"Alas!" I said to myself. "Is this to cost me the only friend I had? Shall we ever be the same again? Will not something, henceforth, be gone from our friendship—something from the pleasant tenor of our intercourse? Poor as I was before this night, am I now poorer still? God grant that it may not be so. He did not love me. It is not possible that he should love me! Seeing me so desolate, he generously sought the right to protect me. Good, chivalrous, gentle heart! He knows now that that right can never be his; and he knows it without offense to his pride, or pain to his friendship. Then why can we not meet to-morrow, as if this interview had never been? If, indeed, he had really loved me—but he did not. No, he certainly did not love me!"

Having reasoned myself into this persuasion, I alternately reproached myself for the anger into which I had been betrayed, and consoled myself by thinking of all that I would say to him on the morrow, before parting. In the midst of my reverie, Goody came in with the coffee.

"My blessed lamb," said she, looking strangely disturbed; "nothing's the matter, is there? Just tell me if any thing's the matter, my deary?"

"No—that is to say, not much. Why do you ask?"

"Because—because, my dear lamb, it's given me such a turn, that I'm all of a tremble."

"What has given you a turn?" I asked, quickly. "Is any thing wrong?"

"I—I don't know, my deary. I suppose so; else why should he be taking on like that?"

"He? Who? The Professor?"

"To be sure, deary. Who else? Then, you see, I didn't know him at first, coming upon him in the dark, at the foot of the staircase."

"When was this?"

"Not two minutes ago, as I was bringing in the sugar for your coffee, darling."

"Not two minutes ago?" I repeated, going toward the door. "Then he is there still!"

"No, no, my lamb; he's far enough by this time. He just pulled his hat over his eyes and ran away like a madman, when he saw me."

"But what was he doing, Goody?"

"Doing, my deary? Just leaning his poor head down upon the banisters, and sobbing fit to break his heart."

My own heart sank within me. I turned cold from head to foot. Oh, was it love, then, after all?

The next morning I found a note on my breakfast table, containing these words :—

"By the time this reaches you, I shall be many leagues away. I keep my word. I do not leave Rome 'to-morrow;' I leave to-night, by the courier. I feel that it is best. I do not wish to see you again, till this dream has become a painless memory. I did love you. I do love you. It is the first, last, only love of my life. Let this truth excuse my presumption, and be then forgotten. To love you is now a crime, to be lived down and expiated. When I feel that I have conquered, and dare dwell in your presence again, I will return to Rome and watch over you till I die. I have left a balance of a few hundred scudi at Pakenham's bank, which I entreat you to borrow if you need money. I have entered it in your name, to save trouble; and you shall pay it back by and by, when you are prosperous. God bless you!"

CHAPTER LVII.

THE SECRET THAT CAME WITH THE SUMMER.

"MAY bien vestu d'habit reverdissant
Semé de fleurs."—FRANCOIS I.

THE spring came; the languid, fragrant, joyous Italian spring, all sunshine and perfume, and singing of birds, and blossoming of flowers. The Easter festivals were past, and the strangers dispersed and gone. The snow faded suddenly from the summit of Soracte. The Colosseum hung out its banners of fresh green. The Campagna glowed under the midday sun, like a Persian carpet—one wilderness of poppies and hare-bells, buttercups, daisies, wild convolvuli, and purple hyacinths. Every crumbling ruin burst into blossom, like a garden. Every cultivated patch within the city walls ran over, as it were, spontaneously, with the delicious products of the spring. Every stall at the shady corner of every quiet piazza was piled high with early fruits; and the flower-girls sat all day long on the steps of the Trinità de' Monti. Even the sullen pulses of the Tiber seemed stirred by a more genial current as they eddied round the broken piers of the Ponte Rotto. Even the solemn sepulchers of the Appian Way put forth long feathery grasses from each mouldering cranny, and the wild eglantine struck root among the shattered urns of the road-side columbarium. Now, too, the transparent nights, all spangled with fire-flies, were even more balmy than the days. And now the moon shone down on troops of field-laborers encamped under the open sky against the city walls; and the nightingales sang as if inspired, among the shadowy cypresses of the Protestant burial-ground.

A happy, gentle time, fruitful in promise and tender in peace!—a gracious time, full of balm for wounded hearts, and hope for troubled souls—a time when the weariest sufferer was for a moment at rest, and the bitterest questions were hushed on the lips of the despairing! A blessed, blessed time, never to be recalled without tears of prayer and thanksgiving!

It had been first a doubt—then a hope—now

a certainty. It had haunted me for months, by day and night, at my work, and in my dreams. It had flashed upon me, quite suddenly, when I was not alone, making my heart beat, and my cheek vary from pale to crimson. It had waked me, over and over again, in the dead waste and middle of the night, forbidding sleep from my eyes, and conjuring before me such visions of possible joy that I scarcely dared to let my thoughts dwell on them. I remember how I used to lie in bed in the darkness, with closed eyes and folded hands, centering all my being in the one supreme act of prayer; and how I sometimes broke down under an overwhelming sense of my own weakness, and wept till I fell asleep. And now it was certainty — a wonderful, enrapturing, bewildering certainty; and the world was suddenly transfigured; and I walked upon roses; and the air I breathed was liquid sunshine!

It was my secret. I was a miser, and kept it to myself. I loved to be alone, that I might exult in it, and dwell upon it, and repeat it a hundred times, and again a hundred times, and find fresh music in the words at every utterance! I could not work when the knowledge first became mine. I went daily to the Sciarra Palace; took my usual seat; mixed the colors on the pallet; and then sat idle, lost in delicious dreams. As the day advanced, I generally gave up the useless effort, and wandered out to some quiet place where I could sit in the shade of trees and dream again. Thus for several days in succession, I haunted the secluded alleys of the Quirinal Gardens, and the ruins of the Baths of Caracalla; sometimes roaming restlessly to and fro, but oftenest sitting still, in a kind of passive ecstasy, wondering how the world had suddenly become so beautiful. Nothing now seemed as it was before. A little while ago, and day followed day mechanically; and the sun shone, or the rain fell, and I heeded not; and the flowers blossomed by the wayside, and I passed them unobservant. Now I saw every thing, as if for the first time; and drank in delight from each sight and sound of spring.

And all this arose out of my secret; and that secret—ah! that priceless secret lay close, close to my heart, doubling each fond pulsation in a tender, mysterious harmony; blending life with life, and love with love, and irradiating all the future with a light direct from heaven. My child — dear God! how the words thrilled my very brain, when I whispered them softly to my self! Was there ever such melody in words before? Was there ever such consolation? Was there ever such wealth? Only those who had lived with nothing to live for, only those who have worked with nothing to work for, can tell what my secret was to me.

It informed every thought, and influenced every act of my daily life. It revived the ambition of art which had so long been dead within me. It awakened the sense of beauty which had so long lain dormant. It created a new interest in every earth-born thing, inanimate or animate, and linked it with a thousand happy projects. I could not see the wild flowers in the grass without thinking how sweet it would be, by and by, to gather them for tiny hands to play with. I could not hear the lark's song over head, without some fancy of how I might train that baby ear to love sweet sounds, and all God's happy creatures. I even overleaped the chasm of years, and, sitting among the ponderous arches of the ancient baths, planned how I would study the history and language of this vanished people, and teach them to my child amid the scenes of their greatness.

Thus, building my fairy castles in the air, the sunny hours went by, and evening came, and I went home through the dusky streets with heaven in my heart. Sometimes I turned aside for a few moments, to enter the open door of some church and listen to the chanting. I remember that even the tawdry images of the Virgin and Child at the corners of the public thoroughfares touched me now with something of a poetical significance which they had never possessed before.

I always went home, at this time, with reluctance. I was in love with solitude, and, egotist that I was! grew impatient of dear old Goody's harmless prattle. Ah, how unwilling I was to share my secret with her! How I put it off from day to day, and dreaded lest she should discover it for herself!

Henceforth I was to be no more alone. Henceforth, the highest and holiest of all earthly love, and the tenderest of all earthly companionship, was to be mine. This thought was my crowning happiness—not a wholly unalloyed and unshadowed happiness, even then; for how could I, even in the first flush of my new joy, forget that my child must enter life legally dishonored, and never know the father from whom its being came? Alas! the father—the father whom I still loved so dearly—whose portrait I should look for, presently, in a baby face—whose tone I should by and by listen for in a baby voice—whom I must try to love henceforward as a mere memory, dead, and forgiven, and passed away.

And this was my secret that came with the summer.

<hr>

CHAPTER LVIII.

AN OLD FRIEND.

"I HAVE had playmates, I have had companions
In my days of childhood, in my joyful school-days."
C. LAMB.

THE summer went by in work, and hope, and tender expectation. My task finished at the Sciarra Palace, I found myself "passing rich," with a capital of two hundred scudi, and a fresh commission. This time it was a cabinet painting by Giulio Romano, and the original was intrusted to my care, to copy at home. I now made myself a little studio by partitioning off half my sitting-room, with a large folding screen, and used to paint there all day long close against the partly darkened window, with the warm orange-scented air creeping in from the gardens beyond. Here Goody would sit by with her needle-work, or chat to me from the other side of the screen while she prepared our modest dinner; and on the outer loggia we loitered many an hour after dusk, watching the fire-flies circling to and fro, and whispering to each other of the guests to come. As the later heats drew on, a silence fell upon the Roman streets, and all who could afford to leave the city emigrated to the seaside or the mountains. But I had no desire to follow the general example, and no means; unless by borrowing from the Professor's fund, to which nothing short of necessity should have compelled me. I loved Rome best in its season of solitude; and, less fearful of recognition than at other times, ventured occasionally into the public gardens and galleries, and sometimes indulged myself with an afternoon among the delicious glades of the Borghese grounds.

Thus July and August passed, and September came with rumors of the vintage on the hills—September, so full of hope, and promise; so rich in giving; so long in coming; so welcome at last!

The Professor wrote seldom, and very briefly. Early in September, while the hope of which he knew nothing was yet unfulfilled, I received a letter from him which informed me that my old friend and school-companion, Ida Saxe, was on her way to Rome. Promoted to the sub-professorship which I had left vacant, and having been twice successful in competition for the medal, she had now received a small grant from the Academic fund, to enable her to prosecute her studies in Italy. "She has already spent some weeks in Florence," wrote Professor Metz; "and by the time you receive my letter, will probably have arrived in Rome. You can learn her address, if you choose, at the Hotel Minerva. I do not ask you to seek her. I have kept your secret faithfully, and it is for yourself to judge whether you will in this case depart from your prescribed line of conduct. If I might advise you, I should say, 'Go to her.' A student in Rome, like yourself, traversing the same streets, frequenting the same galleries, and devoted to the same pursuits, it is impossible that she should not, some day, encounter you. It is not likely that she will stay less than three years; and it is most unlikely that for three years you can succeed in avoiding her. If, however, you prefer removing to Florence, by all means do so. I can give you an introduction to a dealer on the Lung' Arno, and may venture, I think, to promise that you will do as well there as in Rome. I shall be glad to know your decision by an early post. Ever yours, etc., etc."

My decision was speedily made. I put my work aside; and, having first looked at a large airy upper room for which my landlady required a tenant, went at once to the Albergo de la Minerva, and inquired if the signora Saxe had arrived.

"Sì, signora, by the Siena diligence, about an hour ago," replied the waiter; and showed me up four flights of stairs, to a little gloomy room against the roof, where I found her sitting in the midst of her boxes, pale, weary and disconsolate.

"Ida," I said, lifting my vail. "Do you remember me?"

She rose, looked at me, hesitated, changed color, and then, with a cry of surprise and joy, sprang into my arms.

"Barbara!" she exclaimed. "Meine geliebte Barbara! Is it really, really thyself?"

And with this she wept and laughed, and kissed me over and over again, and could scarcely believe that it was not all a dream.

"Ah, what years have gone by!" she said, presently, as we sat hand in hand. "What long, long years! I never thought to see you

again, Barbara. We heard that you had married; but we knew not even your name. Why did you never write? Why did you never come to see us again? Alas! you forgot us — you forgot your poor Ida, who loved you so dearly, and whose easel stood beside your own for so many years! Are you living in Rome? Is your husband a painter? How did you know I was here? Who told you? How good of you to come so soon! I have not been here an hour, and I was so lonely!"

To which I replied—

"Meine liebe Ida, you ask more questions in a breath than I can answer in a day. Tell me first what your plans are?"

"Plans?" said she. "I have none, except to study hard."

"But where do you propose to live?"

"I have no idea."

"Have you no friends in Rome?"

"I thought not, an hour ago."

"Would you like to live with me? My padrona has a room to let, and——"

"What happiness! I would rather live with you than with any one in the world."

"Then I can assure you, my darling, that you are the only person in the world whom I would take to live with me. Your boxes, I see, are not even uncorded; so, if you please, we will send for a vettura, and go at once."

"But your husband — are you sure that he will be pleased to—to have a stranger——"

"My husband, dear, is not in Rome, and I have but my own pleasure to consult in taking you to my home. Are you too tired to go with me now?"

"Tired? The sight of your face has banished all my fatigue. How far have we to go?"

"About half a mile. If you prefer to walk, we can send the luggage by a facchino."

"I would much rather walk, if—if you——"

"It will not fatigue me," I replied, hastily. "I walk out every day at this time, when the dusk is coming on, and the heat of the afternoon is past. It will do me good to stroll quietly homeward through this sweet evening air."

So we groped our way down the four dark flights of stairs, and, having left the necessary directions, emerged into the piazza at the back of the Pantheon.

"And this is Rome!" said Ida, as we went along. "And this the Pantheon, where Raffaelle lies buried! And this Barbara, whom I thought I had lost forever! I feel as if I must wake presently, and find myself in my own little dormitory at Zollenstrasse-am-Main. Tell me, Barbara, am I really awake?"

"Indeed, I believe so," I replied, smiling.

"But I can not prove it."

"It is not in the least like the Rome of my dreams," continued she. "I was not prepared for shops, and cabs, and modern streets like these. I had pictured a sort of Palmyra — a wilderness of majestic ruins in the midst of the Campagna, with a kind of modern suburb, out of sight, where people lived, and slept, and ate, and drank, like other common mortals. Mercy! what strange creature is that, with the ruff and the striped stockings? He looks as if he had stepped out of a medieval German picture."

"It is one of the Pope's Swiss Guard," I replied, amused by her naïve volubility. "And now we are in the Corso—the heart of modern Rome."

"How cheerful it is here!" said she; "how much fuller of life than Florence! I have just come from Florence—I was there five weeks, in a gloomy boarding-house, in a still more gloomy street. I was so miserable! I don't know what I should have done, if it had not been for a dear, kind, disagreeable old English lady, who liked me, and took me out sometimes for a drive in the lovely country outside the walls. She was such a dear old lady. She contradicted every body, and she hated every thing foreign, and she made me laugh so! They all detested her in the boarding-house—except myself. At last she went away to join her niece in Pisa; and then the place became so intolerable that I would stay no longer."

"But the galleries and the churches—surely those delighted you?"

"Delighted me? They bewildered me. I wandered through them, like Aladdin in the garden of jewels. If I were to tell you how I felt when I first saw Michael Angelo's David standing out in the open air against the Ducal palace, or how I almost wept for joy when I found myself in presence of the Venus and the Fornarina, you would laugh at me! Was there ever such a painter's Paradise as the Uffizii? Do you remember the first long corridor, full of religious subjects of the early Tuscan school? Do you remember all those sad-looking Madonnas, each with her head a little on one side; and those stiff golden-haired angels, that hold up their hands in quaint adoration, never bending a finger? Do you remember how wonderfully the velvets and embroideries were painted? Do you remember the queer old medieval saints in court dresses, looking so like Louis the Eleventh; the St. Johns and St. Stephens in red velvet shoes, and jeweled baldrics, and elaborate doublets, each with a golden plate of glory miraculously suspended an inch above his head?"

"Indeed I do; and the amazing landscapes in the background, where uncomfortable red castles are perched on inaccessible peaks of bright blue rock, and the world seems made of nothing but coral and carbonate of copper!"

"And then the Niobe, and the Madonna della Seggiola, and the frescoes of Giotto—is it not something to have lived for, when one has seen all these? But there! one can not take up one's abode in churches and galleries; and Florence is a dreary place after three o'clock in the afternoon! Every house looks like a prison; and a *pension* full of uncongenial strangers is worse than no society at all. I often wished myself back at the College, in spite of the Raffaelles and Giottos. But you have not yet told me how you heard of my arrival in Rome?"

"By a letter which I received to-day from Professor Metz."

"Professor Metz! Then he knew where you were, and—why, to be sure, he was in Rome a few months ago! So, I suppose he met you and—how stupid of me not to have guessed that at first! How strange of him, never to tell us one word about you! And by the by, *liebe*, I do not yet know your married name. I know you only as my fellow-student, Barbara Churchill."

"Then you must know me now, dear Ida, as Barbara Carlyon," I replied.

"Barbara Carlyon! What a pretty name! Ah, dear, I always thought you would marry the Herr Farquhar, and be a grand lady, ever so much richer and finer than our Grand Duchess. I am almost disappointed that you are Mrs. Carlyon, instead. And now tell me something about your husband; but you look vexed! What have I said?"

"Nothing, dear—nothing, at least, that you could help, or I avoid. So—you like the name of Carlyon? It is one that has brought me much grief. We will not talk of my—my husband or myself, dear, just at present. The subject is a painful one, and—and—this is the Piazza di Spagna, and the church at the top of that noble flight of steps is the Trinità de' Monti. This is quite the English quarter of Rome. Up yonder lies the French Academy. We have but a few yards farther to go now."

Ida pressed my arm affectionately, and made no reply. Her joyous flow of talk was all checked, and I could see that her kind heart was troubled. As we approached the corner of the Via della Croce, we came upon a little crowd gathered round a street-singer, who was chanting some simple ballad to the accompaniment of a cracked guitar. The man's voice was deep and musical, and he wore a scarlet cap, and a long black beard, frosted here and there with silver.

"What a picturesque fellow!" exclaimed Ida. "How I should like to make a study of his head!"

"Then do so, by all means," I replied. "He would sit to you, no doubt, for a few pauls."

But she was shy, and would not speak before the bystanders; so, after lingering a moment, we passed on.

"It is strange," I said, more to myself than her; "but I seem to have seen that face before —somewhere—long ago—and yet there is something changed about it. Where could it have been? And where?"

"Perhaps in a picture," suggested Ida.

"Very likely. I dare say he has sat as a model many a time; and yet—well, Ida, this is the Vicolo d'Aliberti, and this little house with the green shutters is—home."

Thus I took my old school-friend to dwell with me in my humble lodging in the Vicolo d'Aliberti, and made her welcome; and by and by we had coffee together upon the loggia, and talked of old times till the moon rose over the brow of the Pincio. But that very night the angels of life and death stood on my threshold; and for hours it seemed doubtful whether the Almighty One would send a soul to earth, or gather two to heaven. But as suffering came with darkness, so came joy with the rising of the sun; and as the morning light poured in at the window, a little tender blossom of life was laid in my arms.

CHAPTER LIX.

THE MODEL.

"As mine own shadow was this child to me
A second self, far dearer and more fair,
Which clothed in undissolving radiancy
All those steep paths which languor and despair
Of human things, had made so dark and bare."
　　　　　　　　　SHELLEY.

MY little living flower, so fair, so placid, so fragile; to whom my love was providence, my life nourishment, my arms the world! I adored him; and he was mine—utterly mine. I was never weary of repeating this to myself, and whispering it upon his lips between the kisses—those rose-leaf lips of which I was so jealous, that, when another mouth had touched them, I hastened to kiss the stranger-kiss away, and make them once more all my own.

I was almost ashamed, at first, to let them see how I worshiped my idol. If he smiled in any face but mine, I was ready to weep with vexation. I never yielded him from my embrace without a secret pang. Only to lie and watch him as he slept on the pillow by my side was perfect content; but to lean above him when he waked—to meet the wanderings of his tiny hands—to gaze down into the clear unconscious depths of his blue eyes, was ecstasy and joy unspeakable. Day by day I beheld the sweet mystery of his growth, and entered some fresh record upon the tablets of my memory. Day by day I watched the everlasting miracle of life unfolding itself for my adoration and delight, till my heart ached with the fullness of its love, and every thought became a poem, and every act a prayer. Thus the first weeks went by, and each week my "wonder-flower" bloomed into new loveliness and strength. His beauty at first was but that angelic baby-beauty of perfect fairness and purity that almost seems to give confirmation to the poet's theory of how "Heaven lies about us in our infancy;" but before the first month of his little life was all lived out, there came a change which spoke to no heart, and was visible to no eyes but mine—a dawning of the father in his infant face, which made him, if that could be, more beloved than ever; and yet thrilled all my pleasure with a sense of bitter pain. It was not always there. When I looked for it, I could seldom see it. It came and went in flashes; an indefinable, inexplicable something no sooner seen than it vanished.

In the mean time Ida had become established as part of our little household. She tenanted the large room up-stairs; Goody acted as cook and general purveyor; and we all three took our meals together without distinction of precedence, like King Arthur and his knights of the Round Table. For the first few weeks, Ida staid almost constantly at home, surrounding me with loving cares, and indifferent to all the wonders of Rome. I with difficulty prevailed upon her once or twice to go as far as St. Peter's, or the Colosseum, or the little church of the Cappucini, where Guido's masterpiece lights all the sordid chancel, like a window opening to the sun; but I could not prevail upon her to visit the Vatican without me. She had promised herself, she said, not to see the Transfiguration, or the School of Athens, or the Communion of St. Jerome, or the Last Judgment, till we looked

upon them together; and though it were three months hence, she was determined to wait for me. From this resolution I could not move her. Meanwhile, she occupied my little studio, and painted from whatever model she could find. Of these there were always plenty haunting about the corners of the Piazza di Spagna, and the steps of the Trinità de' Monti—fierce brigands purchasable at two pauls the hour; Trasteverini Madonnas with little brown babies; majestic patriarchs whose venerable heads were the common property of all the artists in Rome; and Pifferari who were willing, for a consideration, to "pipe to the spirit ditties of no tone," at the pleasure of the hirer. Better than all these, however, she one day chanced again upon the bearded guitar-singer of the Via della Croce, and brought him home in triumph. After a sitting of two hours, she dismissed him with an appointment for the following morning, and came to me with her sketch in her hand, and her head full of projects.

"See, Barbara," said she; "it is but roughly laid in, yet what an effect already! He has a charming head—so refined, so melancholy! I have the greatest mind in the world to undertake a large picture at once, and make him my principal figure. It would do to send over to Zollenstrasse for the competition next spring; and if I do not secure this model while I can get him, I shall lose him altogether; for he is going away, he tells me, before long. What think you of Galileo before the council of Inquisitors; or Columbus laying his project before Ferdinand and Isabella? Both are good subjects; and I have studies for both in my portfolio. One is expected, you see, to do something ambitious in Rome; and—and if you do not think I should be venturing out of my depth——"

"Who dares nothing, achieves nothing," I replied, smiling. "Let me see your studies."

She ran and fetched them, radiant with excitement. Both were unusually clever; but of the two, I preferred the Columbus.

"And you really think I may venture to undertake it?" said Ida, breathlessly.

"I do, truly."

"And my model?"

"I do not see how you could have found a better. It is the face of one who has thought and suffered; the very type of the contemplative, intellectual, heroic navigator. Strange! the more I look at it, the more familiar it seems. I am certain I have seen that man somewhere—a long time ago."

"I will run at once to Dovizielli's, and order the canvas," said Ida, and was gone in a moment.

The model came again next morning at ten o'clock, and found Ida waiting for him with a canvas measuring six feet by three. I was sitting out upon the loggia in a great lounge chair, enjoying the balmy October air and the shade of the flickering vine-leaves that roofed in the trellis over head. An open book lay unread in my lap; my baby slept in his cradle at my feet; and Goody sat opposite, cutting beans for dinner.

"*Buon giorno, signore,*" said the model, taking off his cap, and bowing to each of us in succession.

"*Buon giorno,*" replied Ida. "I am going to put you in a large picture, *amico;* and I hope you will stay in Rome long enough to let me complete it."

"I hope so, signora."

"How soon shall you be leaving?"

"I do not know, signora."

"In six weeks, do you think?"

"I can not tell, signora. It does not depend on myself."

"On what does it depend, then?" asked Ida, somewhat impatiently.

The model looked grave.

"On God's will, signora," replied he, and came to the open window, outside which I was sitting.

"*Che bello fanciullo!*" he said, bending toward the cradle: "*è la sua, signora?*"

"Yes," I answered, with a flush of pride and pleasure. "He is my baby."

"He is like a snow-drop," said the model, in his musical Italian; and sighed, and turned away.

In that instant I recognized him. It was the ballad-singer of the forest of Vincennes. He looked older, and sadder, and wore a beard reaching midway to his waist; but I knew him, for all that. The recognition came upon me like a shock, bringing with it a throng of associations. I closed my eyes, and the green woods were once more waving around me, and Hugh's warm kiss was glowing on my lips. Then I remembered how I had seen the same man a few weeks later in the Champs Elysées, the very evening before my wedding-day. My husband never explained his wild conduct of that evening; and till this moment I had forgotten it as though it had never been. Ah, *dolce tempo passato!* How much joy and how much sorrow had been mine, since then! The burning tears welled up, and dropped down, one by one. No one saw them. Ida had placed the model and begun her charcoal outline; and Goody was busy with her household task. Presently my boy woke, smiling, and turned his blue eyes to the light. I snatched him to my bosom, and covered him with kisses. My poor boy, who would never know any parent's love but mine—who had not even the right to bear his father's ancient name!

Her beans finished, Goody rose and went in, leaving me alone on the loggia. I plucked a bunch of vine leaves, and, turning somewhat aside that I might not be disturbed by the sight of the model, played with my baby till the tears on my cheeks "took sunshine from his eyes." A burst of military music presently filled the air, and I saw a file of bayonets scintillating above the level of the road wall leading up to the Pincio. The tiny creature in my lap laughed and moved its little arms. I fancied he was listening to the joyous clang, and my heart throbbed tumultuously, believing that in these indications I beheld the first awakenings of the intelligent soul.

Suddenly, in the very flush of my rapture, I heard a name that seemed to stop my pulses and my breathing, and freeze the smile upon my lips.

"Capri."

Sitting there like one stunned, I lost what immediately followed. The next words which bore meaning to my ear were spoken by Ida.

"You are quite sure of what you tell me, *amico?*"

"*Certo, certo, signora.*"

"How is it that you know so much about the rigging of a vessel?"

"Signora, I have been a sailor."

"But this is a Spanish galleon of more than three hundred years ago."

"*Fa niente*, signora. No vessel lying in port would be rigged like that vessel in your picture. It is impossible. Where did the signora see the ship which she has taken for a model?"

"In an old Spanish engraving."

"And was the ship at anchor alongside the quays?"

"No; the engraving represented a fleet of galleons at sea."

"*Eccolà!* If the vessel were under way, the signora would be absolutely right; but she may rely upon it that all these ropes would be slack, and these sails furled, in harbor. I beg the signora's pardon for my boldness in naming it."

"Pray do no such thing," said Ida. "I am sincerely obliged to you for your information."

And then they were both silent.

He was Italian—he had been a sailor—he had spoken the name of Capri! He might, perhaps, know something of the history of Maddalena—he might be able to tell me something—to make many things clearer to me——Who could tell? It was not impossible. It was worth a trial. What should I do? To question him would be to tell Ida all that my pride had hitherto kept sealed in my own heart. Yet not to question him would be to abandon a chance that might never again present itself. While I was yet confused and hesitating, Ida spoke again.

"How long is it, *amico*," said she, "since you have given up the sea?"

"About three years, signora."

"You find it more profitable, I suppose, to sit to artists as a model."

"To be a model, signora, is not my calling. I told the signora so, when she requested me to sit to her."

"True; I had forgotten it. You are a ballad-singer."

"Yes, signora."

"And why have you given up the sea for street-singing. Do you earn more money by it?"

"On the contrary, signora. Where I earn two pauls by music, I could earn a scudo at sea."

"Then why abandon the sea?"

"Because—because I wished to see foreign countries, signora."

"But a sailor sees foreign countries."

"*È vero*, signora; but he only sees the ports. I wished to travel over land."

"And where have you traveled, then?" asked Ida, evidently interested and amused.

"To Paris and London, signora."

"On foot?"

"Always on foot, signora, and singing for my daily bread."

"How singular! And now, I suppose, having seen the world, you have come home to your native country for the rest of your life?"

"I know not, signora. The world is wide, and I have seen very little of it; and—and the purpose for which I traveled is yet unfulfilled. But I am going home for the present."

"Shall you go to sea again?"

"Yes, signora; I think so."

"You said you were a Neapolitan?"

"A native of Capri, signora."

"The inhabitants of those islands are mostly sailors, are they not?"

"Sailors and fishermen, signora."

"And you are a sailor."

"I am both, signora. That is to say, I am a pilot between Naples and the Grecian Archipelago; and when I am at home for a week or two, I go out fishing like the others."

I trembled—I turned cold—I laid the child down in the cradle, and bent forward with clasped hands and parted lips.

"Are you married?" asked Ida presently, in the abstracted tone of one whose thoughts are more than half engaged elsewhere.

"Yes, signora."

"Did your wife travel with you?"

"Yes, signora."

"Is she now in Rome?"

"No, signora. I sent her back to Capri some weeks since, in a sailing vessel that was leaving Livorno."

"You have no family, I suppose?"

"We had one child, signora," said the model, sadly; "but he died three years ago."

"Poor things!" exclaimed Ida, with ready sympathy. "That must have been a great sorrow for you."

"It was the will of the good God, signora," replied the model.

"Did he die in infancy?"

"No, signora. He lived to be ten years of age —such a fine, brave boy! It was very hard to art from him."

"Alas, how sad!"

"We took him to the best physician in Naples," continued the model, "and his mother made a pilgrimage to the shrine of our Lady of Loretto; but it was of no avail. The hand of God was upon him. The signora is very good to interest herself in our sorrows."

"I can only give you my sympathy, amico," said Ida. "I wish I could do more."

"No one can do more," replied the model, with a sigh.

"It is, however, some comfort to talk now and then of one's troubles."

"I never talk of them, signora. I—I sometimes wish I could. It is only the signora's great kindness and sympathy that have now led me to speak so freely."

Again the conversation dropped.

My agitation had risen to agony. My thoughts leaped from fact to fact, comparing dates, weighing possibilities, marshaling evidence, and uniting link to link, with a clearness and rapidity that seemed independent of my own volition. Maddalena's eldest brother was a pilot in Neapolitan and Greek waters — he was married —his child was born thirteen years ago, and Hugh was present at the baptism. Could all this be coincidence only? Were they never going to speak again? What would be said next? What should I do, if they remained silent! Every moment of suspense seemed like an hour.

At length Ida resumed the subject.

"You have only led this wandering life, then, since you lost your boy?" said she.

"That is all, signora."

"Ah, I understand. You traveled to forget your grief."

He made no reply.

"And shall you now go back to your old home?"

"Yes, signora."

"Will not that be very sad for you?"

"Sì, signora; ma che fare? It was my father's house. His children were born there, and beneath its roof he and our mother died. It is sad, but it is sacred. We islanders do not abandon our homes because our loved ones are gone."

"Who has taken care of the place for you all this time?"

"No one, signora. It is locked up, and the priest has the key. Our neighbors will not suffer the garden to fall to ruin; and there are no robbers in the island. We shall find every thing as we left it."

"But you spoke just now of your father's family. Have you no brothers or sisters to welcome you back?"

The model shook his head.

"I had one brother, signora," said he; "but he has been dead many years. He was drowned at sea."

"Alas!—and no sisters?"

"I—I have neither father nor mother, brother nor sister," replied the model, gloomily. "My wife and I are alone in the world together."

I rose up—sat down again—shuddered from head to foot. Every word that he spoke added confirmation to my suspicions. His very reservations were testimonies. He was Paolo— I knew he was Paolo—the beloved brother of Maddalena, whom Hugh had never seen; whom he twice met, therefore, without recognition. The one drowned at sea was the sullen Jacopo. But the wife—the wife to whom I had given the five-franc piece that evening in the Champs Elysées—Hugh had known her, and hence his agitation when the light fell on her face! I felt that I must question him, cost what it might.!

The next silence was interrupted by the model.

"The signora is not Italian," said he.

"No," replied Ida, "I am Bavarian."

"Bavarian?" repeated he. "I never heard of that nation."

"Bavaria is a part of Germany," said Ida. "A Bavarian is a German; as a Neapolitan is an Italian."

"Capito, signora," replied he, thoughtfully; and then, after a pause, added, "I—I thought the signora might be English. There are so many English in Rome."

"Yes, very many," rejoined Ida, absorbed in her work. "The head a little more toward the left shoulder, if you please. No—that is too much—there—just so."

"The signora has, perhaps, been in England?" pursued the model.

"No, never — do not move, pray — why do you ask?"

"Oh — it is of no consequence, signora."

"My friend here is English," said Ida, "and a Londoner."

I could resist the impulse no longer.

"Ida!" I said. "Ida, come here—come to me, liebe."

She laid down her brush, and came directly.

"Ach, lieber Gott! how pale you are. What is the matter?"

"I want to speak to that man, Ida—alone."

"To the model?" stammered she, amazed.

"To the model, darling. I — I think I know something of his family — his private history. Will you stay here while I speak to him?"

"I will go up-stairs to my room, if you please."

"No need, *liebe*. Take care of baby while I am gone."

And with this I went in, closing the window after me, and, taking Ida's seat, said —

"I am English, *amico*. Can I do any thing for you? Have you any friends in my country about whom I can help you to inquire?"

He colored up, and paused a moment before replying.

"*Grazie*, signora," he said. "I have a friend who—who went to England—who may be in England now, if she yet lives. But I have lost sight of her."

"Was she a relation?"

"Yes, signora."

"Your sister, perhaps?"

"Ye—yes, signora."

"Then it was in search of her, I suppose, that you undertook the journey of which I heard you speaking just now?"

He bent his head somewhat reluctantly, as if annoyed at having to confess it.

"How long is it since she went to England?"

"I—I can not tell, signora. I only know that she has been in England since she—left Capri?"

"How long is it, then, since she left Capri?"

"About thirteen years. But it is of no use, lady. You can not help us. She is gone, and we shall never see her or hear of her again."

"You can not tell. The lost sometimes reappear when we least expect to find traces of them. How do you know that your sister has been in England?"

"She wrote to me, signora; and the letter bore the English post-mark."

"Did she give you no address?"

"None."

"How long since was this?"

"About five years ago, signora."

"Why did she leave Capri, and with whom?"

"Pardon, signora. Those questions I can not answer."

"Nay, how can I hope to help you, if you will not freely tell me all?"

"I—I can not, signora."

I rose, and looked out from the loggia. Ida had withdrawn to the farthest corner with my baby in her arms, and was playing with him as if he were a child herself. Satisfied that she heard nothing, I resumed my seat.

"Listen," I said. "I once heard of a young girl—the sister of two sailors whose home was in the island of Capri—as it might be your sister, and your home. One of these brothers was married, as you might be; and the young sister, and the young wife, and the two brothers, all dwelt under the same roof, and were one family. The elder brother was a pilot, as you say you were. He went to sea, and while he was at sea, his wife brought a little infant into the world."

The model lifted his head sharply, and uttered a suppressed guttural exclamation.

"There came to Capri about this time," I continued, "a rich English gentleman. The young girl fell in love with him, and——"

"*Ah, Dio!* her name? Her name?"

"Maddalena."

He sprang forward—he fell at my feet—he kissed the hem of my garment.

"Signora—for the love of God! Where is she, dear signora, blessed signora, *la sorellina mia*—my sister, whom I have sought with bleeding feet and aching heart? Speak, signora, where is she?"

"Alas!" I said, almost as much agitated as himself, "that I can not tell you. I only know that she was living and well, a year ago."

"Did you see her?"

"A friend of mine who had seen her, told me her story."

"Was she unhappy?"

"No—she was melancholy; very studious; very quiet; a student of many books."

"And poor, signora?"

"No, not poor."

"And that *maladetto Inglese*—what of him? Had he abandoned her?"

"Abandoned her? No—that could not be. She was his wife."

"His wife?"

"Yes—he married her."

Paolo sprang to his feet, and laughed bitterly.

"Impossible," said he. "She was married already."

My heart leaped up in my bosom—my whole being was flooded with a tide of inexpressible joy.

"Married already?" I repeated. "But—but perhaps a divorce——"

"No, no, no, signora. Our church knows no divorce. Besides, her husband is still living in Capri."

I shaded my face with my hand, lest it should betray me. I was dizzy with happiness.

"No," continued Paola, sternly. "He seduced her—he stole her away from a good man and an honorable home. She might have been a happy woman now, but for him, with children's faces about her hearth."

"But are you sure that he stole her away?" I faltered.

"What does the signora mean?"

"I—I have heard that she fled to him of her own will, for protection—that he found her hidden on board his vessel after he had put to sea; and that, in short, she—threw herself upon his mercy."

Paola struck a heavy blow upon the table with his clenched fist.

"I do not believe it," he said violently.

"I also heard that she abhorred the man to whom she was married."

"I do not believe that either. I can understand that she did not love him. He was old—old enough to be her father; but she need not have married him. I would not believe it, signora, unless she told me so herself."

"And supposing that she did tell you so herself?"

"Then I should despise her."

"Nay, you would forgive and pity her."

He paused, and passed his hand across his brow.

"Well—I suppose I should, signora," he said, slowly. "She was my darling. She was like my own child. Our father, with his last breath, bade me love and cherish her. Yes, poor Maddalena—I should forgive her, and pity her."

"And—and you would forgive him, too?"

"The Englishman?"

"Yes, the Englishman."

"I took an oath that I would be revenged upon him," said Paolo. "We are not mere peasants, signora. We are untaught, and we are poor; but our father's father could count back for generations, to the time when our name was noble, and half the island was ours. We prize our honor, signora, as jealously as if we were noble still; and I swore to avenge our disgrace upon Maddalena's lover, if I ever met him, face to face."

"But if the fault were hers?"

"The disgrace is still ours, signora."

"Then punish the one who brought it upon you—Maddalena herself."

"She is punished long since," replied Paolo. "*Povera* Maddalena!"

"But——"

"But my oath, signora."

"To keep that oath would be more wicked than to break it. Are you a Christian?"

"Signora, I am an Italian."

"Enough," I said, rising in anger. "You shall never find your sister."

"Signora!"

"I know who that Englishman is. He is the dear friend of my friend, and I will not betray him to your ignorant vengeance. I could have helped you. Now it is over. They shall be warned of you; and you will never see Maddalena's face again."

He turned pale, and the tears rose to his eyes.

"*Cara signora*," he stammered, "*per pietà* ——"

I turned to the window; but he caught my hand.

"I—I will promise what you please," he cried; "if—if she confesses that she fled to him unasked—I will forego my oath—I will do anything, if you but give me Maddalena!"

"I can not give her to you," I said. "I can but cause inquiry to be made. I know no more where she is at this moment than yourself."

"Then will you inquire, signora?"

"I do not know. How can I be sure that you will keep faith with me?"

"I swear it, signora."

"That is not enough."

He took a little metal cross from his bosom, fell on his knees, and kissed it devoutly.

"By my belief in the mercy of God, and the intercession of the blessed mother of Christ; by my hopes of forgiveness in the world to come; by my faith in the holy Saint Paolo, my patron saint; and by the memory of my father and mother, whose souls I trust are in heaven."

The solemnity with which he uttered this pledge left no room for doubt.

"I believe you," I said; "and I will do what I can. In the mean time, go back to Capri, and leave all in my hands. If any living soul can help you to find your sister, I am that person. Be satisfied with this assurance, and be patient. It may be months before I succeed in even hearing of her; for I can only use remote and circuitous means. But such means as I can command shall be employed. This you may rely upon."

He rose, and kissed my hand.

"I will pray for you, signora, night and day," said he.

"Then we understand each other?"

"Wholly, signora."

"And you consent to all my conditions?"

"All, and absolutely."

I was about to open the window and recall Ida, when another thought occurred to me, and I paused with my hand upon the lock.

"What was the name of this Englishman?" I asked.

"Does not the signora know it?"

"I can—ascertain it; but it might save time if you could give it to me correctly."

"Alas! signora, I can not. My brother and wife called him Signor Hugo; but that was only his baptismal name. His other name was harsh and difficult, and they could not remember it."

"Well, we must try to do without it."

"Stay, signora, I have this book—he left it at our cottage, and there is writing in it. I have always carried it about with me, in the hope that it might some day be of use. See—here are words in pencil!"

It was a tiny volume of the Georgics of Virgil, bound in old stained vellum, with the initials H. F. on the title-page, and a few explanatory notes in his careless hand, scrawled here and there upon the margins.

"Is this the only proof you have?"

"Yes, signora."

"You had better leave it with me. To one who knew his writing, it might perhaps help to identify him; but you are not even sure, I suppose, that it is his writing?"

"I believe it, signora; but I can not be sure."

"*Ebbene*, we must have patience."

"I have had patience for so many years, signora, that I can well be patient now. You have given me hope, *gentilissima signora*, and I was well-nigh despairing."

"Hope, then, friend Paolo; and believe that I will do all I can to restore your lost sister to her home."

"The saints bless and watch over you, signora."

I opened the window, recalled Ida, took my baby from her arms, and with a hasty kiss and a whispered "thanks, *liebe*," ran to my bedroom, and locked the door. There my first impulse was to lay him down upon a sofa, fall on my knees beside him, and cover him with kisses and tears of joy.

No stain now upon his birth—no shame attaching to his innocent life—my boy, my darling, my own! Some day he shall bear his ancient name—some day, though I may not live to see it, he shall hold his own under his ancestral roof, and keep up the olden dignity of Farquhar of Broomhill! Oh, blessed, blessed certainty! What a bright world it had become within the short space of this last half-hour; and yet—and yet the tears, the foolish, hot, rebellious tears kept raining down, as if I were not, even now, as happy as I ought to be.

Were they tears of joy?

A difficult question. They were not tears of sorrow; and yet there was sorrow in the joy, and bitter mingling with the sweet, and shadow with the sunshine. Possibly there may also have been something of self-questioning as to the past. At all events I wept, and could not stay from weeping.

CHAPTER LX.

THE TORSO OF THE BELVEDERE.

How was I to keep my promise to Paolo? This question "teased me out of thought;" haunted me by day, and troubled my sleep by night. If the disclosure of my real position toward my husband had been productive of great comfort, it was also fruitful in anxieties. I had, in truth, undertaken a task which I knew not how to fulfill. I had no one to counsel me; no one to aid me. If I sought advice I betrayed my secret. If I set inquiries on foot by opening a correspondence with any of my friends or family, I betrayed my incognito. My pride forbade that I should take any steps which might seem to pave the way toward a reconciliation with my husband. My poverty made it impossible that I should employ expensive and secret means for the prosecution of such inquiries as were necessary. At the same time, I desired Maddalena's removal with a passionate eagerness that only made the powerlessness of my position doubly bitter. Tormented by doubts, and wearied out by vain thinking, I sadly needed some wise friend upon whose judgment I could rest. My own passions were my only advisers; and from such counselors as pride, resentment, jealousy, and wounded love, what temperate verdict could be expected to result? In this painful incertitude some weeks went by; and still nothing was done. Anxiety began to tell upon me, and I grew daily paler and thinner. As for Paolo, I avoided him as though he were my creditor, and shrunk from his questioning face like a guilty creature. Alas! how—how was I to keep my promise?

About this time, when my boy was nearly three months old, and my perplexities were at their hight, I fulfilled another promise, long-delayed, and went with Ida to the Vatican. We chose a private day, locked up our rooms, and took Goody with us to carry the baby.

It was a delicious day, mild and sunny; the date, I think, the second of December; the atmosphere May; the sky a cloudless dome of infinite blue, softened by a tender haze that melted into gray on the horizon. We crossed the courtyard, in which three or four carriages were waiting, and began with the gallery of inscriptions, and the Musco Chiaramonti; neither of which possessed any attraction for my impatient companion. Her desires were winged, and flew direct to the Transfiguration, and the Stanze of Raffaelle. She longed to run, that she might be there the sooner. Thus we came to the vestibule of the Torso, and stood in presence of that grand fragment, the divine ideal of all physical power, which confers eternal glory upon the name of "Apollonius, son of Nestor of Athens." Here she forgot her impatience, and wandered round and round the wondrous ruin, silent in admiration. Then we talked of Michael Angelo, and his worshiping study of it, and of all he said he owed to it through life. And then I told Ida of how, when he was old and blind, he used to cause himself to be led into the room where it stood, that he might pass his wise hands over it and feel the beauty that he could no longer see.

"C'est joli," said a grave voice, close by.

"Question de goût!" replied something rustling past in silks and perfumes.

"Well!" ejaculated a third, "I call it frightful rubbish, and I don't care who says to the contrary."

"I declare, Barbara, it's my dear disagreeable old lady of Pisa!" exclaimed Ida.

But I had recognized her for myself already. Turning involuntarily at the sound of those well-known accents, I found myself face to face with—Mrs. Sandyshaft.

"Eh? What? Mercy alive! Hilda—Hilda, look here! Bab, as I live and breathe!"

"My dear aunt!"

"Dear aunt—dear aunt, indeed! Dear fiddlestick! There, what's the good of kissing, when you've—you've—you've half broken my heart, you—somebody give me a smelling-bottle—I'm making a fool of myself."

We both made fools of ourselves, if to laugh, cry, kiss, and speak, all in a breath, be the way to do it. The truth was that we loved each other dearly; hardly conscious of how much till we were parted, and never demonstrating it unless under the influence of strong emotion. Now, however, we clung together as though we never meant to be parted again.

"Well, Barbara," said Hilda, wiping away a natural tear or two, "I must say I am very glad to have found you at last; but how could you do such a—such an excessively vulgar thing as to run away in this ridiculous manner?"

"Yes; my Goodness Gracious, yes! What on earth made you run away, you little fool?" gasped my aunt, wiping her eyes with one hand, and holding me fast with the other. "Why, in heaven's name, have you made us all miserable for a whole twelvemonth?—costing us a fortune in advertising, and what not; and dragging me out of my comfortable home into all manner of filthy, barbarous, uncivilized foreign countries, where soap and water's an unknown luxury, and the beds mere sacks of fleas, if not worse! And at my time of life too! You ought to be ashamed of yourself, and I hope you are; and if you're not, you're worse than I took you to be!"

At which moment, the Count de Chaumont, who had discreetly retired into the background, came forward, solemnly polite as ever, and raising his hat a quarter of an inch from his head, said—

"Madame, j'ai l'honneur de vous saluer."

"I'll tell you what it is, Bab," said my aunt, when the first shock of our meeting was somewhat over, "now I've caught you, I don't mean to lose sight of you. You must come home with me to my hotel, and there I shall keep you; and we'll go at once, too, and have our talk out; for I must have the whole story of your vagabondizing, you little idiot, from beginning to end."

"But I have a friend with me," I began, "and——"

"You must give your friend her dismissal for to-day," interrupted my aunt, "and tell her you live in future at the Hôtel d'Angleterre, where she may come to see you, if she likes."

"But we live in lodgings together——"

"Live in fiddlesticks together! Don't I tell you, child, you live with me? I won't be contradicted. Where's your friend? Oh, I see—

that young woman over yonder. Well, go and tell her that I'm your aunt, and I've taken lawful possession of you, and you're going home with me straightway."

"If I do," said I, desperately, "I must bring the baby.

"The WHAT?" shrieked my aunt.

"The baby."

"*Whose* baby?"

"Mine."

My aunt said not another word, but deliberately sat down on an antique colossal foot near which she happened to be standing, and shut her eyes in silence.

"This is too much," she said faintly, after a pause of several seconds. "I had not expected this of you, Bab. To—to run away was bad enough; but to commit the additional folly of a baby—Ugh! is the monster here?"

"He's not a monster!" I replied, indignantly. "He's the most beautiful baby you ever saw in your life!"

"Bring him here," said my aunt, still with her eyes shut.

I beckoned to Goody to come forward.

"Now look, if you please, aunt, and see if he deserves to be called a—what I can not bring my lips to call him again."

"Is he there?"

"Yes."

My aunt opened one eye cautiously; then the other; stared at him as if he were some strange invention; touched his cheek with the extreme tip of her forefinger, as if she feared he might explode like a grenade; and said nothing.

"Really, a very fine child," observed Hilda, patronizingly. "How old is he, dear?"

"Nearly three months."

"*Madame,*" said the Count, sententiously, "*je vous en fais mes compliments.*"

But still my aunt said nothing.

I felt piqued; and, not caring to linger there for her opinion on my darling, turned away, and went over to where Ida was sitting quietly in a corner, waiting till I should have time to remember her presence. A few words of explanation sufficed. We shook hands; said farewell for the day—and behold, on turning suddenly round, I caught my aunt in the very act of surreptitiously kissing the baby, when she thought I was not looking!

CHAPTER LXI.

MRS. SANDYSHAFT IN THE CHARACTER OF A MEDIATOR.

"AND now," said my aunt, drawing her chair opposite to mine, and settling herself for a thorough cross-examination;" now that we are alone and quiet, be so good as to tell me, Bab, what you think of yourself?"

Sitting there, face to face with Mrs. Sandyshaft, in that dreary private sitting-room of the Hôtel d'Angleterre, with Goody and the baby banished to an adjoining bedroom, and a searching semi-judicial process coming on, I felt myself fortified by an unwonted spirit of resistance, and made up my mind on no account to say what I did think of myself, whatever the provocation.

"In what way do you mean, my dear aunt?" I asked, smiling.

"In every way. As a niece, for instance—as a daughter—as a wife. You did not suppose it would be very pleasant for me to have you run away, heaven only knew where, and be living, heaven only knew how—did you? You did not suppose your father would be particularly delighted to have a public scandal attaching to his daughter's name—did you? You did not suppose you were acting up to your marriage vows, or doing much in the way of loving, honoring, and obeying your lawful husband, when you took it into your head to desert his roof—did you? A pretty dance you have led all your friends, to be sure; and a pretty goose you have made of yourself, into the bargain!"

"My dear, dear aunt," I said, "that *you* should have missed me, and grieved for me, and sought for me—that *you* should have departed from the habits of a long life, surmounted the prejudices of years, and encountered all the discomforts of foreign travel for my sake——"

"Discomforts enough and to spare, goodness knows!" ejaculated my aunt, parenthetically.

"—touches me to a degree that I hardly know how to express to you in words. It fills me with so much gratitude—I might almost say, with so much remorse——"

"Ay, you may say it indeed. Plenty of room for it!" muttered my aunt.

"—to think that any conduct of mine (however justifiable on other grounds) should have been the cause of all this pain to you, that I feel I can only offer you, in compensation, the devotion and companionship of my life. I will never leave you again, dear, if you care to have me!"

"Humph!" said my aunt, softened, but dubious.

"As for my father," I continued, "his pride alone has suffered in my disappearance. He has loved me so little all my life, that I must confess I attach but trifling importance to any effect my conduct may have produced upon him."

"Well, so far, that's all well and good," replied my aunt, "but as for your husband——"

"As for Mr. Farquhar, aunt, you are, certainly, the last person by whom I should expect to be called to account in this question of separation."

"And why so, pray?" asked she, sharply.

"Because you never liked him—at least, never since he became my husband."

"I've liked him a vast deal better, poor fellow! since your misconduct toward him," said she, with a resolute shake of the head.

"And because you were so annoyed and disappointed, on learning the choice I had made."

"No reason why I should not wish you to conduct yourself like a respectable married woman, when once you had made it!"

"And because, whenever you found the opportunity, you said every thing in your power to unsettle my faith in his stability, and my respect for himself."

"More fool I!" said my aunt. "I ought to have known better."

I did not contradict her. I had come to the end of my retort in all its clauses, and waited for what she should say next.

"And pray where have you been these twelve months?" asked she, after a brief pause.

"Here—in Rome."

"Humph! and what have you been doing?"

"Well, I had a brain-fever, to begin with, and lay ill at Civita Vecchia for several weeks. Since then, I have supported myself by copying the old masters."

"Are you in debt?"

"Not a farthing—stay; I must not forget that I owe my old servant fifty pounds, which were the savings of her whole life, and which she lent to me when we left—Broomhill."

"She shall have them back to-day," said Mrs. Sandyshaft, promptly. "And now, ma'am, may I make so bold as to inquire what your name may have been all this time; for if it had been either Farquhar or Churchill, I must have found you long since."

"I have called myself Mrs. Carlyon."

"Carlyon," repeated she, musingly. "Carlyon—I'm sure I've heard the name somewhere. Bless you! I have had the passport books searched at all the principal ports, and the Lord knows what besides; but it was no good. Nobody could tell me any thing about you; and here you turn up, at last, by chance! Just like your perversity."

"You would rather have hunted me down, I suppose, in fair chase," said I, with a laugh.

"I would rather have had something for my money," replied Mrs. Sandyshaft. "Why, Bab, you scamp, you've cost me—well, never mind what you've cost me. More than you're worth from head to foot, I can tell you. As for Hugh, he's spent hundreds in the search."

"Indeed?"

"Indeed!" echoed my aunt, angrily. "You may curl up your lip, and drawl 'indeed' as superciliously as you please; but he's worth a dozen of you, for all that! And you've never once asked for him yet! You don't know whether he's alive or dead, I suppose? No—not you. He may be dead twice over, for aught you can tell."

"He may be dead, my dear aunt," said I, affecting a profound indifference; "but I do not really see how he could possibly be so twice over."

"We all die twice," replied she. "The first time is when we simply cease to be; the second, when we are forgotten."

"Dear aunt," I exclaimed, "that is very well said!"

"Well said, or ill said, it's nothing to the purpose," she retorted sharply. "You needn't trouble to compliment me. I don't value it one farthing. I value good feeling, and common-sense, and principle, a mighty deal more than compliments, I can tell you."

"I hope," said I, turning red and feeling somewhat nettled, "that you do not think me wanting in either good feeling or principle?"

"Indeed I do, though. A woman who runs away from her husband for no reasonable cause——"

"I beg your pardon. I had what seemed to me an absolutely reasonable cause."

"Fiddlededee! you acted on mad impulse. Reason had nothing whatever to do with it."

"Again, I must beg your pardon——"

"You'd better beg your husband's pardon," interrupted my aunt.

"You can not tell under what impressions I acted or what provocation I received."

"Then you're just wrong; for I know all about it, from beginning to end."

"How——"

"Hold your tongue, Bab, and I'll tell you. The night you came home from Lord Bayham's ball, you overheard a conversation between your husband and—somebody else. You interpreted what you heard according to your notions. You asked for no explanations. You sought nobody's advice. You 'reasoned' about as much as a child that's frightened by a shadow. The consequence was that you acted like a fool, and ran away. I dare say you thought it very fine, and heroic, and dramatic, and all that sort of thing. Nobody else did; that's one comfort."

"But how do you know that I overheard that conversation, and how can you tell what that conversation was about?"

"You goose, you dropped something down by the door at which you listened—some trinket or another, that was found there afterward by the servants, and given to your husband. Of course, the mystery of your flight was at once explained. He remembered all that had been said, and guessed the wise conclusions to which you had jumped. It was as plain as a pikestaff."

"And then, I suppose, went to you with the story of his wrongs," said I, bitterly.

"He came to me," replied my aunt, very gravely, "believing that I knew where to find you—full of regret for all his past follies, and of self-reproach for every weak concession of which he had been guilty. Full of love and pity for you, also—which you didn't deserve. You heard her ask him to call her wife, and he was ass enough to do it. She was no more his wife than I'm his grandmother."

"I know that now," said I; "but I would not believe an angel from heaven who should tell me she was never his mistress!"

"Of course she was his mistress—he doesn't deny it; but that was twelve or thirteen years ago."

"He seduced her away from a good husband and a respectable home," said I, quoting Paolo, "and brought her——"

"He did no such a thing," interposed my aunt. "She fell in love with him, and hid herself on board his yacht, like a bold hussy as she was!"

"Oh, of course you defend him, if only to blame me!" I exclaimed, working myself up to a pitch of genuine anger. "Perhaps you are of opinion that an English gentleman may with propriety maintain his wife and his mistress under the same roof?"

"I think nothing of the kind. I can not so much blame him for having yielded to the first temptation, when he was young, and free, and the woman threw herself at his feet. No man could have helped himself in such a case—unless it was Saint Anthony; and I'm not one of those who believe in your miracles of virtue. But what I blame him for, was letting her remain at Broomhill after he had brought you home. There was his great fault."

"A fault which nothing can excuse."

"Humph! I won't say that, Bab. I won't say that. The poor thing was nothing to him but a woman who had loved him to her own cost and suffering—who had been nothing to him for years and years before he cared for you—who had given all her mind up to books and study;

and whose only happiness in life was to live like a mouse under a corner of his roof, and take care of his library, and kiss the dust he trod upon, if he would but let her. He hadn't the heart to turn her out, Bab. It was weak. It was culpably weak; but the last straw breaks the camel's back, Bab—and the last blow sometimes breaks a woman's heart. She might have died, Bab; and that wouldn't have been a pleasant thought for Hugh Farquhar, all the rest of his life."

"Hugh Farquhar seems to have found an excellent advocate," said I, steeling myself against compassion.

"That was his first great fault," continued Mrs. Sandyshaft, taking no notice of my observation. "The second was just such another piece of weakness. When you found out that she lived in the house, he should have trusted to your generosity, and told you all. Half-truths often do more mischief than lies. If that's a proverb, it's one of my own making. It's true anyhow, and here's a case in point."

"Any other woman would have felt and believed as I did."

"Very likely; but she wouldn't have run away as you did, without waiting to ask whether her beliefs and feelings were founded on facts."

"I—I confess that I acted hastily," said I, reluctantly.

"The first word of sense you've spoken yet."

"I'm much obliged to you."

"Bab—will you listen to good advice if one takes the trouble to offer it?"

"Certainly."

"Then just sit down at my desk yonder, and write to your husband. You confess you acted hastily—confess it to him. Say you're sorry for your own follies, and ready to forgive his; and make an end of the matter."

"I'll do no such thing—I would die first!"

"And why, pray?"

"Because it is he who has been in the wrong from first to last. I committed an error of precipitation—he a deliberate offense. You seem to forget, aunt, how my pride has been insulted, and my trust deceived!"

"I grant he was a great fool to keep her there, and worse than a fool not to admit all while he was about it; but there! he's suffered enough for his faults, goodness knows."

"He deserved to suffer," said I; "but what have his sufferings been, compared with mine?"

"Pretty equal, I should say," observed my aunt, coolly.

"Nay, this is too much! Has he suffered jealousy, fever, despair, exile, shame? Has he believed our marriage illegal? Has he undergone the misery of toiling for his daily bread under every pressure of mental unrest and physical weakness?"

"He has been ill both in body and mind; and as for unrest, one would think the poor man had St. Vitus's dance, to see him always pacing up and down the room; getting up from his chair as soon as he has sat down; wandering about the park and the roads in all weathers; off to-day to London; back again to-morrow at Broomhill; off to Dover, or Calais, or Marseilles the next day; coming back after having traveled day and night for a week, with his clothes all covered with mud and dust, and his hat so battered that

you wouldn't pick it out of the gutter, and his neckcloth tied all on one side, as if he was going to be hanged by it! I'm sure I've often thought he looked more like a maniac than a man in his senses. And then he begins a sentence and stops, forgetting what he meant to say next; and then pulls a map out of his pocket, and begins to show you how his wife must have gone in this direction, or that; and how, if he had only thought of it sooner, he must have overtaken her! Then he looks twenty years older; for what with his bad nights, and his gray hairs——"

"Gray hairs?" I exclaimed. "Hugh Farquhar gray?"

"As a badger," replied my aunt; "and as thin and pallid as if he had lived on opium all his life. Nobody who hadn't seen him within the last year would know him in the street. Why, the perpetual traveling would alone have killed most men. He's been twice to Zollenstrasse; ever so many times to Paris; once here, as far as Rome, even—and never with any reward for his pains. But what's the good of telling you all this? You don't care to hear it!"

"I do care, indeed," I said, unable to control the faltering of my voice, and turning away, so as to shade my face with my hand.

"Humph! if you did, you'd write the letter."

"No, Aunt Sandyshaft," I replied, struggling to speak firmly. "I would not write the letter., I—I can not but grieve at the picture you put before me. It wrings my heart to know that the husband whom I have so much loved—whom I still so much love—should be so changed and shattered; but—but if my heart were to break for it, nothing should induce me to write that letter. Nothing—so it is mere waste of time to ask me."

"All very fine," said my aunt; "but what does it mean? I suppose you don't intend to stay in Rome all the rest of your days, and live by copying the old masters, as you call 'em?"

"I did not say that."

"What do you say then? Speak plain English, Bab; for I don't understand heroics."

"It means this, aunt—that before I touch his hand again in reconciliation, before I cross his threshold as his wife, that woman must be given back to her own people, and banished out of my sight forever. As to tolerating her beneath my roof——"

"Nobody's asked you to tolerate her," interrupted Mrs. Sandyshaft. "Of course she'll be sent away, neck and crop. Do you think I'd let you go back, with that hussy in the house?"

"Let all this be done; and let him ask my pardon for not having done it before I ever passed the gates of Broomhill, and then——"

"And then, when there's nothing left to write about, and he's probably rushed off to Rome as if he'd been shot out of a cannon, you'll condescend to write. Is that it, Bab?"

"Yes."

"Oh, very well; then we understand each other. But in the mean time somebody must inform him that your ladyship is found, and communicate your high and mighty conditions—eh?"

"Clearly; but I must dictate the letter."

"Who's to write it?"

"Nobody so fit as yourself."

"Then I write it my own way—that's flat."

"Nonsense, my dear aunt! In a matter so utterly concerning myself——"

"I'm not a puppet," said Mrs. Sandyshaft, with an obstinate jerk of the head. "I've capacity enough to write a simple letter, I should hope; and I won't write at any body's dictation, if I know it."

"But this is not a 'simple' letter. It is a very important letter; and a great deal depends on the way in which it is worded. My own dignity and self-respect demand that——"

"Bother your dignity and self-respect! Think a little less about both, Bab, and more about that poor, miserable fellow, who's never known a moment's peace, day or night, since you left him. And as for the letter, tell me what you want said, and I'll say it; but I won't have it dictated."

"Then I won't have it written."

"Oh, very well! Please yourself."

"And, remember, Aunt Sandyshaft, that it is you, now, who are raising up obstacles."

"Fiddlededee!"

"And—and some day," sobbed I, "you'll perhaps, be sorry that—that you re—re—fused—"

"Bab, this is temper—temper and nothing else. It won't do with me. You may write your letter yourself, if you like; or you may get Hilda to write it. But if I do it, I do it my own way, and there's an end of it."

At this moment there came a gentle tap at the door, and Goody looked in.

"It's past three o'clock, deary, and asking your pardon, ma'am, for the intrusion, but the dear blessed little angel is very restless; and it's getting dusk already; and out after dark, my lamb, he should not be."

"That's quite true, Goody, and I was a cruel, thoughtless creature to forget it. There, you see, I've only my bonnet to put on, and I'm ready in a moment. Good-by, Aunt Sandyshaft —here is my address, if you care to come and see me. It's close by—not a quarter of a mile hence; and—and if, after I am gone, you think better of your decision, and like to come round and take tea with me at seven o'clock, we can talk over the subject of the letter. I am sure you will think differently when you have time to reflect. Give my love to Hilda, and tell her I hope to see her again to-morrow. Here, Goody —give the darling to me. I will carry him downstairs myself."

And with this, I hurried away, down the great stone staircase, and home by the back streets and short cuts, as fast as I could walk; pausing only once, for a couple of minutes, at the English baker's in the Via Condotti, to buy some English muffins for my aunt's tea.

For I felt certain she would come.

How slowly the hours of that afternoon went by! How restless I was, and how my certainty faded away and diminished as seven o'clock drew near!

"She is so obstinate," thought I. "She never can see that she has been in the wrong. But then she is just, after all; and she must admit that I have a right to the principal voice in a matter so vitally concerning myself. Will she come? Or will she pique herself on staying away, and making me go to her first? If she meant to come, she would surely be here now! and yet——"

I went to the bedroom window every moment. I heaped fresh logs on the fire; placed her chair ready in the warmest corner; trimmed the lamp; peeped at the muffins; solaced myself every now and then with a cautious glance at my darling sleeping in his little cot; and listened, with a beating heart, to every sound upon the stairs. At last, just as my watch pointed to a quarter past the time, and I was ready to sit down and weep for disappointment, the door opened and my aunt walked in.

I sprang to meet her with a cry of delight— kissed her—helped her off with her cloak—ran to fetch a stool for her feet—poured out our first cups of tea, and, having helped her to a slice of muffin, took her by both hands, and said—

"Now, you dear old thing, since you have been so nice, and kind, and good, and have yielded this point so sweetly, I'll yield a point too. You shall write the letter your own way, while you're here to-night; and I'll just look over your shoulder, and put in a word here and there."

"Humph! the post went out at four, my dear," replied my aunt, drily, "and my letter with it. But I thought I'd come and tell you— and, upon my word, this is the first drop of tea, deserving the name of tea, that I've tasted since I left England."

CHAPTER LXII.

SUSPENSE.

HUGH, it appeared, was on the point of starting for Chambery when my aunt last heard from him, and had requested her, in case of emergency, to write to him at that place. He was led thither, it seemed, by some vague report, hoping against hope, but prepared for the inevitable disappointment which always awaited him. "I go," he wrote, "but I know beforehand that I go in vain. She is lost to me forever. Some day, perhaps, when I am quite worn out with long seeking, I may find her grave in some solitary spot, among the graves of strangers. God grant it! I would fain die there, and be laid beside her." My aunt gave me this letter. I carried it in my bosom by day; slept with it under my pillow at night; blistered it all over with my tears. Mine was a mere make-believe stoicism, surface-deep and sadly transparent, after all.

From Rome to Chambery:—I looked in the map, and was dismayed to see how far apart they lay, and what a world of mountains lay between. I went down to the post-office, and was told that letters to Chambery might be dispatched via Turin or Marseilles. In either case they would take from five to six days—as long as if sent to London! I then made my way to the Hôtel d'Angleterre, to ask Mrs. Sandyshaft by which route she had directed her letter to be forwarded; and received for answer that she "hadn't troubled her head about routes, or branches either. Not she. She had just put Post Office, Chambery, Savoy—and quite enough. The Where was all that concerned her; the How she left to those whose business it was to convey it."

Thus poorly comforted, I could only sit down patiently, counting out each lagging hour of the six long days, and feeding my imagination with conjectures of every possible calamity that might befall my aunt's letter.

Supposing, now, that the address was illegible! A hand more essentially crabbed and distort, when written in haste, it would be difficult to conceive. And she must have written in haste; for it was past three when I left her, and the letter had to be posted by four o'clock. Supposing, on the other hand, that it went *viâ* Turin, and the mail was robbed among the mountains — or by sea, and the steamer were lost? Supposing, even, that it arrived safely at Chambery, and Hugh were gone before it came? Would it, in that case, be forwarded to Broomhill? or would it lie there month after month, dusty and unclaimed, with its words of hope and comfort all unread?

Thus five days went by. On the fifth, I said, "To-morrow he will receive it." On the sixth, "To-day it is his." I fancied him calling listlessly at the post-office as he passed by; or finding it in the morning on his breakfast-table. I pictured to myself the impatient sigh with which he would toss it aside, incredulous of any good it might contain — the reluctance with which he would presently break the seal — the sudden flash lighting up his poor pale face — the bound that he would make to the bell; the ringing voice in which he would call for post-horses; the instantaneous transition from apathy to energy, from that state of hope deferred which maketh the heart sick, to hope fulfilled, glowing, radiant, and instinct with vitality.

As the day advanced, and the evening drew on, I said to myself, "He is on his way. He will travel day and night. Every mile will seem a league to his impatience, and every hour a week." Then I calculated how long the journey would take him, if he came by Turin, Genoa, and the sea; and found that he might quite possibly arrive by the evening of the third day. At this thought, I trembled and turned pale.

Only two days more! I could not believe it. My aunt came to sit with me in the morning, while I was painting; and Hilda brought her carriage to take me for a drive, later in the day. I forgot where we went, or what was said or done by the way. I thought of nothing but Hugh.

Only one day more! I went through my morning's work mechanically, breaking off, every now and then, to kiss my baby, and whisper in his little uncomprehending ear — " to-morrow, to-morrow, my angel, thou shalt lie in thy father's arms!" To Paolo I said, "Wait with patience. We shall soon have news of Maddalena."

The last day passed as if in a dream. I could neither paint, nor talk, nor sit still; and so stole away quietly to the gardens of the Pincio, and wandered about the sunny walks alone. At dinner, I literally fasted. In the evening, my nervous excitement became so painfully uncontrollable that if only the ashes collapsed on the hearth, or the windows shook, I trembled from head to foot. He would go direct to my aunt, at the Hôtel d'Angleterre; and she would send him on to the Vicolo d'Aliberti. Fancy his footsteps on the stairs! Fancy the joy of being folded once more in his arms, and weeping out the last of so many bitter tears upon his bosom! Then

came the painful remembrance of how altered he must be; and I tried to prepare myself for the cruel lines channeled on his brow, and the gray hairs sprinkling his dark locks, once so free from change. Thus the evening hours trailed slowly by, and midnight came and no Hugh. At one o'clock, Ida stole down-stairs, entreating me to go to bed; but of what avail would it have been to do so, with every nerve of body and brain strung to the keenest wakefulness? Finding persuasion useless, she sat up with me, prepared to retreat at the first intimation of his coming. Thus the night wore on, and the expectations which, a few hours since, had been certainties, turned to doubts and apprehensions. At length six o'clock struck; and, worn out with watching, I waked Ida, who had fallen asleep in her chair, and we both went to bed.

I slept heavily for a few hours, and woke to find Mrs. Sandyshaft at my bedside.

"Is he come?" were the words that sprung instantaneously to my lips.

"No, child. He hasn't wings."

"But it is now three days and three nights since he received the letter!"

"You goose! Suppose he finds the mountain roads blocked up with snow between Chambery and Lyons? Suppose, when he gets to Marseilles, he finds no steamer ready to start? Suppose he had left Chambery for some other place — say Paris — when the letter arrived, and it had to be forwarded—what then?"

What then, indeed! I sank back upon my pillow with a weary sigh, and said—

"Well—any of these things might be; but in such case, when—when will he come?"

"Impossible to say—but within a week, no doubt."

"A week! Another long week!"

"And in the mean time," added she, "I'd advise you not to make it your practice to sit up every night. It won't bring him one bit the sooner."

"How long is it, Aunt Sandyshaft, since you last saw him?" I asked, presently.

"Not since I made up my mind to join Hilda and her precious Count out here in Italy. He came with me as far as Marseilles—and I'm sure I don't know what would have become of me on the way, if he hadn't—and saw me safe on board the Leghorn boat before he left me."

"That was kind of him!" I said, warmly.

"Humph! it was civil; but nothing wonderful," replied my aunt, with a sharp side-glance at me.

"And then what did he do?"

"Went back to England, I believe. At all events, his first letter to me was dated from Broomhill."

"And you have only had two from him, you say?"

"Only two, one of which you have."

"And the other you destroyed. Are you *quite* sure you destroyed it, aunt?"

"Bless my heart, yes; and saw the sparks fly up the chimney. I only kept this one, for fear I should forget the name of the place. Rubbish-storing, Bab, has never been a failing of mine."

Rubbish! She called his letter rubbish!

"I suppose," I said, after another pause, "he concludes you are in Rome by this time?"

"I don't see how that's likely, for I hadn't

concluded it myself when I replied to his letter. The De Chaumonts, at that time, talked of spending the winter in Naples; but Hilda, as usual, changed her mind at the last moment, and came here instead. To me, one place was the same as another; and you were as likely to be found in Rome as in Naples, if in either. As for Hugh Farquhar, if he supposes any thing, he supposes I'm in South Italy, scrambling up Mount Vesuvius. By the by, Bab, did I tell you that your father had settled in Brussels?"

"No—you had not mentioned it."

"He has, then. They have taken rooms in a fashionable quarter; and go to court; and drive out every day in their own barouche (jobbing the horses,) and give fortnightly receptions, with nothing to eat; and are mighty fine folks, indeed, in a small way. That just suits your father. Edmund Churchill, Esquire, was always a grand man, in his own opinion. But you don't listen?"

"Yes—oh, yes—I listen."

"Like the man in the song—'My body's in Segovia, my heart is in Madrid.' Oh, Bab, Bab, you're made of the same stuff as other people, in spite of the airs you give yourself when you're dignified. Mercy on us! don't cry. What good can crying do to you, or any body?"

"I—I feel as if he wouldn't come now at all!" sobbed I, fairly breaking down, and hiding my face in the pillows. "I was so full of hope all these ten days; and now the hope is all gone—all gone!"

"Because he is twelve hours after the time you had fixed upon, out of your own wise head! Bab, don't be a fool. Suppose he is a week after the time—what then? He's sure to come at last."

"A week—what shall I do for a whole week, not knowing where he is, or whether he's had the letter? He—he may be ill—or gone all the way back to England—who can tell?"

My aunt rose up, very deliberately, and put on her gloves.

"If you ask me, Bab, what you are to do for a whole week," said she, "I'd advise you to do what he has done for a whole year. Bear it."

"You're—you're very cruel!"

"Perhaps I am. It was your turn last, and it's mine now. However, to show you that I'm not a miracle of wickedness, I'll tell you what I'm now going home to do—to write three letters; one to Hugh Farquhar, addressed to his own house at Broomhill; one to his housekeeper, desiring her to forward that letter to him, wherever he may be; and the third to the postmaster at Naples, requesting that any thing which may have arrived for me there shall be at once sent on to Rome. Now, what d'ye say to that?"

"My dearest, kindest aunt——"

"Oh, I'm kind now, am I? I was cruel two minutes ago. There, cheer up, Bab; and make haste to dress and have your breakfast, and be all right by two o'clock, when I'll bring a carriage round, and take you and that infant monster for a drive. Good by."

I did cheer up, by a great effort, for that and several succeeding days; but my heart was heaviest when I smiled most; and my nights were spent in tears. Thus the prescribed week went by, and then another week; and still he neither came nor wrote. There had been time, and more than time, for the letter to be forwarded from Chambery to Broomhill, and from Broomhill back to Chambery. At length the suspense became intolerable, and I made up my mind to bear it no longer. I went to Mrs. Sandyshaft, and announced my determination to start for Chambery the following day.

"The stupidest thing you could do, Bab," said she. "That's precisely the way to miss him. Where two people are looking for each other, one should always stop still."

"How can I tell that he is not that one? How can I tell that he is not lying on a bed of sickness?"

"If he were, he would have had his letter; and either have written himself, or caused somebody to write."

"Well—these are but conjectures; and I mean to go. I shall at least have the satisfaction of hearing whatever there is to hear; and at all events I shall not be breaking my heart in idleness here in Rome."

"Your mind's made up?"

"Firmly. I am now going to secure my place to Civita Vecchia."

"No need. If you *must* go, I'll go with you —under protest—and we'll take post-horses. What about the monster?"

"Baby and Goody must go, of course."

"A pretty piece of folly, to be sure; and the day after to-morrow, the first of January! Bab, Bab, you're a greater idiot than I took you to be —the greatest idiot I ever knew, except myself."

CHAPTER LXIII.

WHITHER?

"I THANK you, valiant Cassio.
What tidings can you tell me of my lord?"—OTHELLO.

FROM Rome to Civita Vecchia with post-horses; from Civita Vecchia to Marseilles by steamer, with a bitter wind blowing from the north-east, and brief but sudden storms of snow and rain sweeping over the sea; from Marseilles to Lyons by railway; and from Lyons by post-chaise to Chambery. A dreary journey of many days' duration, intensely cold and comfortless, and made doubly difficult by the helplessness of my companions. The last day was the worst of all. We were fifteen hours on the road; six of which were spent in snow and darkness, struggling slowly up among mountain roads rendered almost impassable by several days of bad weather. Worn out with fatigue and cold, we reached Chambery an hour after midnight, and were driven to the Hôtel du Petit Paris. Here my first inquiry was for Hugh. The sleepy waiter knew nothing of the name. I described him; but he was confident that no such gentleman had been there. I asked what other hotels there were in the town. He replied that there were several; but none so good as the Petit Paris. There was La Poste; and there was L'Aigle Noir. Madame might inquire at both to-morrow; but it was unlikely that any English traveler would prefer either to the Hôtel du Petit Paris. As for the other inns, they were *auberges*, and out of the question. With this I was obliged to be content till morning.

L

I was so weary that I slept heavily, and never woke till between nine and ten o'clock the following day. The sunlight met my eye like a reproach. It was a glorious morning, cold but brilliant, with something hopeful and reassuring in the very air. I rose, confident of success, and went to the post-office before breakfast. A young man lounging at the door, with a cigar in his mouth, followed me into the office, and took his place at the bureau. I asked if he could give me the address of an English gentleman, Farquhar by name, who I had reason to believe was staying, or had been staying, in Chambery.

The clerk shook his head. · He knew of no such person.

"There are, perhaps, some letters awaiting Mr. Farquhar's arrival?"

"No, Madame. None."

"Nay, one I think there must be; for I know that it was dispatched nearly a month since. Will Monsieur oblige me by looking?"

Monsieur retired, reluctantly, to a distant corner of the bureau; took a packet of letters from a pigeon-hole in a kind of little cupboard between the windows, shuffled them as if they were cards, tossed them back into the pigeon-hole, and returned with the same shake of the head. There were no letters for Madame's friend. Absolutely none.

I turned away, disappointed, but incredulous. At the threshold, I paused. It might be a mere mistake of pronunciation, after all. I took out my pocket-book, pencilled the words "Hugh Farquhar, Esquire," very plainly on a blank leaf, and handed it to the clerk. His face lighted up directly.

"Ah, *that* name?" said he. "*Mais, oui ; je crois qu'il y a des lettres.* I beg Madame's pardon a thousand times; but Madame said an English gentleman, and this name is surely Polish or Russian?"

"No, no, English," I replied impatiently, my eyes fixed on the pigeon-hole.

He returned to it; took out the letters; sorted them, oh, how slowly! laid one aside; sorted them again, to make sure that he had omitted none; replaced the packet; paused to dust the letter before bringing it to the counter; and then, instead of placing it in my eager hand, said :

"Madame has brought Monsieur Farquhar's passport?"

"No—how can I bring it when I do not even know that he is here?"

"Then I can not surrender the letter."

"But, Monsieur—I am his wife."

"The postal law does not permit letters to be delivered unless on exhibition of the passport of the individual to whom they are addressed."

"Then, Monsieur will, at least, permit me to see the letter?"

He would not trust it across the counter; but held it jealously, in such a manner that I could read the address. It was directed in Mrs. Sandyshaft's handwriting to Hugh Farquhar, Esq., Broomhill, and re-directed to Chambery by Mrs. Fairhead. The back was almost covered with English, French, and Italian postmarks of various dates. It was evidently the second letter, written on the tenth day after the first. Where, then, was the first?

"Are you sure, Monsieur, that there is no other?"

"*Madame, j'en suis bien sûr.*"

"And there have been no others?"

He hesitated.

"I can not say, Madame. If so, they have been delivered."

I felt myself flush scarlet with impatience.

"But, good heavens ! monsieur, this is a matter of deep importance. Can you not remember what letters you have given out, or to whom you gave them ?"

He shrugged his shoulders, and replied, with a half-impertinent smile—

"Madame asks impossibilities. I do not say that there may not have been other letters. I believe there were; but I can not undertake to remember them. Perhaps my colleague may recollect having delivered them. Madame had better inquire of him."

"Where is monsieur's colleague to be found ?" I asked, haughtily.

"He is at present gone out to breakfast—*ah, le voilà !*"

At this moment another young man entered the office, short, brisk, black-eyed; a thorough man of business. They exchanged a few words in an undertone. Then the new comer came forward, and took the other's place at the little counter.

"Madame demands if there have been other letters delivered from this office to Monsieur—Monsieur——"

"Hugh Farquhar."

"Precisely. *Eh bien*, madame, there have been others. I can not tell how many. Three or four—perhaps six. They have all been delivered; except the last, which has been shown to madame, and is yet unclaimed."

"Delivered to himself ?"

"To himself some; and some to his messenger, on exhibition of monsieur's passport."

"How long since, Monsieur ?"

"Three weeks, I should think—or a month."

"Then he has left Chambery ?"

"It would seem so, madame; but if you will take the trouble to inquire at the Hôtel de la Poste——"

"At the Hôtel de la Poste ! Was he staying there ?"

"I conclude so, madame, since the garçon from La Poste came once or twice for letters."

"It would be in vain, I suppose, to ask if monsieur can remember whether a letter directed in the same handwriting as the one now lying here, was delivered to Monsieur Farquhar on or about the twelfth of December ?"

The clerk took up Mrs. Sandyshaft's letter, carefully scrutinized the superscription, and said—

"So many letters pass through our hands, madame, that I should be unwilling to hazard a decided opinion; but I think I have observed this writing before, and on a letter addressed to the same party. If so, it was somewhere about the time which madame specifies, and——"

"Was it delivered to himself, monsieur ?"

"I was just about to say, madame, that, in that case, I rather incline to the belief that I delivered that letter to a lady."

"To a lady ?"

"On exhibition of monsieur's passport."

I leaned upon the counter for a moment, quite faint and speechless ; then, pulling my vail down upon my face, said, quickly and tremulously,—"Thanks, monsieur,"—and hurried out of the office.

A little way up the road there stood a clump of trees, a fountain, and a stone bench. I made my way to the bench and sat down, feeling very giddy. My mind was all confused. I felt as if some great misfortune had befallen me; though I scarcely comprehended the nature of it. Presently some young girls came up, chattering and laughing, to fill their pitchers from the fountain. I saw them look at me and whisper together. I shuddered, rose, and turned away. Walking on, as it were, instinctively, I crossed an open space surrounded by public buildings, and entering a street which opened off by one of the angles, found myself immediately opposite a large white house, across the front of which was painted the words, "Hôtel de la Poste." A respectable-looking man was standing at the door, with his hands in his pockets. I paused, advanced a step, and asked if I could speak to the landlord. To which he replied, with a bow—

"*Madame, je suis le maître d'hôtel.* Be pleased to walk in."

"No, thank you, monsieur, I—I only wish to make an inquiry."

"At your service, madame."

"I am anxious to know, monsieur, whether an English gentleman named Farquhar has been staying lately at your hotel?"

"Not very lately, madame. He has been gone nearly a month."

"May I ask how long he remained here?"

"About a fortnight, madame."

"Can you tell me if he is gone back to England?"

"If madame will take the trouble to accept a seat in the bureau, I will refer to the visitor's book, and see if monsieur left any address."

I stepped into the landlord's little parlor and sat down, while he turned over the pages of a large book that lay upon a side-table. Presently his forefinger, which had been rapidly running down column after column, stopped at a certain entry, like a pointer.

"No address left, madame," said he. "But monsieur, I think, took post-horses from here. I will refer to my books, and see in what direction he traveled."

And the obliging maître d'hôtel took down a ledger from his bookshelves, and resumed the same process of search. Again the swift forefinger came to a sudden halt.

"Monsieur F.—*numéros, quatre, trois, cinq, et six*," said he, running rapidly over the items of the various entries. "*Appartments,* so much; dinners, breakfast, wine, etc.—*post-horses to Grenoble*—Monsieur went from here to Grenoble."

"To Grenoble?" I repeated. "Thanks, monsieur—and left no address?"

"None, madame."

"Monsieur Farquhar traveled—alone?"

"Monsieur arrived alone, Madame—*c'est à dire*, accompanied by his colored servant; and was joined here by Mademoiselle, his sister."

"By—by his—sister?"

"Yes, Madame. Mademoiselle arrived the day before they started for Grenoble. *Mon Dieu, Madame! Vous—vous trouvez malade?*"

"Thank you—" I said, pressing my hand to my forehead. "I—I feel somewhat faint. A

long journey—and—and the fatigue of walking before breakfast——"

"Allow me to call for a glass of wine——"

"No, thank you—a little water. You are very good."

The landlord ran himself to a filter standing in the hall, and brought me a tumblerful of fresh water. Refreshed and steadied by the cool draught, I rose, and bade him good morning. He attended me to the door, and, seeing me hesitate, asked in what direction I wished to go.

"To the Hotel du Petit Paris."

"Straight on, madame, till you come to the end of the street, and then turn to the left. The Petit Paris will be straight before you. You can not miss your way."

"I am much obliged, Monsieur; good morning."

"Madame, I have the honor to wish you good morning."

———

"Bab, my dear," said my aunt, "we can do no more than we have done. We must just sit down now, and be patient."

"Patient!" I echoed, with a bitter sigh.

"Well, what's to be gained by impatience? Here's Grenoble; yonder's the railway station; and to-day is the eighth of January. Six-and-twenty days ago, a traveler leaves this hotel, bag and baggage; goes to that railway station; takes tickets for somewhere or another; and disappears. Who's to tell in what direction he went—east, west, north, or south? The cleverest detective in Bow Street couldn't track a man on such a clue as that. I defy him. Much less three women and a baby."

"Yet it is so hard to give up, now that we are on his very footsteps——"

"Fiddlesticks, Bab. Footsteps don't help one six-and-twenty days after date. One might go to New-York and back in the time."

My aunt was sitting in an easy chair by the fire; I was standing by the window, looking over toward the Alps and the sunset. We had followed on as far as Grenoble, and here all traces of Hugh and his companions disappeared. They had left by railway the morning after their arrival, and were gone no one knew whither. Reluctant as I was to admit it, I knew that my aunt was right, and further search useless.

"Well?" said she, presently. "What's to be done?"

"What you please," I replied listlessly.

"Humph! if I did what I pleased, I should go back to Suffolk at once, and take you with me. Will you go?"

"To Suffolk? Oh, no—never, never again, unless——"

"Unless what, pray?"

"Unless with him."

"That's a ridiculous condition, Bab."

"Let him make every thing clear to me—let him——let him explain how it is that this woman is again with him——"

"That's easily explained. She has followed him, I've no doubt, like a dog."

"Perhaps; but that is not all. That's not enough."

"Well, Bab—your fittest home, for the present, is my home. Decline it, if you please; but that's where you ought to be. In the mean time, we can't stay in this out-of-the-world place—can we?"

"Certainly not. We must go back to Rome. Perhaps he is already there, awaiting our return."

"I'll be bound, if so, that *he* won't be such a fool as to run off to Chambery after *us*," said my aunt. "But I don't believe we shall find him there."

"Nor I," I replied, hopelessly.

My aunt stood up, and came over to the window.

"Shall we trudge off again to-morrow then?" said she, laying her hand kindly on my shoulder. "Do you feel strong enough—eh ?"

"Oh, yes—quite strong enough."

"And you'd rather go to Rome ?"

"Of course. It is our only chance."

"Very well—Rome it shall be. And as for that letter—well, well, I've my own suspicions; but never mind. Time will show. We must play the game of patience, now ; but we hold all the best cards in our own hands, my dear, and win we must—some day. Poor Bab!"

We stood there for several minutes quite silently, and watched the round red sun sink slowly down behind the farthest peaks. The broad plain lay below, all dusk and mysterious. The lowest mountains became violet in shade, and the loftiest crimson in light; and the great glaciers flashed like fire on the remotest horizon. I thought of the time when Hugh and I traveled together in the mighty Oberland, and my eyes grew dim, and my heart heavy, with the remembrance.

"How grand it is," I said sadly.

"Yes, it's grand, of course it's grand," replied Mrs. Sandyshaft. "But the truth is, my dear, I've no taste for the sublime. Mountains are all very well in their way; but give me Suffolk!"

The next morning, we took the railway back again to Marseilles, and embarked on board the French boat for Civita Vecchia.

───◆───

CHAPTER LXIV.

THE OLD, OLD STORY.

"He is but a landscape painter,
And a village maiden she."

　　　　　　　　　　　TENNYSON.

JANUARY, February, March went by; April came ; and still there was no sign or word from Hugh. Hilda went off to Naples with her obedient husband, for the fashionable season. Ida completed her large picture, and dispatched it to Zollenstrasse for the approaching competition. Paolo, after lingering in Rome week after week, lost faith in my ability to help him, and went back to his wife and home in Capri. In the mean time my aunt came to live with us in the Vicolo d'Aliberti, and we engaged all the upper portion of the house, and a couple of good servants for her accommodation. In the mean time, also, my darling throve like a young plant in the sunshine, drinking in strength and beauty from every fragrant breath that stirred the opening blossoms of the spring. He knew me now —held out his little arms when he saw me from afar off—smiled when I smiled; and testified his love in a thousand fond and helpless ways, scarcely intelligible to any eyes but mine.

"Methought his looks began to talk with me; .
And no articulate sounds, but something sweet
His lips would frame."

Heaven knows I needed all the unconscious comfort his baby heart could give ! I was very wretched.

It was the mystery that made my life so miserable—the painful, oppressive, entangling mystery, that haunted me perpetually, sleeping or waking, till my brain ached, and my very soul was weary.

The letter had been delivered—that was certain. Immediately after its delivery, Hugh had left Chambery for Grenoble—that also was certain. From Grenoble he had taken his departure, after one night's delay, by railway ; and from this point all trace of him disappeared. He had left no address. He had neither written to Mrs. Sandyshaft, nor to any of his own people at Broomhill. He had totally, unaccountably, mysteriously vanished ; and with him had also vanished Tippo and Maddalena. Sometimes I thought he must have been murdered by banditti, and buried where he fell. Sometimes I asked myself if Maddalena could have poisoned him in some fierce passion of jealousy and despair ? She was Italian, and her black eyes had in them "something dangerous." Again, I questioned if he had ever received Mrs. Sandyshaft's letter. The clerk believed that he had delivered it to a lady. That lady must have been Maddalena; and what if she had destroyed it ? Supposing this, would he not have marveled at my aunt's long silence, and have written to her at the Neapolitan office ?

These questions tormented me ; pursued me ; poisoned the very air and sunshine around me; and made my life one long, sickening, heartbreaking suspense. In vain those around me preached the wisdom and necessity of patience. I could endure, and I could suffer ; but there was no patience for such a burthen of anxiety as mine.

Thus the slow weeks dragged past, and hope gradually died away, and I made up my mind that I should never see him more.

And now my turn had come to grow pale and absent—to pore upon the map, and say "If I had taken this direction, I should have met him ;" or "If I had gone at once, I should have found him"—to rack my brain with suppositions, and my heart with bitter reproaches. It was retribution, terrible, literal, torturing. Retribution dealt out even-handed ; measure for measure ; cup for cup, to the last drop of the draught. My aunt never reproached me now ; but my self-condemnation was enough. In every pang that I suffered, I remembered those which my flight had inflicted on him. In every dark conjecture that sent a shudder through my whole being, I recognized his anguish. It was a woeful time ; and any fault that had been mine in the past was expiated to the utmost.

One afternoon, very early in April, Ida came to me in my little painting-room, and sat down on a stool at my feet. I was alone, and had been brooding over my grief for hours in silence. She took my hand, and laid her cheek upon it, tenderly.

"My poor Barbara," said she, "you have been solitary. Where is Mrs. Sandyshaft ?"

"Out, dear. She dines to-day at her banker's,

after accompanying them in a drive to Antemnæ and Fidenæ."

"Had I known that, I would have staid at home. It is not good for you to be alone."

"Nay, dear, it makes little difference " I replied, sadly.

"You have not been painting?"

"No."

"Nor reading?"

"No."

"Nor walking?"

"I walked on the Pincio this morning before breakfast, with Goody and the child."

"You must not always call him 'the child,' and 'the baby,'" said Ida coaxingly. "You must accustom yourself, dear, to give him his own pretty name. I should love to call him Hugh, if I were you—little Hugh—Ugolino."

"No, no—not yet. I can not."

"Well then, may I?"

"No, darling—I can not bear it yet. By and by, perhaps—when I am stronger——"

"Enough—I will not tease you. And now—and now, do you not wonder where I have been all day?"

"Ay, dear," was my listless answer. "Where?"

"Well, I went first to Plowden's to inquire if there were yet any news from Zollenstrasse respecting the safe arrival of my picture. I told you I was going there, when I went out."

"I had forgotten it."

"And then I thought I would step in at Piale's, to see if he had yet procured that Hand-book of Rome for Mrs. Sandyshaft, which she ordered several days ago."

"That was thoughtful and kind, my Ida."

"And—and at Piale's, I met the gentleman, dear, whom I told you I encountered once or twice before—do you remember?"

"To be sure. The English artist who lodged in your father's house in Munich; and who was so good to you when you were a child."

"To whom I owe my first beginnings of art, and who procured me my presentation to the Zollenstrasse College," said Ida warmly.

"He has been, indeed, a good friend," I replied, trying to fix my wandering attention. "So you met him again to-day at Piale's?"

"Yes—he was in the reading-room; but—he rose up when he saw me, and shook hands so kindly; and—and asked me if I would like to go to the Campana Museum, for which he had a permission of entry. Now, you know, dear, the Campana collection is one of the great difficulties of Rome. It is almost impossible to procure admission, and——"

"And you went, I suppose?"

"I was very glad to avail myself of the opportunity—and I thought there could be no objection to the escort of a—a gentleman whom I had known since I was a little girl——"

"Surely not, my dear Ida. I am glad you have seen the collection. It is very beautiful."

"Indeed it is," replied Ida. "He asked me with whom I was living. I find he knows you, Barbara."

"Knows me?" I repeated. "How should that be?"

"He has met you, dear—at a pic-nic."

"Ah—that is possible. I have forgotten his name?"

"Penwarne—Alfred Penwarne. Is it not a grand name?"

"Yes—it is a good name. I remember him now. He is very satirical."

"He is very witty," said Ida, coloring up, and speaking somewhat emphatically.

"Nay, dear child—I mean no unkindness of your friend. So he remembers to have seen me at Tivoli?"

"Yes; and he asked me if you were one of the Carylons of Pen—Pen—something, in Cornwall; and then he said that Carlyon was a Cornish name, and that he himself was a Cornish man. I was so confused, Barbara; and yet I could scarcely keep from laughing."

"Poor Ida! it was very annoying for you."

"Oh, it was nothing. Well, dear—we went all through the Campana gallery; and then, on coming out, Mr. Penwarne proposed that we should take a turn on the Pincio. And—and then——"

She paused; and I was startled to find how her hand trembled in mine.

"Why, Ida," I exclaimed, "you are nervous, child! Your cheek is flushed—you tremble—what is it?"

"I—I scarcely know whether to laugh or cry," faltered she; "but—but it is all so strange—I seem as if I could not believe it——"

"Could not believe what, my darling?"

"What he told me in—in the gardens."

A sudden light flashed upon me. I stooped over her where she sat at my feet, and taking her pretty head between my hands, turned her face toward me.

"What did he tell you, my little Ida?" I said, smiling. "That he had never forgotten you, all these years—and that Ida Penwarne would sound far prettier for a lady's name than Ida Saxe?"

She flung her arms round my neck, and buried her blushing face in my bosom.

"He said that—that he had always thought of me with kindness," whispered she, "and that —since the first day he met me here in Rome, he—he loved me!"

"And you, Liebe—what did you reply?"

"I hardly remember——I—I think I said I was very glad not to have been—forgotten—by him."

"But, my dear child, is not all this strangely precipitate? You have not seen Mr. Penwarne more than twice before to-day, and how can you tell whether——"

"I have seen him a great many times," said Ida, guiltily. "I—I couldn't help it. I suppose that, knowing where I lived——"

"He contrived to meet you, by accident—eh?"

"Perhaps; and then——"

"And then, what?"

"He lived in our house for more than two years. It is not as if we were strangers."

"That is true."

"And—and besides, Barbara, I—I think I loved him a little, before I came to Zollenstrasse at all!"

Pretty, artless Ida! Her long-hidden secret was told at last, and all the rest of her life's innocent romance was soon poured out. It was the old, old story, of which the world is never weary—the old story of how admiration and gratitude became love in a simple maiden's heart, dwelling there, an unwritten poem, year after year; unfostered by a single hope; untainted by a single regret; pure as her own soul, and sacred as her religion. She had so much to tell, and yet it was so little when told! How he first came to live at her father's cottage by the banks of the Isar; how he took kindly notice of her from the first; how she loved to linger near when he was painting, and with what eager wonder she watched the daily progress of his work; how he took her, one day, to the museum of pictures; how, another day, he made a little portrait of her in oils, and gave it to her mother; how, at last, he offered to teach her something of drawing; and what a happy time it was when she used to go out with him into the fields behind the house, and sketch the pine rafts that came down the river, the great elms that fringed the opposite bank, and all the homely subjects round about—these, and the like simple incidents, made the substance of her little story; yet every detail interested me, and I listened to it from first to last with a tender sympathy that caused me, for the time, to forget my trouble in her happiness.

Thus we sat talking till the early dusk drew on, and the red glow of the embers on the hearth became the only light by which we saw each other's face; and then Ida went up to her own room, and I was alone again.

The wind had risen within the last hour, and came, every now and then, in sudden gusts against the window. I rose, and looked out. A few stars gleamed between the rifts of ragged cloud that drifted across the sky, and an occasional blot of rain came with the wind. I turned from the cheerless prospect with a shudder; and, resuming my former seat, fell back upon the old train of thought, as if nothing had occurred to interrupt it. Presently my boy waked in his little cot, with that sweet, impatient, inarticulate cry that was so eloquent to my ear. I hastened to throw on a fresh log and a couple of pine-cones, to make the room bright for him; then took him in my arms; danced him to and fro before the fire to the tune of a quaint, old-fashioned Italian lullaby; kissed him; talked to him; and watched how his great blue eyes were turned toward the leaping flame in wonder and delight. These were my happy moments—my only happy moments now—and even these were often overcast by sudden clouds of anguish.

All at once the door opened, and Goody, with a startled look upon her face, peeped in.

"My deary," said she, "there's a lady waiting to see you."

"A lady?"

"And—and she asked for Mrs. Farquhar, my deary," added the old servant, apprehensively.

"My name?" I stammered, seized with a vague terror. "Who knows my name?"

"She's quite a stranger," said Goody, "and—she's here!"

I rose as my visitor appeared on the threshold. She came in—closed the door—lifted her vail.

It was Maddalena.

————

CHAPTER LXV.

MADDALENA'S CONFESSION.

"FACE to face in my chamber, my silent chamber, I saw her!
God, and she and I only."—MRS. BROWNING.

MY first impulse was one of terror—unmixed, overmastering terror. I turned cold from head to foot, and my heart failed within me. For a moment, we stood there, face to face, in the firelight; both silent. Maddalena was the first to speak.

"At last we meet," she said, in a low, distinct tone. "At last!"

I shuddered. I so well remember that vibrating, melancholy voice, with its slightly foreign intonation.

"Whose child is that?"

I clasped my boy closer to my bosom. My lips moved, but uttered no sound.

"Whose child is that?" she repeated.

"Mine."

She took a step forward; but as she did so, I sprang back, laid my baby in his cot, and stood before it, trembling but desperate, like some wild creature at bay.

"Keep off!" I cried, vehemently. "You shall not touch him."

She looked at me with eyes that dilated as she spoke.

"Fool!" she said, scornfully. "Do you think I would harm your child?"

Then her face grew gentle and her voice softened, as she added:

"Is it not *his*, also?"

"His!" I echoed, my terror rapidly giving place to indignation. "Do you presume to name my husband to my face?"

"I come here to-night for no other purpose than to speak of him."

"In that case," I said, controlling my voice to a steady coldness as I went on, "you will be so good as to remember that you address Mr. Farquhar's wife."

She smiled, disdainfully.

"His wife?" she repeated. "Ay—I am not likely to forget it."

"What have you to say to me?"

"Much," she replied, leaning against the table, and pressing her hand to her side, as if in pain. "Truths bitter to tell—so bitter that, three weeks ago, I would have torn my tongue out, sooner than utter them. Yet I am here to-night to tell them to—*you*."

She paused again, as if for breath, and I saw that she looked very ill. I pointed, almost involuntarily, to a chair that was standing by; but she took no notice of the gesture.

'Listen,' she said, in a voice so resolutely defiant that it seemed to mock the quivering of her lips; "listen, you, his lady-wife, to a peasant who was his mistress. He never sought me. It was I who fled to him, and laid myself at his feet. He never loved me. The love was mine; the pity and indulgence his. He never married me. Such was the chivalry of his nature, that he would have made me his wife if he could; simply because I was a woman, and had given myself to him. But I was already married; and so that could not be. Yet, in the rashness of his generosity, he gave me a solemn promise that he would never wed another. It was a promise that he should never have given. It was a promise that he had not strength to keep. He has told me since how he suffered and struggled under temptation; how he even fled from that temptation before he yielded. You know that, better than I can tell you."

Indeed, I did know it. I bowed my head in silence. I could not speak—I could only listen. It was as if my life and all my future hung upon her lips; while, at every word she uttered, some cloud seemed to roll away from the past.

"I never knew that promise was broken," she continued, "till a few days before he brought —his wife—to Broomhill. It had been my home up to that time, and he had vowed it should be mine while I lived. I then learned that I must either leave the shelter of his roof; or dwell beneath it a voluntary prisoner. I chose the latter, and, for his sake, endured——"

She checked herself, and flashing a hasty glance at me, said:

"No matter what I endured. I loved him—and love him. A hundred wives could do no more. Not one in a hundred thousand would have done so much."

"Hush," I said, gently. "These are comparisons which it neither becomes you to make, nor me to hear."

She waved her hand impatiently.

"My precautions," said she, "were in vain. Fate guided you. Step by step, you discovered all. You, however, rejected some truths; and too literally accepted the purport of words which —which were not for your ear. Do you understand me?"

"Perfectly. But my husband—Mr. Farquhar —tell me where——"

"Patience. I have a confession to make first."

"A confession?" I repeated; all my fears flooding back at once upon my heart.

She turned even paler than before, and fiercely clenched the hand that rested on the table.

"You fled," said she, in a deep low tone; "and your flight sealed my fate. Sooner or later you must return — I knew that. I also knew that the day of your return would be the day of my banishment. I had hated you before, but from that hour I hated you with tenfold bitterness. Ay, you may well shrink! We Southerns hate as we love — to madness. There was a time, and that not long since, when I could have taken your life without pity."

I listened, as if in a terrible dream.

"You fled," she went on to say, breathing with difficulty, and speaking in short, sharp sentences, like one in pain. "You fled, and I was again free. But my peace was gone. He suffered; and his sufferings were my sufferings—his restlessness, my restlessness. Life lost its last charm for me. I loathed even Broomhill—Broomhill, once so calm and pleasant! Thus a year passed."

Again she broke off abruptly. Her brow contracted, and the veins rose like cords upon the back of her thin, resolute hand. It was as if she could not bring herself to utter what she had next to say.

"He went abroad," she continued. "He wrote to me. It was his wish that I should remain no longer at Broomhill. He—he had resolved to provide me with a home far away;

and he bade me join him—at Chambery. That letter came to me like my death-warrant. I had expected it; but the blow fell none the less heavily. I obeyed without a murmur. Had he bidden me die by slow poison, I should have obeyed as literally. I went. He told me that I was to live henceforth at Nice, where he had bought a villa for me by the sea. He thought kindly for me, even in this. It was my own climate, my own sea, the land of my own tongue. But it was banishment—banishment!"

"But when you left Chambery," I began, trembling with eagerness to know more, "when you left Chambery, in what——"

"Patience," she said again. "You shall hear all in its course. I joined him at Chambery. He made it appear there that I was his sister. I arrived on the Sunday afternoon. It was arranged that we should begin our journey the following day. I rose early the next morning, and went out before breakfast; for I was very restless. He asked me to call at the Post-office, and leave directions that all letters should be forwarded to him at the Bureau Restante, Nice. He also gave me his passport to show, in case any should have arrived by that morning's mail. I made up my mind, as I went along, that I would not leave his address. There was always danger that news of yourself might come at last, and my only hope hung on your absence. They were just opening the bag when I went in, and at once handed me a letter for him. I recognized Mrs. Sandyshaft's writing. I had often seen it at Broomhill. I had no sooner taken that letter in my hand than I felt a presentiment of evil. I wandered out beyond the town, and sat down in a solitary place to examine it. The more I looked at it, the more I was convinced that it contained some fatal intelligence. My destiny trembled in the balance. It was in my own power to turn the scale. I—I hesitated long. The temptation was all-powerful, and yet I—I struggled against it——"

"You destroyed the letter!" I exclaimed.

"I was desperate," she replied, starting into sudden energy. "It was my only stake—and I played it. Yes, I confess it—I opened the letter—read it—tore it into a thousand fragments, and sent it floating down the stream that hurried by. There, you know it now — all the black and bitter truth."

"Alas, poor Hugh!" I faltered, tearfully.

Maddalena opened her dark eyes full upon me, half in wonder, half in scorn. She had expected a torrent of reproaches. She could not comprehend how grief and pity should take precedence of resentment in my heart.

"We left Chambery," she resumed hastily, "and went to Nice. There he consented to rest awhile, and repair his shattered strength. It had been agreed that Mrs. Sandyshaft should only write in case she had something definite to communicate. Day after day, he waited and hoped. At last he wrote to her at Naples. I intercepted that letter also, and it remained unanswered. At length the climate, which at first had done him good, began to fail of its effect. As the spring advanced, he fell gradually more and more out of health. I saw him declining daily—not from disease; but because he was too weary of life to bear the burden of living. Then my punishment began."

"Wretch!" I cried, "you let him die! You let him die, when a word would have saved him! Oh, it was murder—murder!"

She smiled—a strange, agonized, terrible smile.

"You have been well avenged," she said, "in all that I have suffered."

I fell on my knees beside the little cot, in a paroxysm of despair and horror. I could not weep. I could only struggle for breath, and grasp the woodwork frame with both hands, convulsively.

"My child!" I gasped. "My poor, fatherless baby! Dead—oh, God! dead—dead!"

Maddalena came over swiftly and silently, and laid her cold hand on mine.

"Be comforted," she said. "Your husband lives."

I looked at her. My lips moved, but my tongue was dumb. I felt as if her words had some meaning which my sense failed to compass.

"He lives," she repeated. "I have come to take you to him."

The reäction was too much. I had not strength to bear the sudden joy. I uttered a faint cry; felt myself falling forward, powerless to put out a hand in self help; and lapsed into utter unconsciousness.

CHAPTER LXVI.

THE OSTERIA DELLA FOSSA.

"Quite dumb? Dead, dead."—Shakspeare.

"Where is she?"

They were the first words I uttered, when my memory came back and I had strength to speak.

"Hush, Bab," said my aunt, putting her finger to her lip. "You mustn't talk. What's-her-name's gone this three quarters of an hour, and—mercy on us! you mustn't try to sit up, child! Lie down and be quiet, or we shall have you going off again, as sure as fate."

"Gone? Gone without me?" I cried, struggling to an upright posture, in spite of my aunt's well-meant efforts to pin me to the sofa.

"Without you?—well, I should think so. Here you've been in a dead faint, ever since they fetched me home. You wouldn't have had her put you in a coach and carry you off like that, I suppose? But do lie down, Bab, and hold your tongue, and be rational."

I fell back, silenced and exhausted.

"Besides, we've got the address," added my aunt. "Ida has it all written out upon a card. Hotel—hotel—whatever is the name of the place, my dear? I'm sure I can't remember."

"Osteria della Fossa," replied Ida, smoothing my hair back, tenderly.

"Where is it?" I whispered.

"Some little way beyond La Storta, Liebchen, on the Florence road—not far, I believe, from Veii."

I closed my eyes and lay still for several minutes, during which my aunt insisted on prescribing sal-volatile and water, while Goody busied herself in the preparation of some strong "English" tea.

"What o'clock is it?" was my next question.

"Nearly ten, darling; and a wild dreary night."

My aunt looked up, sharply.

"It's of no use, Bab," said she. "I know what you're thinking of; but it can't be done. You don't stir an inch before to-morrow, I promise you—and not then, unless you're a vast deal better."

I made no reply; but I pressed Ida's hand significantly, and she returned the pressure.

"And Hugh won't expect you, either," continued my aunt. "She'll tell him you're not well; and it won't kill him to wait twelve hours longer!"

"He will not wait till to-morrow,". I said, confidently. "He will be here himself before midnight."

"Here himself? No, no, my dear—love can do a good deal, I've no doubt; but I don't believe in miracles. Love won't give a man strength to rise from a sick-bed, on which——"

"A sick-bed?" I cried, starting upright in a moment. "Merciful heaven! he is ill, and you never told me!"

"Never told you?" stammered my aunt. "But she——didn't she tell you?"

"Not a word. Oh, speak—speak—quickly—the truth—let me have the truth?"

My aunt hesitated, and looked as if she would fain recall her words.

"He—he was ill when he started, you know," she began.

"I did not know it!"

"But he would come, when he once knew you were in Rome. He was too ill to venture by sea, so they traveled post——"

"All the way from Nice?"

"No, from the baths of Lucca, where he had gone for change of air, about ten days before."

"Go on—go on!"

"Well, my dear, there's not much more to tell. He ought to have been in his bed when he started; but nothing would keep him. He knocked up half-way, at a place called—called——"

"Bolseno," suggested Ida.

"Where he was obliged to put up for half a day, and a night," continued my aunt. "But the next morning he would go on again. He got worse and worse, the farther he went; and at this place—what d'ye call it—Fossa?—within twelve or fourteen miles of Rome, was forced to give in, and do what any sensible man would have done at first; namely, take to his bed, and send for you and a doctor."

"And she told you all this?"

"After a deal of cross-examination; but you know, my dear, when I question folks I will be answered. Mercy on us, child! what are you about?"

"I am going to my husband," I replied, firmly. "Nay, aunt, no opposition can stay me. I will go. Let a carriage and post-horses be sent for instantly."

"But you're ill yourself, Bab, and——"

"I am well—quite well, now."

"It's midsummer madness, I tell you!"

"Let it be madness, then—I mean to be at the Osteria della Fossa by midnight."

My aunt threw up her hands in indignant protest, while Ida glided quietly from the room, to see that my orders were obeyed.

"Mind this, Bab," said Mrs. Sandyshaft; "if any harm comes of it, remember I set my face

against it. Why, you may be waylaid by banditti on the road! Who ever heard of such a
thing as a lady going across that horrible desert
outside Rome, at night, and unprotected? Besides, how can you leave the child?"

"I shall take him with me."

"Oh, if you want to kill the child, I have no
more to say," exclaimed my aunt, very angrily.
"You know better than I do, what effect the
pestilent night-air of the Campagna is likely to
take upon a poor little infant like that. It's a
wicked tempting of Providence—God forgive
me, that I should say so of my own niece; but
that's what I think. Please yourself!"

I did please myself. I knew that on a night
when the atmosphere was purified by heavy rain,
there would be no danger from miasmata; and
I also knew that I could carry my boy from his
bed to the carriage, and so, most probably, all
the way, without once awaking him. I said so,
briefly but very decidedly, and left Mrs. Sandyshaft to cool down while I dressed for the journey. When I came back from my bedroom, I
found her with her bonnet on, and a ponderous
old horse-pistol lying before her on the table.

"There, my dear," said she, nodding very
good-temperedly, and taking up this weapon
with an air of great satisfaction, "that's to keep
off the banditti. It always hung over my bedroom chimney-piece at Stoneycroft Hall; and
when I came abroad, I brought it in the drawer
of my dressing-case, where other folks carry
jewelry. None of your foreign spies thought
of looking there; and catch me traveling about
the world without some means of self-defense!"

Night; darkness; the wind howling round the
empty piazzas; the rain dashing against the
carriage-windows; the blurred lamps flaring at
the street-corners; the long, lonely thoroughfares echoing to our wheels as we rattle past—
every revolution of those wheels, every clatter
of our horses' hoofs on the wet stones, every
lagging second of every minute carrying us
nearer and nearer! Now we cross the Piazza
del Popolo, with the solemn old Egyptian obelisk dimly seen in the midst; and are stopped
for a moment at the gate, where some half-dozen
soldiers and a customs official are loitering inside, by a blazing wood-fire. Now we are out
upon the walled road beyond; and overhead all
is pitchy darkness, and around us the driving,
blinding rain.

Mrs. Sandyshaft sits beside me, and my baby
sleeps sweetly in my arms. We are both silent.
The postillion shouts to his horses and cracks his
whip. Once we meet a traveling carriage with
blazing lamps, and once overtake a lumber-
ing diligence escorted by a couple of dragoons.
These are the only incidents of our journey.
By and by the walls and outlying villas are left
behind; and we traverse a black, mysterious expanse of open country, over which our road
seems sometimes to rise, and sometimes to fall,
as if the ground were hilly. Thus the weary
minutes ebb away; and still every turn of the
wheels carries us nearer and nearer.

Now we reach La Storta, the first post from
Rome, and take fresh horses. The change is
effected, no doubt, as quickly as usual; but the
delay, to my impatience, seems interminable. I
throw a liberal buono mano to the last postillion; the new one springs into his saddle; we

dash away at a gallant pace; and through the
gloom of the night, something like the outlines
of near hills are now and then vaguely dis-
tinguishable. More than two thirds of the distance are now past. In about twenty minutes
more——I turn hot and cold by turns. I can
scarcely breathe. The wildest apprehensions flit
across my mind. What if he were dead when
I arrive? What if he should only live to sigh
out his last breath in my arms? What if Maddalena knew that he was dying; and so brought
me hither to gratify a last, subtle, pitiless, profound revenge? I strive to recall her face as I
saw it just before I fainted. It looked pale, and
strange, and full of meaning. She said, "your
husband lives;"—not "he will live." Alas!

The road takes an abrupt turn. Then comes
a break in the stormy canopy of clouds, and a
faint gleam shows that we have entered a steep
ravine. The brawl of a torrent mingles with
the hoarse murmuring of the wind.

"Just the place for banditti," mutters my
aunt, peering suspiciously from side to side.

All at once, a light is seen gleaming some
little distance ahead. Our postillion spurs his
horses—shouts—cracks his whip—pulls up before a low, wide-fronted wayside inn—the Osteria della Fossa!

The landlord (a mere peasant in a sheep-skin
jacket) comes hurrying out with a lighted pine-
torch in his hand, and bows us into a tiny, comfortless parlor with a paved floor, and a handful of smoldering ashes on the hearth.

"I'll wait here, Bab, and take care of the
child," says my aunt, flurriedly; "and, for
mercy's sake, keep as cool as you can. Remember, he's very ill, and excitement can only
do him mischief. There now, keep up a good
heart, and God bless you."

"Is he awake?" I ask, tremulously.

"Dimanderò, signora," replies the landlord,
moving toward the stairs.

I sprang after him.

"No, no," I cried, snatching the lamp from
the table. "Show me the way."

"Up-stairs, signora—the second door to the
right. Permetta——"

"Enough—I will go up alone."

I went alone. At the landing I paused;
dreading, longing to go forward; a wild fluttering at my heart; a weight of lead upon my feet.
Another two or three steps, and the first door is
passed. Before I reach the second, I pause
again. Is it only shadow, or do I see something
dark against the threshold?

The shadow moves—moans—lifts a white face
to the light, and, crawling toward me along the
sordid passage, grovels in piteous supplication.

"If you have a woman's heart in your
breast—if you hope for God's pity in your last
need, speak for me!"

"Maddalena?"

"Only to see him once more—to kiss his
hand—to hear his voice, and know myself forgiven! Only this! only this!"

"Poor soul! what has happened?"

"He will not see me—he will not speak to
me! I lie at his threshold, dying—dying—
dying, because he hates me!"

"Nay, you are not dying, and he does not
hate you. Be calm. You shall see him, and he
shall forgive you—for my sake. There, rise—

rise and go down to the fireside. Your hands are like ice."

"You promise?"

"I promise. It shall be my first prayer to him, and I know he will grant it. How long is it since he refused to see you? What have you done to anger him?"   .

"Confessed — confessed every thing! Till this evening, I had never told him all. I did not dare. I pretended I had news of you from a stranger. It was to save his life. I knew he would die without you. But I could not bear to deceive him longer. I told him; and when I told him, he—ah, Dio! he cursed me!"

"He will recall the curse. Let me go to him, Maddalena, and, by the love I bear toward my child, he shall pardon you."

"God in heaven bless you!"

"But you must go down to the fire, and be patient awhile. It may be an hour before I call you."

"An hour? Oh, no—no—not an hour!"

I comforted her with such assurance of speed as I could give; helped her to rise; saw her totter feebly down the stairs, a step at a time; and then turned to the door of the second chamber; opened it softly, and went in.

I saw a bed, screened by a single curtain; a table, on which a small oil-lamp was burning; and a young peasant woman dozing in a chair beside the window. I hesitated a moment, considering what was best to be done; then crossed the room noiselessly; woke her by a gentle touch; laid my finger to my lips; and pointed first to my wedding-ring, and then to the door. She opened her dark eyes—looked startled—then puzzled — then intelligent; whispered "capisco;" and crept out of the room.

I sat down in her vacant chair—alone with him.

His watch lay on the table—his dear familiar watch; and with it a little plain gold locket that I had once given him, containing my portrait. It seemed so strange to see them here! I held my breath, and listened for his breathing. I could not hear it. My terrors rushed back upon me. I had meant to sit there quietly till he woke; but it was impossible. I felt that I *must* look upon him, be the risk what it might!

I rose, shading the lamp with my hand, and stole over to the bedside. His face was turned to the wall; his hair fell on the pillow in long, wild locks; and he lay with one arm above his head, and the other thrown carelessly back. What a wasted hand it was, and how the veins throbbed on it, as I gazed!

The blinding tears welled up from my heart to my eyes, and dropped heavily, one by one, upon the coverlet, like drops of summer rain. He stirred; and I moved back, quickly.

Then he sighed; muttered something to himself; stirred again; and said:

"Che ora è?"

I stammered—

"Mezza-notte, signore."

He drew his breath quickly; seemed to listen for a moment; then sat up all at once—tore the curtain aside—cried, "Barbara! my wife!" —and we were once more folded in each other's arms.

Once more, after so many bitter, bitter months of parting. Oh, the joy of that moment! the bewildering, overwhelming, intoxicating joy; never to be forgotten, and yet never to be perfectly remembered. Tears, kisses, questions, sobs, broken exclamations—who can recall or record them? They are sacred, and dwell vaguely upon the memory, like a half-forgotten perfume.

    .   .   .   .   .   .

"I am better—I know that I am better. The dead weight is gone from my heart, and the springs of life are renewed in my veins. Ah, Barbarina—my little Barbarina, how sweet to live again! How weary the world has been without thee! Methinks I hardly knew all the depths of my own tenderness for thee, till I had lost thee."

"We will never part again, my beloved."

"Never, till death—but we won't talk of death, my darling. There—let me lay my head upon your bosom; let me feel your breath upon my forehead. God be thanked for all this happiness!"

"Amen, husband."

"Hast thou missed me, my little one?"

"Day and night; sleeping and waking; in every act, and thought, and effort of my life."

He smiled, and closed his eyes. An ineffable peace stole over his features, and he fell asleep.

I dared not move—I scarcely dared to breathe; for his head was resting on my bosom, and my arms supported him. Alas! how weak he was —how weak and pale, and sorrow-worn and wan! A long time, or what seemed a long time, went by thus. He slept like an infant; and, as he slept, I saw with rapture the faint color returning to his parted lips, and the deadly pallor fading from his cheeks and brow. Then my position began to grow intensely painful. My limbs became cramped; my head swam; my hands and feet lost sensation; and I felt as if I might at any moment make some involuntary movement which would wake him. But my strong self-control prevailed. I bore it, agony as it was, till it ceased to be agony, and became a mere physical numbness, easy to endure.

The house all this time was profoundly quiet. I could hear the horses pawing now and then in the stable outside, and every tick of a clock somewhere on the ground-floor below. Once I fancied I heard a footstep on the stairs; but it was only for an instant. At length, when my eyes were beginning to close, despite my efforts to keep them open, he awoke.

"Then it is true!" said he. "No dream, after all!"

"Utterly true, my husband."

"And I have been asleep, sweetheart—asleep in thy dear arms! Such sleep is life. I feel well — quite well, already — and quite happy. Another kiss, my Barbara — let me hold your hand—so!——"

And he fell asleep again.

As he slept, his grasp relaxed, and I was enabled gradually to disengage my hand. His head was now resting on the pillow. His breathing was gentle and regular. His hands were cool; and the smile with which he had last spoken yet lingered on his lips. Such sleep was life, indeed! He was saved—I knew that he was saved; and I knelt down by his bedside, and offered up a silent thanksgiving to Him who "giveth his beloved sleep."

Then I rose, took the lamp, and stole across the room. I opened the door. Something dark lay stretched across the threshold. It was Maddalena, crouched in her old place, with her face buried in her hands. Poor Maddalena! I had almost forgotten her.

Fearing to rouse her while the door was yet open, I stepped cautiously over her feet; closed the door behind me; and then touched her on the shoulder.

"Maddalena," I whispered. "Wake, Maddalena!"

She neither stirred nor spoke. I stooped, and took her hand. It was cold, like marble, and as heavy. An icy shiver ran through me at the touch.

"Maddalena!" I repeated, "are you asleep?" She still made no reply. I held the lamp to her face—she was dead.

———

My story is told. I believed, when I began to write, that I had "the labor of many months" before me. That was just six years ago. Wealth and happiness are no friends to industry. I have loitered over my task till its latest incidents have already become things of the far past, and more than one of the actors who figure in its pages have passed away forever from the stage of life. Who are those vanished ones? Nay; I will assume the story-teller's license, and be silent. What need to jar our viols with the echo of a passing bell? What need, indeed, to follow farther the fortunes of any of those who, having played their parts, now make their exits as the curtain falls? Paolo sailing sadly homeward over the sapphire fields of the Tyrrhene sea, bearing his sister's body to its last rest in the little lonely graveyard of her native Capri—the good Professor merging his whole life and pouring his whole soul into his work; climbing steadily on toward ever loftier aims and broader views; less anxious for personal fame than for the development of truth in art, yet winning the one for himself and the other for his disciples by the force of his own rugged, resolute genius—Hilda ruling her dull husband as if he were a lackey in her service; carrying her imperious beauty from court to court; dissatisfied at heart, and weary of even the wealth and homage for which she had staked all the freshness of her youth—Mrs. Sandyshaft exulting once more in English roast-beef and the society of her hundred pigs; hating foreigners and the fine arts with an undying bitterness; quarreling with Dr. Topham, playing piquet with Hugh, and persisting in calling all babies monsters, without exception or favor—Ida and her husband leading their pleasant artist-life close against that spot where "the antique house in which Raphael lived, casts its long brown shadow down into the heart of modern Rome"—what are all these but pictures which each reader will long ago have conceived for himself, and which no coloring of mine can bring before him more vividly?

For my own part, in the golden years that have gone by since these times of which I have been writing, I can add nothing. Great happiness, like deep grief, is sacred. Words mock it. Its peace is too profound, its joy too perfect, to bear the gross translation. Let those who love, realize the poem of our lives. To all other ears, its music would be discord; its language unintelligible. The hazel wand that brings to light the treasures of the earth, hath no magic save in the hand of the Diviner.